KU-696-117

VII

ENGLISH

Russell

Thomas Hardy.

Vol. 7-8, frontis.

THE

Masterpiece Library of Short Stories

The Thousand Best Complete Tales of all Times and all Countries

Selected by

AN INTERNATIONAL BOARD OF EMINENT CRITICS

Sir William Robertson Nicoll, LL.D.

Sir Arthur Quiller-Couch
Sir Frederick Wedmore
Clement Shorter
Sir Edmund Gosse, C.B., LL.D.
George Saintsbury, LL.D.
W. P. Trent, LL.D.
Richard le Gallienne
Carl Van Doren
Brander Matthews, Litt.D.
Thomas Seccombe

Edited by

Sir J. A. Hammerton

VII. ENGLISH

LONDON
THE EDUCATIONAL BOOK COMPANY LIMITED

Special Edition in 10 double-volumes issued by Allied Newspapers, Ltd., in association with The Educational Book Co. Ltd.

Editorial Board

Editorial Note

A SHORT story may be a mere anecdote of three hundred words or a work of ten or fifteen thousand. In content it may be anything from a glimpse of character, an incident, to a highly finished picture of life. But it should be a complete work of imagination, its effect achieved with a minimum of personages and events.

TO select the best thousand examples was a task that could be achieved only on arbitrary lines. As to length, three thousand words was the ideal average, but this excluded some of the finest stories, so exceptions had to be allowed. National characteristics also had consideration. Another test was the value of a story as illustrating the development of the art.

PROBLEMS of arrangement were not entirely solved by classification according to the country of each writer's origin. This puts Richard Steele into the Irish volume and separates those ideal literary partners Agnes and Egerton Castle. But it is the best possible arrangement for the work, and the index makes reference easy. The inclusion of a series of stories of the War became possible when the War itself ruled out all modern German work.

A WORD as to the method of selection. The General Editor prepared a trial list of titles which were submitted to all the members of the Editorial Board, who rejected and added according to their individual tastes and knowledge. These individual lists were then collated and the final list evolved. The thousand stories selected are therefore representative of the combined opinion of the whole group of editors. A very few modifications of the final list were made necessary by difficulties of copyright and considerations of Anglo-Saxon taste in certain translations from foreign literatures.

MOST of the foreign stories have been specially translated, and all copyrights, in both stories and translations, the use of which authors and publishers have courteously permitted, are duly credited at the end of each volume. J. A. H.

Contents of Volume VII

THE ENGLISH STORY-TELLERS

From Sir Thomas Elyot to Charles Dickens

NOTHING in the wide field of literary research is at once so fascinating and so baffling as an inquiry into the history of prose fiction. Whole libraries full of curious learning have been written about its origins. Scholars have found its dim beginnings in the antique apologues of the distant Orient and followed their migration across the deserts of Arabia to ancient Greece and Rome. Its relation to the satirical fabliaux of old France, the legends of Scandinavia and the heroic romances of Celt and Teuton has been the theme of many devoted pens.

Roughly, very roughly, the so-called schools of prose fiction have been classified into three main divisions: didactic, romantic and realistic; but since the pollen of the apologue first fell on the fertile soil of the faery garden of Boccaccio and was carried thence to northern Europe and America, no literary Linnæus has succeeded in naming and codifying the infinite variety of its developments.

The history of the English short story is no less difficult to trace than that of other branches of the subject. Its rise was singularly slow and obscure. The Elizabethans, so masterful in all else, failed to do much more in short-story form than translate or paraphrase the Italian novelle and the picaresque pleasantries of Spain. Not only the drama and poetry, but the novel itself, attained a permanent shape or structure in England long before the short story, otherwise than as a kind of digression in longer works, emerged from its early stage as an anecdote, didactic or satirical, told alternately in verse and prose.

The art of short-story writing called for qualities of observation, invention, style and constructive skill in which the best of the Elizabethan authors of novels and romances—Lyly, Sidney, Deloney, Greene, Lodge and Nash—were deficient. They are dead and their works are the prey of the book-worm and the philologist. They were pioneers who merit the warm regard of posterity, but they left no immediate followers. Apart from the merits or demerits of their work there were two causes for this.

In the first place, just as the Wars of the Roses closed on the promise of the *Canterbury Tales*, so the Civil War, while it eclipsed the genius of Shakespeare and his contemporary singers, robbed the sixteenth-century prose story of quick fruition. In the second place, the short story called for a special medium. This is ultimately found in the periodical, of which Defoe's *Review* was the parent, the magazine, the miscellany and the keepsake. Thus the eighteenth century was well under way before the short story became established in our midst; and it was not until the nineteenth century that native genius touched it and it lived.

In this volume the reader will be able to follow the growth of the English short story from its crude beginnings in two of the old jest-books, through the intermediate stage of imitation and translation, to the standardising of the art in the works of Thackeray and Dickens.

A HUNDRED MERRY TALES

The *Hundred Merry Tales*, whence the young lord of Padua ironically suggested that the volatile Beatrice had "got her good wit," and from which "The Welshman's Confession" and "The Overmasterful Husband" are taken—these forming numbers xiv and lxiv of the collection—is the most original of our jest-books, and such of its contents as reflect contemporary life are of more than passing value. In plan it is not unlike the *Gesta Romanorum*, being set out with "morals" as is the *Gesta*, but with a racy Rabelaisian touch in its treatment of the friars, the Welsh and women. First printed by Rastell, brother-in-law of Sir Thomas More, himself a humorist, in 1526, the only perfect copy of the original known to exist is in the Royal Library at Göttingen. The one (imperfect) copy in England was recovered in 1815 from sheets used by a binder as pasteboard for another book. The best tale against the friars is xlviii: "Of the Friar that told the Three Children's Fortunes." The mother is informed that of her family one will be a beggar, the second a thief, and the third an assassin ; but advised to make the potential beggar a friar, the potential thief a lawyer, and he who was destined to be an assassin a physician. When these tales were collected Shakespeare's Ancient Pistol had not eaten his leek, and the popular English conception of the Welsh seems to have been based on the notion that under the Tudors the Welsh had too many favours bestowed upon them by the Court.

TITUS AND GISIPPUS

A romance, the theme of which is coeval with the dawn of imaginative literature, lives in the works of Greek dramatist and Roman historian, and was rejuvenated by the genius of Boccaccio, is enshrined in " The Wonderful History of Titus and Gisippus," which forms chapter xii of the second part of *The Boke named The Governour devised by Sir Thomas Elyot, Knight.* Sir Thomas Elyot was a friend (on this side the scaffold) of Sir Thomas More and an ambassador of Henry VIII, to whom *The Governour* was dedicated. His book enjoys the distinction of being the first on the subject of education written and printed in the English language ; and the story given from it is one of the earliest renderings in English of any of the tales in the *Decameron*, the whole of which was not translated till 1619, eighty-eight years after the publication of *The Governour*.

Elyot introduced the story to " recreate " his readers and " minister to their singular pleasure," and the dramatic old fable still grips the imagination of both writers and readers, and will continue to do so while the gift of friendship is preserved to humanity. Of Eastern origin, in its earliest printed form it appears in the twelfth-century miscellany, *De Claricali Disciplina* by Petrus Alfonsus, whence it found its way into the *Gesta Romanorum*, the version in which inspired a Latin poem by Lydgate ; but Boccaccio's " Tito and Gesippo " (Novel 8, Day x of the *Decameron*), the beauty of which is reflected in no small degree by Elyot, is admittedly the most eloquent of its companions if not the most beautiful short story in the Italian language. A bald statement of its origin and analogues would fill more than twice the space allotted to this Introduction, but it may be added that the story has been dramatised in Italy, France and Germany as well as in England, and that Goldsmith paraphrased it in his " Alcander and Septimius," in the first number of a short-lived weekly paper called *The Bee*.

THE STORY OF THE UNKIND KING

The next story comes, in happy sequence, from Sir Philip Sidney, whose friendships—with Languet and Fulke Greville particularly—belong to the more enduring and attractive personalia of the literary life of his time. In addition the story affords an instructive object lesson in the development of spirit, flexibility and fluency in English prose style, and in Sidney's power of differentiation of character. His characters live and have a being of their own. It was from "The Story of the Unkind Paphlagonian King and his Kind Son" (Book ii, chapter x of *The Arcadia*) that Shakespeare drew the underplot of Gloster and his two sons in *King Lear*.

Published after Sidney's death, *The Arcadia* ran through fifteen editions before the close of the seventeenth century, and was translated into French and German. The Greek of Heliodorus, the Italian of Sannazaro, and the Spanish of Montemayor furnished its inspiration, but the style is the author's own, the man himself, who was no Puritan; and the work, it has been well said, "reflects Sidney's tendency to turn in spirit from the world of things as they were to the world of things as they might be." It was Sidney who laid down the golden rule for every author who aims at truth:

> Biting my truant pen, beating myself for spite,
> "Fool," said my muse to me, "Look in thy heart and write."

THE WAKING MAN'S DREAM

"King Lewis and the Husbandman" is No. xxiii in the second of the curious jest-books so popular in the sixteenth century—*Mery Tales, Wittie Questions and Quicke Answeres, Very pleasant to be Readde*, containing anecdotes and ana from the pages of Plutarch, Livy, Valerius Maximus, and from Eastern, French and Italian sources, put into homely English. The germ of the example given is to be found in Lane's *Arabian Tales and Anecdotes*. For the anonymous tale entitled "The Waking Man's Dream," another parable with an Oriental origin, we are indebted to a discovery by H. G. Norton, who in 1845 found what he believed to be a portion of a 1620 reprint of some black-letter stories by Richard Edwards, and so arrived at a 1570 source of the Introduction to the old play of *The Taming of a Shrew* (1594), which served as a foundation-play for Shakespeare's *The Taming of the Shrew*.

"The Waking Man's Dream" is an expanded version of a story in the *Admirable and Memorable Histories*, translated in 1607 from the French of Goulart. The "moral" in the last-named work is rather more piquant than that in the version given in the pages ensuing: "The dissolute spend the night, yea the last night, in false joys. O man, this stately usage of the above-named Artisan is like unto a dream that passeth, and his goodly day, and the years of a wicked life, differ nothing but in more or less. He slept four-and-twenty hours; other wicked men sometimes four-and-twenty thousands of hours. It is a little or a great dream: and nothing more."

THE FISHWIFE OF STRAND-ON-THE-GREEN

"The Tale Told by the Fishwife of Strand-on-the-Green" is from an old chap-book which forms an early and popular example in English of the adaptation of the narrative framework of the *Decameron*, a device as old as "The Seven Wise Masters" and "The Thousand and One Nights." The plan was one that Defoe and Addison adopted when they invented the one a Club for his *Review* and the other a Club for *The Spectator*. The full title of the chap-book, which was published in 1620, is as follows: "Westward for Smelts: The Waterman's-Fare of Mad Merry Western Wenches whose Tongues, albeit like Bell-clappers they never leave Ringing, yet their Tales are Sweet and will much Content You. Written by Kind Kit of Kingston." The reader is asked to suppose that a company of fishwives, who had made a good market, while being rowed homeward from Queenhithe to Brentford, Strand-on-the-Green, Richmond, Twickenham, Kingston and Hampton, "with their heads full of wine and their purses full of coin," requite the waterman for a song by telling a series of tales, of which our example is the second, and a free rendering (the first in English) of Boccaccio's "Bernabo da Genovo" (*Decameron*, Novel 9, Day ii). This was derived from two thirteenth-century French romances and a mediaeval French play; and these, with Holinshed's *Chronicle*, furnished Shakespeare with material for *Cymbeline*. The story is to be found very widely spread in the folklore of many nations both East and West, including the tale of "Taliesin" in the *Mabinogion* and the Scottish ballad of "The Twa Knights."

DANIEL DEFOE

With the stories of Daniel Defoe we reach one of the most remarkable stages in the history of English prose fiction, the coming of realism in its simplest, most direct and most convincing form. Though he suffered the pillory for being "found out" in duping the public by his *Shortest Way with the Dissenters*, Defoe went on to pour out a voluminous stream of fictitious tales so meticulously resembling narratives of actual experience that his *Journal of the Plague Year*, for example, was quoted as authentic by George II's physician, Dr. Mead, while Lord Chatham did not hesitate to commend the *Memoirs of a Cavalier* as the best account of the Civil War. No other man's fiction, unless it be Edgar Allan Poe's, has been so often mistaken for fact. Even to-day it is difficult for many to believe that *Robinson Crusoe* is as much a work of the imagination as Jules Verne's *From the Earth to the Moon.*

His ghost story, "The Apparition of Mrs. Veal"—"A True Relation of the Apparition of One Mrs. Veal, the Next Day after Her Death, to One Mrs. Bargrave, at Canterbury, the 8th of September 1705, which Apparition recommends the Perusal of Drelincourt's Book of Consolations against the Fear of Death" (1705)—appeared as a pamphlet in 1706. According to tradition it was written for the publisher of Drelincourt's deadly quarto, and surely no advertisement has ever excelled it in efficacy. Scott, in his *Life of Defoe*, gives an acute analysis of the story, the qualities of verisimilitude in which are displayed to advantage also in "The Ghost of Dorothy Dingley." To both of these essays in the "plausible style" Scott's remark aptly applies: "Could the thing have happened in reality, so it would have been told."

ADDISON—FIELDING

"The Vision of Mirzah" (No. 159 of *The Spectator*) reminds one that Addison was, like Defoe, given to "visions," though these were visions of a better state of society rather than of human credulity. "The Vision of Mirzah" was presented as a translation from an Oriental manuscript picked up at Grand Cairo, with a promise of its continuation, which went unfulfilled. It is one of the most popular of *The Spectator* Essays, and exhibits Addison's style at its best. Of the famous Coverley papers Sir Walter Raleigh declares that all that is wanting to make of them a serial novel of a very high order is a greater unity and continuity of scheme, a view supported by the remarkable "Preface" by Sir J. G. Frazer to his notable edition of the *Essays of Joseph Addison* (1915). "The History of Leonora, or The Unfortunate Jilt" is an episode, complete in itself, from Henry Fielding's *History of the Adventures of Joseph Andrews and his Friend Abraham Adams, Written in Imitation of the Manner of Cervantes, Author of "Don Quixote,"* which appeared two years after Richardson's *Pamela.* Started with a view to satirise the last-named book, *Joseph Andrews* developed into a masterpiece, the real foundation-stone of modern English fiction, just as *Don Quixote* grew into the glory of Spanish literature.

COLERIDGE—LAMB

We now come to two names linked inseparably in the annals of literary friendship: Samuel Taylor Coleridge and Charles Lamb. The former's infinitely pathetic "Maria Schöning," which depicts an orphan girl's tragic struggle against ill-fortune and reflects human sympathy, guile, cruelty and superstition, is based on a story heard by Coleridge in Germany. Charles Lamb's "Dream-Children: a Reverie" is one of the most graceful examples of his unique gift for blending humour and pathos, and was among the essays, signed "Elia," that, at the age of forty-five, he began to contribute in 1820 to the newly-founded *London Magazine*. "Juke Judkins' Courtship" is not included in Canon Ainger's edition of Lamb's works, but, with Mr. Birrell, "we could have put up better with his presence than his absence" from that generally admirable edition. The story first appeared in the *New Monthly Magazine*, and as an example of artistic satire stands by itself.

JAMES MORIER—MARY MITFORD

In "Hajji Baba and the Stolen Money" we are again surrounded by an atmosphere of Eastern adventure. It is taken from James Morier's *Adventures of Hajji Baba of Ispahan* (1824–28), the hero of which has been happily described as a sort of Persian Gil Blas, clever, unscrupulous and always amusing. The author lived for the greater part of his life in the Orient. Mary Russell Mitford made for herself a lasting reputation by *Our Village*, the source of "The Election." *Our Village*, which evidenced the influence of both Crabbe and Jane Austen, and the only counterpart to which in English fiction is Mrs. Gaskell's *Cranford*, commenced in the *Lady's Magazine* of 1819, and then appeared in parts. The village is Three Miles Cross, near Reading. Miss Mitford's work is characterised by the writer's sterling sympathy, which won the hearts as well as the minds of her readers.

BARHAM—MARRYAT

"Thomas Ingoldsby" (Canon Harris Richard Barham) was the author of two forgotten novels, one beautiful poem ("As I Laye A-Thynkynge"), and a series of burlesque tales, mostly metrical, which, soon after they began to appear in *Bentley's Miscellany* in 1837, under the editorship of Charles Dickens, won a world-wide vogue. Of these droll and clever rhymes "The Jackdaw of Rheims" is a classic of its kind. "The Lady Rohesia" is a diverting example of the author's mock-heroic humour in prose. Frederick Marryat, a naval captain who served under Lord Cochrane, derived not a little of his vigour and animal fun from Smollett. Writing with a ready pen, he possessed a fair sense of humour, of which "S.W. and by W. ¾ W." (from *Olla Podrida*) affords a good criterion, a sound workable knowledge of human nature, and a far from negligible command of pathos. He remains the prose laureate of the British sailor.

MARY SHELLEY—TOM HOOD

Mary Wollstonecraft Shelley, daughter of William Godwin and second wife of Percy Bysshe Shelley, was a writer whose gifts fell little if at all short of genius. Her *Frankenstein*, which added a word to everyday English imagery and was written when she was nineteen, was described by Lamb as " the most extraordinary realisation of the idea of a being out of nature which had ever been offered." She is represented in the following pages by " The Sisters of Albano," a moving tale of love and lawlessness with an Italian setting ; and an artistically told legend of Margaret of Navarre, " The False Rhyme," taken from *The Keepsake* of 1829 and 1830 respectively. The haunting fragment, " A Tale of Terror," by Thomas Hood, appeared in the *New Monthly Magazine* when Theodore Hook was editor. It is as vivid as the waking recollection of a distressing nightmare, but its general effect is inimitably humorous.

MRS. GORE—DOUGLAS JERROLD

Mrs. Catherine Grace Gore was a voluminous writer, whose witty and caustic novels were mainly of fashionable life. Her " Ehrenbreitstein " is a sample of the Gothic romance style of fiction which appears to have been specially acceptable to readers of the once popular *Keepsake*. She has been described as " the wittiest woman of her age." Both Thomas Hood and Douglas Jerrold are in a sense descendants of the writers of our old jest-books, though with a real rather than an assumed moral fervour. " The Tragedy of the Till : Told by the Hermit of Bellyfulle," is from what Jerrold, not without justification, regarded as his best work—*Chronicles of Clovernook*. A like wholesome vein of homely philosophy distinguishes his " Jacques Cocast," a contribution to the *New Monthly* of 1841.

BENJAMIN DISRAELI—SAMUEL WARREN

If Benjamin Disraeli's gift for novel-writing was made subservient to his ambitions as a politician, he began to write quite early and retained his passion for writing throughout the rest of his life. He was, to use his own words, " born in a library," and that interesting proof of his intellectual precocity, " A True Story," appeared in Leigh Hunt's *Indicator* in 1820, when its author was in his fifteenth year. His first novel, *Vivian Grey*, was published in 1826–27 ; his last,

Endymion, in 1880, the year before that in which he died. Acquaintance with his novels as well as his statesmanship is essential to the historian of his times. Samuel Warren's *Passages from the Diary of a Late Physician*, from which " The Resurrectionist " is taken, owes something to the method introduced by Defoe. He certainly studied medicine before he was called to the Bar, but, with that qualifying exception, he was no more a physician than Defoe was a Cavalier. However, his work met with a remarkable success on its appearance in *Blackwood's* and long afterwards, many attributing it to this or that well-known doctor. The *Diary* has an importance as originating a type. Its author scored another success with " Ten Thousand a Year," an amusing tale of an ignorant but pretentious linen-draper's shopman, Mr. Tittlebat Titmouse, who becomes a man of fortune.

MRS. GASKELL

Mrs. Elizabeth Cleghorn Gaskell, the biographer of Charlotte Brontë, was as much at her ease in the novel as in the short story. Her exquisite art is distinguished by rare qualities of humour as well as of pathos, and, most of all, by sympathy. She depicted with unerring skill the rights and wrongs of the modern industrial system and the charms of the English countryside. " The Squire's Story," a model of its class, is a resetting of an episode in the bygone history of her childhood's home, Knutsford, a little town on the Lancashire borders of Cheshire. It appeared originally in the Christmas Number of *Household Words* for 1853. " The Half-Brothers," a tragedy of the Fells, which few can read unmoved, was first published in the *Dublin University Magazine* of November 1858.

THACKERAY—DICKENS

William Makepeace Thackeray is one of the greatest masters of English prose, one of our greatest satirists, critics and parodists, as Charles Dickens is one of the greatest masters of English humour. Of the two Thackeray is the more admired as Dickens is the more loved—and the more read. With representative examples from the works of these two immortals we close this our first volume of English short stories. " Dennis Haggarty's Wife " (*Men's Wives*) is a scathing indictment of an unlovable feminine type and a story of a life's devotion unrewarded. " A Gambler's Death " (*Paris Sketch-Book*), another study drawn from military life, also carries a moral; and a comparison between these morals and those of the old jest-books is in its way a measure of the growth of the subject-matter of this volume.

"A Little Dinner in Bittlestone Street" is a deliciously diverting story from the *Book of Snobs*. "The Princess's Tragedy" is from the "Memoirs of Barry Lyndon," Thackeray's first essay in sustained composition and a masterpiece of intellectual power. It was printed in *Fraser's Magazine* in 1844. "Dimond Cut Dimond" represents his early satirical work in the *Yellowplush Papers*.

Of the seven stories by Dickens "The Bagman's Story" is from the *Pickwick Papers* (1836–37); "The Poor Relation's Story" from *Household Words*, 1852; "The Story of Richard Doubledick," Dickens's one excursion into the romance of war, from *Household Words*, 1854; "Boots at the Holly-Tree" from the same periodical of 1855; "Dr. Manette's MS." from *A Tale of Two Cities* (1859); "To be taken with a Grain of Salt" from *All the Year Round*, 1865; and "The Signalman" from *All the Year Round*, 1866. The selection may fairly be regarded as an index to the wide range of the author's sympathies and the style characterising his work as a short-story writer.

W. F. A.

"HUNDRED MERRY TALES"
15TH CENTURY

THE WELSHMAN'S CONFESSION

A WELSHMAN dwelling in a wild place in Wales came to his Curate in the time of Lent and was confessed ; and when his confession was in manner at the end, the Curate asked him whether he had any other thing to say that grieved his conscience, which, sore abashed, answered no word a great while.

At last, by exhortation of his ghostly father, he said that there was one thing in his mind that greatly grieved his conscience, which he was ashamed to utter, for it was so grievous that he trowed God would never forgive him.

To whom the Curate answered and said that God's mercy was above all, and bade him not despair in the mercy of God, for, whatsoever it was, if he were repentant, God would forgive him.

And so, by long exhortation, at the last he showed it, and said thus :

" Sir, it happened once, that as my wife was making a cheese on a Friday I would have said whether it had been salt or fresh, and took a little of the whey in my hand and put it in my mouth, and, or I was ware, part of it went down my throat against my will, and so I brake my fast."

To whom the Curate said, " If there be none other thing, I warrant God shall forgive thee."

So when he had well comforted him with the mercy of God the Curate prayed him to answer a question and to tell him truth.

The Curate said that there were robberies and murders done nigh the place where he dwelt, and divers men found slain, and asked him whether he were consenting to any of them.

To whom he answered and said " Yes " ; and said he was party to many of them, and did help to rob and to slay divers of them.

Then the Curate asked him why he did not confess him thereof.

The Welshman answered and said he took it for no sin, for it was a custom among them that when any booty came of any rich merchant riding, it was but a good neighbour's deed one to help another when one called another, and so they took that but for good fellowship and neighbourhood.

Here ye may see that some have remorse of conscience of small venial sins, and fear not to do great offences without shame of the world or dread of God: and as the common proverb is, they stumble at a straw and leap over a block.

"HUNDRED MERRY TALES"

THE OVERMASTERFUL HUSBAND

A YOUNG man late married to a wife thought it was good policy to get the mastery of her in the beginning.

Came to her, the pot seething over the fire, although the meat therein was not cooked enough, suddenly commanded her to take the pot from the fire.

Which answered and said, that the meat was not ready to eat.

And he said again, " I will have it taken off, for my pleasure."

This good woman, loth yet to offend him, set the pot beside the fire as he bade.

And anon after he commanded her to set the pot behind the door, and she said thereto again, " Ye be not wise therein."

But he precisely said, it should be so as he bade.

And she gently again did his commandment.

This man, yet not satisfied, commanded her to set the pot ahigh upon the hen-roost.

" What ! " quoth the wife again ; " I trow ye be mad."

And he fiercely then commanded her to set it there, or else, he said, she should repent.

She, somewhat afeared to move his patience, took a ladder and set it to the roost, and went herself up the ladder, and took the pot in her hand, praying her husband then to hold the ladder fast, for sliding ; which so did.

And when the husband looked up and saw the pot stand there on height he said thus, " So now standeth the pot there as I would have it."

This wife, hearing that, suddenly poured the hot pottage on his head, and said thus, " And now ben the pottage there as I would have them."

By this tale men may see that it is no wisdom for a man to attempt a meek woman's patience too far, lest it turn to his own hurt and damage.

SIR THOMAS ELYOT

1499–1546

THE WONDERFUL HISTORY OF TITUS AND GISIPPUS

THERE was in the city of Rome a noble senator, named Fulvius, who sent his son, called Titus, being a child, to the city of Athens, in Greece (which was the fountain of all manner of doctrine), there to learn good letters : and caused him to be hosted with a worshipful man of that city, called Chremes.

This Chremes happened to have also a son named Gisippus, who not only was equal to the said young Titus in years, but also in stature, proportion of body, favour, and colour of visage, countenance, and speech. The two children were so like, that without much difficulty it could not be discerned of their proper parents, which was Titus from Gisippus, or Gisippus from Titus.

These two young gentlemen, as they seemed to be one in form and personage, so shortly after acquaintance, the same nature wrought in their hearts such a mutual affection, and their wills and appetites daily more and more so confederated themselves, that it seemed none other, when their names were declared, but that they had only changed their places, issuing (as I might say) out of the one body, and entering into the other. They together, and at one time went to their learning and study, at one time to their meals and refection, they delighted both in one doctrine, and profited equally therein ; finally, they together increased in doctrine, that within a few years few within Athens might be compared unto them.

At the last died Chremes, which was not only to his son, but also to Titus cause of much sorrow and heaviness. Gisippus, by the goods of his father, was known to be a man of great substance : wherefore there were offered to him great and rich marriages. And he then being of ripe years, and of an able and goodly personage, his friends, kin, and allies exhorted him busily to take a wife, to the intent he might increase his lineage and progeny. But the young man, having his heart already wedded to his friend Titus, and his mind fixed to the study of philosophy, fearing that marriage should be the occasion to sever him both from the one and the other, refused of long time to be persuaded, until at the last, partly by the importunate calling on of his kinsmen, partly by the consent and advice of his dear friend Titus, thereto by other desired, he assented to marry such a one as should like him.

What shall need any words ? His friends found a young gentlewoman, which in equality of years, virtuous conditions, nobility of blood, beauty, and sufficient riches, they thought was for such a young man apt and convenient. And when they and her friends upon the covenants of marriage were thoroughly accorded, they counselled Gisippus to repair unto the maiden, and to behold how her person contented him : and he so doing found her in every form and condition according to his expectation and appetite, whereat he much rejoiced, and became of her amorous, insomuch as many and oftentimes leaving Titus at his study, he secretly repaired unto her.

Notwithstanding, the fervent love that he had to his friend Titus at the last surmounted his shamefacedness, wherefore he disclosed to him his secret journeys, and what delectation he took in beholding the excellent beauty of her whom he intended to marry, and how with her good manners and sweet entertainment, she had constrained him to be her lover. And on a time he, having with him his friend Titus, went to his lady, of whom he was received most joyously.

But Titus forthwith as he beheld so heavenly a personage, adorned with beauty inexplicable, in whose visage was a most amiable countenance, mixed with maidenly shamefacedness, and the rare and sober words and well couched, which issued out of her pretty mouth, Titus was thereat abashed, and had the heart through pierced with the fiery dart of blind Cupid, of the which wound the anguish was so exceeding and vehement, that neither the study of philosophy, neither the remembrance of his dear friend Gisippus, who so much loved and trusted him, could anything withdraw him from that unkind appetite, but that of force he must love inordinately that lady, whom his said friend had determined to marry. Albeit with incredible pains he kept his thoughts secret until that he and Gisippus were returned unto their lodgings.

Then the miserable Titus, withdrawing him as it were to his study, all tormented and oppressed with love, threw himself on a bed, and there rebuking his own most despiteful unkindness, which by the sudden sight of a maiden, he had conspired against his most dear friend Gisippus, against all humanity and reason, cursed his fate or constellation, and wished that he had never come to Athens. And therewith sent he out from the bottom of his heart deep and cold sighs, in such plenty, that it lacked but little that his heart was not riven in pieces.

In dolour and anguish tossed he himself by a certain space, but to no man would he discover it. But at the last, the pain became so intolerable, that would he or no, he was enforced to keep his bed, being for lack of sleep and other natural sustenance, brought in such feebleness, that his legs might not sustain his body.

Gisippus missing his dear friend Titus, was much abashed, and hearing that he lay sick in his bed, had forthwith his heart pierced with heaviness, and with all speed came to him, where he lay. And beholding the rosial colour, which was wont to be in his visage, turned into sallow, the residue pale, his ruddy lips wan, and his eyes leaden and hollow, might unneth [1] keep himself from weeping: but to the intent he would not discomfort his friend Titus, dissimulated his heaviness, and with a comfortable countenance demanded of Titus, what was the cause of his disease, blaming him of unkindness, that he so long had sustained it, without giving him knowledge, that he might for him have provided some remedy, if any might have been got, though it were with the dispensing of all his substance.

With which words the mortal sighs renewed in Titus, and the salt tears burst out of his eyen in such abundance, as it had been a land flood running down of a mountain after a storm. That beholding Gisippus, and being also resolved into tears, most heartily desired him, and (as I might say) conjured him, for the fervent and entire love that had been, and yet was between them, that he would no longer hide from him his grief, and that there was nothing to him so dear and precious (although it were his own life) that might restore Titus to health, but that he would gladly, and without grudging employ it, with which words, obtestations, and tears of Gisippus, Titus constrained, all blushing and ashamed, holding down his head, brought forth with great difficulty his words in this wise:

"My dear and most loving friend, withdraw your friendly offers, cease of your courtesy, refrain your tears and regrettings, take rather your knife, and slay me here where I lie, or otherwise take vengeance on me, most miserable and false traitor unto you, and of all other most worthy to suffer shameful death. For where as God of nature, like as He hath given to us similitude in all the parts of our body, so hath He conjoined our wills, studies, and appetites together in one, so that between men was never like concord and love, as I suppose. And now notwithstanding, only with the look of a woman, those bonds of love be dissolved, reason oppressed, friendship is excluded, there availeth no wisdom, no doctrine, no fidelity or trust: yea, your trust is the cause that I have conspired against you this treason.

"Alas! Gisippus, what envious spirit moved you to bring me to her, whom you have chosen to be your wife, where I received this poison? I say, Gisippus, where was then your wisdom, that ye

[1] *Unneth*, First English, "uneath," not easily.

remembered not the fragility of our common nature? what need ye to call me for a witness of your private delights? why would ye have me see that, which you yourself could not behold without ravishing of mind and carnal appetite? Alas, why forgot ye, that our minds and appetites were ever one? and that also what so ye liked was ever to me in like degree pleasant. What will ye more? Gisippus, I say your trust is the cause that I am entrapped. The rays or beams issuing from the eyen of her whom ye have chosen, with the remembrance of her incomparable virtues, hath thrilled throughout the midst of my heart, and in such wise burneth it, that above all things I desire to be out of this wretched and most unkind life, which is not worthy the company of so noble and loving a friend as ye be."

And therewith Titus concluded his confession, with so profound and bitter a sigh, received with tears, that it seemed that all his body should be dissolved and relented into salt drops.

But Gisippus, as he were therewith nothing astonished or discontented, with an assured countenance, and merry regard, embracing Titus, and kissing him, answered in this wise:

"Why, Titus, is this your only sickness and grief that ye so uncourteously have so long concealed, and with much more unkindness kept from me, than ye have conceived it? I acknowledge my folly wherewith ye have with good right upbraided me, that in showing to you her whom I loved, I remembered not the common estate of our nature, neither the agreeableness, or (as I might say) the unity of our two appetites. Surely that default can be by no reason excused, wherefore it is only I that have offended. For who may by right prove that ye have trespassed, that by the inevitable stroke of Cupid's dart are thus bitterly wounded? Think ye me such a fool or ignorant person, that I know not the power of Venus, where she liketh to show her importable[1] violence? Have not ye well resisted against such a goddess, that for my sake have striven with her almost to the death? What more loyalty or truth can I require of you? Am I of that virtue, that I may resist against celestial influence, preordinate by providence divine? If I so thought, what were my wits? where were my study so long time spent in noble philosophy? I confess to you, Titus, I love that maiden as much as any wise man might possible: and took in her company more delight and pleasure than of all the treasure and lands that my father left me, which ye know was right abundant.

"But now I perceive that the affection of love toward her surmounteth in you above measure, what, shall I think it of a wanton lust, or sudden appetite in you, whom I have ever known of grave and sad disposition, inclined alway to honest doctrine, flying all vain dalliance and dishonest pastime? Shall I imagine to be in

[1] *Importable*, unbearable.

you any malice or fraud, since from the tender time of our childhood, I have alway found in you, my sweet friend Titus, such a conformity with all my manners, appetites, and desires, that never was seen between us any manner of contention? May God forbid, that in the friendship of Gisippus and Titus should happen any suspicion: or that any fantasy should pierce my head whereby that honourable love between us should be the mountenance of a crumb[1] perished. Nay, nay, Titus, it is as I said, the only providence of God: she was by Him from the beginning prepared to be your lady and wife. For such fervent love entereth not into the heart of a wise man and virtuous, but by a divine disposition: whereat if I should be discontented or grudge, I should not only be unjust to you, withholding that from you which is undoubtedly yours, but also obstinate and repugnant against the determination of God, which shall never be found in Gisippus.

"Therefore, gentle friend Titus, dismay you not at the chance of love, but receive it joyously with me, that am with you nothing discontented, but marvellous glad, since it is my hap to find for you such a lady, with whom ye shall live in felicity, and receive fruit to the honour and comfort of all your lineage. Here I renounce to you clearly all my title and interest, that I now have or might have in the fair maiden. Call to your pristinate courage, wash clean your visage and eyes thus bewept, and abandon all heaviness. The day appointed for our marriage approacheth: let us consult how, without difficulty, ye may wholly attain your desires. Take heed this mine advice: ye know well that we two be so like, that being apart, and in one apparel, few men do know us. Also ye do remember that the custom is that, notwithstanding any ceremony done at the time of the espousals, the marriage, notwithstanding is not confirmed until at night that the husband putteth a ring on the finger of his wife, and unlooseth her girdle. Therefore, I myself will be present with my friends, and perform all the parts of a bridegroom. And ye shall abide in a place secret, where I shall appoint you, until it be night. And then shall ye quickly convey yourself into the maiden's chamber, and for the similitude of our personages, and of our apparel, ye shall not be espied of the women, which have none of us any acquaintance, and shortly get you to bed, and put your own ring on the maiden's finger, and undo the girdle of virginity, and do all other thing that shall be to your pleasure.

"Be now of good cheer, Titus, and comfort yourself with good reflections and solace, that this wan and pale colour, and your cheeks meagre and lean, be not the cause of your discovering. I know well, that, ye having your purpose, I shall be in obloquy and derision of all men, and so hated of all my kindred, that they shall seek

[1] *The mountenance of a crumb*, to the amount of a crumb.

occasion to expulse me out of this city, thinking me to be a notable reproach to all my family. But let God therein work, I force not [1] what pain that I abide, so that ye, my friend Titus, may be safe, and pleasantly enjoy your desires, to the increasing of your felicity."

With these words Titus began to move, as it were, out of a dream, and doubting whether he heard Gisippus speak, or else saw but a vision, lay still as a man abashed. But when he beheld the tears trickling down by the face of Gisippus, he then comforted him, and thanking him for his incomparable kindness, refused the benefit that he offered, saying that it were better that a hundred such unkind wretches as he was should perish, than so noble a man as was Gisippus should sustain reproach or damage.

But Gisippus eftesoones comforted Titus, and therewith sware and protested, that with free and glad will he would that this thing should be in form aforesaid accomplished, and therewith embraced and sweetly kissed Titus. Who perceiving the matter sure, and not feigned, as a man not sick, but only awaked out of his sleep, set himself up in his bed ; the quick blood somewhat resorted unto his visage, and after a little good meats and drinks taken, he was shortly, and in a few days, restored into his old fashion and figure.

To make the tale short : the day of marriage was come. Gisippus, accompanied with his allies and friends, came to the house of the damosel, where they were honourably and joyously feasted. And between him and the maiden was a sweet entertainment, which to behold, all that were present, took much pleasure and comfort, praising the beauty, goodliness, virtue, and courtesy, which in this couple were excellent above all other that they had ever seen. What shall I say more ? The covenants were read and sealed, the dower appointed, and all other bargains concluded, and the friends of either part took their leave and departed : the bride with a few women (as was the custom) brought into her chamber ; then, as it was before agreed, Titus conveyed himself, after Gisippus returned to his house, or perchance to the chamber appointed for Titus, nothing sorrowful, although that he heartily loved the maiden, but with a glad heart and countenance that he had so recovered his friend from death, and so well brought him to the effect of his desire. . . . The morrow is come. Gisippus, thinking it expedient that the truth should be discovered, assembled all the nobility of the city at his own house, where also by appointment was Titus, who among them had these words that do follow :—

" My friends, Athenians, there is at this time showed among you an example, almost incredible, of the divine power of honourable love, to the perpetual renown and commendation of this noble city of Athens, whereof he ought to take excellent comfort, and therefore

[1] *I force not*, I care not.

give due thanks to God, if there remain among you any token of the ancient wisdom of your most noble progenitors. For what more praise may be given to people that benevolence, faithfulness, and constancy ? without whom all countries and cities be brought unto desolation and ruin, like as by them they become prosperous and in most high felicity. What, shall I long tarry you in conjecturing mine intent and meaning ? Ye all know from whence I came unto this city, that of adventure I found in the house of Chremes his son Gisippus, of mine own age, and in everything so like to me that neither his father nor any other man could discern of us the one from the other, but by our own insignment or showing : in so much as there were put about our necks laces of sundry colours to declare our personages. What mutual agreement and love have been alway between us during the eight years that we have been together, ye all be witnesses, that have been beholders and wonderers of our most sweet conversation and consent of appetites, wherein was never any discord or variance.

" And, as for my part, after the decease of my father, notwithstanding that there was descended and happened unto me great possessions, fair houses, with abundance of riches ; also I being called home by the desirous and importunate letters of mine allies and friends, which be of the most noble of all the senators, offered the advancement to the highest dignities in the public weal, I will not remember the lamentations of my most natural mother, expressed in her tender letters, all besprent and blotted with abundance of tears, wherein she accuseth me of unkindness, for my long tarrying, and especially now in her most discomfort. But all this could not remove me the breadth of my nail from my dear friend, Gisippus. And but by force could not I, nor yet may be drawn from his sweet company, but if he thereto will consent. I choosing rather to live with him as his companion and fellow, yea, and as his servant rather than to be Consul of Rome. Thus my kindness hath been well acquitted (or as I might say), redoubled, delivering me from the death, yea from the most cruel and painful death of all other.

" I perceive ye wonder hereat, noble Athenians, and no marvel. For what person should be so hardy to attempt any such thing against me, being a Roman, and of the noble blood of the Romans ? Or who should be thought so malicious to slay me, who (as all ye be my judges) never trespassed against any person within this city. Nay, nay, my friends, I have none of you all therein suspected. I perceive you desire and hearken to know what he was that presumed to do so cruel and great an enterprise. It was love, noble Athenians, the same love which, as your poets do remember, did wound the more part of all the gods, that ye do honour, that constrained Jupiter to transform himself in a swan, a bull, and divers other likenesses :

the same love that caused Hercules, the vanquisher and destroyer of monsters and giants, to spin on a rock, sitting among maidens in a woman's apparel: the same love that caused to assemble all the noble princes of Asia and Greece in the fields of Troy: the same love, I say, against whose assaults may be found no defence or resistance, hath suddenly and unaware stricken me unto the heart with such vehemence and might, that I had in short space died with most fervent torments had not the incomparable friendship of Gisippus holpen me. I see you would fain know who she is that I loved.

"I will no longer delay you, noble Athenians. It is Sophronia, the lady whom Gisippus had chosen to have to his wife, and whom he most entirely loved. But when his most gentle heart perceived that my love was in a much higher degree than his toward that lady, and that it proceeded neither of wantonness, neither of long conversation, nor of any other corrupt desire or fantasy, but in an instant, by the only look, and with such fervence, that immediately I was so cruciate, that I desired, and in all that I mought provoked death to take me. He by his wisdom soon perceived (as I doubt not but that ye do) that it was the very provision of God that she should be my wife and not his: whereto he giving place, and more esteeming true friendship than the love of a woman, whereunto he was induced by his friends and not by violence of Cupid constrained, as I am, hath willingly granted to me the interest that he had in the damosel. And it is I, Titus, that have verily wedded her, I have put the ring on her finger, I have undone the girdle of her shamefacedness: what will ye more? I have lain with her, and confirmed the matrimony, and made her a wife."

At these words all they that were present began to murmur, and to cast a disdainous and grievous look upon Gisippus. Then spake again Titus:

"Leave your grudgings and menacing countenance towards Gisippus; he hath done to you all honour, and no need of reproach. I tell you he hath accomplished all the parts of a friend: that love, which was most certain, hath he continued. He knew he might find in Greece another maiden, and fair and as rich as this that he had chosen, and one, perchance, that he mought love better. But such a friend as I was, having respect to our similitude, the long approved concord, also mine estate and condition, he was sure to find never none. Also the damosel suffereth no disparagement in her blood, or hindrance in her marriage, but is much rather advanced (no dispraise to my dear friend Gisippus).

"Also consider, noble Athenians, that I took her not my father living, when ye mought have suspected that as well her riches as her beauty should have thereto allured me: but soon after my father's decease, when I far exceeded her in possessions and substance, when the most notable men of Rome and Italy desired mine alliance ; ye have therefore all cause to rejoice and thank Gisippus, and not to be angry, and also to extol his wonderful kindness toward me, whereby he hath won me and all my blood, such friends to you and your city, that ye may be assured, to be by us defended against all the world : which being considered, Gisippus hath well deserved a statue or image of gold, to be set on a pillar, in the midst of your city, for an honourable monument, in the remembrance of our incomparable friendship, and of the good that thereby may come to your city.

" But if this persuasion cannot satisfy you, but that ye will imagine anything to the damage of my dear friend Gisippus after my departing, I make my vow unto God, creator of all thing, that as I shall have knowledge thereof, I shall forthwith resort hither, with the invincible power of the Romans, and revenge him in such wise against his enemies that all Greece shall speak of it to their perpetual dishonour, shame, and reproach."

And therewith Titus and Gisippus rose, but the other for fear of Titus dissembleth their malice, making semblant as they had been with all thing contented.

Soon after, Titus, being sent for by the authority of the Senate and people of Rome, prepared to depart out of Athens, and would fain have had Gisippus to have gone with him, offering to divide with him all his substance and fortune. But Gisippus, considering how necessary his counsel should be to the city of Athens, would not depart out of his country. Notwithstanding that above all earthly things he most desired the company of Titus : which above also, for the said consideration, Titus approved.

Titus with his lady is departed towards the city of Rome, where, at their coming, they were of the mother of Titus, his kinsmen, and of all the Senate and people joyously received. And there lived Titus with his lady in joy inexplicable, and had by her many fair children : and for his wisdom and learning was so highly esteemed that there was no dignity or honourable office within the city that he had not with much favour and praise achieved and occupied.

But now let us resort to Gisippus, who immediately upon the departing of Titus was so maligned at, as well by his own kinsmen as by the friends of the lady, that he, to their seeming, shamefully abandoned, leaving her to Titus, that they spared not daily to vex him with all kinds of reproach that they could devise or imagine : and first they excluded him out of their council, and prohibited him from all honest company.

And yet not being therewith satisfied, finally they adjudged him unworthy to enjoy any possessions or goods left to him by his parents whom he (as they supposed) by his indiscreet friendship had so distained. Wherefore they despoiled him of all things, and almost naked, expelled him out of the city.

Thus is Gisippus, late wealthy, and one of the most noble men of Athens, for his kind heart, banished his country for ever, and as a man dismayed, wandering hither and thither, finding no man that would succour him. At the last remembering in what pleasure his friend lived with his lady, for whom he suffered these damages, concluded to go to Rome, and declare his infortune to his said friend Titus. What shall need a long tale? In conclusion, with much pain, cold, hunger, and thirst, he is come to the city of Rome, and diligently enquiring for the house of Titus, at the last he came to it: but beholding it so beautiful, large and princely, he was ashamed to approach nigh to it, being in so simple estate and unclad, but standeth by, that in case Titus came forth out of his house, he might present himself to him.

He being in this thought, Titus, holding his lady by the hand, issued out from his door, and taking their horses to solace themselves, beheld Gisippus, and beholding his vile apparel, regarded him not, but passed forth on their way, wherewith Gisippus was so wounded to the heart, thinking Titus had contemned his fortune, that oppressed with mortal heaviness, fell in a sownde,[1] but being recovered by some that stood by, thinking him to be sick, forthwith departed, intending not to abide any longer, but as a wild beast to wander abroad in the world. But for weariness he was constrained to enter into an old barn without the city; where he, casting himself on the bare ground with weeping and dolorous crying, bewaileth his fortune; but most of all accusing the ingratitude of Titus, for whom he suffered all that misery, the remembrance whereof was so intolerable that he determined no longer to live in that anguish and dolour. And therewith drew his knife, purposing to have slain himself. But ever wisdom (which he by the study of philosophy had attained) withdrew him from that desperate act. And in this contention between wisdom and will, fatigued with long journeys in watch, or as God would have it, he fell into a deep sleep. His knife (wherewith he would have slain himself) falling down by him.

In the meantime, a common and notable ruffian or thief, which had robbed and slain a man, was entered into the barn where Gisippus lay, to the intent to sojourn there all that night. And seeing Gisippus bewept, and his visage replenished with sorrow, and also the naked knife by him, perceived well that he was a man desperate, and surprised with heaviness of heart, was weary of his life: which the said ruffian taking for a good occasion to escape, took the knife of Gisippus, and putting it in the wound of him that was slain, put

[1] *Sownde*, swoon.

it all bloody in the hand of Gisippus, being fast asleep, and so departed.

Soon after, the dead man being found, the officers made diligent search for the murderer : at the last they entering into the barn, and finding Gisippus asleep, with the bloody knife in his hand, awaked him ; wherewith he entered again into his old sorrows, complaining his evil fortune. But when the officers laid unto him the death of the man, and the having of the bloody knife, thereat rejoiced, thanking God that such occasion was happened, whereby he should suffer death by the laws, and escape the violence of his own hands.

Wherefore he denied nothing that was laid to his charge, desiring the officers to make haste that he might be shortly out of his life. Whereat they marvelled. Anon, report came to the Senate that a man was slain, and that a stranger, and a Greek born, was found in such form as is before-mentioned. They forthwith commanded him to be brought unto their presence, sitting there at that time, Titus being then Consul, or in other like dignity. The miserable Gisippus was brought to the bar, with bills and staves like a felon, of whom it was demanded if he slew the man that was founden dead. He nothing denied, but in most sorrowful manner cursed his fortune, naming himself of all other most miserable.

At the last one demanding him of what country he was, he confessed to be an Athenian, and therewith he cast his sorrowful eye upon Titus with much indignation, and burst out into sighs and tears abundantly. That beholding Titus, and espying by a little sign in his visage, which he knew, that it was his dear friend Gisippus, and anon considering that he was brought into despair by some misadventure, rose out of his place where he sat, and falling on his knees before the judges, said that he had slain the man for old malice that he bare toward him, and that Gisippus, being a stranger, was guiltless, and all men mought perceive that the other was a desperate person. Wherefore to abbreviate his sorrows, he confessed the act whereof he was innocent, to the intent that he would finish his sorrows with death, wherefore Titus desired the judges to give sentence on him according to his merits. But Gisippus, perceiving his friend Titus (contrary to his expectation) to offer himself to the death for his safeguard, more importunately cried to the Senate to proceed in their judgment on him, that was the very offender.

Titus denied, and affirmed with reasons and arguments that he was the murderer, and not Gisippus. Thus they of long time, with abundance of tears, contended which of them should die for the other, whereat all the Senate and people were wonderfully abashed, not knowing what it meant. The murderer in deed happened to be in the prease [1] at that time, who, perceiving the marvellous conten-

[1] *Prease*, press, crowd.

tion of these two persons, which were both innocent, and that it proceeded of an incomparable friendship, was vehemently provoked to discover the truth. Wherefore he brake through the prease, and coming before the Senate, spake in this wise :

" Noble fathers, I am such a person, whom ye know have been a common barrator [1] and thief by a long space of years : ye know also, that Titus is of a noble blood, and is approved to be alway a man of excellent virtue and wisdom, and never was malicious. This other stranger seemeth to be a man full of simplicity, and that more is desperate for some grievous sorrow that he hath taken, as it is to you evident. I say to you, fathers, they both be innocent ; I am that person that slew him that is founden dead by the barn, and robbed him of his money. And when I found in the barn this stranger lying asleep, having by him a naked knife, I, the better to mine offence, did put the knife into the wound of the dead man, and so all bloody laid it again by this stranger. This was my mischievous desire to escape your judgment. Whereunto now I remit me wholly, rather than this noble man Titus, or this innocent stranger, should unworthily die."

Hereat all the Senate and people took comfort, and the noise of rejoicing hearts filled all the court. And when it was further examined, Gisippus was discovered ; the friendship between him and Titus was throughout the city published, extolled, and magnified. Wherefore the Senate consulted of this matter, and finally, at the instance of Titus and the people, discharged the felon. Titus recognised his negligence in forgetting Gisippus.

And Titus, being advertised of the exile of Gisippus, and the despiteful cruelty of his kindred, was therewith wonderful wroth, and having Gisippus home to his house (where he was with incredible joy received of the lady, whom some time he should have wedded) honourably apparelled him ; and there Titus offered to him to use all his goods and possessions at his own pleasure and appetite. But Gisippus desiring to be again in his proper country, Titus, by the consent of the Senate and people, assembled a great army, and went with Gisippus unto Athens, where he, having delivered to him all those which were causers of banishing and despoiling of his friend Gisippus, did on them sharp execution ; and restoring to Gisippus his lands and substance, stablished him in perpetual quietness, and so returned to Rome.

[1] *Barrator*, mischief-maker.

SIR PHILIP SIDNEY
1554–1586

THE STORY OF THE UNKIND KING

It was in the kingdome of Galacia, the season being (as in the depth of winter) very cold, and as then sodainely growne to so extreame and foule a storme, that never any winter (I thinke) brought foorth a fowler child ; so that the princes were even compelled by the haile, that the pride of the winde blew into their faces, to seeke some shrowding place within a certain hollow rocke offering it unto them, they made it their shield against the tempests furie.

And so staying there, till the violence thereof was passed, they heard the speach of a couple, who not perceiving them (being hidde within that rude canapy) helde a straunge and pitifull disputation which made them steppe out ; yet in such sort, as they might see unseene. There they perceaved an aged man, and a young, scarcely come to the age of a man, both poorely arayed, extreamely weather beaten ; the olde man blinde, the young man leading him : and yet, through all those miseries, in both these seemed to appeare a kind of noblenesse, nut sutable to that affliction.

But the first words they heard, were these of the old man.

" Well, Leonatus " (said he), " since I cannot perswade thee to leade me to that which should end my griefe, and my trouble, let me now entreat thee to leave me : feare not, my miserie cannot be greater then it is, and nothing doth become me but miserie ; feare not the danger of my blind steps, I cannot fall worse then I am. And doo not, I pray thee, doo not obstinately continue to infect thee with my wretchedness. But flie, flie from this region, onely worthy of me."

" Deare father " (answered he), " doo not take away from me the onely remnant of my happinesse : while I have power to doo you service, I am not wholly miserable."

" Ah, my sonne " (saide he, and with that he groned, as if sorrow strave to breake his herte), " how eville fits it me to have such a sonne, and how much doth thy kindness unbraide my wickednesse ? "

These dolefull speeches, and some others to like purpose (well shewing they had not been borne to the fortune they were in) moved the princes to goe out unto them, and aske the younger what they were.

"Sirs" (answered he, with a good grace, and made the more agreable by a certaine noble kinde of pitiousnes), "I see well you are straungers, that know not our miserie so well here knowne, that no man dare know, but that we must be miserable. In deede, our state is such, as though nothing is so needfull unto us as pittie, yet nothing is more daungerous unto us, then to make our selves so knowne as may stirre pittie. But your presence promiseth that cruelty shall not over-runne hate. And if it did, in truth our state is soncke below the degree of feare.

"This old man (whom I leade) was lately rightfull prince of this countrie of Paphlagonia, by the hard-harted ungratefulnes of a sonne of his, deprived, not onely of his kingdome (whereof no forraine forces were able to spoyle him) but of his sight, the riches which nature graunts to the poorest creatures. Whereby, and by other his unnaturall dealings, he hath bin driven to such griefe, as even now he would have had me to have led him to the toppe of this rocke, thence to cast himself headlong to death: and so would have made me (who received my life of him) to be the worker of his destruction. But, noble gentlemen (said he), if either of you have a father, and feele what duetifull affection is engraffed in a sonnes hart, let me intreate you to convey this afflicted prince to some place of rest and securitie. Amongst your worthie actes it shall be none of the least, that a king, of such might and fame, and so unjustly oppressed, is in any sort by you relieved."

But before they could make him answere, his father began to speake:

"Ah, my sonne" (said he), "how evill an historian are you, that leave out the chiefe knotte of all the discourse: my wickednes, my wickednes. And if thou doest it to spare my eares (the onely sense nowe left me proper for knowledge) assure thy selfe thou dost mistake me. And I take witnesse of that sunne which you see (with that he cast up his blinde eyes, as if he would hunt for light), and wish my selfe in worse case then I do wish my selfe, which is as evill as may be, if I speake untruely; that nothing is so welcome to my thoughts as the publishing of my shame. Therefore, know you, gentlemen (to whom from my harte I wish that it may not prove ominous foretoken of misfortune to have mettle with such a miser as I am), that whatsoever my sonne (O God, that trueth binds me to reproach him with the name of my sonne) hath said, is true.

"But, besides those truthes, this is also true: that, having had in lawful mariage, of a mother fitte to beare royall children, this sonne (suche one as partly you see, and better shall knowe by my shorte declaration), and so enjoyed the expectations in the world of him, till he was growen to justifie their expectations (so as I needed envie no father for the chiefe comfort of mortalitie, to leave an other ones-selfe after me), I was caried by a bastarde sonne of mine (if, at least, I be bounde to beleeve the words of that base woman my concubine, his mother) first to mislike, then to hate, lastly to destroy, to doo my best to destroy, this sonne (I thinke you thinke) undeserving destruction. What waies he used to bring me to it, if I should tell you, I should tediously trouble you with as much poysonous hypocrisie, desperate fraud, smoothe malice, hidden ambition, and smiling envie, as in any living person could be harbored. But I list it not, no remembrance of naughtines delights me, but mine own: and, methinks, the accusing his traines might in some manner excuse my fault, which certainly I loth to doo. But the conclusion is, that I gave order to some servants of mine, whom I thought as apte for such charities as my selfe, to leade him out into a forrest, and there to kill him.

"But those theeves (better natured to my sonne then my selfe) spared his life, letting him goe, to learn to live poorely: which he did, giving himselfe to be a private soldier, in a countrie hereby. But as he was redy to be greatly advanced for some noble peeces of service which he did, he hearde newes of me: who (dronke in my affection to that unlawfull and unnaturall sonne of mine) suffered my selfe so to be governed by him, that all favors and punishments passed by him, all offices, and places of importance, distributed to his favourites; so that ere I was aware, I had left my selfe nothing but the name of a king: which he shortly wearie of too, with many indignities (if any thing may be called an indignity which was laid upon me), threw me out of my seat, and put out my eies; and then (proud in his tyrannie) let me goe, neither imprisoning, nor killing me: but rather delighting to make me feele my miserie; miserie, indeed, if ever there were any; full of wretchednes, fuller of disgrace, and fullest of guiltines.

"And as he came to the crowne by so unjust meanes, as unjustlie he kept it, by force of stranger souldiers in cittadels, the nestes of tyranny, and murderers of libertie; disarming all his own countrimen, that no man durst shew himself a welwiller of mine: to say the trueth (I think) few of them being so (considering my cruell follie to my good sonne, and foolish kindnes to my unkinde bastard): but if there were any who fell to pitie of so great a fall, and had yet any sparkes of unstained duety lefte in them towardes me, yet durst they not shewe it, scarcely with giving me alms at their doores; which yet was the onelie sustenaunce of my distressed life, no bodie daring to shewe so much charitie as to lende me a handle to guide my darke steppes: till this sonne of mine (God knowes, woorthie of a more vertuous, and more fortunate father) forgetting my abhominable wrongs, not recking danger, and neglecting the present good way he was in doing himselfe good, came hether to doo this kind office you see him performe towards me, to my unspeakable griefe; not onelie because his kindnes is a glasse even to my blind eyes, of my naughtines, but that above all griefes, it greeves me he should desperatly adventure the losse of his well-deserving life for mine, that yet owe more to fortune for my deserts, as if he would cary mudde in a chest of christall. For well I know, he that now raigneth, how much soever (and with good reason) he despiseth me, of all men despised; yet he will not let slippe any advantage to make away with him, whose just title (ennobled by courage and goodnes) may one day shake the seat of a never secure tyrannie. And for this cause I craved of him to leade me to the toppe of this rocke, indeede I must confesse, with meaning to free him from so serpentine a companion as I am. But he finding what I purposed, onelie therein since he was borne, shewed himselfe disobedient unto me.

"And now, gentlemen, you have the true storie, which I pray you publish to the world, that my mischievous proceedings may be the glorie of his filiall pietie the onelie reward now left for so great a merite. And if it may be, let me obtaine that of you, which my sonne denies me; for never was there more pitie in saving any, then in ending me; both because therein my agonies shall ende, and so shall you preserve this excellent young man, who els wilfully followes his owne ruine."

The matter, in itself lamentable, lamentably expressed by the old prince (which needed not take to himselfe the gestures of pitie, since his face could not put of the markes thereof) greatly moved the two princes to compassion, which could not stay in such harts as theirs without seeking remedie. But by and by the occasion was presented: for Plexirtus (so was the bastard called) came thether with fortie horse, onelie of purpose to murder this brother; of whose comming he had soone advertisement, and thought no eyes of sufficient credite in such a matter, but his owne; and therefore came himselfe to be actor, and spectator.

And as soone as he came, not regarding the weake (as he thought) garde of but two men, commaunded some of his followers to set their handes to his, in the killing of Leonatus. But the young prince (though not otherwise armed but with a sworde), how falsely soever he was dealt with by others, would not betray himselfe: but bravely drawing it out, made the death of the first that assayled him, warne his fellowes to come more warily after him. But then Pyrocles and Musidorus were quickly become parties (so just a defence deserving as much as old friendship), and so did behave them among that companie (more injurious then valiant) that many of them lost their lives for their wicked maister.

Yet perhaps had the number of them at last prevailed, if the King of Pontus (lately by them made so) had not come unlooked for to their succour. Who (having had a dreame which had fixt his imagination vehemently upon some great daunger, presently to follow those two princes whom he most deerely loved) was come in all hast, following as well as he could their tracke with a hundreth horses in that countrie, which he thought (considering who then raigned) a fit place inough to make the stage of any tragedie.

But then the match had ben so ill made for Plexirtus, that his ill-led life, and worse-gotten honour, should have tumbled together to destruction: had there not come in Tydeus and Telenor, with fortie or fiftie in their suit, to the defence of Plexirtus. These two were brothers, of the noblest house of that country, brought up from their infancie with Plexirtus: men of such prowesse as not to know feare in themselves, and yet to teach it others that should deale with them: for they had often made their lives triumph over most terrible daungers; never dismayed, and ever fortunate; and truely no more settled in their valure, then disposed to goodnesse and justice, if either they had lighted on a better friend, or could have learned to make friendship a child, and not the father vertue.

But, bringing up (rather then choise) having first knit their minds unto him (indeed, craftie inough, eyther to hide his faults, or never to shewe them, but when they might pay home) they willingly held out the course, rather to satisfie him, then all the world; and rather to be good friendes then good men: so, as though they did not like the evill he did, yet they liked him that did the evill, and, though not councellors of the offence, yet protectors of the offender.

Now, they having heard of this sodaine going out, with so small a company, in a country full of evil-wishing minds toward him (though they knew not the cause), followed him; till they found him in such case as they were to venture their lives, or else he to loose his: which they did with such force of minde and bodie, that truly I may justly say, Pyrocles and Musidorus had never till then found any that could make them so well repeate their hardest lesson in the feates of armes. And briefly so they did, that, if they overcame not, yet were they not overcome, but caried away that ungratefull maister of theirs to a place of securitie; howsoever the princes laboured to the contrary.

But this matter being thus far begun, it became not the constancie of the princes so to leave it; but in all hast making forces both in Pontus and Phrygia, they had in fewe dayes lefte him but only that one strong place where he was.

For feare having bene the onelie knot that had fastened his people unto him, that once untied by a greater force, they all scattered from him, like so many birdes, whose cage had bene broken.

In which season the blind king (having in the chief citie of his realme set the crowne upon his sonne Leonatus' head) with many teares (both of joy and sorrow) setting forth to the people his owne fault and his sonnes vertue, after he had kist him, and forst his sonne to accept honour of him (as of his newe-become subject) even in a moment died, as it should seeme: his hart broken with unkindnes and affliction, stretched so farre beyond his limits with this excesse of comfort, as it was able no longer to keep safe his vitall spirits.

But the new king (having no lesse lovingly performed all duties to him dead, then alive) pursued on the siege of his unnatural brother, inasmuch for the revenge of his father, as for the establishing of his owne quiet. In which siege, truly I cannot but acknowledge the prowesse of those two brothers, then whom the princes never found in all their travell two men of greater habilitie to performe, nor of habler skill for conduct.

But Plexirtus, finding that, if nothing else, famin would at last bring him to destruction, thought better by humblenes to creepe, where by pride he could not march. For certainly so had nature formed him, and the exercise of craft conformed him to all turnings of sleights, that, though no man had lesse goodnes in his soule then he, no man could find better the places whence arguments might grow of goodnesse to another: though no man felt lesse pitie, no man could tel better how to stir pitie: no man more impudent to deny, where proofes were not manifest; no man more ready to confesse with a repenting manner of aggravating his owne evill, where denial would but make the fault fowler.

Now, he tooke this way, that, having gotten a pasport for one (that pretended he would put Plexirtus alive into his hands) to speak with the king his brother, he himselfe (though much against the minds of the valiant brothers, who rather wished to die in brave defence) with a rope about his neck, barefooted, came to offer himselfe to the discretion of Leonatus.

Where what submission he used, how cunningly in making greater the fault he made the faultines the lesse, how artificially he could set out the torments of his own conscience, with the burdensome comber he had found of his ambitious desires; how finely seeming to desire nothing but death, as ashamed to live, he begd life in the refusing it, I am not cunning inough to be able to expresse: but so fell out of it, that though, at first sight, Leonatus saw him with no other eie then as the murderer of his father; and anger already began to paint revenge in many colours, ere long he had not only gotten pitie, but pardon; and if not an excuse of the fault past, yet an opinion of a future amendment: while the poor villaines (chiefe ministers of his wickednes, now betraied by the author thereof) were delivered to many cruell sorts of death; he so handling it, that it rather seemed he had rather come into the defence of an unremediable mischiefe already committed, then that they had done it at first by his consent.

In such sort the princes left these reconciled brothers (Plexirtus in all his behavious carying him in far lower degree of service than the ever-noble nature of Leonatus would suffer him), and taking likewise their leaves of their good friend the King of Pontus (who returned to enjoy their benefite, both of his wife and kingdome), they privately went thence, having onelie with them the two valiant brothers, who would needs accompanie them through divers places; they foure dooing actes more daungerous, though lesse famous, because they were but privat chivalries: till hearing of the faire and vertuous Queen Erona of Lycia, besieged by the puissant King of Armenia, they bent themselves to her succour, both because the weaker (and weaker as being a ladie), and partly, because they heard the King of Armenia had in his company three of the most famous men living for matters of armes, that were knowe to be in the worlde.

Whereof one was the Prince Plangus (whose name was sweetened by your breath, peerlesse ladie, when the last daie it pleased you to mention him unto me), the other two were two great princes (though holding of him), Barzanes and Euardes, men of giant-like both hugenes and force: in which two especially the trust the King had of victory was reposed. And of them, those two brothers of Tydeus and Telenor (sufficient judges in warlike matters) spake so high commendations, that the two young princes had even a youthfull longing to have some triall of their vertue. And, therefore, as soone as they were entred into Lycia, they joyned themselves with them that faithfully served the poore Queene, at that time besieged: and, ere long, animated in such sort of their almost over-throwne harts, that they went by force to relieve the towne, though they were deprived of a great part of their strength by the parting of the two brothers, who were sent for in all hast to returne to their old friend and maister, Plexirtus: who (willingly hoodwinking themselves from seeing his faultes, and binding themselves to beleeve what he said) often abused the vertue of courage to defend his fowle vice of injustice. But now they were sent for to advaunce a conquest he was about; while Pyrocles and Musidorus pursued the deliverie of the Queene Erona.

"MERY TALES, WITTIE QUESTIONS AND QUICK ANSWERES" 16TH CENTURY

KING LEWIS AND THE HUSBANDMAN

WHAT time King Lewis of France the XI. of that name, because of the trouble that was in the realm kept himself in Burgoyne, he chanced, by occasion of hunting, to become acquainted with one Conon, a homely husbandman and a plain-meaning fellow, in which manner of men the high princes greatly delight them.

To this man's house the king oft resorted from hunting, and with great pleasure he would eat radish roots with him.

Within a while after, when Lewis was restored home and had the governance of France in his hand, this husbandman was counselled by his wife to take a goodly sort of radish roots and to go and give them to the king, and put him in mind of the good cheer that he had made him at his house. Conon would not assent thereto.

"What, foolish woman!" quoth he; "the great princes remember not such small pleasures."

But for all that she would not rest till Conon took out a great sight of the fairest roots and took his journey toward the Court. But as he went by the way he ate up all the radishes save one of the greatest.

Conon peaked into the Court, and stood where the king should pass by; by and by the king knew him and called him to him. Conon stepped to the king and presented his root with a glad cheer.

And the king took it more gladly, and bade one that was nearest to him to lay it up among those jewels that he loved best; and then commanded Conon to dine with him.

When dinner was done, he thanked Conon: and when the king saw that he would depart home, he commanded to give him a thousand crowns of gold for his radish root.

When this was known in the king's house, one of the Court gave the king a proper minion horse. The king perceiving that he did it because of the liberality showed unto Conon, with very glad cheer he took the gift, and counselled with his lords how and with what gift he might recompense the horse that was so goodly and fair.

This meanwhile the pickthank had a marvellous great hope, and, thought in his mind thus: If he so well recompensed the radish root that was given of a rustical man, how much more largely will he recompense such an horse, that is given of me that am of the Court?

When every man had said his mind as though the king had counselled about a great weighty matter, and that they had long fed the pickthank with vain hope, at last the king said:

"I remember now what we shall give him"; and so he called one of his lords, and bade him in his ear go fetch him that that he found in his chamber (and told him the place where) featly folded up in silk.

Anon he came and brought the radish root, and even as it was folded up the king gave it with his own hand to the courtier, saying:

"We suppose your horse is well recompensed with this jewel, for it hath cost us a thousand crowns."

The courtier went his way never so glad, and when he had unfolded it, he found none other treasure but the radish root almost withered.

ANONYMOUS

1570

THE WAKING MAN'S DREAM

In the time that Phillip Duke of Burgundy (who by the gentlenesse and curteousnesse of his carriage purchaste the name of good) guided the reines of the country of Flanders, this prince, who was of an humour pleasing, and full of judicious goodnesse, rather then silly simplicity, used pastimes which for their singularity are commonly called the pleasures of Princes: after this manner he no lesse shewed the quaintnesse of his wit then his prudence.

Being in Bruxelles with all his court, and having at his table discoursed amply enough of the vanities and greatnesse of this world, he let each one say his pleasure on this subject, whereon was alleadged grave sentences and rare examples: walking towards the evening in the towne, his head full of divers thoughts, he found a Tradesman lying in a corner sleeping very soundly, the fumes of Bacchus having surcharged his braine. I describe this man's drunkenesse in as good manner as I can to the credit of the party. This vice is so common in both the superior and inferiour Germany, that divers, making glory and vaunting of their dexterity in this art, encrease their praise thereby, and hold it for a brave act. The good Duke, to give his followers an example of the vanity of all the magnificence with which he was invironed, devised a meanes farre lesse dangerous than that which Dionysius the Tyrant used towards Democles, and which in pleasantnesse beares a marvellous utility. He caused his men to carry away this sleeper, with whom, as with a blocke, they might doe what they would, without awaking him; he caused them to carry him into one of the sumptuosest parts of his Pallace, into a chamber most state-like furnished, and makes them lay him on a rich bed. They presently strip him of his bad cloathes, and put him on a very fine and cleane shirt, instead of his own, which was foule and filthy. They let him sleepe in that place at his ease, and whilest he settles his drinke the Duke prepares the pleasantest pastime that can be imagined.

In the morning, this drunkard being awake drawes the curtaines of this brave rich bed, sees himselfe in a chamber adorned like a Paradice, he considers the rich furniture with an amazement such as you may imagine: he beleeves not his eyes, but layes his fingers on them, and feeling them open, yet perswades himselfe they are shut by sleep, and that all he sees is but a pure dreame.

As soone as he was knowne to be awake, in comes the officers of the Dukes house, who were instructed by the Duke what they should do. There were pages bravely apparelled, Gentlemen of the chamber, Gentleman waiters, and the High Chamberlaine, who, all in faire order and without laughing, bring cloathing for this new guest: they honour him with the same reverences as if he were a Soveraigne Prince; they serve him bare headed, and aske him what suite he will please to weare that day.

This fellow, affrighted at the first, beleeving these things to be inchantment or dreames, reclaimed by these submissions, tooke heart, and grew bold, and setting a good face on the matter, chused amongst all the apparell that they presented unto him that which he liked best, and which he thought to be fittest for him: he is accommodated like a King, and served with such ceremonies, as he had never seene before, and yet beheld them without saying anything, and with an assured countenance. This done, the greatest Nobleman in the Dukes Court enters the chamber with the same reverence and honour to him as if he had been their Soveraigne Prince (Phillip with Princely delight beholds this play from a private place); divers of purpose petitioning him for pardons, which he grants with such a continuance and gravity, as if he had had a Crowne on his head all his life time.

Being risen late, and dinner time approaching, they asked him if he were pleased to have his tables covered. He likes that very well. The table is furnished, where he is set alone, and under a rich Canopie; he eates with the same ceremony which was observed at the Dukes meales; he made good cheere, and chawed with all his teeth, but only drank with more moderation then he could have wisht, but the Majesty which he represented made him refraine. All taken away, he was entertained with new and pleasant things; they led him to walk about the great Chambers, Galleries, and Gardens of the Pallace (for all this merriment was played within the gates, they being shut only for recreation to the Duke and the principall of his Court): they shewed him all the richest and most pleasantest things therein, and talked to him thereof as if they had all beene his, which he heard with an attention and contentment beyond measure, not saying one word of his base condition, or declaring that they tooke him for another. They made him passe the afternoone in all kinds of sports; musicke, dancing, and a

Comedy, spent some part of the time. They talked to him of some State matters, whereunto he answered according to his skill, and like a right Twelftetide King.

Super time approaching, they aske this new created Prince if he would please to have the Lords and Ladies of his Court to sup and feast with him; whereat he seemed something unwilling, as if he would not abase his dignity unto such familiarity; neverthelesse, counterfeiting humanity and affability, he made signes that he condiscended thereunto: he then, towards night, was led with sound of Trumpets and Hoboyes into a faire hall, where long tables were set, which were presently covered with divers sorts of dainty meates, the Torches shined in every corner, and made a day in the midst of a night: the Gentlemen and Gentlewomen were set in fine order, and the Prince at the upper end in a higher seat. The service was magnificent; the musicke of voyces and instruments fed the eare, whilest mouthes found their food in the dishes. Never was the imaginary Duke at such a feast: carousses begin after the manner of the Country; the Prince is assaulted on all sides, as the Owle is assaulted by all the Birds, when he begins to soare. Not to seeme uncivill, he would doe the like to his good and faithfull subjects. They serve him with very strong wine, good Hipocras, which he swallowed downe in great draughts, and frequently redoubled; so that, charged with so many extraordinaryes, he yeelded to deaths cousin german, sleep, which closed his eyes, stopt his eares, and made him loose the use of his reason and all his other sences.

Then the right Duke, who had put himselfe among the throng of his Officers to have the pleasure of this mummery, commanded that this sleeping man should be stript out of his brave cloathes, and cloathed againe in his old ragges, and so sleeping carried and layd in the same place where he was taken up the night before. This was presently done and there did he snort all the night long, not taking any hurt either from the hardnesse of the stones or the night ayre, so well was his stomacke filled with good preservatives. Being awakened in the morning by some passenger, or it may bee by some that the good Duke Phillip had thereto appointed, "Ha!" said he, "my friends, what have you done? You have rob'd mee of a Kingdome, and have taken mee out of the sweetest and happiest dreame that ever man could have fallen into."

Then, very well remembring all the particulars of what had passed the day before, he related unto them, from point to point, all that had happened unto him, still thinking it assuredly to bee a dreame. Being returned home to his house, he entertaines his wife, neighbours, and friends, with this his dreame, as he thought: the truth whereof being at last published by the mouthes of those Courtiers who had been present at this pleasant recreation, the good man could not beleeve it, thinking that for sport they had framed this history upon his dreame ; but when Duke Phillip, who would have the full contentment of this pleasant tricke, had shewed him the bed wherein he lay, the cloathes which he had worne, the persons who had served him, the Hall wherein he had eaten, the gardens and galleries wherein he had walked, hardly could he be induced to beleeve what he saw, imagining that all this was meere inchantment and illusion.

The Duke used some liberality towards him for to helpe him in the poverty of his family ; and, taking an occasion thereon to make an Oration unto his Courtiers concerning the vanity of this worlds honours, he told them that all that ambitious persons seeke with so much industry is but smoake, and a meere dreame, and that they are strucken with that pleasant folly of the Athenian, who imagined that all the riches that arrived by shipping in the haven of Athens to be his, and that all the Marchants were but his factors: his friends getting him cured by a skilfull Physitian of the debility of his brain, in lieu of giving them thanks for this good office, he reviled them, saying that, whereas he was rich in conceit, they had by this cure made him poore and miserable in effect.

Harpaste, a foole that Senecaes wife kept, and whose pleasant imagination this grave Phylosopher doth largely relate, being growne blind, could not perswade herselfe that she was so, but continually complained that the house wherein she dwelt was dark, that they would not open the windowes, and that they hindred her from setting light, to make her beleeve she could see nothing: hereupon this great Stoick made this fine consideration, that every vitious man is like unto this foole, who, although he be blind in his passion, yet thinks not himself to be so, casting all his defect on false surmises, whereby he seeks not only to have his sinne worthy of excuse and pardon, but even of praise: the same say the covetous, ambitious, and voluptuous persons, in defence of their imperfections ; but in fine (as the Psalmist saith) all that must passe awaye, and the images thereof come to nothing, as the dreame of him that awaketh from sleepe.

If a bucket of water be as truly water, as all the sea, the difference only remaining in the quantity, not in the quality, why shall we not say, that our poore Brabander was a Soveraigne Prince for the space of fowre and twenty houres, being that he received all the honours and commodities thereof: how many Kings and Popes have not lasted longer, but have dyed on the very day of their Elections or Coronations ? As for those other pompes, which have lasted longer, what are they else but longer dreames ? This vanity of worldly things is a great sting to a well composed soule, to helpe it forward towards the heavenly kingdome.

ANONYMOUS
1620

THE TALE TOLD BY THE FISHWIFE OF STRAND-ON-THE-GREEN

In the troublesome raigne of King Henry the sixt, there dwelt in Waltam (not farre from London) a gentleman, which had to wife a creature most beautifull: so that in her time there were few found that matched her (none at all that excelled her), so excellent were the gifts that nature had bestowed on her. In body was she not onely so rare, and unparalleled, but also in her gifts of minde: so that this creature, it seemed, that Grace and Nature strove who should excell each other in their gifts toward her.

The gentleman her husband thought himselfe so happy in his choise, that he beleeved, in choosing her, he tooke hold of that blessing which heaven proffereth every man once in his life. Long did not this opinion hold for currant, for in his height of love he began so to hate her, that he sought her death: the cause I will tell you.

Having businesse one day to London, he took his leave very kindly of his wife, and accompanied with one man, he rode to London: being toward night, he tooke up his inne, and, to be briefe, he went to supper amongst other gentlemen. Amongst other talke at table, one tooke occasion to speake of women, and what excellent creatures they were, so long as they continued loyall to man. To whom answered one, saying:

"This is truth, Sir: so is the Divell so long as he doth no harme, which is neaver: his goodnes and women's loyaltie will come both in one yeere, but it is so farre off, that none in this age shall live to see it."

This gentleman loving his wife dearely (and knowing her to be free from this uncivill gentleman's generall taxation of women) in her behalfe, saide:

"Sir, you are too bitter against the sexe of women, and doe ill (for some one's sake that hath proved false to you) to taxe the generalitie of women-kinde with lightnesse ; and but I would not be counted uncivill amongst these gentlemen, I would give you the reply that approved untruth deserveth, you know my meaning, Sir : construe my words as you please : excuse me, gentlemen, if I be uncivill : I answere in the behalfe of one who is as free from disloyaltie as the sunne from darknes, or the fire from the cold."

" Pray, Sir," said the other, " since wee are opposite in opinions, let us rather talke like lawyers, that wee may be quickly friends again, then like souldiers which end their wordes with blowes. Perhaps this woman that you answer for is chaste, but yet against her will : for many women are honest 'cause they have not the means and opportunitie to bee dishonest (so is a thiefe true in prison 'cause he hath nothing to steale) : had I but opportunitie, and knew this same saint you so adore, I would pawne my life and whole estate, in a short while to bring you some manifest token of her disloyaltie. Sir, you are yong in the knowledge of women's slights, your want of experience makes you too credulous ; therefore be not abused."

This speech of his made the gentleman more out of patience then before, so that with much adoe he held himselfe from offering violence ; but his anger beeing a little over, he said :

"Sir, I doe verily beleeve that this vaine speech of yours proceedeth rather from a loose and ill manner'd minde, then of any experience you have had of women's loosenes : and since you thinke your selfe so cunning in that (divellish art) of corrupting women's chastitie, I will lay downe heere a hundred pounds, against which you shall lay fifty pounds, and before these gentlemen I promise you, if that within a month's space you bring me anie token of this gentlewoman's disloyaltie (for whose sake I have spoken in the behalfe of all women) I doe freely give you leave to enjoy the same ; conditionally you not performing it, I may enjoy your money. If that it be a match, speake, and I will acquaint you where she dwelleth : and besides, I vow, as I am a gentleman, not to give her notice of any such intent that is toward her."

" Sir," quoth the man, " your proffer is faire, and I accept the same " : so the money was delivered into the oast of the house his hands, and the sitters by were witnesses : so drinking together like friends, they went every man in his chamber.

The next day this man having knowledge of the place, rid thither, leaving the gentleman at the inne, who being assured of his wives chastitie, made no other account but to winne the wager, but it fell out otherwise : for the other vowed either by force, policie, or free will to get some jewell or other toy from her, which was enough to perswade the gentleman that he was a cuckold and win the wager he had laid. This villaine (for he deserved no better stile) lay at Waltam a whole day, before he came to the sight of her: at last he espyed her in the fields, to whom he went and kissed her (a thing no modest woman can deny): after his salutation, he said:

"Gentlewoman, I pray pardon me if I have beene too bold: I was intreated by your husband which is at London (I riding this way) to come and see you: by me he hath sent his commends to you, with a kinde intreat that you would not be discontented for his long absence, it being serious businesse that keepes him from your sight."

The gentlewoman very modestly bade him welcome, thanking him for his kindnes, withall telling him that her husband might command her patience as long as he pleased. Then intreated shee him to walke homeward, where shee gave him such entertainment as was fit for a gentleman, and her husband's friend.

In the time of his abiding at her house, he oft would have singled her in private talke, but she perceiving the same (knowing it to bee a thing not fitting a modest woman) would never come in his sight but at meales, and then were there so many at boord, that it was no time to talke of love-matters; therefore he saw he must accomplish his desire some other way, which he did in this maner:—

He having layne two nights at her house, and perceiving her to bee free from lustfull desires, the third night he fained himselfe to be something ill, and so went to bed timelier then he was wont. When he was alone in his chamber, he began to think with himselfe that it was now time to do that which he determined; for if he tarried any longer, they might have cause to think that he came for some ill intent, and waited opportunity to execute the same: therefore he resolved to doe something that night, that might winne him the wager, or utterly bring him in despaire of the same.

With this resolution he went to her chamber, which was but a paire of staires from his, and finding the doore open, he went in, placing himselfe under the bed: Long had he not lyne there, but in came the gentlewoman with her maiden; who having been at prayers with her household, was going to bed. She preparing herselfe to bedward, laid her head-tyre and those jewels she wore on a little table thereby: at length he perceived her to put off a littel crucifix of gold, which dayly she wore next to her heart, this jewell he thought fittest for his turne, and therefore observed where she did lay the same. At length the gentlewoman having untyred her selfe, went to bed: her maid then bolting of the doore, took the candle, and went to bed in a withdrawing roome onely separated with arras. This villaine lay still under the bed, listening if he could heare her draw her breath long: then thought he all sure, and like a cunning villaine rose without noise, going straight to the table, where, finding of the crucifix, he lightly went to the doore, which he cunningly unbolted; all this performed he with so little noise, that neither the mistris nor the maid heard him.

Having gotten into his chamber, he wished for day, that he might carry this jewell to her husband as signe of his wives disloyaltie; but seeing his wishes but in vaine, he laid him downe to sleepe: happy had she beene had his bed proved his grave.

In the morning, so soone as the folkes were stirring, he rose and went to the horse-keeper, praying him to helpe him to his horse, telling him that he had took his leave of his mistris the last night. Mounting his horse, away rid he to London, leaving the gentlewoman in bed; who, when she rose, attiring her selfe hastily ('cause some one tarried to speake with her) missed not her crucifix: so passed she the time away, as shee was wont other dayes to doe, no whit troubled in mind, though much sorrow was toward her; onely she seemed a little discontented that her ghest went away so unmannerly, she using him so kindely.

So leaving her, I will speake of him, who the next morning was betimes at London; and comming to the inne, he asked for the gentleman, who then was in bed, but he quickly rose and came downe to him, who seeing him return'd so suddenly he thought he came to have leave to release himselfe of his wager; but this chanced otherwise: for having saluted him, he said in this manner:

"Sir, did not I tell you that you were too yong in experience of woman's subtilties, and that no woman was longer good then she had cause, or time to doe ill? this you beleeved not, and thought it a thing so unlikely, that you gave me a hundred pounds for the knowledge of it. In brief know your wife is a woman, and therefore a wanton, a changeling: to confirme that I speake, see heere (shewing him the crucifix), know you this? if this be not sufficient proofe, I wil fetch you more."

At the sight of this, his blood left his face, running to comfort his faint heart, which was ready to breake at the sight of this crucifix, which he knew she alwayes wore next to her heart, and therefore he must (as he thought) goe something neere, which stole so private a jewell. But remembering himselfe, he cheeres his spirits, seeing that was sufficient proofe and he had wonne the wager, which he commanded should be given to him.

Thus was the poore gentleman abused, who went into his chamber, and beeing weary of this world (seeing where he had put onely his trust, he was deceived) he was minded to fall upon his sword, and so end all his miseries at once: but his better genius perswaded him contrary, and not so (by laying violent hands on himselfe) to leape into the Divel's mouth.

Thus being in many mindes, but resolving no one thing, at last he concluded to punish her with death, which had deceived his trust, and himselfe utterly to forsake his house and lands, and follow the fortunes of King Henry.

To this intent he called his man, to whom he said:

" George, thou knowest I have ever held thee deare, making more account of thee then thy other fellowes, and thou hast often told me that thou diddest owe thy life to me, which at any time thou wouldest bee ready to render up to doe me good."

" True, Sir (answered his man), I said no more then, then I will now at any time, whensoever you please, performe."

" I beleeve thee, George (replyed he): but there is no such need: I onely would have thee doe a thing for me, in which is no great danger, yet the profit which thou shalt have thereby shall amount to my wealth: for the love that thou bearest to me, and for thy own good, will thou do this ?"

" Sir (answered George), more for your love, then any reward, I will doe it (and yet money makes many men valiant); pray tell me what it is ?"

" George (said his master), this it is, thou must goe home, praying thy mistris to meete me halfe the way to London; but having her by the way, in some private place kill her: I meane as I speake; kill her, I say, this is my command, which thou hast promised to performe, which if thou performest not, I vow to kill thee the next time thou commest in my sight. Now for thy reward it shall be this: Take my ring, and when thou hast done my command, by vertue of it, doe thou assume my place till my returne, at which time thou shalt know what my reward is, till then govern my whole estate: and for thy mistris absence, and mine own, make what excuse thou please: so be gone."

" Well, Sir (said George), since it is your will, tho unwilling I am to doe it, yet I will performe it."

So went he his way towards Waltam, and his master presently rid to the court, where he abode with King Henry, who a little before was inlarged by the Earle of Warwicke, and placed in the throne againe.

George beeing come to Waltam, did his dutie to his mistris, who wondred to see him, and not her husband, for whom she demanded of George: he answered her, that he was at Enfield, and did request her to meet him there.

To which shee willingly agreed, and presently rode with him toward Enfield.

At length they being come into a by-way, George began to speake with her in this manner:

" Mistris, I pray you tel me what that wife deserves, who through some lewd behaviour of hers, hath made her husband to neglect his estate, and meanes of life, seeking by all meanes to dye, that he might be free from the shame which her wickednesse hath purchased him ?"

"Why, George (quoth shee), hath thou met with some such creature ? Be it whomsoever might I be her judge, I should thinke her worthy of death : how thinkest thou ?"

"Faith, mistris (said he), I thinke so too, and am so fully perswaded that her offence deserveth that punishment, that I purpose to bee executioner to such a one my selfe. Mistris, you are this woman : you have so offended my master (you know best how your selfe) that he hath left his house, vowing never to see the same till you be dead, and I am the man appointed by him to kill you ; therefore, those words which you meane to utter, speake them presently, for I cannot stay."

Poor gentlewoman, at the report of these unkinde words (ill-deserved at her hands) she looked as one dead, and uttering aboundance of teares, she at last spake these words :

"And can it bee, that my kindnes and loving obedience hath merited no other reward at his hands then death ? It cannot be ; I know thou onely tryest me, how patiently I would endure such an unjust command. I'le tell thee heere, thus with body prostrate on the earth, and hands lift up to heaven, I would pray for his preservation, those should be my worst words : for death's fearfull visage shewes pleasant to that soule that is innocent."

"Why, then, prepare your selfe (said George), for by heaven I doe not jest."

With that shee prayed him stay, saying :

"And is it so ? then, what should I desire to live, having lost his favour (and without offence) whom I so dearly loved, and in whose sight my happiness did consist ? come, let me die. Yet, George, let mee have so much favour at thy hands, as to commend me in these few words to him : Tell him my death I willingly embrace, for I have owed him my life (yet no otherwise but by a wives obedience) ever since I call'd him husband ; but that I am guilty of the least fault toward him, I utterly deny, and doe (at this houre of my death) desire that heaven would powre down vengeance upon me, if ever I offended him in thought. Intreat him that he would not speake ought that were ill on mee, when I am dead, for in good troth I have deserved none. Pray heaven blesse him. I am prepared now ; strike, prethee, home, and kill me and my griefes at once."

George, seeing this, could not withhold himselfe from shedding teares, and with pitie he let fall his sword, saying :

"Mistris, that I have used you so roughly, pray pardon me, for I was commanded so by my master, who hath vowed, if I let you live, to kill me. But I being perswaded that you are innocent, I will rather undergoe the danger of his wrath, then to staine my hands with the bloud of your cleere and spotlesse brest: Yet let mee intreat you (so much) that you would not come in his sight (lest in his rage he turne your butcher), but live in some disguise till time have opened the cause of his mistrust, and shewed you guiltlesse, which (I hope) will not be long."

To this she willingly granted (being loth to die causelesse), and thanked him for his kindnes: so parted they both, having teares in their eyes. George went home, where he shewed his master's ring for the government of the house till his master and mistris returne, which he said lived a while at London, 'cause the time was so troublesome, and that was a place where they were more secure then in the countrey. This his fellowes beleeved, and were obedient to his will, amongst whom he used himselfe so kindely, that he had all their loves.

This poore gentlewoman (mistris of the house) in short time got man's apparell for her disguise; so wandred she up and downe the countrey, for she could get no service, because the time was so dangerous that no man knew whom he might trust; onely she maintained her selfe with the price of those jewels which she had, all which she sold. At the last, being quite out of money, and having nothing left (which she could well spare) to make money of, she resolved rather to starve, then so much to debase herself to become a beggar: with this resolution she went to a solitary place beside Yorke, where shee lived the space of two dayes on hearbs, and such things as shee could there finde.

In this time it chanced that King Edward (beeing come out of France, and lying thereabout with the small forces hee had) came that way with some two or three noblemen, with an intent to discover if any ambushes were laid to him at an advantage. He seeing there this gentlewoman, whom he supposed to be a boy, asked her what she was, and what she made there in that private place? To whom shee very wisely and modestly withall answered, that she was a poore boy, whose bringing up had bin better then her outward parts then shewed, but at that time she was both friendlesse, and comfortlesse, by reason of the late warre.

He being moved to see one so well featur'd (as she was) to want, entertained her for one of his pages, to whom she shewed her selfe so dutifull and loving, that (in short time) shee had his love above all her fellows. Still followed she the fortunes of King Edward, hoping at last (as not long after it did fall out) to be reconciled to her husband.

After the battell at Barnet (where King Edward got the best), she going up and downe amongst the slaine men (to know whether her husband, which was on King Henries side, were dead or escaped) happened to see the other, who had been her ghest, lying there for dead: she remembring him, and thinking him to be one whom her husband loved, went to him, and finding him not dead, she caused one to helpe her with him to a house there-by: where opening of his brest to dresse his wounds, she espied her crucifix; at sight of which her heart was joyfull (hoping by this to find him that was the originall of her disgrace), for she remembring her selfe, found that she had lost that crucifix ever since that morning he departed from her house so suddenly.

But saying nothing of it at that time, she caused him to be carefully looked unto, and brought up to London after her, whither she went with the king, carrying the crucifix with her.

On a time when he was a little recovered, shee went to him, giving him the crucifix which shee had taken from about his neckc: to whom he said:

"Good, gentle youth, keep the same; for now in my misery of sicknes, when the sight of that picture should be most comfortable, it is to me most uncomfortable, and breedeth such horrour in my conscience (when I think how wrongfully I got the same), that so long as I see it, I shall never be in rest."

Now knew she that he was the man that caused the separation twixt her husband and her selfe; yet said shee nothing, using him as respectively as shee had before; only shee caused the man, in whose house he lay, to remember the words he had spoken concerning the crucifix.

Not long after, she being alone, attending on the king, beseeched his grace to doe her justice on a villain that had been the cause of all the misery she had suffered. He loving her (above all his other pages) most dearely, said:

"Edmund (for so had she named herself), thou shalt have what right thou wilt on thy enemy; cause him to be sent for, and I will be thy judge myself."

She being glad of this (with the king's authority) sent for her husband, whom she heard was one of the prisoners that was taken at the battell of Barnet, she appointing the other, now recovered, to be at the court at the same time.

They being both come (but not one seeing of the other), the king sent for the wounded man into the presence; before whom the page asked him how he came by the crucifix? He, fearing that his villany would come forth, denyed the words he had said before his oast, affirming he bought it. With that shee called in the oast of the house where he lay, bidding him boldly speake what he had heard this man say concerning the crucifix.

The oast then told the king, that in the presence of this page he heard him intreat that the crucifix might be taken from his sight, for it did wound his conscience to thinke how wrongfully he had gotten the same. These words did the page averre ; yet he utterly denyed the same, affirming that he bought it, and that if he did speake such words in his sicknesse, they proceeded from the lightnesse of his braine, and were untruthes.

Shee, seeing this villain's impudency, sent for her husband in, to whom she shewed the crucifix, saying :

" Sir, doe you know, doe you know this ? "

" Yes," answered hee, " but would God I ne're had knowne the owner of it ! It was my wives, a woman vertuous, till this divell (speaking to the other) did corrupt her purity, who brought me this crucifix as a token of her inconstancie."

With that the king said :

" Sirra, now you are found to be a knave ; did you not even now affirm that you bought it ? " To whom he answered (with fearful countenance) :

" And it like your grace, I said so, to preserve this gentleman's honour, and his wives, which by my telling of the truth would have been much indamag'd ; for indeed she being a secret friend of mine, gave me this, as a testimony of her love."

The gentlewoman, not being able longer to cover herself in that disguise, said :

" And it like your majesty, give mee leave to speake, and you shall see me make this villaine confesse, how he hath abused that good gentleman."

The king having given her leave, she said :

" First, sir, you confessed before your oast, and myself, that you had wrongfully got this jewell ; then, before his majestie you affirmed you bought it, so denying your former words ; now you have denyed that which you so boldly affirmed before, and have said it was this gentleman's wives gift. (With his majesties leave) I say thou art a villaine, and this is likewise false : (with that she discovered herself to be a woman, saying), Hadst thou (villaine) ever any strumpet's favour at my hands ? Did I (for any sinfull pleasure I received from thee) bestow this on thee ? Speake, and if thou have any goodnes left in thee, speake the truth."

With that, he, being daunted at her sudden sight, fell on his knees before the king, beseeching his grace to be mercifull unto him, for he had wronged that gentlewoman : therewith told he the king of the match betweene the gentleman and himselfe, and how he stole the crucifix from her, and by that meanes perswaded her husband that she was a wanton.

The king wondred how he durst (knowing God to bee just) commit so great villany, but more admired he to see his page to turn a gentlewoman : but ceasing to admire, he said :

" Sir (speaking to her husband), you did the part of an unwise man to lay so foolish a wager, for which offence the remembrance of your folly is punishment inough ; but seeing it concernes me not, your wife shall be your judge."

With that mistris Dorrill (thanking his majestie) went to her husband, saying :

" All my anger to you I lay downe with this kisse."

He, wondring all this while to see this strange and unlooked-for change, wept for joy, desiring her to tell him how shee was preserved, wherein shee satisfied him at full.

The king was likewise glad that he had preserved this gentlewoman from wilfull famine, and gave judgment on the other in this manner : That he should restore the money treble which he had wrongfully got from him ; and so was to have a yeeres imprisonment.

So this gentleman and his wife went (with the king's leave) lovingly home, where they were kindly welcomed by George, to whom for recompense he gave the money which he received. So lived they ever after in great content.

DANIEL DEFOE
1659–1731

THE APPARITION OF MRS. VEAL

THIS thing is so rare in all its circumstances, and on so good authority, that my reading and conversation has not given me anything like it. It is fit to gratify the most ingenious and serious inquirer.

Mrs. Bargrave is the person to whom Mrs. Veal appeared after her death; she is my intimate friend, and I can avouch for her reputation for these last fifteen or sixteen years, on my own knowledge; and I can confirm the good character she had from her youth to the time of my acquaintance; though since this relation she is calumniated by some people that are friends to the brother of Mrs. Veal who appeared, who think the relation of this appearance to be a reflection, and endeavour what they can to blast Mrs. Bargrave's reputation and to laugh the story out of countenance. But by the circumstances thereof, and the cheerful disposition of Mrs. Bargrave, notwithstanding the unheard-of ill-usage of a very wicked husband, there is not the least sign of dejection in her face; nor did I ever hear her let fall a desponding or murmuring expression; nay, not when actually under her husband's barbarity, which I have been witness to, and several other persons of undoubted reputation.

Now you must know Mrs. Veal was a maiden gentlewoman of about thirty years of age, and for some years last past had been troubled with fits, which were perceived coming on her by her going off from her discourse very abruptly to some impertinence. She was maintained by an only brother, and kept his house in Dover. She was a very pious woman, and her brother a very sober man, to all appearance; but now he does all he can to null or quash the story. Mrs. Veal was intimately acquainted with Mrs. Bargrave from her childhood. Mrs. Veal's circumstances were then mean; her father did not take care of his children as he ought, so that they were exposed to hardships; and Mrs. Bargrave in those days had as unkind a father, though she wanted neither for food nor clothing, while Mrs. Veal wanted for both; so that it was in the power of Mrs. Bargrave to be very much her friend in several instances, which mightily endeared Mrs. Veal; insomuch that she would often say: "Mrs. Bargrave, you are not only the best, but the only friend I have in the world; and no circumstance in life shall ever dissolve my friendship." They would often condole each other's adverse fortune, and read together Drelincourt upon Death, and other good books; and so, like two Christian friends, they comforted each other under their sorrow.

Some time after, Mr. Veal's friends got him a place in the Custom House at Dover, which occasioned Mrs. Veal, by little and little, to fall off from her intimacy with Mrs. Bargrave, though there was never any such thing as a quarrel; but an indifferency came on by degrees, till at last Mrs. Bargrave had not seen her in two years and a half; though above a twelvemonth of the time Mrs. Bargrave had been absent from Dover, and this last half-year had been in Canterbury about two months of the time, dwelling in a house of her own.

In this house, on the 8th of September last, viz. 1705, she was sitting alone, in the forenoon, thinking over her unfortunate life, and arguing herself into a due resignation to Providence, though her condition seemed hard. "And," said she, "I have been provided for hitherto, and doubt not but I shall be still; and am well satisfied that my afflictions shall end when it is most fit for me"; and then took up her sewing-work, which she had no sooner done but she hears a knocking at the door. She went to see who it was there, and this proved to be Mrs. Veal, her old friend, who was in a riding-habit: at that moment of time the clock struck twelve at noon.

"Madam," says Mrs. Bargrave, "I am surprised to see you, you have been so long a stranger"; but told her she was glad to see her, and offered to salute her, which Mrs. Veal complied with, till their lips almost touched; and then Mrs. Veal drew her hand across her own eyes and said: "I am not very well," and so waived it. She told Mrs Bargrave she was going a journey, and had a great mind to see her first.

"But," says Mrs. Bargrave, "how came you to take a journey alone? I am amazed at it, because you have so fond a brother."

"Oh," says Mrs. Veal, "I gave my brother the slip, and came away, because I had so great a desire to see you before I took my journey." So Mrs. Bargrave went in with her into another room within the first, and Mrs. Veal set her down in an elbow-chair, in which Mrs. Bargrave was sitting when she heard Mrs. Veal knock. Then says Mrs. Veal:

"My dear friend, I am come to renew our old friendship again, and beg your pardon for my breach of it; and if you can forgive me, you are one of the best of women."

"Oh," says Mrs. Bargrave, "don't mention such a ting; I have not had an uneasy thought about it; I can easily forgive it."

"What did you think of me?" said Mrs. Veal.

Says Mrs. Bargrave: "I thought you were like the rest of the world, and that prosperity had made you forget yourself and me."

Then Mrs. Veal reminded Mrs. Bargrave of the many friendly offices she did her in former days, and much of the conversation they had with each other in the time of their adversity; what books they read, and what comfort in particular they received from Drelincourt's *Book of Death*, which was the best, she said, on that subject ever wrote. She also mentioned Dr. Sherlock, and two Dutch books which were translated, wrote upon death, and several others; but Drelincourt, she said, had the clearest notions of death and of the future state of any who handled that subject.

Then she asked Mrs. Bargrave whether she had Drelincourt. She said: "Yes." Says Mrs. Veal: "Fetch it." And so Mrs. Bargrave goes upstairs and brings it down. Says Mrs. Veal:

"Dear Mrs. Bargrave, if the eyes of our faith were as open as the eyes of our body, we should see numbers of angels about us for our guard. The notions we have of heaven now are nothing like what it is, as Drelincourt says. Therefore be comforted under your afflictions, and believe that the Almighty has a particular regard to you, and that your afflictions are marks of God's favour; and when they have done the business they are sent for, they shall be removed from you. And believe me, my dear friend, believe what I say to you, one minute of future happiness will infinitely reward you for all your sufferings; for I can never believe [and claps her hand upon her knee with great earnestness, which indeed ran through most of her discourse] that ever God will suffer you to spend all your days in this afflicted state; but be assured that your afflictions shall leave you, or you them in a short time." She spake in that pathetical and heavenly manner, that Mrs. Bargrave wept several times, she was so deeply affected with it.

Then Mrs. Veal mentioned Dr. Horneck's *Ascetick*, at the end of which he gives an account of the lives of the primitive Christians. Their pattern she recommended to our imitation, and said their conversation was not like this of our age; "for now," says she, "there is nothing but frothy, vain discourse, which is far different from theirs. Theirs was to edification, and to build one another up in faith; so that they were not as we are, nor are we as they were; but," said she, "we might do as they did. There was a hearty friendship among them; but where is it now to be found?"

Says Mrs. Bargrave: "'Tis hard indeed to find a true friend in these days."

Says Mrs. Veal: " Mr. Norris has a fine copy of verses, called *Friendship in Perfection,* which I wonderfully admire. Have you seen the book ? " says Mrs. Veal.

" No," says Mrs. Bargrave, " but I have the verses of my own writing out."

" Have you ? " says Mrs. Veal ; " fetch them then." Which she did from above-stairs, and offered them to Mrs. Veal to read, who refused, and waived the thing, saying, holding down her head would make it ache ; and then desired Mrs. Bargrave to read them to her, which she did.

As they were admiring *Friendship* Mrs. Veal said: " Dear Mrs. Bargrave I shall love you forever." In the verses there is twice used the word Elysian. " Ah ! " says Mrs. Veal, " these poets have such names for heaven ! " She would often draw her hand across her own eyes and say: " Mrs. Bargrave, don't you think I am mightily impaired by my fits ? "

" No," says Mrs. Bargrave, " I think you look as well as ever I knew you."

After all this discourse, which the apparition put in words much finer than Mrs. Bargrave said she could pretend to, and was much more than she can remember (for it cannot be thought that an hour and three-quarters' conversation could all be retained, though the main of it she thinks she does), she said to Mrs. Bargrave she would have her write a letter to her brother, and tell him she would have him give rings to such and such, and that there was a purse of gold in her cabinet, and that she would have two broad pieces given to her cousin Watson.

Talking at this rate, Mrs. Bargrave thought that a fit was coming upon her, and so placed herself in a chair just before her knees, to keep her from falling to the ground, if her fit should occasion it (for the elbow-chair, she thought, would keep her from falling on either side) ; and to divert Mrs. Veal, as she thought, she took hold of her gown-sleeve several times and commended it. Mrs. Veal told her it was a scoured silk, and newly made up. But for all this, Mrs. Veal persisted in her request, and told Mrs. Bargrave she must not deny her ; and she would have her tell her brother all their conversation when she had an opportunity.

" Dear Mrs. Veal," said Mrs. Bargrave, " this seems so impertinent that I cannot tell how to comply with it ; and what a mortifying story will our conversation be to a young gentleman ! "

" Well," says Mrs. Veal, " I must not be denied."

" Why," says Mrs. Bargrave, " 'tis much better, methinks, to do it yourself."

" No," says Mrs. Veal, " though it seems impertinent to you now, you will see more reason for it hereafter."

Mrs. Bargrave then, to satisfy her importunity, was going to fetch a pen and ink; but Mrs. Veal said: "Let it alone now, and do it when I am gone; but you must be sure to do it"; which was one of the last things she enjoined her at parting; and so she promised her.

Then Mrs. Veal asked for Mrs. Bargrave's daughter. She said she was not at home: "but if you have a mind to see her," says Mrs. Bargrave, "I'll send for her."

"Do," says Mrs. Veal. On which she left her, and went to a neighbour's to send for her; and by the time Mrs. Bargrave was returning, Mrs. Veal was got without the door in the street, in the face of the beast-market, on a Saturday (which is market-day), and stood ready to part as soon as Mrs. Bargrave came to her.

She asked her why she was in such haste. She said she must be going, though perhaps she might not go her journey until Monday; and told Mrs. Bargrave she hoped she should see her again at her cousin Watson's before she went whither she was a-going. Then she said she would take her leave of her, and walked from Mrs. Bargrave in her view, till a turning interrupted the sight of her, which was three-quarters after one in the afternoon.

Mrs. Veal died the 7th of September, at twelve o'clock at noon, of her fits, and had not above four hours' senses before death, in which time she received the sacrament.

The next day after Mrs. Veal's appearance, being Sunday, Mrs. Bargrave was mightily indisposed with a cold and a sore throat, that she could not go out that day; but on Monday morning she sends a person to Captain Watson's to know if Mrs. Veal were there. They wondered at Mrs. Bargrave's inquiry, and sent her word that she was not there, nor was expected.

At this answer, Mrs. Bargrave told the maid she had certainly mistook the name, or made some blunder. And though she was ill, she put on her hood, and went herself to Captain Watson's, though she knew none of the family, to see if Mrs. Veal was there or not. They said they wondered at her asking, for that she had not been in town; they were sure, if she had, she would have been there. Says Mrs. Bargrave: "I am sure she was with me on Saturday almost two hours." They said it was impossible; for they must have seen her, if she had.

In comes Captain Watson while they are in dispute, and said that Mrs. Veal was certainly dead, and her escutcheons were making. This strangely surprised Mrs. Bargrave, who went to the person immediately who had the care of them, and found it true.

Then she related the whole story to Captain Watson's family, and what gown she had on, and how striped, and that Mrs. Veal told her it was scoured. Then Mrs. Watson cried out: "You have seen her indeed, for none knew but Mrs. Veal and myself that the gown was scoured." And Mrs. Watson owned that she described the gown exactly; "for," said she, "I helped her to make it up." This Mrs. Watson blazed all about the town, and avouched the demonstration of the truth of Mrs. Bargrave's seeing Mrs. Veal's apparition; and Captain Watson carried two gentlemen immediately to Mrs. Bargrave's house to hear the relation from her own mouth.

And then it spread so fast that gentlemen and persons of quality, the judicious and sceptical part of the world, flocked in upon her, which at last became such a task that she was forced to go out of the way; for they were in general extremely satisfied of the truth of the thing, and plainly saw that Mrs. Bargrave was no hypochondriac, for she always appears with such a cheerful air and pleasing mien, that she has gained the favour and esteem of all the gentry, and 'tis thought a great favour if they can but get the relation from her own mouth.

I should have told you before that Mrs. Veal told Mrs. Bargrave that her sister and brother-in-law were just come down from London to see her.

Says Mrs. Bargrave: "How came you to order matters so strangely?"

"It could not be helped," says Mrs. Veal. And her sister and brother did come to see her, and entered the town of Dover just as Mrs. Veal was expiring.

Mrs. Bargrave asked her whether she would drink some tea. Says Mrs. Veal: "I do not care if I do; but I'll warrant this mad fellow [meaning Mrs. Bargrave's husband] has broke all your trinkets."

"But," says Mrs. Bargrave, "I'll get something to drink in for all that." But Mr. Veal waived it, and said: "It is no matter; let it alone"; and so it passed.

All the time I sat with Mrs. Bargrave, which was some hours, she recollected fresh sayings of Mrs. Veal. And one material thing more she told Mrs. Bargrave—that old Mr. Breton allowed Mrs. Veal ten pounds a year, which was a secret, and unknown to Mrs. Bargrave till Mrs. Veal told it her.

Mrs. Bargrave never varies in her story, which puzzles those who doubt the truth, or are unwilling to believe it. A servant in a neighbour's yard adjoining to Mrs. Bargrave's house heard her talking to somebody an hour of the time Mrs. Veal was with her.

Mrs. Bargrave went out to her next neighbour's the very moment she parted with Mrs. Veal, and told what ravishing conversation she had with an old friend, and told the whole of it. Drelincourt's *Book of Death* is, since this happened, bought up strangely. And it is to be observed that, notwithstanding all this trouble and fatigue Mrs. Bargrave has undergone upon this account, she never took the value of a farthing, nor suffered her daughter to take anything of anybody, and therefore can have no interest in telling the story.

But Mr. Veal does what he can to stifle the matter, and said he would see Mrs. Bargrave ; but yet it is certain matter of fact that he has been at Captain Watson's since the death of his sister, and yet never went near Mrs. Bargrave ; and some of her friends report her to be a great liar, and that she knew of Mr. Breton's ten pounds a year. But the person who pretends to say so has the reputation of a notorious liar among persons whom I know to be of undoubted repute.

Now, Mr. Veal is more a gentleman than to say she lies, but says a bad husband has crazed her ; but she needs only to present herself, and it will effectually confute that pretence. Mr. Veal says he asked his sister on her deathbed whether she had a mind to dispose of anything, and she said : "No." Now, the things which Mrs. Veal's apparition would have disposed of were so trifling, and nothing of justice aimed at in their disposal, that the design of it appears to me to be only in order to make Mrs. Bargrave so to demonstrate the truth of her appearance, as to satisfy the world of the reality thereof as to what she had seen and heard, and to secure her reputation among the reasonable and understanding part of mankind.

And then again, Mr. Veal owns that there was a purse of gold ; but it was not found in her cabinet, but in a comb-box. This looks improbable ; for that Mrs. Watson owned that Mrs. Veal was so very careful of the key of her cabinet, that she would trust nobody with it ; and if so, no doubt she would not trust her gold out of it. And Mrs. Veal's often drawing her hand over her eyes, and asking Mrs. Bargrave whether her fits had not impaired her, looks to me as if she did it on purpose to remind Mrs. Bargrave of her fits, to prepare her not to think it strange that she should put her upon writing to her brother to dispose of rings and gold, which looked so much like a dying person's request ; and it took accordingly with Mrs. Bargrave, as the effects of her fits coming upon her ; and was one of the many instances of her wonderful love to her, and care of her, that she should not be affrighted ; which indeed appears in her whole management, particularly in her coming to her in the day-time, waiving the salutation, and when she was alone ; and then the manner of her parting, to prevent a second attempt to salute her.

Now, why Mr. Veal should think this relation a reflection (as 'tis plain he does by his endeavouring to stifle it) I can't imagine, because the generality believe her to be a good spirit, her discourse was so heavenly. Her two great errands were to comfort Mrs. Bargrave in her affliction, and to ask her forgiveness for her breach of friendship, and with a pious discourse to encourage her. So that, after all, to suppose that Mrs. Bargrave could hatch such an invention as this from Friday noon till Saturday noon (supposing that she knew of Mrs. Veal's death the very first moment), without jumbling circumstances, and without any interest too, she must be more witty, fortunate, and wicked too, than any indifferent person, I dare say, will allow.

I asked Mrs. Bargrave several times if she was sure she felt the gown. She answered modestly: "If my senses be to be relied on, I am sure of it." I asked her if she heard a sound when she clapped her hand upon her knee. She said she did not remember she did; and she said: "She appeared to be as much a substance as I did, who talked with her; and I may," said she, "be as soon persuaded that your apparition is talking to me now as that I did not really see her; for I was under no manner of fear; I received her as a friend, and parted with her as such. I would not," says she, "give one farthing to make any one believe it; I have no interest in it. Nothing but trouble is entailed upon me for a long time, for aught I know; and had it not come to light by accident, it would never have been made public."

But now she says she will make her own private use of it, and keep herself out of the way as much as she can; and so she has done since. She says she had a gentleman who came thirty miles to her to hear the relation, and that she had told it to a room full of people at a time. Several particular gentlemen have had the story from Mrs. Bargrave's own mouth.

This thing has very much affected me, and I am as well satisfied as I am of the best grounded matter of fact. And why we should dispute matter of fact because we cannot solve things of which we have no certain or demonstrative notions, seems strange to me. Mrs. Bargrave's authority and sincerity alone would have been undoubted in any other case.

DANIEL DEFOE

THE GHOST OF DOROTHY DINGLEY

In the beginning of this year, a disease happened in this town of Launceston, and some of my scholars died of it. Among others who fell under the malignity then triumphing, was John Elliot, the eldest son of Edward Elliot of Treherse, Esq., a stripling of about sixteen years of age, but of more than common parts and ingenuity. At his own particular request, I preached at the funeral, which happened on the 20th day of June 1665. In my discourse (*ut mos reique locique postulabat*), I spoke some words in commendation of the young gentleman; such as might endear his memory to those that knew him, and, withal, tended to preserve his example to the fry which went to school with him, and were to continue there after him. An ancient gentleman, who was then in the church, was much affected with the discourse, and was often heard to repeat, the same evening, an expression I then used out of Virgil:—

Et puer ipse fuit cantari dignus.

The reason why this grave gentleman was so concerned at the character, was a reflection he made upon a son of his own, who being about the same age, and, but a few months before, not unworthy of the like character I gave of the young Mr. Elliot, was now, by a strange accident, quite lost as to his parent's hopes and all expectation of any further comfort by him.

The funeral rites being over, I was no sooner come out of the church, but I found myself most courteously accosted by this old gentleman; and with an unusual importunity almost forced against my humour to see his house that night; nor could I have rescued myself from his kindness, had not Mr. Elliot interposed and pleaded title to me for the whole of the day, which, as he said, he would resign to no man.

Hereupon I got loose for that time, but was constrained to leave a promise behind me to wait upon him at his own house the Monday following. This then seemed to satisfy, but before Monday came I had a new message to request me that, if it were possible, I would be there on the Sunday. The second attempt I resisted, by answering that it was against my convenience, and the duty which mine own people expected from me.

Yet was not the gentleman at rest, for he sent me another letter on the Sunday, by no means to fail on the Monday, and so to order my business as to spend with him two or three days at least. I was indeed startled at so much eagerness, and so many dunnings for a visit, without any business; and began to suspect that there must needs be some design in the bottom of all this excess of courtesy. For I had no familiarity, scarce common acquaintance with the gentleman or his family; nor could I imagine whence should arise such a flush of friendship on the sudden.

On the Monday I went, and paid my promised devoir, and met with entertainment as free and plentiful as the invitation was importunate. There also I found a neighbouring minister who pretended to call in accidentally, but by the sequel I suppose it otherwise. After dinner this brother of the coat undertook to show me the gardens, where, as we were walking, he gave me the first discovery of what was mainly intended in all this treat and compliment.

First he began to tell the infortunity of the family in general, and then gave an instance in the youngest son. He related what a hopeful, sprightly lad he lately was, and how melancholic and sottish he was now grown. Then did he with much passion lament, that his ill-humour should so incredibly subdue his reason; for, says he, the poor boy believes himself to be haunted with ghosts, and is confident that he meets with an evil spirit in a certain field about half a mile from this place, as often as he goes that way to school.

In the midst of our twaddle, the old gentleman and his lady (as observing their cue exactly) came up to us. Upon their approach, and pointing me to the arbour, the parson renews the relation to me; and they (the parents of the youth) confirmed what he said, and added many minute circumstances, in a long narrative of the whole. In fine, they all three desired my thoughts and advice in the affair.

I was not able to collect thoughts enough on the sudden to frame a judgment upon what they had said, only I answered, that the thing which the youth reported to them was strange, yet not incredible, and that I knew not then what to think or say of it; but if the lad would be free to me in talk, and trust me with his counsels, I had hopes to give them a better account of my opinion the next day.

I had no sooner spoken so much, but I perceived myself in the springe their courtship had laid for me; for the old lady was not able to hide her impatience, but her son must be called immediately.

This I was forced to comply with and consent to, so that drawing off from the company to an orchard near by, she went herself and brought him to me, and left him with me.

It was the main drift of all these three to persuade me that either the boy was lazy, and glad of any excuse to keep from the school, or that he was in love with some wench and ashamed to confess it ; or that he had a fetch upon his father to get money and new clothes, that he might range to London after a brother he had there ; and therefore they begged of me to discover the root of the matter, and accordingly to dissuade, advise, or reprove him, but chiefly, by all means, to undeceive him as to the fancy of ghosts and spirits.

I soon entered into a close conference with the youth, and at first was very cautious not to displease him, but by smooth words to ingratitate myself and get within him, for I doubted he would be too distrustful or too reserved. But we had scarcely passed the first situation, and begun to speak to the business, before I found that there needed no policy to screw myself into his breast ; for he most openly and with all obliging candour did aver, that he loved his book, and desired nothing more than to be bred a scholar ; that he had not the least respect for any of womankind, as his mother gave out ; and that the only request he would make to his parents was, that they would but believe his constant assertions concerning the woman he was disturbed with, in the field called the Higher-Broom Quartils. He told me with all naked freedom, and a flood of tears, that his friends were unkind and unjust to him, neither to believe nor pity him ; and that if any man (making a bow to me) would but go with him to the place, he might be convinced that the thing was real, etc.

By this time he found me apt to compassionate his condition, and to be attentive to his relation of it, and therefore he went on in this way :—

" This woman which appears to me," saith he, " lived a neighbour here to my father, and died about eight years since ; her name, Dorothy Dingley, of such a stature, such age, and such complexion. She never speaks to me, but passeth by hastily, and always leaves the footpath to me, and she commonly meets me twice or three times in the breadth of the field.

" It was about two months before I took any notice of it, and though the shape of the face was in my memory, yet I did not recall the name of the person, but without more thoughtfulness, I did suppose it was some woman who lived thereabout, and had frequent occasion that way. Nor did I imagine anything to the contrary before she began to meet me constantly, morning and evening, and always in the same field, and sometimes twice or thrice in the breadth of it.

"The first time I took notice of her was about a year since, and when I first began to suspect and believe it to be a ghost, I had courage enough not to be afraid, but kept it to myself a good while, and only wondered very much about it. I did often speak to it, but never had a word in answer. Then I changed my way, and went to school the Under Horse Road, and then she always met me in the narrow lane, between the Quarry Park and the Nursery, which was worse.

"At length I began to be terrified at it, and prayed continually that God would either free me from it or let me know the meaning of it. Night and day, sleeping and waking, the shape was ever running in my mind, and I often did repeat these places of Scripture (with that he takes a small Bible out of his pocket), Job vii. 14: 'Thou scarest me with dreams, and terrifiest me through visions.' And Deuteronomy xxviii. 67: 'In the morning, thou shalt say, Would God it were even; and at even thou shalt say, Would God it were morning; for the fear of thine heart, wherewith thou shalt fear, and for the sight of thine eyes, which thou shalt see.'"

I was very much pleased with the lad's ingenuity in the application of these pertinent Scriptures to his condition, and desired him to proceed.

"When," says he, "by degrees, I grew very pensive, inasmuch that it was taken notice of by all our family; whereupon, being urged to it, I told my brother William of it, and he privately acquainted my father and mother, and they kept it to themselves for some time.

"The success of this discovery was only this; they did sometimes laugh at me, sometimes chide me, but still commanded me to keep to my school, and put such fopperies out of my head. I did accordingly go to school often, but always met the woman in the way."

This, and much more to the same purpose, yea, as much as held a dialogue of near two hours, was our conference in the orchard, which ended with my proffer to him, that, without making any privy to our intents, I would next morning walk with him to the place, about six o'clock. He was even transported with joy at the mention of it, and replied, "But will you, sure, sir? Will you, sure, sir? Thank God! Now I hope I shall be relieved."

From this conclusion we retired into the house.

The gentleman, his wife, and Mr. Sam were impatient to know the event, insomuch that they came out of the parlour into the hall to meet us; and seeing the lad look cheerfully, the first compliment from the old man was, "Come, Mr. Ruddle, you have talked with him; I hope now he will have more wit. An idle boy! an idle boy!"

At these words, the lad ran up the stairs to his own chamber, without replying, and I soon stopped the curiosity of the three expectants by telling them I had promised silence, and was resolved to be as good as my word ; but when things were riper they might know all. At present, I desired them to rest in my faithful promise, that I would do my utmost in their service, and for the good of their son. With this they were silenced ; I cannot say satisfied.

The next morning before five o'clock, the lad was in my chamber, and very brisk. I arose and went with him. The field he led me to I guessed to be twenty acres, in an open country, and about three furlongs from any house. We went into the field, and had not gone about a third part, before the spectrum, in the shape of a woman, with all the circumstances he had described her to me in the orchard the day before (as much as the suddenness of its appearance and evanition would permit me to discover), met us and passed by. I was a little surprised at it, and though I had taken up a firm resolution to speak to it, yet I had not the power, nor indeed durst I look back ; yet I took care not to show any fear to my pupil and guide, and therefore only telling him that I was satisfied in the truth of his complaint, we walked to the end of the field and returned, nor did the ghost meet us that time above once. I perceived in the young man a kind of boldness, mixed with astonishment : the first caused by my presence, and the proof he had given of his own relation, and the other by the sight of his persecutor.

In short, we went home : I somewhat puzzled, he much animated. At our return, the gentlewoman, whose inquisitiveness had missed us, watched to speak with me. I gave her a convenience, and told her that my opinion was that her son's complaint was not to be slighted, nor altogether discredited ; yet, that my judgment in his case was not settled. I gave her caution, moreover, that the thing might not take wind, lest the whole country should ring with what we had yet no assurance of.

In this juncture of time I had business which would admit no delay ; wherefore I went for Launceston that evening, but promised to see them again next week. Yet I was prevented by an occasion which pleaded a sufficient excuse, for my wife was that week brought home from a neighbour's house very ill. However, my mind was upon the adventure. I studied the case, and about three weeks after went again, resolving, by the help of God, to see the utmost.

The next morning, being the 27th day of July 1665, I went to the haunted field by myself, and walked the breadth of the field without any encounter. I returned and took the other walk, and then the spectrum appeared to me, much about the same place where I saw it before, when the young gentleman was with me. In my thoughts, it moved swifter than the time before, and about ten feet distance from me on my right hand, insomuch that I had not time to speak, as I had determined with myself beforehand.

The evening of this day, the parents, the son, and myself being in the chamber where I lay, I propounded to them our going all together to the place next morning, and after some asseveration that there was no danger in it, we all resolved upon it. The morning being come, lest we should alarm the family of servants, they went under the pretence of seeing a field of wheat, and I took my horse and fetched a compass another way, and so met at the stile we had appointed.

Thence we all four walked leisurely into the Quartils, and had passed above half the field before the ghost made appearance. It then came over the stile just before us, and moved with that swiftness that by the time we had gone six or seven steps it passed by. I immediately turned head and ran after it, with the young man by my side; we saw it pass over the stile by which we entered, but no farther. I stepped upon the hedge at one place, he at another, but could discern nothing; whereas, I dare aver, that the swiftest horse in England could not have conveyed himself out of sight in that short space of time. Two things I observed in this day's appearance. 1. That a spaniel dog, who followed the company unregarded, did bark and run away as the spectrum passed by; whence it is easy to conclude that it was not our fear or fancy which made the apparition. 2. That the motion of the spectrum was not gradation, or by steps, and moving of the feet, but a kind of gliding, as children upon the ice, or a boat down a swift river, which punctually answers the description the ancients gave of their *Lemures*, which was Κατὰ ῥύμτω ἀέριον καὶ ὁρμὴν ἄπζαποδισον (Heliodorus).

But to proceed. This ocular evidence clearly convinced, but, withal, strangely frightened the old gentleman and his wife, who knew this Dorothy Dingley in her lifetime, were at her burial, and now plainly saw her features in this present apparition. I encouraged them as well as I could, but after this they went no more. However, I was resolved to proceed, and use such lawful means as God hath discovered, and learned men have successfully practised in these irregular cases.

The next morning being Thursday, I went out very early by myself, and walked for about an hour's space in meditation and prayer in the field next adjoining to the Quartils. Soon after five I stepped over the stile into the disturbed field, and had not gone above thirty or forty paces before the ghost appeared at the farther stile. I spoke to it with a loud voice, in some such sentences as the way of these dealings directed me, whereupon it approached, but slowly, and when I came near, it moved not. I spake again, and it answered, in a voice neither very audible nor intelligible. I was not in the least terrified, and therefore persisted until it spake again, and gave me satisfaction. But the work could not be finished at this time; wherefore the same evening, an hour after sunset, it met me again near the same place, and after a few words on each side, it quietly vanished, and neither doth appear since, nor ever will more to any man's disturbance. The discourse in the morning lasted about a quarter of an hour.

These things are true, and I know them to be so, with as much certainty as eyes and ears can give me; and until I can be persuaded that my senses do deceive me about their proper object, and by that persuasion deprive myself of the strongest inducement to believe the Christian religion, I must and will assert that these things in this paper are true.

As for the manner of my proceeding, I find no reason to be ashamed of it, for I can justify it to men of good principles, discretion, and recondite learning, though in this case I choose to content myself in the assurance of the thing, rather than be at the unprofitable trouble to persuade others to believe it; for I know full well with what difficulty relations of so uncommon a nature and practice obtain relief. He that tells such a story may expect to be dealt withal as a traveller in Poland by the robbers, viz., first murdered and then searched,—first condemned for a liar, or superstitious, and then, when it is too late, have his reasons and proofs examined. This incredulity may be attributed—

1. To the infinite abuses of the people, and impositions upon their faith by the cunning monks and friars, etc., in the days of darkness and popery; for they made apparitions as often as they pleased, and got both money and credit by quieting the *terriculamenta vulgi*, which their own artifice had raised.

2. To the prevailing of Somatism and the Hobbean principle in these times, which is a revival of the doctrine of the Sadducees; and as it denies the nature, so it cannot consist with the apparition of spirits; of which, see *Leviathan*, p. 1, c. 12.

3. To the ignorance of men in our age, in this peculiar and mysterious part of philosophy and of religion, namely, the communication between spirits and men. Not one scholar in ten thousand (though otherwise of excellent learning) knows anything of it or the way how to manage it. This ignorance breeds fear and abhorrence of that which otherwise might be of incomparable benefit to mankind.

But I being a clergyman and young, and a stranger in these parts, do apprehend silence and secrecy to be my best security.

In rebus abstrusissimis abundans cautela non nocet.

JOSEPH ADDISON

1672–1719

THE VISION OF MIRZAH

When I was at Grand Cairo, I picked up several oriental manuscripts, which I have still by me. Among others I met with one entitled *The Visions of Mirzah*, which I have read over with great pleasure. I intend to give it to the public when I have no other entertainment for them, and shall begin with the first vision, which I have translated word for word as follows:

"On the fifth day of the moon, which, according to the custom of my forefathers, I always kept holy, after having washed myself, and offered up my morning devotions, I ascended the high hills of Bagdat, in order to pass the rest of the day in meditation and prayer. As I was here airing myself on the tops of the mountains, I fell into a profound contemplation on the vanity of human life; and passing from one thought to another, 'Surely,' said I, 'man is but a shadow, and life a dream.' Whilst I was thus musing, I cast my eyes towards the summit of a rock that was not far from me, where I discovered one in the habit of a shepherd, with a little musical instrument in his hand. As I looked upon him, he applied it to his lips, and began to play upon it. The sound of it was exceeding sweet, and wrought into a variety of tunes that were inexpressibly melodious, and altogether different from anything I had ever heard: they put me in mind of those heavenly airs that are played to the departed souls of good men upon their first arrival in Paradise, to wear out the impressions of the last agonies, and qualify them for the pleasures of that happy place. My heart melted away in secret raptures.

"I had been often told that the rock before me was the haunt of a genius, and that several had been entertained with music who had passed by it, but never heard that the musician had before made himself visible. When he had raised my thoughts by those transporting airs which he played, to taste the pleasures of his conversation, as I looked upon him like one astonished, he beckoned to me, and by the waving of his hand directed me to approach the place where he sat. I drew near with that reverence that is due to a superior nature; and as my heart was entirely subdued by the captivating strains I had heard, I fell down at his feet and wept. The genius smiled upon me with a look of compassion and affability that familiarised him to my imagination, and at once dispelled all the fears and apprehensions with which I approached him. He lifted me from the ground, and taking me by the hand, 'Mirzah,' said he, 'I have heard thee in thy soliloquies; follow me.'

"He then led me to the highest pinnacle of the rock, and placing me on the top of it, 'Cast thy eyes eastward,' said he, 'and tell me what thou seest.' 'I see,' said I, 'a huge valley, and a prodigious tide of water rolling through it.' 'The valley that thou seest,' said he, 'is the vale of misery, and the tide of water that thou seest is part of the great tide of eternity.' 'What is the reason,' said I, 'that the tide I see rises out of a thick mist at one end, and again loses itself in a thick mist at the other?' 'What thou seest,' said he, 'is that portion of eternity which is called time, measured out by the sun, and reaching from the beginning of the world to its consummation. Examine now,' said he, 'this sea that is thus bounded with darkness at both ends, and tell me what thou discoverest in it.' 'I see a bridge,' said I, 'standing in the midst of the tide.' 'That bridge thou seest,' said he, 'is human life: consider it attentively.' Upon a more leisurely survey of it, I found that it consisted of threescore and ten entire arches, with several broken arches, which, added to those that were entire, made up the number about an hundred. As I was counting the arches, the genius told me that this bridge consisted at first of a thousand arches; but that a great flood swept away the rest, and left the bridge in the ruinous condition I now beheld it. 'But tell me further,' said he, 'what thou discoverest on it.' 'I see multitudes of people passing over it,' said I, 'and a black cloud hanging on each end of it.' As I looked more attentively, I saw several of the passengers dropping through the bridge, into the great tide that flowed underneath it; and upon further examination, perceived there were innumerable trap-doors that lay concealed in the bridge, which the passengers no sooner trod upon, but they fell through into the tide, and immediately disappeared. These hidden pitfalls were set very thick at the entrance of the bridge, so that throngs of people no sooner broke through the cloud, but many of them fell into them. They grew thinner towards the middle, but multiplied and lay closer together towards the end of the arches that were entire.

"There were indeed some persons, but their number was very small, that continued a kind of hobbling march on the broken arches, but fell through one after another, being quite tired and spent with so long a walk.

"I passed some time in the contemplation of this wonderful

structure, and the great variety of objects which it presented. My heart was filled with a deep melancholy to see several drooping unexpectedly in the midst of mirth and jollity, and catching at everything that stood by them to save themselves. Some were looking up towards the heavens in a thoughtful posture, and in the midst of a speculation stumbled and fell out of sight. Multitudes were very busy in the pursuit of bubbles that glittered in their eyes and danced before them, but often, when they thought themselves within the reach of them, their footing failed, and down they sank. In this confusion of objects, I observed some with scimitars in their hands, and others with pill-boxes, who ran to and fro upon the bridge, thrusting several persons on trap-doors which did not seem to lie in their way, and which they might have escaped had they not been thus forced upon them.

"The genius, seeing me indulge myself in this melancholy prospect, told me I had dwelt long enough upon it; 'Take thine eyes off the bridge,' said he, 'and tell me if thou yet seest anything thou dost not comprehend.' Upon looking up, 'What mean,' said I, 'those great flights of birds that are perpetually hovering about the bridge, and settling upon it from time to time? I see vultures, harpies, ravens, cormorants, and among many other feathered creatures several little winged boys, that perch in great numbers upon the middle arches.' 'These,' said the genius, 'are envy, avarice, superstition, despair, love, with the like cares and passions that infest human life.'

"I here fetched a deep sigh; 'Alas,' said I, 'man was made in vain! how is he given away to misery and mortality! tortured in life, and swallowed up in death!' The genius, being moved with compassion towards me, bid me quit so uncomfortable a prospect. 'Look no more,' said he, 'on man in the first stage of his existence, in his setting out for eternity; but cast thine eye on that thick mist into which the tide bears the several generations of mortals that fall into it.' I directed my sight as I was ordered, and (whether or no the good genius strengthened it with a supernatural force, or dissipated part of the mist that was before too thick for the eye to penetrate) I saw the valley opening at the further end, and spreading forth into an immense ocean, that had a huge rock of adamant running through the midst of it, and dividing it into two equal parts. The clouds still rested on one half of it, insomuch that I could discover nothing in it: but the other appeared to me a vast ocean planted with innumerable islands, that were covered with fruits and flowers, and interwoven with a thousand little shining seas that ran among them. I could see persons dressed in glorious habits, with garlands upon their heads, passing among the trees, lying down by the sides of the fountains, or resting on beds of flowers; and could hear a confused harmony of singing birds, falling waters, human voices, and musical instruments. Gladness grew in me upon the discovery of so delightful a scene. I wished for the wings of an eagle, that I might fly away to those happy seats ; but the genius told me there was no passage to them, except through the gates of death that I saw opening every moment upon the bridge. ' The islands,' said he, ' that lie so fresh and green before thee, and with which the whole face of the ocean appears spotted as far as thou canst see, are more in number than the sands on the sea-shore ; there are myriads of islands behind those which thou here discoverest, reaching farther than thine eye or even thine imagination can extend itself. These are the mansions of good men after death, who, according to the degree and kinds of virtue in which they excelled, are distributed among these several islands, which abound with pleasures of different kinds and degrees, suitable to the relishes and perfections of those who are settled in them ; every island is a paradise accommodated to its respective inhabitants. Are not these, O Mirzah, habitations worth contending for ? Does life appear miserable, that gives thee opportunities of earning such a reward ? is death to be feared, that will convey thee to so happy an existence ? Think not man was made in vain, who has such an eternity reserved for him.' I gazed with inexpressible pleasure on these happy islands. At length, said I, ' Show me now, I beseech thee, the secrets that lie hidden under those dark clouds which cover the ocean on the other side of the rock of adamant.' The genius making me no answer, I turned about to address him a second time, but I found that he had left me. I then turned again to the vision which I had been so long contemplating ; but instead of the rolling tide, the arched bridge, and the happy islands, I saw nothing but the long hollow valley of Bagdat, with oxen, sheep, and camels grazing upon the sides of it."

HENRY FIELDING
1707–1754

THE HISTORY OF LEONORA, OR THE UNFORTUNATE JILT

LEONORA was the daughter of a gentleman of fortune: she was tall and well-shaped, with a sprightliness in her countenance, which often attracts beyond more regular features, joined with an insipid air: nor is this kind of beauty less apt to deceive than allure, the good humour which it indicates being often mistaken for good nature, and the vivacity for true understanding.

Leonora, who was now at the age of eighteen, lived with an aunt of hers, in a town in the north of England. She was an extreme lover of gaiety, and very rarely missed a ball or any other public assembly, where she had frequent opportunities of satisfying a greedy appetite of vanity, with the preference which was given her by the men to almost every other woman present.

Among many young fellows who were particular in their gallantries towards her, Horatio soon distinguished himself in her eyes beyond all his competitors: she danced with more than ordinary gaiety when he happened to be her partner; neither the fairness of the evening, nor the music of the nightingale, could lengthen her walk like his company. She affected no longer to understand the civilities of others, whilst she inclined so attentive an ear to every compliment of Horatio, that she often smiled even when it was too delicate for her comprehension.

Horatio was a young gentleman of a good family, bred to the law, and had been some few years called to the degree of a barrister. His face and person were such as the generality allowed handsome, but he had a dignity in his air very rarely to be seen. His temper was of the saturnine complexion and without the least taint of moroseness. He had wit and humour, with an inclination to satire, which he indulged rather too much.

This gentleman, who had contracted the most violent passion for Leonora, was the last person who perceived the probability of its success. The whole town had made the match for him before he himself had drawn a confidence from her actions sufficient to mention his passion to her ; for it was his opinion, and perhaps he was there in the right, that it is highly impolitic to talk seriously of love to a woman before you have made such progress in her affections that she herself expects and desires to hear it.

But whatever diffidence the fears of a lover may create, which are apt to magnify every favour conferred on a rival, and to see the little advances towards themselves through the other end of the perspective, it was impossible that Horatio's passion should so blind his discernment as to prevent his conceiving hopes from the behaviour of Leonora, whose fondness for him was now as visible to an indifferent person in their company as his for her.

It was in the midst of a gay conversation in the walks one evening, when Horatio whispered Leonora that he was desirous to take a turn or two with her in private ; for that he had something to communicate to her of great consequence.

" Are you sure it is of consequence ? " said she, smiling.

" I hope," answered he, " you will think so too, since the whole future happiness of my life must depend on the event."

Leonora, who very much suspected what was coming, would have deferred it till another time ; but Horatio, who had more than half conquered the difficulty of speaking by the first motion, was so very importunate that she at last yielded, and, leaving the rest of the company, they turned aside into an unfrequented walk.

They had retired far out of sight of the company, both maintaining a strict silence. At last, Horatio made a full stop, and taking Leonora, who stood pale and trembling, gently by the hand, he fetched a deep sigh, and then, looking on her eyes with all the tenderness imaginable, he cried out, in a faltering accent :

" O Leonora ! is it necessary for me to declare to you on what the future happiness of my life must be founded ? Must I say there is something belonging to you which is a bar to my happiness, and which, unless you will part with, I must be miserable ! "

" What can that be ? " replied Leonora.

" No wonder," said he, " you are surprised that I should make an objection to anything which is yours : yet sure you may guess, since it is the only one which the riches of the world, if they were mine, should purchase of me. Oh, it is that which you must part with to bestow all the rest ! Can Leonora, or rather, will she, doubt longer ? Let me, then, whisper it in her ears.—It is your name, madam. It is by parting with that, by your condescension to be for ever mine, which must at once prevent me from being the most miserable, and will render me the happiest of mankind."

Leonora, covered with blushes, and with as angry a look as she could possibly put on, told him, that had she suspected what his declaration would have been, he should not have decoyed her from her company; that he had so surprised and frighted her, that she begged him to convey her back as quick as possible; which he, trembling very near as much as herself, did.

Many weeks had not passed after this interview before Horatio and Leonora were what they call on a good footing together. All ceremonies, except the last, were now over; the writings were now drawn, and everything was in the utmost forwardness, preparative to the putting Horatio in possession of all his wishes. I will, if you please, repeat you a letter from each of them, and which will give you no small idea of their passion on both sides.

"*Horatio to Leonora.*

"How vain, most adorable creature, is the pursuit of pleasure in the absence of an object to which the mind is entirely devoted, unless it has some relation to that object! I was last night condemned to the society of men of wit and learning, which, however agreeable it might have formerly been to me, now only gave me a suspicion that they imputed my absence in conversation to the true cause. For which reason, when your engagements forbid me the ecstatic happiness of seeing you, I am always desirous to be alone; since my sentiments for Leonora are so delicate that I cannot bear the apprehension of another's prying into those delightful endearments with which the warm imagination of a lover will sometimes indulge him, and which I suspect my eyes then betray.

"To fear this discovery of our thoughts may, perhaps, appear too ridiculous a nicety to minds not susceptible of all the tenderness of this delicate passion; and surely we shall suspect there are few such when we consider that it requires every human virtue to exert itself in its full extent; since the beloved, whose happiness it ultimately respects, may give us charming opportunities of being brave in her defence, generous to her wants, compassionate to her afflictions, grateful to her kindness; and, in the same manner, of exercising every other virtue, which he, who would not do to any degree, and that with the utmost rapture, can never deserve the name of a lover. It is therefore with a view to the delicate modesty of your mind that I cultivate it so purely in my own; and it is that which will sufficiently suggest to you the uneasiness I bear from those liberties which men, to whom the world allow politeness, will sometimes give themselves on these occasions.

"Can I tell you with what eagerness I expect the arrival of that blessed day when I shall experience the falsehood of a common assertion that the greatest human happiness consists in hope?—a doctrine which no person had ever stronger reason to believe than myself at present, since none ever tasted such bliss as fires my bosom with the thoughts of spending my future days with such a companion, and that every action of my life will have the glorious satisfaction of conducing to your happiness."

"*Leonora to Horatio.*

"The refinement of your mind has been so evidently proved by every word and action, ever since I had the first pleasure of knowing you, that I thought it impossible my good opinion of Horatio could have been heightened to any additional proof of merit. This very thought was my amusement when I received your last letter, which, when I opened, I confess I was surprised to find the delicate sentiments expressed there so far exceeded what I thought could come even from you (although I know all the generous principles human nature is capable of are centred in your breast) that words cannot paint what I feel on the reflection that my happiness shall be the ultimate end of all your actions.

"O Horatio! what a life must that be where the meanest domestic cares are sweetened by the pleasing consideration that the man on earth who best deserves, and to whom you are most inclined to give your affections, is to reap either profit or pleasure from all you do! In such a case toils must be turned into diversions, and nothing but the unavoidable inconveniences of life can make us remember that we are mortal.

"If the solitary turn of your thoughts and the desire of keeping them undiscovered make even the conversation of men of wit and learning tedious to you, what anxious hours must I spend, who am condemned by custom to the conversation of women, whose natural curiosity leads them to pry into all my thoughts, and whose envy can never suffer Horatio's heart to be possessed by anyone, without forcing them into malicious designs against the person who is so happy as to possess it? But, indeed, if ever envy can possibly have any excuse, or even alleviation, it is in this case, where the good is so great that it must be equally natural to all to wish for it for themselves; nor am I ashamed to own it: and to your merit, Horatio, I am obliged, that prevents my being in that most uneasy of all the situations I can figure in my imagination, of being led by inclination to love the person whom my own judgment forces me to condemn."

Matters were in so great forwardness between this fond couple that the day was fixed for their marriage, and was now within a fortnight, when the sessions chanced to be held for that county in a town about twenty miles' distance from that which is the scene of our story. It seems it is usual for the young gentlemen of the bar to repair to these sessions, not so much for the sake of profit, as to show their parts, and learn the law of the justices of peace; for which purpose one of the wisest and gravest of all the justices is appointed speaker, or chairman as they modestly call it, and he reads them a lecture, and instructs them in the true knowledge of the law.

Hither repaired Horatio, who, as he hoped by his profession to advance his fortune, which was not at present very large, for the sake of his dear Leonora, resolved to spare no pains, nor lose any opportunity of improving or advancing himself in it.

The same afternoon in which he left the town, as Leonora stood at her window, a coach and six passed by, which she declared to be the completest, genteelest, prettiest equipage she ever saw; adding these remarkable words: "Oh, I am in love with that equipage!" which, though her friend Florella at that time did not greatly regard, she has since remembered.

In the evening an assembly was held, which Leonora honoured with her company; but intended to pay her Horatio the compliment of refusing to dance in his absence. Oh, why have not women as good resolution to maintain their vows as they have often good inclinations in making them!

The gentleman who owned the coach and six came to the assembly. His clothes were as remarkably fine as his equipage could be. He soon attracted the eyes of the company; all the smarts, all the silk waistcoats with silver and gold edgings, were eclipsed in an instant. I have been told he had on a cut velvet coat of a cinnamon colour lined with a pink satin, embroidered all over with gold; his waistcoat, which was cloth of silver, was embroidered with gold likewise. I cannot be particular as to the rest of his dress, but it was all in the French fashion; for Bellarmine, that was his name, was just arrived from Paris.

This fine figure did not more entirely engage the eyes of every lady in the assembly than Leonora did his. He had scarce beheld her but he stood motionless and fixed as a statue, or at least would have done so if good breeding had permitted him. However, he carried it so far, before he had power to correct himself, that every person in the room easily discovered where his admiration was settled. The other ladies began to single out their former partners, all perceiving who would be Bellarmine's choice, which they however endeavoured by all possible means to prevent, many of them saying to Leonora, "O madam! I suppose we sha'n't have the pleasure of seeing you dance to-night!" and then crying out, in Bellarmine's hearing, "Oh, Leonora will not dance, I assure you: her partner is not here."

One maliciously attempted to prevent her, by sending a disagreeable fellow to ask her, that so she might be obliged either to dance with him, or sit down; but this scheme proved abortive.

Leonora saw herself admired by the fine stranger and envied by every woman present. Her little heart began to flutter within her, and her head was agitated with a convulsive motion ; she seemed as if she would speak to several of her acquaintance, but had nothing to say, for as she would not mention her present triumph, so she could not disengage her thoughts one moment from the contemplation of it. She had never tasted anything like this happiness. She had before known what it was to torment a single woman, but to be hated and secretly cursed by a whole assembly was a joy reserved for this blessed moment. As this vast profusion of ecstasy had confounded her understanding, so there was nothing so foolish as her behaviour : she played a thousand childish tricks, distorted her person into several shapes, and her face into several laughs, without any reason.

In a word, her carriage was as absurd as her desires, which were to affect an insensibility of the stranger's admiration, and at the same time a triumph, from that admiration, over every woman in the room.

In this temper of mind, Bellarmine, having inquired who she was, advanced to her, and with a low bow begged the honour of dancing with her, which she, with as low a curtsey, immediately granted. She danced with him all night, and enjoyed perhaps the highest pleasure that she was capable of feeling.

Leonora retired about six in the morning, but not to rest ; she tumbled and tossed in her bed, with very short intervals of sleep, and those entirely filled with dreams of the equipage and fine clothes she had seen, and the balls, operas and ridottos which had been the subject of their conversation.

In the afternoon Bellarmine, in the dear coach and six, came to wait on her. He was indeed charmed with her person, and was, on inquiry, as well pleased with the circumstances of her father—for he himself, notwithstanding all his finery, was not quite so rich as a Crœsus or an Attalus.

He was so pleased that he resolved to make his addresses to her directly. He did so accordingly, and that with so much warmth and briskness that he quickly baffled her weak repulses, and obliged the lady to refer him to her father, who, she knew, would quickly declare in favour of a coach and six.

Thus what Horatio had by sighs and tears, love and tenderness, been so long obtaining, the French-English Bellarmine with gaiety and gallantry possessed himself of in an instant ; in other words, what modesty had employed a full year in raising, impudence demolished in twenty-four hours.

From the opening of the assembly till the end of Bellarmine's visit Leonora had scarce one thought of Horatio ; but he now began, though an unwelcome guest, to enter into her mind. She wished she had seen the charming Bellarmine and his charming equipage before matters had gone so far.

"Yet why," says she, "should I wish to have seen him before? or what signifies it that I have seen him now? Is not Horatio my lover, almost my husband? Is he not as handsome, nay handsomer, than Bellarmine? Ay, but Bellarmine is the genteeler and the finer man; yes, that he must be allowed: yes, yes, he is that, certainly. But did not I, no longer ago than yesterday, love Horatio more than all the world? Ay, but yesterday I had not seen Bellarmine. But does not Horatio dote on me, and may he not in despair break his heart if I abandon him? Well, and has not Bellarmine a heart to break too? Yes, but I promised Horatio first; but that was poor Bellarmine's misfortune; if I had seen him first, I should certainly have preferred him. Did not the dear creature prefer me to every woman in the assembly, when every she was laying out for him? When was it in Horatio's power to give me such an instance of affection? Can he give me an equipage, or any of those things which Bellarmine will make me mistress of? How vast is the difference between being the wife of a poor counsellor, and the wife of one of Bellarmine's fortune! If I marry Horatio I shall triumph over no more than one rival, but by marrying Bellarmine I shall be the envy of all my acquaintance. What happiness! But can I suffer Horatio to die? for he has sworn he cannot survive my loss; but perhaps he may not die; if he should, can I prevent it? Must I sacrifice myself to him? Besides, Bellarmine may be as miserable for me too."

She was thus arguing with herself, when some young ladies called her to the walks, and a little relieved her anxiety for the present.

The next morning Bellarmine breakfasted with her in presence of her aunt, whom he sufficiently informed of his passion for Leonora. He was no sooner withdrawn than the old lady began to advise her niece on this occasion.

"You see, child," says she, "what fortune has thrown in your way; and I hope you will not withstand your own preferment."

Leonora, sighing, begged her not to mention any such things when she knew her engagements to Horatio.

"Engagements to a fig!" cried the aunt; "you should thank Heaven, on your knees, that you have it in your power to break them. Will any woman hesitate a moment whether she shall ride in a coach or walk on foot all the days of her life? But Bellarmine drives six, and Horatio not even a pair."

"Yes, but, madam, what will the world say?" answered Leonora; "will not they condemn me?"

"The world is always on the side of prudence," cries the aunt, "and would surely condemn you if you sacrified your interest to any motive whatever. Oh, I know the world very well; and you show your ignorance, my dear, by your objection. On my conscience, the world is wiser: I have lived longer in it than you; and, I assure you, there is not anything worth our regard besides money; nor did I ever know one person who married from other considerations who did not afterwards heartily repent it. Besides, if we examine the two men, can you prefer a sneaking fellow who has been bred at the university to a fine gentleman just come from his travels? All the world must allow Bellarmine to be a fine gentleman,—positively a fine gentleman, and a handsome man."

"Perhaps, madam, I should not doubt, if I knew how to be handsomely off with the other."

"Oh, leave that to me," says the aunt; "you know your father has not been acquainted with the affair. Indeed, for my part, I thought it might do well enough, not dreaming of such an offer; but I'll disengage you: leave me to give the fellow an answer. I warrant you shall have no further trouble."

Leonora was at length satisfied with her aunt's reasoning; and Bellarmine supping with her that evening, it was agreed he should the next morning go to her father and propose the match, which she consented should be consummated at his return.

The aunt retired soon after supper; and the lovers being left together, Bellarmine began in the following manner:

"Yes, madam; this coat, I assure you, was made at Paris, and I defy the best English tailor even to imitate it. There is not one of them can cut, madam; they can't cut. If you observe how this skirt is turned, and this sleeve; a clumsy English rascal can do nothing like it. Pray, how do you like my liveries?"

Leonora answered, she thought them very pretty.

"All French," says he, "I assure you, except the great coats: I never trust anything more than a great coat to an Englishman. You know one must encourage our own people what one can, especially as before I had a place I was in the country interest: he, he, he! But for myself, I would see the dirty island at the bottom of the sea, rather than wear a single rag of English work about me; and I am sure, after you have made one tour to Paris, you will be of the same opinion with regard to your own clothes. You can't conceive what an addition a French dress would be to your beauty; I positively assure you, at the first opera I saw since I came over, I mistook the English ladies for chambermaids: he, he, he!"

With such sort of polite discourse did the gay Bellarmine entertain his beloved Leonora, when the door opened on a sudden, and Horatio entered the room. Here it is impossible to express the surprise of Leonora.

A long silence prevailed in the whole company. If the familiar entrance of Horatio struck the greatest astonishment into Bellarmine, the unexpected presence of Bellarmine no less surprised

Horatio. At length Leonora, collecting all the spirit she was mistress of, addressed herself to the latter, and pretended to wonder at the reason of so late a visit.

"I should, indeed," answered he, "have made some apology for disturbing you at this hour, had not my finding you in company assured me I do not break in upon your repose."

Bellarmine rose from his chair, traversed the room in a minuet step, and hummed an opera tune; while Horatio, advancing to Leonora, asked her, in a whisper, if that gentleman was not a relation of hers; to which she answered with a smile, or rather sneer:

"No, he is no relation yet"; adding, she could not guess the meaning of his question.

Horatio told her softly it did not arise from jealousy.

"Jealousy! I assure you, it would be very strange in a common acquaintance to give himself any of those airs."

These words a little surprised Horatio; but before he had time to answer, Bellarmine danced up to the lady, and told her, he feared he interrupted some business between her and the gentleman.

"I have no business," said she, "with the gentleman, nor any other, which need be any secret to you."

"You'll pardon me," said Horatio, "if I desire to know who this gentleman is, who is to be entrusted with all our secrets."

"You'll know soon enough," cried Leonora; "but I can't guess what secrets can ever pass between us of such mighty consequence."

"No, madam!" cries Horatio; "I'm sure you would not have me understand you in earnest."

"'Tis indifferent to me," says she, "how you understand me; but I think so unseasonable a visit is difficult to be understood at all, at least when people find one engaged; though one's servants do not deny one, one may expect a well-bred person should soon take the hint."

"Madam," said Horatio, "I did not imagine any engagement with a stranger, as it seems this gentleman is, would have made my visit impertinent, or that any such ceremonies were to be preserved between persons in our situation."

"Sure you are in a dream," says she, "or would persuade me that I am in one. I know no pretensions a common acquaintance can have to lay aside the ceremonies of good breeding."

"Sure," says he, "I am in a dream; for it is impossible I should be really esteemed a common acquaintance by Leonora, after what has passed between us."

"Passed between us! Do you intend to affront me before this gentleman?"

"D—n me, affront the lady?" says Bellarmine, cocking his hat, and strutting up to Horatio; "does any man dare affront this lady before me, d—n me ? "

" Harkee, sir," says Horatio, " I would advise you to lay aside that fierce air ; for I am mightily deceived if this lady has not a violent desire to get your worship a good drubbing."

" Sir," said Bellarmine, " I have the honour to be her protector ; and d—n me, if I understand your meaning."

" Sir," answered Horatio, " she is rather your protectress ; but give yourself no more airs, for you see I am prepared for you " (shaking his whip at him).

" *Oh! serviteur très humble,*" says Bellarmine ; " *je vous entend parfaitement bien.*"

At which time, the aunt, who had heard of Horatio's visit, entered the room, and soon satisfied all his doubts. She convinced him that he was never more awake in his life, and that nothing more extraordinary had happened in his three days' absence, than a small alteration in the affections of Leonora, who now burst into tears, and wondered what reason she had given him to use her in so barbarous a manner.

Horatio desired Bellarmine to withdraw with him ; but the ladies prevented it, by laying violent hands on the latter ; upon which the former took his leave without any great ceremony, and departed, leaving the lady with his rival to consult for his safety, which Leonora feared her indiscretion might have endangered ; but the aunt comforted her with assurances, that Horatio would not venture his person against so accomplished a cavalier as Bellarmine : and that, being a lawyer, he would seek revenge in his own way, and the most they had to apprehend from him was an action.

They at length therefore agreed to permit Bellarmine to retire to his lodgings, having first settled all matters relating to the journey which he was to undertake in the morning, and their preparations for the nuptials at his return. But, alas ! as wise men have observed, the seat of valour is not the countenance ; and many a grave and plain man will, on a just provocation, betake himself to that mischievous metal, cold iron ; while men of a fiercer brow, and sometimes with that emblem of courage, a cockade, will more prudently decline it.

Leonora was awaked in the morning, from a visionary coach and six, with the dismal account that Bellarmine was run through the body by Horatio ; that he lay languishing at an inn, and the surgeon had declared the wound mortal. She immediately leaped out of the bed, danced about the room in a frantic manner, tore her hair and beat her breast in all the agonies of despair ; in which sad condition her aunt, who likewise arose at the news, found her.

The good old lady applied her utmost art to comfort her niece. She told her, while there was life there was hope ; but that if he should die, her affliction would be of no service to Bellarmine, and would only expose herself, which might probably keep her some time without any future offer; that as matters had happened, her wisest way would be to think no more of Bellarmine, but to endeavour to regain the affections of Horatio.

"Speak not to me," cried the disconsolate Leonora; "is it not owing to me that poor Bellarmine has lost his life? Have not these cursed charms" (at which words she looked steadfastly in the glass) "been the ruin of the most charming man of this age? Can I ever bear to contemplate my own face again?" (with her eyes still fixed on the glass). "Am I not the murderess of the finest gentleman? No other woman in the town could have made any impression on him."

"Never think of things past," cries the aunt; "think of regaining the affections of Horatio."

"What reason," said the niece, "have I to hope he would forgive me? No, I have lost him as well as the other, and it was your wicked advice which was the occasion of all: you seduced me, contrary to my inclinations, to abandon poor Horatio" (at which words she burst into tears); "you prevailed upon me, whether I would or no, to give up my affections for him: had it not been for you, Bellarmine never would have entered into my thoughts: had not his addresses been backed by your persuasions, they never would have made any impression on me; I should have defied all the fortune and equipage in the world: but it was you, it was you, who got the better of my youth and simplicity, and forced me to lose my dear Horatio for ever."

The aunt was almost borne down with this torrent of words; she, however, rallied all the strength she could, and, drawing her mouth up in a purse, began:

"I am not surprised, niece, at this ingratitude. Those who advise young women for their interest must always expect such a return: I am convinced my brother will thank me for breaking off your match with Horatio at any rate."

"That may not be in your power yet," answered Leonora, "though it is very ungrateful in you to desire or attempt it, after the presents you have received from him."

For indeed true it is, that many presents, and some pretty valuable ones, had passed from Horatio to the old lady; but as true it is, that Bellarmine, when he breakfasted with her and her niece, had complimented her with a brilliant from his finger, of much greater value than all she had touched of the other.

The aunt's gall was on float to reply, when a servant brought a letter into the room; which Leonora, hearing it came from Bellarmine, with great eagerness opened, and read as follows:

"Most divine Creature—The wound which I fear you have heard I received from my rival is not like to be so fatal as those shot into my heart, which have been fired from your eyes, tout brilliant. Those are the only cannons by which I am to fall; for my surgeon gives me hopes of being soon able to attend your ruelle; till when, unless you would do me an honour which I have scarcely the hardiesse to think of, your absence will be the greatest anguish which can be felt by, madam, avec tout le respect, in the world, your most obedient, most absolute dévoté, Bellarmine."

As soon as Leonora perceived such hopes of Bellarmine's recovery, and that the gossip Fame had, according to custom, so enlarged his danger, she presently abandoned all further thoughts of Horatio, and was soon reconciled to her aunt, who received her again into favour with a more Christian forgiveness than we generally meet with. Indeed, it is possible she might be a little alarmed at the hints which her niece had given her concerning the presents: she might apprehend such rumours, should they get abroad, might injure a reputation, which, by frequenting church twice a day, and preserving the utmost rigour and strictness in her countenance and behaviour for many years, she had established.

Leonora's passion returned now for Bellarmine with greater force, after its small relaxation, than ever. She proposed to her aunt to make him a visit in his confinement, which the old lady, with great and commendable prudence, advised her to decline:

"For," says she, "should any accident intervene to prevent your intended match, too forward a behaviour with this lover may injure you in the eyes of others. Every woman, till she is married, ought to consider of, and provide against, the possibility of the affair's breaking off."

Leonora said she should be indifferent to whatever might happen in such a case: for she had now so absolutely placed her affections on this dear man (so she called him), that, if it was her misfortune to lose him, she should for ever abandon all thoughts of mankind. She therefore resolved to visit him, notwithstanding all the prudent advice of her aunt to the contrary, and that very afternoon executed her resolution.

Leonora, having once broken through the bounds which custom and modesty impose on her sex, soon gave an unbridled indulgence to her passion. Her visits to Bellarmine were more constant, as well as longer, than his surgeon's: in a word, she became absolutely his nurse; made his water-gruel, administered him his medicines, and, notwithstanding the prudent advice of her aunt to the contrary, almost entirely resided in her wounded lover's apartment.

The ladies of the town began to take her conduct under consideration: it was the chief topic of discourse at their tea-tables, and was severely censured by the most part, especially by Lindamira, a lady, whose discreet and starch carriage, together with a constant attendance at church three times a day, had utterly defeated many malicious attacks on her own reputation; for such was the envy that Lindamira's virtue had attracted, that, notwithstanding her own strict behaviour, and strict inquiry into the lives of others, she had not been able to escape being the mark of some arrows herself, which, however, did her no injury; a blessing, perhaps, owed by her to the clergy, who were her chief male companions, and with two or three of whom she had been barbarously and unjustly calumniated.

The extreme delicacy of Lindamira's virtue was cruelly hurt by those freedoms which Leonora allowed herself: she said it was an affront to her sex; that she did not imagine it consistent with any woman's honour to speak to the creature, or to be seen in her company; and that, for her part, she should always refuse to dance at an assembly with her, for fear of contamination by taking her by the hand.

But to return to my story: as soon as Bellarmine was recovered, which was somewhat within a month from his receiving the wound, he set out, according to agreement, for Leonora's father, in order to propose the match, and settle all matters with him, touching settlements, and the like.

A little before his arrival, the old gentleman had received an intimation of the affair by the following letter, which I can repeat verbatim, and which, they say, was written neither by Leonora nor her aunt, though it was in a woman's hand. The letter was in these words:

"Sir—I am sorry to acquaint you, that your daughter Leonora has accepted one of the basest, as well as most simple parts, with a young gentleman to whom she has engaged herself, and whom she has (pardon the word) jilted for another of inferior fortune, notwithstanding his superior figure. You may take what measures you please on this occasion: I have performed what I thought my duty; as I have, though unknown to you, a very great respect for your family."

The old gentleman did not give himself the trouble to answer this kind epistle; nor did he take any notice of it after he had read it, till he saw Bellarmine. He was, to say the truth, one of those fathers who look on children as an unhappy consequence of their youthful pleasures; which, as he would have been delighted not to have had attended them, so was he no less pleased with any opportunity to rid himself of the encumbrance. He passed, in the world's language, as an exceeding good father; being not only so rapacious as to rob and plunder all mankind to the utmost of his power, but even to deny himself the conveniences, and almost necessaries of life; which his neighbours attributed to a desire of raising immense fortunes for his children; but, in fact, it was not so: he heaped up money for its own sake only, and looked on his children as his rivals, who were to enjoy his beloved mistress when he was incapable of possessing her; and which he would have been much more charmed with the power of carrying along with him: nor had his children any other security of being his heirs than that the law would constitute them such without a will, and that he had not affection enough for any one living to take the trouble of writing one.

To this gentleman came Bellarmine on the errand I have mentioned. His person, his equipage, his family, and his estate, seemed to the father to make him an advantageous match for his daughter; he, therefore, very readily, accepted his proposals: but when Bellarmine imagined the principal affair concluded, and began to open the incidental matters of fortune, the old gentleman presently changed his countenance saying, he resolved never to marry his daughter on a Smithfield match; that whoever had love for her to take her, would, when he died, find her share of his fortune in his coffers; but he had seen such examples of undutifulness happen from the too early generosity of parents, that he had made a vow never to part with a shilling whilst he lived.

He commended the saying of Solomon, "He that spareth the rod, spoileth the child"; but added, he might have likewise asserted, that he that spares the purse saves the child. He then ran into a discourse on the extravagance of the youth of the age; whence he launched into a dissertation on horses; and came at length to commend those Bellarmine drove.

That fine gentleman, who at another season would have been well enough pleased to dwell a little on that subject, was now very eager to resume the circumstance of fortune. He said he had a very high value for the young lady, and would receive her with less than he would any other whatever; but that even his love to her made some regard to worldly matters necessary; for it would be a most distracting sight for him to see her, when he had the honour to be her husband, in less than a coach and six.

The old gentleman answered, "Four will do, four will do," and then took a turn from horses to extravagance, and from extravagance to horses, till he came round to the equipage again; whither he was no sooner arrived, than Bellarmine brought him back to the point; but all to no purpose: he made his escape from that subject in a minute; till at last the lover declared, that, in the present situation of his affairs, it was impossible for him, though he loved Leonora more than *tout le monde*, to marry her without any fortune.

To which the father answered, he was sorry then his daughter must lose so valuable a match; that if he had an inclination, at present it was not in his power to advance a shilling; that he had had great losses, and been at great expense on projects, which, though he had great expectations from them, had yet produced him nothing; that he did not know what might happen hereafter, as on the birth of a son, or such accident; but he would make no promise, nor enter into any article; for he would not break his vow for all the daughters in the world.

In short, Bellarmine, having tried every argument and persuasion which he could invent, and finding them all ineffectual, at length took his leave, but not in order to return to Leonora: he proceeded directly to his own seat, whence, after a few days' stay, he returned to Paris, to the great delight of the French and the honour of the English nation. But as soon as he arrived at his home, he presently despatched a messenger with the following epistle to Leonora:

"ADORABLE AND CHARMANTE—I am sorry to have the honour to tell you I am not the heureux person destined for your divine arms. Your papa has told me so with a politesse not often seen on this side Paris; you may, perhaps, guess his manner of refusing me. Ah, mon Dieu! you will certainly believe me, madam, incapable myself of delivering this triste message, which I intend to try the French air, to cure the consequence of. A jamais! Cœur! Ange! Au diable! If your papa obliges you to a marriage, I hope we shall see you at Paris; till when, the wind that flows from thence will be the warmest dans le monde, for it will consist almost entirely of my sighs. Adieu, ma princesse! Ah l'amour!

BELLARMINE."

I shall not attempt to describe Leonora's condition when she received this letter; it is a picture of horror, which I should have as little pleasure in drawing as you in beholding. She immediately left the place where she was the subject of conversation and ridicule, and retired to the country, where she has ever since led a disconsolate life, and deserves, perhaps, pity for her misfortunes, more than our censure for a behaviour to which the artifices of her aunt very probably contributed, and to which very young women are often rendered too liable by that blameable levity in the education of their sex.

SAMUEL TAYLOR COLERIDGE

1772–1834

MARIA SCHÖNING

Maria Eleonora Schöning was the daughter of a Nuremberg wine-drawer. She received her unhappy existence at the price of her mother's life, and at the age of seventeen she followed, as the sole mourner, the bier of her remaining parent. From her thirteenth year she had passed her life at her father's sick-bed, the gout having deprived him of the use of his limbs ; and beheld the arch of heaven only when she went to fetch food or medicines. The discharge of her filial duties occupied the whole of her time and all her thoughts. She was his only nurse, and for the last two years they lived without a servant. She prepared his scanty meals, she bathed his aching limbs, and though weak and delicate from constant confinement and the poison of melancholy thoughts, she had acquired an unusual power in her arms, from the habit of lifting her old and suffering father out of and into his bed of pain.

Thus passed away her early youth in sorrow : she grew up in tears, a stranger to the amusements of youth and its more delightful schemes and imaginations. She was not, however, unhappy ; she attributed indeed, no merit to herself for her virtues, but for that reason were they the more her reward.

The peace which passeth all understanding disclosed itself in all her looks and movements. It lay on her countenance, like a steady unshadowed moonlight ; and her voice, which was naturally at once sweet and subtle, came from her like the fine flute-tones of a masterly performer, which still floating at some uncertain distance, seem to be created by the player rather than to proceed from the instrument. If you had listened to it in one of those brief sabbaths of the soul, when the activity and discursiveness of the thoughts are suspended, and the mind quietly eddies round, instead of flowing onward—(as at late evening in the spring I have seen a bat wheel in silent circles round and round a fruit-tree in full blossom, in the midst of which, as within a close tent of the purest white, an unseen nightingale was piping its sweetest notes)—in such a mood you might have half fancied, half felt, that her voice had a separate being of its own; that it was a living something, whose mode of existence was for the ear only: so deep was her resignation, so entirely had it become the unconscious habit of her nature, and in all she did or said, so perfectly were both her movements and her utterance without effort, and without the appearance of effort! Her dying father's last words, addressed to the clergyman who attended him, were his grateful testimony, that during his long and sore trial his good Maria had behaved to him like an angel; that the most disagreeable offices, and the least suited to her age and sex, had never drawn an unwilling look from her, and that whenever his eye had met hers he had been sure to see in it either the tear of pity or the sudden smile expressive of her affection and wish to cheer him.

"God," said he, "will reward the good girl for all her long dutifulness to me!"

He departed during the inward prayer which followed these his last words. His wish will be fulfilled in eternity; but for this world the prayer of the dying man was not heard!

Maria sat and wept by the grave which now contained her father, her friend, the only bond by which she was linked to life. But while yet the last sound of his death-bell was murmuring away in the air, she was obliged to return with two revenue officers, who demanded entrance into the house, in order to take possession of the papers of the deceased, and from them to discover whether he had always given in his income, and paid the yearly income-tax according to his oath and in proportion to his property.

After the few documents had been looked through and collated with the registers, the officers found, or pretended to find, sufficient proofs that the deceased had not paid his tax proportionably, which imposed on them the duty to put all the effects under lock and seal. They therefore desired the maiden to retire to an empty room, till the ransom office had decided on the affair. Bred up in suffering, and habituated to immediate compliance, the affrighted and weeping maiden obeyed. She hastened to the empty garret, while the revenue officers placed the lock and seal upon the other doors, and finally took away the papers to the ransom office.

Not before evening did the poor faint Maria, exhausted with weeping, rouse herself with the intention of going to her bed; but she found the door of her chamber sealed up, and that she must pass the night on the floor of the garret. The officers had had the humanity to place at the door the small portion of food that happened to be in the house.

Thus passed several days, till the officers returned with an order that Maria Eleonora Schöning should leave the house without delay, the commission court having confiscated the whole property to the city treasury. The father before he was bedridden had never possessed any considerable property ; but yet, by his industry, had been able not only to keep himself free from debt, but to lay up a small sum for the evil day. Three years of evil days, three whole years of sickness, had consumed the greatest part of this ; yet still enough remained not only to defend his daughter from immediate want, but likewise to maintain her till she could get into some service or employment, and should have recovered her spirits sufficiently to bear up against the hardships of life. With this thought her dying father comforted himself, and this hope too proved vain !

A timid girl, whose past life had been made up of sorrow and privation, she went indeed to solicit the commissioners in her own behalf ; but these were, as is mostly the case on the Continent, advocates—the most hateful class, perhaps, of human society, hardened by the frequent sight of misery, and seldom superior in moral character to English pettifoggers or Old Bailey attorneys.

She went to them, indeed, but not a word could she say for herself ! Her tears and inarticulate sounds—for these her judges had no ears or eyes. Mute and confounded, like an unfledged dove fallen out from its mother's nest, Maria betook herself to her home, and found the house door too now shut upon her. Her whole wealth consisted in the clothes she wore. She had no relations to whom she could apply, for those of her mother had disclaimed all acquaintance with her, and her father was a Nether Saxon by birth. She had no acquaintance, for all the friends of old Schöning had forsaken him in the first year of his sickness. She had no playfellow, for who was likely to have been the companion of a nurse in the room of a sick man ?

Surely, since the creation never was a human being more solitary and forsaken than this innocent poor creature, that now roamed about friendless in a populous city, to the whole of whose inhabitants her filial tenderness, her patient domestic goodness, and all her soft yet difficult virtues, might well have been the model.

> But homeless near a thousand homes she stood,
> And near a thousand tables pined, and wanted food !

The night came, and Maria knew not where to find a shelter. She tottered to the churchyard of the St. James' Church in Nuremberg, where the body of her father rested. Upon the yet grassless grave she threw herself down ; and could anguish have prevailed over youth, that night she had been in heaven.

The day came, and, like a guilty thing, this guiltless, this good being stole away from the crowd that began to pass through the churchyard, and hastening through the streets to the city gate, she hid herself behind a garden hedge just beyond it, and there wept away the second day of her desolation.

The evening closed in; the pang of hunger made itself felt amid the dull aching of self-wearied anguish, and drove the sufferer back again into the city.

Yet what could she gain there? She had not the courage to beg, and the very thought of stealing never occurred to her innocent mind. Scarce conscious whither she was going, or why she went, she found herself once more by her father's grave, as the last relic of evening faded away in the horizon. I have sat for some minutes with my pen resting; I can scarce summon the courage to tell, what I scarce know whether I ought to tell. Were I composing a tale of fiction the reader might justly suspect the purity of my own heart, and most certainly would have abundant right to resent such an incident, as an outrage wantonly offered to his imagination.

As I think of the circumstance, it seems more like a distempered dream! but alas! what is guilt so detestable other than a dream of madness, that worst madness, the madness of the heart? I cannot but believe that the dark and restless passions must first have drawn the mind in upon themselves, and as with the confusion of imperfect sleep, have in some strange manner taken away the sense of reality, in order to render it possible for a human being to perpetrate what it is too certain that human beings have perpetrated. The churchyards in most of the German cities, and too often, I fear, in those of our own country, are not more injurious to health than to morality. Their former venerable character is no more. The religion of the place has followed its superstitions, and their darkness and loneliness tempt worse spirits to roam in them than those whose nightly wanderings appalled the believing hearts of our brave forefathers! It was close by the new-made grave of her father that the meek and spotless daughter became the victim to brutal violence, which weeping and watching and cold and hunger had rendered her utterly unable to resist. The monster left her in a trance of stupefaction, and into her right hand, which she had clenched convulsively, he had forced a half-dollar.

It was one of the darkest nights of autumn: in the deep and dead silence the only sounds were the slow blunt ticking of the church clock, and now and then the sinking down of bones in the nigh charnel-house. Maria, when she had in some degree recovered her senses, sat upon the grave near which—not her innocence had been sacrificed, but—that which, from the frequent admonitions and almost the dying words of her father, she had been accustomed to consider as such.

Guiltless, she felt the pangs of guilt, and still continued to grasp the coin which the monster had left in her hand, with an anguish as sore as if it had been indeed the wages of voluntary prostitution. Giddy and faint from want of food, her brain becoming feverish from sleeplessness, and in this unexampled concurrence of calamities, this complication and entanglement of misery in misery, she imagined that she heard her father's voice bidding her leave his sight.

His last blessings had been conditional, for in his last hours he had told her that the loss of her innocence would not let him rest quiet in his grave. His last blessings now sounded in her ear like curses, and she fled from the churchyard as if a demon had been chasing her; and hurrying along the streets, through which it is probable her accursed violater had walked with quiet and orderly step to his place of rest and security, she was seized by the watchmen of the night—a welcome prey, as they receive in Nuremberg half a gulden from the police chest for every woman that they find in the streets after ten o'clock at night. It was midnight, and she was taken to the next watch-house.

The sitting magistrate before whom she was carried the next morning prefaced his first question with the most opprobrious title that ever belonged to the most hardened street-walkers, and which man born of woman should not address even to these, were it but for his own sake. The frightful name awakened the poor orphan from her dream of guilt, it brought back the consciousness of her innocence, but with it the sense likewise of her wrongs and of her helplessness. The cold hand of death seemed to grasp her, she fainted dead away at his feet and was not without difficulty recovered.

The magistrate was so far softened, and only so far, as to dismiss her for the present, but with a menace of sending her to the House of Correction if she were brought before him a second time. The idea of her own innocence now became uppermost in her mind; but mingling with the thought of her utter forlornness, and the image of her angry father, and doubtless still in a state of bewilderment, she formed the resolution of drowning herself in the river Pegnitz—in order (for this was the shape which her fancy had taken) to throw herself at her father's feet, and to justify her innocence to him in the world of spirits. She hoped that her father would speak for her to the Saviour, and that she should be forgiven.

But as she was passing through the suburb she was met by a soldier's wife, who during the lifetime of her father had been occasionally employed in the house as a charwoman. This poor woman was startled at the disordered apparel and more disordered looks of her young mistress, and questioned her with such an anxious and heartfelt tenderness, as at once brought back the poor orphan to her natural feelings and the obligations of religion. As a frightened child throws itself into the arms of its mother, and hiding its head on her breast, half tells amid sobs what has happened to it, so did she throw herself on the neck of the woman who had uttered the first words of kindness to her since her father's death, and with loud weeping she related what she had endured and what she was about to have done, told her all her affliction and her misery, the wormwood and the gall! Her kind-hearted friend mingled tears with tears; pressed the poor forsaken one to her heart; comforted her with sentences out of the hymn-book; and with the most affectionate entreaties conjured her to give up her horrid purpose, for that life was short, and heaven was for ever.

Maria had been bred up in the fear of God; she now trembled at the thought of her former purpose, and followed her friend Harlin, for that was the name of her guardian angel, to her home hard by. The moment she entered the door she sank down and lay at her full length, as if only to be motionless in a place of shelter had been the fulness of delight. As when a withered leaf, that has been long whirled about by the gusts of autumn, is blown into a cave or hollow tree, it stops suddenly, and all at once looks the very image of quiet—such might this poor orphan appear to the eye of a meditative imagination.

A place of shelter she had attained, and a friend willing to comfort her in all that she could; but the noble-hearted Harlin was herself a daughter of calamity, one who from year to year must lie down in weariness and rise up to labour; for whom this world provides no other comfort but the sleep which enables them to forget it; no other physician but death, which takes them out of it! She was married to one of the city guards, who, like Maria's father, had been long sick and bedridden. Him, herself, and two little children, she had to maintain by washing and charing; and some time after Maria had been domesticated with them, Harlin told her that she herself had been once driven to a desperate thought by the cry of her hungry children, during a want of employment, and that she had been on the point of killing one of the little ones, and of then surrendering herself into the hands of justice.

In this manner, she had conceived, all would be well provided for; the surviving child would be admitted, as a matter of course, into the Orphan House, and her husband into the Hospital; while she herself would have atoned for her act by a public execution, and, together with the child that she had destroyed, would have passed into a state of bliss. All this she related to Maria, and those tragic ideas left but too deep and lasting impression on her mind. Weeks after, she herself renewed the conversation, by expressing to her benefactress her inability to conceive how it was possible for one human being to take away the life of another, especially that of an innocent little child.

"For that reason," replied Harlin, "because it was so innocent and so good, I wished to put it out of this wicked world. Thinkest thou, then, that I would have my head cut off for the sake of a wicked child? Therefore it was little Nan that I meant to have taken with me, who, as you see, is always so sweet and patient; little Frank has already his humours and naughty tricks, and suits better for this world."

This was the answer. Maria brooded a while over it in silence, then passionately snatched the children up in her arms, as if she would protect them against their own mother.

For one whole year the orphan lived with the soldier's wife, and by their joint labours barely kept off absolute want. As a little boy (almost a child in size though in his thirteenth year) once told me of himself, as he was guiding me up the Brocken, in the Hartz Forest, they had but "little of that, of which a great deal tells but for little."

But now came the second winter, and with it came bad times, a season of trouble for this poor and meritorious household. The wife now fell sick: too constant and too hard labour, too scanty and too innutritious food, had gradually wasted away her strength. Maria redoubled her efforts in order to provide bread, and fuel for their washing which they took in; but the task was above her powers. Besides, she was so timid and so agitated at the sight of strangers, that sometimes, with the best good-will, she was left without employment. One by one, every article of the least value which they possessed was sold off, except the bed on which the husband lay. He died just before the approach of spring; but about the same time the wife gave signs of convalescence.

The physician, though almost as poor as his patients, had been kind to them: silver and gold had he none, but he occasionally brought a little wine, and often assured them that nothing was wanting to her perfect recovery but better nourishment and a little wine every day. This, however, could not be regularly procured, and Harlin's spirits sank, and as her bodily pain left her she became more melancholy, silent, and self-involved. And now it was that Maria's mind was incessantly racked by the frightful apprehension, that her friend might be again meditating the accomplishment of her former purpose. She had grown as passionately fond of the two children as if she had borne them under her own heart; but the jeopardy in which she conceived her friend's salvation to stand—this was her predominant thought. For all the hopes and fears, which under a happier lot would have been associated with the objects of the senses, were transferred, by Maria, to her notions and images of a future state.

In the beginning of March, one bitter cold evening, Maria started up and suddenly left the house. The last morsel of food had been divided between the two children for their breakfast; and for the last hour or more the little boy had been crying for hunger, while his gentle sister had been hiding her face in Maria's lap, and pressing her little body against her knees, in order by that mechanic pressure to dull the aching from emptiness. The tender-hearted and visionary maiden had watched the mother's eye, and had interpreted several of her sad and steady looks according to her preconceived apprehensions. She had conceived all at once the strange and enthusiastic thought that she would in some way or other offer her own soul for the salvation of the soul of her friend. The money, which had been left in her hand, flashed upon the eye of her mind, as a single unconnected image; and faint with hunger and shivering with cold, she sallied forth—in search of guilt!

Awful are the dispensations of the Supreme, and in His severest judgments the hand of mercy is visible. It was a night so wild with wind and rain, or rather rain and snow mixed together, that a famished wolf would have stayed in his cave, and listened to a howl more fearful than his own. Forlorn Maria! thou wert kneeling in pious simplicity at the grave of thy father, and thou becamest the prey of a monster! Innocent thou wert, and without guilt didst thou remain. Now thou goest forth of thy own accord—but God will have pity on thee! Poor bewildered innocent; in thy spotless imagination dwelt no distinct conception of the evil which thou wentest forth to brave! To save the soul of thy friend was the dream of thy feverish brain, and thou wert again apprehended as an outcast of shameless sensuality, at the moment when thy too spiritualised fancy was busied with the glorified forms of thy friend and of her little ones interceding for thee at the throne of the Redeemer!

At this moment her perturbed fancy suddenly suggested to her a new means for the accomplishment of her purpose; and she replied to the night-watch—who with a brutal laugh bade her expect on the morrow the unmanly punishment, which to the disgrace of human nature the laws of Protestant states (alas! even those of our own country) inflict on female vagrants—that she came to deliver herself up as an infanticide.

She was instantly taken before the magistrate, through as wild and pitiless a storm as ever pelted on a houseless head! through as black and tyrannous a night as ever aided the workings of a heated brain! Here she confessed that she had been delivered of an infant by the soldier's wife, Harlin, that she deprived it of life in the presence of Harlin, and according to a plan preconcerted with her, and that Harlin had buried it somewhere in the wood, but where she knew not. During this strange tale she appeared to listen, with a mixture of fear and satisfaction, to the howling of the wind; and never sure could a confession of real guilt have been accompanied by a more dreadfully appropriate music!

At the moment of her apprehension she had formed the scheme of helping her friend out of the world in a state of innocence. When the soldier's widow was confronted with the orphan, and the latter had repeated her confession to her face, Harlin answered in these words, "For God's sake, Maria! how have I deserved this of thee?" Then turning to the magistrate, said, "I know nothing of this."

This was the sole answer which she gave, and not another word could they extort from her. The instruments of torture were brought, and Harlin was warned, that if she did not confess of her own accord, the truth would be immediately forced from her. This menace convulsed Maria Schöning with affright; her intention had been to emancipate herself and her friend from a life of unmixed suffering, without the crime of suicide in either, and with no guilt at all on the part of her friend. The thought of her friend's being put to the torture had not occurred to her.

Wildly and eagerly she pressed her friend's hands, already bound in preparation for the torture—she pressed them in agony between her own, and said to her, "Anna! confess it! Anna, dear Anna! it will then be well with all of us! all, all of us! and Frank and little Nan will be put into the Orphan House!"

Maria's scheme now passed, like a flash of lightning, through the widow's mind; she acceded to it at once, kissed Maria repeatedly, and then serenely turning her face to the judge, acknowledged that she had added to the guilt by so obstinate a denial, that all her friend had said was true, save only that she had thrown the dead infant into the river, and not buried it in the wood.

They were both committed to prison, and as they both persevered in their common confession, the process was soon made out and the condemnation followed the trial: and the sentence, by which they were both to be beheaded with the sword, was ordered to be put in force on the next day but one. On the morning of the execution the delinquents were brought together, in order that they might be reconciled with each other, and join in common prayer for forgiveness of their common guilt.

But now Maria's thoughts took another turn. The idea that her benefactress, that so very good a woman, should be violently put out of life, and this with an infamy on her name which would cling for ever to the little orphans, overpowered her. Her own excessive desire to die scarcely prevented her from discovering the whole plan; and when Harlin was left alone with her, and she saw her friend's calm and affectionate look, her fortitude was dissolved; she burst into loud and passionate weeping, and throwing herself into her friend's arms, with convulsive sobs she entreated her forgiveness.

Harlin pressed the poor agonised girl to her arms; like a tender mother, she kissed and fondled her wet cheeks, and in the most solemn and emphatic tones assured her that there was nothing to forgive. On the contrary, she was her greatest benefactress, and the instrument of God's goodness to remove her at once from a miserable world and from the temptation of committing a heavy crime. In vain! Her repeated promises, that she would answer before God for them both, could not pacify the tortured conscience of Maria, till at length the presence of the clergyman and the preparations for receiving the sacrament occasioned the widow to address her thus: "See, Maria! this is the Body and Blood of Christ, which takes away all sin! Let us partake together of this holy repast with full trust in God and joyful hope of our approaching happiness."

These words of comfort, uttered with cheering tones, and accompanied with a look of inexpressible tenderness and serenity, brought back peace for a while to her troubled spirit. They communicated together, and on parting, the magnanimous woman once more embraced her young friend; then stretching her hand toward heaven, said, "Be tranquil, Maria! by to-morrow morning we are there, and all our sorrows stay here behind us."

I hasten to the scene of the execution; for I anticipate my reader's feelings in the exhaustion of my own heart. Serene and with unaltered countenance the lofty-minded Harlin heard the strokes of the death-bell, stood before the scaffold while the staff was broken over her, and at length ascended the steps, all with a steadiness and tranquillity of manner which was not more distant from fear than from defiance and bravado. Altogether different was the state of poor Maria: with shattered nerves and an agonising conscience that incessantly accused her as the murderess of her friend, she did not walk but staggered towards the scaffold and stumbled up the steps.

While Harlin, who went first, at every step turned her head round and still whispered to her, raising her eyes to heaven, "But a few minutes, Maria! and we are there!"

On the scaffold she again bade her farewell, again repeating, "Dear Maria! but one minute now, and we are together with God."

But when she knelt down and her neck was bared for the stroke, the unhappy girl lost all self-command, and with a loud and piercing shriek she bade them hold and not murder the innocent "She is, innocent! I have borne false-witness! I alone am the murderess!"

She rolled herself now at the feet of the executioner, and now at those of the clergymen, and conjured them to stop the execution: declaring that the whole story had been invented by herself; that she had never brought forth, much less destroyed, an infant; that for her friend's sake she made this discovery; that for herself she wished to die, and would die gladly, if they would take away her friend, and promise to free her soul from the dreadful agony of having murdered her friend by false-witness.

The executioner asked Harlin if there were any truth in what Maria Schöning had said.

The heroine answered with manifest reluctance: "Most assuredly she hath said the truth; I confessed myself guilty, because I wished to die and thought it best for both of us; and now that my hope is on the moment of its accomplishment, I cannot be supposed to declare myself innocent for the sake of saving my life—but any wretchedness is to be endured rather than that poor creature should be hurried out of the world in a state of despair."

The outcry of the attending populace prevailed to suspend the execution: a report was sent to the assembled magistrates, and in the meantime one of the priests reproached the widow in bitter words for her former false confession.

"What," she replied, sternly but without anger, "what would the truth have availed? Before I perceived my friend's purpose I did deny it: my assurance was pronounced an impudent lie; I was already bound for the torture, and so bound that the sinews of my hands started, and one of their worships in the large white peruke, threatened that he would have me stretched till the sun shone through me! and that then I should cry out, Yes, when it was too late."

The priest was hard-hearted or supersitious enough to continue his reproofs, to which the noble woman condescended no further answer.

The other clergyman, however, was both more rational and more humane. He succeeded in silencing his colleague, and the former half of the long hour, which the magistrate took in making speeches on the improbability of the tale instead of re-examining the culprits in person, he employed in gaining from the widow a connected account of all the circumstances, and in listening occasionally to Maria's passionate descriptions of all her friend's goodness and magnanimity. For she had gained an influx of life and spirit from the assurance in her mind, both that she had now rescued Harlin from death and was about to expiate the guilt of her purpose by her own execution.

For the latter half of the time the clergyman remained in silence, lost in thought, and momentarily expecting the return of the messenger. All that during the deep silence of this interval could be heard was one exclamation of Harlin to her unhappy friend :

"Oh ! Maria ! Maria ! couldst thou but have kept up thy courage but for another minute, we should have been now in heaven ! "

The messenger came back with an order from the magistrates to proceed with the execution ! With reanimated countenance Harlin placed her neck on the block, and her head was severed from her body amid a general shriek from the crowd. The executioner fainted after the blow, and the under-hangman was ordered to take his place.

He was not wanted. Maria was already gone : her body was found as cold as if she had been dead for some hours. The flower had been snapt in the storm, before the scythe of violence could come near it.

CHARLES LAMB
1775–1834

DREAM-CHILDREN
A REVERIE

CHILDREN love to listen to stories about their elders when *they* were children ; to stretch their imagination to the conception of a traditionary great-uncle, or grandame, whom they never saw. It was in this spirit that my little ones crept about me the other evening to hear about their great-grandmother Field, who lived in a great house in Norfolk (a hundred times bigger than that in which they and papa lived), which had been the scene—so at least it was generally believed in that part of the country—of the tragic incidents which they had lately become familiar with from the ballad of the *Children in the Wood*.

Certain it is, that the whole story of the children and their cruel uncle was to be seen fairly carved out in the wood upon the chimney-piece of the great hall—the whole story down to the Robin Red-breasts—till a foolish rich person pulled it down to set up a marble one of modern invention in its stead, with no story upon it. Here Alice put out one of her dear mother's looks, too tender to be called upbraiding.

Then I went on to say how religious and how good their great-grandmother Field was, how beloved and respected by everybody, though she was not, indeed, the mistress of this great house, but had only the charge of it (and yet in some respects she might be said to be the mistress of it too) committed to her by the owner, who preferred living in a newer and more fashionable mansion, which he had purchased somewhere in the adjoining county ; but still she lived in it in a manner as if it had been her own, and kept up the dignity of the great house in a sort while she lived, which afterwards came to decay, and was nearly pulled down, and all its old ornaments stripped and carried away to the owner's other house, where they were set up, and looked as awkward as if some one were to carry away the old tombs they had seen lately at the Abbey, and stick them up in Lady C.'s tawdry gilt drawing-room.

Here John smiled, as much as to say, "That would be foolish indeed."

And then I told how, when she came to die, her funeral was attended by a concourse of all the poor, and some of the gentry too, of the neighbourhood, for many miles round, to show their respect for her memory, because she had been such a good and religious woman—so good, indeed, that she knew all the Psalter by heart, aye, and a great part of the Testament besides.

Here little Alice spread her hands. Then I told what a tall, upright, graceful person their great-grandmother Field once was; and how in her youth she was esteemed the best dancer—here Alice's little right foot played an involuntary movement, till, upon my looking grave, it desisted—the best dancer, I was saying, in the county, till a cruel disease, called a cancer, came, and bowed her down with pain; but it could never bend her good spirits, or make them stoop; but they were still upright, because she was so good and religious.

Then I told how she was used to sleep by herself in a lone chamber of the great lone house; and how she believed that an apparition of two infants was to be seen at midnight gliding up and down the great staircase near where she slept; but she said, "Those innocents would do her no harm"; and how frightened I used to be, though in those days I had my maid to sleep with me, because I was never half so good or religious as she, and yet I never saw the infants.

Here John expanded all his eyebrows, and tried to look courageous. Then I told how good she was to all her grandchildren, having us to the great house in the holidays, where I in particular used to spend many hours by myself in gazing upon the old busts of the twelve Caesars, that had been emperors of Rome, till the old marble heads would seem to live again, or I to be turned into marble with them; how I never could be tired with roaming about that huge mansion, with its vast empty rooms, with their worn-out hangings, fluttering tapestry, and carved oaken panels, with the gilding almost rubbed out—sometimes in the spacious old-fashioned gardens, which I had almost to myself, unless when now and then a solitary gardening man would cross me—and how the nectarines and peaches hung upon the walls without my ever offering to pluck them, because they were forbidden fruit, unless now and then,—and because I had more pleasure in strolling about among the old melancholy-looking yew-trees, or the firs, and picking up the red berries, and the fir-apples, which were good for nothing but to look at—or in lying about upon the fresh grass, with all the fine garden smells around me—or basking in the orangery, till I could almost fancy myself ripening too along with the oranges and the limes, in that grateful warmth—or in watching the dace that darted to and fro in the fish-pond, at the bottom of the garden, with here and there a great sulky pike hanging midway down the water in silent state, as if it mocked at their impertinent friskings,—I had more pleasure in these busy-idle diversions than in all the sweet flavours of peaches, nectarines, oranges, and such-like common baits of children.

Here John slily deposited back upon the plate a bunch of grapes, which, not unobserved by Alice, he had meditated dividing with her, and both seemed willing to relinquish them for the present as irrelevant. Then, in somewhat a more heightened tone, I told how, though their great-grandmother Field loved all her grandchildren, yet, in an especial manner, she might be said to love their uncle, John L——, because he was so handsome and spirited a youth, and a king to the rest of us; and, instead of moping about in solitary corners like some of us, he would mount the most mettlesome horse he could get, when but an imp no bigger than themselves, and make it carry him half over the county in a morning, and join the hunters when there were any out—and yet he loved the old great house and gardens too, but had too much spirit to be always pent up within their boundaries—and how their uncle grew up to man's estate as brave as he was handsome, to the admiration of everybody, but of their great-grandmother Field most especially; and how he used to carry me upon his back when I was a lame-footed boy—for he was a good bit older than me—many a mile when I could not walk for pain;—and how, in after-life, he became lame-footed too, and I did not always (I fear) make allowances enough for him when he was impatient, and in pain, nor remember sufficiently how considerate he had been to me when I was lame-footed; and how, when he died, though he had not been dead an hour it seemed as if he had died a great while ago, such a distance there is betwixt life and death; and how I bore his death, as I thought, pretty well at first, but afterwards it haunted and haunted me; and though I did not cry or take it to heart as some do, and as I think he would have done if I had died, yet I missed him all day long, and I knew not till then how much I had loved him.

I missed his kindness, and I missed his crossness, and wished him to be alive again, to be quarrelling with him (for we quarrelled sometimes), rather than not have him again, and was as uneasy without him as he, their poor uncle, must have been when the doctor took off his limb.

Here the children fell a-crying, and asked if their little mourning which they had on was not for Uncle John, and they looked up, and prayed me not to go on about their uncle, but to tell them some stories about their pretty dead mother.

Then I told how, for seven long years, in hope sometimes, sometimes in despair, yet persisting ever, I courted the fair Alice W—n;

and, as much as children could understand, I explained to them what coyness, and difficulty, and denial meant in maidens, when suddenly turning to Alice, the soul of the first Alice looked out at her eyes, with such a reality of representment that I became in doubt which of them stood there before me, or whose that bright hair was; and while I stood gazing, both the children gradually grew fainter to my view, receding, and still receding, till nothing at last but two mournful features were seen in the uttermost distance, which, without speech, strangely impressed upon me the effects of speech:

"We are not of Alice, nor of thee, nor are we children at all. The children of Alice call Bartrum father. We are nothing; less than nothing, and dreams. We are only what might have been, and must wait upon the tedious shores of Lethe millions of ages before we have existence and a name"——and immediately awaking, I found myself quietly seated in my bachelor arm-chair, where I had fallen asleep with the faithful Bridget unchanged by my side.

CHARLES LAMB

JUKE JUDKINS' COURTSHIP

I AM the only son of a considerable brazier in Birmingham, who, dying in 1803, left me successor to the business, with no other encumbrance than a sort of rent-charge, which I am enjoined to pay out of it, of ninety-three pounds sterling *per annum*, to his widow, my mother: and which the improving state of the concern, I bless God, has hitherto enabled me to discharge with punctuality. (I say, I am enjoined to pay the said sum, but not strictly obligated: that is to say, as the will is worded, I believe the law would relieve me from the payment of it; but the wishes of a dying parent should in some sort have the effect of law.) So that, though the annual profits of my business, on an average of the last three or four years, would appear to an indifferent observer, who should inspect my shop-books, to amount to the sum of one thousand three hundred and three pounds, odd shilling, the real proceeds in that time have fallen short of that sum to the amount of the aforesaid payment of ninety-three pounds sterling annually.

I was always my father's favourite. He took a delight to the very last in recounting the little sagacious tricks and innocent artifices of my childhood. One manifestation thereof I never heard him repeat without tears of joy trickling down his cheeks. It seems, that when I quitted the parental roof (Aug. 27, 1788), being then six years and not quite a month old, to proceed to the Free School at Warwick, where my father was a sort of trustee, my mother—as mothers are usually provident on these occasions—had stuffed the pockets of the coach, which was to convey me and six more children of my own growth that were going to be entered along with me at the same seminary, with a prodigious quantity of gingerbread, which I remembered my father said was more than was needed: and so indeed it was; for, if I had been to eat it all myself, it would have got stale and mouldy before it had been half spent. The consideration whereof set me upon my contrivances how I might secure to myself as much of the gingerbread as would keep good for the next two or three days, and yet none of the rest in manner be wasted. I had a little pair of pocket-compasses, which I usually carried about me for the purpose of making draughts and measurements, at which I was always very ingenious, of the various engines and mechanical inventions in which such a town as Birmingham abounded.

By means of these, and a small penknife which my father had given me, I cut out the one half of the cake, calculating that the remainder would reasonably serve my turn ; and subdividing it into many little slices, which were curious to see for the neatness and niceness of their proportion, I sold it out in so many pennyworths to my young companions as served us all the way to Warwick, which is a distance of some twenty miles from this town : and very merry, I assure you, we made ourslves with it, feasting all the way. By this honest stratagem I put double the prime cost of the gingerbread into my purse, and secured as much as I thought would keep good and moist for my next two or three days' eating.

When I told this to my parents on their first visit to me at Warwick, my father (good man), patted me on the cheek, and stroked my head, and seemed as if he could never make enough of me ; but my mother unaccountably burst into tears, and said, " it was a very niggardly action," or some such expression, and that " she would rather it would please God to take me "—meaning (God help me) that I should die—" than that she should live to see me grow up *a mean man*," which shows the difference of parent from parent, and how some mothers are more harsh and intolerant to their children than some fathers ; when we might expect quite the contrary.

My father, however, loaded me with presents from that time, which made me the envy of my school-fellows. As I felt this growing disposition in them, I naturally sought to avert it by all the means in my power ; and from that time I used to eat my little packages of fruit, and other nice things, in a corner, so privately that I was never found out. Once, I remember, I had a huge apple sent me, of that sort which they call *cats'-heads*. I concealed this all day under my pillow ; and at night, but not before I had ascertained that my bed-fellow was sound asleep,—which I did by pinching him rather smartly two or three times, which he seemed to perceive no more than a dead person, though once or twice he made a motion as if he would turn, which frightened me,—I say, when I had made all sure, I fell to work upon my apple ; and, though it was as big as an ordinary man's two fists, I made shift to get through it before it was time to get up. And a more delicious feast I never made ; thinking all night what a good parent I had (I mean my father) to send me so many nice things, when the poor lad that lay by me had no parent or friend in the world to send him anything nice ; and thinking of his desolate condition, I munched and munched as silently as I could, that I might not set him a-longing if he overheard me.

And yet, for all this considerateness and attention to other people's feelings, I was never much a favourite with my school-fellows; which I have often wondered at, seeing that I never defrauded any one of them of the value of a halfpenny, or told stories of them to their master, as some little lying boys would do, but was ready to do any of them all the services in my power, that were consistent with my own well-doing. I think nobody can be expected to go farther than that.

But I am detaining my reader too long in recording my juvenile days. It is time I should go forward to a season when it became natural that I should have some thoughts of marrying, and, as they say, settling in the world. Nevertheless, my reflections on what I may call the boyish period of my life may have their use to some readers. It is pleasant to trace the man in the boy; to observe shoots of generosity in those young years; and to watch the progress of liberal sentiments, and what I may call a genteel way of thinking, which is discernible in some children at a very early age, and usually lays the foundation of all that is praiseworthy in the manly character afterwards.

With the warmest inclinations towards that way of life, and a serious conviction of its superior advantages over a single one, it has been the strange infelicity of my lot never to have entered into the respectable estate of matrimony.

Yet I was once very near it.

I courted a young woman in my twenty-seventh year; for so early I began to feel symptoms of the tender passion! She was well-to-do in the world, as they call it; but yet not such a fortune as, all things considered, perhaps I might have pretended to. It was not my own choice altogether; but my mother very strongly pressed me to it. She was always putting it to me, that I had "comings-in sufficient,"—that I "need not stand upon a portion"; though the young woman, to do her justice, had considerable expectations, which yet did not quite come up to my mark, as I told you before.

My mother had this saying always in her mouth, that I had "money enough"; that it was time I enlarged my housekeeping, and to show a spirit befitting my circumstances. In short, what with her importunities, and my own desires in part co-operating,—for, as I said, I was not yet quite twenty-seven,—a time when the youthful feelings may be pardoned if they show a little impetuosity,—I resolved, I say, upon all these considerations, to set about the business of courting in right earnest. I was a young man then; and having a spice of romance in my character (as the reader has doubtless observed long ago), such as that sex is apt to be taken with, I had reason in no long time to think that my addresses were anything but disagreeable. Certainly the happiest part of a young man's life is the time when he is going a-courting. All the generous impulses are then awake, and he feels a double existence in participating his hopes and wishes with another being.

Return yet again for a brief moment, ye visionary views, transient enchantments! ye moonlight rambles with Cleora in the Silent Walk at Vauxhall (*N.B.*—About a mile from Birmingham, and resembling the gardens of that name near London, only that the price of admission is lower), when the nightingale has suspended her notes in June to listen to our loving discourses, while the moon was overhead! (for we generally used to take our tea at Cleora's mother's before we set out, not so much to save expenses as to avoid the publicity of a repast in the gardens,—coming in much about the time of half-price, as they call it,) ye soft intercommunions of soul, when, exchanging mutual vows, we prattled of coming felicities! The loving disputes we have had under those trees, when this house (planning our future settlement) was rejected, because, though cheap, it was dull; and the other house was given up, because, though agreeably situated, it was too high-rented!—one was too much in the heart of the town, another was too far from business.

These minutiae will seem impertinent to the aged and prudent. I write them only to the young. Young lovers, and passionate as being young (such were Cleora and I then), alone can understand me. After some weeks wasted, as I may now call it, in this sort of amorous colloquy, we at length fixed upon the house in the High Street, No. 203, just vacated by the death of Mr. Hutton of this town, for our future residence. I had all the time lived in lodgings (only renting a shop for business), to be near my mother,—near, I say: not in the same house: for that would have been to introduce confusion into our housekeeping, which it was desirable to keep separate. Oh, the loving wrangles, the endearing differences, I had with Cleora, before we could quite make up our minds to the house that was to receive us!—I pretending, for argument's sake, the rent was too high, and she insisting that the taxes were moderate in proportion; and love at last reconciling us in the same choice. I think at that time, moderately speaking, she might have had anything out of me for asking. I do not, nor shall ever, regret that my character at that time was marked with a tinge of prodigality. Age comes fast enough upon us, and, in its good time, will prune away all that is inconvenient in these excesses. Perhaps it is right that it should do so.

Matters, as I said, were ripening to a conclusion between us, only the house was yet not absolutely taken, some necessary arrangements, which the ardour of my youthful impetuosity could hardly brook at that time (love and youth will be precipitate),—some preliminary arrangements, I say, with the landlord, respecting fixtures,—very necessary things to be considered in a young man about to settle in the world, though not very accordant with the impatient state of my then passions,—some obstacles about the valuation of the fixtures,—had hitherto precluded (and I shall always think providentially) my final closes with his offer ; when one of those accidents, which, unimportant in themselves, often arise to give a turn to the most serious intentions of our life, intervened, and put an end at once to my projects of wiving, and of housekeeping.

I was never much given to theatrical entertainments ; that is, at no time of my life was I ever what they call a regular play-goer : but on some occasion of a benefit-night, which was expected to be very productive, and indeed turned out so, Cleora expressing a desire to be present, I could do no less than offer, as I did very willingly, to squire her and her mother to the pit. At that time it was not customary in our town for tradesfolk, except some of the very topping ones, to sit, as they now do, in the boxes.

At the time appointed I waited upon the ladies, who had brought with them a young man, a distant relation, whom, it seems, they had invited to be of the party. This a little disconcerted me, as I had about me barely silver enough to pay for our three selves at the door, and did not at first know that their relation had proposed paying for himself. However, to do the young man justice, he not only paid for himself, but for the old lady besides ; leaving me only to pay for two, as it were. In our passage to the theatre the notice of Cleora was attracted to some orange wenches that stood about the doors vending their commodities. She was leaning on my arm ; and I could feel her every now and then giving me a nudge, as it is called, which I afterwards discovered were hints that I should buy some oranges.

It seems, it is a custom at Birmingham, and perhaps in other places, when a gentleman treats ladies to the play,—especially when a full night is expected, and that the house will be inconveniently warm,—to provide them with this kind of fruit, oranges being esteemed for their cooling property. But how could I guess at that, never having treated ladies to a play before, and being, as I said, quite a novice at entertainments of this kind ?

At last, she spoke plain out, and begged that I would buy some of " those oranges," pointing to a particular barrow. But, when I came to examine the fruit, I did not think the quality of it was answerable to the price. In this way I handled several baskets of them ; but something in them all displeased me. Some had thin rinds, and some were plainly over-ripe, which is as great a fault as not being ripe enough ; and I could not (what they call) make a bargain.

While I stood haggling with the woman, secretly determining to put off my purchase till I should get within the theatre, where I expected we should have better choice, the young man, the cousin (who, it seems had left us without my missing him), came running to us with his pockets stuffed out with oranges, inside and out, as they say. It seems, not liking the look of the barrow-fruit any more than myself, he had slipped away to an eminent fruiterer's, about three doors distant, which I never had the sense to think of, and had laid out a matter of two shillings in some of the best St. Michael's, I think I ever tasted.

What a little hinge, as I said before, the most important affairs in life may turn upon! The mere inadvertence to the fact that there was an eminent fruiterer's within three doors of us, though we had just passed it without the thought once occurring to me, which he had taken advantage of, lost me the affection of my Cleora. From that time she visibly cooled towards me; and her partiality was as visibly transferred to this cousin. I was long unable to account for this change in her behaviour; when one day, accidently discoursing of oranges to my mother, alone, she let drop a sort of reproach to me, as if I had offended Cleora by my *nearness* as she called it, that evening.

Even now, when Cleora has been wedded some years to that same officious relation, as I may call him, I can hardly be persuaded that such a trifle could have been the motive for her inconstancy; for could she suppose that I would sacrifice my dearest hopes in her to the paltry sum of two shillings, when I was going to treat her to the play, and her mother too (an expense of more than four times that amount), if the young man had not interfered to pay for the latter, as I mentioned?

But the caprices of the sex are past finding out: and I begin to think my mother was in the right; for doubtless women know women better than we can pretend to know them.

JAMES MORIER
1780–1849

HAJJI BABA AND THE STOLEN MONEY

My father having died without a will, I was, of course, proclaimed his sole heir without any opposition, and consequently all those who had aspired to be sharers of his property, baulked by my unexpected appearance, immediately withdrew to vent their disappointment in abusing me. They represented me as a wretch devoid of all respect for my parents, as one without religion, an adventurer in the world, and the companion of lûties and wandering dervishes.

As I had no intention of remaining at Ispahan, I treated their endeavours to hurt me with contempt, and consoled myself by giving them a full return of all their scurrility, by expressions which neither they nor their fathers had ever heard—expressions which I had picked up from amongst the illustrious characters with whom I had passed the first years of my youth.

When we were left to ourselves, my mother and I, after having bewailed in sufficiently pathetic language, she the death of a husband, I the loss of a father, the following conversation took place :

" Now tell me, O my mother—for there can be no secrets between us—tell me what was the state of Kerbelai Hassan's concerns. He loved you, and confided in you, and you must therefore be better acquainted with them than any one else."

" What do I know of them, my son ? " said she, in great haste, and seeming confusion.

I stopped her, to continue my speech. " You know that, according to the law, his heir is bound to pay his debts : they must be ascertained. Then, the expenses of the funeral are to be defrayed ; they will be considerable ; and at present I am as destitute of means as on the day you gave me birth. To meet all this, money is necessary, or else both mine and my father's name will be disgraced among men, and my enemies will not fail to overcome me. He must have been reputed wealthy, or else his deathbed would never have been surrounded by that host of blood-suckers and time-servers which have been driven away by my presence. You, my mother, must tell me where he was accustomed to deposit his ready cash ; who were, or who are likely to be, his debtors ; and what might be his possessions, besides those which are apparent."

"Oh, Allah !" exclaimed she, "what words are these ? Your father was a poor, good man, who had neither money nor possessions. Money, indeed ! We had dry bread to eat, and that was all ! Now and then, after the arrival of a great caravan, when heads to be shaved were plentiful, and his business brisk, we indulged in our dish of rice, and our skewer of kabob, but otherwise we lived like beggars. A bit of bread, a morsel of cheese, an onion, a basin of sour curds—that was our daily fare ; and, under these circumstances can you ask me for money, ready money too ? There is this house, which you see and know ; then his shop, with its furniture ; and when I have said that, I have nearly said all. You are just arrived in time, my son, to step into your father's shoes, and take up his business ; and *Inshallah,* please God, may your hand be fortunate ! may it never cease wagging, from one year's end to the other !"

"This is very strange !" exclaimed I, in my turn. "Fifty years', and more, hard and unceasing toil ! and nothing to show for it ! This is incredible ! We must call in the diviners."

"The diviners ?" said my mother, in some agitation ; "of what use can they be ? They are only called in when a thief is to be discovered. You will not proclaim your mother a thief, Hajji, will you ? Go, make inquiries of your friend, and your father's friend, the *âkhon* [schoolmaster]. He is acquainted with the whole of the concerns, and I am sure he will repeat what I have said."

"You do not speak amiss, mother," said I. "The âkhon probably does know what were my father's last wishes, for he appeared to be the principal director in his dying moments ; and he may tell me, if money there was left, where it is to be found."

Accordingly I went straightway to seek the old man, whom I found seated precisely in the very same corner of the little parish mosque, surrounded by his scholars, in which some twenty years before I myself had received his instructions. As soon as he saw me he dismissed his scholars, saying that my footsteps were fortunate, and that others, as well as himself, should partake of the pleasure which I was sure to dispense wherever I went.

"Ahi, âkhon," said I, "do not laugh at my beard. My good fortune has entirely forsaken me ; and even now, when I had hoped that my destiny, in depriving me of my father, had made up the loss by giving me wealth, I am likely to be disappointed, and to turn out a greater beggar than ever."

"*Allah kerim,* God is merciful," said the schoolmaster ; and lifting up his eyes to heaven, whilst he placed his hands on his knees, with their palms uppermost, he exclaimed, " Oh, Allah, whatever is, thou art it." Then addressing himself to me, he said, " Yes, my son, such is the world, and such will it ever be, as long as man shuts not up his heart from all human desires. Want nothing, seek nothing, and nothing will seek you."

" How long have you been a Sûfi," said I, " that you talk after this manner ? I can speak on that subject also, since my evil star led me to Kom, but now I am engrossed with other matters." I then informed him of the object of my visit, and requested him to tell me what he knew of my father's concerns.

Upon this question he coughed, and, making up a face of great wisdom, went through a long string of oaths and professions, and finished by repeating what I had heard from my mother ; namely, that he believed my father to have died possessed of no (*nagd*) ready cash (for that, after all, was the immediate object of my search) ; and what his other property was, he reminded me that I knew as well as himself.

I remained mute for some time with disappointment, and then expressed my surprise in strong terms. My father, I was aware, was too good a Mussulman to have lent out his money upon interest ; for I recollected a circumstance, when I was quite a youth, which proved it. Osman Aga, my first master, wanting to borrow a sum from him, for which he offered an enormous interest, my father put his conscience into the hands of a rigid mollah, who told him that the precepts of the Koran entirely forbade it. Whether since that time he had relaxed his principles, I could not say ; but I was assured that he always set his face against the unlawful practice of taking interest, and that he died as he had lived, a perfect model of a true believer.

I left the mosque in no very agreeable mood, and took my way to the spot where I had made my first appearance in life—namely, my father's shop—turning over in my mind as I went what steps I should take to secure a future livelihood. To remain at Ispahan was out of the question—the place and the inhabitants were odious to me ; therefore, it was only left me to dispose of everything that was now my own, and to return to the capital, which, after all, I knew to be the best market for an adventurer like myself. However, I could not relinquish the thought that my father had died possessed of some ready money, and suspicions would haunt my mind in spite of me, that foul play was going on somewhere or other. I was at a loss to whom to address myself, unknown as I was in the city, and I was thinking of making my case known to the cadi, when, approaching the gate of the caravanserai, I was accosted by the old capiji.

" Peace be unto you, Aga ! " said he ; " may you live many years, and may your abundance increase! My eyes are enlightened by seeing you."

"Are your spirits so well wound up, Ali Mohamed," said I, in return, "that you choose to treat me thus? As for the abundance you talk of, 'tis abundance of grief, for I have none other that I know of. Och!" said I, sighing, "my liver has become water, and my soul has withered up."

"What news is this?" said the old man. "Your father (peace be unto him!) is just dead—you are his heir—you are young, and, *Mashallah!* you are handsome—your wit is not deficient: what do you want more?"

"I am his heir, 'tis true; but what of that—what advantage can accrue to me, when I only get an old mud-built house, with some worn-out carpets, some pots and pans, and decayed furniture, and yonder shop with a brass basin and a dozen of razors? Let me spit upon such an inheritance."

"But where is your money, your ready cash, Hajji? Your father (God be with him!) had the reputation of being as great a niggard of his money as he was liberal of his soap. Everybody knows that he amassed much, and never passed a day without adding to his store."

"That may be true," said I; "but what advantage will that be to me, since I cannot find where it was deposited? My mother says that he had none—the âkhon repeats the same—I am no conjurer to discover the truth. I had it in my mind to go to the cadi."

"To the cadi?" said Ali Mohamed. "Heaven forbid! Go not to him—you might as well knock at the gate of this caravanserai when I am absent, as try to get justice from him, without a heavy fee. No, he sells it by the miscal, at a heavy price, and very light weight does he give after all. He does not turn over one leaf of the Koran until his fingers have been well plated with gold, and if those who have appropriated your father's sacks are to be your opponents, do not you think that they will drain them into the cadi's lap, rather than he should pronounce in your favour?"

"What then is to be done?" said I. "Perhaps the diviners might give me some help."

"There will be no harm in that," answered the doorkeeper. "I have known them make great discoveries during my service in this caravanserai. Merchants have frequently lost their money, and found it again through their means. It was only in the attack of the Turcomans, when much property was stolen, that they were completely at their wits' end. Ah! that was a strange event. It brought much misery on my head; for some were wicked enough to say that I was their accomplice, and, what is more extraordinary, that you were amongst them, Hajji!—for it was on account of your name, which the dog's son made use of to induce me to open the gate, that the whole mischief was produced."

Lucky was it for me that old Ali Mohamed was very dull of sight, or else he would have remarked strange alterations in my features when he made these observations. However, our conference ended by his promising to send me the most expert diviner of Ispahan; "a man," said he, "who would entice a piece of gold out of the earth if buried twenty gez deep, or even if it was hid in the celebrated well of Kashan."

The next morning, soon after the first prayers, a little man came into my room, whom I soon discovered to be the diviner. He was a humpback, with an immense head, with eyes so wonderfully brilliant, and a countenance so intelligent, that I felt he could look through and through me at one glance. He wore a dervish's cap, from under which flowed a profusion of jet-black hair, which, added to a thick bush of a beard, gave an imposing expression to his features. His eyes, which by a quick action of his eyelid (whether real or affected, I know not) twinkled like stars, made the monster, who was not taller than a good bludgeon, look like a little demon.

He began by questioning me very narrowly; made me relate every circumstance of my life—particularly since my return to Ispahan—inquired who were my father's greatest apparent friends and associates, and what my own suspicions led me to conclude. In short, he searched into every particular, with the same scrutiny that a doctor would in tracing and unravelling an intricate disorder.

When he had well pondered over everything that I had unfolded, he then required to be shown the premises which my father principally inhabited. My mother having gone that morning to the bath, I was enabled, unknown to her, to take him into her apartments, where he requested me to leave him to himself, in order that he might obtain a knowledge of the localities necessary to the discoveries which he hoped to make. He remained there a full quarter of an hour, and when he came out requested me to collect those who were in my father's intimacy, and in the habit of much frequenting the house, and that he would return, they being assembled, and begin his operations.

Without saying a word to my mother about the diviner, I requested her to invite her most intimate friends for the following morning, it being my intention to give them a breakfast; and I myself begged the attendance of the âkhon, the capiji, my father's nephew by his first wife, and a brother of my mother, with others who had free entrance into the house.

They came punctually; and when they had partaken of such fare as I could place before them, they were informed of the predicament in which I stood, and that I had requested their attendance to be witnesses to the endeavours of the diviner to discover where my father was wont to keep his money, of the existence of which, somewhere or other, nobody who knew him could doubt. I looked into each man's face as I made this speech, hoping to remark some expression which might throw a light upon my suspicions, but everybody seemed ready to help my investigation, and maintained the most unequivocal innocence of countenance.

At length the dervish, Teez Negah (for that was the name of the conjurer), was introduced, accompanied by an attendant who carried something wrapt up in a handkerchief. Having ordered the women in the anderûn to keep themselves veiled, because they would probably soon be visited by men, I requested the dervish to begin his operations.

He first looked at every one present with great earnestness, but more particularly fixed his basilisk eyes upon the âkhon, who evidently could not stand the scrutiny, but exclaimed "*Allah il Allah!*"—there is but one God,—stroked down his face and beard, and blew first over one shoulder and then over the other, by way of keeping off the evil spirit. Some merriment was raised at his expense; but he did not appear to be in a humour to meet any one's jokes.

After this, the dervish called to his attendant, who from the handkerchief drew forth a brass cup of a plain surface, but written all over with quotations from the Koran, having reference to the crime of stealing, and defrauding the orphan of his lawful property. He was a man of few words, and simply saying, "In the name of Allah, the All-wise, and All-seeing," he placed the cup on the floor, treating it with much reverence, both in touch and in manner.

He then said to the lookers-on, "*Inshallah*, it will lead us at once to the spot where the money of the deceased Kerbelai Hassan (may God show him mercy!) is, or was, deposited."

We all looked at each other, some with expressions of incredulity, others with unfeigned belief, when he bent himself towards the cup, and with little shoves and pats of his hand he impelled it forwards, exclaiming all the time, "See, see, the road it takes. Nothing can stop it. It will go in spite of me. *Mashallah, Mashallah!*"

We followed him until he reached the door of the harem, where we knocked for admittance. After some negotiation it was opened, and there we found a crowd of women (many of whom had only loosely thrown on their veils) waiting with much impatience to witness the feats which this wonderful cup was to perform.

"Make way," said the diviner to the women who stood in his path, as he took his direction towards a corner of the court, upon which the windows of the room opened—"Make way; nothing can stop my guide."

A woman whom I recognised to be my mother, stopped his progress several times, until he was obliged to admonish her, with some bitterness, to keep clear of him.

"Do you not see," said he, "we are on the Lord's business? Justice will be done in spite of the wickedness of man."

At length he reached a distant corner, where it was plain that the earth had been recently disturbed, and there he stopped.

"*Bismillah*, in the name of Allah," said he, "let all present stand around me, and mark what I do." He dug into the ground with his dagger, clawed the soil away with his hands, and discovered a place in which were the remains of an earthen vessel, and the marks near it of there having been another.

"Here," said he, "here the money was, but is no more." Then taking up his cup, he appeared to caress it, and make much of it, calling it his little uncle and his little soul.

Every one stared. All cried out, "*ajaib*," wonderful; and the little humpback was looked upon as a supernatural being.

The capiji, who was accustomed to such discoveries, was the only one who had the readiness to say, "But where is the thief? You have shown us where the game lay, but we want you to catch it for us: the thief and the money, or the money without the thief—that is what we want."

"Softly, my friend," said the dervish to the capiji, "don't jump so soon from the crime to the criminal. We have a medicine for every disorder, although it may take some time to work."

He then cast his eyes upon the company present, twinkling them all the while in quick flashes, and said, "I am sure every one here will be happy to be clear of suspicion, and will agree to what I shall propose. The operation is simple and soon over."

"*Elbettah*," certainly; "*Belli*," yes; "*Een che har est?*" what word is this? was heard to issue from every mouth, and I requested the dervish to proceed.

He called again to his servant, who produced a small bag, whilst he again took the cup under his charge.

"This bag," said the diviner, "contains some old rice. I will put a small handful of it into each person's mouth, which they will forthwith chew. Let those who cannot break it beware, for Eblis is near at hand."

Upon this, placing us in a row, he filled each person's mouth with rice, and all immediately began to masticate. Being the complainant, of course I was exempt from the ordeal; and my mother, who chose to make common cause with me, also stood out of the ranks. The quick-sighted dervish would not allow of this, but made her undergo the trial with the rest, saying, "The property we seek is not yours, but your son's. Had he been your husband, it would be another thing." She agreed to his request, though with bad grace, and then all the jaws were set to wagging, some looking upon it as a good joke, others thinking it a hard trial to the nerves. As fast as each person had ground his mouthful, he called to the dervish and showed the contents of his mouth.

All had now proved their innocence excepting the âkhon and my mother. The former, whose face exhibited the picture of an affected cheerfulness with great nervous apprehension, kept mumbling his rice, and turning it over between his jaws, until he cried out in a querulous tone, " Why do you give me this stuff to chew ? I am old, and have no teeth : it is impossible for me to reduce the grain " ; and then he spat it out. My mother, too, complained of her want of power to break the hard rice, and did the same thing. A silence ensued, which made us all look with more attention than usual upon them, and it was only broken by a time-server of my mother, an old woman, who cried out, " What child's play is this ? Who has ever heard of a son treating his mother with this disrespect, and his old schoolmaster, too ? Shame, shame !—let us go—he is probably the thief himself."

Upon this the dervish said, " Are we fools and asses, to be dealt with in this manner ?—either there was money in that corner, or there was not—either there are thieves in the world, or there are not. This man and this woman," pointing to the âkhon and my mother, " have not done that which all the rest have done. Perhaps they say the truth, they are old, and cannot break the hard grain. Nobody says that they stole the money—they themselves know that best," said he, looking at them through and through ; " but the famous diviner, Hezarfun, he who was truly called the bosom friend to the Great Bear, and the confidant of the planet Saturn,—he who could tell all that a man has ever thought, thinks, or will think,—he hath said that the trial by rice among cowards was the best of all tests of a man's honesty. Now, my friends, from all I have remarked, none of you are slayers of lions, and fear is easily produced among you. However, if you doubt my skill in this instance, I will propose a still easier trial—one which commits nobody, which works like a charm upon the mind, and makes the thief come forward of his own accord, to ease his conscience and purse of its ill-gotten wealth, at one and the same time. I propose the *Hak reezî*, or the heaping up earth. Here in this corner I will make a mound, and will pray so fervently this very night, that, by the blessing of Allah, the Hajji," pointing to me, " will find his money buried in it to-morrow at this hour. Whoever is curious, let them be present, and if something be not discovered, I will give him a miscal of hair from my beard."

He then set to work, and heaped up earth in a corner, whilst the lookers-on loitered about, discussing what they had just seen ; some examining me and the dervish as children of the evil spirit, whilst others again began to think as much of my mother and the schoolmaster. The company then dispersed, most of them promising to return the following morning, at the appointed time, to witness the search into the heap of earth.

I must own that I began now to look upon the restoration of my property as hopeless. The diviner's skill had certainly discovered that money had been buried in my father's house, and he had succeeded in raising ugly suspicions in my mind against two persons whom I felt it to be a sin to suspect ; but I doubted whether he could do more.

However, he appeared again on the following morning, accompanied by the capiji, and by several of those who had been present at the former scene. The âkhon, however, did not appear, and my mother was also absent, upon pretext of being obliged to visit a sick friend. We proceeded in a body to the mound, and the dervish having made a holy invocation, he approached it with a sort of mysterious respect.

" Now we shall see," said he, " whether the Gins and the Peris have been at work this night " ; and, exclaiming " *Bismillah !* " he dug into the earth with his dagger.

Having thrown off some of the soil, a large stone appeared, and having disengaged that, to the astonishment of all, and to my extreme delight, a canvas bag, well filled, was discovered.

" Oh, my soul ! oh, my heart ! " exclaimed the humpback, as he seized upon the bag, " you see that the dervish Teez Negah is not a man to lose a hair of his beard. There, there," said he, putting it into my hand, " there is your property : go, and give thanks that you have fallen into my hands, and do not forget my *hak sai* or my commission."

Everybody crowded round me, whilst I broke open the wax that was affixed to the mouth of the bag, upon which I recognised the impression of my father's seal ; and eagerness was marked on all their faces as I untied the twine with which it was fastened. My countenance dropped woefully when I found that it contained only silver, for I had made up my mind to see gold. Five hundred reals was the sum of which I became the possessor, out of which I counted fifty, and presented them to the ingenious discoverer of them. " There," said I, " may your house prosper ! If I were rich I would give you more : and although this is evidently but a small part of what my father (God be with him !) must have accumulated, still, again I say, may your house prosper, and many sincere thanks to you."

The dervish was satisfied with my treatment of him, and took his leave, and I was soon after left by the rest of the company, the capiji alone remaining. " Famous business we have made of it this morning," said he. " Did I not say that these diviners performed wonders ? "

" Yes," said I, " yes, it is wonderful, for I never thought his operations would have come to anything."

Impelled by a spirit of cupidity, now that I had seen money glistening before me, I began to complain that I had received so little, and again expressed to Ali Mohamed my wish of bringing the case before the cadi ; " for," said I, " if I am entitled to these five hundred reals, I am entitled to all my father left ; and you will acknowledge that this must be but a very small part of his savings."

" Friend," said he, " listen to the words of an old man. Keep what you have got, and be content. In going before the cadi, the first thing you will have to do will be to give of your certain, to get at that most cursed of all property, the uncertain. Be assured that, after having drained you of your four hundred and fifty reals, and having got five hundred from your opponents, you will have the satisfaction to hear him tell you both to ' go in peace, and do not trouble the city with your disputes.' Have not you lived long enough in the world to have learnt this common saying—' Every one's teeth are blunted by acids, except the cadi's, which are by sweets ' ? The cadi who takes five cucumbers as a bribe will admit any evidence for ten beds of melons."

After some deliberation, I determined to take the advice of the capiji ; for it was plain that, if I intended to prosecute any one, it could only be my mother and the âkhon ; and to do that, I should raise such a host of enemies, and give rise to such unheard-of scandal, that perhaps I should only get stoned by the populace for my pains.

MARY RUSSELL MITFORD

1787–1855

THE ELECTION

A FEW years back, a gentleman of the name of Danby came to reside in a small decayed borough town—whether in Wiltshire or Cornwall matters not to our story, although in one of those counties the aforesaid town was probably situate, being what is called a close borough, the joint property of two noble families.

Mr. Danby was evidently a man of large fortune, and that fortune as evidently acquired in trade—indeed he made no more secret of the latter circumstance than the former. He built himself a large, square, red house, equally ugly and commodious, just without the town; walled in a couple of acres of ground for a kitchen-garden; kept a heavy one-horse chaise, a stout pony, and a brace of greyhounds; and having furnished his house solidly and handsomely, and arranged his domestic affairs to his heart's content, began to look about amongst his neighbours; scraped acquaintance with the lawyer, the apothecary, and the principal tradesmen; subscribed to the reading-room and the billiard-room; became a member of the bowling-green and the cricket club, and took as lively an interest in the affairs of his new residence as if he had been born and bred in the borough.

Now this interest, however agreeable to himself, was by no means equally conducive to the quiet and comfort of the place. Mr. Danby was a little, square, dark man, with a cocked-up nose, a good-humoured but very knowing smile, a pair of keen black eyes, a loud voluble speech, and a prodigious activity both of mind and body. His very look betokened his character—and that character was one not uncommon among the middle ranks of Englishmen.

In short, besides being, as he often boasted, a downright John Bull, the gentleman was a reformer, zealous and uncompromising as ever attended a dinner at the Crown and Anchor, or made a harangue in Palace Yard. He read Cobbett; had his own scheme for the redemption of tithes; and a plan, which, not understanding, I am sorry I cannot undertake to explain, for clearing off the national debt without loss or injury to anybody.

Besides these great matters, which may rather be termed the theorique than the practique of reform, and which are at least perfectly inoffensive, Mr. Danby condescended to smaller and more worrying observances, and was, indeed, so strict and jealous a guardian of the purity of the corporation, and the incorruptibility of the vestry, that an alderman could not wag a finger, or a church-warden stir a foot, without being called to account by this vigilant defender of the rights, liberties, and purses of the people.

He was beyond a doubt the most troublesome man in the parish, and that is a wide word. In the matter of reports and inquiries Mr. Hume was but a type of him. He would mingle economy with a parish dinner, and talk of retrenchment at the mayor's feast; brought an action under the Turnpike Act against the clerk and treasurer of the commissioners of the road; commenced a suit in Chancery with the trustees of the charity school; and, finally, threatened to open the borough—that is to say, to support any candidate who should offer to oppose the nominees of the two great families, the one Whig, and the other Tory, who now possessed the two seats in parliament as quietly as their own hereditary estates;—an experiment which recent instances of successful opposition in other places rendered not a little formidable to the noble owners.

What added considerably to the troublesome nature of Mr. Danby's inquisitions was the general cleverness, ability, and information of the individual. He was not a man of classical education, and knew little of books; but with things he was especially conversant. Although very certain that Mr. Danby had been in business, nobody could guess what that business had been. None came amiss to him. He handled the rule and the yard with equal dexterity; astonished the butcher by his insight into the mysteries of fattening and dealing; and the grocer by his familiarity with the sugar and coffee markets; disentangled the perplexities of the confused mass of figures in the parish books with the dexterity of a sworn accountant; and was so great upon points of law, so ready and accurate in quoting reports, cases, and precedents, that he would certainly have passed for a retired attorney, but for the zeal and alertness with which, at his own expense, he was apt to rush into lawsuits.

With so remarkable a genius for turmoil, it is not to be doubted that Mr. Danby, in spite of many excellent and sterling qualities, succeeded in drawing upon himself no small degree of odium. The whole corporation were officially his enemies; but his principal opponent, or rather the person whom he considered as his principal opponent, was Mr. Cardonnel, the rector of the parish, who, besides several disputes pending between them (one especially respecting the proper situation of the church organ, the placing of which harmonious instrument kept the whole town in discord for a twelvemonth), was married to the Lady Elizabeth, sister of the Earl of B., one of the patrons of the borough ; and being, as well as his wife, a very popular and amiable character, was justly regarded by Mr. Danby as one of the chief obstacles to his projected reform. Whilst, however, our reformer was, from the most patriotic motives, doing his best or his worst to dislike Mr. Cardonnel, events of a very different nature were gradually operating to bring them together.

Mr. Danby's family consisted of a wife—a quiet lady-like woman, with very ill-health, who did little else than walk from her bed to her sofa, eat water-gruel and drink soda-water—and of an only daughter, who was, in a word, the very apple of her father's eye.

Rose Danby was indeed a daughter of whom any father might have been proud. Of middle height and exquisite symmetry, with a rich, dark, glowing complexion, a profusion of glossy, curling, raven hair, large affectionate black eyes, and a countenance at once so sweet and so spirited, that its constant expression was like that which a smile gives to other faces.

Her temper and understanding were in exact keeping with such a countenance—playful, gentle, clever, and kind ; and her accomplishments and acquirements of the very highest order. When her father entered on his new residence she had just completed her fifteenth year ; and he, unable longer to dispense with the pleasure of her society, took her from the excellent school near London, at which she had hitherto been placed, and determined that her education should be finished by masters at home.

It so happened, that this little town contained one celebrated artist, a professor of dancing, who kept a weekly academy for young ladies, which was attended by half the families of gentility in the county. M. Le Grand (for the dancing master was a little lively Frenchman) was delighted with Rose. He declared that she was his best pupil, his very best, the best that ever he had in his life.

" Mais voyez, donc, Monsieur ? " said he one day to her father, who would have scorned to know the French for " how d'ye do " ; " Voyez, comme elle met de l'aplomb, de la force, de la nettete, dans ses entrechats ! Qu'elle est leste, et legere, et petrie de graces, la petite ! "

And Mr. Danby, comprehending only that the artist was praising his darling, swore that Monsieur was a good fellow, and returned the compliment after the English fashion, by sending him a haunch of venison the next day.

But M. Le Grand was not the only admirer whom Rose met with at the dancing-school. It chanced that Mr. Cardonnel also had an only daughter, a young person about the same age, bringing up under the eye of her mother, and a constant attendant at the professor's academy. The two girls, nearly of a height, and both good dancers, were placed together as partners; and being almost equally prepossessing in person and manner (for Mary Cardonnel was a sweet, delicate, fair creature, whose mild blue eyes seemed appealing to the kindness of every one they looked upon), took an immediate and lasting fancy to each other; shook hands at meeting and parting, smiled whenever their glances chanced to encounter; and soon began to exchange a few kind and hurried words in the pauses of the dance, and to hold more continuous chat at the conclusion.

And Lady Elizabeth, almost as much charmed with Rose as her daughter, seeing in the lovely little girl everything to like, and nothing to disapprove, encouraged and joined in the acquaintance; attended with a motherly care to her cloaking and shawling; took her home in her own carriage when it rained; and finally waylaid Mr. Danby, who always came himself to fetch his darling, and with her bland and gracious smile requested the pleasure of Miss Danby's company to a party of young people, which she was about to give on the occasion of her daughter's birthday. I am afraid that our sturdy reformer was going to say, No! But Rose's "Oh, papa!" was irresistible; and to the party she went.

After this the young people became every day more intimate. Lady Elizabeth waited on Mrs. Danby, and Mrs. Danby returned the call; but her state of health precluded visiting, and her husband, who piqued himself on firmness and consistency, contrived, though with some violence to his natural kindness of temper, to evade the friendly advances and invitations of the rector.

The two girls, however, saw one another almost every day. It was a friendship like that of Rosalind and Celia, whom, by the way, they severally resembled in temper and character—Rose having much of the brilliant gaiety of the one fair cousin, and Mary the softer and gentler charm of the other. They rode, walked, and sung together; were never happy asunder; played the same music; read the same books; dressed alike; worked for each other; and interchanged their own little property of trinkets and flowers, with a generosity that seemed only emulous which should give most.

At first, Mr. Danby was a little jealous of Rose's partiality to the rectory; but she was so fond of him, so attentive to his pleasures, that he could not find in his heart to check hers; and when, after a long and dangerous illness, with which the always delicate Mary was affected, Mr. Cardonnel went to him, and with tears streaming down his cheeks, told him he believed that, under Providence, he owed his daughter's life to Rose's unwearying care, the father's heart was fairly vanquished; he wrung the good rector's hand, and never grumbled at her long visits again.

Lady Elizabeth, also, had her share in producing this change of feeling, by presenting him in return for innumerable baskets of peaches and melons and hot-house grapes (in the culture of which he was curious) with a portrait of Rose, drawn by herself—a strong and beautiful likeness, with his own favourite greyhound at her feet; a picture which he would not have exchanged for the "Transfiguration."

Perhaps, too, consistent as he thought himself, he was not without an unconscious respect for the birth and station which he affected to despise, and was, at least, as proud of the admiration which his daughter excited in those privileged circles, as of the sturdy independence which he exhibited by keeping aloof from them in his own person. Certain it is, that his spirit of reformation insensibly relaxed, particularly towards the rector; and that he not only ceded the contested point of the organ, but presented a splendid set of pulpit-hangings to the church itself.

Time wore on; Rose had refused half the offers of gentility in the town and neighbourhood; her heart appeared to be invulnerable. Her less affluent and less brilliant friend was generally understood (and as Rose, on hearing the report, did not contradict it, the rumour passed for certainty) to be engaged to a nephew of her mother's, Sir William Frampton, a young gentleman of splendid fortune, who had lately passed much time at his fair place in the neighbourhood.

Time wore on; and Rose was now nineteen, when an event occurred which threatened a grievous interruption to her happiness. The Earl of B.'s member died; his nephew, Sir William Frampton, supported by his uncle's powerful interest, offered himself for the borough; an independent candidate started at the same time; and Mr. Danby felt himself compelled, by his vaunted consistency, to insist on his daughter's renouncing her visits to the rectory, at least until after the termination of the election. Rose wept and pleaded, pleaded and wept, in vain. Her father was obdurate; and she, after writing a most affectionate note to Mary Cardonnel, retired to her own bedroom in very bad spirits, and, perhaps, for the first time in her life, in very bad humour.

About half an hour afterwards, Sir William Frampton and Mr. Cardonnel called at the red house.

"We are come, Mr. Danby," said the rector, "to solicit your interest."

"Nay, nay, my good friend," returned the reformer, "you know that my interest is promised, and that I cannot with any consistency——"

"To solicit your interest with Rose——" resumed his reverence.

"With Rose!" interrupted Mr. Danby.

"Ay—for the gift of her heart and hand—that being, I believe, the suffrage which my good nephew here is most anxious to secure," rejoined Mr. Cardonnel.

"With Rose," again ejaculated Mr. Danby: "why, I thought that your daughter——"

"The gipsy has not told you, then!" replied the rector. "Why, William and she have been playing the parts of Romeo and Juliet for these six months past."

"My Rose!" again exclaimed Mr. Danby. "Why, Rose! Rose! I say!" and the astonished father rushed out of the room, and returned the next minute, holding the blushing girl by the arm. "Rose, do you love this young man?"

"Oh, papa!" said Rose.

"Will you marry him?"

"Oh, papa!"

"Do you wish me to tell him that you will not marry him?"

To this question Rose returned no answer; she only blushed the deeper, and looked down with a half smile. "Take her, then," resumed Mr. Danby; "I see the girl loves you. I can't vote for you, though, for I've promised, and, you know, my good sir, that an honest man's word——"

"I don't want your vote, my dear sir," interrupted Sir William Frampton; "I don't ask for your vote, although the loss of it may cost me my seat, and my uncle his borough. This is the election that I care about, the only election worth caring about. Is it not, my own sweet Rose?—the election, of which the object lasts for life, and the result is happiness. That's the election worth caring about. Is it not, mine own Rose!"

And Rose blushed an affirmative; and Mr. Danby shook his intended son-in-law's hand, until he almost wrung it off, repeating at every moment, "I can't vote for you, for a man must be consistent, but you're the best fellow in the world, and you shall have my Rose. And Rose will be a great lady," continued the delighted father; "my little Rose will be a great lady after all!"

THOMAS INGOLDSBY
(R. H. BARHAM)
1788–1845

THE LADY ROHESIA

THE Lady Rohesia lay on her death-bed !

So said the doctor, and doctors are generally allowed to be judges in these matters ; besides, Doctor Butts was the Court Physician : he carried a crutch-handled staff, with its cross of the blackest ebony —*raison de plus*.

" Is there no hope, Doctor ? " said Beatrice Grey.

" Is there no hope ? " said Everard Ingoldsby.

" Is there no hope ? " said Sir Guy de Montgomeri. He was the Lady Rohesia's husband ; he spoke the last.

The doctor shook his head. He looked at the disconsolate widower *in posse,* then at the hour-glass ; its waning sand seemed sadly to shadow forth the sinking pulse of his patient. Dr. Butts was a very learned man. " *Ars longa, vita brevis !* " said Doctor Butts.

" I am very sorry to hear it," quoth Sir Guy de Montgomeri.

Sir Guy was a brave knight, and a tall ; but he was no scholar.

" Alas ! my poor sister ! " sighed Ingoldsby.

" Alas ! my poor mistress ! " sobbed Beatrice.

Sir Guy neither sighed nor sobbed ; his grief was too deep-seated for outward manifestation.

" And how long, Doctor—— ? " The afflicted husband could not finish the sentence.

Dr. Butts withdrew his hand from the wrist of the dying lady. He pointed to the horologe ; scarcely a quarter of its sand remained in the upper moiety. Again he shook his head ; the eye of the patient waxed dimmer, the rattling in the throat increased.

" What's become of Father Francis ? " whimpered Beatrice.

" The last consolations of the church——" suggested Everard.

A darker shade came over the brow of Sir Guy.

" Where *is* the Confessor ? " continued his grieving brother-in-law.

" In the pantry," cried Marion Hacket pertly, as she tripped downstairs in search of that venerable ecclesiastic ;—" in the pantry, I warrant me." The bower-woman was not wont to be in the wrong ; in the pantry was the holy man discovered—at his devotions.

" *Pax vobiscum !* " said Father Francis, as he entered the chamber of death.

" *Vita brevis !* " retorted Doctor Butts. He was not a man to be browbeat out of his Latin—and by a paltry Friar Minim, too. Had it been a Bishop, indeed, or even a mitred Abbot,—but a miserable Franciscan !

" *Benedicite !* " said the Friar.

" *Ars longa !* " returned the Leech.

Doctor Butts adjusted the tassels of his falling band ; drew his short sad-coloured cloak closer around him ; and, grasping his cross-handled walking-staff, stalked majestically out of the apartment. Father Francis had the field to himself.

The worthy chaplain hastened to administer the last rites of the church. To all appearance he had little time to lose ; as he concluded, the dismal toll of the passing-bell sounded from the belfry tower ;—little Hubert, the bandy-legged sacristan, was pulling with all his might. It was a capital contrivance that same passing-bell, —which of the Urbans or Innocents invented it is a query ; but, whoever he was, he deserved well of his country and of Christendom.

Ah ! our ancestors were not such fools, after all, as we, their degenerate children, conceit them to have been. The passing-bell ! a most solemn warning to imps of every description, is not to be regarded with impunity ; the most impudent *Succubus* of them all dare as well dip his claws in holy water as come within the verge of its sound. Old Nick himself, if he sets any value at all upon his tail, had best convey himself clean out of hearing, and leave the way open to Paradise. Little Hubert continued pulling with all his might,—and St. Peter began to look out for a customer.

The knell seemed to have some effect even upon the Lady Rohesia ; she raised her head slightly ; inarticulate sounds issued from her lips,—inarticulate, that is, to the profane ears of the laity. Those of Father Francis, indeed, were sharper ; nothing, as he averred, could be more distinct than the words, " A thousand marks to the priory of St. Mary Rouncival."

Now the Lady Rohesia Ingoldsby had brought her husband broad lands and large possessions ; much of her ample dowry, too, was at her own disposal ; and nuncupative wills had not yet been abolished by Acts of Parliament.

" Pious soul ! " ejaculated Father Francis. " A thousand marks, she said——"

" If she did, I'll be shot ! " said Sir Guy de Montgomeri.

" —A thousand marks ! " continued the Confessor, fixing his cold grey eye upon the knight, as he went on heedless of the interruption ;—" a thousand marks ! and as many *Aves* and *Paters* shall be duly said—as soon as the money is paid down."

Sir Guy shrank from the monk's gaze ; he turned to the window, and muttered to himself something that sounded like " Don't you wish you may get it ? "

———

The bell continued to toll. Father Francis had quitted the room, taking with him the remains of the holy oil he had been using for Extreme Unction. Everard Ingoldsby waited on him down stairs.

" A thousand thanks ! " said the latter.

" A thousand marks ! " said the friar.

" A thousand devils ! " growled Sir Guy de Montgomeri, from the top of the landing-place.

But his accents fell unheeded ; his brother-in-law and the friar were gone ; he was left alone with his departing lady and Beatrice Grey.

Sir Guy de Montgomeri stood pensively at the foot of the bed ; his arms were crossed upon his bosom, his chin was sunk upon his breast ; his eyes were filled with tears ; the dim rays of the fading watchlight gave a darker shade to the furrows on his brow, and a brighter tint to the little bald patch on the top of his head—for Sir Guy was a middle-aged gentleman, tall and portly withal, with a slight bend in his shoulders, but that not much ; his complexion was somewhat florid, especially about the nose ; but his lady was *in extremis*, and at this particular moment he was paler than usual.

" Bim ! bome ! " went the bell. The knight groaned audibly ; Beatrice Grey wiped her eye with her little square apron of lace de Malines ; there was a moment's pause, a moment of intense affliction ; she let it fall—all but one corner, which remained between her finger and thumb. She looked at Sir Guy ; drew the thumb and forefinger of her other hand slowly along its border, till they reached the opposite extremity. She sobbed aloud. " So kind a lady ! " said Beatrice Grey.—" So excellent a wife ! " responded Sir Guy.—" So good ! " said the damsel.—" So dear ! " said the knight.—" So pious ! " said she.—" So humble ! " said he.—" So good to the poor ! "—" So capital a manager ! "—" So punctual at matins ! "—" Dinner dished to moment ! "—" So devout ! " said Beatrice.—" So fond of me ! " said Sir Guy.—" And of Father Francis ! "—" What the devil do you mean by that ? " said Sir Guy de Montgomeri.

The knight and the maiden had rung their antiphonic changes on the fine qualities of the departing Lady, like the *Strophe* and *Antistrophe* of a Greek play. The cardinal virtues once disposed of, her minor excellences came under review. She would drown a witch, drink lambs' wool at Christmas, beg Dominie Dumps's boys a holiday, and dine upon sprats on Good Friday ! A low moan from the subject of these eulogies seemed to intimate that the enumeration of her good deeds was not altogether lost on her,—that the parting spirit felt and rejoiced in the testimony.

" She was too good for earth ! " continued Sir Guy.

" Ye-ye-yes ! " sobbed Beatrice.

" I did not deserve her ! " said the knight.

" No-o-o-o ! " cried the damsel.

" Not but that I made her an excellent husband, and a kind ; but she is going, and—and—where, or when, or how—shall I get such another ? "

" Not in broad England—not in the whole wide world ! " responded Beatrice Grey ; " that is, not *just* such another ! " Her voice still faltered, but her accents on the whole were more articulate ; she dropped the corner of her apron, and had recourse to her handkerchief ; in fact, her eyes were getting red—and so was the tip of her nose.

Sir Guy was silent : he gazed for a few moments steadfastly on the face of his lady. The single word, " Another ! " fell from his lips like a distant echo ; it is not often that the viewless nymph repeats more than is necessary.

" Bim ! bome ! " went the bell. Bandy-legged Hubert had been tolling for half an hour ; he began to grow tired, and St. Peter fidgety.

" Beatrice Grey ! " said Sir Guy de Montgomeri, " what's to be done ? What's to become of Montgomeri Hall ?—and the buttery —and the servants ? And what—what's to become of *me*, Beatrice Grey ? " There was pathos in his tones, and a solemn pause succeeded. " I'll turn monk myself ! " said Sir Guy.

" Monk ? " said Beatrice.

" I'll be a Carthusian ! " repeated the knight, but in a tone less assured : he relapsed into a reverie. Shave his head !—he did not so much mind that, he was getting rather bald already ; but, beans for dinner—and those without butter—and then a horse-hair shirt !

The knight seemed undecided : his eye roamed gloomily around the apartment ; it paused upon different objects, but as if it saw them not ; its sense was shut, and there was no speculation in its glance : it rested at last upon the fair face of the sympathising damsel at his side, beautiful in her grief.

Her tears had ceased ; but her eyes were cast down, mournfully fixed upon her delicate little foot, which was beating the devil's tattoo.

There is no talking to a female when she does not look at you. Sir Guy turned round : he seated himself on the edge of the bed ;

and, placing his hand beneath the chin of the lady, turned up her face in an angle of fifteen degrees.

" I don't think I shall take the vows, Beatrice ; but what's to become of me ? Poor, miserable, old—that is poor, miserable, middle-aged man that I am !—No one to comfort, no one to care for me ! " Beatrice's tears flowed afresh, but she opened not her lips. " 'Pon my life ! " continued he, " I don't believe there is a creature now would care a button if I were hanged to-morrow ! "

" Oh ! don't say so, Sir Guy ! " sighed Beatrice ; " you know there's—there's Master Everard, and—and Father Francis—"

" Pish ! " cried Sir Guy, testily.

" And—there's your favourite old bitch."

" I am not thinking of old bitches ! " quoth Sir Guy de Montgomeri.

Another pause ensued : the knight had released her chin, and taken her hand ; it was a pretty little hand, with long taper fingers and filbert-formed nails, and the softness of the palm said little for its owner's industry.

" Sit down, my dear Beatrice," said the knight, thoughtfully ; " you must be fatigued with your long watching. Take a seat, my child." Sir Guy did not relinquish her hand ; but he sidled along the counterpane, and made room for his companion between himself and the bed-post.

Now this is a very awkward position for two people to be placed in, especially when the right hand of the one holds the right hand of the other : in such an attitude, what the deuce can the gentleman do with his left ? Sir Guy closed his till it became an absolute fist, and his knuckles rested on the bed a little in the rear of his companion.

" Another ! " repeated Sir Guy, musing ; " if, indeed, I could find such another ! " He was talking to his thought, but Beatrice Grey answered him.

" There's Madam Fitzfoozle."—" A frump ! " said Sir Guy.

" Or the Lady Bumbarton."—" With her hump ! " muttered he.

" There's the Dowager——"

" Stop—stop ! " said the knight, " stop one moment ! " He paused ; he was all on the tremble ; something seemed rising in his throat, but he gave a great gulp, and swallowed it. " Beatrice," said he, " what think you of "—his voice sank into a most seductive softness,—" what think you of—Beatrice Grey ? "

The murder was out : the knight felt infinitely relieved ; the knuckles of his left hand unclosed spontaneously ; and the arm he had felt such a difficulty in disposing of, found itself—nobody knows how—all at once, encircling the jimp waist of the pretty Beatrice. The young lady's reply was expressed in three syllables. They were,

"Oh, Sir Guy!" The words might be somewhat indefinite, but there was no mistaking the look. Their eyes met; Sir Guy's left arm contracted itself spasmodically: when the eyes meet—at least as theirs met—the lips are very apt to follow the example. The knight had taken one long, loving kiss—nectar and ambrosia! He thought on Doctor Butts and his *repetatur haustus*—a prescription Father Francis had taken infinite pains to translate for him: he was about to repeat it, but the dose was interrupted *in transitu*. Doubtless the adage,

> There's many a slip
> 'Twixt the cup and the lip,

hath reference to medicine. Sir Guy's lip was again all but in conjunction with that of his bride-elect.

It has been hinted already that there was a little round polished patch on the summit of the knight's *pericranium*, from which his locks had gradually receded; a sort of *oasis*—or rather a *Mont Blanc* in miniature, rising above the highest point of vegetation. It was on this little spot, undefended alike by Art and Nature, that at this interesting moment a blow descended, such as we must borrow a term from the Sister Island adequately to describe: it was a "Whack!"

Sir Guy started upon his feet; Beatrice Grey started upon hers: but a single glance to the rear reversed her position,—she fell upon her knees and screamed.

The knight, too, wheeled about, and beheld a sight which might have turned a bolder man to stone. It was She!—the all-but-defunct Rohesia—there she sat, bolt upright!—her eyes no longer glazed with the film of impending dissolution, but scintillating like flint and steel; while in her hand she grasped the bed-staff—a weapon of mickle might, as her husband's bloody coxcomb could now well testify. Words were yet wanting, for the quinsy, which her rage had broken, still impeded her utterance; but the strength and rapidity of her guttural intonations augured well for her future eloquence.

Sir Guy de Montgomeri stood for a while like a man distraught; this resurrection—for such it seemed—had quite overpowered him. "A husband oft-times makes the best physician," says the proverb; he was a living personification of its truth. Still it was whispered he had been content with Dr. Butts; but this lady was restored to bless him for many years. Heavens, what a life he led!

The Lady Rohesia mended apace; her quinsy was cured; the bell was stopped; and little Hubert, the sacristan, kicked out of the chapelry. St. Peter opened his wicket, and looked out; there was nobody there ; so he flung-to the gate in a passion, and went back to his lodge, grumbling at being hoaxed by a runway ring.

Years rolled on. The improvement of Lady Rohesia's temper did not keep pace with that of her health ; and one fine morning Sir Guy de Montgomeri was seen to enter the *porte-cochère* of Durham House, at that time the town residence of Sir Walter Raleigh. Nothing more was ever heard of him ; but a boat full of adventurers was known to have dropped down with the tide that evening to Deptford Hope, where lay the good ship the *Darling*, commanded by Captain Keymis, who sailed next morning on the Virginia voyage.

A brass plate, some eighteen inches long, may yet be seen in Denton chancel, let into a broad slab of Bethersden marble ; it represents a lady kneeling, in her wimple and hood ; her hands are clasped in prayer, and beneath is an inscription in the characters of the age—

'Praie for ye sowle of ye Lady Royse,
And for alle Christen sowles !'

The date is illegible ; but it appears that she survived King Henry the Eighth, and that the dissolution of monasteries had lost St. Mary Rouncival her thousand marks. As for Beatrice Grey, it is well known that she was alive in 1559, and then had virginity enough left to be a maid of honour to " good Queen Bess."

CAPTAIN MARRYAT
1792–1848

S.W. AND BY W. ¾ W.

JACK LITTLEBRAIN was, physically considered, as fine grown, and moreover as handsome a boy as ever was seen, but it must be acknowledged that he was not very clever. Nature is, in most instances, very impartial; she has given plumage to the peacock, but, as every one knows, not the slightest ear for music. Throughout the feathered race it is almost invariably the same; the homeliest clad are the finest songsters. Among animals the elephant is certainly the most intelligent, but, at the same time, he cannot be considered as a beauty.

Acting upon this well-ascertained principle, nature imagined that she had done quite enough for Jack when she endowed him with such personal perfection; and did not consider it was at all necessary that he should be very clever; indeed, it must be admitted not only that he was not very clever, but (as the truth must be told) remarkably dull and stupid.

However, the Littlebrains have been for a long while a well-known, numerous, and influential family, so that, if it were possible that Jack could have been taught anything, the means were forthcoming: he was sent to every school in the country; but it was in vain. At every following vacation he was handed over from the one pedagogue to the other, of those whose names were renowned for the Busbian system of teaching by stimulating both ends: he was horsed every day and still remained an ass, and at the end of six months, if he did not run away before that period was over, he was invariably sent back to his parents as incorrigible and unteachable. What was to be done with him? The Littlebrains had always got on in the world, somehow or another, by their interest and connections; but here was one who might be said to have no brains at all. After many pros and cons, and after a variety of consulting letters had passed between the various members of his family, it was decided, that as his maternal uncle, Sir Theophilus Blazers, G.C.B., was at that time second in command in the Mediterranean, he should be sent to sea under his command; the admiral having, in reply to a letter on the subject, answered that it was hard indeed if he did not lick him into some shape or another; and that, at all events, he'd warrant that Jack should be able to box the compass before he had been three months nibbling the ship's biscuit; further, that it was very easy to get over the examination necessary to qualify him for lieutenant, as a turkey and a dozen of brown stout sent in the boat with him on the passing day, as a present to each of the passing captains, would pass him, even if he were as incompetent as a camel (or, as they say at sea, a cable) to pass through the eye of a needle; that having once passed, he would soon have him in command of a fine frigate, with a good nursing first lieutenant; and that if he did not behave himself properly, he would make his signal to come on board of the flag-ship, take him into the cabin, and give him a sound horse-whipping, as other admirals have been known to inflict upon their own sons under similar circumstances. The reader must be aware that, from the tenor of Sir Theophilus' letter, the circumstances which we are narrating must have occurred some fifty years ago.

When Jack was informed that he was to be a midshipman, he looked up in the most innocent way in the world (and innocent he was, sure enough), turned on his heels, and whistled as he went for want of thought. For the last three months he had been at home, and his chief employment was kissing and romping with the maids, who declared him to be the handsomest Littlebrain that the country had ever produced. Our hero viewed the preparations made for his departure with perfect indifference, and wished everybody good-bye with the utmost composure. He was a happy, good-tempered fellow; who never calculated, because he could not; never decided, for he had not wit enough to choose; never foresaw, although he could look straight before him; and never remembered, because he had no memory. The line, "If ignorance is bliss, 'tis folly to be wise," was certainly made especially for Jack; nevertheless he was not totally deficient: he knew what was good to eat or drink, for his taste was perfect, his eyes were very sharp, and he could discover in a moment if a peach was ripe on the wall; his hearing was quick, for he was the first in the school to detect the footsteps of his pedagogue; and he could smell anything savoury nearly a mile off, if the wind lay the right way. Moreover, he knew that if he put his fingers in the fire that he would burn himself; that knives cut severely; that birch tickled; and several other little axioms of this sort which are generally ascertained by children at an early age, but which Jack's capacity had not received until at a much later date. Such as he was, our hero went to sea; his stock in his sea-chest being very abundant, while his stock of ideas was proportionably small.

We will pass over the trans-shipments of Jack until he was

eventually shipped on board the *Mendacious*, then lying at Malta, with the flag of Sir Theophilus Blazers at the fore—a splendid ship carrying 120 guns, and nearly 120 midshipmen of different calibres. (I pass over captain, lieutenant, and ship's company, having made mention of her most valuable qualifications.) Jack was received with a hearty welcome by his uncle, for he came in pudding-time, and was invited to dinner; and the admiral made the important discovery, that if his nephew was a fool in other points, he was certainly no fool at his knife and fork. In a short time his messmates found out that he was no fool at his fists, and his knock-down arguments ended much disputation. Indeed, as the French would say, Jack was perfection in the *physique*, although so very deficient in the *morale*.

But if Pandora's box proved a plague to the whole world, Jack had his individual portion of it, when he was summoned to *box* the compass by his worthy uncle Sir Theophilus Blazers; who, in the course of six months, discovered that he could not make his nephew box it in the three, which he had warranted in his letter; every day our hero's ears were boxed, but the compass never. It required all the cardinal virtues to teach him the cardinal points during the forenoon, and he made a point of forgetting them before the sun went down. Whenever they attempted it (and various were the teachers employed to drive the compass into Jack's head), his head drove round the compass; and try all he could, Jack never could compass it. It appeared, as some people are said only to have one idea, as if Jack could only have one *point* in his head at a time, and to that point he would stand like a well-broken pointer. With him the wind never changed till the next day. His uncle pronounced him to be a fool, but that did not hurt his nephew's feelings; he had been told so too often already.

I have said that Jack had a great respect for good eating and drinking, and, moreover, was blessed with a good appetite: every person has his peculiar fancies, and if there was anything which more titillated the palate and olfactory nerves of our hero, it was a roast goose with sage and onions. Now it so happened, that having been about seven months on board of the *Mendacious*, Jack had one day received a summons to dine with the admiral, for the steward had ordered a roast goose for dinner, and knew not only that Jack was partial to it, but also that Jack was the admiral's nephew, which always goes for something on board of a flag-ship. Just before they were sitting down to table, the admiral wishing to know how the wind was, and having been not a little vexed with the slow progress of his nephew's nautical acquirements, said, " Now, Mr. Littlebrain, go up and bring me down word how the wind is; and mark me, as, when you are sent, nine times out of ten you make a mistake, I shall now bet you five guineas against your dinner that you make a mistake this time: so now be off and we will soon ascertain whether you lose your dinner or I lose my money. Sit down, gentlemen, we will not wait for Mr. Littlebrain."

Jack did not much admire this bet on the part of his uncle, but still less did he like the want of good manners in not waiting for him. He had just time to see the covers removed, to scent a whiff of the goose, and was off.

"The admiral wants to know how the wind is, sir," said Jack to the officer of the watch.

The officer of the watch went to the binnacle, and setting the wind as nearly as he could, replied, "Tell Sir Theophilus that it is *S.W. and by W. $\frac{3}{4}$ W.*"

"That's one of those confounded long points that I never can remember," cried Jack in despair.

"Then you'll 'get goose,' as the saying is," observed one of the midshipmen.

"No; I'm afraid that I shan't get any," replied Jack, despondingly. "What did he say, S.W. and by N. $\frac{3}{4}$ E.?"

"Not exactly," replied his messmate, who was a good-natured lad, and laughed heartily at Jack's version. "S.W. and by W. $\frac{3}{4}$ W."

"I never can remember it," cried Jack. "I'm to have five guineas if I do, and no dinner if I don't; and if I stay here much longer, I shall get no dinner at all events, for they are all terribly peckish, and there will be none left."

"Well, if you'll give me one of the guineas, I'll show you how to manage it," said the midshipman.

"I'll give you two, if you'll only be quick and the goose a'n't all gone," replied Jack.

The midshipman wrote down the point from which the wind blew, at full length, upon a bit of paper, and pinned it to the rim of Jack's hat. "Now," said he, "when you go into the cabin, you can hold your hat so as to read it without their perceiving you."

"Well, so I can; I never should have thought of that," said Jack.

"You hav'n't wit enough," replied the midshipman.

"Well, I see no wit in the compass," replied Jack.

"Nevertheless, it's full of point," replied the midshipman: "now be quick."

Our hero's eyes served him well if his memory was treacherous; and as he entered the cabin door he bowed over his hat very politely, and said, as he read it off, "S.W. and by W. $\frac{3}{4}$ W.," and then he added, without reading at all, "if you please, Sir Theophilus."

"Steward," said the admiral, "tell the officer of the watch to step down."

"How's the wind, Mr. Growler?"

"S.W. and by W. $\frac{3}{4}$ W.," replied the officer.

"Then, Mr. Littlebrain, you have won your five guineas, and may now sit down and enjoy your dinner."

Our hero was not slow in obeying the order, and ventured, upon the strength of his success, to send his plate twice for goose. Having eaten their dinner, drunk their wine, and taken their coffee, the officers, at the same time, took the hint which invariably accompanies the latter beverage, made their bows and retreated. As Jack was following his seniors out of the cabin, the admiral put the sum which he had staked into his hands, observing that "it was an ill wind that blew nobody good."

So thought Jack, who, having faithfully paid the midshipman the two guineas for his assistance, was now on the poop keeping his watch, as midshipmen usually do; that is, stretched out on the signal lockers and composing himself to sleep after the most approved fashion, answering the winks of the stars by blinks of his eyes, until at last he shut them to keep them warm. But, before he had quite composed himself, he thought of the goose and the five guineas. The wind was from the same quarter, blowing soft and mild; Jack lay in a sort of reverie as it fanned his cheek, for the weather was close and sultry.

"Well," muttered Jack to himself, "I do love that point of the compass, at all events, and I think that I never shall forget S.W. by W. $\frac{3}{4}$ W. No I never—never liked one before, though——"

"Is that true?" whispered a gentle voice in his ear; "do you love 'S.W. and by W. $\frac{3}{4}$ W.,' and will you, as you say, never forget her?"

"Why, what's that?" said Jack, opening his eyes and turning half round on his side.

"It's me—'S.W. and by W. $\frac{3}{4}$ W.,' that you say you love."

Littlebrain raised himself and looked round; there was no one on the poop except himself and two or three of the after-guard, who were lying down between the guns.

"Why, who was it that spoke?" said Jack, much astonished.

"It was the wind you love and who has long loved you," replied the same voice; "do you wish to see me?"

"See you—see the wind?—I've been already sent on that message by the midshipmen," thought Jack.

"Do you love me as you say, and as I love you?" continued the voice.

"Well, I like you better than any other point of the compass, and I'm sure I never thought I should like one of them," replied Jack.

"That will not do for me; will you love only me?"

"I'm not likely to love the others," replied Jack, shutting his eyes again; "I *hate* them all."

" And love me ? "

" Well, I do love you, that's a fact," replied Jack as he thought of the goose and the five guineas.

" Then look round and you shall see me," said the soft voice.

Jack, who hardly knew whether he was asleep or awake, did at this summons once more take the trouble to open his eyes, and beheld a fairy female figure, pellucid as water, yet apparently possessing substance ; her features were beautifully soft and mild, and her outline trembled and shifted as it were, waving gently to and fro. It smiled sweetly, hung over him, played with his chestnut curls, softly touched his lips with her own, passed her trembling fingers over his cheeks, and its warm breath appeared as if it melted into his. Then it grew more bold—embraced his person, searched into his neck and collar, as if curious to examine him.

Jack felt a pleasure and gratification which he could not well comprehend ; once more the charmer's lips trembled upon his own, now remaining for a moment, now withdrawing, again returning to kiss and kiss again, and once more did the soft voice put the question :

" Do you love me ? "

" Better than goose," replied Jack.

" I don't know who goose may be," replied the fairy form, as she tossed about Jack's waving locks ; " you must love only me, promise me that before I am relieved."

" What, have you got the first watch, as well as me ? " replied Jack.

" I am on duty just now, but I shall not be so long. We southerly winds are never kept long in one place ; some of my sisters will probably be sent here soon."

" I don't understand what you talk about," replied Jack. " Suppose you tell me who you are, and what you are, and I'll do all I can to keep awake ; I don't know how it is, but I've felt more inclined to go to sleep since you have been fanning me about than I did before."

" Then I will remain by your side while you listen to me. I am, as I told you, a wind——"

" That's puzzling," said Jack, interrupting her.

" My name is ' S.W. and by W. $\frac{3}{4}$ W.' "

" Yes, and a very long name it is. If you wish me to remember you, you should have had a shorter one."

This ruffled the wind a little, and she blew rather sharp into the corner of Jack's eye ; however, she proceeded :

" You are a sailor, and of course you know all the winds on the compass by name."

" I wish I did ; but I don't," replied Littlebrain ; " I can recollect you, and not one other."

Again the wind trembled with delight on his lips, and she proceeded: " You know that there are thirty-two points on the compass, and these points are divided into quarters; so that there are, in fact, 128 different winds."

" There are more than I could ever remember; I know that," said Jack.

" Well, we are in all 128. All the winds which have northerly in them are coarse and ugly; all the southerly winds are pretty."

" You don't say so?" replied our hero.

" We are summoned to blow, as required, but the hardest duty generally falls to the northerly winds, as it should do, for they are the strongest; although we southerly winds can blow hard enough when we choose. Our characters are somewhat different. The most unhappy in disposition, and I may say the most malevolent, are the north and easterly winds; the N.W. winds are powerful, but not unkind; the S.E. winds vary, but, at all events, we of the S.W. are considered the mildest and most beneficent. Do you understand me?"

" Not altogether. You're going right round the compass, and I never could make it out, that's a fact. I hear what you say, but I cannot promise to recollect it; I can only recollect S.W. and by W. $\frac{3}{4}$ W."

" I care only for your recollecting me; if you do that, you may forget all the rest. Now you see we South-Wests are summer winds, and are seldom required but in this season; I have often blown over your ship these last three months, and I always have lingered near you, for I loved you."

" Thank you—now go on, for seven bells have struck some time, and I shall be going to turn in. Is your watch out?"

" No, I shall blow for some hours longer. Why will you leave me—why won't you stay on deck with me?"

" What, stay on deck after my watch is out? No, if I do, blow me! We midshipmen never do that—but I say, why can't you come down with me, and turn in my hammock? It's close to the hatchway, and you can easily do it."

" Well, I will, upon one promise. You say that you love me; now I'm very jealous, for we winds are always supplanting one another. Promise me that you will never mention any other wind in the compass but me; for if you do, they may come to you, and if I hear of it I'll blow the masts out of your ship, that I will."

" You don't say so?" replied Jack, surveying her fragile, trembling form.

" Yes, I will, and on a lee-shore too; so that the ship shall go to pieces on the rocks, and the admiral and every soul on board her be drowned."

" No, you wouldn't, would you?" said our hero, astonished.

"Not if you promise me. Then I'll come to you and pour down your windsails, and dry your washed clothes as they hang on the rigging, and just ripple the waves as you glide along, and hang upon the lips of my dear love, and press him in my arms. Promise me, then, on no account ever to recollect or mention any other wind but me."

"Well, I think I may promise that," replied Jack, "I'm very clever at forgetting; and then you'll come to my hammock, won't you, and sleep with me? You'll be a nice cool bedfellow these warm nights."

"I can't sleep on my watch as midshipmen do; but I'll watch you while you sleep, and I'll fan your cheeks, and keep you cool and comfortable, till I'm relieved."

"And when you go, when will you come again?"

"That I cannot tell—when I'm summoned; and I shall wait with impatience, that you may be sure of."

"There's eight bells," said Jack, starting up; "I must go down and call the officer of the middle watch; but I'll soon turn in, for my relief is not so big as myself, and I can thrash him."

Littlebrain was as good as his word; he cut down his relief, and then thrashed him for venturing to expostulate. The consequence was, that in ten minutes he was in his hammock, and "S.W. and by W. $\frac{3}{4}$ W." came gently down the hatchway and rested in his arms. Jack soon fell fast asleep, and when he was wakened up the next morning by the quarter-master, his bedfellow was no longer there. A mate inquiring how the wind was, was answered by the quarter-master that they had a fresh breeze from the N.N.W., by which Jack understood that his sweetheart was no longer on duty.

Our hero had passed such a happy night with his soft and kind companion that he could think of nothing else; he longed for her to come again, and, to the surprise of everybody, was now perpetually making inquiries as to the wind which blew. He thought of her continually, and in fact was as much in love with "S.W. and by W. $\frac{3}{4}$ W." as he possibly could be. She came again—once more did he enjoy her delightful company; again she slept with him in his hammock, and then, after a short stay, she was relieved by another.

We do not intend to accuse the wind of inconstancy, as that was not her fault; nor of treachery, for she loved dearly; nor of violence, for she was all softness and mildness; but we do say that "S. W. and by W. $\frac{3}{4}$ W." was the occasion of Jack being very often in a scrape, for our hero kept his word; he forgot all other winds, and with him there was no other except his dear "S.W. and by W. $\frac{3}{4}$ W." It must be admitted of Jack that, at all events, he showed great perseverance, for he stuck to his point.

Our hero would argue with his messmates, for it is not those who are most capable of arguing who are most fond of it ; and, like all arguers not very brilliant, he would flounder and diverge away right and left, just as the flaws of ideas came into his head.

"What nonsense it is your talking that way," would his opponent say ; "why don't you come to the point ?"

"And so I do," cried Jack.

"Well, then, what is your point ?"

"S.W. and by W. ¾ W.," replied our hero.

Who could reply to this ? But in every instance, and through every difficulty, our hero kept his promise, until his uncle, Sir Theophilus, was very undecided whether he should send him home to be locked up in a lunatic asylum, or bring him on in the service to the rank of post-captain. Upon mature consideration, however, as a man in Bedlam is a very useless member of society, and a teetotal non-productive, whereas a captain in the navy is a responsible agent, the admiral came to the conclusion that Littlebrain must follow up his destiny.

At last Jack was set down as the greatest fool in the ship, and was pointed out as such. The ladies observed that such might possibly be the case, but at all events he was the handsomest young man in the Mediterranean fleet. We believe that both parties were correct in their assertions.

Time flies—even a midshipman's time, which does not fly quite so fast as his money—and the time came for Mr. Littlebrain's examination. Sir Theophilus, who now commanded the whole fleet, was almost in despair. How was it possible that a man could navigate a ship with only one quarter point of the compass in his head ?

Sir Theophilus scratched his wig ; and the disposition of the Mediterranean fleet, so important to the country, was altered according to the dispositions of the captains who commanded the ships. In those days there were martinets in the service ; officers who never overlooked an offence, or permitted the least deviation from strict duty ; who were generally hated, but at the same time were most valuable to the service. As for his nephew passing his examination before any of those of the first or second, or even of the third degree, the admiral knew that it was impossible. The consequence was, that one was sent away on a mission to Genoa about nothing ; another to watch for vessels, never expected, off Sardinia ; two more to cruise after a French frigate which had never been built : and thus, by degrees, did the admiral arrange, so as to obtain a set of officers sufficiently pliant to allow his nephew to creep under the gate which barred his promotion, and which he never could have vaulted over. So the signal was made—our hero went on board—his uncle had not forgotten the propriety of a little *douceur* on the occasion ;

and, as the turkeys were all gone, three couple of geese were sent in the same boat, as a present to each of the three passing captains. Littlebrain's heart failed him as he pulled to the ship; even the geese hissed at him, as much as to say, "If you were not such a stupid ass, we might have been left alive in our coops." There was a great deal of truth in that remark, if they did say so.

Nothing could have been made more easy for Littlebrain than his examination. The questions had all been arranged beforehand; and some kind friend had given him all the answers written down. The passing captains apparently suffered from the heat of the weather, and each had his hand on his brow, looking down on the table, at the time that Littlebrain gave his answers, so that of course they did not observe that he was reading them off. As soon as Littlebrain had given his answer, and had had sufficient time to drop his paper under the table, the captains felt better and looked up again.

There were but eight questions for our hero to answer. Seven had been satisfactorily got through; then came the eighth, a very simple one:—"What is your course and distance from Ushant to the Start?" This question having been duly put, the captains were again in deep meditation, shrouding their eyes with the palms of their hands.

Littlebrain had his answer—he looked at the paper. What could be more simple than to reply? and then the captains would have all risen up, shaken him by the hand, complimented him upon the talent he had displayed, sent their compliments to the commander-in-chief and their thanks for the geese. Jack was just answering, "North——"

"Recollect your promise!" cried a soft voice, which Jack well recollected.

Jack stammered—the captains were mute—and waited patiently.

"I must say it," muttered Jack.

"You shan't," replied the little Wind.

"Indeed I must," said Jack, "or I shall be turned back."

The captains, surprised at this delay and the muttering of Jack, looked up, and one of them gently inquired if Mr. Littlebrain had not dropped his handkerchief or something under the table? And then they again fixed their eyes upon the green cloth.

"If you dare, I'll never see you again," cried "S.W. and by W. $\frac{3}{4}$ W."—"never come to your hammock—but I'll blow the ship on shore, every soul shall be lost, admiral and all; recollect your promise!"

"Then I shall never pass," replied Jack.

"Do you think that any other point in the compass shall pass you except me?—never! I am too jealous for that. Come now, dearest!" and the Wind again deliciously trembled upon the lips of our hero, who could no longer resist.

"S.W. and by W. ¾ W.," exclaimed Jack firmly.

"You have made a slight mistake, Mr. Littlebrain," said one of the captains. "*Look* again—I meant to say, *think* again."

"S.W. and by W. ¾ W.," again repeated Jack.

"Dearest, how I love you!" whispered the soft Wind.

"Why, Mr. Littlebrain," said one of the captains—for Jack had actually laid the paper down on the table—"what's in the wind now?"

"She's obstinate," replied Jack.

"You appear to be so, at all events," replied the captain. "Pray, try once more."

"I have it!" thought Jack, who tore off the last answer from his paper. "I gained five guineas by that plan once before." He then handed the bit of paper to the passing captain. "I believe that's right, sir," said our hero.

"Yes, that is right; but could you not have said it instead of writing it, Mr. Littlebrain?"

Jack made no reply; his little sweetheart pouted a little, but said nothing; it was an evasion which she did not like. A few seconds of consultation then took place, as a matter of form. Each captain asked of the other if he was perfectly satisfied as to Mr. Littlebrain's capabilities, and the reply was in the affirmative; and they were perfectly satisfied that he was either a fool or a madman. However, as we have had both in the service by way of precedent, Jack was added to the list, and the next day was appointed lieutenant.

Our hero did his duty as lieutenant of the forecastle; and as all the duty of that officer is, when hailed from the quarter-deck, to answer, "*Ay, ay, sir,*" he got on without making many mistakes. And now he was very happy; no one dared to call him a fool except his uncle; he had his own cabin, and many was the time that his dear little "S.W. and by W. ¾ W." would come in by the scuttle and nestle by his side.

"You won't see so much of me soon, dearest," said she, one morning, gravely.

"Why not, my soft one?" replied Jack.

"Don't you recollect that the winter months are coming on?"

"So they are," replied Jack. "Well, I shall long for you back."

And Jack did long, and long very much, for he loved his dear wind and the fine weather which accompanied her. Winter came on, and heavy gales and rain, and thunder and lightning; nothing but double-reefed top-sails and wearing in succession; and our hero walked the forecastle and thought of his favourite wind. The N.E. winds came down furiously, and the weather was bitter cold.

The officers shook the rain and spray off their garments when their watch was over, and called for grog.

" Steward, a glass of grog," cried one ; " and let it be strong."

" The same for me," said Jack ; " only, I'll mix it myself."

Jack poured out the rum till the tumbler was half full.

" Why, Littlebrain," said his messmate, " that is a dose ; that's what we call a regular *Nor-wester*."

" Is it ? " replied Jack. " Well, then, Nor-westers suit me exactly, and I shall stick to them like cobblers' wax."

And during the whole of the winter months our hero showed a great predilection for Nor-westers.

It was in the latter end of February that there was a heavy gale ; it had blown furiously from the northward for three days, and then it paused and panted as if out of breath—no wonder ! And then the wind shifted and shifted again, with squalls and heavy rain, until it blew from every quarter of the compass.

Our hero's watch was over, and he came down and called for a " Nor-wester " as usual.

" How is the wind now ? " asked the first lieutenant of the master, who came down dripping wet.

" S.S.W., but drawing now fast to the westward," said old Spun-yarn.

And so it was ; and it veered round until " S.W. and by W. ¾ W.," with an angry gust, came down the skylight, and blowing strongly into our hero's ear, cried :

" Oh, you false one ! "

" False ! " exclaimed Jack. " What ! you here, and so angry too ? What's the matter ? "

" What's the matter !—do you think I don't know ? What have you been doing ever since I was away, comforting yourself during my absence with *Nor-westers* ? "

" Why, you a'n't jealous of a Nor-wester, are you ? " replied Littlebrain. " I confess I'm rather partial to them."

" What !—this to my face !—I'll never come again, without you promise me that you will have nothing to do with them, and never call for one again. Be quick—I cannot stay more than two minutes ; for it is hard work now, and we relieve quick—say the word."

" Well, then," replied Littlebrain, " you've no objection to *half-and-half* ? "

" None in the world ; that's quite another thing, and has nothing to do with the wind."

" It has, though," thought Jack, " for it gets a man in the wind ; but I won't tell her so ; and," continued he, " you don't mind a raw nip, do you ? "

" No—I care for nothing except a Nor-wester."

"I'll never call for one again," replied Jack; "it is but making my grog a little stronger; in future it shall be *half-and-half*."

"That's a dear! Now I'm off—don't forget me"; and away went the wind in a great hurry.

It was about three months after this short visit, the fleet being off Corsica, that our hero was walking the deck, thinking that he soon should see the object of his affections, when a privateer brig was discovered at anchor a few miles from Bastia. The signal was made for the boats of the fleet to cut her out; and the admiral, wishing that his nephew should distinguish himself somehow, gave him the command of one of the finest boats. Now Jack was as brave as brave could be; he did not know what danger was; he hadn't wit enough to perceive it, and there was no doubt but he would distinguish himself. The boats went on the service. Jack was the very first on board, cheering his men as he darted into the closed ranks of his opponents. Whether it was that he did not think that his head was worth defending, or that he was too busy in breaking the heads of others to look after his own, this is certain, that a tomahawk descended upon it with such force as to bury itself in his skull (and his was a thick skull too). The privateer's men were overpowered by numbers, and then our hero was discovered under a pile of bodies, still breathing heavily. He was hoisted on board and taken into his uncle's cabin; the surgeon shook his head when he had examined that of our hero.

"It must have been a most tremendous blow," said he to the admiral, "to have penetrated——"

"It must have been, indeed," replied the admiral, as the tears rolled down his cheeks; for he loved his nephew.

The surgeon, having done all that his art would enable him to do, left the cabin to attend to the others who were hurt; the admiral also went on the quarter-deck, walking to and fro for an hour in a melancholy mood. He returned to the cabin and bent over his nephew; Jack opened his eyes.

"My dear fellow," said the admiral, "how's your head now?"

"*S.W. and by W. ¾ W.*," faintly exclaimed our hero, constant in death, as he turned a little on one side and expired.

It was three days afterwards, as the fleet were on a wind making for Malta, that the bell of the ship tolled, and a body, sewed up in a hammock and covered with the Union Jack, was carried to the gangway by the admiral's bargemen. It had been a dull, cloudy day, with little wind; the hands were turned up, the officers and men stood uncovered; the admiral in advance with his arms folded, as the chaplain read the funeral service over the body of our hero,—and as the service proceeded, the sails flapped, for the wind had shifted a little; a motion was made, by the hand of the officer of the watch, to the man at the helm to let the ship go off the wind, that the service might not be disturbed, and a mizzling soft rain descended. The wind had shifted to our hero's much-loved *point*, his fond mistress had come to mourn over the loss of her dearest, and the rain that descended were the tears which she shed at the death of her handsome but not over-gifted lover.

MARY WOLLSTONECRAFT SHELLEY
1797–1851

THE SISTERS OF ALBANO

And near Albano's scarce divided waves
Shine from a sister valley ;—and afar
The Tiber winds, and the broad ocean laves
The Latian coast where sprang the Epic war,
" Arms and the Man," whose re-ascending star
Rose o'er an empire ; but beneath thy right
Tully reposed from Rome ; and where yon bar
Of girding mountains intercepts the sight
The Sabine farm was till'd, the weary bard's delight.

It was to see this beautiful lake that I made my last excursion before quitting Rome. The spring had nearly grown into summer, the trees were all in full but fresh green foliage, the vine-dresser was singing, perched among them, training his vines : the cicala had not yet begun her song, the heats therefore had not commenced ; but at evening the fireflies gleamed among the hills, and the cooing aziolo assured us of what in that country needs no assurance, fine weather for the morrow. We set out early in the morning to avoid the heats, breakfasted at Albano, and till ten o'clock passed our time in visiting the Mosaic, the villa of Cicero, and other curiosities of the place. We reposed during the middle of the day in a tent elevated for us at the hill-top, whence we looked on the hill-embosomed lake, and the distant eminence crowned by a town with its church. Other villages and cottages were scattered among the foldings of mountains, and beyond we saw the deep blue sea of the southern poets, which received the swift and immortal Tiber, rocking it to repose among its devouring waves. The Coliseum falls and the Pantheon decays—the very hills of Rome are perishing—but the Tiber lives for ever, flows for ever, and for ever feeds the land-encircled Mediterranean with fresh waters.

Our summer and pleasure-seeking party consisted of many : to me the most interesting person was the Countess Atanasia D——, who was as beautiful as an imagination of Raphael, and good as the ideal of a poet. Two of her children accompanied her, with animated looks and gentle manners, quiet, yet enjoying. I sat near her, watching the changing shadows of the landscape before us. As the sun descended, it poured a tide of light into the valley of the lake, deluging the deep bank formed by the mountain with liquid gold. The domes and turrets of the far town flashed and gleamed, the trees were dyed in splendour ; two or three slight clouds, which had drunk the radiance till it became their essence, floated golden islets in the lustrous empyrean. The waters, reflecting the brilliancy of the sky and the fire-tinted banks, beamed a second heaven, a second irradiated earth, at our feet. The Mediterranean, gazing on the sun—as the eyes of a mortal bride fail and are dimmed when reflecting her lover's glances—was lost, mixed in his light, till it had become one with him. Long (our souls, like the sea, the hills, and lake, drinking in the supreme loveliness) we gazed, till the too full cup overflowed, and we turned away with a sigh.

At our feet there was a knoll of ground that formed the foreground of our picture ; two trees lay basking against the sky, glittering with the golden light, which like dew seemed to hang amid their branches; a rock closed the prospect on the other side, twined round by creepers, and redolent with blooming myrtle ; a brook, crossed by huge stones, gushed through the turf, and on the fragments of rock that lay about sat two or three persons, peasants, who attracted our attention. One was a hunter, as his gun, lying on a bank not far off, demonstrated ; yet he was a tiller of the soil : his rough straw hat, and his picturesque but coarse dress, belonged to that class. The other was some contadina, in the costume of her country, returning, her basket on her arm, from the village to her cottage home. They were regarding the stores of a pedlar, who with doffed hat stood near: some of these consisted of pictures and prints—views of the country, and portraits of the Madonna. Our peasants regarded these with pleased attention.

"One might easily make a story for that pair," I said : "his gun is a help to the imagination, and we may fancy him a bandit with his contadina love, the terror of all the neighbourhood, except of her, the most defenceless being in it."

"You speak lightly of such a combination," said the lovely countess at my side, "as if it must not in its nature be the cause of dreadful tragedies. The mingling of love with crime is a dread conjunction, and lawless pursuits are never followed without bringing on the criminal, and all allied to him, ineffable misery. I speak with emotion, for your observation reminds me of an unfortunate girl, now one of the Sisters of Charity in the convent of Santa Chiara at Rome, whose unhappy passion for a man such as you mention spread destruction and sorrow widely around her."

I entreated my lovely friend to relate the history of the nun ; for a long time she resisted my entreaties, as not willing to depress the spirit of a party of pleasure by a tale of sorrow. But I urged her, and she yielded. Her sweet Italian phraseology now rings in my ears, and her beautiful countenance is before me. As she spoke, the sun set, and the moon bent her silver horn in the ebbing tide of glory he had left. The lake changed from purple to silver, and the trees, before so splendid, now in dark masses, just reflected from their tops the mild moonlight. The fire-flies flashed among the rocks; the bats circled round us: meanwhile thus commenced the Countess Atanasia:

The nun of whom I speak had a sister older than herself; I can remember them when as children they brought eggs and fruit to my father's villa. Maria and Anina were constantly together. With their large straw hats to shield them from the scorching sun, they were at work in their father's *podere* all day, and in the evening, when Maria, who was the elder by four years, went to the fountain for water, Anina ran at her side. Their cot—the folding of the hill conceals it—is at the lake-side opposite; and about a quarter of a mile up the hill is the rustic fountain of which I speak. Maria was serious, gentle, and considerate; Anina was a laughing, merry little creature, with the face of a cherub. When Maria was fifteen, their mother fell ill, and was nursed at the convent of Santa Chiara at Rome. Maria attended her, never leaving her bedside day or night. The nuns thought her an angel, she deemed them saints: her mother died, and they persuaded her to make one of them; her father could not but acquiesce in her holy intention, and she became one of the Sisters of Charity, the nun-nurses of Santa Chiara. Once or twice a year she visited her home, gave sage and kind advice to Anina, and sometimes wept to part from her; but her piety and her active employments for the sick reconciled her to her fate. Anina was more sorry to lose her sister's society. The other girls of the village did not please her: she was a good child, and worked hard for her father, and her sweetest recompense was the report he made of her to Maria, and the fond praises and caresses the latter bestowed on her when they met.

It was not until she was fifteen that Anina showed any diminution of affection for her sister. Yet I cannot call it diminution, for she loved her perhaps more than ever, though her holy calling and sage lectures prevented her from reposing confidence, and made her tremble lest the nun, devoted to heaven and good works, should read in her eyes, and disapprove of the earthly passion that occupied her. Perhaps a part of her reluctance arose from the reports that were current against her lover's character, and certainly from the disapprobation and even hatred of him that her father frequently expressed. Ill-fated Anina! I know not if in the north your peasants love as ours; but the passion of Anina was entwined with the roots of her being, it was herself: she could die, but not cease to love. The dislike of her father for Domenico made their intercourse clandestine. He was always at the fountain to fill her pitcher, and lift it on her head. He attended the same mass; and when her father went to Albano, Velletri, or Rome, he seemed to learn by instinct the exact moment of his departure, and joined her in the *podere*, labouring with her and for her, till the old man was seen descending the mountain-path on his return. He said he worked for a contadino near Nemi. Anina sometimes wondered that he could spare so much time for her; but his excuses were plausible, and the result too delightful not to blind the innocent girl to its obvious cause.

Poor Domenico! the reports spread against him were too well founded: his sole excuse was that his father had been a robber before him, and he had spent his early years among these lawless men. He had better things in his nature, and yearned for the peace of the guiltless. Yet he could hardly be called guilty, for no dread crime stained him; nevertheless, he was an outlaw and a bandit, and now that he loved Anina these names were the stings of an adder to pierce his soul. He would have fled from his comrades to a far country, but Anina dwelt amid their very haunts. At this period also, the police established by the French government, which then possessed Rome, made these bands more alive to the conduct of their members, and rumours of active measures to be taken against those who occupied the hills near Albano, Nemi, and Velletri, caused them to draw together in tighter bonds. Domenico would not, if he could, desert his friends in the hour of danger.

On a *festa* at this time—it was towards the end of October—Anina strolled with her father among the villagers, who all over Italy make holiday, by congregating and walking in one place. Their talk was entirely of the *laddri* and the French, and many terrible stories were related of the extirpation of banditti in the kingdom of Naples, and the mode by which the French succeeded in their undertaking was minutely described. The troops scoured the country, visiting one haunt of the robbers after the other, and dislodging them, tracked them, as in those countries they hunt the wild beasts of the forest, till drawing the circle narrower, they enclosed them in one spot. They then drew a cordon round the place, which they guarded with the utmost vigilance, forbidding any to enter it with provisions, on pain of instant death. And as this menace was rigorously executed, in a short time the besieged bandits were starved into a surrender. The French troops were now daily expected, for they had been seen at Velletri and Nemi; at the same time it was affirmed that several outlaws had taken up their abode at Rocca Giovane, a deserted village on the summit of one of these hills, and it was supposed that they would make that place the scene of their final retreat.

The next day, as Anina worked in the *podere*, a party of French horse passed by along the road that separated her garden from the lake. Curiosity made her look at them; and her beauty was too great not to attract: their observations and address soon drove her away—for a woman in love consecrates herself to her lover, and deems the admiration of others to be profanation. She spoke to her father of the impertinence of these men, and he answered by rejoicing at their arrival and the destruction of the lawless bands that would ensue. When, in the evening, Anina went to the fountain, she looked timidly around, and hoped that Domenico would be at his accustomed post, for the arrival of the French destroyed her feeling of security. She went rather later than usual, and a cloudy evening made it seem already dark; the wind roared among the trees, bending hither and thither even the stately cypresses; the waters of the lake were agitated into high waves, and dark masses of thunder-cloud lowered over the hill-tops, giving a lurid tinge to the landscape. Anina passed quickly up the mountain-path: when she came in sight of the fountain, which was rudely hewn in the living rock, she saw Domenico leaning against a projection of the hill, his hat drawn over his eyes, his *tabaro* fallen from his shoulders, his arms folded in an attitude of dejection. He started when he saw her; his voice and phrases were broken and unconnected; yet he never gazed on her with such ardent love, nor solicited her to delay her departure with such impassioned tenderness.

"How glad I am to find you here!" she said: "I was fearful of meeting one of the French soldiers: I dread them even more than the banditti."

Domenico cast a look of eager inquiry on her, and then turned away, saying, "Sorry am I that I shall not be here to protect you. I am obliged to go to Rome for a week or two. You will be faithful, Anina mia; you will love me, though I never see you more?"

The interview, under these circumstances, was longer than usual: he led her down the path till they nearly came in sight of her cottage; still they lingered: a low whistle was heard among the myrtle underwood at the lake side; he started; it was repeated, and he answered it by a similar note: Anina, terrified, was about to ask what this meant, when, for the first time, he pressed her to his heart, kissed her roseate lips, and, with a muttered "Carissima addio," left her, springing down the bank; and as she gazed in wonder, she thought she saw a boat cross a line of light made by the opening of a cloud. She stood long absorbed in reverie, wondering and remembering with thrilling pleasure the quick embrace and impassioned farewell of her lover. She delayed so long that her father came to seek her.

Each evening after this Anina visited the fountain at the Ave Maria; he was not there; each day seemed an age; and incomprehensible fears occupied her heart. About a fortnight after, letters arrived from Maria. They came to say that she had been ill of the malaria fever, that she was now convalescent, but that change of air was necessary for her recovery, and that she had obtained leave to spend a month at home at Albano. She asked her father to come the next day to fetch her. These were pleasant tidings for Anina; she resolved to disclose everything to her sister, and during her long visit she doubted not but that she would contrive her happiness. Old Andrea departed the following morning, and the whole day was spent by the sweet girl in dreams of future bliss. In the evening Maria arrived, weak and wan, with all the marks of that dread illness about her; yet, as she assured her sister, feeling quite well.

As they sat at their frugal supper several villagers came in to inquire for Maria; but all their talk was of the French soldiers and the robbers, of whom a band of at least twenty was collected in Rocca Giovane, strictly watched by the military.

"We may be grateful to the French," said Andrea, "for this good deed: the country will be rid of these ruffians."

"True, friend," said another; "but it is horrible to think what these men suffer; they have, it appears, exhausted all the food they brought with them to the village, and are literally starving. They have not an ounce of macaroni among them; and a poor fellow who was taken and executed yesterday was a mere anatomy; you could tell every bone in his skin."

"There was a sad story the other day," said another, "of an old man from Nemi, whose son, they say, is among them at Rocca Giovane: he was found within the lines with some *baccalà* under his *pastrano*, and shot on the spot."

"There is not a more desperate gang," observed the first speaker, "in the states and the regno put together. They have sworn never to yield but upon good terms: to secure these, their plan is to waylay passengers and make prisoners, whom they keep as hostages for mild treatment from the government. But the French are merciless; they are better pleased that the bandits wreak their vengeance on these poor creatures than spare one of their lives."

"They have captured two persons already," said another; "and there is old Betta Tossi half frantic, for she is sure her son is taken: he has not been at home these ten days."

"I should rather guess," said an old man, "that he went there with good will: the young scapegrace kept company with Domenico Baldi of Nemi."

" No worse company could he have kept in the whole country," said Andrea : " Domenico is the bad son of a bad race. Is he in the village with the rest ? "

" My own eyes assured me of that," replied the other. " When I was up the hill with eggs and fowls to the piquette there, I saw the branches of an ilex move ; the poor fellow was weak, perhaps, and could not keep his hold ; presently he dropt to the ground ; every musket was levelled at him, but he started up and was away like a hare among the rocks. Once he turned, and then I saw Domenico as plainly, though thinner, poor lad, by much than he was, as plainly as I now see——Santa Virgine ! what is the matter with Nina ? "

She had fainted ; the company broke up, and she was left to her sister's care. When the poor child came to herself she was fully aware of her situation, and said nothing, except expressing a wish to retire to rest. Maria was in high spirits at the prospect of her long holiday at home, but the illness of her sister made her refrain from talking that night, and blessing her, as she said good-night, she soon slept. Domenico starving !—Domenico trying to escape and dying through hunger was the vision of horror that wholly possessed poor Anina. At another time the discovery that her lover was a robber might have inflicted pangs as keen as those which she now felt ; but this at present made a faint impression, obscured by worse wretchedness. Maria was in a deep and tranquil sleep. Anina rose, dressed herself silently, and crept down stairs. She stored her market-basket with what food there was in the house, and, unlatching the cottage-door, issued forth, resolved to reach Rocca Giovane and to administer to her lover's dreadful wants. The night was dark, but this was favourable, for she knew every path and turn of the hills, every bush and knoll of ground between her home and the deserted village which occupies the summit of that hill : you may see the dark outline of some of its houses about two hours' walk from her cottage. The night was dark, but still ; the libeccio brought the clouds below the mountain-tops, and veiled the horizon in mist ; not a leaf stirred ; her footsteps sounded loud in her ears, but resolution overcame fear. She had entered yon ilex grove, her spirits rose with her success, when suddenly she was challenged by a sentinel : no time for escape ; fear chilled her blood ; her basket dropped from her arm ; its contents rolled out on the ground ; the soldier fired his gun and brought several others around him ; she was made prisoner.

In the morning, when Maria awoke, she missed her sister from her side. I have overslept myself, she thought, and Nina would not disturb me. But when she came down stairs and met her father, and Anina did not appear, they began to wonder. She was not in the *podere* ; two hours passed, and then Andrea went to seek her.

Entering the near village, he saw the contadini crowding together, and a stifled exclamation of " Ecco il padre ! " told him that some evil had betided. His first impression was that his daughter was drowned ; but the truth, that she had been taken by the French carrying provisions within the forbidden line, was still more terrible. He returned in frantic desperation to his cottage, first to acquaint Maria with what had happened and then to ascend the hill to save his child from her impending fate. Maria heard his tale with horror ; but an hospital is a school in which to learn self-possession and presence of mind. " Do you remain, my father," she said : " I will go. My holy character will awe these men, my tears move them : trust me ; I swear that I will save my sister." Andrea yielded to her superior courage and energy.

The nuns of Santa Chiara when out of their convent do not usually wear their monastic habit, but dress simply in a black gown. Maria, however, had brought her nun's habiliments with her, and thinking thus to impress the soldiers with respect, she now put it on. She received her father's benediction, and asking that of the Virgin and the saints, she departed on her expedition. Ascending the hill, she was soon stopped by the sentinels. She asked to see their commanding officer, and being conducted to him, she announced herself as the sister of the unfortunate girl who had been captured the night before. The officer, who had received her with carelessness, now changed countenance ; his serious look frightened Maria, who clasped her hands, exclaiming, " You have not injured the child ? she is safe ? "

" She is safe—now," he replied with hesitation ; " but there is no hope of pardon."

" Holy Virgin, have mercy on her ! what will be done to her ? "

" I have received strict orders ; in two hours she dies."

" No ! no ! " exclaimed Maria impetuously, " that cannot be ! you cannot be so wicked as to murder a child like her."

" She is old enough, madame," said the officer, " to know that she ought not to disobey orders ; mine are so strict that were she but nine years old, she dies."

These terrible words stung Maria to fresh resolution : she entreated for mercy ; she knelt ; she vowed that she would not depart without her sister ; she appealed to Heaven and the saints. The officer, though cold-hearted, was good natured and courteous, and he assured her with the utmost gentleness that her supplications were of no avail ; that were the criminal his own daughter he must enforce his orders. As a sole concession, he permitted her to see her sister. Despair inspired the nun with energy ; she almost ran up the hill, outspeeding her guide ; they crossed a folding of the hills to a little sheep-cot, where sentinels paraded before the door.

There was no glass to the windows, so the shutters were shut, and when Maria first went in from the bright daylight she hardly saw the slight figure of her sister leaning against the wall, her dark hair fallen below her waist, her head sunk on her bosom, over which her arms were folded. She started wildly as the door opened, saw her sister, and sprung with a piercing shriek into her arms.

They were left alone together: Anina uttered a thousand frantic exclamations, beseeching her sister to save her, and shuddering at the near approach of her fate. Maria had felt herself, since their mother's death, the natural protectress and support of her sister, and she never deemed herself so called on to fulfil this character as now that the trembling girl clasped her neck, her tears falling on her cheeks and her choked voice entreating her to save her. The thought—O could I suffer instead of you! was in her heart, and she was about to express it, when it suggested another idea, on which she was resolved to act. First she soothed Anina by her promises, then glanced round the cot; they were quite alone: she went to the window, and through a crevice saw the soldiers conversing at some distance. "Yes, dearest sister," she cried, "I will—I can save you—quick—we must change dresses—there is no time to be lost!—you must escape in my habit."

"And you remain to die?"

"They dare not murder the innocent, a nun! Fear not for me—I am safe."

Anina easily yielded to her sister, but her fingers trembled; every string she touched she entangled. Maria was perfectly self-possessed, pale, but calm. She tied up her sister's long hair, and adjusted her veil over it so as to conceal it; she unlaced her bodice, and arranged the folds of her own habit on her with the greatest care; then, more hastily, she assumed the dress of her sister, putting on, after a lapse of many years her native contadina costume. Anina stood by, weeping and helpless, hardly hearing her sister's injunctions to return speedily to their father, and under his guidance seek sanctuary. The guard now opened the door. Anina clung to her sister in terror, while she, in soothing tones, entreated her to calm herself.

The soldier said they must delay no longer, for the priest had arrived to confess the prisoner.

To Anina the idea of confession associated with death was terrible; to Maria it brought hope. She whispered in a smothered voice, "The priest will protect me—fear not—hasten to our father!"

Anina almost mechanically obeyed: weeping with her handkerchief placed unaffectedly before her face, she passed the soldiers; they closed the door on the prisoner, who hastened to the window and saw her sister descend the hill with tottering steps, till she was lost behind some rising ground. The nun fell on her knees—cold dew bathed her brow, instinctively she feared: the French had shown small respect for the monastic character; they destroyed the convents and desecrated the churches. Would they be merciful to her, and spare the innocent? Alas! was not Anina innocent also? Her sole crime had been disobeying an arbitrary command, and she had done the same.

"Courage!" cried Maria; "perhaps I am fitter to die than my sister is. Gesu, pardon me my sins, but I do not believe that I shall outlive this day!"

In the meantime, Anina descended the hill slowly and tremblingly. She feared discovery, she feared for her sister, and above all, at the present moment, she feared the reproaches and anger of her father. By dwelling on this last idea, it became exaggerated into excessive terror, and she determined, instead of returning to her home, to make a circuit among the hills, to find her way by herself to Albano, where she trusted to find protection from her pastor and confessor. She avoided the open paths, and following rather the direction she wished to pursue than any beaten road, she passed along nearer to Rocca Giovane than she anticipated. She looked up at its ruined houses and bell-less steeple, straining her eyes to catch a glimpse of him, the author of all her ills. A low but distinct whistle reached her ear, not far off; she started—she remembered that on the night when she last saw Domenico a note like that had called him from her side; the sound was echoed and re-echoed from other quarters; she stood aghast, her bosom heaving, her hands clasped. First she saw a dark and ragged head of hair, shadowing two fiercely gleaming eyes, rise from beneath a bush. She screamed, but before she could repeat her scream three men leapt from behind a rock, secured her arms, threw a cloth over her face, and hurried her up the acclivity. Their talk, as she went along, informed her of the horror and danger of her situation.

Pity, they said, that the holy father and some of his red stockings did not command the troops: with a nun in their hands, they might obtain any terms. Coarse jests passed as they dragged their victim towards their ruined village. The paving of the street told her when they arrived at Rocca Giovane, and the change of atmosphere that they entered a house. They unbandaged her eyes: the scene was squalid and miserable, the walls ragged and black with smoke, the floor strewn with offals and dirt; a rude table and broken bench was all the furniture; and the leaves of Indian corn, heaped high in one corner, served, it seemed for a bed, for a man lay on it, his head buried in his folded arms. Anina looked round on her savage hosts: their countenances expressed every variety of brutal ferocity now rendered more dreadful from gaunt famine and suffering.

"O there is none who will save me!" she cried. The voice startled the man who was lying on the floor; he leapt up—it was Domenico: Domenico, so changed, with sunk cheeks and eyes, matted hair, and looks whose wildness and desperation differed little from the dark countenances around him. Could this be her lover?

His recognition and surprise at her dress led to an explanation. When the robbers first heard that their prey was no prize, they were mortified and angry; but when she related the danger she had incurred by endeavouring to bring them food, they swore with horrid oaths that no harm should befall her, but that if she liked she might make one of them in all honour and equality. The innocent girl shuddered. "Let me go," she cried; "let me only escape and hide myself in a convent for ever!"

Domenico looked at her in agony. "Yes, poor child," he said, "go, save yourself: God grant no evil befall you; the ruin is too wide already." Then turning eagerly to his comrades, he continued: "You hear her story. She was to have been shot for bringing food to us: her sister has substituted herself in her place. We know the French; one victim is to them as good as another: Maria dies in their hands. Let us save her. Our time is up; we must fall like men, or starve like dogs: we have still ammunition, still some strength left. To arms! let us rush on the poltroons, free their prisoner, and escape or die!"

There needed but an impulse like this to urge the outlaws to desperate resolves. They prepared their arms with looks of ferocious determination. Domenico, meanwhile, led Anina out of the house, to the verge of the hill, inquiring whither she intended to go. On her saying, to Albano, he observed, "That were hardly safe; be guided by me, I entreat you: take these piastres, hire the first conveyance you find, hasten to Rome, to the convent of Santa Chiara: for pity's sake, do not linger in this neighbourhood."

"I will obey your injunctions, Domenico," she replied, "but I cannot take your money; it has cost you too dear: fear not, I shall arrive safely at Rome without that ill-fated silver."

Domenico's comrades now called loudly to him: he had no time to urge his request; he threw the despised dollars at her feet.

"Nina, adieu for ever," he said: "may you love again more happily!"

"Never!" she replied. "God has saved me in this dress; it were sacrilege to change it: I shall never quit Santa Chiara."

Domenico had led her a part of the way down the rock; his comrades appeared at the top, calling to him.

"Gesu save you!" cried he: "reach the convent—Maria shall join you there before night. Farewell!" He hastily kissed her hand, and sprang up the acclivity to rejoin his impatient friends.

The unfortunate Andrea had waited long for the return of his children. The leafless trees and bright clear atmosphere permitted every object to be visible, but he saw no trace of them on the hill-side ; the shadows of the dial showed noon to be passed, when, with uncontrollable impatience, he began to climb the hill, towards the spot where Anina had been taken. The path he pursued was in part the same that this unhappy girl had taken on her way to Rome. The father and daughter met : the old man saw the nun's dress, and saw her unaccompanied : she covered her face with her hands in a transport of fear and shame ; but when, mistaking her for Maria, he asked in a tone of anguish for his youngest darling, her arms fell ; she dared not raise her eyes, which streamed with tears.

" Unhappy girl ! " exclaimed Andrea, " where is your sister ? "

She pointed to the cottage prison, now discernible near the summit of a steep acclivity. " She is safe," she replied : " she saved me ; but they dare not murder her."

" Heaven bless her for this good deed," exclaimed the old man, fervently ; " but you hasten on your way, and I will go in search of her."

Each proceeded on an opposite path. The old man wound up the hill, now in view, and now losing sight of the hut where his child was captive ; he was aged, and the way was steep. Once, when the closing of the hill hid the point towards which he for ever strained his eyes, a single shot was fired in that direction ; his staff fell from his hands, his knees trembled and failed him ; several minutes of dead silence elapsed before he recovered himself sufficiently to proceed : full of fears he went on, and at the next turn saw the cot again. A party of soldiers were on the open space before it, drawn up in a line as if expecting an attack. In a few moments from above them shots were fired, which they returned, and the whole was enveloped and veiled in smoke. Still Andrea climbed the hill, eager to discover what had become of his child : the firing continued quick and hot. Now and then, in the pauses of musketry and the answering echoes of the mountains, he heard a funereal chant ; presently, before he was aware, at a turning of the hill, he met a company of priests and contadini, carrying a large cross and a bier. The miserable father rushed forward with frantic impatience ; the awe-struck peasants set down their load—the face was uncovered, and the wretched man fell senseless on the corpse of his murdered child.

The countess Atanasia paused, overcome by the emotions inspired by the history she related. A long pause ensued : at length one of the party observed, " Maria, then, was the sacrifice to her goodness."

"The French," said the countess, "did not venerate her holy vocation; one peasant girl to them was the same as another. The immolation of any victim suited their purpose of awe-striking the peasantry. Scarcely, however, had the shot entered her heart, and her blameless spirit been received by the saints in Paradise, when Domenico and his followers rushed down the hill to avenge her and themselves. The contest was furious and bloody; twenty French soldiers fell, and not one of the banditti escaped, Domenico, the foremost of the assailants, being the first to fall."

I asked, "And where are now Anina and her father?"

"You may see them, if you will," said the countess, "on your return to Rome. She is a nun of Santa Chiara. Constant acts of benevolence and piety have inspired her with calm and resignation. Her prayers are daily put up for Domenico's soul, and she hopes, through the intercession of the Virgin, to rejoin him in the other world.

"Andrea is very old; he has outlived the memory of his sufferings, but he derives comfort from the filial attentions of his surviving daughter. But when I look at his cottage on this lake, and remember the happy laughing face of Anina among the vines, I shudder at the recollection of the passion that has made her cheeks pale, her thoughts for ever conversant with death, her only wish to find repose in the grave."

MARY WOLLSTONECRAFT SHELLEY

THE FALSE RHYME

On a fine July day, the fair Margaret, Queen of Navarre, then on a visit to her royal brother, had arranged a rural feast for the morning following, which Francis declined attending. He was melancholy; and the cause was said to be some lover's quarrel with a favourite dame. The morrow came, and dark rain and murky clouds destroyed at once the schemes of the courtly throng. Margaret was angry, and she grew weary: her only hope for amusement was in Francis, and he had shut himself up—an excellent reason why she should the more desire to see him. She entered his apartment: he was standing at the casement, against which the noisy shower beat, writing with a diamond on the glass. Two beautiful dogs were his sole companions. As Queen Margaret entered, he hastily let down the silken curtain before the window, and looked a little confused.

"What treason is this, my liege," said the queen, "which crimsons your cheek? I must see the same."

"It is treason," replied the king, "and therefore, sweet sister, thou mayest not see it."

This the more excited Margaret's curiosity, and a playful contest ensued: Francis at last yielded: he threw himself on a huge high-backed settee; and as the lady drew back the curtain with an arch smile, he grew grave and sentimental as he reflected on the cause which had inspired his libel against all womankind.

"What have we here?" cried Margaret: "nay, this is *lèse majesté*—

Souvent femme varie,
Bien fou qui s'y fie!

Very little change would greatly amend your couplet:—would it not run better thus—

Souvent homme varie,
Bien folle qui s'y fie?

I could tell you twenty stories of man's inconstancy."

"I will be content with one true tale of woman's fidelity," said

Francis drily ; " but do not provoke me. I would fain be at peace with the soft Mutabilities, for thy dear sake."

" I defy your Grace," replied Margaret rashly, " to instance the falsehood of one noble and well-reputed dame."

" Not even Emilie de Lagny ? " asked the King.

This was a sore subject for the Queen. Emilie had been brought up in her own household, the most beautiful and the most virtuous of her maids of honour. She had long loved the Sire de Lagny, and their nuptials were celebrated with rejoicings but little ominous of the result. De Lagny was accused but a year after of traitorously yielding to the Emperor a fortress under his command, and he was condemned to perpetual imprisonment. For some time Emilie seemed inconsolable, often visiting the miserable dungeon of her husband, and suffering on her return from witnessing his wretchedness such paroxysms of grief as threatened her life. Suddenly, in the midst of her sorrow, she disappeared ; and inquiry only divulged the disgraceful fact, that she had escaped from France, bearing her jewels with her, and accompanied by her page, Robinet Leroux. It was whispered that, during their journey, the lady and the stripling often occupied one chamber ; and Margaret, enraged at these discoveries, commanded that no further quest should be made for her lost favourite.

Taunted now by her brother, she defended Emilie, declaring that she believed her to be guiltless, even going so far as to boast that within a month she would bring proof of her innocence.

" Robinet was a pretty boy," said Francis, laughing.

" Let us make a bet," cried Margaret : " if I lose, I will bear this vile rhyme of thine as a motto to my shame to my grave ; if I win——"

" I will break my window, and grant thee whatever boon thou askest."

The result of this bet was long sung by troubadour and minstrel. The Queen employed a hundred emissaries—published rewards for any intelligence of Emilie—all in vain. The month was expiring, and Margaret would have given many bright jewels to redeem her word. On the eve of the fatal day, the jailor of the prison in which the Sire de Lagny was confined sought an audience of the Queen ; he brought her a message from the knight to say, that if the Lady Margaret would ask his pardon as her boon, and obtain from her royal brother that he might be brought before him, her bet was won. Fair Margaret was very joyful, and readily made the desired promise. Francis was unwilling to see his false servant, but he was in high good humour, for a cavalier had that morning brought intelligence of a victory over the Imperialists. The messenger himself was lauded in the despatches as the most fearless and bravest knight in

France. The King loaded him with presents, only regretting that a vow prevented the soldier from raising his visor or declaring his name.

That same evening, as the setting sun shone on the lattice on which the ungallant rhyme was traced, Francis reposed on the same settee, and the beautiful Queen of Navarre, with triumph in her bright eyes, sat beside him. Attended by guards, the prisoner was brought in; his frame was attenuated by privation, and he walked with tottering steps. He knelt at the feet of Francis, and uncovered his head; a quantity of rich golden hair then escaping, fell over the sunken cheeks and pallid brow of the suppliant.

"We have treason here!" cried the King: "sir jailor, where is your prisoner?"

"Sire, blame him not," said the soft faltering voice of Emilie; "wiser men than he have been deceived by woman. My dear lord was guiltless of the crime for which he suffered. There was but one mode to save him: I assumed his chains—he escaped with poor Robinet Leroux in my attire—he joined your army: the young and gallant cavalier who delivered the despatches to your Grace, whom you overwhelmed with honours and reward, is my own Enguerrard de Lagny. I waited but for his arrival with testimonials of his innocence to declare myself to my lady, the Queen. Has she not won her bet? And the boon she asks——"

"Is de Lagny's pardon," said Margaret, as she also knelt to the King: "spare your faithful vassal, sire, and reward this lady's truth."

Francis first broke the false-speaking window, then he raised the ladies from their supplicatory posture.

In the tournament given to celebrate this "Triumph of Ladies," the Sire de Lagny bore off every prize; and surely there was more loveliness in Emilie's faded cheek, more grace in her emaciated form—types as they were of truest affection—than in the prouder bearing and fresher complexion of the most brilliant beauty in attendance on the courtly festival.

THOMAS HOOD
1799–1845

A TALE OF TERROR

THE following story I had from the lips of a well-known Aeronaut, and nearly in the same words.

It was on one of my ascents from Vauxhall, and a gentleman of the name of Mavor had engaged himself as a companion in my aerial excursion. But when the time came his nerves failed him, and I looked vainly round for the person who was to occupy the vacant seat in the car. Having waited for him till the last possible moment, and the crowd in the gardens becoming impatient, I prepared to ascend alone; and the last cord that attached me to the earth was about to be cast off, when suddenly a strange gentleman pushed forward and volunteered to go up with me into the clouds. He pressed the request with so much earnestness that, having satisfied myself, by a few questions, of his respectability and received his promise to submit in every point to my directions, I consented to receive him in lieu of the absentee; whereupon he stepped with evident eagerness and alacrity into the machine. In another minute we were rising above the trees; and in justice to my companion I must say, that in all my experience no person at a first ascent had ever shown such perfect coolness and self-possession. The sudden rise of the machine, the novelty of the situation, the real and exaggerated dangers of the voyage, and the cheering of the spectators are apt to cause some trepidation, or at any rate excitement, in the boldest individuals; whereas the stranger was as composed and comfortable as if he had been sitting quite at home in his own library chair. A bird could not have seemed more at ease, or more in its element, and yet he solemnly assured me, upon his honour, that he had never been up before in his life. Instead of exhibiting any alarm at our great height from the earth, he evinced the liveliest pleasure whenever I emptied one of my bags of sand, and even once or twice urged me to part with more of the ballast. In the meantime, the wind, which was very light, carried us gently along in a north-east direction, and the day being particularly bright and clear, we enjoyed a delightful bird's-eye view of the great metropolis and the surrounding country. My companion listened with great interest while I pointed out to him the various objects over which we passed, till I happened casually to observe that the balloon must be directly over Hoxton. My fellow-traveller then for the first time betrayed some uneasiness, and anxiously inquired whether I thought he could be recognised by any one at our then distance from the earth. It was, I told him, quite impossible. Nevertheless he continued very uneasy, frequently repeating, "I hope they don't see," and entreating me earnestly to discharge more ballast. It then flashed upon me for the first time that his offer to ascend with me had been a whim of the moment, and that he feared the being seen at that perilous elevation by any member of his own family. I therefore asked him if he resided at Hoxton, to which he replied in the affirmative ; urging again, and with great vehemence, the emptying of the remaining sandbags.

This, however, was out of the question, considering the altitude of the balloon, the course of the wind, and the proximity of the sea-coast. But my comrade was deaf to these reasons ; he insisted on going higher, and on my refusal to discharge more ballast deliberately pulled off and threw his hat, coat, and waistcoat overboard.

"Hurrah, that lightened her !" he shouted ; "but it's not enough yet," and he began unloosening his cravat.

"Nonsense," said I, "my good fellow, nobody can recognise you at this distance, even with a telescope."

"Don't be too sure of that," he retorted rather simply ; "they have sharp eyes at Miles's."

"At where ?"

"At Miles's Madhouse !"

Gracious Heaven !—the truth flashed upon me in an instant. I was sitting in the frail car of a balloon, at least a mile above the earth with a Lunatic ! The horrors of the situation, for a minute, seemed to deprive me of my own senses. A sudden freak of a distempered fancy, a transient fury, the slightest struggle might send us both, at a moment's notice, into eternity ! In the meantime the Maniac, still repeating his insane cry of "higher, higher, higher," divested himself, successively, of every remaining article of clothing, throwing each portion, as soon as taken off, to the winds. The inutility of remonstrance, or rather the probability of its producing a fatal irritation, kept me silent during these operations : but judge of my terror when, having thrown his stockings overboard, I heard him say, "We are not yet high enough by ten thousand miles—one of us must throw out the other."

To describe my feelings at this speech is impossible. Not only the awfulness of my position, but its novelty, conspired to bewilder me, for certainly no flight of imagination—no, not the wildest nightmare dream—had ever placed me in so desperate and forlorn a situation. It was horrible, horrible! Words, pleadings, remonstrances were useless, and resistance would be certain destruction. I had better have been unarmed, in an American Wilderness, at the mercy of a savage Indian! And now, without daring to stir a hand in opposition, I saw the Lunatic deliberately heave first one and then the other bag of ballast from the car, the balloon, of course, rising with proportionate rapidity. Up, up, up it soared—to an altitude I had never even dared to contemplate; the earth was lost to my eyes, and nothing but the huge clouds rolled beneath us! The world was gone, I felt, for ever! The Maniac, however, was still dissatisfied with our ascent, and again began to mutter.

"Have you a wife and children?" he asked abruptly.

Prompted by a natural instinct, and with a pardonable deviation from truth, I replied that I was married, and had fourteen young ones who depended on me for their bread!

"Ha! ha! ha!" laughed the Maniac, with a sparkling of his eyes that chilled my very marrow. "I have three hundred wives and five thousand children; and if the balloon had not been so heavy by carrying double, I should have been home to them by this time."

"And where do they live?" I asked, anxious to gain time by any question that first occurred to me.

"In the moon," replied the Maniac; "and when I have lightened the car, I shall be there in no time."

I heard no more, for suddenly approaching me, and throwing his arms round my body——

MRS. CATHERINE GRACE GORE
1799–1861

EHRENBREITSTEIN

In the course of the campaigns immediately following the French Revolution the fortress of Ehrenbreitstein, on the banks of the Rhine, experienced, on more than one occasion, the unequal fortunes of war ; and was compelled to submit to the superior force, or superior skill, of a conquering army. After the passage of the French troops under Hoche, effected at Weisse Thurm, in 1797, a blockade, which endured until the peace of Leoben, harassed its devoted garrison. It was then abandoned to the possession of the troops of the Elector of Mayence ; and although the little town of Thal, situated at its base, had been sacrificed in the course of the siege, Coblentz, whose position on the opposite bank, at the confluence of the Moselle with the Rhine, derives its best security from the fortress, was thus restored to tranquillity, and a hope of happier times.

The confusion of an ill-disciplined and inexperienced army had indeed rendered abortive to the Rhenish shores those local advantages by which they ought to have been secured from devastation ; and the prolonged disorganisation and disunion prevalent in the adjacent provinces had, by the most impolitic inconsistency, embarrassed every branch of public business, and while agriculture was driven from the ravaged plains, and commerce from the ensanguined waves of the Rhine, civil discord had embroiled the citizens of almost every town of mark along its course.

But affairs were now beginning to wear a more promising aspect. The Congress of Rastadt had already opened its negotiations, and despair on one side, and exhaustion or weariness on the other, had succeeded in cooling the heat of those national feuds which had brought the ruinous footsteps of advancing and retreating armies to trample the bosom of an afflicted country. That there were some among its sons over-eager to avenge the deep scars thus inflicted, the murder of the French deputies at the very gates of Rastadt terribly attests.

It chanced that some days previous to the opening of the Congress, a French noble—the Count D'Aubigny—with his wife and son, had been arrested, on their return to their native country, by the authorities of Coblentz; who, judging from the passports and papers in his possession that he had high influence, and an important connection with the Directory, secured him in the fortress of Ehrenbreitstein as a valuable hostage for the interests of their city.

The Count, who had sought safety in emigration during the short supremacy of one of the earlier and more furious factions of the republic, had been recently recalled to fill an appointment of dignity and honour under the new government. Galling as it was to his feelings to be thus thwarted and restrained upon the very threshold of France, yet his trust in the efficacy of an appeal which he had forwarded to the Congress prevented him from giving way to the natural impatience of his mind. A deeper feeling, however—a feeling of horror and desperation—soon superseded his irritation and regrets: a body of French troops presented itself before the fortress, menacing its garrison and luckless inhabitants with all the horrors of a protracted siege.

It was in vain that D'Aubigny recalled to his own mind, and whispered to his fair companion, that the fortress was bomb-proof and casemated with unequal art; and still more vain were his entreaties to Colonel Faber, its brave but sturdy commandant, that his wife and child might be conveyed under a flag of truce to Coblentz. The colonel, to whom his prisoner was both nationally and individually an object of distrust, persisted that the interest of his command forbade the concession.

"Your ladies of France," said he, "God give them grace!—are too nimble-tongued to be trusted in an enemy's camp, and Moritz Faber will scarcely be tempted to enable the fair Countess to carry tidings of the nakedness of the land, and of the impoverished resources of the fort, unto a band which bears the tri-coloured rag as its ensign, and treachery as its password. No, no!—abide in the old eagle's nest. Our galleries are a surety from your friends in the valley; and when our provisions fail—which fail they shall ere I yield the charge committed to my hand unto a gang of marauding cut-throats—the Countess and her son shall honourably share our fare and our famine. Perhaps the plea of a lady's sufferings may more promptly disperse your gentle countrymen yonder, who write themselves *preux chevaliers*, than falconet or culverin!"

Count D'Aubigny, finding persuasion fruitless, and knowing that resistance might even less avail him, could only pray, that either the return of his own *estafette* from Rastadt, or of that despatched by Colonel Faber, might bring a mandate of intelligence between the besieging and besieged. A few days sufficed to show him, and the expiration of several weeks tended most horribly to prove, that the fortress had been surprised in an hour of security and consequent destitution; he looked tremblingly to the result, and marked the daily diminution of their apportionment of provisions, with a sense of dread he dared not reveal to his companions in misfortune.

If any woman, however, could be gifted to receive with fortitude an announcement of evil, severe as that anticipated by the Count, it was Eveline—his lovely and most beloved wife: for her mind was as firm and elevated in its character as her demeanour and disposition were femininely gentle: and her attachment to the young Eugene, the son of D'Aubigny by a former marriage, partook of a conscientious devotion to his interests, such as the mere tenderness of maternal love could not have alone suggested.

It was for him—it was for that fair boy, who had loved her so fondly—that her first apprehensions of the horror of their position became terrible to her mind. Eugene was frail and delicate, and had been nurtured with the softest tending; he had attained neither the strength of body nor mind essential to the endurance of an evil from which his high condition might have seemed to secure him; and his parents, for they were equally so in affection for the child, had not courage to forewarn and inure him to the approaching calamity.

They saw him from the first reject with silent but evident loathing the coarse food tendered for his support. They marked his soft cheek grow wan under the deprivation, his little voice gradually weaken, his step bound less playfully along the rude pavement of their chamber; and they looked into each other's faces with fearful eyes as they first noted the change; but dared not interrogate the boy, or utter one audible comment. Soon, however, fatally soon, the miserable fact became too loudly a matter of comment in the garrison for even the child to remain in ignorance of their threatened destiny. Day after day passed, and brought nothing but sights of death and sounds of lamentation; and the wasting strength of the prisoners rendered their minds still more susceptible of terror and despair; but neither their wants nor the murmurs of the soldiery could influence by the weight of a feather the stern determination of the commandant to yield but in his hour of death.

Let those who limit their consciousness of the pangs of hunger by the loss of an occasional meal, which may have rendered restless their luxurious couch, affect to underrate the agonies of starvation, and to attemper according to Adam Smith's theory of morality their arguments for the indecency of bewailing a vulgar lack of food. But the actual sense of famine,—the gnawing, irritating sense, which confuses the ears with strange sounds—the body with sickness—the heart with perturbation—the head with dizzy bewilderment—these are sufferings which defy the mastery of mental fortitude!

D'Aubigny was the first to give utterance to his feelings, for they were solely urged by the suppressed torments he was condemned to witness. "My Eveline," said he, "my sweet, my heavenly-minded wife, could I have believed when I sought your hand, amid the lofty pomp of your high estate, that I should but win it to share in the horrors of my evil destiny—could I have dreamed, when I wept my first glad tears over this boy's cradle, that I should live to wish him unborn—to see him perish—slowly—horribly——"

"Hush! D'Aubigny, he sleeps; his head hath sunk upon my knee."

"No! mother," said the boy very faintly, "I am not sleeping; I am listening quietly to my kind father's voice."

"It is exhaustion! by the God of mercy! it is exhaustion which hath bowed his head!" exclaimed the Count, taking his son into his arms and gazing with an indescribable thrill upon his attenuated countenance, then rushing forwards in despite of the outcry and resistance of the various sentries, he forced himself into the presence of Colonel Faber, still straining his child to his bosom.

"Look at him!" said he, with a voice broken by sobs; "'tis my only child,—look upon him,—and if you have the heart of a man, deny not my petition. It is not yet too late,—send him from Ehrenbreitstein."

"It cannot be," answered Faber resolutely, although the manifest condition of the lovely boy brought a deep flush even to his temples. "I will give him up my own share of provision with pleasure, Count D'Aubigny; but not a living soul must leave the fortress!—I am deeply responsible to my country: and the famishing condition of my soldiers—*my children*—might otherwise prompt me to desert a trust which the Congress of Rastadt appear so little interested to protect. My duty, sir, is one of sternness; I *cannot* grant your request."

"Do not weep, father," murmured the child faintly, "I never saw tears of thine before; do not let them fall for Eugene. I *will* be better; I *will* feed heartily on the food we can still procure;—do not weep, father."

And with an effort mighty at his age the child did indeed force between his lips the loathsome morsels which fell scantily to their share. Every domestic animal within the walls had been sacrificed; and the obscene flesh of dogs and horses had become a delicacy beyond the soldiers' power of purchase! and on such revolting aliments did Eveline force herself to feed, in order to entice and deceive the boy's enfeebled appetite. But all would not do;—already many of the least hardy of the garrison had fallen a sacrifice to want of wholesome food;—and the failing strength and tremulous lips of Eugene and his mother proclaimed that they were soon to follow. Yes, they were dying of starvation!

Again the Count attempted to move the feelings of Faber in their behalf ; but he no longer bore denial with resignation. Moved beyond his patience, he raved, threatened, and even attempted violence ; and as the scene had many witnesses, the commandant felt it due to himself to punish the offender with solitary confinement.

" Thus, too," thought the staunch old soldier, " I shall spare this unfortunate parent the misery of looking upon sufferings which he cannot alleviate."

The wretched chamber inhabited by the Countess D'Aubigny was situated in one of the loftiest and most secure towers of the fortress ; and when the sun, which had lost its power to cheer the desponding prisoners, dawned through the arrow-slits on the day succeeding that of D'Aubigny's imprisonment, Eveline rose to drag her failing, quivering limbs towards the morning air, and resting her head beside the narrow opening, looking down upon the blue, glassy, dancing, *free* waters of the Rhine, that rippled far, far below the fortress, and prayed that they might rise and overwhelm her. But she instantly reproved the thought, as she had already done the proposal of her husband, that they should anticipate their inevitable and horrible end.

" This child," she had replied, " is a sacred deposit in our hands ; we have no right to leave him orphaned, to his sorrow ; and you could not—no ! you could not attempt *his* little life ! "

" What seest thou yonder, mother ? " faltered the boy, whom her movement had disturbed, but who was now too weak to approach the *soupirail* for refreshment.

" I see Heaven's mighty sunshine, dear Eugene, bright as if it shone upon no human misery. I see the white city of Coblentz, backed by its green plantations, and sending up the smoke of a thousand hearths. Beside them there is happiness, Eugene,—smiles and food, child,—and with *us* abideth nought save trust in the mercy of God. Think upon it—think, beloved child, that we shall soon be free from pain and grief ! "

" I cannot, think, mother ; my head swims strangely. But there is still feeling in my heart,—and it is all for thee and for my father."

" Eugene, should we survive this peril, and thou hast the strength of youth in thy favour, let this remembrance become a pledge for the tender mercies of thy future life ; so that the poor and the hungry may not plead to thee in vain."

" Mother, thy words reach not my failing ears ; draw nearer, mother, for I would die with my hand in thine."

On that very day the destines of the fortress were accomplished ; and the sacrifice which had been made was made in vain :—the fiat of the Congress of Rastadt commanded the brave Faber to open its gates to the enemy of his country. The noble brother of Eveline

D'Aubigny, whose anxiety for her liberation had motived in a great measure the blockade of Ehrenbreitstein, was the first to rush into the chamber of the captive. No living thing stirred there. The boy had died first, for his face was covered and his limbs composed; and Eveline—if the fair wasted thing which lay beside him might claim that name—had perished in the effort of executing that last duty!

DOUGLAS JERROLD
1803–1857

THE TRAGEDY OF THE TILL

Told by the Hermit of Bellyfulle

"It is a strange tale, but it hath the recommendation of brevity. Some folks may see nothing in it but tricksiness of an extravagant spirit; and some, perchance, may pluck a heart of meaning out of it. However, be it as it may, you shall hear it, sir.

"There was a man called Isaac Pugwash, a dweller in a miserable slough of London, a squalid denizen of one of the foul nooks of that city of Plutus. He kept a shop, which, though small as a cabin, was visited as granary and store-house by half the neighbourhood. All the creature-comforts of the poor—from bread to that questionable superfluity, small-beer—were sold by Isaac. Strange it was that with such a trade Pugwash grew not rich. He had many bad debts, and of all shopkeepers was most unfortunate in false coin. Certain it is he had neither eye not ear for bad money. Counterfeit semblances of majesty beguiled him out of bread and butter, and cheese, and red herring, just as readily as legitimate royalty struck at the Mint. Malice might impute something of this to the political principles of Pugwash, who, as he had avowed himself again and again, was no lover of a monarchy.

"Nevertheless, I cannot think Pugwash had so little regard for the countenance of majesty as to welcome it as readily when silvered copper as when sterling silver. No, a wild foolish enthusiast was Pugwash, but in the household matter of good and bad money he had very wholesome prejudices. He had a reasonable wish to grow rich, yet was entirely ignorant of the by-ways and short-cuts to wealth. He would have sauntered through life with his hands in his pockets and a daisy in his mouth; and dying with just enough in his house to pay the undertaker, would have thought himself a fortunate fellow; he was, in the words of Mrs. Pugwash, such a careless, foolish, dreaming creature. He was cheated every hour by a customer of some kind; and yet to deny credit to anybody—he would as soon have denied the wife of his bosom. His customers knew the weakness and failed not to exercise it.

"To be sure, now and then, fresh from conjugal counsel, he would refuse to add a single herring to a debtor's score; no, he would not be sent to the workhouse by anybody. A quarter of an hour after, the denied herring, with an added small loaf, was given to the little girl sent to the shop by the rejected mother, —'he couldn't bear to see poor children wanting anything.'

"Pugwash had another unprofitable weakness. He was fond of what he called nature, though in his dim, close shop he could give her but a stifling welcome. Nevertheless, he had the earliest primroses on his counter,—'they threw,' he said, 'such a nice light about the place.' A sly, knavish customer presented Issaac with a pot of polyanthuses, and, won by the flowery gift, Pugwash gave the donor ruinous credit. The man with wall-flowers regularly stopped at Isaac's shop, and for only sixpence Pugwash would tell his wife he had made the place a Paradise. 'If we can't go to nature, Sally, isn't it a pleasant thing to be able to bring nature to us?'

"Whereupon Mrs. Pugwash would declare that a man with at least three children to provide for had no need to talk of nature. Nevertheless, the flower-man made his weekly call. Though at many a house the penny could not every week be spared to buy a hint, a look of nature for the darkened dwellers, Isaac, despite of Mrs. Pugwash, always purchased. It is a common thing, an old familiar cry," said the Hermit—"to see the poor man's florist, to hear his loud-voiced invitation to take his nosegays, his penny-roots; and yet is it a call, a conjuration of the heart of man overlaboured and desponding—walled in by the gloom of a town—divorced from the fields and their sweet healthful influences—almost shut out from the sky that reeks in vapour over him;—it is a call that tells him there are things of the earth beside food and covering to live for; and that God in His great bounty hath made them for all men. Is it not so?" asked the Hermit.

"Most certainly," we answered; "it would be the very sinfulness of avarice to think otherwise."

"Why, sir," said the Hermit, benevolently smiling, "thus considered, the loud-lunged city bawler of roots and flowers becomes a high benevolence, a peripatetic priest of nature. Adown dark lanes and miry alleys he takes sweet remembrances—touching records of the loveliness of earth, that with their bright looks and balmy odours cheer and uplift the dumpish heart of man; that make his soul stir within him, and acknowledge the beautiful. The penny, the ill-spared penny—for it would buy a wheaten roll—the poor housewife pays for root of primrose, is her offering to the hopeful loveliness of nature; is her testimony of the soul struggling with the blighting, crushing circumstance of sordid earth, and sometimes yearning towards earth's sweetest aspects. Amidst the violence, the coarseness, and the suffering that may surround and defile the wretched there must be moments when the heart escapes, craving for the innocent and lovely; when the soul makes for itself even of a flower a comfort and a refuge."

The Hermit paused a moment, and then in blither voice resumed. "But I have strayed a little from the history of our small tradesman, Pugwash. Well, sir, Isaac for some three or four years kept on his old way, his wife still prophesying in loud and louder voice the inevitable workhouse. He would so think and talk of nature when he should mind his shop; he would so often snatch a holiday to lose it in the fields, when he should take stock and balance his books. What was worse, he every week lost more and more by bad money. With no more sense than a buzzard, as Mrs. Pugwash said, for a good shilling, he was the victim of those laborious folks who make their money with a fine independence of the state, out of their own materials. It seemed the common compact of a host of coiners to put off their base-born offspring upon Isaac Pugwash; who, it must be confessed, bore the loss and the indignity like a Christian martyr.

"At last, however, the spirit of the man was stung. A guinea, as Pugwash believed of statute gold, was found to be of little less value than a brass button. Mrs. Pugwash clamoured and screamed as though a besieging foe was in her house; and Pugwash himself felt that further patience would be pusillanimity. Whereupon, sir, what think you Isaac did? Why, he suffered himself to be driven by the voice and vehemence of his wife to a conjurer, who in a neighbouring attic was a sideral go-between to the neighbourhood—a vender of intelligence from the stars to all who sought and duly fee'd him. This magician would declare to Pugwash the whereabout of the felon coiner, and—the thought was anodyne to the hurt mind of Isaac's wife—the knave would be law-throttled.

"With sad indignant spirit did Isaac Pugwash seek Father Lotus; for so, sir, was the conjurer called. He was none of your common wizards. Oh no! he left it to the mere quack-salvers and mountebanks of his craft to take upon them a haggard solemnity of look, and to drop monosyllables, heavy as bullets, upon the ear of the questioner. The mighty and magnificent hocuspocus of twelvepenny magicians was scorned by Lotus. There was nothing in his look or manner that showed him the worse for keeping company with spirits: on the contrary, perhaps, the privileges he enjoyed of them served to make him only the more blithe and jocund. He might have passed for a gentleman, at once easy and cunning in the law; his sole knowledge, that of labyrinthine sentences made expressly to wind poor common sense on parchment. He had an eye like a snake, a constant smile upon his lip, a cheek coloured like an apple, and an activity of movement wide away from the solemnity of the conjurer.

He was a small eel-figured man of about sixty, dressed in glossy black, with silver buckles and flowing periwig.

"It was impossible not to have a better opinion of sprites and demons seeing that so nice, so polished a gentleman was their especial pet. And then his attic had no mystic circle, no curtain of black, no death's head, no mummy of apocryphal dragon—the vulgar catchpennies of fortune-telling trader. There was not even a pack of cards to elevate the soul of man into the regions of the mystic world. No, the room was plainly yet comfortably set out. Father Lotus reposed in an easy chair, nursing a snow-white cat upon his knee; now tenderly patting the creature with one hand, and now turning over a little Hebrew volume with the other. If a man wished to have dealings with sorry demons, could he desire a nicer little gentleman than Father Lotus to make the acquaintance for him? In a few words Isaac Pugwash told his story to the smiling magician. He had, amongst much other bad money, taken a counterfeit guinea; could Father Lotus discover the evil-doer?

"'Yes, yes, yes,' said Lotus, smiling, 'of course—to be sure; but that will do but little: in your present state—but let me look at your tongue.' Pugwash obediently thrust the organ forth. 'Yes, yes, as I thought. 'Twill do you no good to hang the rogue; none at all. What we must do is this—we must cure you of the disease.'

"'Disease!' cried Pugwash. 'Bating the loss of my money, I was never better in all my days.'

"'Ha! my poor man,' said Lotus, 'it is the benevolence of nature that she often goes on, quietly breaking us up, ourselves knowing no more of the mischief than a girl's doll when the girl rips up its seams. Your malady is of the perceptive organs. Leave you alone and you'll sink to the condition of a baboon.'

"'God bless me!' cried Pugwash.

"'A jackass with sense to choose a thistle from a toadstool will be a reasoning creature to you! for consider, my poor soul,' said Lotus in a compassionate voice, 'in this world of tribulation we inhabit, consider what a benighted nincompoop is man if he cannot elect a good shilling from a bad one.'

"'I have not a sharp eye for money,' said Pugwash modestly. 'It's a gift, sir; I'm assured it's a gift.'

"'A sharp eye! An eye of horn,' said Lotus. 'Never mind, I can remedy all that; I can restore you to the world and to yourself. The greatest physicians, the wisest philosophers have, in the profundity of their wisdom, made money the test of wit. A man is believed mad; he is a very rich man, and his heir has very good reason to believe him lunatic; whereupon the heir, the madman's careful friend, calls about the sufferer a company of wizards to sit in judgment on the suspected brain and report a verdict thereupon.

Well, ninety-nine times out of the hundred, what is the first question put, as test of reason? Why, a question of money. The physician, laying certain pieces of current coin in his palm, asks of the patient their several value. If he answer truly, why truly there is hope; but if he stammer or falter at the coin, the verdict runs, and wisely runs, mad—incapably mad.'

"'I'm not so bad as that,' said Pugwash, a little alarmed.

"'Don't say how you are—it's presumption in any man,' cried Lotus. 'Nevertheless, be as you may, I'll cure you if you'll give attention to my remedy.'

"'I'll give my whole soul to it,' exclaimed Pugwash.

"'Very good, very good; I like your earnestness, but I don't want all your soul,' said Father Lotus, smiling—'I want only part of it: that, if you confide in me, I can take from you with no danger. Ay, with less peril than the pricking of a whitlow. Now, then, for examination. Now, to have a good stare at this soul of yours.' Here Father Lotus gently removed the white cat from his knee, for he had been patting her all the time he talked, and turned full round upon Pugwash. 'Turn out your breeches' pockets,' said Lotus; and the tractable Pugwash immediately displayed the linings. 'So!' cried Lotus, looking narrowly at the brown holland whereof they were made—'very bad, indeed; very bad; never knew a soul in a worse state in all my life.'

"Pugwash looked at his pockets and then at the conjurer: he was about to speak, but the fixed earnest look of Father Lotus held him in respectful silence.

"'Yes, yes,' said the wizard, still eyeing the brown holland, 'I can see it all; a vagabond soul; a soul wandering here and there like a pauper without a settlement; a ragamuffin soul.'

"Pugwash found confidence and breath. 'Was there ever such a joke?' he cried; 'know a man's soul by the linings of his breeches' pockets!' and Pugwash laughed, albeit uncomfortably.

"Father Lotus looked at the man with philosophic compassion. 'Ha, my good friend!' he said, 'that all comes of your ignorance of moral anatomy.'

"'Well, but, Father Lotus——'

"'Peace,' said the wizard, 'and answer me. You'd have this soul of yours cured?'

"'If there's anything the matter with it,' answered Pugwash. 'Though not of any conceit I speak it, yet I think it as sweet and as healthy a soul as the souls of my neighbours. I never did wrong to anybody.'

"'Pooh!' cried Father Lotus.

"'I never denied credit to the hungry,' continued Pugwash.

"'Fiddle-de-dee!' said the wizard very nervously.

" 'I never laid out a penny in law upon a customer; I never refused small-beer to——'

" 'Silence!' cried Father Lotus; 'don't offend philosophy by thus bragging of your follies. You are in a perilous condition; still you may be saved. At this very moment, I much fear it, gangrene has touched your soul: nevertheless, I can separate the sound from the mortified parts and start you new again as though your lips were first wet with mother's milk.'

" Pugwash merely said—for the wizard began to awe him—'I'm very much obliged to you.'

" 'Now,' said Lotus, 'answer a few questions and then I'll proceed to the cure. What do you think of money?'

" 'A very nice thing,' said Pugwash, 'though I can do with as little of it as most folks.'

" Father Lotus shook his head. 'Well, and the world about you?'

" 'A beautiful world,' said Pugwash; 'only the worst of it is, I can't leave the shop as often as I would to enjoy it. I'm shut in all day long, I may say, a prisoner to brick-dust, herrings, and bacon. Sometimes, when the sun shines and the cobbler's lark over the way sings as if he'd split his pipe, why then, do you know, I do so long to get into the fields; I do hunger for a bit of grass like any cow.'

" The wizard looked almost hopelessly on Pugwash. 'And that's your religion and business? Infidel of the counter! Saracen of the till! However—patience,' said Lotus, 'and let us conclude.—And the men and women of the world, what do you think of them?'

" 'God bless 'em, poor souls!' said Pugwash. 'It's a sad scramble some of 'em have, isn't it?'

" 'Well,' said the conjurer, 'for a tradesman, your soul is in a wretched condition. However, it is not so hopelessly bad that I may not yet make it profitable to you. I must cure it of its vagabond desires and above all make it respectful of money. You will take this book.' Here Lotus took a little volume from a cupboard and placed it in the hand of Pugwash. 'Lay it under your pillow every night for a week, and on the eighth morning let me see you.'

" 'Come, there's nothing easier than that,' said Pguwash with a smile, and reverently putting the volume in his pocket—(the book was closed by metal clasps, curiously chased)—he descended the garret stairs of the conjurer.

" On the morning of the eighth day Pugwash again stood before Lotus.

" 'How do you feel now?' asked the conjurer with a knowing look.

" 'I haven't opened the book—'tis just as I took it,' said Pugwash, making no further answer.

" 'I know that,' said Lotus; 'the clasps be thanked for your ignorance.' Pugwash slightly coloured; for, to say the truth, both he and his wife had vainly pulled and tugged and fingered and coaxed the clasps that they might look upon the necromantic page. 'Well, the book has worked,' said the conjurer; 'I have it.'

" 'Have it! what?' asked Pugwash.

" 'Your soul,' answered the sorcerer. 'In all my practice,' he added gravely, 'I never had a soul come into my hands in worse condition.'

" 'Impossible!' cried Pugwash. 'If my soul is, as you say, in your own hands, how is it that I'm alive? How is it that I can eat, drink, sleep, walk, talk, do everything, just like anybody else?'

" 'Ha!' said Lotus, 'that's a common mistake. Thousands and thousands would swear, ay, as they'd swear to their own noses, that they have their souls in their own possession; bless you,' and the conjurer laughed maliciously, 'it's a popular error. Their souls are altogether out of 'em.'

" 'Well,' said Pugwash, 'if it's true that you have, indeed, my soul, I should like to have a look at it.'

" 'In good time,' said the conjurer; 'I'll bring it to your house and put it in its proper lodging. In another week I'll bring it to you; 'twill then be strong enough to bear removal.'

" 'And what am I to do all the time without it?' asked Pugwash in a tone of banter. 'Come,' said he, still jesting, 'if you really have my soul, what's it like—what's its colour; if indeed souls have colours?'

" 'Green—green as a grasshopper when it first came into my hands,' said the wizard; 'but 'tis changing daily. More: it was a skipping, chirping, giddy soul; 'tis every hour mending. In a week's time, I tell you, it will be fit for the business of the world.'

" 'And pray, good father—for the matter has till now escaped me—what am I to pay you for this pain and trouble, for this precious care of my miserable soul?'

" 'Nothing,' answered Lotus, 'nothing whatever. The work is too nice and precious to be paid for; I have a reward you dream not of for my labour. Think you that men's immortal souls are to be mended like iron pots, at tinker's price? Oh, no! they who meddle with souls go for higher wages.'

" After further talk Pugwash departed, the conjurer promising to bring him home his soul at midnight that night week. It seemed strange to Pugwash, as the time passed on, that he never seemed to miss his soul; that, in very truth, he went through the labours of the day with even better gravity than when his soul possessed him. And more: he began to feel himself more at home in his shop; the cobbler's lark over the way continued to sing, but awoke in Isaac's heart no thought of the fields: and then for flowers and plants, why, Isaac began to think such matters fitter the thoughts of children and foolish girls than the attention of grown men with the world before them. Even Mrs. Pugwash saw an alteration in her husband; and though to him she said nothing, she returned thanks to her own sagacity that made him seek the conjurer.

"At length the night arrived when Lotus had promised to bring home the soul of Pugwash. He sent his wife to bed, and sat with his eyes upon the Dutch clock, anxiously awaiting the conjurer. Twelve o'clock struck, and at the same moment Father Lotus smote the door-post of Isaac Pugwash.

"'Have you brought it?' asked Pugwash.

"'Or wherefore should I come?' said Lotus. 'Quick; show a light to the till, that your soul may find itself at home.'

"'The till!' cried Pugwash; 'what the devil should my soul do in the till?'

"'Speak not irreverently,' said the conjurer, 'but show a light.'

"'May I live for ever in darkness if I do!' cried Pugwash.

"'It is no matter,' said the conjurer: and then he cried, 'Soul, to your earthly dwelling-place! Seek it—you know it.' Then turning to Pugwash, Lotus said, 'It is all right. Your soul's in the till.'

"'How did it get there?' cried Pugwash in amazement.

"'Through the slit in the counter,' said the conjurer; and ere Pugwash could speak again the conjurer had quitted the shop.

"For some minutes Pugwash felt himself afraid to stir. For the first time in his life he felt himself ill at ease, left as he was with no other company save his own soul. He at length took heart and went behind the counter that he might see if his soul was really in the till. With trembling hand he drew the coffer, and there, to his amazement, squatted like a tailor, upon a crown-piece, did Pugwash behold his own soul, which cried out to him in notes no louder than a cricket's—'How are you? *I* am comfortable.' It was a strange yet pleasing sight to Pugwash to behold what he felt to be his own soul embodied in a figure no bigger than the top joint of his thumb. There it was, a stark-naked thing with the precise features of Pugwash; albeit the complexion was of a yellower hue. 'The conjurer said it was green,' cried Pugwash: 'as I live, if that be my soul—and I begin to feel a strange odd love for it—it is yellow as a guinea. Ha! ha! Pretty, precious, darling soul!' cried Pugwash as the creature took up every piece of coin in the till and rang it with such a look of rascally cunning that sure I am Pugwash would in past times have hated the creature for the trick.

"But every day Pugwash became fonder and fonder of the creature in the till: it was to him such a counsellor and such a blessing. Whenever the old flower-man came to the door, the soul of Pugwash from the till would bid him pack with his rubbish : if a poor woman —an old customer it might be—begged for the credit of a loaf, the Spirit of the Till, calling through the slit in the counter, would command Pugwash to deny her. More : Pugwash never again took a bad shilling. No sooner did he throw the pocket-piece down upon the counter than the voice from the till would denounce its worthlessness. And the soul of Pugwash never quitted the till. There it lived, feeding upon the colour of money, and capering, and rubbing its small scoundrel hands in glee as the coin dropped—dropped in. In time the soul of Pugwash grew too big for so small a habitation, and then Pugwash moved his soul into an iron box ; and some time after he sent his soul to his banker's—the thing had waxed so big and strong on gold and silver."

"And so," said we, "the man flourished, and the conjurer took no wages for all he did to the soul of Pugwash ?"

"Hear the end," said the Hermit. "For some time it was a growing pleasure to Pugwash to look at his soul, as it always was with the world-buying metals. At length he grew old, very old ; and every day his soul grew uglier. Then he hated to look upon it ; and then his soul would come to him and grin its deformity at him. Pugwash died, almost as rich as an Indian king ; but he died, shrieking in his madness to be saved from the terrors of his own soul."

"And such the end," we said ; "such the Tragedy of the Till ? A strange romance."

"Romance," said the Sage of Bellyfulle ; "sir, 'tis a story true as life. For at this very moment how many thousands, blind and deaf to the sweet looks and voice of nature, live and die with their souls in a Till ?"

DOUGLAS JERROLD

JACQUES COCAST, THE HUNCHBACK PHILOSOPHER

"THANK God for my hunch!" cried Jacques Cocast, then eleven years old, and escaped from the pitying hands of Martin Fleau the miller, who, casting a compassionate glance at Cocast's unseemly load, exclaimed:

"Well, the saints have burthened thee enough—go, I wouldn't beat a hunchback."

"Thank God for my hunch!" were the grateful words of the apple-stealing Jacques, and he followed his lighter-heeled companions, who, on the first alarm, had scampered safely off from the miller's orchard, leaving the deformed co-mate to the vengeance of the despoiled. The miller, as we have shown, was merciful, and Jacques Cocast, the hunchback, went his way unbruised.

Jacques Cocast grew up, the living plaything of the boys of the village. He was their drudge, their jest, their scapegoat. His good-humour turned bitterness itself to merriment, and with at times the tears starting to his eyes he would laugh them down, and without knowing it play the practical philosopher.

"Out, ye imp of deformity!" cried Cocast's stepmother at least once a day; whereupon Jacques, to the increasing ire of his father's wife, would meekly cry:

"Thank God for my hunch!"

Left to himself, now spurned, and now at least endured by his growing companions, Jacques Cocast made a friend of his book, and found the exceeding reward of such friendship. He could read, write, and cypher to the shame of many of his seniors. Jacques Cocast's father took sudden pride in his own misshapen flesh, and Cocast's wife stormed at her stepson with increasing vigour.

The notary wanted a clerk. All eyes were turned upon Jacques as the very lad for the office. The notary himself condescended to canvass the pretensions of Jacques to the dignity. Already Jacques felt himself installed, when a slim, fair-haired, pink-complexioned youth was preferred to Cocast, the notary's wife having pithily informed her obedient husband that his house should be no dwelling-place for a hunchback.

Jacques Cocast sighed as he turned from the notary's door, and his heart beat heavily as he crawled to his paternal home. In two or three days, however, the hunchback smiled and laughed as before, and the clerkship was forgotten in sweet communings with his book.

Some four years passed on,—when oh, shame to the notary's wife —shame to the fair-haired youth—the faithless woman fled from the bosom of her husband, taking with her in her flight her husband's clerk! Great was the consternation throughout the village—loud and deep the revilings of every honest spouse. Jacques Cocast joined in no abuse; but with a fine charity for the inexperience of youth, with even a tenderness towards the sin of the unfaithful wife, and considering within himself the subtle powers of the tempter, he felt grateful for his escape, and breathed his gratitude in his wonted syllables:

"Thank God for my hunch!"

Jacques Cocast was now a painstaking, philosophic tailor; and from no high elevation than his shop-board could look down on many of the vanities of human life. He was now twenty, and increasing years had only served to mellow his rich heart and make him feel a lessening load upon his shoulders. Jacques would make one at all village holidays, led thereto by his own light-heartedness, and of late, furthermore urged to each festival by the blue eyes of Félicité, the baker's daughter.

Luckless Jacques Cocast! Fly the sweet perdition! You know not the falsehood of those azure lights—the venom of that pouting, pulpy lip; Félicité laughs with a witch's laugh at the love of the hunchback—whilst he, poor innocent—exalted, sublimated by his passion, lives in an atmosphere of balm and sun—vaults like a grasshopper about the earth, and gives his heart and soul to the tyranny that rejoices him. Jacques Cocast knew not vanity. He would clothe himself in the humblest weed, and then think that the best wardrobe which drew to itself the least notice. Now was it otherwise. The eyes of Félicité had smiled upon the tailor, and Jacques Cocast should henceforth be the best and the most critical customer of Jacques Cocast. If Félicité had looked with favour on his body, he would take the hitherto despised article under his future care and habit it worthy of her who had elected it as her own. As for his hump, that was gone, yea, vanished, melted in the sunlight of Félicité's eyes. With these rejoicing thoughts Jacques Cocast would array himself finely as the finest caterpillar; his vestments now barred, and spotted, and burnished with a hundred hues. And as he basked in the smiles of Félicité, the baker's wicked daughter would laugh in her hollow heart and the folks of the village would confidentially clap their fingers to their noses and wink towards the tailor.

For a month or more was Jacques Cocast the blissful Adam of this fool's paradise. For a full month did he breathe Elysium. At length the eyes of Jacques Cocast were opened and he saw his forlornness. It was the day of a *ducasse*. In the pride of his heart, and in all the glory of his trade, did the hunchback array himself to dance with Félicité, the baker's daughter. She had of late been so loving, so complying, so tender! The next dance might be at their own wedding. At all events, how they would dance on the coming Sunday! He, the hunchback, buoyed by his loving heart, would foot it so lightly that not a blade of grass should bend beneath him—not a dew-drop be scattered by his mercurial toe.

The dancers are assembled. The fiddles sound. Jacques Cocast, in all the glory of a new suit, burning like a peacock in a conflict of colours, and in the triumph of a gladdened soul, advances to lead out Félicité, the baker's daughter. Already he has his hand upon her hand when a gigantic thumb and finger with vice-like power grips the nose of Jacques Cocast and whirls him from his partner. A laugh that drowns the fiddles bursts from the merry-makers. Jacques Cocast, with lightning in his eyes, and all the blood in his body rushing to his nose, looked for his assailant.

Hercule Grossetête, a rival of six feet, French measure, with fierce eyes and parrot nose, glaring and protruding from between raven whiskers, with arms akimbo, stands before the tailor. Nevertheless, the soul of Jacques Cocast is mighty, and he is meditating how he may best spring upon the giant and tear his iron heart from his body, when—oh, ye daughters of Eve! oh, ye rosy wickednesses, ye honied poisons!—Félicité, the baker's daughter, advanced to Hercule, and curtseying, and putting her hand in his—in his hand, yet warm from the outraged nose of her doating lover, signified that she was ready to dance, that she had looked with eyes of favour on the punishment of the tailor. Then sank the heart of Jacques Cocast. He quitted the scene of his past happiness, and in an agony of despair wandered, a very lunatic.

Foolish Jacques Cocast! Who would pity the despair of a hunchback? Who compassionate a love-broken heart, if accompanied by overladen shoulders? What is a beautiful sentiment with a straight backed, comely man, is a thing for a jest, an excellent joke with a hunchback. And so, Jacques Cocast, go home. Sleep not in the fields at nights. Lie not under the window of the baker's daughter, and waste not away until, as you complain, your head has grown too little for your hat,—but up, man, and to your comfortable abode. Shave yourself, change your linen, leap upon your shop-board, thread your needle, heat your goose, and defy love! A friendly

Genius whispered some such advice to Jacques Cocast, for ere a month had passed, the tailor had once more taken to his sober attire, was seated smiling at his work, and if a thought of the cruel baker's daughter would sometimes intrude, he would banish the unwelcome guest by the very vehemence of stitching.

Months passed away, and the time of drawing for the conscription arrived. Mothers looked anxious—plighted maidens would sigh frequently and look with tender gaze upon their future husband—the young men would laugh, laugh louder than was their wont to hush the secret care that preyed upon them. But what was the conscription, with the banishment, the danger, the wounds and death combined in the word to Jacques Cocast ? He was a hunchback. His shoulders were exempt by nature from a knapsack. He was not a comely morsel for glory ; he was not worthy of the powder and shot bestowed upon prettier men. No, he was secure in his deformity ; his heart started not at the muttering of the beaten sheepskin. Hence Jacques Cocast, without one throb, save for the fate of some old acquaintance, might linger about the town-hall of the arrondissement, and learn the fortune of his fellow-villagers.

The day of drawing came. There was the shriek of triumph as one sprang into his mother's arms—as his sister clung about his neck—as his plighted wife, and *now* their wedding-day was certain—there were bursts of joy and tears of happiness as the exempt sprang among the crowd ; and there were cries of despair, and sobbings as among breaking hearts as the new conscripts told the fate that tore them from their homes.

" Thank God for my hunch ! " cried Jacques Cocast twenty times as he saw the wretchedness of the conscript soldier.

Among those drawn to wear future laurels was Hercule Grossetête. He looked savage as a snubbed ogre ; and the baker's beautiful daughter hung on his arm, and was crying her heart out, and vowing between her sobs that for the sake of her dear Hercule she would try to live and die a maid : and Hercule, with his fancy listening to the whistling bullets, smiled vacantly on the magnanimity of Félicité, and bade Heaven help her in all her trials.

And did the heart of Jacques Cocast rejoice at this ? By no means—he felt no triumph at the calamity of Grossetête—no pleasure at the grief of his fair, false baker's daughter ; but with a gush of gratitude he exclaimed :

" Thank God for my hunch ! "

Hercule Grossetête went to the wars. Fortune, that had heaped such obloquy upon the shoulders of Cocast, had fitted Grossetête for the dignity of a grenadier. He quitted the village, left the baker's daughter, and was soon marching, and perhaps day-dreaming of pillage and epaulettes. We know not what struggles Félicité endured to keep her pledge to Hercule; they must have been severe and manifold; for it was at least six months after the departure of her grenadier that she wedded the son of the village grocer, the grocer father opportunely dying and leaving his stock and business to his only son. All the world—that is, all the village—believed in the conjugal bliss of the grocer and his wife. Pierre Chandelles was so meek, so gentle a soul, any woman must be happy with him.

Again, Félicité was always the sweetest-tempered girl: there had been curious tales of her sudden passion, but such tales had been trumped up by the ugliest girls of the village.

Three months had passed since Pierre and Félicité were one; and Jacques Cocast—for in the magnanimity of his soul he did not withdraw his custom from Pierre on account of his wife; besides, Pierre's was the only shop in the village—modestly tapped a sou on Pierre's counter, it being the intention of the tailor to dispense that coin in beeswax. Suddenly there was a noise within; Jacques recognised the voice of Félicité, albeit he had never before heard it at so high a pitch. Another minute, and Pierre rushes into the shop followed by his wife, who, heedless of the wants of a customer, heedless of the cries of her husband, demolished an earthen pipkin, unluckily in her hand, upon her lord and sovereign's head. No sheep ever bled with more meekness than did Pierre Chandelles the grocer.

"What did you want?" asked Pierre, with still a vigilant eye to business.

"I'll call again when your wounds are dressed," said Jacques Cocast; "in the meantime, thank God for my hunch!"

Years went on, and Jacques Cocast gathered about him the small comforts of the world, and keeping the spirit of his youth, was blithe as a bird.

One autumn evening, wandering a mile or two on the road from the village, and thinking he knew not upon what, Jacques Cocast was suddenly startled in his reflections by a loud voice.

"For the love of the saints, if you have it, give me a pinch of snuff."

The prayer proceeded from a blind soldier, seated on a tree felled near the roadside.

"With all my heart," cried Cocast. "Here, empty my box."

"Alas, good sir!" said the soldier, "look at me again."

Cocast looked and saw that the man had lost both his arms.

"You must, indeed, *give* me the snuff," said the soldier.

"With all my heart, I say again," cried Cocast, and with the most delicate care he supplied the nostrils of the mutilated veteran.

"Good Heavens!" suddenly exclaimed Cocast, "why, you are Hercule Grossetête."

"I am," answered the soldier. "And what have you to say to that?"

"What!" Jacques Cocast, looking at the eyeless, armless victim of glory, could only say:

"*Thank God for my hunch!*"

Almost all men have a hunch of some kind. Let them, with Jacques Cocast, thank God for it.

BENJAMIN DISRAELI
1804–1881

A TRUE STORY

When I was a young boy I had delicate health, and was somewhat of a pensive and contemplative turn of mind : it was my delight in the long summer evenings to slip away from my noisy and more robust companions, that I might walk in the shade of a venerable wood, my favourite haunt, and listen to the cawing of the old rooks, who seemed as fond of this retreat as I was.

One evening I sat later than usual, though the distant sound of the cathedral clock had more than once warned me to my home. There was a stillness in all nature that I was unwilling to disturb by the least motion.

From this reverie I was suddenly startled by the sight of a tall, slender female who was standing by me, looking sorrowfully and steadily in my face. She was dressed in white, from head to foot, in a fashion I had never seen before ; her garments were unusually long and flowing, and rustled as she glided through the low shrubs near me as if they were made of the richest silk. My heart beat as if I was dying, and I knew not that I could have stirred from the spot ; but she seemed so very mild and beautiful, I did not attempt it. Her pale brown hair was braided round her head, but there were some locks that strayed upon her neck ; and altogether she looked like a lovely picture, but not like a living woman. I closed my eyes forcibly with my hands, and when I looked again she had vanished.

I cannot exactly say why I did not on my return speak of this beautiful appearance, nor why, with a strange mixture of hope and fear, I went again and again to the same spot that I might see her. She always came, and often in the storm and the plashing rain, that never seemed to touch or to annoy her, and looked sweetly at me, and silently passed on ; and though she was so near to me, that once the wind lifted those light straying locks, and I felt them against my cheek, yet I never could move or speak to her. I fell ill ; and when I recovered my mother closely questioned me of the tall lady, of whom, in the height of my fever, I had so often spoken.

I cannot tell you what a weight was taken from my boyish spirits when I learnt that this was no apparition, but a most lovely woman; not young, though she had kept her young looks, for the grief which had broken her heart seemed to have spared her beauty.

When the rebel troops were retreating after their total defeat, in that very wood I was so fond of, a young officer, unable any longer to endure the anguish of his wounds, sunk from his horse, and laid himself down to die. He was found there by the daughter of Sir Henry R——, and conveyed by a trusty domestic to her father's mansion. Sir Henry was a loyalist; but the officer's desperate condition excited his compassion, and his many wounds spoke a language a brave man could not misunderstand. Sir Henry's daughter with many tears pleaded for him, and pronounced that he should be carefully and secretly attended. And well she kept that promise, for she waited upon him (her mother being long dead) for many weeks, and anxiously watched for the first opening of eyes, that, languid as he was, looked brightly and gratefully upon his young nurse.

You may fancy better than I can tell you, as he slowly recovered, all the moments that were spent in reading, and low-voiced singing, and gentle playing on the lute, and how many fresh flowers were brought to one whose wounded limbs would not bear him to gather them for himself, and how calmly the days glided on in the blessedness of returning health and in that sweet silence so carefully enjoined him.

I will pass by this to speak of one day, which, bright and pleasanter than others, did not seem more bright or more lovely than the looks of the young maiden, as she gaily spoke of " a little festival " which (though it must bear an unworthier name) she meant really to give in honour of her guest's recovery; " and it is time, lady," said he, " for that guest so tended and so honoured, to tell you his whole story, and speak to you of one who will help him to thank you; may I ask you, fair lady, to write a little billet for me, which even in these times of danger I may find some means to forward? "

To his mother, no doubt, she thought, as with light steps and a lighter heart she seated herself by his couch, and smilingly bade him dictate; but, when he said " My dear wife," and lifted up his eyes to be asked for more, he saw before him a pale statue, that gave him one look of utter despair, and fell, for he had no power to help her, heavily at his feet.

Those eyes never truly reflected the pure soul again, or answered by answering looks the fond enquiries of her poor old father.

She lived to be as I saw her,—sweet and gentle, and delicate always; but reason returned no more. She visited till the day of her death the spot where she first saw that young soldier, and dressed herself in the very clothes that he said so well became her.

SAMUEL WARREN
1807–1877

THE RESURRECTIONIST

My gentle reader—start not at learning that I have been, in my time, a resurrectionist! Let not this appalling word, this humiliating confession, conjure up in your fancy a throng of vampire-like images and associations, or earn your "Physician's" dismissal from your hearts and hearths. It is your own groundless fears, my fair trembler!—your own superstitious prejudices—that have driven me, and will drive many others of my brethren, to such dreadful doings as those hereafter detailed. Come, come—let us have one word of reason between us on the abstract question—and then for my tale. You expect us to cure you of disease, and yet deny us the only means of learning *how*! You would have us bring you the ore of skill and experience, yet forbid us to break the soil or sink a shaft! Is this fair, *fair* reader? Is this reasonable?

What I am now going to describe was my first and last exploit in the way of body-stealing. It was a grotesque if not a ludicrous scene, and occurred during the period of my "walking the hospitals," as it is called, which occupied the two seasons immediately after my leaving Cambridge. A young and rather interesting female was admitted a patient at the hospital I attended; her case baffled all our skill, and her symptoms even defied diagnosis. *Now*, it seemed an enlargement of the heart—now, an ossification—then this, that, and the other; and at last it was plain we knew nothing at all about the matter—no, not even whether her disorder was organic or functional, primary or symptomatic—or whether it *was* really the heart that was at fault. She received no benefit at all under the fluctuating schemes of treatment we pursued, and at length fell into dying circumstances. As soon as her friends were apprised of her situation, and had an inkling of our intention to open the body, they insisted on removing her immediately from the hospital, that she might "die at home."

In vain did Sir —— and his dressers expostulate vehemently with them, and represent, in exaggerated terms, the imminent peril attending such a step. Her two brothers avowed their apprehension of our designs, and were inflexible in exercising their right of removing their sister. I used all my rhetoric on the occasion, but in vain; and at last said to the young men, "Well, if you are afraid only of our *dissecting* her, we can get hold of her, if we are so disposed, as easily if she die with you as with us."

"Well—we'll *troy* that, measter," replied the elder, while his Herculean fist oscillated somewhat significantly before my eyes. The poor girl was removed accordingly to her father's house, which was at a certain village about five miles from London, and survived her arrival scarcely ten minutes! We soon contrived to receive intelligence of the event; and as I and Sir ——'s two dressers had taken great interest in the case throughout, and felt intense curiosity about the real nature of the disease, we met together and entered into a solemn compact, that, come what might, we would have her body out of the ground. A trusty spy informed us of the time and exact place of the girl's burial; and on expressing to Sir —— our determination about the matter, he patted me on the back, saying, "Ah, my fine fellow!—IF you have SPIRIT enough—dangerous," etc. etc.

Was it not skilfully said? The baronet further told us, he felt himself so curious about the matter that if fifty pounds would be of use to us in furthering our purpose, they were at our service. It needed not this, nor a glance at the *éclat* with which the successful issue of the affair would be attended among our fellow-students, to spur our resolves.

The notable scheme was finally adjusted at my rooms in the Borough. M—— and E——, Sir ——'s dressers, and myself, with an experienced "*grab*"—that is to say, a *professional* resurrectionist—were to set off from the Borough about nine o'clock the next evening—which would be the third day after the burial—in a glass coach provided with all "appliances and means to boot." During the day, however, our friend the grab suffered so severely from an overnight's excess as to disappoint us of his invaluable assistance. This unexpected *contretempts* nearly put an end to our project; for the few other grabs we knew were absent on *professional tours*! Luckily, however, I bethought me of a poor Irish porter—a sort of "ne'er-do-weel" hanger-on at the hospital—whom I had several times hired to go on errands. This man I sent for to my room, and, in the presence of my two coadjutors, persuaded, threatened, and bothered into acquiescence, promising him half-a-guinea for his evening's work—and as much whisky as he could drink prudently. As Mr. Tip—that was the name he went by—had some personal acquaintance with the sick grab, he succeeded in borrowing his chief tools; with which, in a sack large enough to contain our expected prize, he repaired to my rooms about nine o'clock, while the coach was standing at the door. Our Jehu had received a quiet douceur in addition to the hire of himself and coach.

As soon as we had exhibited sundry doses of Irish cordial to our friend Tip—under the effects of which he became quite " bouncible," and *ranted* about the feat he was to take a prominent part in—and equipped ourselves in our worst clothes, and white top-coats, we entered the vehicle—four in number—and drove off. The weather had been exceedingly capricious all the evening—moonlight, rain, thunder, and lightning, fitfully alternating. The only thing we were anxious about was the darkness, to shield us from all possible observation. I must own that, in analysing the feelings that prompted me to undertake and go through with this affair, the mere love of adventure operated quite as powerfully as the wish to benefit the cause of anatomical science. A midnight expedition to the tombs !—It took our fancy amazingly ; and then Sir ——'s cunning hint about the " danger "—and our " spirit " !

The garrulous Tip supplied us with amusement all the way down—rattle, rattle, rattle, incessantly ; but as soon as we had arrived at that part of the road where we were to stop, and caught sight of —— church, with its hoary steeple—glistening in the fading moonlight, as though it were standing sentinel over the graves around it, one of which we were going so rudely to violate—Tip's spirits began to falter a little. He said little—and that at intervals.

To be very candid with the reader, *none* of us felt over-much at our ease. Our expedition began to wear a somewhat hare-brained aspect, and to be environed with formidable contingencies which we had not taken sufficiently into our calculations. What, for instance, if the two stout fellows, the brothers, should be out watching their sister's grave ? They were not likely to stand on much ceremony with us. And then the manual difficulties ! E—— was the only one of us that had ever assisted at the exhumation of a body—and the rest of us were likely to prove but bungling workmen. However, we had gone too far to think of retreating. We none of us *spoke* our suspicions, but the silence that reigned within the coach was tolerably significant. In contemplation, however, of some such contingency we had put a bottle of brandy in the coach pocket ; and before we drew up, had all four of us drunk pretty deeply of it. At length the coach turned down a by-lane to the left, which led directly to the churchyard wall ; and after moving a few steps down it, in order to shelter our vehicle from the observation of highway passengers, the coach stopped, and the driver opened the door.

" Come, Tip," said I, " out with you."

" Get out, did you say, sir ? To be sure I will—Och ! to be sure I will." But there was small show of alacrity in his movements as he descended the steps ; for while I was speaking I was interrupted by the solemn clangour of the church clock announcing the hour of midnight. The sounds seemed to *warn* us against what we were going to do.

" 'Tis a cowld night, yer honours," said Tip, in an undertone, as we successively alighted, and stood together, looking up and down the dark lane, to see if anything was stirring but ourselves. " 'Tis a cowld night—and—and—and," he stammered.

" Why, you cowardly old scoundrel," grumbled M——, " are you frightened already ? What's the matter, eh ? Hoist up the bag on your shoulders directly, and lead the way down the lane."

" Och, but yer honours—och ! by the mother that bore me, but 'tis a murtherous cruel thing, I'm thinking, to wake the poor cratur from her last sleep."

He said this so querulously, that I began to entertain serious apprehensions, after all, of his defection ; so I insisted on his taking a little more brandy, by way of bringing him up to par. It was of no use, however. His reluctance increased every moment—and it even dispirited *us*. I verily believe the turning of a straw would have decided us all on jumping into the coach again, and returning home without accomplishing our errand. Too many of the students, however, were apprised of our expedition, for us to think of terminating it so ridiculously. As it were by mutual consent, we stood and paused a few moments, about half-way down the lane. M—— whistled with infinite spirit and distinctness ; E—— remarked to me that he always " thought a churchyard at midnight was the gloomiest object imaginable " ; and I talked about *business*— " soon be over "—" shallow grave "—etc. etc.

" Confound it—what if those two brothers of hers SHOULD be there ? " said M—— abruptly, making a dead stop, and folding his arms on his breast.

" Powerful fellows, both of them ! " muttered E——. We resumed our march—when Tip, our advanced guard—a title he earned by anticipating our steps about three inches—suddenly stood still, let down the bag from his shoulders, elevated both hands in a listening attitude, and exclaimed, " Whisht !—whisht !—By my soul, *what* was that ? "

We all paused in silence, looking palely at one another—but could hear nothing except the drowsy flutter of a bat wheeling away from us a little overhead.

" Fait—an' wasn't it somebody *spaking* on the far side o' the hedge I heard ? " whispered Tip.

" Poh—stuff, you idiot ! " I exclaimed, losing my temper. " Come, M—— and E——, it's high time we had done with all this cowardly nonsense ; and if we mean really to *do* anything, we must make haste. 'Tis past twelve—day breaks about four—and it is coming on wet, you see." Several large drops of rain, pattering heavily among the leaves and branches, corroborated my words, by announcing a coming shower, and the air was sultry enough to warrant the expectation of a thunderstorm. We therefore buttoned up our greatcoats to the chin, and hurried on to the churchyard wall, which ran across the bottom of the lane. This wall we had to climb over to get into the churchyard, and it was not a very high one.

Here Tip annoyed us again. I told him to lay down his bag, mount the wall, and look over into the yard, to see whether all was clear before us; and, as far as the light would enable him, to look about for a new-made grave. Very reluctantly he complied, and contrived to scramble to the top of the wall. He had hardly time, however, to peer over into the churchyard, when a fluttering streak of lightning flashed over us, followed, in a second or two, by a loud burst of thunder! Tip fell in an instant to the ground, like a cockchafer shaken from an elm-tree, and lay crossing himself, and muttering paternosters. We could scarcely help laughing at the manner in which he tumbled down, simultaneously with the flash of lightning. "Now, look ye, gintlemen," said he, still squatting on the ground, "do you mane to give the poor cratur Christian burial, when ye've done wid her? An' will you put her back again as ye found her? 'Case, if you won't, blood an' oons"——

"Hark ye now, Tip," said I sternly, taking out one of a brace of *empty* pistols I had put into my greatcoat pocket, and presenting it to his head, "we have hired you on this business, for the want of a better, you wretched fellow! and if you give us any more of your nonsense, by —— I'll send a bullet through your brain! Do you hear me, Tip?"

"Och, aisy, aisy wid ye! don't murther me! Bad luck to me that I ever cam wid ye! Och, and if ivver I live to die, won't I see and bury my ould body out o' the rache of all the docthers in the world? If I don't, divel burn me!" We all laughed aloud at Tip's truly Hibernian expostulation.

"Come, sir, mount! over with you!" said we, helping to push him upwards. "Now, drop this bag on the other side," we continued, giving him the sack that contained our implements. We all three of us then followed, and alighted safely in the churchyard. It poured with rain; and, to enhance the dreariness and horrors of the time and place, flashes of lightning followed in quick succession, shedding a transient awful glare over the scene, revealing the white tombstones, the ivy-grown venerable church, and our own figures, a shivering group, come on an unhallowed errand! I perfectly well recollect the lively feelings of apprehension—"the compunctious visitings of remorse"—which the circumstances called forth in my own breast, and which, I had no doubt, were shared by my companions.

As no time, however, was to be lost, I left the group, for an instant, under the wall to search out the grave. The accurate instructions I had received enabled me to pitch on the spot with little difficulty; and I returned to my companions, who immediately followed me to the scene of operations. We had no umbrellas, and our greatcoats were saturated with wet; but the brandy we had recently taken did us good service, by exhilarating our spirits and especially those of Tip. He untied the sack in a twinkling, and shook out the hoes and spades, etc.; and taking one of the latter himself, he commenced digging with such energy that we had hardly prepared ourselves for work before he had cleared away nearly the whole of the mound. The rain soon abated, and the lightning ceased for a considerable interval, though thunder was heard occasionally grumbling sullenly in the distance, as if expressing anger at our unholy doings—at least I felt it so. The pitchy darkness continued, so that we could scarcely see one another's figures. We worked on in silence, as fast as our spades could be got into the ground; taking it in turns, two by two, as the grave would not admit of more. On—on—on we worked till we had hollowed out about three feet of earth. Tip then hastily joined together a long iron screw or borer, which he thrust into the ground, for the purpose of ascertaining the depth at which the coffin yet lay from us.

To our vexation, we found a distance of three feet remained to be got through.

"Sure, and by the soul of St. Patrick, but we'll not be done by the morning!" said Tip, as he threw down the instrument and resumed his spade.

We were all discouraged. Oh, how earnestly I wished myself at home, in my snug little bed in the Borough! How I cursed the Quixotism that had led me into such an undertaking! I had no time, however, for reflection, as it was my turn to relieve one of the diggers; so into the grave I jumped, and worked away as lustily as before. While I was thus engaged, a sudden noise, close to our ears, so startled me, that I protest I thought I should have dropped down dead in the grave I was robbing.

I and my fellow-digger let fall our spades, and all four stood still for a second or two in an ecstasy of fearful apprehension. We could not see more than a few inches around us, but heard the grass trodden by approaching feet! They proved to be those of an ass, that was turned at night into the churchyard, and had gone on eating his way towards us; and, while we were standing in mute expectation of what was to come next, opened on us with an astounding hee-haw! hee-haw! hee-haw! Even after we had discovered the ludicrous nature of the interruption, we were too agitated to laugh. The brute was actually close upon us, and had *given tongue* from under poor Tip's elbow, having approached him from behind as he stood leaning on his spade. Tip started suddenly backward against the animal's head, and fell down.

Away sprang the jackass, as much confounded as Tip, kicking and scampering like a mad creature among the tombstones, and hee-hawing incessantly, as if a hundred devils had got into it for the purpose of discomfiting us. I felt so much fury and fear lest the noise should lead to our discovery I could have killed the brute if it had been within my reach, while Tip stammered, in an affrightened whisper—" Och, the baste ! Och, the baste ! The big black divel of a baste ! The murtherous, thundering " —— and a great many epithets of the same sort. We gradually recovered from the agitation which this provoking interruption had occasioned ; and Tip, under the promise of two bottles of whisky as soon as we arrived safe at home with our prize, renewed his exertions, and dug with such energy that we soon cleared away the remainder of the superincumbent earth, and stood upon the bare lid of the coffin. The grapplers, with ropes attached to them, were then fixed in the sides and extremities, and we were in the act of raising the coffin, when the sound of a human voice, accompanied with footsteps, fell on our startled ears. We heard both distinctly, and crouched down close over the brink of the grave, awaiting in breathless suspense a corroboration of our fears. After a pause of two or three minutes, however, finding that the sounds were not renewed, we began to breathe freer, persuaded that our ears must have deceived us.

Once more we resumed our work, succeeded in hoisting up the coffin—not without a slip, however, which nearly precipitated it down again to the bottom, with all four of us upon it—and depositing it on the graveside. Before proceeding to use our screws or wrenches, we once more looked and listened, and listened and looked ; but neither seeing nor hearing anything we set to work, prized off the lid in a twinkling, and a transient glimpse of moonlight disclosed to us the shrouded inmate—all white and damp. I removed the face-cloth, and unpinned the cap, while M—— loosed the sleeves from the wrists. Thus were we engaged, when E——, who had hold of the feet, ready to lift them out, suddenly let them go—gasped, " Oh, my God ! there they are ! " and placed his hand on my arm. He shook like an aspen leaf. I looked towards the quarter whither his eyes were directed, and, sure enough, saw the figure of a man—if not two—moving stealthily towards us. " Well, we're discovered, that's clear," I whispered as calmly as I could.

" We shall be murdered ! " groaned E——.

" Lend me one of the pistols you have with you," said M—— resolutely ; " by ——, I'll have a shot for my life, however ! "

As for poor Tip, who had heard every syllable of this startling colloquy, and himself seen the approaching figures, he looked at me in silence, the image of black horror! I could have laughed even then, to see his staring black eyes—his little cocked ruby-tinted nose—his chattering teeth.

"Hush—hush!" said I, cocking my pistol, while M—— did the same; for none but myself knew that they were unloaded. To add to our consternation, the malignant moon withdrew the small scantling of light she had been doling out to us, and sank beneath a vast cloud, "black as Erebus," but not before we had caught a glimpse of two more figures moving towards us in an opposite direction. "Surrounded!" two of us muttered in the same breath. We all rose to our feet, and stood together, not knowing what to do—unable in the darkness to see one another distinctly. Presently we heard a voice say, in a subdued tone, "Where are they? where? *Sure* I saw them! Oh, there they are. Halloa—halloa!"

That was enough—the signal of our flight. Without an instant's pause, or uttering another syllable, off we sprung, like small-shot from a gun's mouth, all of us in different directions, we knew not whither. I heard the report of a gun—mercy on me! and pelted away, scarcely knowing what I was about, dodging among the graves—now coming full-butt against a plaguy tombstone, then tumbling on the slippery grass—while some one followed close at my heels, panting and puffing, but whether friend or foe I knew not.

At length I stumbled against a large tombstone; and, finding it open at the two ends, crept under it, resolved there to abide the issue. At the moment of my ensconcing myself the sound of the person's footsteps who had followed me suddenly ceased. I heard a splashing sound, then a kicking and scrambling, a faint stifled cry of "Ugh—oh ugh!" and all was still. Doubtless it must be one of my companions, who had been wounded. What could I do, however? I did not know in what direction he lay—the night was pitch-dark—and if I crept from my hiding-place, for all I knew, I might be shot myself. I shall never forget that hour—no, never! There was I, squatting like a tod on the wet grass and weeds, not daring to do more than breathe! Here was a predicament! I could not conjecture how the affair would terminate.

Was I to lie where I was till daylight, that then I might step into the arms of my captors? What was become of my companions? While turning these thoughts in my mind, and wondering that all was so quiet, my ear caught the sound of the splashing of water, apparently at but a yard or two's distance, mingled with the sounds of a half-smothered human voice—"Ugh! ugh! Och, murther! murther! murther!"—another splash—"and isn't it dead, and drowned, and kilt I am"——

Whew! *Tip* in trouble, thought I, not daring to speak. Yes—

it was poor Tip, I afterwards found—who had followed at my heels, scampering after me as fast as fright could drive him, till his career was unexpectedly ended by his tumbling—souse—head over heels, into a newly-opened grave in his path, with more than a foot of water in it. There the poor fellow remained, after recovering from the first shock of his fall, not daring to utter a word for some time, lest he should be discovered—straddling over the water with his toes and elbows stuck into the loose soil on each side, to support him. This was his interesting position, as he subsequently informed me, at the time of uttering the sounds which first attracted my attention. Though not aware of his situation at the time, I was almost choked with laughter as he went on with his soliloquy, somewhat in this strain :—

"Och, Tip, ye ould divel! Don't it sarve ye right, ye fool? Ye villainous ould coffin-robber! Won't ye burn for this hereafter, ye sinner? Ulaloo! When ye are dead yourself, may ye be trated like that poor cratur—and yourself alive to see it! Och, hubbaboo! hubbaboo! Isn't it sure that I'll be drowned, an' then it's kilt I'll be!" A loud splash, and a pause for a few moments, as if he were readjusting his footing—"Och! an' I'm catching my dith of cowld! Fait, an' it's a divel a drop o' the two bottles o' whisky I'll ever see—Och, och, och!"—another splash—"och, an' isn't this uncomfortable! Murther and oons!—if ever I come out of this—sha'n't I be dead before I do?"

"Tip—Tip—Tip!" I whispered in a low tone. There was a dead silence. "Tip, Tip, where are you? What's the matter, eh?" No answer; but he muttered in a low tone to himself—"*Where am I!* by my soul! Isn't it dead, and kilt, and drowned, and murthered I am—that's all!"

"Tip—Tip—Tip!" I repeated, a little louder.

"Tip, indeed! Fait, ye may call, bad luck to ye—whoever ye are—but it's divel a word I'll be after spaking to ye."

"Tip, you simpleton! It's I—Mr. ——."

In an instant there was a sound of jumping and splashing, as if surprise had made him slip from his standing again, and he called out, "Whoo! whoo! an' is't you, sweet Mr. ——! What is the matter wid ye? Are ye kilt? Where are they all? Have they taken ye away, every mother's son of you?" he asked eagerly, in a breath.

"Why, what are *you* doing, Tip? Where are *you*?"

"Fait, an' it's being *washed* I am, in the feet, and in the queerest *tub* your honour ever saw!" A noise of scuffling not many yards off, silenced us both in an instant.

Presently I distinguished the voice of E——, calling out, "Help, M——!" (my name)—"Where are you?" The noise increased, and seemed nearer than before. I crept from my lurking place, and aided at Tip's resurrection, when both of us hurried towards the spot whence the sound came. By the faint moonlight I could just see the outlines of two figures violently struggling and grappling together. Before I could come up to them both fell down, locked in each other's arms, rolling over each other, grasping one another's collars, gasping and panting as if in mortal struggle. The moon suddenly emerged, and who do you think, reader, was E——'s antagonist? Why, the person whose appearance had so discomfited and affrighted us all—OUR COACHMAN.

That worthy individual, alarmed at our protracted stay, had, contrary to our injunctions, left his coach to come and search after us. He it was whom we had seen stealing towards us; his step—his voice had alarmed us, for he could not see us distinctly enough to discover whether we were his fare or not. He was on the point of whispering my name, it seems—when we must all have understood one another—when lo! we all started off in the manner which has been described; and he himself, not knowing that he was the reason of it, had taken to his heels, and fled for his life! He supposed we had fallen into a sort of ambuscade. He happened to hide himself behind the tombstone next but one to that which sheltered E——. Finding all quiet, he and E——, as if by mutual consent, were groping from their hiding-places, when they unexpectedly fell foul of one another—each too affrighted to speak—and hence the scuffle.

After this satisfactory dénouement we all repaired to the grave's mouth, and found the corpse and coffin precisely as we had left them. We were not many moments in taking out the body, stripping it, and thrusting it into the sack we had brought. We then tied the top of the sack, carefully deposited the shroud, etc., in the coffin, re-screwed down the lid—fearful, impious mockery!—and consigned it once more to its resting-place, Tip scattering a handful of earth on the lid, and exclaiming reverently—"An' may the Lord forgive us for what we have done to ye!" The coachman and I then took the body between us to the coach, leaving M——, and E——, and Tip to fill up the grave.

Our troubles were not yet ended, however. Truly it seemed as though Providence were throwing every obstacle in our way. Nothing went right. On reaching the spot where we had left the coach, behold it lay several yards farther in the lane, tilted into the ditch—for the horses, being hungry, and left to themselves, in their anxiety to graze on the verdant bank of the hedge, had contrived to overturn the vehicle in the ditch—and one of the horses was kicking vigorously when we came up—the whole body off the ground—and resting on that of his companion. We had considerable difficulty in righting the coach, as the horses were inclined to be obstreperous. We succeeded, however—deposited our unholy spoil within, turned the horses' heads towards the high road, and then, after enjoining Jehu to keep his place on the box, I went to see how my companions were getting on. They had nearly completed their task, and told me that "shovelling *in* was surprisingly easier than shovelling *out*!"

We took great pains to leave everything as neat and as nearly resembling what we found it as possible, in order that our visit might not be suspected. We then carried away each our own tools, and hurried as fast as possible to our coach, for the dim twilight had already stolen a march upon us, devoutly thankful that, after so many interruptions, we had succeeded in effecting our object.

It was broad daylight before we reached town, and a wretched coach company we looked, all wearied and dirty—Tip especially, who nevertheless snored in the corner as comfortably as if he had been warm in his bed. I heartily resolved with him, on leaving the coach, that it should be "the devil's own dear self only that should timpt me out again *body-snatching*!"

MRS. GASKELL
1810–1865

THE SQUIRE'S STORY

In the year 1769 the little town of Barford was thrown into a state of great excitement by the intelligence that a gentleman (and "quite the gentleman," said the landlord of the George Inn) had been looking at Mr. Clavering's old house. This house was neither in the town nor in the country. It stood on the outskirts of Barford, on the roadside leading to Derby. The last occupant had been a Mr. Clavering—a Northumberland gentleman of good family—who had come to live in Barford while he was but a younger son; but when some elder branches of the family died, he had returned to take possession of the family estate. The house of which I speak was called the White House, from its being covered with a greyish kind of stucco. It had a good garden to the back, and Mr. Clavering had built capital stables, with what were then considered the latest improvements. The point of good stabling was expected to let the house, as it was in a hunting county; otherwise it had few recommendations. There were many bedrooms; some entered through others, even to the number of five, leading one beyond the other; several sitting-rooms of the small and poky kind, wainscoted round with wood, and then painted a heavy slate colour; one good dining-room, and a drawing-room over it, both looking into the garden, with pleasant bow-windows.

Such was the accommodation offered by the White House. It did not seem to be very tempting to strangers, though the good people of Barford rather piqued themselves on it, as the largest house in the town; and as a house in which "townspeople" and "county people" had often met at Mr. Clavering's friendly dinners. To appreciate this circumstance of pleasant recollection, you should have lived some years in a little country town, surrounded by gentlemen's seats. You would then understand how a bow or a courtesy from a member of a county family elevates the individuals who receive it almost as much, in their own eyes, as the pair of blue garters fringed with silver did Mr. Bickerstaff's ward. They trip lightly on air for a whole day afterwards. Now Mr. Clavering was gone, where could town and county mingle ?

I mention these things that you may have an idea of the desirability of the letting of the White House in the Barfordites' imagination ; and to make the mixture thick and slab, you must add for yourselves the bustle, the mystery, and the importance which every little event either causes or assumes in a small town ; and then, perhaps, it will be no wonder to you that twenty ragged little urchins accompanied the " gentleman " aforesaid to the door of the White House ; and that, although he was above an hour inspecting it under the auspices of Mr. Jones, the agent's clerk, thirty more had joined themselves on to the wondering crowd before his exit, and awaited such crumbs of intelligence as they could gather before they were threatened or whipped out of hearing distance. Presently out came the " gentleman " and the lawyer's clerk. The latter was speaking as he followed the former over the threshold. The gentleman was tall, well-dressed, handsome ; but there was a sinister cold look in his quick-glancing, light blue eye, which a keen observer might not have liked. There were no keen observers among the boys and ill-conditioned gaping girls. But they stood too near ; inconveniently close ; and the gentleman, lifting up his right hand, in which he carried a short riding-whip, dealt one or two sharp blows to the nearest, with a look of savage enjoyment on his face as they moved away whimpering and crying. An instant after, his expression of countenance had changed.

" Here ! " said he, drawing out a handful of money, partly silver, partly copper, and throwing it into the midst of them. " Scramble for it ! fight it out, my lads ! Come this afternoon, at three, to the George, and I'll throw you out some more."

So the boys hurrahed for him as he walked off with the agent's clerk. He chuckled to himself, as over a pleasant thought. " I'll have some fun with those lads," he said ; " I'll teach 'em to prowling and prying about me. I'll tell you what I'll do. I'll make the money so hot in the fire-shovel that it shall burn their fingers. You come and see the faces and the howling. I shall be very glad if you will dine with me at two ; and by that time I may have made up my mind respecting the house."

Mr. Jones, the agent's clerk, agreed to come to the George at two, but, somehow, he had a distaste for his entertainer. Mr. Jones would not like to have said, even to himself, that a man with a purse full of money, who kept many horses, and spoke familiarly of noblemen—above all, who thought of taking the White House—could be anything but a gentleman ; but still the uneasy wonder as to who this Mr. Robinson Higgins could be, filled the clerk's mind long after Mr. Higgins, Mr. Higgins's servants, and Mr. Higgins's stud had taken possession of the White House.

The White House was re-stuccoed (this time of a pale yellow colour), and put into thorough repair by the accommodating and delighted landlord ; while his tenant seemed inclined to spend any amount of money on internal decorations, which were showy and effective in their character, enough to make the White House a nine days' wonder to the good people of Barford. The slate-coloured paints became pink, and were picked out with gold ; the old-fashioned banisters were replaced by newly gilt ones ; but, above all, the stables were a sight to be seen. Since the days of the Roman Emperor never was there such provision made for the care, the comfort, and the health of horses. But every one said it was no wonder, when they were led through Barford, covered up to their eyes, but curving their arched and delicate necks, and prancing with short high steps, in repressed eagerness.

Only one groom came with them ; yet they required the care of three men. Mr. Higgins, however, preferred engaging two lads out of Barford ; and Barford highly approved of his preference. Not only was it kind and thoughtful to give employment to the lounging lads themselves, but they were receiving such a training in Mr. Higgins's stables as might fit them for Doncaster or Newmarket.

The district of Derbyshire in which Barford was situated was too close to Leicestershire not to support a hunt and a pack of hounds. The master of the hounds was a certain Sir Harry Manley, who was *aut* a huntsman *aut nullus*. He measured a man by the " length of his fork," not by the expression of his countenance or the shape of his head. But, as Sir Harry was wont to observe, there was such a thing as too long a fork, so his approbation was withheld until he had seen a man on horseback ; and if his seat there was square and easy, his hand light, and his courage good, Sir Harry hailed him as a brother.

Mr. Higgins attended the first meet of the season, not as a subscriber but as an amateur. The Barford huntsmen piqued themselves on their bold riding ; and their knowledge of the country came by nature ; yet this new strange man, whom nobody knew, was in at the death, sitting on his horse, both well breathed and calm, without a hair turned on the sleek skin of the latter, supremely addressing the old huntsman as he hacked off the tail of the fox ; and he, the old man, who was testy even under Sir Harry's slightest rebuke, and flew out on any other member of the hunt that dared to utter a word against his sixty years' experience as stable-boy, groom, poacher, and what not—he, old Isaac Wormeley, was meekly listening to the wisdom of this stranger, only now and then giving one of his quick, up-turning, cunning glances, not unlike the sharp o'er-canny looks of the poor deceased Reynard, round whom the hounds were howling, unadmonished by the short whip, which was now tucked into Wormeley's well-worn pocket.

When Sir Harry rode into the copse—full of dead brushwood and wet tangled grass—and was followed by the members of the hunt, as one by one they cantered past, Mr. Higgins took off his cap and bowed—half deferentially, half insolently—with a lurking smile in the corner of his eye at the discomfited looks of one or too of the laggards.

"A famous run, sir," said Sir Harry. "The first time you have hunted in our country; but I hope we shall see you often."

"I hope to become a member of the hunt, sir," said Mr. Higgins.

"Most happy—proud, I'm sure, to receive so daring a rider among us. You took the Cropper-gate, I fancy; while some of our friends here"—scowling at one or two cowards by way of finishing his speech. "Allow me to introduce myself—master of the hounds." He fumbled in his waistcoat pocket for the card on which his name was formally inscribed. "Some of our friends here are kind enough to come home with me to dinner; might I ask for the honour?"

"My name is Higgins," replied the stranger, bowing low. "I am only lately come to occupy the White House at Barford, and I have not as yet presented my letters of introduction."

"Hang it!" replied Sir Harry; "a man with a seat like yours, and that good brush in your hand, might ride up to any door in the county (I'm a Leicestershire man!) and be a welcome guest. Mr. Higgins, I shall be proud to become better acquainted with you over my dinner-table."

Mr. Higgins knew pretty well how to improve the acquaintance thus begun. He could sing a good song, tell a good story, and was well up in practical jokes; with plenty of that keen worldly sense, which seems like an instinct in some men, and which in this case taught him on whom he might play off such jokes, with impunity from their resentment, and with a security of applause from the more boisterous, vehement, or prosperous. At the end of twelve months Mr. Robinson Higgins was, out-and-out, the most popular member of the Barford hunt; had beaten all the others by a couple of lengths, as his first patron, Sir Harry, observed one evening, when they were just leaving the dinner-table of an old hunting squire in the neighbourhood.

"Because, you know," said Squire Hearn, holding Sir Harry by the button—"I mean, you see, this young spark is looking sweet upon Catherine; and she's a good girl, and will have ten thousand pounds down, the day she's married, by her mother's will; and—excuse me, Sir Harry—but I should not like my girl to throw herself away."

Though Sir Harry had a long ride before him, and but the early and short light of a new moon to take it in, his kind heart was so much touched by Squire Hearn's trembling, tearful anxiety, that he stopped and turned back into the dining-room to say, with more asseverations than I care to give:

"My good Squire, I may say I know that man pretty well by this time, and a better fellow never existed. If I had twenty daughters he should have the pick of them."

Squire Hearn never thought of asking the grounds for his old friend's opinion of Mr. Higgins; it had been given with too much earnestness for any doubts to cross the old man's mind as to the possibility of its not being well founded. Mr. Hearn was not a doubter, or a thinker, or suspicious by nature; it was simply love for Catherine, his only daughter, that prompted his anxiety in this case; and, after what Sir Harry had said, the old man could totter with an easy mind, though not with very steady legs, into the drawing-room, where his bonny, blushing daughter Catherine and Mr. Higgins stood close together on the hearth-rug—he whispering, she listening with downcast eyes.

She looked so happy, so like what her dead mother had looked when the Squire was a young man, that all his thought was how to please her most. His son and heir was about to be married, and bring his wife to live with the Squire; Barford and the White House were not distant an hour's ride; and, even as these thoughts passed through his mind, he asked Mr. Higgins if he could not stay all night—the young moon was already set—the roads would be dark—and Catherine looked up with a pretty anxiety, which, however, had not much doubt in it, for the answer.

With every encouragement of this kind from the old Squire, it took everybody rather by surprise when one morning it was discovered that Miss Catherine Hearn was missing; and when, according to the usual fashion in such cases, a note was found, saying that she had eloped with "the man of her heart," and gone to Gretna Green, no one could imagine why she could not quietly have stopped at home and been married in the parish church. She had always been a romantic, sentimental girl; very pretty and very affectionate, and very much spoiled, and very much wanting in common sense. Her indulgent father was deeply hurt at this want of confidence in his never-varying affection; but when his son came, hot with indignation from the Baronet's (his future father-in-law's house, where every form of law and of ceremony was to accompany his own impending marriage), Squire Hearn pleaded the cause of the young couple with imploring cogency, and protested that it was a piece of spirit in his daughter, which he admired and was proud of.

However, it ended with Mr. Nathaniel Hearn's declaring that he and his wife would have nothing to do with his sister and her husband.

"Wait till you've seen him, Nat!" said the old Squire, trembling with his distressful anticipations of family discord; "he's an excuse for any girl. Only ask Sir Harry's opinion of him."

"Confound Sir Harry! So that a man sits his horse well, Sir Harry cares nothing about anything else. Who is this man—this fellow? Where does he come from? What are his means? Who are his family?"

"He comes from the south—Surrey or Somersetshire, I forget which; and he pays his way well and liberally. There's not a tradesman in Barford but says he cares no more for money than for water; he spends like a prince, Nat. I don't know who his family are, but he seals with a coat of arms, which may tell you if you want to know—and he goes regularly to collect his rents from his estates in the south. Oh, Nat! if you would but be friendly, I should be as well pleased with Kitty's marriage as any father in the county."

Mr. Nathaniel Hearn gloomed, and muttered an oath or two to himself. The poor old father was reaping the consequences of his weak indulgence to his two children. Mr. and Mrs. Nathaniel Hearn kept apart from Catherine and her husband; and Squire Hearn durst never ask them to Levison Hall, though it was his own house. Indeed, he stole away as if he were a culprit whenever he went to visit the White House; and if he passed a night there, he was fain to equivocate when he returned home the next day; an equivocation which was well interpreted by the surly, proud Nathaniel. But the younger Mr. and Mrs. Hearn were the only people who did not visit at the White House.

Mr. and Mrs. Higgins were decidedly more popular than their brother and sister-in-law. She made a very pretty, sweet-tempered hostess, and her education had not been such as to make her intolerant of any want of refinement in the associates who gathered round her husband. She had gentle smiles for townspeople as well as county people; and unconsciously played an admirable second in her husband's project of making himself universally popular.

But there is some one to make ill-natured remarks, and draw ill-natured conclusions from very simple premises, in every place; and in Barford this bird of ill-omen was a Miss Pratt. She did not hunt—so Mr. Higgins's admirable riding did not call out her admiration. She did not drink—so the well-selected wines, so lavishly dispensed among his guests, could never mollify Miss Pratt. She could not bear comic songs, or buffo stories—so, in that way, her approbation was impregnable. And these three secrets of popularity constituted Mr. Higgins's great charm.

Miss Pratt sat and watched. Her face looked immovably grave

at the end of any of Mr. Higgins's best stories ; but there was a keen, needle-like glance of her unwinking little eyes, which Mr. Higgins felt rather than saw, and which made him shiver, even on a hot day, when it fell upon him. Miss Pratt was a dissenter, and, to propitiate this female Mordecai, Mr. Higgins asked the dissenting minister whose services she attended, to dinner ; kept himself and his company in good order ; gave a handsome donation to the poor of the chapel.

All in vain—Miss Pratt stirred not a muscle more of her face towards graciousness ; and Mr. Higgins was conscious that, in spite of all his open efforts to captivate Mr. Davis, there was a secret influence on the other side, throwing in doubts and suspicions, and evil interpretations of all he said or did. Miss Pratt, the little, plain old maid, living on eighty pounds a year, was the thorn in the popular Mr. Higgins's side, although she had never spoken one uncivil word to him ; indeed, on the contrary, had treated him with a stiff and elaborate civility.

The thorn—the grief to Mrs. Higgins was this. They had no children ! Oh ! how she would stand and envy the careless, busy motion of half a dozen children ; and then, when observed, move on with a deep, deep sigh of yearning regret. But it was as well.

It was noticed that Mr. Higgins was remarkably careful of his health. He ate, drank, took exercise, rested, by some secret rules of his own ; occasionally bursting into an excess, it is true, but only on rare occasions—such as when he returned from visiting his estates in the south, and collecting his rents. That unusual exertion and fatigue—for there were no stage-coaches within forty miles of Barford, and he, like most country gentlemen of that day, would have preferred riding if there had been—seemed to require some strange excess to compensate for it ; and rumours went through the town that he shut himself up, and drank enormously for some days after his return. But no one was admitted to these orgies.

One day—they remembered it well afterwards—the hounds met not far from the town; and the fox was found in a part of the wild heath, which was beginning to be enclosed by a few of the more wealthy townspeople, who were desirous of building themselves houses rather more in the country than those they had hitherto lived in.

Among these the principal was a Mr. Dudgeon, the attorney of Barford, and the agent for all the county families about. The firm of Dudgeon had managed the leases, the marriage-settlements, and the wills of the neighbourhood for generations. Mr. Dudgeon's father had the responsibility of collecting the landowners' rents just as the present Mr. Dudgeon had at the time of which I speak : and as his son and his son's son have done since. Their business was an hereditary estate to them ; and with something of the old feudal feeling was mixed a kind of proud humility at their position towards the squires whose family secrets they had mastered, and the mysteries of whose fortunes and estates were better known to the Messrs. Dudgeon than to themselves.

Mr. John Dudgeon had built himself a house on Wildbury Heath—a mere cottage, as he called it; but though only two storeys high, it spread out far and wide, and workpeople from Derby had been sent for on purpose to make the inside as complete as possible. The gardens too were exquisite in arrangement, if not very extensive; and not a flower was grown in them but of the rarest species.

It must have been somewhat of a mortification to the owner of this dainty place when, on the day of which I speak, the fox, after a long race, during which he had described a circle of many miles, took refuge in the garden; but Mr. Dudgeon put a good face on the matter when a gentleman hunter, with the careless insolence of the squires of those days and that place, rode across the velvet lawn, and tapping at the window of the dining-room with his whip-handle, asked permission—no! that is not it—rather, informed Mr. Dudgeon of their intention—to enter his garden in a body, and have the fox unearthed. Mr. Dudgeon compelled himself to smile assent, with the grace of a masculine Griselda; and then he hastily gave orders to have all that the house afforded of provision set out for luncheon, guessing rightly enough that a six hours' run would give even homely fare an acceptable welcome.

He bore without wincing the entrance of the dirty boots into his exquisitely clean rooms; he only felt grateful for the care with which Mr. Higgins strode about, laboriously and noiselessly moving on the tip of his toes, as he reconnoitred the rooms with a curious eye.

"I'm going to build a house myself, Dudgeon; and, upon my word, I don't think I could take a better model than yours."

"Oh! my poor cottage would be too small to afford any hints for such a house as you would wish to build, Mr. Higgins," replied Mr. Dudgeon, gently rubbing his hands nevertheless at the compliment.

"Not at all! not at all! Let me see. You have dining-room, drawing-room"—he hesitated, and Mr. Dudgeon filled up the blank as he expected.

"Four sitting-rooms and the bedrooms. But allow me to show you over the house. I confess I took some pains in arranging it, and, though far smaller than what you would require, it may, nevertheless, afford you some hints."

So they left the eating gentlemen with their mouths and their plates quite full, and the scent of the fox overpowering that of the hasty rashers of ham; and they carefully inspected all the ground-floor rooms. Then Mr. Dudgeon said:

"If you are not tired, Mr. Higgins—it is rather my hobby, so you must pull me up if you are—we will go upstairs, and I will show you my sanctum."

Mr. Dudgeon's sanctum was the centre room, over the porch, which formed a balcony, and which was carefully filled with choice flowers in pots. Inside, there were all kinds of elegant contrivances for hiding the real strength of all the boxes and chests required by the particular nature of Mr. Dudgeon's business: for although his office was in Barford, he kept (as he informed Mr. Higgins) what was the most valuable here, as being safer than an office which was locked up and left every night.

But, as Mr. Higgins reminded him with a sly poke in the side, when next they met, his own house was not over-secure. A fortnight after the gentlemen of the Barford hunt lunched there, Mr. Dudgeon's strong-box—in his sanctum upstairs, with the mysterious spring-bolt to the window invented by himself, and the secret of which was only known to the inventor and a few of his most intimate friends, to whom he had proudly shown it;—this strong-box, containing the collected Christmas rents of half a dozen landlords (there was then no bank nearer than Derby), was rifled; and the secretly rich Mr. Dudgeon had to stop his agent in his purchases of paintings by Flemish artists, because the money was required to make good the missing rents.

The Dogberries and Verges of those days were quite incapable of obtaining any clue to the robber or robbers; and though one or two vagrants were taken up and brought before Mr. Dunover and Mr. Higgins, the magistrates who usually attended in the court-room at Barford, there was no evidence brought against them, and after a couple of nights' durance in the lock-ups they were set at liberty. But it became a standing joke with Mr. Higgins to ask Mr. Dudgeon, from time to time, whether he would recommend him a place of safety for his valuables; or if he had made any more inventions lately for securing houses from robbers.

About two years after this time—about seven years after Mr. Higgins had been married—one Tuesday evening, Mr. Davis was sitting reading the news in the coffee-room of the George Inn. He belonged to a club of gentlemen who met there occasionally to play at whist, to read what few newspapers and magazines were published in those days, to chat about the market at Derby, and prices all over the country.

This Tuesday night it was a black frost; and few people were in the room. Mr. Davis was anxious to finish an article in the *Gentleman's Magazine*; indeed, he was making extracts from it, intending to answer it, and yet unable with his small income to purchase a copy. So he stayed late; it was past nine, and at ten o'clock the room was closed.

But while he wrote, Mr. Higgins came in. He was pale and haggard with cold; Mr. Davis, who had had for some time sole possession of the fire, moved politely on one side, and handed to the new-comer the sole London newspaper which the room afforded.

Mr. Higgins accepted it, and made some remark on the intense coldness of the weather; but Mr. Davis was too full of his article, and intended reply, to fall into conversation readily. Mr. Higgins hitched his chair nearer to the fire, and put his feet on the fender, giving an audible shudder. He put the newspaper on one end of the table near him, and sat gazing into the red embers of the fire, crouching down over them as if his very marrow were chilled. At length he said:

"There is no account of the murder at Bath in that paper?"

Mr. Davis, who had finished taking his notes, and was preparing to go, stopped short, and asked:

"Has there been a murder at Bath? No! I have not seen anything of it—who was murdered?"

"Oh! it was a shocking, terrible murder!" said Mr. Higgins, not raising his look from the fire, but gazing on with his eyes dilated till the whites were seen all round them. "A terrible, terrible murder! I wonder what will become of the murderer? I can fancy the red glowing centre of that fire—look and see how infinitely distant it seems, and how the distance magnifies it into something awful and unquenchable."

"My dear sir, you are feverish; how you shake and shiver!" said Mr. Davis, thinking privately that his companion had symptoms of fever, and that he was wandering in his mind.

"Oh, no!" said Mr. Higgins, "I am not feverish. It is the night which is so cold."

And for a time he talked with Mr. Davis about the article in the *Gentleman's Magazine*, for he was rather a reader himself, and could take more interest in Mr. Davis's pursuits than most of the people at Barford. At length it drew near to ten, and Mr. Davis rose up to go home to his lodgings.

"No, Davis, don't go. I want you here. We will have a bottle of port together, and that will put Saunders into good humour. I want to tell you about this murder," he continued, dropping his voice, and speaking hoarse and low. "She was an old woman, and he killed her, sitting reading her Bible by her own fireside!" He looked at Mr. Davis with a strange searching gaze, as if trying to find some sympathy in the horror which the idea presented to him.

"Who do you mean, my dear sir? What is this murder you are so full of? No one has been murdered here."

"No, you fool! I tell you it was in Bath!" said Mr. Higgins, with sudden passion; and then calming himself to most velvet-smoothness of manner, he laid his hand on Mr. Davis's knee, there, as they sat by the fire, and gently detaining him, began the narration of the crime he was so full of; but his voice and manner were constrained to a stony quietude: he never looked in Mr. Davis's face; once or twice, as Mr. Davis remembered afterwards, his grip tightened like a compressing vice.

"She lived in a small house in a quiet old-fashioned street, she and her maid. People said she was a good old woman; but for all that she hoarded and hoarded, and never gave to the poor. Mr. Davis, it is wicked not to give to the poor—wicked—wicked, is it not? I always give to the poor, for once I read in the Bible that 'Charity covereth a multitude of sins.' The wicked old woman never gave, but hoarded her money, and saved, and saved. Some one heard of it; I say she threw a temptation in his way, and God will punish her for it. And this man—or it might be a woman, who knows?—and this person—heard also that she went to church in the mornings, and her maid in the afternoons; and so—while the maid was at church, and the street and the house quite still, and the darkness of a winter afternoon coming on—she was nodding over the Bible—and that, mark you! is a sin, and one that God will avenge sooner or later; and a step came in the dusk up the stair, and that person I told you of stood in the room. At first he—no! At first, it is supposed—for, you understand, all this is mere guess-work—it is supposed that he asked her civilly enough to give him her money, or to tell him where it was; but the old miser defied him, and would not ask for mercy and give up her keys, even when he threatened her, but looked him in the face as if he had been a baby—Oh, God! Mr. Davis, I once dreamt when I was a little innocent boy that I should commit a crime like this, and I wakened up crying; and my mother comforted me—that is the reason I tremble so now—that and the cold, for it is very very cold!"

"But did he murder the old lady?" asked Mr. Davis. "I beg your pardon, sir, but I am interested by your story."

"Yes! he cut her throat; and there she lies yet in her quiet little parlour, with her face upturned and all ghastly white, in the middle of a pool of blood. Mr. Davis, this wine is no better than water; I must have some brandy!"

Mr. Davis was horror-struck by the story, which seemed to have fascinated him as much as it had done his companion.

"Have they got any clue to the murderer?" said he. Mr. Higgins drank down half a tumber of raw brandy before he answered.

"No! no clue whatever. They will never be able to discover him, and I should not wonder—Mr. Davis—I should not wonder if he repented after all, and did bitter penance for his crime; and if so—will there be mercy for him at the last day?"

" God knows ! " said Mr. Davis, with solemnity. " It is an awful story," continued he, rousing himself ; " I hardly like to leave this warm light room and go out into the darkness after hearing it. But it must be done," buttoning on his great-coat—" I can only say I hope and trust they will find out the murderer and hang him.—If you'll take my advice, Mr. Higgins, you'll have your bed warmed, and drink a treacle-posset just the last thing ; and, if you'll allow me, I'll send you my answer to Philologus before it goes up to old Urban."

The next morning Mr. Davis went to call on Miss Pratt, who was not very well ; and by way of being agreeable and entertaining, he related to her all he had heard the night before about the murder at Bath ; and really he made a very pretty connected story out of it, and interested Miss Pratt very much in the fate of the old lady—partly because of a similarity in their situations ; for she also privately hoarded money, and had but one servant, and stopped at home alone on Sunday afternoons to allow her servant to go to church.

" And when did all this happen ? " she asked.

" I don't know if Mr. Higgins named the day ; and yet I think it must have been on this very last Sunday."

" And to-day is Wednesday. Ill news travels fast."

" Yes, Mr. Higgins thought it might have been in the London newspaper."

" That it could never be. Where did Mr. Higgins learn all about it ? "

" I don't know, I did not ask ; I think he only came home yesterday ; he had been south to collect his rents, somebody said."

Miss Pratt grunted. She used to vent her dislike and suspicions of Mr. Higgins in a grunt whenever his name was mentioned.

" Well, I sha'n't see you for some days. Godfrey Merton has asked me to go and stay with him and his sister ; and I think it will do me good. Besides," added she, " these winter evenings—and these murderers at large in the country—I don't quite like living with only Peggy to call to in case of need."

Miss Pratt went to stay with her cousin, Mr. Merton. He was an active magistrate, and enjoyed his reputation as such. One day he came in, having just received his letters.

" Bad account of the morals of your little town here, Jessy ! " said he, touching one of his letters. " You've either a murderer among you, or some friend of a murderer. Here's a poor old lady at Bath had her throat cut last Sunday week ; and I've a letter from the Home Office, asking to lend them ' my very efficient aid,' as they are pleased to call it, towards finding out the culprit. It seems he must have been thirsty, and of a comfortable jolly turn ; for before going to his horrid work he tapped a barrel of ginger wine the old lady had set by to work ; and he wrapped the spigot round with a piece of a letter taken out of his pocket, as may be supposed ; and this piece of a letter was found afterwards ; there are only these letters on the outside, '*ns, Esq., -arford, -egworth,*' which some one has ingeniously made out to mean Barford, near Kegworth. On the other side there is some allusion to a racehorse, I conjecture, though the name is singular enough : 'Church-and-King-and-down-with-the-Rump.' "

Miss Pratt caught at this name immediately ; it had hurt her feelings as a dissenter only a few months ago, and she remembered it well.

" Mr. Nat Hearn has—or had (as I am speaking in the witness-box, as it were, I must take care of my tenses)—a horse with that ridiculous name."

" Mr. Nat Hearn," repeated Mr. Merton, making a note of the intelligence ; then he recurred to his letter from the Home Office again.

" There is also a piece of a small key, broken in the futile attempt to open a desk—well, well. Nothing more of consequence. The letter is what we must rely upon."

" Mr. Davis said that Mr. Higgins told him——" Miss Pratt began.

" Higgins ! " exclaimed Mr. Merton, " *ns*. Is it Higgins, the blustering fellow that ran away with Nat Hearn's sister ? "

" Yes ! " said Miss Pratt. " But though he has never been a favourite of mine——"

" *ns*," repeated Mr. Merton. " It is too horrible to think of ; a member of the hunt—kind old Squire Hearn's son-in-law ! Who else have you in Barford with names that end in *ns* ? "

" There's Jackson, and Higginson, and Blenkinsop, and Davis, and Jones. Cousin ! One thing strikes me—how did Mr. Higgins know all about it to tell Mr. Davis on Tuesday what had happened on Sunday afternoon ? "

There is no need to add much more. Those curious in lives of the highwaymen may find the name of Higgins as conspicuous among those annals as that of Claude Duval. Kate Hearn's husband collected his rents on the highway, like many another " gentleman " of the day ; but, having been unlucky in one or two of his adventures, and hearing exaggerated accounts of the hoarded wealth of the old lady at Bath, he was led on from robbery to murder, and was hanged for his crime at Derby in 1775.

He had not been an unkind husband ; and his poor wife took lodgings in Derby to be near him in his last moments—his awful last moments. Her old father went with her everywhere, but into her husband's cell; and wrung her heart by constantly accusing himself of having promoted her marriage with a man of whom he knew so little. He abdicated his squireship in favour of his son Nathaniel. Nat was prosperous, and the helpless silly father could be of no use to him; but to his widowed daughter the foolish old man was all in all; her knight, her protector, her companion—her most faithful loving companion. Only he ever declined assuming the office of her counsellor—shaking his head sadly, and saying:

"Ah! Kate, Kate! if I had had more wisdom to have advised thee better, thou need'st not have been an exile here in Brussels, shrinking from the sight of every English person as if they knew thy story."

I saw the White House not a month ago; it was to let, perhaps for the twentieth time since Mr. Higgins occupied it; but still the tradition goes in Barford that once upon a time a highwayman lived there, and amassed untold treasures; and that the ill-gotten wealth yet remains walled up in some unknown concealed chamber; but in what part of the house no one knows.

THE HALF-BROTHERS

My mother was twice married. She never spoke of her first husband, and it is only from other people that I have learnt what little I know about him. I believe she was scarcely seventeen when she was married to him: and he was barely one-and-twenty. He rented a small farm up in Cumberland, somewhere towards the sea-coast; but he was perhaps too young and inexperienced to have the charge of land and cattle; anyhow, his affairs did not prosper, and he fell into ill-health, and died of consumption before they had been three years man and wife, leaving my mother a young widow of twenty, with a little child only just able to walk, and the farm on her hands for four years more by the lease, with half the stock on it dead, or sold off one by one to pay the more pressing debts, and with no money to purchase more, or even to buy the provisions needed for the small consumption of every day. There was another child coming, too; and sad and sorry, I believe, she was to think of it.

A dreary winter she must have had in her lonesome dwelling, with never another near it for miles around; her sister came to bear her company, and they two planned and plotted how to make every penny they could raise go as far as possible. I can't tell you how it happened that my little sister, whom I never saw, came to sicken and die; but, as if my poor mother's cup was not full enough, only a fortnight before Gregory was born the little girl took ill of scarlet fever, and in a week she lay dead.

My mother was, I believe, just stunned with this last blow. My aunt has told me that she did not cry; Aunt Fanny would have been thankful if she had; but she sat holding the poor wee lassie's hand, and looking in her pretty, pale, dead face, without so much as shedding a tear. And it was all the same, when they had to take her away to be buried. She just kissed the child, and sat her down in the window-seat to watch the little black train of people (neighbours—my aunt, and one far-off cousin, who were all the friends they could muster) go winding away amongst the snow, which had fallen thinly over the country the night before.

When my aunt came back from the funeral, she found my mother in the same place, and as dry-eyed as ever. So she continued until after Gregory was born; and, somehow, his coming seemed to loosen the tears, and she cried day and night, day and night, till my aunt and the other watcher looked at each other in dismay, and would fain have stopped her if they had but known how. But she bade them let her alone, and not be over-anxious, for every drop she shed eased her brain, which had been in a terrible state before for want of the power to cry. She seemed after that to think of nothing but her new little baby; she hardly appeared to remember either her husband or her little daughter that lay dead in Brigham churchyard—at least so Aunt Fanny said; but she was a great talker, and my mother was very silent by nature, and I think Aunt Fanny may have been mistaken in believing that my mother never thought of her husband and child just because she never spoke about them.

Aunt Fanny was older than my mother, and had a way of treating her like a child; but, for all that, she was a kind, warm-hearted creature, who thought more of her sister's welfare than she did of her own; and it was on her bit of money that they principally lived, and on what the two could earn by working for the great Glasgow sewing-merchants. But by-and-by my mother's eyesight began to fail. It was not that she was exactly blind, for she could see well enough to guide herself about the house, and to do a good deal of domestic work; but she could no longer do fine sewing and earn money. It must have been with the heavy crying she had had in her day, for she was but a young creature at this time, and as pretty a young woman, I have heard people say, as any on the country-side.

She took it sadly to heart that she could no longer gain anything towards the keep of herself and her child. My Aunt Fanny would fain have persuaded her that she had enough to do in managing their cottage and minding Gregory; but my mother knew that they were pinched, and that Aunt Fanny herself had not as much to eat, even of the commonest kind of food, as she could have done with; and as for Gregory, he was not a strong lad, and needed, not more food—for he always had enough, whoever went short—but better nourishment, and more flesh-meat.

One day—it was Aunt Fanny who told me all this about my poor mother, long after her death—as the sisters were sitting together, Aunt Fanny working, and my mother hushing Gregory to sleep, William Preston, who was afterwards my father, came in.

He was reckoned an old bachelor; I suppose he was long past forty, and he was one of the wealthiest farmers thereabouts, and had known my grandfather well, and my mother and my aunt in their more prosperous days. He sat down, and began to twirl his hat by way of being agreeable; my Aunt Fanny talked, and he listened and looked at my mother. But he said very little, either on that visit, or on many another that he paid before he spoke out what had been the real purpose of his calling so often all along, and from the very first time he came to their house.

One Sunday, however, my Aunt Fanny stayed away from church, and took care of the child, and my mother went alone. When she came back, she ran straight upstairs, without going into the kitchen to look at Gregory or speak any word to her sister, and Aunt Fanny heard her cry as if her heart was breaking; so she went up and scolded her right well through the bolted door, till at last she got her to open it. And then she threw herself on my aunt's neck, and told her that William Preston had asked her to marry him, and had promised to take good charge of her boy, and to let him want for nothing, neither in the way of keep nor of education, and that she had consented.

Aunt Fanny was a good deal shocked at this; for, as I have said, she had often thought that my mother had forgotten her first husband very quickly, and now here was proof positive of it, if she could so soon think of marrying again. Besides, as Aunt Fanny used to say, she herself would have been a far more suitable match for a man of William Preston's age than Helen, who, though she was a widow, had not seen her four-and-twentieth summer.

However, as Aunt Fanny said, they had not asked her advice; and there was much to be said on the other side of the question. Helen's eyesight would never be good for much again, and as William Preston's wife she would never need to do anything, if she chose to sit with her hands before her; and a boy was a great charge to a widowed mother; and now there would be a decent, steady man to see after him. So, by-and-by, Aunt Fanny seemed to take a brighter view of the marriage than did my mother herself, who hardly ever looked up, and never smiled after the day when she promised William Preston to be his wife. But much as she had loved Gregory before, she seemed to love him more now. She was continually talking to him when they were alone, though he was far too young to understand her moaning words, or give her any comfort, except by his caresses.

At last William Preston and she were wed; and she went to be mistress of a well-stocked house, not above half an hour's walk from where Aunt Fanny lived. I believe she did all that she could to please my father; and a more dutiful wife, I have heard him himself say, could never have been. But she did not love him, and he soon found it out. She loved Gregory, and she did not love him.

Perhaps, love would have come in time, if he had been patient enough to wait; but it just turned him sour to see how her eye brightened and her colour came at the sight of that little child, while for him who had given her so much, she had only gentle words as cold as ice. He got to taunt her with the difference in her manner, as if that would bring love: and he took a positive dislike to Gregory,—he was so jealous of the ready love that always gushed out like a spring of fresh water when he came near. He wanted her to love him more, and perhaps that was all well and good; but he wanted her to love her child less, and that was an evil wish.

One day, he gave way to his temper, and cursed and swore at Gregory, who had got into some mischief, as children will; my mother made some excuse for him; my father said it was hard enough to have to keep another man's child, without having it perpetually held up in its naughtiness by his wife, who ought to be always in the same mind that he was; and so from little they got to more; and the end of it was, that my mother took to her bed before her time, and I was born that very day.

My father was glad, and proud, and sorry, all in a breath; glad and proud that a son was born to him; and sorry for his poor wife's state, and to think how his angry words had brought it on. But he was a man who liked better to be angry than sorry, so he soon found out that it was all Gregory's fault, and owed him an additional grudge for having hastened my birth.

He had another grudge against him before long. My mother began to sink the day after I was born. My father sent to Carlisle for doctors, and would have coined his heart's blood into gold to save her, if that could have been; but it could not.

My Aunt Fanny used to say sometimes, that she thought that Helen did not wish to live, and so just let herself die away without trying to take hold on life; but when I questioned her, she owned that my mother did all the doctors bade her do, with the same sort of uncomplaining patience with which she had acted through life. One of her last requests was to have Gregory laid in her bed by my side, and then she made him take hold of my little hand. Her husband came in while she was looking at us so, and when he bent tenderly over her to ask her how she felt now, and seemed to gaze on us two little half-brothers, with a grave sort of kindliness, she looked up in his face and smiled, almost her first smile at him; and such a sweet smile! as more besides Aunt Fanny have said.

In an hour she was dead. Aunt Fanny came to live with us. It was the best thing that could be done. My father would have been glad to return to his old mode of bachelor life, but what could he do with two little children? He needed a woman to take care of him, and who so fitting as his wife's elder sister? So she had the charge of me from my birth; and for a time I was weakly, as was but natural, and she was always beside me, night and day watching over me, and my father nearly as anxious as she. For his land had come down from father to son for more than three hundred years, and he would have cared for me merely as his flesh and blood that was to inherit the land after him.

But he needed something to love, for all that, to most people, he was a stern, hard man, and he took to me as, I fancy, he had taken to no human being before—as he might have taken to my mother, if she had had no former life for him to be jealous of. I loved him back again right heartily. I loved all around me, I believe, for everybody was kind to me. After a time, I overcame my original weakliness of constitution, and was just a bonny, strong-looking lad whom every passer-by noticed, when my father took me with him to the nearest town.

At home I was the darling of my aunt, the tenderly-beloved of my father, the pet and plaything of the old domestic, the "young master" of the farm-labourers, before whom I played many a lordly antic, assuming a sort of authority which sat oddly enough, I doubt not, on such a baby as I was.

Gregory was three years older than I. Aunt Fanny was always kind to him in deed and in action, but she did not often think about him, she had fallen so completely into the habit of being engrossed by me, from the fact of my having come into her charge as a delicate baby. My father never got over his grudging dislike to his stepson, who had so innocently wrestled with him for the possession of my mother's heart. I mistrust me, too, that my father always considered him as the cause of my mother's death and my early delicacy; and utterly unreasonable as this may seem, I believe my father rather cherished his feeling of alienation to my brother as a duty, than strove to repress it.

Yet not for the world would my father have grudged him anything that money could purchase. That was, as it were, in the bond when he had wedded my mother. Gregory was lumpish and loutish, awkward and ungainly, marring whatever he meddled in, and many a hard word and sharp scolding did he get from the people about the farm, who hardly waited till my father's back was turned before they rated the stepson.

I am ashamed—my heart is sore to think how I fell into the fashion of the family, and slighted my poor orphan step-brother. I don't think I ever scouted him, or was wilfully ill-natured to him; but the habit of being considered in all things, and being treated as something uncommon and superior, made me insolent in my prosperity, and I exacted more than Gregory was always willing to grant, and then, irritated, I sometimes repeated the disparaging words I had heard others use with regard to him, without fully understanding their meaning. Whether he did or not I cannot tell. I am afraid he did. He used to turn silent and quiet—sullen and sulky, my father thought it; stupid, Aunt Fanny used to call it.

But every one said he was stupid and dull, and this stupidity and dulness grew upon him. He would sit without speaking a word, sometimes, for hours; then my father would bid him rise and do some piece of work, maybe, about the farm. And he would take three or four tellings before he would go. When we were sent to school, it was all the same. He could never be made to remember his lessons; the schoolmaster grew weary of scolding and flogging, and at last advised my father just to take him away, and set him to some farmwork that might not be above his comprehension. I think he was more gloomy and stupid than ever after this, yet he was not a cross lad; he was patient and good-natured, and would try to do a kind turn for any one, even if they had been scolding or cuffing him not a minute before. But very often his attempts at kindness ended in some mischief to the very people he was trying to serve, owing to his awkward, ungainly ways.

I suppose I was a clever lad; at any rate, I always got plenty of praise; and was, as we called it, the cock of the school. The schoolmaster said I could learn anything I chose, but my father, who had no great learning himself, saw little use in much for me, and took me away betimes, and kept me with him about the farm. Gregory was made into a kind of shepherd, receiving his training under old Adam, who was nearly past his work. I think old Adam was almost the first person who had a good opinion of Gregory. He stood to it that my brother had good parts, though he did not rightly know how to bring them out; and, for knowing the bearings of the Fells, he said he had never seen a lad like him. My father would try to bring Adam round to speak of Gregory's faults and shortcomings; but, instead of that, he would praise him twice as much as soon as he found out what was my father's object.

One winter-time, when I was about sixteen, and Gregory nineteen, I was sent by my father on an errand to a place about seven miles distant by the road, but only about four by the Fells. He bade me return by the road, whichever way I took in going, for the evenings closed in early, and were often thick and misty; besides which, old Adam, now paralytic and bedridden, foretold a downfall of snow before long.

I soon got to my journey's end, and soon had done my business; earlier by an hour, I thought, than my father had expected, so I took the decision of the way by which I would return into my own hands, and set off back again over the Fells, just as the first shades of evening began to fall. It looked dark and gloomy enough; but everything was so still that I thought I should have plenty of time to get home before the snow came down.

Off I set at a pretty quick pace. But night came on quicker. The right path was clear enough in the daytime, although at several points two or three exactly similar diverged from the same place; but when there was a good light, the traveller was guided by the sight of distant objects,—a piece of rock,—a fall in the ground—which were quite invisible to me now. I plucked up a brave heart, however, and took what seemed to me the right road. It was wrong, however, and led me whither I knew not, but to some wild boggy moor where the solitude seemed painful, intense, as if never footfall of man had come thither to break the silence.

I tried to shout,—with the dimmest possible hope of being heard—rather to reassure myself by the sound of my own voice; but my voice came husky and short, and yet it dismayed me; it seemed so weird and strange in that noiseless expanse of black darkness. Suddenly the air was filled thick with dusky flakes, my face and hands were wet with snow. It cut me off from the slightest knowledge of where I was, for I lost every idea of the direction from which I had come, so that I could not even retrace my steps; it hemmed me in, thicker, thicker, with a darkness that might be felt. The boggy soil on which I stood quaked under me if I remained long in one place, and yet I dared not move far.

All my youthful hardiness seemed to leave me at once. I was on the point of crying, and only very shame seemed to keep it down. To save myself from shedding tears, I shouted—terrible, wild shouts for bare life they were. I turned sick as I paused to listen; no answering sound came but the unfeeling echoes. Only the noiseless, pitiless snow kept falling thicker, thicker—faster, faster! I was growing numb and sleepy. I tried to move about, but I dared not go far, for fear of the precipices which, I knew, abounded in certain places on the Fells. Now and then, I stood still and shouted again; but my voice was getting choked with tears, as I thought of the desolate, helpless death I was to die, and how little they at home, sitting round the warm, red, bright fire, wotted what was become of me,—and how my poor father would grieve for me—it would surely kill him—it would break his heart, poor old man! Aunt Fanny too—was this to be the end of all her cares for me?

I began to review my life in a strange kind of vivid dream, in which the various scenes of my few boyish years passed before me like visions. In a pang of agony, caused by such remembrance of my short life, I gathered up my strength and called out once more, a long, despairing, wailing cry, to which I had no hope of obtaining any answer, save from the echoes around, dulled as the sound might be by the thickened air.

To my surprise, I heard a cry—almost as long, as wild as mine—so wild that it seemed unearthly, and I almost thought it must be the voice of some of the mocking spirits of the Fells, about whom I had heard so many tales. My heart suddenly began to beat fast and loud. I could not reply for a minute or two. I nearly fancied I had lost the power of utterance.

Just at this moment a dog barked. Was it Lassie's bark—my brother's collie?—an ugly enough brute, with a white, ill-looking face, that my father always kicked whenever he saw it, partly for its own demerits, partly because it belonged to my brother. On such occasions, Gregory would whistle Lassie away, and go off and sit with her in some outhouse.

My father had once or twice been ashamed of himself, when the poor collie had yowled out with the suddenness of the pain, and had relieved himself of his self-reproach by blaming my brother, who, he said, had no notion of training a dog, and was enough to ruin any collie in Christendom with his stupid way of allowing them to lie by the kitchen fire. To all which Gregory would answer nothing, nor even seem to hear, but go on looking absent and moody. Yes! there again! It was Lassie's bark! Now or never! I lifted up my voice and shouted "Lassie! Lassie! For God's sake, Lassie!"

Another moment, and the great white-faced Lassie was curving and gambolling with delight round my feet and legs, looking, however, up in my face with her intelligent, apprehensive eyes, as if fearing lest I might greet her with a blow, as I had done oftentimes before. But I cried with gladness, as I stooped down and patted her. My mind was sharing in my body's weakness, and I could not reason, but I knew that help was at hand. A grey figure came more and more distinctly out of the thick, close-pressing darkness. It was Gregory wrapped in his maud.

"Oh, Gregory!" said I, and I fell upon his neck, unable to speak another word. He never spoke much, and made me no answer for some little time. Then he told me we must move, we must walk for the dear life—we must find our road home, if possible; but we must move or we should be frozen to death.

"Don't you know the way home?" asked I.

"I thought I did when I set out, but I am doubtful now. The snow blinds me, and I am feared that in moving about just now I have lost the right gait homewards."

He had his shepherd's staff with him, and by dint of plunging it before us at every step we took—clinging close to each other, we went on safely enough, as far as not falling down any of the steep rocks, but it was slow, dreary work. My brother, I saw, was more guided by Lassie and the way she took than anything else, trusting to her instinct. It was too dark to see far before us; but he called her back continually, and noted from what quarter she returned, and shaped our slow steps accordingly. But the tedious motion scarcely kept my very blood from freezing. Every bone, every fibre in my body seemed first to ache, and then to swell, and then to turn numb with the intense cold. My brother bore it better than I, from having been more out upon the hills. He did not speak, except to call Lassie. I strove to be brave, and not complain; but now I felt the deadly fatal sleep stealing over me.

"I can go no farther," I said, in a drowsy tone. I remember I suddenly became dogged and resolved. Sleep I would, were it only for five minutes. If death were to be the consequence, sleep I would. Gregory stood still. I suppose he recognised the peculiar phase of suffering to which I had been brought by the cold.

"It is of no use," said he, as if to himself. "We are no nearer home than we were when we started, as far as I can tell. Our only chance is in Lassie. Here! roll thee in my maud, lad, and lay thee down on this sheltered side of this bit of rock. Creep close under it, lad, and I'll lie by thee, and strive to keep the warmth in us. Stay! hast gotten aught about thee they'll know at home?"

I felt him unkind thus to keep me from slumber, but on his repeating the question, I pulled out my pocket-handkerchief, of some showy pattern, which Aunt Fanny had hemmed for me—Gregory took it, and tied it round Lassie's neck.

"Hie thee, Lassie, hie thee home!" And the white-faced, ill-favoured brute was off like a shot in the darkness. Now I might lie down—now I might sleep. In my drowsy stupor I felt that I was being tenderly covered up by my brother; but what with I neither knew nor cared—I was too dull, too selfish, too numb to think and reason, or I might have known that in that bleak bare place there was naught to wrap me in, save what was taken off another. I was glad enough when he ceased his cares and lay down by me. I took his hand.

"Thou canst not remember, lad, how we lay together thus by our dying mother. She put thy small, wee hand in mine—I reckon she sees us now; and belike we shall soon be with her. Anyhow, God's will be done."

"Dear Gregory," I muttered, and crept nearer to him for warmth. He was talking still, and again about our mother, when I fell asleep. In an instant—or so it seemed—there were many voices about me—many faces hovering round me—the sweet luxury of warmth was stealing into every part of me. I was in my own little bed at home. I am thankful to say, my first word was "Gregory?"

A look passed from one to another—my father's stern old face strove in vain to keep its sternness; his mouth quivered, his eyes filled slowly with unwonted tears.

"I would have given him half my land—I would have blessed him as my son,—oh God! I would have knelt at his feet, and asked him to forgive my hardness of heart."

I heard no more. A whirl came through my brain, catching me

back to death. I came slowly to my consciousness, weeks afterwards. My father's hair was white when I recovered, and his hands shook as he looked into my face.

We spoke no more of Gregory. We could not speak of him ; but he was strangely in our thoughts. Lassie came and went with never a word of blame ; nay, my father would try to stroke her, but she shrank away ; and he, as if reproved by the poor dumb beast, would sigh, and be silent and abstracted for a time.

Aunt Fanny—always a talker—told me all. How, on that fatal night, my father, irritated by my prolonged absence, and probably more anxious than he cared to show, had been fierce and imperious, even beyond his wont, to Gregory : had upbraided him with his father's poverty, his own stupidity which made his services good for nothing—for so, in spite of the old shepherd, my father always chose to consider them.

At last, Gregory had risen up, and whistled Lassie out with him—poor Lassie, crouching underneath his chair for fear of a kick or a blow. Some time before, there had been some talk between my father and my aunt respecting my return ; and when Aunt Fanny told me all this, she said she fancied that Gregory might have noticed the coming storm, and gone out silently to meet me. Three hours afterwards, when all were running about in wild alarm, not knowing whither to go in search of me—not even missing Gregory, or heeding his absence, poor fellow—poor, poor fellow !—Lassie came home, with my handkerchief tied round her neck. They knew and understood, and the whole strength of the farm was turned out to follow her, with wraps, and blankets, and brandy, and everything that could be thought of. I lay in chilly sleep, but still alive, beneath the rock that Lassie guided them to. I was covered over with my brother's plaid, and his thick shepherd's coat was carefully wrapped round my feet. He was in his shirt-sleeves—his arm thrown over me—a quiet smile (he had hardly ever smiled in life) upon his still, cold face.

My father's last words were, " God forgive me my hardness of heart towards the fatherless child ! "

And what marked the depth of his feeling of repentance, perhaps more than all, considering the passionate love he bore my mother, was this : we found a paper of directions after his death, in which he desired that he might lie at the foot of the grave in which, by his desire, poor Gregory had been laid with OUR MOTHER.

WILLIAM MAKEPEACE THACKERAY

1811–1863

DENNIS HAGGARTY'S WIFE

THERE was an odious Irishwoman and her daughter who used to frequent the "Royal Hotel" at Leamington some years ago, and who went by the name of Mrs. Major Gam. Gam had been a distinguished officer in his Majesty's service, whom nothing but death and his own amiable wife could overcome. The widow mourned her husband in the most becoming bombazeen she could muster, and had at least half an inch of lampblack round the immense visiting-tickets which she left at the houses of the nobility and gentry her friends.

Some of us, I am sorry to say, used to call her Mrs. Major Gammon; for if the worthy widow had a propensity, it was to talk largely of herself and family (of her own family, for she held her husband's very cheap), and of the wonders of her paternal mansion, Molloyville, county of Mayo. She was of the Molloys of that county; and though I never heard of the family before, I have little doubt, from what Mrs. Major Gam stated, that they were the most ancient and illustrious family of that part of Ireland. I remember there came down to see his aunt a young fellow with huge red whiskers and tight nankeens, a green coat, and an awful breastpin, who, after two days' stay at the Spa, proposed marriage to Miss S——, or, in default, a duel with her father; and who drove a flash curricle with a bay and a grey, and who was presented with much pride by Mrs. Gam as Castlereagh Molloy of Molloyville. We all agreed that he was the most insufferable snob of the whole season, and were delighted when a bailiff came down in search of him.

Well, this is all I know personally of the Molloyville family; but at the house, if you met the Widow Gam, and talked on any subject in life, you were sure to hear of it. If you asked her to have pease at dinner, she would say, "Oh, sir, after the pease at Molloyville, I really don't care for any others—do I, dearest Jemima? We always had a dish in the month of June, when my father gave his head gardener a guinea (we had three at Molloyville), and sent him with his compliments and a quart of pease to our neighbour, dear Lord Marrowfat. What a sweet place Marrowfat Park is! isn't it, Jemima?" If a carriage passed by the window, Mrs. Major Gammon would be sure to tell you that there were three carriages at Molloyville—"the barouche, the chawiot, and the covered cyar." In the same manner she would favour you with the number and names of the footmen of the establishment; and on a visit to Warwick Castle (for this bustling woman made one in every party of pleasure that was formed from the hotel), she gave us to understand that the great walk by the river was altogether inferior to the principal avenue of Molloyville Park. I should not have been able to tell so much about Mrs. Gam and her daughter, but that, between ourselves, I was particularly sweet upon a young lady at the time, whose papa lived at the "Royal," and was under the care of Dr. Jephson.

The Jemima appealed to by Mrs. Gam in the above sentence was, of course, her daughter, apostrophised by her mother, "Jemima, my soul's darling!" or "Jemima, my blessed child!" or, "Jemima, my own love!" The sacrifices that Mrs. Gam had made for that daughter were, she said, astonishing. The money she had spent in masters upon her, the illnesses through which she had nursed her, the ineffable love the mother bore her, were only known to Heaven, Mrs. Gam said. They used to come into the room with their arms round each other's waists; at dinner, between the courses, the mother would sit with one hand locked in her daughter's; and if only two or three young men were present at the time, would be pretty sure to kiss her Jemima more than once during the time whilst the bohea was poured out.

As for Miss Gam, if she was not handsome, candour forbids me to say she was ugly. She was neither one no t'other. She was a person who wore ringlets and a band round her forehead; she knew four songs, which became rather tedious at the end of a couple of months' acquaintance; she had excessively bare shoulders; she inclined to wear numbers of cheap ornaments, rings, brooches, *ferronnières*, smelling-bottles, and was always, we thought, very smartly dressed: though old Mrs. Lynx hinted that her gowns and her mother's were turned over and over again, and that her eyes were almost put out by darning stockings.

These eyes Miss Gam had very large, though rather red and weak, and used to roll them about at every eligible unmarried man in the place. But though the widow subscribed to all the balls; though she hired a fly to go to the meet of the hounds; though she was constant at church, and Jemima sang louder than any person there except the clerk; and though, probably, any person who made her a happy husband would be invited down to enjoy the three footmen, gardeners, and carriages at Molloyville, yet no English gentleman was found sufficiently audacious to propose. Old Lynx used to say that the pair had been at Tunbridge, Harrogate, Brighton, Ramsgate, Cheltenham, for this eight years past; where they had met, it seemed, with no better fortune. Indeed, the widow looked rather high for her blessed child; and as she looked with the contempt which no small number of Irish people feel upon all persons who get their bread by labour or commerce, and as she was a person whose energetic manners, costume, and brogue were not much to the taste of quiet English country gentlemen, Jemima—sweet, spotless flower—still remained on her hands, a thought withered, perhaps, and seedy.

Now at this time the 120th Regiment was quartered at Weedon Barracks, and with the corps was a certain Assistant-Surgeon Haggarty, a large, lean, tough, raw-boned man, with big hands, knock-knees, and carroty whiskers, and, withal, as honest a creature as ever handled a lancet. Haggarty, as his name imports, was of the very same nation as Mrs. Gam; and, what is more, the honest fellow had some of the peculiarities which belonged to the widow, and bragged about his family almost as much as she did. I do not know of what particular part of Ireland they were kings, but monarchs they must have been, as have been the ancestors of so many thousand Hibernian families; but they had been men of no small consideration in Dublin, "where my father," Haggarty said, "is as well known as King William's statue, and where he 'rowls his carriage, too,' let me tell ye."

Hence, Haggarty was called by the wags "Rowl the carriage," and several of them made inquiries of Mrs. Gam regarding him. "Mrs. Gam, when you used to go up from Molloyville to the Lord-Lieutenant's balls, and had your town-house in Fitzwilliam Square, used you to meet the famous Doctor Haggarty in society?"

"Is it Surgeon Haggarty of Gloucester Street, ye mean? The black Papist! D'ye suppose that the Molloys would sit down to table with a creature of that sort?"

"Why, isn't he the most famous physician in Dublin, and doesn't he rowl his carriage there?"

"The horrid wretch! He keeps a shop, I tell ye, and sends his sons out with the medicine. He's got four of them off into the army—Ulick and Phil, and Terence and Denny; and now it's Charles that takes out the physic. But how should I know about these odious creatures? Their mother was a Burke, of Burke's Town, County Cavan, and brought Surgeon Haggarty two thousand pounds. She was a Protestant, and I am surprised how she could have taken up with a horrid, odious, Popish apothecary!"

From the extent of the widow's information, I am led to suppose that the inhabitants of Dublin are not less anxious about their neighbours than are the natives of English cities; and I think it is very probable that Mrs. Gam's account of the young Haggartys who carried out the medicine is perfectly correct, for a lad in the 120th made a caricature of Haggarty coming out of a chemist's shop with an oil-cloth basket under his arm, which set the worthy surgeon in such a fury that there would have been a duel between him and the ensign could the fiery doctor have had his way.

Now Dionysius Haggarty was of an exceedingly inflammable temperament, and it chanced that of all the invalids, the visitors, the young squires of Warwickshire, the young manufacturers from Birmingham, the young officers from the barracks—it chanced, unluckily for Miss Gam and himself, that he was the only individual who was in the least smitten by her personal charms. He was very tender and modest about his love, however; for it must be owned that he respected Mrs. Gam hugely, and fully admitted, like a good simple fellow as he was, the superiority of that lady's birth and breeding to his own. How could he hope that he, a humble assistant-surgeon, with a thousand pounds his Aunt Kitty left him for all his fortune—how could he hope that one of the race of Molloyville would ever condescend to marry him?

Inflamed, however, by love, and inspired by wine, one day, at a picnic at Kenilworth, Haggarty, whose love and raptures were the talk of the whole regiment, was induced by his waggish comrades to make a proposal in form.

"Are you aware, Mr. Haggarty, that you are speaking to a Molloy?" was all the reply majestic Mrs. Gam made when, according to the usual formula, the fluttering Jemima referred her suitor to "mamma." She left him with a look which was meant to crush the poor fellow to earth; she gathered up her cloak and bonnet, and precipitately called for her fly. She took care to tell every single soul in Leamington that the son of the odious Papist apothecary had had the audacity to propose for her daughter (indeed, a proposal, coming from whatever quarter it may, does no harm), and left Haggarty in a state of extreme depression and despair.

His down-heartedness, indeed, surprised most of his acquaintances in and out of the regiment; for the young lady was no beauty, and a doubtful fortune, and Dennis was a man outwardly of an unromantic turn, who seemed to have a great deal more liking for beef-steak and whisky-punch than for women, however fascinating.

But there is no doubt this shy, uncouth, rough fellow had a warmer and more faithful heart hid within him than many a dandy who is as handsome as Apollo. I, for my part, never can understand why a man falls in love, and heartily give him credit for so doing, never mind with what or whom. *That* I take to be a point quite as much beyond an individual's own control as the catching of the small-pox or the colour of his hair. To the surprise of all, Assistant-Surgeon Dionysius Haggarty was deeply and seriously in love ; and I am told that one day he very nearly killed the before-mentioned young ensign with a carving-knife for venturing to make a second caricature representing Lady Gammon and Jemima in a fantastical park, surrounded by three gardeners, three carriages, three footmen, and the covered cyar. He would have no joking concerning them. He became moody and quarrelsome of habit. He was for some time much more in the surgery and hospital than in the mess. He gave up the eating, for the most part, of those vast quantities of beef and pudding for which his stomach had used to afford such ample and swift accommodation ; and when the cloth was drawn, instead of taking twelve tumblers, and singing Irish melodies as he used to do in a horrible cracked yelling voice, he would retire to his own apartment, or gloomily pace the barrack-yard, or madly whip and spur a grey mare he had on the road to Leamington, where his Jemima (although invisible for him) still dwelt.

The season at Leamington coming to a conclusion by the withdrawal of the young fellows who frequented that watering-place, the Widow Gam retired to her usual quarters for the other months of the year. Where these quarters were, I think we have no right to ask ; for I believe she had quarrelled with her brother at Molloyville, and, besides, was a great deal too proud to be a burden on anybody.

Not only did the widow quit Leamington, but very soon afterwards the 120th received its marching orders, and left Weedon and Warwickshire. Haggarty's appetite was by this time partially restored ; but his love was not altered, and his humour was still morose and gloomy. I am informed that at this period of his life he wrote some poems relative to his unhappy passion—a wild set of verses of several lengths, and in his handwriting, being discovered upon a sheet of paper in which a pitch-plaster was wrapped up, which Lieutenant and Adjutant Wheezer was compelled to put on for a cold.

Fancy, then, three years afterwards, the surprise of all Haggarty's acquaintances on reading in the public papers the following announcement :—

"Married, at Monkstown, on the 12th instant, Dionysius Haggarty, Esq., of H.M. 120th Foot, to Jemima Amelia Wilhelmina Molloy, daughter of the late Major Lancelot Gam, R.M., and granddaughter of the late, and niece of the present, Burke Bodkin Blake Molloy, Esq., Molloyville, County Mayo."

"Has the course of true love at last begun to run smooth?" thought I, as I laid down the paper, and the old times, and the old leering, bragging widow, and the high shoulders of her daughter, and the jolly days with the 120th, and Dr. Jephson's one-horse chaise, and the Warwickshire hunt, and—and Louisa S——, but never mind *her*—came back to my mind. "Has that good-natured, simple fellow at last met with his reward? Well, if he has not to marry the mother-in-law, too, he may get on well enough."

Another year announced the retirement of Assistant-Surgeon Haggarty from the 120th, where he was replaced by Assistant-Surgeon Angus Rothsay Leech, a Scotchman, probably, with whom I have not the least acquaintance, and who has nothing whatever to do with this little history.

Still more years passed on, during which time I will not say that I kept a constant watch upon the fortunes of Mr. Haggarty and his lady; for, perhaps, if the truth were known, I never thought for a moment about them, until one day, being at Kingstown, near Dublin, dawdling on the beach and staring at the Hill of Howth, as most people at that watering-place do, I saw coming towards me a tall gaunt man, with a pair of bushy red whiskers, of which I thought I had seen the like in former years, and a face which could be no other than Haggarty's. It was Haggarty, ten years older than when we last met, and greatly more grim and thin. He had on one shoulder a young gentleman in a dirty tartan costume, and a face exceedingly like his own peeping from under a battered plume of black feathers, while with his other hand he was dragging a light green go-cart, in which reposed a female infant of some two years old. Both were roaring with great power of lungs.

As soon as Dennis saw me, his face lost the dull, puzzled expression which had seemed to characterise it. He dropped the pole of the go-cart from one hand and his son from the other, and came jumping forward to greet me with all his might, leaving his progeny roaring in the road.

"Bless my sowl," says he, "sure it's Fitz-Boodle! Fitz, don't you remember me? Dennis Haggarty of the 120th? Leamington, you know?—Molloy, my boy, hould your tongue and stop your screeching, and Jemima's, too; d'ye hear?—Well, it does good to sore eyes to see an old face. How fat you're grown, Fitz; and were ye ever in Ireland before? and a'n't ye delighted with it? Confess, now, isn't it beautiful?"

This question regarding the merits of their country, which I have remarked is put by most Irish persons, being answered in a satisfactory manner, and the shouts of the infants appeased from an apple-stall hard by, Dennis and I talked of old times; and I congratulated him on his marriage with the lovely girl whom we all admired, and hoped he had a fortune with her, and so forth. His appearance, however, did not bespeak a great fortune. He had an old grey hat, short old trousers, an old waistcoat with regimental buttons, and patched Blucher boots, such as are not usually sported by persons in easy life.

"Ah!" says he, with a sigh, in reply to my queries, "times are changed since them days, Fitz-Boodle. My wife's not what she was—the beautiful creature you knew her.—Molloy, my boy, run off in a hurry to your mamma, and tell her an English gentleman is coming home to dine;—for you'll dine with me, Fitz, in course?" And I agreed to partake of that meal; though Master Molloy altogether declined to obey his papa's orders with respect to announcing the stranger.

"Well, I must announce you myself," says Haggarty, with a smile. "Come, it's just dinner-time, and my little cottage is not a hundred yards off." Accordingly, we all marched in procession to Dennis's little cottage, which was one of a row and a half of one-storied houses, with little courtyards before them, and mostly with very fine names on the door-posts of each. "Surgeon Haggarty" was emblazoned on Dennis's gate, on a stained green copper-plate; and, not content with this, on the door-post above the bell was an oval with the inscription of "New Molloyville." The bell was broken, of course; the court, or garden path, was mouldy, weedy, seedy; there were some dirty rocks, by way of ornament, round a faded grass-plot in the centre; some clothes and rags hanging out of most part of the windows of New Molloyville, the immediate entrance to which was by a battered scraper, under a broken trellis-work, up which a withered creeper declined any longer to climb.

"Small, but snug," says Haggarty. "I'll lead the way, Fitz. Put your hat on the flower-pot there, and turn to the left into the drawing-room." A fog of onions and turf-smoke filled the whole of the house, and gave signs that dinner was not far off. Far off? You could hear it frizzling in the kitchen, where the maid was also endeavouring to hush the crying of a third refractory child. But as we entered, all three of Haggarty's darlings were in full war.

"Is it you, Dennis?" cried a sharp raw voice, from a dark corner in the drawing-room to which we were introduced, and in which a dirty tablecloth was laid for dinner, some bottles of porter and a cold mutton-bone being laid out on a rickety grand piano hard by. "Ye're always late, Mr. Haggarty. Have you brought the whisky from Nowlan's? I'll go bail ye've not now."

"My dear, I've brought an old friend of yours and mine to take pot-luck with us to-day," said Dennis.

" When is he to come ? " said the lady. At which speech I was rather surprised, for I stood before her.

" Here he is, Jemima, my love," answered Dennis, looking at me. " Mr. Fitz-Boodle ; don't you remember him in Warwickshire, darling ? "

" Mr. Fitz-Boodle ! I am very glad to see him," said the lady, rising and curtseying with much cordiality.

Mrs. Haggarty was blind !

Mrs. Haggarty was not only blind, but it was evident that small-pox had been the cause of her loss of vision. Her eyes were bound with a bandage, her features were entirely swollen, scarred, and distorted by the horrible effects of the malady. She had been knitting in a corner when we entered, and was wrapped in a very dirty bed-gown. Her voice to me was quite different from that in which she addressed her husband. She spoke to Haggarty in broad Irish : she addressed me in that most odious of all languages—Irish-English, endeavouring to the utmost to disguise her brogue, and to speak with the true dawdling *distingué* English air.

" Are you long in I-a-land ? " said the poor creature in this accent. " You must faind it a sad ba'ba'ous place, Mr. Fitz-Boodle, I'm shu-ah ! It was vary kaind of you to come upon us *en famille*, and accept a dinner *sans cérémonie*.—Mr. Haggarty, I hope you'll put the waine into aice ; Mr. Fitz-Boodle must be melted with this hot weathah."

For some time she conducted the conversation in this polite strain, and I was obliged to say, in reply to a query of hers, that I did not find her the least altered, though I should never have recognised her but for this rencontre. She told Haggarty with a significant air to get the wine from the cellah, and whispered to me that he was his own butlah ; and the poor fellow, taking the hint, scudded away into the town for a pound of veal cutlets and a couple of bottles of wine from the tavern.

" Will the childhren get their potatoes and butther here ? " said a barefoot girl, with long black hair flowing over her face, which she thrust in at the door.

" Let them sup in the nursery, Elizabeth, and send—ah ! Edwards to me."

" Is it cook you mane, ma'am ? " said the girl.

" Send her at once ! " shrieked the unfortunate woman ; and the noise of frying presently ceasing, a hot woman made her appearance, wiping her brows with her apron, and asking, with an accent decidedly Hibernian, what the misthress wanted.

" Lead me up to my dressing-room, Edwards ; I really am not fit to be seen in this dishabille by Mr. Fitz-Boodle."

" Fait' I can't ! " says Edwards. " Sure the masther's out at the butcher's, and can't look to the kitchen-fire!"

"Nonsense, I must go!" cried Mrs. Haggarty; and so Edwards, putting on a resigned air, and giving her arm and face a further rub with her apron, held out her arm to Mrs. Dennis, and the pair went upstairs.

She left me to indulge my reflections for half an hour, at the end of which period she came downstairs dressed in an old yellow satin, with the poor shoulders exposed just as much as ever. She had mounted a tawdry cap, which Haggarty himself must have selected for her. She had all sorts of necklaces, bracelets, and ear-rings in gold, in garnets, in mother-of-pearl, in ormolu. She brought in a furious savour of musk, which drove the odours of onions and turf-smoke before it; and she waved across her wretched, angular, mean, scarred features an old cambric handkerchief with a yellow lace border.

"And so you would have known me anywhere, Mr. Fitz-Boodle?" said she, with a grin that was meant to be most fascinating. "I was sure you would; for though my dreadful illness deprived me of my sight, it is a mercy that it did not change my features or complexion at all!"

This mortification had been spared the unhappy woman; but I don't know whether, with all her vanity, her infernal pride, folly, and selfishness, it was charitable to leave her in her error.

Yet why correct her? There is a quality in certain people which is above all advice, exposure, or correction. Only let a man or woman have DULNESS sufficient, and they need bow to no extant authority. A dullard recognises no betters; a dullard can't see that he is in the wrong; a dullard has no scruples of conscience, no doubts of pleasing, or succeeding, or doing right—no qualms for other people's feelings, no respect but for the fool himself. How can you make a fool perceive that he is a fool? Such a personage can no more see his own folly than he can see his own ears. And the great quality of dulness is to be unalterably contented with itself. What myriads of souls are there of this admirable sort—selfish, stingy, ignorant, passionate, brutal; bad sons, mothers, fathers, never known to do kind actions!

To pause, however, in this disquisition, which was carrying us far off Kingstown, New Molloyville, Ireland—nay, into the wide world wherever Dulness inhabits—let it be stated that Mrs. Haggarty, from my brief acquaintance with her and her mother, was of the order of persons just mentioned. There was an air of conscious merit about her, very hard to swallow along with the infamous dinner poor Dennis managed, after much delay, to get on the table. She did not fail to invite me to Molloyville, where she said her cousin would be charmed to see me; and she told me almost as many anecdotes about that place as her mother used to impart in former days. I observed, moreover, that Dennis cut her the favourite pieces of the beef-steak, that she ate thereof with great gusto, and that she drank with similar eagerness of the various strong liquors at table. "We Irish ladies are all fond of a leetle glass of punch," she said, with a playful air; and Dennis mixed her a powerful tumbler of such violent grog as I myself could swallow only with some difficulty. She talked of her suffering a great deal, of her sacrifices, of the luxuries to which she had been accustomed before marriage—in a word, of a hundred of those themes on which some ladies are in the custom of enlarging when they wish to plague some husbands.

But honest Dennis, far from being angry at this perpetual, wearisome, impudent recurrence to her own superiority, rather encouraged the conversation than otherwise. It pleased him to hear his wife discourse about her merits and family splendours. He was so thoroughly beaten down and henpecked that he, as it were, gloried in his servitude, and fancied that his wife's magnificence reflected credit on himself. He looked towards me, who was half sick of the woman and her egotism, as if expecting me to exhibit the deepest sympathy, and flung me glances across the table as much as to say, "What a gifted creature my Jemima is, and what a fine fellow I am to be in possession of her!" When the children came down she scolded them, of course, and dismissed them abruptly (for which circumstance, perhaps, the writer of these pages was not in his heart very sorry); and, after having sat a preposterously long time, left us, asking whether we would have coffee there or in her boudoir.

"Oh! here, of course," said Dennis, with rather a troubled air; and in about ten minutes the lovely creature was led back to us again by "Edwards," and the coffee made its appearance. After coffee her husband begged her to let Mr. Fitz-Boodle hear her voice. "He longs for some of his old favourites."

"No! *do* you?" said she, and was led in triumph to the jingling old piano, and with a screechy, wiry voice sung those very abominable old ditties which I had heard her sing at Leamington ten years back.

Haggarty, as she sang, flung himself back in his chair delighted. Husbands always are, and with the same song—one that they have heard when they were nineteen years old, probably; most Englishmen's tunes have that date, and it is rather affecting, I think, to hear an old gentleman of sixty or seventy quavering the old ditty that was fresh when *he* was fresh and in his prime. If he has a musical wife, depend on it he thinks her old songs of 1788 are better than any he has heard since—in fact he has heard *none* since. When the old couple are in high good-humour, the old gentleman will take the old lady round the waist, and say, "My dear, do sing me one of your own songs" ; and she sits down and sings with her old voice, and, as she sings, the roses of her youth bloom again for a moment. Ranelagh resuscitates, and she is dancing a minuet in powder and a train.

This is another digression. It was occasioned by looking at poor Dennis's face while his wife was screeching (and, believe me, the former was the most pleasant occupation). Bottom tickled by the fairies could not have been in greater ecstasies. He thought the music was divine ; and had further reason for exulting in it, which was, that his wife was always in a good-humour after singing, and never would sing but in that happy frame of mind. Dennis had hinted so much in our little colloquy during the ten minutes of his lady's absence in the "boudoir" ; so, at the conclusion of each piece, we shouted "Bravo!" and clapped our hands like mad.

Such was my insight into the life of Surgeon Dionysius Haggarty and his wife ; and I must have come upon him at a favourable moment too, for poor Dennis has spoken subsequently of our delightful evening at Kingstown, and evidently thinks to this day that his friend was fascinated by the entertainment there. His inward economy was as follows : he had his half-pay, a thousand pounds, about a hundred a year that his father left, and his wife had sixty pounds a year from the mother—which the mother, of course, never paid. He had no practice, for he was absorbed in attention to his Jemima and the children, whom he used to wash, to dress, to carry out, to walk, or to ride, as we have seen, and who could not have a servant, as their dear blind mother could never be left alone. Mrs. Haggarty, a great invalid, used to lie in bed till one, and have breakfast, and hot luncheon there. A fifth part of his income was spent in having her wheeled about in a chair, by which it was his duty to walk daily for an allotted number of hours. Dinner would ensue, and the amateur clergy, who abound in Ireland, and of whom Mrs. Haggarty was a great admirer, lauded her everywhere as a model of resignation and virtue, and praised beyond measure the admirable piety with which she bore her sufferings.

Well, every man to his taste. It did not certainly appear to me that *she* was the martyr of the family.

"The circumstances of my marriage with Jemima," Dennis said to me in some after-conversations we had on this interesting subject, "were the most romantic and touching you can conceive. You saw what an impression the dear girl had made upon me when we were at Weedon ; for from the first day I set eyes on her, and heard her sing her delightful song of 'Dark-eyed Maiden of Araby,' I felt, and said to Turniquet of ours that very night, that *she* was the dark-eyed maid of Araby for *me*—not that she was, you know, for she was born in Shropshire. But I felt that I had seen the woman who was to make me happy or miserable for life. You know how I proposed for her at Kenilworth, and how I was rejected, and how I almost shot myself in consequence—no, you don't know that, for I said nothing about it to any one ; but I can tell you it was a very near thing, and a very lucky thing for me I didn't do it, for—would you believe it ?—the dear girl was in love with me all the time."

" Was she really ? " said I, who recollected that Miss Gam's love of those days showed itself in a very singular manner ; but the fact is, when women are most in love they most disguise it.

" Over head and ears in love with poor Dennis," resumed that worthy fellow, " who'd ever have thought it ? But I have it from the best authority, from her own mother, with whom I'm not over and above good friends now ; but of this fact she assured me, and I'll tell you when and how.

" We were quartered at Cork three years after we were at Weedon, and it was our last year at home ; and a great mercy that my dear girl spoke in time, or where should we have been *now* ? Well, one day, marching home from parade, I saw a lady seated at an open window by another who seemed an invalid ; and the lady at the window, who was dressed in the profoundest mourning, cried out with a scream, ' Gracious heavens ! it's Mr. Haggarty of the 120th.'

" ' Sure I know that voice,' says I to Whiskerton.

" ' It's a great mercy you don't know it a deal too well,' says he ; ' it's Lady Gammon. She's on some husband-hunting scheme, depend on it, for that daughter of hers. She was at Bath last year on the same errand, and at Cheltenham the year before, where, Heaven bless you ! she's as well known as the " Hen and Chickens." '

" ' I'll thank you not to speak disrespectfully of Miss Jemima Gam,' said I to Whiskerton ; ' she's of one of the first families in Ireland, and whoever says a word against a woman I once proposed for, insults me—do you understand ? '

" ' Well, marry her, if you like,' says Whiskerton, quite peevish ; ' marry her, and be hanged ! '

" Marry her ! the very idea of it set my brain a-whirling, and made me a thousand times more mad than I am by nature.

" You may be sure I walked up the hill to the parade-ground that afternoon, and with a beating heart, too. I came to the widow's house. It was called ' New Molloyville,' as this is. Wherever she takes a house for six months, she calls it ' New Molloyville ' ; and has had one in Mallow, in Bandon, in Sligo, in Castlebar, in Fermoy, in Drogheda, and the deuce knows where besides. But the blinds were down, and though I thought I saw somebody behind 'em, no notice was taken of poor Denny Haggarty, and I paced up and down all mess-time in hopes of catching a glimpse of Jemima, but in vain.

The next day I was on the ground again ; I was just as much in love as ever, that's the fact. I'd never been in that way before, look you ; and when once caught, I knew it was for life.

" There's no use in telling you how long I beat about the bush, but when I *did* get admittance to the house (it was through the means of young Castlereagh Molloy, whom you may remember at Leamington, and who was at Cork for the regatta, and used to dine at our mess, and had taken a mighty fancy to me)—when I *did* get into the house, I say, I rushed *in medias res* at once. I couldn't keep myself quiet ; my heart was too full.

" Oh, Fitz ! I shall never forget the day—the moment I was inthrojuiced into the dthrawing-room " (as he began to be agitated, Dennis's brogue broke out with greater richness than ever ; but though a stranger may catch, and repeat from memory, a few words, it is next to impossible for him to *keep up a conversation* in Irish, so that we had best give up all attempts to imitate Dennis). " When I saw old Mother Gam," said he, " my feelings overcame me all at once. I rowled down on the ground, sir, as if I'd been hit by a musket-ball. ' Dearest madam,' says I, ' I'll die if you don't give me Jemima.'

" ' Heavens, Mr. Haggarty !' says she, ' how you seize me with surprise !—Castlereagh, my dear nephew, had you not better leave us ? ' and away he went, lighting a cigar, and leaving me still on the floor.

" ' Rise, Mr. Haggarty,' continued the widow. ' I will not attempt to deny that this constancy towards my daughter is extremely affecting, however sudden your present appeal may be. I will not attempt to deny that, perhaps, Jemima may have a similar feeling ; but, as I said, I never could give my daughter to a Catholic.'

" ' I'm as good a Protestant as yourself, ma'am,' says I ; ' my mother was an heiress, and we were all brought up her way.'

" ' That makes the matter very different,' says she, turning up the whites of her eyes. ' How could I ever have reconciled it to my conscience to see my blessed child married to a Papist ? How could I ever have taken him to Molloyville ? Well, this obstacle being removed, *I* must put myself no longer in the way between two young people. *I* must sacrifice myself, as I always have when my darling girl was in question. You shall see her, the poor dear, lovely, gentle sufferer, and learn your fate from her own lips.'

" ' The sufferer, ma'am,' says I ; ' has Miss Gam been ill ? '

" ' What ! haven't you heard ? ' cried the widow. ' Haven't you heard of the dreadful illness which so nearly carried her from me ? For nine weeks, Mr. Haggarty, I watched her day and night without taking a wink of sleep—for nine weeks she lay trembling between death and life ; and I paid the doctor eighty-three guineas. She is restored now, but she is the wreck of the beautiful creature she was. Suffering, and, perhaps, *another disappointment*—but we won't mention that *now*—have so pulled her down. But I will leave you, and prepare my sweet girl for this strange, this entirely unexpected visit.'

"I won't tell you what took place between me and Jemima, to whom I was introduced as she sat in the darkened room, poor sufferer! nor describe to you with what a thrill of joy I seized (after groping about for it) her poor, emaciated hand. She did not withdraw it; I came out of that room an engaged man, sir; and *now* I was enabled to show her that I had always loved her sincerely, for there was my will made three years back in her favour—that night she refused me, as I told ye. I would have shot myself, but they'd have brought me in *non compos*, and my brother Mick would have contested the will; and so I determined to live, in order that she might benefit by my dying. I had but a thousand pounds then; since that my father has left me two more. I willed every shilling to her, as you may fancy, and settled it upon her when we married, as we did soon after. It was not for some time that I was allowed to see the poor girl's face, or indeed was aware of the horrid loss she had sustained. Fancy my agony, my dear fellow, when I saw that beautiful wreck!"

There was something not a little affecting to think, in the conduct of this brave fellow, that he never once, as he told his story, seemed to allude to the possibility of his declining to marry a woman who was not the same as the woman he loved, but that he was quite as faithful to her now as he had been when captivated by the poor, tawdry charms of the silly Miss of Leamington. It was hard that such a noble heart as this should be flung away upon yonder foul mass of greedy vanity. Was it hard, or not, that he should remain deceived in his obstinate humility, and continue to admire the selfish, silly being whom he had chosen to worship?

"I should have been appointed surgeon of the regiment," continued Dennis, "soon after, when it was ordered abroad to Jamaica, where it now is. But my wife would not hear of going, and said she would break her heart if she left her mother. So I retired on half-pay, and took this cottage; and in case any practice should fall in my way—why, there is my name on the brass plate, and I'm ready for anything that comes. But the only case that ever *did* come was one day when I was driving my wife in the chaise; and another, one night, of a beggar with a broken head. My wife makes me a present of a baby every year, and we've no debts; and between you and me and the post, as long as my mother-in-law is out of the house, I'm as happy as I need be."

"What! you and the old lady don't get on well?" said I.

"I can't say we do; it's not in nature, you know," said Dennis, with a faint grin. "She comes into the house and turns it topsy-turvy. When she's here, I'm obliged to sleep in the scullery. She's never paid her daughter's income since the first year, though she brags about her sacrifices as if she had ruined herself for Jemima; and besides, when she's here, there's a whole clan of the Molloys, horse, foot, and dragoons, that are quartered upon us, and eat me out of house and home."

"And is Molloyville such a fine place as the widow described it?" asked I, laughing, and not a little curious.

"Oh, a mighty fine place entirely!" said Dennis. "There's the oak park of two hundred acres, the finest land ye ever saw, only they've cut all the wood down. The garden in the old Molloy's time, they say, was the finest ever seen in the west of Ireland; but they've taken all the glass to mend the house windows: and small blame to them either. There's a clear rent-roll of three and fifty hundred a year, only it's in the hand of receivers; besides other debts, on which there is no land security."

"Your cousin-in-law, Castlereagh Molloy, won't come into a large fortune?"

"Oh, he'll do very well," said Dennis. "As long as he can get credit, he's not the fellow to stint himself. Faith, I was fool enough to put my name to a bit of paper for him, and as they could not catch him in Mayo, they laid hold of me at Kingstown here. And there was a pretty-to-do. Didn't Mrs. Gam say I was ruining her family, that's all! I paid it by instalments (for all my money is settled on Jemima); and Castlereagh, who's an honourable fellow, offered me any satisfaction in life. Anyhow, he couldn't do more than *that*."

"Of course not; and now you're friends?"

"Yes, and he and his aunt have had a tiff, too; and he abuses her properly, I warrant ye. He says that she carried about Jemima from place to place, and flung her at the head of every unmarried man in England a'most—my poor Jemima, and she all the while dying in love with me! As soon as she got over the small-pox—she took it at Fermoy: God bless her! I wish I'd been by to be her nurse-tender—as soon as she was rid of it, the old lady said to Castlereagh, 'Castlereagh, go to the bar'cks, and find out in the Army List where the 120th is.' Off she came to Cork hot foot. It appears that while she was ill, Jemima's love for me showed itself in such a violent way that her mother was overcome, and promised that, should the dear child recover, she would try and bring us together. Castlereagh says she would have gone after us to Jamaica."

"I have no doubt she would," said I.

"Could you have a stronger proof of love than that?" cried

Dennis. "My dear girl's illness and frightful blindness have, of course, injured her health and her temper. She cannot in her position look to the children, you know, and so they come under my charge for the most part; and her temper is unequal, certainly. But you see what a sensitive, refined, elegant creature she is, and may fancy that she's often put out by a rough fellow like me."

Here Dennis left me, saying it was time to go and walk out the children; and I think his story has matter of some wholesome reflection in it for bachelors who are about to change their condition, or may console some who are mourning their celibacy. Marry, gentlemen, if you like; leave your comfortable dinner at the club for cold mutton and curl-papers at your home; give up your books or pleasures, and take to yourselves wives and children; but think well on what you do first, as I have no doubt you will after this advice and example. Advice is always useful in matters of love; men always take it; they always follow other people's opinions, not their own; they always profit by example. When they see a pretty woman, and feel the delicious madness of love coming over them, they always stop to calculate her temper, her money, their own money, or suitableness for the married life. . . . Ha, ha, ha! Let us fool in this way no more. I have been in love forty-three times with all ranks and conditions of women, and would have married every time if they would have let me. How many wives had King Solomon, the wisest of men? And is not that story a warning to us that Love is master of the wisest? It is only fools who defy him.

I must come, however, to the last, and perhaps the saddest, part of poor Denny Haggarty's history. I met him once more, and in such a condition as made me determine to write this history.

In the month of June last I happened to be at Richmond, a delightful little place of retreat; and there, sunning himself upon the terrace, was my old friend of the 120th. He looked older, thinner, poorer, and more wretched than I had ever seen him. "What! you have given up Kingstown?" said I, shaking him by the hand.

"Yes," says he.

"And is my lady and your family here at Richmond?"

"No," says he, with a sad shake of the head, and the poor fellow's hollow eyes filled with tears.

"Good heavens, Denny! what's the matter?" said I. He was squeezing my hand like a vice as I spoke.

"They've LEFT me!" he burst out with a dreadful shout of passionate grief—a horrible scream which seemed to be wrenched out of his heart. "Left me!" said he, sinking down on a seat, and clenching his great fists, and shaking his lean arms wildly. "I'm a wise man now, Mr. Fitz-Boodle. Jemima has gone away from me; and yet you know how I loved her, and how happy we were! I've got nobody now ; but I'll die soon, that's one comfort, and to think it's she that'll kill me after all ! "

The story, which he told me with a wild and furious lamentation such as is not known among men of our cooler country, and such as I don't like now to recall, was a very simple one. The mother-in-law had taken possession of the house, and had driven him from it. His property at his marriage was settled on his wife. She had never loved him, and told him this secret at last, and drove him out of doors with her selfish scorn and ill-temper. The boy had died ; the girls were better, he said, brought up among the Molloys than they could be with him ; and so he was quite alone in the world, and was living, or rather dying, on forty pounds a year.

His troubles are very likely over by this time. The two fools who caused his misery will never read this history of him—*they* never read godless stories in magazines ; and I wish, honest reader, that you and I went to church as much as they do. These people are not wicked *because* of their religious observances, but *in spite* of them. They are too dull to understand humility, too blind to see a tender and simple heart under a rough ungainly bosom. They are sure that all their conduct towards my poor friend here has been perfectly righteous, and that they have given proofs of the most Christian virtue. Haggarty's wife is considered by her friends as a martyr to a savage husband, and her mother is the angel that has come to rescue her. All they did was to cheat him and desert him. And safe in that wonderful self-complacency with which the fools of this earth are endowed, they have not a single pang of conscience for their villainy towards him, and consider their heartlessness as a proof and consequence of their spotless piety and virtue.

WILLIAM MAKEPEACE THACKERAY

A GAMBLER'S DEATH

ANYBODY who was at C—— school some twelve years since must recollect Jack Attwood. He was the most dashing lad in the place, with more money in his pocket than belonged to the whole fifth form, in which we were companions.

When he was about fifteen, Jack suddenly retreated from C——; and presently we heard that he had a commission in a cavalry regiment, and was to have a great fortune from his father when that old gentleman should die. Jack himself came to confirm these stories a few months after, and paid a visit to his old school-chums. He had laid aside his little school-jacket and inky corduroys, and now appeared in such a splendid military suit as won the respect of all of us. His hair was dripping with oil; his hands were covered with rings; he had a dusky down over his upper lip, which looked not unlike a moustache; and a multiplicity of frogs and braiding on his surtout, which would have sufficed to lace a field-marshal. When old Swishtail, the usher, passed in his seedy black coat and gaiters, Jack gave him such a look of contempt as set us all a-laughing. In fact, it was his turn to laugh now; for he used to roar very stoutly, some months before, when Swishtail was in the custom of belabouring him with his great cane.

Jack's talk was all about the regiment, and the fine fellows in it: how he had ridden a steeplechase with Captain Boldero, and licked him at the last hedge; and how he had very nearly fought a duel with Sir George Grig, about dancing with Lady Mary Slamken at a ball. " I soon made the baronet know what it was to deal with a man of the N—th," said Jack. " Dammee, sir, when I lugged out my barkers, and talked of fighting across the mess-room table, Grig turned as pale as a sheet, or as——"

" Or as you used to do, Attwood, when Swishtail hauled you up," piped out little Hicks, the foundation-boy.

It was beneath Jack's dignity to thrash anybody now but a grown-up baronet; so he let off little Hicks, and passed over the general titter which was raised at his expense. However, he entertained us with his histories about lords and ladies, and so-and-so " of ours," until we thought him one of the greatest men in his Majesty's service, and until the school-bell rung, when, with a heavy heart, we got our books together and marched in to be whacked by old Swishtail. I promise you, he revenged himself on us for Jack's contempt of him. I got that day at least twenty cuts to my share, which ought to have belonged to Cornet Attwood of the N—th Dragoons.

When we came to think more coolly over our quondam school-fellow's swaggering talk and manner, we were not quite so impressed by his merits as at his first appearance among us. We recollected how he used, in former times, to tell us great stories, which were so monstrously improbable that the smallest boy in the school would scout at them ; how often we caught him tripping in facts, and how unblushingly he admitted his little errors on the score of veracity. He and I, though never great friends, had been close companions. I was Jack's form-fellow (we fought with amazing emulation for the *last* place in the class) ; but still I was rather hurt at the coolness of my old comrade, who had forgotten all our former intimacy in his steeplechases with Captain Boldero and his duel with Sir George Grig.

Nothing more was heard of Attwood for some years. A tailor one day came down to C——, who had made clothes for Jack in his schooldays, and furnished him with regimentals. He produced a long bill for one hundred and twenty pounds and upwards, and asked where news might be had of his customer. Jack was in India, with his regiment, shooting tigers and jackals, no doubt. Occasionally, from that distant country some magnificent rumour would reach us of his proceedings. Once I heard that he had been called to a court-martial for unbecoming conduct ; another time, that he kept twenty horses, and won the gold plate at the Calcutta races. Presently, however, as the recollections of the fifth form wore away, Jack's image disappeared likewise, and I ceased to ask or think about my college chum.

A year since, as I was smoking my cigar in the " Estaminet du Grand Balcon "—an excellent smoking-shop, where the tobacco is unexceptionable, and the Hollands of singular merit—a dark-looking, thick-set man, in a greasy well-cut coat, with a shabby hat cocked on one side of his dirty face, took the place opposite me, at the little marble table, and called for brandy. I did not much admire the impudence or the appearance of my friend, nor the fixed stare with which he chose to examine me. At last, he thrust a great greasy hand across the table, and said, " Titmarsh, do you forget your old friend Attwood ? "

I confess my recognition of him was not so joyful as on the day, ten years earlier, when he had come, bedizened with lace and gold rings, to see us at C—— school. A man, in the tenth part of a century, learns a deal of worldly wisdom, and his hand, which goes naturally forward to seize the gloved finger of a millionaire, or a milor, draws instinctively back from a dirty fist, encompassed by a ragged wrist-band and a tattered cuff. But Attwood was in nowise so backward, and the iron squeeze with which he shook my passive paw proved that he was either very affectionate or very poor. You, my dear sir, who are reading this history, know very well the great art of shaking hands. Recollect how you shook Lord Dash's hand the other day, and how you shook *off* poor Blank when he came to borrow five pounds of you.

However, the genial influence of the Hollands speedily dissipated anything like coolness between us ; and, in the course of an hour's conversation, we became almost as intimate as when we were suffering together under the ferule of old Swishtail. Jack told me that he had quitted the army in disgust ; and that his father, who was to leave him a fortune, had died ten thousand pounds in debt. He did not touch upon his own circumstances ; but I could read them in his elbows, which were peeping through his old frock. He talked a great deal, however, of runs of luck, good and bad ; and related to me an infallible plan for breaking all the play-banks in Europe—a great number of old tricks. And a vast quantity of gin-punch was consumed on the occasion ; so long, in fact, did our conversation continue, that (I confess it with shame) the sentiment, or something stronger, quite got the better of me, and I have, to this day, no sort of notion how our palaver concluded. Only, on the next morning, I did not possess a certain five-pound note which on the previous evening was in my sketch-book (by far the prettiest drawing, by the way, in the collection) ; but there, instead, was a strip of paper, thus inscribed :

I O U
Five Pounds. John Attwood,
Late of the N—th Dragoons.

I suppose Attwood borrowed the money, from this remarkable and ceremonious acknowledgment on his part. Had I been sober, I would just as soon have lent him the nose on my face, for, in my then circumstances, the note was of much more consequence to me.

As I lay cursing my ill fortune, and thinking how on earth I should manage to subsist for the next two months, Attwood burst into my little garret—his face strangely flushed—singing and shouting as if it had been the night before. " Titmarsh," cried he, " you are my preserver ! my best friend ! Look here, and here, and here ! " And at every word Mr. Attwood produced a handful of gold, or a glittering heap of five-franc pieces, or a bundle of greasy, dusky bank-notes, more beautiful than either silver or gold. He had won thirteen thousand francs after leaving me, at midnight, in my garret. He separated my poor little all, of six pieces, from this shining and imposing collection ; and the passion of envy entered my soul. I felt far more anxious now than before, although starvation was then staring me in the face ; I hated Attwood for *cheating* me out of all this wealth. Poor fellow ! it had been better for him had he never seen a shilling of it.

However, a grand breakfast at the Café Anglais dissipated my chagrin ; and I will do my friend the justice to say that he nobly shared some portion of his good fortune with me. As far as the creature comforts were concerned, I feasted as well as he, and never was particular as to settling my share of the reckoning.

Jack now changed his lodgings, had cards with " Captain Attwood " engraved on them, and drove about a prancing cab-horse as tall as the giraffe at the Jardin des Plantes ; he had as many frogs on his coat as in the old days, and frequented all the flash restaurateurs' and boarding-houses of the capital. Madame de Saint Laurent, and Madame la Baronne de Vaudrey, and Madame la Comtesse de Don Jonville, ladies of the highest rank, who keep a *société choisie*, and condescend to give dinners at five francs a head, vied with each other in their attentions to Jack. His was the wing of the fowl, and the largest portion of the Charlotte-Russe ; his was the place at the *écarté* table, where the countess would ease him nightly of a few pieces, declaring that he was the most charming cavalier—*la fleur d'Albion*. Jack's society, it may be seen, was not very select ; nor, in truth, were his inclinations ; he was a careless, dare-devil, Macheath kind of fellow, who might be seen daily with a wife on each arm.

It may be supposed that, with the life he led, his five hundred pounds of winnings would not last him long. Nor did they. But for some time his luck never deserted him, and his cash, instead of growing lower, seemed always to maintain a certain level. He played every night.

Of course, such a humble fellow as I could not hope for a continued acquaintance and intimacy with Attwood. He grew overbearing and cool, I thought. At any rate, I did not admire my situation as his follower and dependant, and left his grand dinner for a certain ordinary where I could partake of five capital dishes for ninepence. Occasionally, however, Attwood favoured me with a visit, or gave me a drive behind his great cab-horse. He had formed a whole host of friends besides. There was Fips, the barrister (Heaven knows what he was doing at Paris !) ; and Gortz, the West Indian, who was there on the same business ; and Flapper, a medical student : all these three I met one night at Flapper's rooms, where Jack was invited, and a great " spread " was laid in honour of him.

Jack arrived rather late. He looked pale and agitated ; and

though he ate no supper, he drank raw brandy in such a manner as made Flapper's eyes wink: the poor fellow had but three bottles, and Jack bid fair to swallow them all. However, the West Indian generously remedied the evil; and producing a napoleon, we speedily got the change for it in the shape of four bottles of champagne.

Our supper was uproariously harmonious. Fips sang "The Good Old English Gentleman"; Jack, "The British Grenadiers"; and your humble servant, when called upon, sang that beautiful ditty, "When the Bloom is on the Rye," in a manner that drew tears from every eye—except Flapper's, who was asleep, and Jack's, who was singing "The Bay of Biscay O," at the same time. Gortz and Fips were all the time lunging at each other with a pair of single-sticks, the barrister having a very strong notion that he was Richard the Third. At last Fips hits the West Indian such a blow across his sconce that the other grew furious; he seized a champagne bottle (which was, providentially, empty), and hurled it across the room at Fips. Had that celebrated barrister not bowed his head at the moment, the Queen's Bench would have lost one of its most eloquent practitioners.

Fips stood as straight as he could; his cheek was pale with wrath. "M-m-ister Go-gortz," he said, "I always heard you were a blackguard; now I can pr-pr-peperove it.—Flapper, your pistols! Every ge-ge-genlmn knows what I mean."

Young Mr. Flapper had a small pair of pocket-pistols, which the tipsy barrister had suddenly remembered, and with which he proposed to sacrifice the West Indian. Gortz was nothing loth, but was quite as valorous as the lawyer.

Attwood, who, in spite of his potations, seemed the soberest man of the party, had much enjoyed the scene, until this sudden demand for the weapons. "Pshaw!" said he eagerly, "don't give these men the means of murdering each other. Sit down, and let us have another song." But they would not be still; and Flapper forthwith produced his pistol-case, and opened it, in order that the duel might take place on the spot. There were no pistols there! "I beg your pardon," said Attwood, looking much confused; "I—I took the pistols home with me to clean them!"

I don't know what there was in his tone, or in the words, but we were sobered all of a sudden. Attwood was conscious of the singular effect produced by him, for he blushed, and endeavoured to speak of other things. But we could not bring our spirits back to the mark again, and soon separated for the night. As we issued into the street, Jack took me aside and whispered, "Have you a napoleon, Titmarsh, in your purse?" Alas! I was not so rich. My reply was, that I was coming to Jack, only in the morning, to borrow a similar sum.

He did not make any reply, but turned away homeward. I never heard him speak another word.

. . . .

Two mornings after (for none of our party met on the day succeeding the supper), I was awakened by my porter, who brought a pressing letter from Mr. Gortz:

"DEAR T.,—I wish you would come over here to breakfast. There's a row about Attwood.—Yours truly, SOLOMON GORTZ."

I immediately set forward to Gortz's; he lived in the Rue du Heldes, a few doors from Attwood's new lodging. If the reader is curious to know the house in which the catastrophe of this history took place, he has but to march some twenty doors down from the Boulevard des Italiens, when he will see a fine door, with a naked Cupid shooting at him from the hall, and a Venus beckoning him up the stairs. On arriving at the West Indian's, at about mid-day (it was a Sunday morning), I found that gentleman in his dressing-gown, discussing, in the company of Mr. Fips, a large plate of *bifteck aux pommes*.

"Here's a pretty row!" said Gortz, quoting from his letter. "Attwood's off;—have a bit of beefsteak?"

"What do you mean?" exclaimed I, adopting the familiar phraseology of my acquaintances. "Attwood off?—has he cut his stick?"

"Not bad," said the feeling and elegant Fips—"not such a bad guess, my boy; but he has not exactly *cut his stick*."

"What then?"

"*Why, his throat.*" The man's mouth was full of bleeding beef as he uttered this gentlemanly witticism.

I wish I could say that I was myself in the least affected by the news. I did not joke about it, like my friend Fips—this was more for propriety's sake than for feeling's—but for my old school acquaintance, the friend of my early days, the merry associate of the last few months, I own, with shame, that I had not a tear or a pang. In some German tale there is an account of a creature most beautiful and bewitching, whom all men admire and follow; but this charming and fantastic spirit only leads them, one by one, into ruin, and then leaves them. The novelist, who describes her beauty, says that his heroine is a fairy, and *has no heart*. I think the intimacy which is begotten over the wine-bottle is a spirit of this nature. I never knew a good feeling come from it, or an honest friendship made by it; it only entices men and ruins them; it is only a phantom of friendship and feeling, called up by the delirious blood, and the wicked spells of the wine.

But to drop this strain of moralising (in which the writer is not too anxious to proceed, for he cuts in it a most pitiful figure), we passed sundry criticisms upon poor Attwood's character ; expressed our horror at his death—which sentiment was fully proved by Mr. Fips, who declared that the notion of it made him feel quite faint, and was obliged to drink a large glass of brandy ; and, finally, we agreed that we would go and see the poor fellow's corpse, and witness, if necessary, his burial.

Flapper, who had joined us, was the first to propose this visit. He said he did not mind the fifteen francs which Jack owed him for billiards, but he was anxious to *get back his pistol*. Accordingly, we sallied forth, and speedily arrived at the hotel which Attwood inhabited still. He had occupied, for a time, very fine apartments in this house ; and it was only on arriving there that day that we found he had been gradually driven from his magnificent suite of rooms *au premier*, to a little chamber in the fifth storey. We mounted, and found him. It was a little shabby room, with a few articles of rickety furniture, and a bed in an alcove. The light from the one window was falling full upon the bed and the body. Jack was dressed in a fine lawn shirt—he had kept it, poor fellow, *to die in*, for in all his drawers and cupboards there was not a single article of clothing ; he had pawned everything by which he could raise a penny—desk, books, dressing-case, and clothes ; and not a single halfpenny was found in his possession.[1]

He was lying with one hand on his breast, the other falling towards the ground. There was an expression of perfect calm on the face, and no mark of blood to stain the side towards the light. On the other side, however, there was a great pool of black blood, and in it the pistol : it looked more like a toy than a weapon to take away the life of this vigorous young man. In his forehead, at the side, was a small black wound ; Jack's life had passed through it ; it was little bigger than a mole.

. . . .

" Regardez un peu," said the landlady, " messieurs, il m'a gâté trois matelas, et il me doit quarante quatre francs."

This was all his epitaph : he had spoiled three mattresses, and owed the landlady four-and-forty francs. In the whole world there was not a soul to love him or lament him. We, his friends, were looking at his body more as an object of curiosity, watching it with a kind of interest with which one follows the fifth act of a tragedy, and leaving it with the same feeling with which one leaves the theatre when the play is over and the curtain is down.

[1] In order to account for these trivial details, the reader must be told that the story is, for the chief part, a fact. The letter was likewise a copy from one found in the manner described.

Beside Jack's bed, on his little " table de nuit," lay the remains of his last meal, and an open letter, which we read. It was from one of his suspicious acquaintances of former days, and ran thus:

" Où es-tu, cher Jack ? *why you not come and see me*—tu me dois de l'argent, entends-tu ?—un chapeau, une cachemire, *a box of the Play.* Viens demain soir, je t'attendrai *at eight o'clock,* Passage des Panoramas. *My Sir is at his country.* Adieu à demain.

" Samedi." " FIFINE."

. . . .

I shuddered as I walked through this very Passage des Panoramas, in the evening. The girl was there, pacing to and fro, and looking in the countenance of every passer-by, to recognise Attwood. " ADIEU À DEMAIN ! "—there was a dreadful meaning in the words, which the writer of them little knew. " Adieu à demain ! "—the morrow was come, and the soul of the poor suicide was now in the presence of God. I dare not think of his fate ; for, except in the fact of his poverty and desperation, was he worse than any of us, his companions who had shared his debauches, and marched with him up to the very brink of the grave ?

There is but one more circumstance to relate regarding poor Jack —his burial ; it was of a piece with his death.

He was nailed into a paltry coffin and buried, at the expense of the arrondissement, in a nook of the burial-place beyond the Barrière de l'Etoile. They buried him at six o'clock of a bitter winter's morning, and it was with difficulty that an English clergyman could be found to read a service over his grave. The three men who have figured in this history acted as Jack's mourners ; and as the ceremony was to take place so early in the morning, these men sat up the night through, *and were almost drunk* as they followed his coffin to its resting-place.

MORAL

" When we turned out in our greatcoats," said one of them afterwards, " reeking of cigars and brandy-and-water, d——e, sir, we quite frightened the old buck of a parson ; he did not much like our company." After the ceremony was concluded, these gentlemen were very happy to get home to a warm and comfortable breakfast, and finished the day royally at Frascati's.

WILLIAM MAKEPEACE THACKERAY

A LITTLE DINNER IN BITTLESTONE STREET

In that noble romance called *Ten Thousand a Year,* I remember a profoundly pathetic description of the Christian manner in which the hero, Mr. Aubrey, bore his misfortunes. After making a display of the most florid and grandiloquent resignation, and quitting his country mansion, the writer supposes Aubrey to come to town in a post-chaise and pair sitting bodkin probably between his wife and sister. It is about seven o'clock, carriages are rattling about, knockers are thundering, and tears bedim the fine eyes of Kate and Mrs. Aubrey as they think that in happier times at this hour—their Aubrey used formerly to go out to dinner to the houses of the aristocracy his friends. This is the gist of the passage—the elegant words I forget. But the noble, noble sentiment I shall always cherish and remember. What can be more sublime than the notion of a great man's relatives in tears about—his dinner? With a few touches, what author ever more happily described a Snob?

We were reading the passage lately at the house of my friend, Raymond Gray, Esquire, Barrister-at-Law, an ingenuous youth without the least practice, but who has luckily a great share of good spirits, which enables him to bide his time, and bear laughingly his humble position in the world. Meanwhile, until it is altered, the stern laws of necessity and the expenses of the Northern Circuit oblige Mr. Gray to live in a very tiny mansion in a very queer small square in the airy neighbourhood of Gray's Inn.

What is the more remarkable is, that Gray has a wife there. Mrs. Gray was a Miss Harley Baker: and I suppose I need not say *that* is a respectable family. Allied to the Cavendishes, the Oxfords, the Marrybones, they still, though rather *déchus* from their original splendour, hold their heads as high as any. Mrs. Harley Baker, I know, never goes to church without John behind to carry her prayer-book; nor will Miss Welbeck, her sister, walk twenty yards a shopping without the protection of Figby, her sugar-loaf page; though the old lady is as ugly as any woman in the parish, and as tall and whiskery as a Grenadier. The astonishment is, how Emily Harley Baker could have stooped to marry Raymond Gray. She, who was the prettiest and proudest of the family; she, who refused Sir Cockle Byles, of the Bengal Service; she, who turned up her little nose at Essex Temple, Q.C., and connected with the noble house of Albyn; she, who had but £4000 *pour tout potage,* to marry a man who had scarcely as much more. A scream of wrath and indignation was uttered by the whole family when they heard of this *mésalliance.* Mrs. Harley Baker never speaks of her daughter now but with tears in her eyes, and as a ruined creature. Miss Welbeck says, "I consider that man a villain," and has denounced poor good-natured Mrs. Perkins as a swindler, at whose ball the young people met for the first time.

Mr. and Mrs. Gray, meanwhile, live in Gray's Inn Lane, aforesaid, with a maid-servant and a nurse, whose hands are very full, and in a most provoking and unnatural state of happiness. They have never once thought of crying about their dinner, like the wretchedly puling and Snobbish womankind of my favourite Snob Aubrey, of *Ten Thousand a Year*; but, on the contrary, accept such humble victuals as Fate awards them with a most perfect and thankful good grace—nay, actually have a portion for a hungry friend at times—as the present writer can gratefully testify.

I was mentioning these dinners, and some admirable lemon puddings which Mrs. Gray makes, to our mutual friend the great Mr. Goldmore, the East India Director, when that gentleman's face assumed an expression of almost apoplectic terror, and he gasped out, "What! Do they give dinners?" He seemed to think it a crime and a wonder that such people should dine at all, and that it was their custom to huddle round their kitchen fire over a bone and a crust. Whenever he meets them in society, it is a matter of wonder to him (and he always expresses his surprise very loud) how the lady can appear decently dressed, and the man have an unpatched coat to his back. I have heard him enlarge upon this poverty before the whole room at the Conflagrative Club, to which he and I and Gray have the honour to belong.

We meet at the Club on most days. At half-past four, Goldmore arrives in St. James's Street, from the City, and you may see him reading the evening papers in the bow window of the Club which enfilades Pall Mall—a large plethoric man, with a bunch of seals in a large bow-windowed light waistcoat. He has large coat-tails, stuffed with agents' letters and papers about companies of which he is a Director. His seals jingle as he walks. I wish I had such a man for an uncle, and that he himself were childless. I would love and cherish him, and be kind to him.

At six o'clock in the full season, when all the world is in St. James's Street, and the carriages are cutting in and out among the cabs on the stand, and the tufted dandies are showing their listless faces out of White's ; and you see respectable grey-headed gentlemen waggling their heads to each other through the plate-glass windows of Arthur's : and the red-coats wish to be Briarean, so as to hold all the gentlemen's horses ; and that wonderful red-coated royal porter is sunning himself before Marlborough House ;—at the noon of London time, you see a light-yellow carriage with black horses, and a coachman in a tight floss-silk wig, and two footmen in powder and white and yellow liveries, and a large woman inside in shot silk, a poodle, and a pink parasol, which drives up to the gate of the Conflagrative, and the page goes and says to Mr. Goldmore (who is perfectly aware of the fact, as he is looking out of the windows with about forty other Conflagrative bucks), " Your carriage, sir." G. wags his head. " Remember, eight o'clock precisely," says he to Mulligatawney, the other East India Director, and ascending the carriage plumps down by the side of Mrs. Goldmore for a drive in the Park, and then home to Portland Place. As the carriage whirls off, all the young bucks in the Club feel a secret elation. It is a part of their establishment, as it were. That carriage belongs to their Club, and their Club belongs to them. They follow the equipage with interest ; they eye it knowingly as they see it in the Park. But halt ! we are not come to the Club Snobs yet. O my brave Snobs, what a flurry there will be among you when those papers appear !

Well, you may judge from the above description what sort of a man Goldmore is. A dull and pompous Leadenhall Street Crœsus, good-natured withal, and affable—cruelly affable. " Mr. Goldmore can never forget," his lady used to say, " that it was Mrs. Gray's grandfather who sent him to India ; and though that young woman has made the most imprudent marriage in the world, and has left her station in society, her husband seems an ingenious and laborious young man, and we shall do everything in our power to be of use to him." So they used to ask the Grays to dinner twice or thrice in a season, when, by way of increasing the kindness, Buff, the butler, is ordered to hire a fly to convey them to and from Portland Place.

Of course I am much too good-natured a friend of both parties not to tell Gray of Goldmore's opinion regarding him, and the Nabob's astonishment at the idea of the briefless barrister having any dinner at all. Indeed, Goldmore's saying became a joke against Gray amongst us wags at the Club, and we used to ask him when he tasted meat last ? whether we should bring him home something from dinner ? and cut a thousand other mad pranks with him in our facetious way.

One day, then, coming home from the Club, Mr. Gray conveyed to his wife the astounding information that he had asked Goldmore to dinner.

"My love," says Mrs. Gray, in a tremor, "how could you be so cruel? Why, the dining-room won't hold Mrs. Goldmore."

"Make your mind easy, Mrs. Gray, her ladyship is in Paris. It is only Crœsus that's coming, and we are going to the play afterwards—to Sadler's Wells. Goldmore said at the Club that he thought Shakespeare was a great dramatic poet, and ought to be patronised; whereupon, fired with enthusiasm, I invited him to our banquet."

"Goodness gracious! what *can* we give him for dinner? He has two French cooks; you know Mrs. Goldmore is always telling us about them; and he dines with Aldermen every day."

> "A plain leg of mutton, my Lucy,
> I prythee get ready at three;
> Have it tender, and smoking, and juicy,
> And what better meat can there be?"

says Gray, quoting my favourite poet.

"But the cook is ill; and you know that horrible Pattypan, the pastrycook's——"

"Silence, Frau!" says Gray, in a deep-tragedy voice. "*I* will have the ordering of this repast. Do all things as I bid thee. Invite our friend Snob here to partake of the feast. Be mine the task of procuring it."

"Don't be expensive, Raymond," says his wife.

"Peace, thou timid partner of the briefless one. Goldmore's dinner shall be suited to our narrow means. Only do thou in all things my commands." And seeing by the peculiar expression of the rogue's countenance that some mad waggery was in preparation, I awaited the morrow with anxiety.

Punctual to the hour—(by the way, I cannot omit here to mark down my hatred, scorn, and indignation towards those miserable Snobs who come to dinner at nine, when they are asked at eight, in order to make a sensation in the company. May the loathing of honest folks, the back-biting of others, the curses of cooks, pursue these wretches, and avenge the society on which they trample!)—Punctual, I say, to the hour of five, which Mr. and Mrs. Raymond Gray had appointed, a youth of an elegant appearance, in a neat evening dress, whose trim whiskers indicated neatness, whose light step denoted activity (for in sooth he was hungry, and always is at the dinner hour, whatsoever that hour may be), and whose rich golden hair, curling down his shoulders, was set off by a perfectly new four-and-ninepenny silk hat, was seen wending his way down Bittlestone Street, Bittlestone Square, Gray's Inn. The person in question, I need not say, was Mr. Snob. *He* was never late when invited to dine. But to proceed with my narrative:

Although Mr. Snob may have flattered himself that he made a sensation as he strutted down Bittlestone Street with his richly gilt-knobbed cane (and indeed I vow I saw heads looking at me from Miss Squilsby's, the brass-plated milliner opposite Raymond Gray's, who has three silver-paper bonnets, and two fly-blown French prints of fashion in the window), yet what was the emotion produced by my arrival compared to that with which the little street thrilled, when at five minutes past five the floss-wigged coachman, the yellow hammer-cloth and flunkies, the black horses and blazing silver harness of Mr. Goldmore whirled down the street! It is a very little street, of very little houses, most of them with very large brass plates like Miss Squilsby's. Coal-merchants, architects, and surveyors, two surgeons, a solicitor, a dancing-master, and of course several house-agents, occupy the houses—little two-storeyed edifices with little stucco porticoes. Goldmore's carriage overtopped the roof almost; the first floors might shake hands with Crœsus as he lolled inside; all the windows of those first floors thronged with children and women in a twinkling. There was Mrs. Hammerly in curl-papers; Mrs. Saxby with her front awry; Mr. Wriggles peering through the gauze curtains, holding the while his hot glass of rum-and-water—in fine, a tremendous commotion in Bittlestone Street, as the Goldmore carriage drove up to Mr. Raymond Gray's door.

"How kind it is of him to come with *both* the footmen!" says little Mrs. Gray, peeping at the vehicle too. The huge domestic, descending from his perch, gave a rap at the door which almost drove in the building. All the heads were out; the sun was shining; the very organ-boy paused; the footman, the coach, and Goldmore's red face and white waistcoat were blazing in splendour. The herculean plushed one went back to open the carriage-door.

Raymond Gray opened his—in his shirt-sleeves.

He ran up to the carriage. "Come in, Goldmore," he says. "Just in time, my boy. Open the door Whatdyecallum, and let your master out,"—and Whatdyecallum obeyed mechanically, with a face of wonder and horror, only to be equalled by the look of stupefied astonishment which ornamented the purple countenance of his master.

"Wawt taim will you please have the *cage*, sir," says Whatdyecallum, in that peculiar, unspellable, inimitable, flunkyfied pronunciation which forms one of the chief charms of existence.

"Best have it to the theatre, at night," Gray exclaims; "it is but a step from here to the Wells, and we can walk there. I've got tickets for all. Be at Sadler's Wells at eleven."

" Yes, at eleven," exclaims Goldmore perturbedly, and walks with a flurried step into the house, as if he were going to execution (as indeed he was, with that wicked Gray as a Jack Ketch over him). The carriage drove away, followed by numberless eyes from door-steps and balconies ; its appearance is still a wonder in Bittlestone Street.

" Go in there, and amuse yourself with Snob," says Gray, opening the little drawing-room door. " I'll call out as soon as the chops are ready. Fanny's below, seeing to the pudding."

" Gracious mercy ! " says Goldmore to me, quite confidentially, " How could he ask us ? I really had no idea of this—this utter destitution."

" Dinner, dinner ! " roars out Gray from the dining-room, whence issued a great smoking and frying ; and entering that apartment we find Mrs. Gray ready to receive us, and looking perfectly like a Princess who, by some accident, had a bowl of potatoes in her hand, which vegetables she placed on the table. Her husband was meanwhile cooking mutton-chops on a gridiron over the fire.

" Fanny has made the roly-poly pudding," says he ; " the chops are my part. Here's a fine one ; try this, Goldmore." And he popped a fizzing cutlet on that gentleman's plate. What words, what notes of exclamation can describe the nabob's astonishment ? The table-cloth was a very old one, darned in a score of places. There was mustard in a tea-cup, a silver fork for Goldmore—all ours were iron.

" I wasn't born with a silver spoon in my mouth," says Gray gravely. " That fork is the only one we have. Fanny has it generally."

" Raymond ! " cries Mrs. Gray, in an imploring voice.

" She was used to better things, you know : and I hope one day to get her a dinner service. I'm told the electro-plate is uncommonly good. Where the deuce *is* that boy with the beer ? And now," said he, springing up, " I'll be a gentleman." And so he put on his coat, and sate down quite gravely, with four fresh mutton chops which he had by this time broiled.

" We don't have meat every day, Mr. Goldmore," he continued, " and it's a treat to me to get a dinner like this. You little know, you gentlemen of England, who live at home at ease, what hardships briefless barristers endure."

" Gracious mercy ! " says Mr. Goldmore.

" Where's the half-and-half ? Fanny, go over to the Keys and get the beer. Here's sixpence." And what was our astonishment when Fanny got up as if to go !

" Gracious mercy ! let *me*," cries Goldmore.

" Not for worlds, my dear sir. She's used to it. They wouldn't serve you as well as they serve her. Leave her alone. Law bless you ! " Raymond said with astounding composure. And Mrs. Gray left the room, and actually came back with a tray on which there was a pewter flagon of beer. Little Polly (to whom, at her christening, I had the honour of presenting a silver mug, *ex officio*), followed with a couple of tobacco pipes, and the queerest roguish look in her round little chubby face.

" Did you speak to Tapling about the gin, Fanny, my dear ? " Gray asked, after bidding Polly put the pipes on the chimney-piece, which that little person had some little difficulty in reaching—" The last was turpentine, and even your brewing didn't make good punch of it. You would hardly suspect, Goldmore, that my wife, a Harley Baker, would ever make gin-punch ? I think my mother-in-law would commit suicide if she saw her."

" Don't be always laughing at mamma, Raymond," says Mrs. Gray.

" Well, well, she wouldn't die, and I *don't* wish she would. And you don't make gin-punch, and you don't like it either—and—Goldmore, do you drink your beer out of the glass, or out of the pewter ? "

" Gracious mercy ! " ejaculates Crœsus once more, as little Polly, taking the pot with both her little bunches of hands, offers it smiling to that astonished Director.

And so, in a word, the dinner commenced, and was presently ended in a similar fashion. Gray pursued his unfortunate guest with the most queer and outrageous description of his struggles, misery, and poverty. He described how he cleaned the knives when they were first married ; and how he used to drag the children in a little cart ; how his wife could toss pancakes ; and what parts of his dress she made. He told Tibbits, his clerk (who was in fact the functionary who had brought the beer from the public-house, which Mrs. Fanny had fetched from the neighbouring apartment)—to fetch " the bottle of port wine," when the dinner was over ; and told Goldmore as wonderful a history about the way in which that bottle of wine had come into his hands, as any of his former stories had been. When the repast was all over, and it was near time to move to the play, and Mrs. Gray had retired, and we were sitting ruminating rather silently over the last glasses of port, Gray suddenly breaks the silence by slapping Goldmore on the shoulder, and saying, " Now, Goldmore, tell me something."

" What ? " asks Crœsus.

" Haven't you had a good dinner ? "

Goldmore started, as if a sudden truth had just dawned upon him. He *had* had a good dinner ; and didn't know it until then. The three mutton chops consumed by him were best of the mutton kind :

the potatoes were perfect of their order ; as for the roly-poly, it was too good. The porter was frothy and cool, and the port wine was worthy of the gills of a bishop. I speak with ulterior views ; for there is more in Gray's cellar.

" Well," says Goldmore, after a pause, during which he took time to consider the momentous question Gray put to him—" 'Pon my word—now you say so—I—I have—I really have had a monsous good dinnah—monsous good, upon my ward ! Here's your health, Gray, my boy, and your amiable lady ; and when Mrs. Goldmore comes back, I hope we shall see you more in Portland Place." And with this the time came for the play, and we went to see Mr. Phelps at Sadler's Wells.

The best of this story (for the truth of every word of which I pledge my honour) is, that after this banquet, which Goldmore enjoyed so, the honest fellow felt a prodigious compassion and regard for the starving and miserable giver of the feast, and determined to help him in his profession. And being a Director of the newly established Antibilious Life Assurance Company, he has had Gray appointed standing Counsel, with a pretty annual fee ; and only yesterday, in an appeal from Bombay (Buckmuckjee Bobbachee *v.* Ramchowder-Bahawder) in the Privy Council, Lord Brougham complimented Mr. Gray, who was in the case, on his curious and exact knowledge of the Sanscrit language.

Whether he knows Sanscrit or not, I can't say ; but Goldmore got him the business ; and so I cannot help having a lurking regard for that pompous old Bigwig.

WILLIAM MAKEPEACE THACKERAY

THE PRINCESS'S TRAGEDY

I WAS walking with my Lady Lyndon in the Rotunda at Ranelagh It was in the year 1790; the emigration from France had already commenced, the old counts and marquises were thronging to our shores: not starving and miserable, as one saw them a few years afterwards, but unmolested as yet, and bringing with them some token of their national splendour. I was walking with Lady Lyndon, who, proverbially jealous and always anxious to annoy me, spied out a foreign lady who was evidently remarking me, and of course asked who was the hideous fat Dutch-woman who was leering at me so? I knew her not in the least. I felt I had seen the lady's face somewhere (it was now, as my wife said, enormously fat and bloated); but I did not recognise in the bearer of that face one who had been among the most beautiful women in Germany in her day.

It was no other than Madame de Liliengarten, the mistress, or, as some said, the morganatic wife, of the old Duke of X——, Duke Victor's father. She had left X—— a few months after the elder duke's demise, had gone to Paris, as I heard, where some unprincipled adventurer had married her for her money; but, however, had always retained her quasi-royal title, and pretended, amidst the great laughter of the Parisians who frequented her house, to the honours and ceremonial of a sovereign's widow. She had a throne erected in her state-room, and was styled by her servants and those who wished to pay court to her, or borrow money from her, "Altesse." Report said she drank rather copiously—certainly her face bore every mark of that habit, and had lost the rosy, frank, good-humoured beauty which had charmed the sovereign who had ennobled her.

Although she did not address me in the circle at Ranelagh, I was at this period as well known as the Prince of Wales, and she had no difficulty in finding my house in Berkeley Square; whither a note was next morning despatched to me. "An old friend of Monsieur de Balibari," it stated (in extremely bad French), "is anxious to see the Chevalier again and to talk over old happy times. Rosina de

Liliengarten (can it be that Redmond Balibari has forgotten her ?) will be at her house in Leicester Fields all the morning, looking for one who would never have passed her by *twenty years* ago."

Rosina of Liliengarten it was, indeed—such a full-blown Rosina I have seldom seen. I found her in a decent first-floor in Leicester Fields (the poor soul fell much lower afterwards) drinking tea, which had somehow a very strong smell of brandy in it ; and after salutations, which would be more tedious to recount than they were to perform, and after further straggling conversation, she gave me briefly the following narrative of the events in X——, which I may well entitle the " Princess's Tragedy."

" You remember Monsieur de Geldern, the Police Minister. He was of Dutch extraction, and, what is more, of a family of Dutch Jews. Although everybody was aware of this blot in his scutcheon, he was mortally angry if ever his origin was suspected ; and made up for his father's errors by outrageous professions of religion and the most austere practices of devotion. He visited church every morning, confessed once a week, and hated Jews and Protestants as much as an inquisitor could do. He never lost an opportunity of proving his sincerity, by persecuting one or the other whenever occasion fell in his way.

" He hated the princess mortally ; for her highness in some whim had insulted him with his origin, caused pork to be removed from before him at table, or injured him in some such silly way ; and he had a violent animosity to the old Baron de Magny, both in his capacity of Protestant, and because the latter in some haughty mood had publicly turned his back upon him as a sharper and a spy. Perpetual quarrels were taking place between them in council ; where it was only the presence of his august master that restrained the baron from publicly and frequently expressing the contempt which he felt for the officer of police.

" Thus Geldern had hatred as one reason for ruining the princess, and it is my belief he had a stronger motive still—interest. You remember whom the duke married, after the death of his first wife ?—a princess of the house of F——. Geldern built his fine palace two years after, and, as I feel convinced, with the money which was paid to him by the F—— family for forwarding the match.

" To go to Prince Victor and report to his highness a case which everybody knew, was not by any means Geldern's desire. He knew the man would be ruined for ever in the prince's estimation who carried him intelligence so disastrous. His aim, therefore, was to leave the matter to explain itself to his highness ; and, when the time was ripe, he cast about for a means of carrying his point. He had spies in the houses of the elder and younger Magny ; but this you know, of course, from your experience of Continental customs. We had spies over each other. Your black (Zamar, I think, was his name) used to give me reports every morning ; and I used to entertain the dear old duke with stories of you and your uncle practising picquet and dice in the morning, and with your quarrels and intrigues. We levied similar contributions on everybody in X——, to amuse the dear old man. Monsieur de Magny's valet used to report both to me and Monsieur de Geldern.

" I knew of the fact of the emerald being in pawn ; and it was out of my exchequer that the poor princess drew the funds which were spent upon the odious Löwe, and the still more worthless young chevalier. How the princess could trust the latter as she persisted in doing, is beyond my comprehension ; but there is no infatuation like that of a woman in love : and you will remark, my dear Monsieur de Balibari, that our sex generally fix upon a bad man."

" Not always, madam," I interposed ; " your humble servant has created many such attachments."

" I do not see that that affects the truth of the proposition," said the old lady drily, and continued her narrative. " The Jew who held the emerald had had many dealings with the princess, and at last was offered a bribe of such magnitude that he determined to give up the pledge. He committed the inconceivable imprudence of bringing the emerald with him to X——, and waited on Magny, who was provided by the princess with the money to redeem the pledge, and was actually ready to pay it.

" Their interview took place in Magny's own apartments, when his valet overheard every word of their conversation. The young man, who was always utterly careless of money when it was in his possession, was so easy in offering it, that Löwe rose in his demands, and had the conscience to ask double the sum for which he had previously stipulated.

" At this the chevalier lost all patience, fell on the wretch, and was for killing him ; when the opportune valet rushed in and saved him. The man had heard every word of the conversation between the disputants, and the Jew ran flying with terror into his arms ; and Magny, a quick and passionate, but not a violent man, bade the servant lead the villain downstairs, and thought no more of him.

" Perhaps he was not sorry to be rid of him, and to have in his possession a large sum of money, 4000 ducats, with which he could tempt fortune once more ; as you know he did at your table that night."

" Your ladyship went halves, madam," said I ; " and you know how little I was the better for my winnings."

" The man conducted the trembling Israelite out of the palace, and no sooner had seen him lodged at the house of one of his brethren, where he was accustomed to put up, than he went away to the office of his Excellency the Minister of Police, and narrated every word of the conversation which had taken place between the Jew and his master.

"Geldern expressed the greatest satisfaction at his spy's prudence and fidelity. He gave him a purse of twenty ducats, and promised to provide for him handsomely: as great men do sometimes promise to reward their instruments; but you, Monsieur de Balibari, know how seldom those promises are kept. 'Now, go and find out,' said Monsieur de Geldern, 'at what time the Israelite proposes to return home again, or whether he will repent and take the money.' The man went on this errand. Meanwhile, to make matters sure, Geldern arranged a play-party at my house, inviting you thither with your bank, as you may remember; and finding means, at the same time, to let Maxime de Magny know that there was to be faro at Madame de Liliengarten's. It was an invitation the poor fellow never neglected."

I remembered the facts and listened on, amazed at the artifice of the infernal Minister of Police.

"The spy came back from his message to Löwe, and stated that he had made inquiries among the servants of the house where the Heidelberg banker lodged, and that it was the latter's intention to leave X—— that afternoon. He travelled by himself, riding an old horse, exceedingly humbly attired, after the manner of his people.

"'Johann,' said the Minister, clapping the pleased spy upon the shoulder, 'I am more and more pleased with you. I have been thinking, since you left me, of your intelligence, and the faithful manner in which you have served me; and shall soon find an occasion to place you according to your merits. Which way does this Israelitish scoundrel take?'

"'He goes to R—— to-night.'

"'And must pass by the Kaiserwald. Are you a man of courage, Johann Kerner?'

"'Will your Excellency try me?' said the man, his eyes glittering: 'I served through the Seven Years' War, and was never known to fail there.'

"'Now, listen. The emerald must be taken from that Jew: in the very keeping it the scoundrel has committed high treason. To the man who brings me that emerald I swear I will give five hundred louis. You understand why it is necessary that it should be restored to her highness. I need say no more.'

"'You shall have it to-night, sir,' said the man. 'Of course your Excellency will hold me harmless in case of accident.'

"'Psha!' answered the Minister; 'I will pay you half the money beforehand ; such is my confidence in you. Accident's impossible, if you take your measures properly. There are four leagues of wood; the Jew rides slowly. It will be night before he can reach, let us say, the old Powder-Mill in the wood. What's to prevent you from putting a rope across the road, and dealing with him there ? Be back with me this evening at supper. If you meet any of the patrol, say " foxes are loose,"—that's the word for to-night. They will let you pass them without questions.'

" The man went off quite charmed with his commission ; and when Magny was losing his money at our faro-table, his servant waylaid the Jew at the spot named the Powder-Mill, in the Kaiserwald. The Jew's horse stumbled over a rope which had been placed across the road ; and, as the rider fell groaning to the ground, Johann Kerner rushed out on him, masked, and pistol in hand, and demanded his money. He had no wish to kill the Jew, I believe, unless his resistance should render extreme measures necessary.

" Nor did he commit any such murder ; for, as the yelling Jew roared for mercy, and his assailant menaced him with a pistol, a squad of patrol came up, and laid hold of the robber and the wounded man.

" Kerner swore an oath. ' You have come too soon,' said he to the sergeant of the police. ' *Foxes are loose.*' ' Some are caught,' said the sergeant, quite unconcerned ; and bound the fellow's hands with the rope which he had stretched across the road to entrap the Jew. He was placed behind a policeman on a horse ; Löwe was similarly accommodated, and the party thus came back into the town as the night fell.

" They were taken forthwith to the police quarter ; and, as the chief happened to be there, they were examined by his Excellency in person. Both were rigorously searched ; the Jew's papers and cases taken from him : the jewel was found in a private pocket. As for the spy, the Minister, looking at him angrily, said, ' Why, this is the servant of Chevalier de Magny, one of her highness's equerries ! ' and, without hearing a word in exculpation from the poor frightened wretch, ordered him into close confinement.

" Calling for his horse, he then rode to the prince's apartments at the palace, and asked for an instant audience. When admitted, he produced the emerald. ' This jewel,' said he, ' has been found on the person of a Heidelberg Jew, who has been here repeatedly of late, and has had many dealings with her highness's equerry, the Chevalier de Magny. This afternoon the chevalier's servant came from his master's lodgings, accompanied by the Hebrew ; was heard to make inquiries as to the route the man intended to take on his way homewards ; followed him, or preceded him rather, and was found in the act of rifling his victim by my police in the Kaiserwald. The man will confess nothing; but, on being searched, a large sum in gold was found on his person; and though it is with the utmost pain that I can bring myself to entertain such an opinion, and to implicate a gentleman of the character and name of Monsieur de Magny, I do submit that our duty is to have the chevalier examined relative to the affair. As Monsieur de Magny is in her highness's private service, and in her confidence, I have heard, I would not venture to apprehend him without your highness's permission.'

"The prince's Master of the Horse, a friend of the old Baron de Magny, who was present at the interview, no sooner heard the strange intelligence, than he hastened away to the old general with the dreadful news of his grandson's supposed crime. Perhaps his highness himself was not unwilling that his old friend and tutor in arms should have the chance of saving his family from disgrace; at all events, Monsieur de Hengst, the Master of the Horse, was permitted to go off to the baron undisturbed, and break to him the intelligence of the accusation pending over the unfortunate chevalier.

"It is possible that he expected some such dreadful catastrophe, for, after hearing Hengst's narrative (as the latter afterwards told me), he only said, 'Heaven's will be done!' for some time refused to stir a step in the matter, and then only by the solicitation of his friend was induced to write the letter which Maxime de Magny received at our play-table.

"Whilst he was there, squandering the princess's money, a police visit was paid to his apartments, and a hundred proofs, not of his own guilt with respect to the robbery, but of his guilty connection with the princess, were discovered there,—tokens of her giving, passionate letters from her, copies of his own correspondence to his young friends at Paris,—all of which the Police Minister perused, and carefully put together under seal for his highness, Prince Victor. I have no doubt he perused them, for, on delivering them to the hereditary prince, Gelder said that, *in obedience to his highness's orders,* he had collected the chevalier's papers; but he need not say that, on his honour, he (Geldern) himself had never examined the documents. His difference with Messieurs de Magny was known; he begged his highness to employ any other official person in the judgment of the accusation brought against the young chevalier.

"All these things were going on while the chevalier was at play. A run of luck—you had great luck in those days, Monsieur de Balibari—was against him. He stayed and lost his 4000 ducats. He received his uncle's note, and, such was the infatuation of the wretched gambler, that, on receipt of it, he went down to the courtyard, where the horse was in waiting, absolutely took the money which the poor old gentleman had placed in the saddle-holsters, brought it upstairs, played it, and lost it; and when he issued from the room to fly, it was too late : he was placed in arrest at the bottom of my staircase, as you were upon entering your own home.

" Even when he came in under the charge of the soldiery, sent to arrest him, the old general, who was waiting, was overjoyed to see him, and flung himself into the lad's arms, and embraced him : it was said, for the first time in many years. ' He is here, gentlemen,' he sobbed out,—' thank God he is not guilty of the robbery ! ' and then sank back in a chair in a burst of emotion ; painful, it was said by those present, to witness on the part of a man so brave, and known to be so cold and stern.

" ' Robbery ! ' said the young man, ' I swear before heaven I am guilty of none ! ' and a scene of most touching reconciliation passed between them, before the unhappy young man was led from the guard-house into the prison which he was destined never to quit.

" That night the duke looked over the papers which Geldern had brought to him. It was at a very early stage of the perusal, no doubt, that he gave orders for your arrest ; for you were taken at midnight, Magny at ten o'clock ; after which time the old Baron de Magny had seen his highness, protesting of his grandson's innocence, and the prince had received him most graciously and kindly. His highness said he had no doubt the young man was innocent ; his birth and his blood rendered such a crime impossible ; but suspicion was too strong against him ; he was known to have been that day closeted with the Jew ; to have received a very large sum of money which he squandered at play, and of which the Hebrew had doubtless been the lender,—to have despatched his servant after him, who inquired the hour of the Jew's departure, lay in wait for him, and rifled him. Suspicion was so strong against the chevalier, that common justice required his arrest ; and, meanwhile, until he cleared himself, he should be kept in not dishonourable durance, and every regard had for his name, and the services of his honourable grandfather. With this assurance, and with a warm grasp of the hand, the prince left old General de Magny that night ; and the veteran retired to rest, almost consoled and confident in Maxime's eventual and immediate release.

" But in the morning, before daybreak, the prince, who had been reading papers all night, wildly called to the page, who slept in the next room across the door, bade him get horses, which were always kept in readiness in the stables, and, flinging a parcel of letters into a box, told the page to follow him on horseback with these. The young man (Monsieur de Weissenborn) told this to a young lady who was then of my household, and who is now Madame de Weissenborn, and a mother of a score of children.

" The page described that never was such a change seen as in his august master in the course of that single night. His eyes were blood-shot, his facc livid, his clothes were hanging loose about him, and he who had always made his appearance on parade as precisely dressed as any sergeant of his troops, might have been seen galloping through the lonely streets at early dawn without a hat, his unpowdered hair streaming behind him, like a madman.

" The page, with the box of papers, clattered after his master,— it was no easy task to follow him ; and they rode from the palace to the town, and through it to the general's quarter. The sentinels at the door were scared by the strange figure that rushed up to the general's gate, and, not knowing him, crossed bayonets, and refused him admission. ' Fools,' said Weissenborn, ' it is the prince ! ' And, jangling at the bell, as if for an alarm of fire, the door was at length opened by the porter, and his highness ran up to the general's bed-chamber, followed by the page with the box.

" ' Magny—Magny,' roared the prince, thundering at the closed door, ' get up ! ' And to the queries of the old man from within, answered, ' It is I—Victor—the prince !—get up ! ' And presently the door was opened by the general in his *robe-de-chambre*, and the prince entered. The page brought in the box, and was bidden to wait without, which he did ; but there led from Monsieur de Magny's bedroom into his ante-chamber two doors, the great one which formed the entrance into his room, and a smaller one which led, as the fashion is with our houses abroad, into the closet which communicates with the alcove where the bed is. The door of this was found by M. de Weissenborn to be open, and the young man was thus enabled to hear and see everything which occurred within the apartment.

"The general, somewhat nervously, asked what was the reason of so early a visit from his highness ; to which the prince did not for a while reply, further than by staring at him rather wildly, and pacing up and down the room.

" At last he said, ' Here is the cause ! ' dashing his fist on the box ; and, as he had forgotten to bring the key with him, he went to the door for a moment, saying, ' Weissenborn perhaps has it ' ; but, seeing over the stove one of the general's *couteaux-de-chasse*, he took it down, and said, ' That will do,' and fell to work to burst the red trunk open with the blade of the forest-knife. The point broke, and he gave an oath, but continued haggling on with the broken blade, which was better suited to his purpose than the long, pointed knife, and finally succeeded in wrenching open the lid of the chest.

" ' What is the matter ? ' said he, laughing. ' Here's the matter : —read that !—here's more matter, read that !—here's more—no, not that ; that's somebody else's picture—but here's hers ! Do you know that, Magny ? My wife's—the princess's ! ' Why did you and your cursed race ever come out of France, to plant your infernal wickedness wherever your feet fell, and to ruin honest German homes? What have you and yours ever had from my family but confidence and kindness? We gave you a home when you had none, and here's our reward!' and he flung a parcel of papers down before the old general; who saw the truth at once:—he had known it long before, probably, and sunk down on his chair, covering his face.

"The prince went on gesticulating, and shrieking almost. 'If a man injured you so, Magny, before you begot the father of that gambling, lying villain yonder, you would have known how to revenge yourself. You would have killed him! Yes, would have killed him. But who's to help me to my revenge? I've no equal. I can't meet that dog of a Frenchman,—that pimp from Versailles,—and kill him, as if he had played the traitor to one of his own degree.'

"'The blood of Maxime de Magny,' said the old gentleman, proudly, 'is as good as that of any prince in Christendom.'

"'Can I take it?' cried the prince: 'you know I can't. I can't have the privilege of any other gentleman of Europe. What am I to do? Look here, Magny: I was wild when I came here: I didn't know what to do. You've served me for thirty years; you've saved my life twice: they are all knaves and harlots about my poor old father here—no honest men or women—you are the only one—you saved my life: tell me what am I to do?' Thus, from insulting Monsieur de Magny, the poor distracted prince fell to supplicating him; and, at last, fairly flung himself down, and burst out in an agony of tears.

"Old Magny, one of the most rigid and cold of men on common occasions, when he saw this outbreak of passion on the prince's part, became, as my informant has described to me, as much affected as his master. The old man, from being cold and high, suddenly fell, as it were, into a whimpering querulousness of extreme old age. He lost all sense of dignity: he went down on his knees, and broke out into all sorts of wild, incoherent attempts at consolation; so much so, that Weissenborn said he could not bear to look at the scene, and actually turned away from the contemplation of it.

"But, from what followed in a few days, we may guess the results of the long interview. The prince, when he came away from the conversation with his old servant, forgot his fatal box of papers and sent the page back for them. The general was on his knees praying in the room when the young man entered, and only stirred and looked round wildly as the other removed the packet. The prince rode away to his hunting-lodge at three leagues from X——, and three days after that Maxime de Magny died in prison; having made a confession that he was engaged in an attempt to rob the

Jew, and that he had made away with himself, ashamed of his dishonour.

" But it is not known that it was the general himself who took his grandson poison ; it was said even that he shot him in the prison. This, however, was not the case. General de Magny carried his grandson the draught which was to carry him out of the world ; represented to the wretched youth that his fate was inevitable ; that it would be public and disgraceful unless he chose to anticipate the punishment, and so left him. But *it was not of his own accord*, and not until he had used *every* means of escape, as you shall hear, that the unfortunate being's life was brought to an end.

" As for General de Magny, he quite fell into imbecility a short time after his grandson's death, and my honoured duke's demise. After his highness the prince married the Princess Mary of F——, as they were walking in the English park together they once met old Magny riding in the sun on the easy-chair, in which he was carried commonly abroad after his paralytic fits. ' This is my wife, Magny,' said the prince, affectionately, taking the veteran's hand ; and he added, turning to his princess, ' General de Magny saved my life during the Seven Years' War.'

" ' What, you've taken her back again ? ' said the old man. ' I wish you'd send me back my poor Maxime.' He had quite forgotten the death of the poor Princess Olivia, and the prince, looking very dark indeed, passed away.

" And now," said Madame de Liliengarten, " I have only one more gloomy story to relate to you—the death of the Princess Olivia. It is even more horrible than the tale I have just told you." With which preface the old lady resumed her narrative.

" The kind, weak princess's fate was hastened, if not occasioned, by the cowardice of Magny. He found means to communicate with her from his prison, and her highness, who was not in open disgrace yet (for the duke, out of regard to the family, persisted in charging Magny with only robbery), made the most desperate efforts to relieve him, and to bribe the gaolers to effect his escape. She was so wild that she lost all patience and prudence in the conduct of any schemes she may have had for Magny's liberation ; for her husband was inexorable, and caused the chevalier's prison to be too strictly guarded for escape to be possible. She offered the state jewels in pawn to the court banker ; who of course was obliged to decline the transaction. She fell down on her knees, it is said, to Geldern, the Police Minister, and offered him heaven knows what as a bribe. Finally, she came screaming to my poor dear duke, who, with his age, diseases, and easy habits, was quite unfit for scenes of so violent a nature ; and who, in consequence of the excitement created in his august bosom by her frantic violence and grief, had a fit in which I very nigh lost him. That his dear life was brought to an untimely end by these transactions I have not the slightest doubt ; for the Strasbourg pie, of which they said he died, never, I am sure, could have injured him, but for the injury which his dear gentle heart received from the unusual occurrences in which he was forced to take a share.

" All her highness's movements were carefully, though not ostensibly, watched by her husband, Prince Victor ; who, waiting upon his august father, sternly signified to him that if his highness (*my* duke) should dare to aid the princess in her efforts to release Magny, he, Prince Victor, would publicly accuse the princess and her paramour of high treason, and take measures with the Diet for removing his father from the throne, as incapacitated to reign. Hence, interposition on our part was vain, and Magny was left to his fate.

" It came, as you are aware, very suddenly. Geldern, Police Minister, Hengst, Master of the Horse, and the colonel of the prince's guard, waited upon the young man in his prison two days after his grandfather had visited him there and left behind him the phial of poison which the criminal had not the courage to use. And Geldern signified to the young man that unless he took of his own accord the laurel-water provided by the elder Magny, more violent means of death would be instantly employed upon him, and that a file of grenadiers was in waiting in the courtyard to despatch him. Seeing this, Magny, with the most dreadful self-abasement, after dragging himself round the room on his knees, from one officer to another, weeping and screaming with terror, at last desperately drank off the potion, and was a corpse in a few minutes. Thus ended this wretched young man.

" His death was made public in the *Court Gazette* two days after, the paragraph stating that Monsieur de M——, struck with remorse for having attempted the murder of the Jew, had put himself to death by poison in prison ; and a warning was added to all young noblemen of the duchy to avoid the dreadful sin of gambling, which had been the cause of the young man's ruin, and had brought upon the grey hairs of one of the noblest and most honourable of the servants of the duke irretrievable sorrow.

" The funeral was conducted with decent privacy, the General de Magny attending it. The carriage of the two dukes and all the first people of the court made their calls upon the general afterwards. He attended parade as usual the next day on the Arsenal Place, and Duke Victor, who had been inspecting the building, came out of it leaning on the brave old warrior's arm. He was particularly gracious to the old man, and told his officers the oft-repeated story how at Rosbach, when the X—— contingent served with the troops of the unlucky Soubise, the general had thrown himself in the way of a French dragoon who was pressing hard upon his highness in the rout, had received the blow intended for his master, and killed the assailant. And he alluded to the family motto of 'Magny sans tache,' and said, 'It had always been so with his gallant friend and tutor in arms.' This speech affected all present very much, with the exception of the old general, who only bowed and did not speak; but when he went home he was heard muttering, 'Magny sans tache, Magny sans tache!' and was attacked with paralysis that night, from which he never more than partially recovered.

"The news of Maxime's death had somehow been kept from the princess until now: a *Gazette* even being printed without the paragraph containing the account of his suicide; but it was at length, I know not how, made known to her. And when she heard it, her ladies tell me, she screamed and fell, as if struck dead; then sat up wildly and raved like a madwoman, and was then carried to her bed, where her physician attended her, and where she lay of a brain-fever. All this while the prince used to send to make inquiries concerning her; and from his giving orders that his castle of Schlangenfels should be prepared and furnished, I make no doubt it was his intention to send her into confinement thither; as had been done with the unhappy sister of his Britannic Majesty at Zell.

"She sent repeatedly to demand an interview with his highness; which the latter declined, saying that he would communicate with her highness when her health was sufficiently recovered. To one of her passionate letters he sent back for reply a packet, which, when opened, was found to contain the emerald that had been the cause round which all this dark intrigue moved.

"Her highness at this time became quite frantic; vowed in the presence of all her ladies that one lock of her darling Maxime's hair was more precious to her than all the jewels in the world; rang for her carriage, and said she would go and kiss his tomb; proclaimed the murdered martyr's innocence, and called down the punishment of heaven, the wrath of her family, upon his assassin. The prince, on hearing these speeches (they were all, of course, regularly brought to him), is said to have given one of his dreadful looks (which I remember now), and to have said, 'This cannot last much longer.'

"All that day and the next the Princess Olivia passed in dictating the most passionate letters to the prince her father, to the Kings of France, Naples, and Spain, her kinsmen, and to all other branches of her family, calling upon them in the most incoherent terms to protect her against the butcher and assassin her husband, assailing his person in the maddest terms of reproach, and at the same time confessing her love for the murdered Magny. It was in vain that those ladies who were faithful to her pointed out to her the inutility of these letters, the dangerous folly of the confessions which they made; she insisted upon writing them, and used to give them to her second robe-woman, a Frenchwoman (her highness always affectioned persons of that nation), who had the key of her cassette, and carried every one of these epistles to Geldern.

"With the exception that no public receptions were held, the ceremony of the princess's establishment went on as before. Her ladies were allowed to wait upon her and perform their usual duties about her person. The only men admitted were, however, her servants, her physician and chaplain; and one day when she wished to go into the garden, a heyduc, who kept the door, intimated to her highness that the prince's orders were that she should keep her apartments.

"They abut, as you remember, upon the landing of the marble staircase of Schloss X——; the entrance to Prince Victor's suite of rooms being opposite the princess's on the same landing. This space is large, filled with sofas and benches, and the gentlemen and officers who waited upon the duke used to make a sort of antechamber of the landing-place, and pay their court to his highness there, as he passed out, at eleven o'clock to parade. At such a time, the heyducs within the princess's suite of rooms used to turn out with their halberts and present to Prince Victor—the same ceremony being performed on his own side, when pages came out and announced the approach of his highness. The pages used to come out and say, 'The prince, gentlemen!' and the drums beat in the hall, and the gentlemen rose, who were waiting on the benches that ran along the balustrade.

As if fate impelled her to her death, one day the princess, as her guards turned out, and she was aware that the prince was standing as was his wont, on the landing, conversing with his gentlemen (in the old days he used to cross to the princess's apartment and kiss her hand)—the princess, who had been anxious all the morning, complaining of heat, insisting that all the doors of the apartments should be left open; and giving tokens of an insanity which I think was now evident, rushed wildly at the doors when the guards passed out, flung them open, and before a word could be said, or her ladies could follow her, was in presence of Duke Victor, who was talking as usual on the landing: placing herself between him and the stair, she began apostrophizing him with frantic vehemence:

"'Take notice, gentlemen!' she screamed out, 'that this man is a murderer and a liar; that he lays plots for honourable gentlemen, and kills them in prison! Take notice, that I too am in prison, and fear the same fate: the same butcher who killed Maxime de Magny may, any night, put the knife to my throat. I appeal to you, and to all the kings of Europe, my royal kinsmen. I demand to be set free from this tyrant and villain, this liar and traitor ! I adjure you all, as gentlemen of honour, to carry these letters to my relatives, and say from whom you had them ! ' and with this the unhappy lady began scattering letters about among the astonished crowd.

" '*Let no man stoop !*' cried the prince, in a voice of thunder. ' Madame de Gleim, you should have watched your patient better. Call the princess's physicians : her highness's brain is affected. Gentlemen, have the goodness to retire.' And the prince stood on the landing as the gentlemen went down the stairs, saying fiercely to the guard, ' Soldier, if she moves, strike with your halbert ! ' on which the man brought the point of his weapon to the princess's breast ; and the lady, frightened, shrank back and re-entered her apartments. ' Now, Monsieur de Weissenborn,' said the prince, ' pick up all those papers ' : and the prince went into his own apartments, preceded by his pages, and never quitted them until he had seen every one of the papers burnt.

" The next day the *Court Gazette* contained a bulletin signed by the three physicians, stating that ' her highness the Hereditary Princess laboured under inflammation of the brain, and had passed a restless and disturbed night.' Similar notices were issued day after day. The services of all her ladies, except two, were dispensed with. Guards were placed within and without her doors ; her windows were secured, so that escape from them was impossible : and you know what took place ten days after. The church-bells were ringing all night, and the prayers of the faithful asked for a person *in extremis*. A *Gazette* appeared in the morning, edged with black, and stating that the high and mighty Princess Olivia Maria Ferdinanda, consort of his Serene Highness Victor Louis Emanuel, Hereditary Prince of X——, had died in the evening of the 24th of January 1769.

" But do you know *how* she died, sir ? That, too, is a mystery. Weissenborn, the page, was concerned in this dark tragedy ; and the secret was so dreadful, that never, believe me, till Prince Victor's death did I reveal it.

" After the fatal *esclandre* which the princess had made, the prince sent for Weissenborn, and binding him by the most solemn adjuration to secrecy (he only broke it to his wife many years after : indeed, there is no secret in the world that women cannot know if they will), despatched him on the following mysterious commission.

" ' There lives,' said his highness, ' on the Kehl side of the river, opposite to Strasbourg, a man whose residence you will easily find out from his name, which is *Monsieur de Strasbourg*. You will make your inquiries concerning him quietly, and without occasioning any remark ; perhaps you had better go into Strasbourg for the purpose, where the person is quite well known. You will take with you any comrade on whom you can perfectly rely: the lives of both, remember, depend on your secrecy. You will find out some period when Monsieur de Strasbourg is alone, or only in company of the domestic who lives with him: (I myself visited the man by accident on my return from Paris five years since, and hence am induced to send for him now, in my present emergency). You will have your carriage waiting at his door at night; and you and your comrade will enter his house masked; and present him with a purse of a hundred louis; promising him double that sum on his return from his expedition. If he refuse, you must use force and bring him; menacing him with instant death should he decline to follow you. You will place him in the carriage with the blinds drawn, one or other of you never losing sight of him the whole way, and threatening him with death if he discover himself or cry out. You will lodge him in the Old Tower here, where a room shall be prepared for him; and his work being done, you will restore him to his home in the same speed and secrecy with which you brought him from it.'

" Such were the mysterious orders Prince Victor gave his page; and Weissenborn, selecting for his comrade in the expedition Lieutenant Bartenstein, set out on his strange journey.

" All this while the palace was hushed, as if in mourning; the bulletins in the *Court Gazette* appeared, announcing the continuance of the princess's malady; and though she had but few attendants, strange and circumstantial stories were told regarding the progress of her complaint. She was quite wild. She had tried to kill herself. She had fancied herself to be I don't know how many different characters. Expresses were sent to her family informing them of her state, and couriers despatched *publicly* to Vienna and Paris to procure the attendance of physicians skilled in treating diseases of the brain. That pretended anxiety was all a feint: it was never intended that the princess should recover.

" The day on which Weissenborn and Bartenstein returned from their expedition, it was announced that her highness the princess was much worse; that night the report through the town was that she was at the agony: and that night the unfortunate creature was endeavouring to make her escape.

" She had unlimited confidence in the French chamber-woman who attended her, and between her and this woman the plan of escape was arranged. The princess took her jewels in a casket; a private door, opening from one of her rooms and leading into the outer gate, it was said, of the palace, was discovered for her; and a letter was brought to her, purporting to be from the duke her father-in-law, and stating that a carriage and horses had been provided, and would take her to B——: the territory where she might communicate with her family and be safe.

" The unhappy lady, confiding in her guardian, set out on the expedition. The passages wound through the walls of the modern part of the palace and abutted in effect at the old Owl Tower, as it was called, on the outer wall: the tower was pulled down afterwards, and for good reason.

" At a certain place the candle, which the chamber-woman was carrying, went out; and the princess would have screamed with terror, but her hand was seized, and a voice cried, ' Hush ! ' The next minute a man in a mask (it was the duke himself) rushed forward, gagged her with a handkerchief, her hands and legs were bound, and she was carried swooning with terror into a vaulted room, where she was placed by a person there waiting, and tied in an arm-chair. The same mask who had gagged her, came and bared her neck and said, ' It had best be done now she has fainted.'

" Perhaps it would have been as well; for though she recovered from her swoon, and her confessor, who was present, came forward and endeavoured to prepare her for the awful deed which was about to be done upon her, and for the state into which she was about to enter, when she came to herself it was only to scream like a maniac, to curse the duke as a butcher and tyrant, and to call upon Magny, her dear Magny.

" At this the duke said, quite calmly, ' May God have mercy on her sinful soul ! ' He, the confessor, and Geldern, who were present, went down on their knees; and, as his highness dropped his handkerchief, Weissenborn fell down in a fainting fit; while *Monsieur de Strasbourg,* taking the back hair in his hand, separated the shrieking head of Olivia from her miserable, sinful body. May heaven have mercy upon her soul ! "

. . . .

This was the story told by Madame de Liliengarten, and the reader will have no difficulty in drawing from it that part which affected myself and my uncle; who, after six weeks of arrest, were set at liberty, but with orders to quit the duchy immediately: indeed, with an escort of dragoons to conduct us to the frontier. What property we had we were allowed to sell and realise in money; but none of our play debts were paid to us; and all my hopes of the Countess Ida were thus at an end.

When Duke Victor came to the throne, which he did when, six months after, apolexy carried off the old sovereign his father, all the good old usages of X—— were given up,—play forbidden; the opera and ballet sent to the right-about; and the regiments which the old duke had sold recalled from their foreign service: with them came my countess's beggarly cousin the ensign, and he married her. I don't know whether they were happy or not. It is certain that a woman of such a poor spirit did not merit any very high degree of pleasure.

The now reigning Duke of X—— himself married four years after his first wife's demise, and Geldern, though no longer Police Minister, built the grand house of which Madame de Liliengarten spoke. What became of the minor actors in the great tragedy, who knows? Only Monsieur de Strasbourg was restored to his duties. Of the rest,—the Jew, the chamber-woman, the spy on Magny, I know nothing. Those sharp tools with which great people cut out their enterprises are generally broken in the using: nor did I ever hear that their employers had much regard for them in their ruin.

WILLIAM MAKEPEACE THACKERAY

"DIMOND CUT DIMOND"

From the Memoirs of Chawles Jeames Yellowplush

THE name of my nex master was, if posbil, still more elygant and youfonious than that of my fust. I now found myself boddy servant to the Honrabble Halgernon Percy Deuceace, youngest and fifth son of the Earl of Crabs.

Halgernon was a barrystir—that is, he lived in Pump Cort, Temple; a wulgar naybrood, witch praps my readers don't no. Suffiz it to say, it's on the confines of the citty, and the chosen aboad of the lawyers of this metrappolish.

When I say that Mr. Deuceace was a barrystir, I don't mean that he went sesshums or surcoats (as they call 'em), but simply that he kep chambers, lived in Pump Cort, and looked out for a commitionarship, or a revisinship, or any other place that the Wig guvvyment could give him. His father was a Wig pier (as the landriss told me), and had been a Toary pier. The fack is, his lordship was so poar that he would be anythink or nothink, to get provisions for his sons and an inkum for himself.

I phansy that he aloud Halgernon two hundred a year; and it would have been a very comforable maintenants, only he knever paid him.

Owever, the young genlmn was a genlmn, and no mistake; he got his allowents of nothink a year, and spent it in the most honrabble and fashnabble manner. He kept a kab—he went to Holmax—and Crockfud's—he moved in the most xquizzit suckles, and trubbld the law boox very little, I can tell you. Those fashnabble gents have ways of getten money witch comman pipple doant understand.

Though he only had a therd floar in Pump Cort, he lived as if he had the welth of Cresas. The tenpun notes floo abowt as common as haypince—clarrit and shampang was at his house as vulgar as gin; and verry glad I was, to be sure, to be a valley to a zion of the nobillaty.

Deuceace had, in his sittin-room, a large pictur on a sheet of paper. The names of his family was wrote on it ; it was wrote in the shape of a tree, a-groin out of a man-in-armer's stomick, and the names were on little plates among the bows. The pictur said that the Deuceaces kem into England in the year 1066, along with William Conqueruns. My master called it his podygree. I do bleev it was because he had this pictur, and because he was the *Honrabble* Deuceace, that he mannitched to live as he did. If he had been a common man, you'd have said he was no better than a swinler. It's only rank and buth that can warrant such singularities as my master show'd. For it's no use disgysing it—the Honrabble Halgernon was a GAMBLER. For a man of wulgar family, it's the wust trade that can be ; for a man of common feelinx of honesty, this profession is quite imposbil ; but for a real thoroughbread genlmn, it's the esiest and most prophetable line he can take.

It may praps appear curious that such a fashnable man should live in the Temple ; but it must be recklected that it's not only lawyers who live in what's called the Ins of Cort. Many batchylers, who have nothink to do with lor, have here there loginx ; and many sham barrysters, who never put on a wig and gownd twise in their lives, kip apartments in the Temple, instead of Bon Street, Pickledilly, or other fashnabble places.

Frinstance, on our stairkis (so these houses are called) there was 8 sets of chamberses, and only 3 lawyers. These was bottom floar, Screwson, Hewson, and Jewson, attorneys ; fust floar, Mr. Sergeant Flabber—opsite, Mr. Counslor Bruffy ; and secknd pair, Mr. Haggerstony, an Irish counslor, praktising at the Old Baly, and lickwise what they call reporter to the *Morning Post* nyouspapper. Opsite him was wrote—

MR. RICHARD BLEWITT ;

and on the thud floar, with my master, lived one Mr. Dawkins.

This young fellow was a new comer into the Temple, and unlucky it was for him too—he'd better have never been born ; for it's my firm apinion that the Temple ruined him—that is, with the help of my master and Mr. Dick Blewitt, as you shall hear.

Mr. Dawkins, as I was gave to understand by his young man, had jest left the Universary of Oxford, and had a pretty little fortn of his own—six thousand pound or so—in the stox. He was jest of age, an orfin who had lost his father and mother ; and having distinkwished hisself at Collitch, where he gained seffral prices, was come to town to push his fortn, and study the barryster's bisness.

Not bein of a very high fammly hisself—indeed, I've heard say his father was a chismonger, or something of that lo sort—Dawkins was glad to find his old Oxford friend, Mr. Blewitt, younger son to rich Squire Blewitt, of Listershire, and to take rooms so near him.

Now, tho' there was a considdrable intimacy between me and Mr. Blewitt's gentleman, there was scarcely any betwixt our masters—mine being too much of the aristoxy to associate with one of Mr. Blewitt's sort. Blewitt was what they call a bettin man ; he went reglar to Tattlesall's, kep a pony, wore a white hat, a blue berd's-eye handkercher, and a cut-away coat. In his manners he was the very contrary of my master, who was a slim, ellygant man as ever I see ; he had very white hands, rayther a sallow face, with sharp dark ise, and small wiskus neatly trimmed and as black as Warren's jet ; he spoke very low and soft ; he seemed to be watchin the person with whom he was in convysation, and always flatterd everybody. As for Blewitt, he was quite of another sort. He was always swearin, singing, and slappin people on the back, as hearty as posbill. He seemed a merry, careless, honest cretur, whom one would trust with life and soul. So thought Dawkins, at least ; who, though a quiet young man, fond of his boox, novvles, Byron's poems, floot-playing, and such-like scientafic amusemints, grew hand in glove with honest Dick Blewitt, and soon after with my master, the Honrabble Halgernon. Poor Daw ! he thought he was making good connexions and real friends : he had fallen in with a couple of the most etrocious swinlers that ever lived.

Before Mr. Dawkins's arrivial in our house, Mr. Deuceace had barely condysended to speak to Mr. Blewitt ; it was only about a month after that suckumstance that my master, all of a sudding, grew very friendly with him. The reason was pretty clear—Deuceace *wanted him*. Dawkins had not been an hour in master's company before he knew that he had a pidgin to pluck.

Blewitt knew this too, and bein very fond of pidgin, intended to keep this one entirely to himself. It was amusing to see the Honrabble Halgernon manuvring to get this pore bird out of Blewitt's clause, who thought he had it safe. In fact, he'd brought Dawkins to these chambers for that very porpus, thinking to have him under his eye, and strip him at leisure.

My master very soon found out what was Mr. Blewitt's game. Gamblers know gamblers, if not by instink, at least by reputation ; and though Mr. Blewitt moved in a much lower spear than Mr. Deuceace, they knew each other's dealins and caracters puffickly well.

"Charles, you scoundrel," said Deuceace to me one day (he always spoak in that kind way), "who is this person that has taken the opsit chambers, and plays the flute so industrusly ?"

"It's Mr. Dawkins, a rich young gentleman from Oxford, and a great friend of Mr. Blewittses, sir," says I ; "they seem to live in each other's rooms."

Master said nothink, but he *grin'd*—my eye, how he did grin ! Not the fowl find himself could snear more satannickly.

I knew what he meant :—

Imprimish. A man who plays the floot is a simpleton.

Secknly. Mr. Blewitt is a raskle.

Thirdmo. When a raskle and a simpleton is always together, and when the simpleton is *rich*, one knows pretty well what will come of it.

I was but a lad in them days, but I knew what was what, as well as my master ; it's not gentlemen only that's up to snough. Law bless us ! there was four of us on this stairkes, four as nice young men as you ever see—Mr. Bruffy's young man, Mr. Dawkinses, Mr. Blewitt's, and me ; and we knew what our masters was about as well as they did theirselfs. Frinstance, I can say this for *myself*, there wasn't a paper in Deuceace's desk or drawer, not a bill, a note, or mimerandum, which I hadn't read as well as he : with Blewitt's it was the same—me and his young man used to read 'em all. There wasn't a bottle of wine that we didn't get a glass out of, nor a pound of sugar that we didn't have some lumps of it. We had keys to all the cubbards ; we pipped into all the letters that kem and went ; we pored over all the bill-files ; we'd the best pickens out of the dinners, the livvers of the fowls, the force-mit balls out of the soup, the eggs from the sallit. As for the coals and candles, we left them to the landrisses. You may call this robry. Nonsince ! it's only our rights ; a suvvant's purquizzits is as sacred as the laws of Hengland.

Well, the long and short of it is this. Richard Blewitt, esquire, was sityouated as follows :—He'd an incum of three hunderd a year from his father. Out of this he had to pay one hunderd and, ninety for money borrowed by him at collidge, seventy for chambers, seventy more for his hoss, aty for his suvvant on bord wagis, and about three hunderd and fifty for a sepparat establishmint in the Regency Park ; besides this, his pockit-money, say a hunderd, his eatin, drinkin, and wine-marchant's bill, about two hunderd moar. So that you see he laid by a pretty handsome sum at the end of the year.

My master was diffrent ; and being a more fashnabble man than Mr. B., in course he owed a deal more money. There was fust :—

Account *contray*, at Crockford's	£3,711	0	0
Bills of xchange and I. O. U.'s (but he didn't pay these in most cases)	4,963	0	0
21 tailors' bills, in all	1,306	11	9
3 hossdealers' do.	402	0	0
2 coachbilder	506	0	0
Bills contracted at Cambritch	2,193	6	8
Sundries	987	10	0
	£14,069	8	5

I give this as a curosity—pipple doant know how in many cases fashnabble life is carried on ; and to know even what a real gnlmn *owes* is somethink instructif and agreeable.

But to my tail. The very day after my master had made the inquiries concerning Mr. Dawkins, witch I mentioned already, he met Mr. Blewitt on the stairs ; and byoutiffle it was to see how this gnlmn, who had before been almost cut by my master, was now received by him. One of the sweatest smiles I ever saw was now vizzable on Mr. Deuceace's countenance. He held out his hand, covered with a white kid glove, and said in the most frenly tone of vice posbill, " What ! Mr. Blewitt ? It is an age since we met. What a shame that such near naybors should see each other so seldom ! "

Mr. Blewitt, who was standing at his door, in a pe-green dressing-gown, smoakin a segar, and singin a hunting coarus, looked surprised, flattered, and then suspicious.

" Why, yes," says he, " it is, Mr. Deuceace, a long time."

" Not, I think, since we dined at Sir George Hookey's. By the-bye, what an evening that was—hay, Mr. Blewitt ? What wine ! what capital songs ! I recollect your ' Mayday in the morning '—cuss me, the best comick song I ever heard. I was speaking to the Duke of Doncaster about it only yesterday. You know the duke, I think ? "

Mr. Blewitt said, quite surly, " No, I don't."

" Not know him ! " cries master ; " why, hang it, Blewitt, he knows *you* ; as every sporting man in England does, I should think. Why, man, your good things are in everybody's mouth at New-market."

And so master went on chaffin Mr. Blewitt. That gnlmn at fust answered him quite short and angry ; but, after a little more flummery, he grew as pleased as posbill, took in all Deuceace's flatry and bleeved all his lies. At last the door shut, and they both went into Mr. Blewitt's chambers together.

Of course I can't say what past there ; but in an hour master kem up to his own room as yaller as mustard, and smellin sadly of backo-smoke. I never see any genlmn more sick than he was ; *he'd been smoakin seagars* along with Blewitt. I said nothink, in course, tho I'd often heard him xpress his horrow of backo, and knew very well he would as soon swallow pizon as smoke. But he wasn't a chap to do a thing without a reason : if he'd been smoakin, I warrant he had smoaked to some porpus.

I didn't hear the convysation between 'em ; but Mr. Blewitt's man did : it was—" Well, Mr. Blewitt, what capital seagars ! Have you one for a friend to smoak ? " (The old fox, it wasn't only the *seagars* he was a-smoakin !) " Walk in," says Mr. Blewitt ; and they began a chaffin together—master very ankshous about the young gintleman who had come to live in our chambers, Mr. Dawkins, and always coming back to that subject, saying that people on the same stairkis ot to be frenly ; how glad he'd be, for his part, to know Mr. Dick Blewitt, and *any friend of his*, and so on. Mr. Dick, howsever, seamed quite aware of the trap laid for him. "I really don't no this Dawkins," says he : "he's a chismonger's son, I hear ; and tho I've exchanged visits with him, I doant intend to continyou the acquaintance, not wishin to assoshate with that kind of pipple." So they went on, master fishin, and Mr. Blewitt not wishin to take the hook at no price.

"Confound the vulgar thief!" muttard my master, as he was laying on his sophy, after being so very ill ; "I've poisoned myself with his infernal tobacco, and he has foiled me. The cursed swindling boor! he thinks he'll ruin this poor cheesemonger, does he? I'll step in, and *warn* him."

I thought I should bust a-laffin when he talked in this style. I knew very well what his "warning" meant—lockin the stable-door, but stealin the hoss fust.

Next day, his strattygam for becoming acquainted with Mr. Dawkins we exicuted ; and very pritty it was.

Besides potry and the floote, Mr. Dawkins, I must tell you, had some other parshallities—wiz., he was very fond of good eatin and drinkin. After doddling over his music and boox all day, this young genlmn used to sally out of evenings, dine sumptiously at a tavern, drinkin all sots of wine along with his friend Mr. Blewitt. He was a quiet young fellow enough at fust ; but it was Mr. B. who (for his own porpuses, no doubt) had got him into this kind of life. Well, I needn't say that he who eats a fine dinner, and drinks too much overnight, wants a bottle of soda-water, and a gril, praps, in the morning. Such was Mr. Dawkinses case ; and reglar almost as twelve o'clock came, the waiter from "Dix Coffy-House" was to be seen on our stairkis, bringing up Mr. D.'s hot breakfast.

No man would have thought there was anything in such a trifling cirkumstance ; master did, though, and pounced upon it like a cock on a barlycorn.

He sent me out to Mr. Morell's in Pickledilly, for wot's called a Strasbug-pie—in French, a "*patty defau graw*." He takes a card, and nails it on the outside case (patty defaw graws come generally in a round wooden box, like a drumb) ; and what do you think he writes on it? why, as follos :—"*For the Honourable Algernon Percy Deauceace, &c., &c., &c. With Prince Talleyrand's compliments.*"

Prince Tallyram's complimints, indeed! I laff when I think of it, still, the old surpint! He *was* a surpint, that Deuceace, and no mistake.

Well, by a most extrornary piece of ill-luck, the nex day punctially as Mr. Dawkinses brexfas was coming *up* the stairs, Mr.

Halgernon Percy Deuceace was going *down*. He was as gay as a lark, humming an Oppra tune, and twizzting round his head his hevy gold-headed cane. Down he went very fast, and by a most unlucky axdent struck his cane against the waiter's tray, and away went Mr. Dawkinses gril, kayann, kitchup, soda-water and all! I can't think how my master should have choas such an exact time; to be sure, his windo looked upon the cort, and he could see every one who came into our door.

As soon as the axdent had took place, master was in such a rage as, to be sure, no man ever was in before: he swore at the waiter in the most dreddfle way; he threatened him with his stick, and it was only when he see that the waiter was raythe a bigger man than hisself that he was in the least pazzyfied. He returned to his own chambres; and John, the waiter, went off for more gril to Dixes Coffy-House.

"This is a most unlucky axdent, to be sure, Charles," says master to me, after a few minits paws, during witch he had been and wrote a note, put it into an anvelope, and sealed it with his bigg seal of arms. "But stay—a thought strikes me—take this note to Mr. Dawkins, and that pye you brought yesterday; and hearkye, you scoundrel, if you say where you got it I will break every bone in your skin!"

These kind of prommises were among the few which I knew him to keep; and as I loved boath my skinn and my boans, I carried the noat, and of cors said nothink. Waiting in Mr. Dawkinses chambus for a few minnits, I returned to my master with an anser. I may as well give both of these documence, of which I happen to have taken coppies.

I

THE HON. A. P. DEUCEACE TO T. S. DAWKINS, ESQ.

TEMPLE, *Tuesday*.

"Mr. DEUCEACE presents his compliments to Mr. Dawkins, and begs at the same time to offer his most sincere apologies and regrets for the accident which has just taken place.

"May Mr. Deuceace be allowed to take a neighbour's privilege, and to remedy the evil he has occasioned to the best of his power? If Mr. Dawkins will do him the favour to partake of the contents of the accompanying case (from Strasburg direct, and the gift of a friend, on whose taste as a gourmand Mr. Dawkins may rely), perhaps he will find that it is not a bad substitute for the *plat* which Mr. Deuceace's awkwardness destroyed.

"It will also, Mr. Deuceace is sure, be no small gratification to the original donor of the *pâté*, when he learns that it has fallen into the hands of so celebrated a *bon vivant* as Mr. Dawkins.

"T. S. Dawkins, Esq., etc., etc., etc."

II

FROM T. S. DAWKINS, ESQ., TO THE HON. A. P. DEUCEACE.

"MR. THOMAS SMITH DAWKINS presents his grateful compliments to the Hon. Mr. Deuceace, and accepts with the greatest pleasure Mr. Deuceace's generous proffer.

"It would be one of the *happiest moments* of Mr. Smith Dawkins's life if the Hon. Mr. Deuceace would *extend his generosity* still further, and condescend to partake of the repast which his *munificent politeness* has furnished.

"TEMPLE, *Tuesday*."

Many and many a time, I say, have I grin'd over these letters, which I had wrote from the original by Mr. Bruffy's copyin clark. Deuceace's flam about Prince Tallyram was puffickly successful. I saw young Dawkins blush with delite as he red the note; he toar up for or five sheets before he composed the answer to it, which was as you red abuff, and roat in a hand quite trembling with pleasyer. If you could but have seen the look of triumph in Deuceace's wicked black eyes when he read the noat! I never see a deamin yet, but I can phansy 1, a-holding a writhing soal on his pitch-fork, and smilin like Deuceace. He dressed himself in his very best clothes, and in he went, after sending me over to say that he would xcept with pleasyour Mr. Dawkins's invite.

The pie was cut up, and a most frenly conversation begun betwixt the two genlmin. Deuceace was quite captivating. He spoke to Mr. Dawkins in the most respeckful and flatrin manner—agread in everythink he said—prazed his taste, his furniter, his coat, his classick nolledge, and his playin on the floot; you'd have thought, to hear him, that such a polygon of exlens as Dawkins did not breath—that such a modist, sinsear, honrabble genlmn as Deuceace was to be seen nowhere xcept in Pump Cort. Poor Daw was complitly taken in. My master said he'd introduce him to the Duke of Doncaster, and Heaven knows how many nobs more, till Dawkins was quite intawsicated with pleasyour. I know as a fac (and it pretty well shows the young genlmn's carryter) that he went that very day and ordered 2 new coats, on porpos to be introjuiced to the lords in.

But the best joak of all was at last. Singin, swagrin, and swarink, up stares came Mr. Dick Blewitt. He flung open Mr. Dawkins's door, shouting out, "Daw, my old buck, how are you?" when, all of a sudden, he sees Mr. Deuceace: his jor dropt, he turned chocky white, and then burnin red, and looked as if a stror would knock him down. "My dear Mr. Blewitt," says my master, smiling and offring his hand, "how glad I am to see you! Mr. Dawkins and I were just talking about your pony! Pray sit down."

Blewitt did. And now was the question, who should sit the other out; but, law bless you, Mr. Blewitt was no match for my master: all the time he was fidgetty, silent, and sulky; on the contry, master was charmin. I never herd such a flo of conversatin, or so many wittacisms as he uttered. At last, completely beat, Mr. Blewitt took his leaf; that instant master followed him, and passin his arm through that of Mr. Dick, led him into our chambers, and began talkin to him in the most affabl and affeckshnat manner.

But Dick was too angry to listen: at last, when master was telling him some long story about the Duke of Doncaster, Blewitt burst out,—

"A plague on the Duke of Doncaster! Come, come, Mr. Deuceace, don't you be running your rigs upon me; I an't the man to be bamboozl'd by long-winded stories about dukes and duchesses. You think I don't know you; every man knows you and your line of country. Yes, you're after young Dawkins there, and think to pluck him; but you shan't—no, by ——, you shan't." (The reader must recklect that the oaths which interspussed Mr. B's convysation I have lift out.) Well, after he'd fired a wolley of em, Mr. Deuceace spoke as cool as possbill.

"Heark ye, Blewitt. I know you to be one of the most infernal thieves and scoundrels unhung. If you attempt to hector with me, I will cane you; if you want more, I'll shoot you; if you meddle between me and Dawkins, I will do both. I know your whole life, you miserable swindler and coward. I know you have already won two hunderd pounds of this lad, and want all. I will have half, or you never shall have a penny." It's quite true that master knew things; but how was the wonder.

I couldn't see Mr B..'s face during this dialogue, bein on the wrong side of the door; but there was a considdrable paws after thuse complymints had passed between the two genlmn—one walkin quickly up and down the room; tother, angry and stupid, sittin down, and stampin with his foot.

"Now listen to this, Mr. Blewitt," continues master at last. "If you're quiet, you shall half this fellow's money; but venture to win a shilling from him in my absence or without my consent, and you do it at your peril."

"Well, well, Mr. Deuceace," cried Dick, it's very hard, and I must say not fair: the game was of my startin, and you've no right to interfere with my friend."

"Mr. Blewitt, you are a fool! You professed yesterday not to know this man, and I was obliged to find him out for myself. I should like to know by what law of honour I am bound to give him up to you."

It was charmin to hear this pair of raskles talkin about *honour*. I declare I could have found it in my heart to warn young Dawkins of the precious way in which these chaps were going to serve him. But if *they* didn't know what honour was, *I* did; and never, never did I tell tails about my masters when in their sarvice—*out,* in cors, the hobligation is no longer binding.

Well, the nex day there was a gran dinner at our chambers—white soop, turbit, and lobstir sos; saddil of Scoch muttn, grous, and M'Arony; wines, shampang, hock, maderia, a bottle of poart, and ever so many of clarrit. The compny presint was three—wiz., the Honrabble A. P. Deuceace, R. Blewitt, and Mr. Dawkins, Exquires. My i, how we genlmn in the kitchin did enjy it! Mr. Blewittes man eat so much grous (when it was brot out of the parlor) that I reely thought he would be sik; Mr. Dawkinses genlmn (who was only abowt 13 years of age) grew so il with M'Arony and plumb-puddn as to be obleeged to take sefral of Mr. D's pils, which ½ kild him. But this is all promiscuous: I an't talkin of the survants now, but the masters.

Would you bleeve it? After dinner and praps 8 bottles of wine between the 3, the genlm sat down to *écarty.* It's a game where only 2 plays, and where, in coarse, when there's only 3, one looks on.

Fust they playd crown pints, and a pound the bett. At this game they were wonderful equill; and about suppertime (when grilled am, more shampang, devld biskits, and other things, was brot in) the play stood thus: Mr. Dawkins had won 2 pounds; Mr. Blewitt, 30 shillings; the Honrabble Mr. Deuceace having lost £3 10s. After the devvle and the shampang the play was a little higher. Now it was pound pints, and five pound the bet. I thought, to be sure, after hearing the complymints between Blewitt and master in the morning, that now poor Dawkins's time was come.

Not so: Dawkins won always, Mr. B. betting on his play, and giving him the very best of advice. At the end of the evening (which was abowt five o'clock the nex morning) they stopt. Master was counting up the skore on a card.

"Blewitt," says he, "I've been unlucky. I owe you—let me see—yes, five-and-forty pounds!"

"Five-and-forty," says Blewitt, "and no mistake!"

"I will give you a cheque," says the honrabble genlmn.

"Oh, don't mention it, my dear sir!" But master got a grate. sheet of paper, and drew him a check on Messeers. Pump, Algit and Co., his bankers.

"Now," says master, "I've got to settle with you, my dear Mr. Dawkins. If you had backd your luck, I should have owed you a very handsome sum of money. *Voyons,* thirteen points at a pound—it is easy to calculate"; and drawin out his puss, he clinked over the table 13 goolden suverings, which shon till they made my eyes wink.

So did pore Dawkinses, as he put out his hand, all trembling, and drew them in.

"Let me say," added master, "let me say (and I've had some little experience) that you are the very best *écarté* player with whom I ever sat down."

Dawkinses eyes glistened as he put the money up, and said, "Law, Deuceace, you flatter me."

Flatter him! I should think he did. It was the very think which master ment.

"But mind you, Dawkins," continyoud he, "I must have my revenge; for I'm ruined—positively ruined—by your luck."

"Well, well," says Mr. Thomas Smith Dawkins, as pleased as if he had gained a millium, "shall it be to-morrow?—Blewitt, what say you?"

Mr. Blewitt agreed, in course. My master, after a little demurring, consented too. "We'll meet," says he, "at your chambers. But mind, my dear fello, not too much wine: I can't stand it at any time, especially when I have to play *écarté* with *you*."

Pore Dawkins left our rooms as happy as a prins. "Here, Charles," says he, and flung me a sovring. Pore fellow, pore fellow! I knew what was a-comin!

But the best of it was, that these 13 sovrings which Dawkins won, *master had borrowed them from Mr. Blewitt!* I brought 'em, with 7 more, from that young genlmn's chambers that very morning, for since his interview with master, Blewitt had nothing to refuse him.

Well, shall I continue the tail? If Mr. Dawkins had been the least bit wiser, it would have taken him six months befoar he lost his money; as it was, he was such a confunded ninny that it took him a very short time to part with it.

Nex day (it was Thursday, and master's acquaintance with Mr. Dawkins had only commenced on Tuesday), Mr. Dawkins, as I said, gev his party—dinner at 7. Mr. Blewitt and the two Mr. D.'s as befoar. Play begins at 11. This time I knew the bisness was pretty serious, for we suvvants was packed off to bed at 2 o'clock. On Friday I went to chambers: no master—he kem in for 5 minutes at about 12, made a little toilet, ordered more devvles and soda-water, and back again he went to Mr. Dawkins's.

They had dinner there at 7 again; but nobody seamed to eat, for all the vittls came out to us genlmn: they had in more wine though, and must have drunk at least 2 dozen in the 36 hours.

At ten o'clock, however, on Friday night, back my master came to his chambers. I saw him as I never saw him before—namly, reglar drunk. He staggered about the room, he danced, he hickipd, he swoar, he flung me a heap of silver, and, finely, he sunk down exosted on his bed ; I pullin off his boots and close, and making him comfrabble.

When I had removed his garmints, I did what it's the duty of every servant to do—I emtied his pockets, and looked at his pockit-book and all his letters : a number of axdents have been prevented that way.

I found there, among a heap of things, the following pretty dockyment :—

> I. O. U.
> £4700.
> THOMAS SMITH DAWKINS.
> *Friday, 16th January.*

There was another bit of paper of the same kind—" I.O.U. four hundred pounds.—Richard Blewitt " ; but this, in corse, ment nothink.

. . . .

Nex mornin, at nine, master was up, and as sober as a judg. He drest, and was off to Mr. Dawkins. At 10 he ordered a cab, and the two genlmn went together.

" Where shall he drive, sir ? " says I.

" Oh, tell him to drive to THE BANK."

Pore Dawkins, his eyes red with remors and sleepliss drunkenniss, gave a shudder and a sob, as he sunk back in the wehicle ; and they drove on.

That day he sold out every hapny he was worth, xcept five hundred pounds.

. . . .

Abowt 12 master had returned, and Mr. Dick Blewitt came stridin up the stairs with a sollum and important hair.

" Is your master at home ? " says he.

" Yes, sir," says I ; and in he walks—I, in coars, with my ear to the keyhole, listning with all my mite.

" Well," says Blewitt, " we maid a pretty good night of it, Mr. Deuceace. Yu've settled, I see, with Dawkins."

" Settled ! " says master. " Oh, yes—yes—I've settled with him."

" Four thousand seven hundred, I think ? "

" About that—yes."

" That makes my share—let me see—two thousand three hundred and fifty ; which I'll thank you to fork out."

" Upon my word—why—Mr. Blewitt," says master, " I don't really understand what you mean."

" *You don't know what I mean !* " says, Blewitt, in an axent such as I never before heard—" you don't know what I mean ! Did you not promise me that we were to go shares ? Didn't I lend you twenty sovereigns the other night to pay our losings to Dawkins ? Didn't you swear, on your honour as a gentleman, to give me half of all that might be won in this affair ? "

" Agreed, sir," says Deuceace ; " agreed."

" Well, sir, and now what have you to say ! "

" Why, *that I don't intend to keep my promise !* You infernal fool and ninny ! do you suppose I was labouring for *you* ? Do you fancy I was going to the expense of giving a dinner to that jackass yonder, that you should profit by it ? Get away, sir ! Leave the room, sir ! Or, stop—here—I will give you four hundred pounds —your own note of hand, sir, for that sum, if you will consent to forget all that has passed between us, and that you have never known Mr. Algernon Deuceace."

I've seen pipple angery before now, but never any like Blewitt. He stormed, groaned, belloed, swoar ! At last he fairly began blubbring—now cussing and nashing his teeth, now praying dear Mr. Deuceace to grant him mercy.

At last master flung open the door (Heavn bless us ! it's well I didn't tumble hed over eells into the room), and said, " Charles, show the gentleman downstairs ! " My master looked at him quite steddy. Blewitt slunk down, as misrabble as any man I ever see. As for Dawkins, Heaven knows where he was !

. . . .

" Charles," says my master to me, about an hour afterwards, " I'm going to Paris ; you may come, too, if you please."

CHARLES DICKENS
1812–1870

THE BAGMAN'S STORY

ONE winter's evening, about five o'clock, just as it began to grow dusk, a man in a gig might have been seen urging his tired horse along the road which leads across Marlborough Downs, in the direction of Bristol. I say he might have been seen, and I have no doubt he would have been, if anybody but a blind man had happened to pass that way; but the weather was so bad, and the night so cold and wet, that nothing was out but the water, and so the traveller jogged along in the middle of the road, lonesome and dreary enough. If any bagman of that day could have caught sight of the little neck-or-nothing sort of gig, with a clay-coloured body and red wheels, and the vixenish, ill-tempered, fast-going bay mare, that looked like a cross between a butcher's horse and a two-penny post-office pony, he would have known at once that this traveller could have been no other than Tom Smart, of the great house of Bilson and Slum, Cateaton Street, City. However, as there was no bagman to look on, nobody knew anything at all about the matter; and so Tom Smart and his clay-coloured gig with the red wheels, and the vixenish mare with the fast pace, went on together, keeping the secret among them: and nobody was a bit the wiser.

There are many pleasanter places, even in this dreary world, than Marlborough Downs when it blows hard; and if you throw in beside, a gloomy winter's evening, a miry and sloppy road, and a pelting fall of heavy rain, and try the effect, by way of experiment, in your own proper person, you will experience the full force of this observation.

The wind blew—not up the road or down it, though that's bad enough, but sheer across it, sending the rain slanting down like the lines they used to rule in the copybooks at school, to make the boys slope well. For a moment it would die away, and the traveller would begin to delude himself into the belief that, exhausted with its previous fury, it had quietly lain itself down to rest, when, whoo! he would hear it growling and whistling in the distance, and on it would come rushing over the hill-tops, and sweeping along the plain, gathering sound and strength as it drew nearer, until it dashed with a heavy gust against horse and man, driving the sharp rain into their ears, and its cold damp breath into their very bones ; and past them it would scour, far, far away, with a stunning roar, as if in ridicule of their weakness, and triumphant in the consciousness of its own strength and power.

The bay mare splashed away, through the mud and water, with drooping ears ; now and then tossing her head as if to express her disgust at this very ungentlemanly behaviour of the elements, but keeping a good pace notwithstanding, until a gust of wind, more furious than any that had yet assailed them, caused her to stop suddenly and plant her four feet firmly against the ground to prevent her being blown over. It's a special mercy that she did this, for if she *had* been blown over, the vixenish mare was so light, and the gig was so light, and Tom Smart such a light weight into the bargain, that they must infallibly have all gone rolling over and over together, until they reached the confines of earth, or until the wind fell ; and in either case the probability is, that neither the vixenish mare, nor the clay-coloured gig with the red wheels, nor Tom Smart, would ever have been fit for service again.

"Well, damn my straps and whiskers," says Tom Smart (Tom sometimes had an unpleasant knack of swearing), "Damn my straps and whiskers," says Tom, "if this ain't pleasant, blow me!"

You'll very likely ask me why, as Tom Smart had been pretty well blown already, he expressed this wish to be submitted to the same process again. I can't say—all I know is, that Tom Smart said so—or at least he always told my uncle he said so, and it's just the same thing.

"Blow me," says Tom Smart ; and the mare neighed as if she were precisely of the same opinion.

"Cheer up, old girl," said Tom, patting the bay mare on the neck with the end of his whip. "It won't do pushing on. such a night as this ; the first house we come to we'll put up at, so the faster you go the sooner it's over. Soho, old girl—gently—gently."

Whether the vixenish mare was sufficiently well acquainted with the tones of Tom's voice to comprehend his meaning, or whether she found it colder standing still than moving on, of course I can't say. But I can say that Tom had no sooner finished speaking, than she pricked up her ears, and started forward at a speed which made the clay-coloured gig rattle till you would have supposed every one of the red spokes was going to fly out on the turf of Marlborough Downs ; and even Tom, whip as he was, couldn't stop or check her pace, until she drew up, of her own accord, before a roadside inn on the right-hand side of the way, about half a quarter of a mile from the end of the Downs.

Tom cast a hasty glance at the upper part of the house as he threw the reins to the hostler, and stuck the whip in the box. It was a strange old place, built of a kind of shingle, inlaid, as it were, with cross-beams, with gabled-topped windows projecting completely over the path-way, and a low door with a dark porch, and a couple of steep steps leading down into the house, instead of the modern fashion of half-a-dozen shallow ones leading up to it. It was a comfortable-looking place though, for there was a strong cheerful light in the bar window, which shed a bright ray across the road, and even lighted up the hedge on the other side ; and there was a red flickering light in the opposite window, one moment but faintly discernible, and the next gleaming strongly through the drawn curtains, which intimated that a rousing fire was blazing within. Marking these little evidences with the eye of an experienced traveller, Tom dismounted with as much agility as his half-frozen limbs would permit, and entered the house.

In less than five minutes' time, Tom was ensconced in the room opposite the bar—the very room where he had imagined the fire blazing—before a substantial matter-of-fact roaring fire, composed of something short of a bushel of coals, and wood enough to make half-a-dozen decent gooseberry bushes, piled half-way up the chimney, and roaring and crackling with a sound that of itself would have warmed the heart of any reasonable man. This was comfortable, but this was not all, for a smartly dressed girl, with a bright eye and a neat ankle, was laying a very clean white cloth on the table ; and as Tom sat with his slippered feet on the fender, and his back to the open door, he saw a charming prospect of the bar reflected in the glass over the chimney-piece, with delightful rows of green bottles and gold labels, together with jars of pickles and preserves, and cheeses and boiled hams, and rounds of beef arranged on shelves in the most tempting and delicious array. Well, this was comfortable too ; but even this was not all—for in the bar, seated at tea at the nicest possible little table, drawn close up before the brightest possible little fire, was a buxom widow of somewhere about eight and-forty or thereabouts, with a face as comfortable as the bar, who was evidently the landlady of the house, and the supreme ruler over all these agreeable possessions. There was only one drawback to the beauty of the whole picture, and that was a tall man—a very tall man—in a brown coat and bright basket buttons, and black whiskers and wavy black hair, who was seated at tea with the widow, and who it required no great penetration to discover was in a fair way of persuading her to be a widow no longer, but to confer upon him the privilege of sitting down in that bar, for and during the whole remainder of the term of his natural life.

Tom Smart was by no means of an irritable or envious disposition, but somehow or other the tall man with the brown coat and the bright basket buttons did rouse what little gall he had in his composition, and did make him feel extremely indignant: the more especially as he could now and then observe, from his seat before the glass, certain little affectionate familiarities passing between the tall man and the widow, which sufficiently denoted that the tall man was as high in favour as he was in size. Tom was fond of hot punch—I may venture to say he was *very* fond of hot punch—and after he had seen the vixenish mare well fed and well littered down, and had eaten every bit of the nice little hot dinner which the widow tossed up for him with her own hands, he just ordered a tumbler of it, by way of experiment. Now, if there was one thing in the whole range of domestic art which the widow could manufacture better than another it was this identical article; and the first tumbler was adapted to Tom Smart's taste with such peculiar nicety, that he ordered a second with the least possible delay. Hot punch is a pleasant thing, gentlemen—an extremely pleasant thing under any circumstances—but in that snug old parlour, before the roaring fire, with the wind blowing outside till every timber in the old house creaked again, Tom Smart found it perfectly delightful. He ordered another tumbler, and then another—I am not quite certain whether he didn't order another after that—but the more he drank of the hot punch, the more he thought of the tall man.

"Confound his impudence!" said Tom to himself, "what business has he in that snug bar? Such an ugly villain too!" said Tom. "If the widow had any taste, she might surely pick up some better fellow than that." Here Tom's eye wandered from the glass on the chimney-piece to the glass on the table; and as he felt himself becoming gradually sentimental, he emptied the fourth tumbler of punch and ordered a fifth.

Tom Smart, gentlemen, had always been very much attached to the public line. It had long been his ambition to stand in a bar of his own in a green coat, knee-cords, and tops. He had a great notion of taking the chair at convivial dinners, and he had often thought how well he could preside in a room of his own in the talking way, and what a capital example he could set to his customers in the drinking department. All these things passed rapidly through Tom's mind as he sat drinking the hot punch by the roaring fire, and he felt very justly and properly indignant that the tall man should be in a fair way of keeping such an excellent house, while he, Tom Smart, was as far off from it as ever. So, after deliberating over the two last tumblers whether he hadn't a perfect right to pick a quarrel with the tall man for having contrived to get into the good graces of the buxom widow, Tom Smart at last arrived at the satisfactory conclusion that he was a very ill-used and persecuted individual, and had better go to bed.

Up a wide and ancient staircase the smart girl preceded Tom, shading the chamber candle with her hand, to protect it from the currents of air which in such a rambling old place might have found plenty of room to disport themselves in, without blowing the candle out, but which did blow it out nevertheless ; thus affording Tom's enemies an opportunity of asserting that it was he, and not the wind, who extinguished the candle, and that while he pretended to be blowing it alight again, he was in fact kissing the girl. Be this as it may, another light was obtained, and Tom was conducted through a maze of rooms, and a labyrinth of passages, to the apartment which had been prepared for his reception, where the girl bade him good-night, and left him alone.

It was a good large room with big closets, and a bed which might have served for a whole boarding-school, to say nothing of a couple of oaken presses that would have held the baggage of a small army ; but what struck Tom's fancy was a strange, grim-looking high-backed chair, carved in the most fantastic manner, with a flowered damask cushion, and the round knobs at the bottom of the legs carefully tied up in red cloth, as if it had got the gout in its toes. Of any other queer chair, Tom would only have thought it *was* a queer chair, and there would have been an end of the matter; but there was something about this particular chair, and yet he couldn't tell what it was, so odd and so unlike any other piece of furniture he had ever seen, that it seemed to fascinate him. He sat down before the fire, and stared at the old chair for half an hour ;—Deuce take the chair, it was such a strange old thing, he couldn't take his eyes off it.

" Well," said Tom, slowly undressing himself, and staring at the old chair all the while, which stood with a mysterious aspect by the bedside, " I never saw such a rum concern as that in my days. Very odd," said Tom, who had got rather sage with the hot punch, " Very odd." Tom shook his head with an air of profound wisdom, and looked at the chair again. He couldn't make anything of it though, so he got into bed, covered himself up warm, and fell asleep.

In about half an hour Tom woke up, with a start, from a confused dream of tall men and tumblers of punch ; and the first object that presented itself to his waking imagination was the queer chair.

" I won't look at it any more," said Tom to himself, and he squeezed his eyelids together, and tried to persuade himself he was going to sleep again. No use ; nothing but queer chairs danced before his eyes, kicking up their legs, jumping over each other's backs, and playing all kinds of antics.

" I may as well see one real chair as two or three complete sets of false ones," said Tom, bringing out his head from under the bedclothes. There it was, plainly descernible by the light of the fire looking as provoking as ever.

Tom gazed at the chair; and, suddenly as he looked at it, a most extraordinary change seemed to come over it. The carving of the back gradually assumed the lineaments and expression of an old shrivelled human face; the damask cushion became an antique, flapped waistcoat; the round knobs grew into a couple of feet, encased in red cloth slippers; and the old chair looked like a very ugly old man, of the previous century, with his arms akimbo. Tom sat up in bed, and rubbed his eyes to dispel the illusion. No. The chair was an ugly old gentleman; and what was more, he was winking at Tom Smart.

Tom was naturally a headlong careless sort of dog, and he had had five tumblers of hot punch into the bargain; so, although he was a little startled at first he began to grow rather indignant when he saw the old gentleman winking and leering at him with such an impudent air. At length he resolved that he wouldn't stand it; and as the old face still kept winking away as fast as ever, Tom said, in a very angry tone:

"What the devil are you winking at me for?"

"Because I like it, Tom Smart," said the chair; or the old gentleman, whichever you like to call him. He stopped winking though, when Tom spoke, and began grinning like a superannuated monkey.

"How do you know my name, old nut-cracker face!" inquired Tom Smart, rather staggered;—though he pretended to carry it off so well.

"Come, come, Tom," said the old gentleman, "that's not the way to address solid Spanish Mahogany. Dam'me, you couldn't treat me with less respect if I was veneered." When the old gentleman said this, he looked so fierce that Tom began to grow frightened.

"I didn't mean to treat you with any disrespect, sir," said Tom, in a much humbler tone than he had spoken in at first.

"Well, well," said the old fellow, "perhaps not—perhaps not. Tom——"

"Sir——"

"I know everything about you, Tom; everything. You're very poor, Tom."

"I certainly am," said Tom Smart. "But how came you to know that?"

"Never mind that," said the old gentleman; "you're much too fond of punch, Tom."

Tom Smart was just on the point of protesting that he hadn't tasted a drop since his last birthday, but when his eye encountered that of the old gentleman, he looked so knowing that Tom blushed, and was silent.

"Tom," said the old gentleman, "the widow's a fine woman—remarkably fine woman—eh, Tom?" Here the old fellow screwed up his eyes, cocked up one of his wasted little legs, and looked altogether so unpleasantly amorous, that Tom was quite disgusted with the levity of his behaviour;—at his time of life, too!

"I am her guardian, Tom," said the old gentleman.

"Are you?" inquired Tom Smart.

"I knew her mother, Tom," said the old fellow; "and her grandmother. She was very fond of me—made me this waistcoat, Tom."

"Did she?" said Tom Smart.

"And these shoes," said the old fellow, lifting up one of the red-cloth mufflers; "but don't mention it, Tom. I shouldn't like to have it known that she was so much attached to me. It might occasion some unpleasantness in the family." When the old rascal said this, he looked so extremely impertinent, that, as Tom Smart afterwards declared, he could have sat upon him without remorse.

"I have been a great favourite among the women in my time, Tom," said the profligate old debauchee; "hundreds of fine women have sat in my lap for hours together. What do you think of that, you dog, eh!" The old gentleman was proceeding to recount some other exploits of his youth, when he was seized with such a violent fit of creaking that he was unable to proceed.

"Just serves you right, old boy," thought Tom Smart; but he didn't say anything.

"Ah!" said the old fellow, "I am a good deal troubled with this now. I am getting old, Tom, and have lost nearly all my rails. I have had an operation performed, too—a small piece let into my back—and I found it a severe trial, Tom."

"I dare say you did, sir," said Tom Smart.

"However," said the old gentleman, "that's not the point. Tom! I want you to marry the widow."

"Me, sir!" said Tom.

"You," said the old gentleman.

"Bless your reverend locks," said Tom—(he had a few scattered horse-hairs left)—"bless your reverend locks, she wouldn't have me." And Tom sighed involuntarily, as he thought of the bar.

"Wouldn't she?" said the old gentleman firmly.

"No, no," said Tom; "there's somebody else in the wind. A tall man—a confoundedly tall man—with black whiskers."

"Tom," said the old gentleman, "she will never have him."

"Won't she?" said Tom. "If you stood in the bar, old gentleman, you'd tell another story."

"Pooh, pooh," said the old gentleman. "I know all about that."

" About what ? " said Tom.

" The kissing behind the door, and all that sort of thing, Tom," said the old gentleman. And here he gave another impudent look, which made Tom very wroth, because, as you all know, gentlemen, to hear an old fellow, who ought to know better, talking about these things, is very unpleasant—nothing more so.

" I know all about that, Tom," said the old gentleman. " I have seen it done very often in my time, Tom, between more people than I should like to mention to you ; but it never came to anything after all."

" You must have seen some queer things," said Tom, with an inquisitive look.

" You may say that, Tom," replied the old fellow, with a very complicated wink. " I am the last of my family, Tom," said the old gentleman, with a melancholy sigh.

" Was it a large one ? " inquired Tom Smart.

" There were twelve of us, Tom," said the old gentleman ; " fine straight-backed, handsome fellows as you'd wish to see. None of your modern abortions—all with arms, and with a degree of polish, though I say it that should not, which would have done your heart good to behold."

" And what's become of the others, sir ? " asked Tom Smart.

The old gentleman applied his elbow to his eye as he replied, " Gone, Tom, gone. We had hard service, Tom, and they hadn't all my constitution. They got rheumatic about the legs and arms, and went into kitchens and other hospitals ; and one of 'em, with long service and hard usage, positively lost his senses :—he got so crazy that he was obliged to be burnt. Shocking thing that, Tom."

" Dreadful ! " said Tom Smart.

The old fellow paused for a few minutes, apparently struggling with his feelings of emotion, and then said :

" However, Tom, I am wandering from the point. This tall man, Tom, is a rascally adventurer. The moment he married the widow, he would sell off all the furniture, and run away. What would be the consequence ? She would be deserted and reduced to ruin, and I should catch my death of cold in some broker's shop."

" Yes, but——"

" Don't interrupt me," said the old gentleman. " Of you, Tom, I entertain a very different opinion ; for I well know that if you once settled yourself in a public-house you would never leave it as long as there was anything to drink within its walls."

" I am very much obliged to you for your good opinion, sir," said Tom Smart.

" Therefore," resumed the old gentleman, in a dictatorial tone, " you shall have her, and he shall not."

" What is to prevent it ? " said Tom Smart eagerly.

" This disclosure," replied the old gentleman ; " he is already married."

" How can I prove it ? " said Tom, starting half out of bed.

The old gentleman untucked his arm from his side, and having pointed to one of the oaken presses, immediately replaced it in its old position.

" He little thinks," said the old gentleman, " that in the right-hand pocket of a pair of trousers in that press he has left a letter entreating him to return to his disconsolate wife, with six—mark me, Tom—six babes, and all of them small ones."

As the old gentleman solemnly uttered these words his features grew less and less distinct and his figure more shadowy. A film came over Tom Smart's eyes. The old man seemed gradually blending into the chair, the damask waistcoat to resolve into a cushion, the red slippers to shrink into little red cloth bags. The light faded gently away, and Tom Smart fell back on his pillow and dropped asleep.

Morning aroused Tom from the lethargic slumber into which he had fallen on the disappearance of the old man. He sat up in bed, and for some minutes vainly endeavoured to recall the events of the preceding night. Suddenly they rushed upon him. He looked at the chair ; it was a fantastic and grim-looking piece of furniture, certainly, but it must have been a remarkably ingenious and lively imagination that could have discovered any resemblance between it and an old man.

" How are you, old boy ? " said Tom. He was bolder in the daylight—most men are.

The chair remained motionless, and spoke not a word.

" Miserable morning," said Tom. No. The chair would not be drawn into conversation.

" Which press did you point to ?—you can tell me that," said Tom. Devil a word, gentlemen, the chair would say.

" It's not much trouble to open it, anyhow," said Tom, getting out of bed very deliberately. He walked up to one of the presses. The key was in the lock ; he turned it, and opened the door. There *was* a pair of trousers there. He put his hand into the pocket, and drew forth the identical letter the old gentleman had described !

" Queer sort of thing, this," said Tom Smart, looking first at the chair and then at the press, and then at the letter, and then at the chair again. " Very queer," said Tom. But, as there was nothing in either to lessen the queerness, he thought he might as well dress himself, and settle the tall man's business at once—just to put him out of his misery.

Tom surveyed the rooms he passed through, on his way downstairs, with the scrutinising eye of a landlord; thinking it not impossible that before long they and their contents would be his property. The tall man was standing in the snug little bar, with his hands behind him, quite at home. He grinned vacantly at Tom. A casual observer might have supposed he did it only to show his white teeth; but Tom Smart thought that a consciousness of triumph was passing through the place where the tall man's mind would have been, if he had had any. Tom laughed in his face; and summoned the landlady.

"Good morning, ma'am," said Tom Smart, closing the door of the little parlour as the widow entered.

"Good morning, sir," said the widow. "What will you take for breakfast, sir?"

Tom was thinking how he should open the case, so he made no answer.

"There's a very nice ham," said the widow, "and a beautiful cold larded fowl. Shall I send 'em in, sir?"

These words roused Tom from his reflections. His admiration of the widow increased as she spoke. Thoughtful creature! Comfortable provider!

"Who is that gentleman in the bar, ma'am?" inquired Tom.

"His name is Jinkins, sir," said the widow, slightly blushing.

"He's a tall man," said Tom.

"He is a very fine man, sir," replied the widow, "and a very nice gentleman."

"Ah!" said Tom.

"Is there anything more you want, sir?" inquired the widow, rather puzzled by Tom's manner.

"Why, yes," said Tom. "My dear ma'am, will you have the kindness to sit down for one moment?"

The widow looked much amazed, but she sat down, and Tom sat down too, close beside her. I don't know how it happened, gentlemen—indeed my uncle used to tell me that Tom Smart said *he* didn't know how it happened either—but somehow or other the palm of Tom's hand fell upon the back of the widow's hand, and remained there while he spoke.

"My dear ma'am," said Tom Smart—he had always a great notion of committing the amiable—"My dear ma'am, you deserve a very excellent husband;—you do indeed."

"Lor, sir!" said the widow—as well she might: Tom's mode of commencing the conversation being rather unusual, not to say startling; the fact of his never having set eyes upon her before the previous night being taken into consideration. "Lor, sir!"

"I scorn to flatter, my dear ma'am," said Tom Smart. "You deserve a very admirable husband, and whoever he is, he'll be a very lucky man." As Tom said this his eye involuntarily wandered from the widow's face to the comforts around him.

The widow looked more puzzled than ever, and made an effort to rise. Tom gently pressed her hand, as if to detain her, and she kept her seat. Widows, gentlemen, are not usually timorous, as my uncle used to say.

"I am sure I am very much obliged to you, sir, for your good opinion," said the buxom landlady, half-laughing; "and if ever I marry again——"

"*If*," said Tom Smart, looking very shrewdly out of the right-hand corner of his left eye. "*If*——"

"Well," said the widow, laughing outright this time. "*When* I do, I hope I shall have as good a husband as you describe."

"Jinkins to wit," said Tom.

"Lor, sir!" exclaimed the widow.

"Oh, don't tell me," said Tom, "I know him."

"I am sure nobody who knows him knows anything bad of him," said the widow, bridling up at the mysterious air with which Tom had spoken.

"Hem!" said Tom Smart.

The widow began to think if was high time to cry, so she took out her handkerchief, and inquired whether Tom wished to insult her; whether he thought it like a gentleman to take away the character of another gentleman behind his back; why, if he had got anything to say, he didn't say it to the man, like a man, instead of terrifying a poor weak woman in that way; and so forth.

"I'll say it to him fast enough," said Tom, "only I want you to hear it first."

"What is it?" inquired the widow, looking intently in Tom's countenance.

"I'll astonish you," said Tom, putting his hand in his pocket.

"If it is that he wants money," said the widow, "I know that already, and you needn't trouble yourself."

"Pooh, nonsense, that's nothing," said Tom Smart. "*I* want money. 'Tan't that."

"Oh, dear, what can it be?" exclaimed the poor widow.

"Don't be frightened," said Tom Smart. He slowly drew forth the letter, and unfolded it. "You won't scream?" said Tom doubtfully.

"No, no," replied the widow; "let me see it."

"You won't go fainting away, or any of that nonsense?" said Tom.

"No, no," returned the widow hastily.

"And don't run out, and blow him up," said Tom, "because I'll do all that for you; you had better not exert yourself."

"Well, well," said the widow, "let me see it."

"I will," replied Tom Smart; and, with these words, he placed the letter in the widow's hand.

Gentlemen, I have heard my uncle say that Tom Smart said the widow's lamentations when she heard the disclosure would have pierced a heart of stone. Tom was certainly very tender-hearted, but they pierced his to the very core. The widow rocked herself to and fro, and wrung her hands.

"Oh, the deception and villainy of man!" said the widow.

"Frightful, my dear ma'am; but compose yourself," said Smart.

"Oh, I can't compose myself," shrieked the widow. "I shall never find anyone else I can love so much!"

"Oh yes you will, my dear soul," said Tom Smart, letting fall a shower of the largest sized tears, in pity for the widow's misfortunes. Tom Smart, in the energy of his compassion, had put his arm round the widow's waist; and the widow, in a passion of grief, had clasped Tom's hand. She looked up in Tom's face, and smiled through her tears. Tom looked down in hers, and smiled through his.

I never could find out, gentlemen, whether Tom did or did not kiss the widow at that particular moment. He used to tell my uncle he didn't, but I have my doubts about it. Between ourselves, gentlemen, I rather think he did.

At all events, Tom kicked the very tall man out at the front door half an hour after, and married the widow a month after. And he used to drive about the country, with the clay-coloured gig with red wheels, and the vixenish mare with the fast pace, till he gave up business many years afterwards, and went to France with his wife; and then the old house was pulled down.

CHARLES DICKENS

THE POOR RELATION'S STORY

He was very reluctant to take precedence of so many respected members of the family, by beginning the round of stories they were to relate as they sat in a goodly circle by the Christmas fire; and he modestly suggested that it would be more correct if "John our esteemed host" (whose health he begged to drink) would have the kindness to begin. For as to himself, he said, he was so little used to lead the way that really—— But as they all cried out here, that he must begin, and agreed with one voice that he might, could, would, and should begin, he left off rubbing his hands, and took his legs out from under his arm-chair, and did begin.

I have no doubt (said the poor relation) that I shall surprise the assembled members of our family, and particularly John our esteemed host to whom we are so much indebted for the great hospitality with which he has this day entertained us, by the confession I am going to make. But, if you do me the honour to be surprised at anything that falls from a person so unimportant in the family as I am, I can only say that I shall be scrupulously accurate in all I relate.

I am not what I am supposed to be. I am quite another thing. Perhaps before I go further I had better glance at what I *am* supposed to be.

It is supposed, unless I mistake—the assembled members of our family will correct me if I do, which is very likely (here the poor relation looked mildly about him for contradiction)—that I am nobody's enemy but my own. That I never met with any particular success in anything. That I failed in business because I was unbusiness-like and credulous—in not being prepared for the interested designs of my partner. That I failed in love because I was ridiculously trustful—in thinking it impossible that Christiana could deceive me. That I failed in my expectations from my uncle Chill, on account of not being as sharp as he could have wished in worldly matters. That, through life, I have been rather put upon and disappointed in a general way. That I am at present a bachelor of between fifty-nine and sixty years of age, living on a limited income in the form of a quarterly allowance, to which I see that John our esteemed host wishes me to make no further allusion.

The supposition as to my present pursuits and habits is to the following effect.

I live in a lodging in the Clapham Road—a very clean back room, in a very respectable house—where I am expected not to be at home in the daytime, unless poorly; and which I usually leave in the morning at nine o'clock, on pretence of going to business. I take my breakfast—my roll and butter, and my half-pint of coffee—at the old-established coffee-shop near Westminster Bridge; and then I go into the City—I don't know why—and sit in Garraway's Coffee House, and on 'Change, and walk about, and look into a few offices and counting-houses where some of my relations or acquaintances are so good as to tolerate me, and where I stand by the fire if the weather happens to be cold. I get through the day in this way until five o'clock, and then I dine: at a cost, on the average, of one and threepence. Having still a little money to spend on my evening's entertainment, I look into the old-established coffee-shop as I go home, and take my cup of tea, and perhaps my bit of toast. So, as the large hand of the clock makes its way round to the morning hour again, I make my way round to the Clapham Road again, and go to bed when I get to my lodging—fire being expensive, and being objected to by the family on account of its giving trouble and making a dirt.

Sometimes one of my relations or acquaintances is so obliging as to ask me to dinner. These are holiday occasions, and then I generally walk in the Park. I am a solitary man, and seldom walk with anybody. Not that I am avoided because I am shabby; for I am not at all shabby, having always a very good suit of black on (or rather Oxford mixture, which has the appearance of black and wears much better); but I have got into a habit of speaking low, and being rather silent, and my spirits are not high, and I am sensible that I am not an attractive companion.

The only exception to this general rule is the child of my first cousin, Little Frank. I have a particular affection for that child, and he takes very kindly to me. He is a diffident boy by nature; and in a crowd he is soon run over, as I may say, and forgotten. He and I, however, get on exceedingly well. I have a fancy that the poor child will in time succeed to my peculiar position in the family. We talk but little; still, we understand each other. We walk about, hand in hand; and without much speaking he knows what I mean, and I know what he means. When he was very little indeed, I used to take him to the windows of the toy-shops, and show him the toys inside. It is surprising how soon he found out that I would have made him a great many presents if I had been in circumstances to do it.

Little Frank and I go and look at the outside of the Monument—he is very fond of the Monument—and at the Bridges, and at all the sights that are free. On two of my birthdays, we have dined on *à-la-mode* beef, and gone at half-price to the play, and been deeply interested. I was once walking with him in Lombard Street, which we often visit on account of my having mentioned to him that there are great riches there—he is very fond of Lombard Street—when a gentleman said to me as he passed by, " Sir, your little son has dropped his glove." I assure you, if you will excuse my remarking on so trivial a circumstance, this accidental mention of the child as mine quite touched my heart and brought the foolish tears into my eyes.

When Little Frank is sent to school in the country I shall be very much at a loss what to do with myself, but I have the intention of walking down there once a month and seeing him on a half-holiday. I am told he will then be at play upon the Heath ; and if my visits should be objected to, as unsettling the child, I can see him from a distance without his seeing me, and walk back again. His mother comes of a highly genteel family, and rather disapproves, I am aware, of our being so much together. I know that I am not calculated to improve his retiring disposition ; but I think he would miss me beyond the feeling of the moment if we were wholly separated.

When I die in the Clapham Road I shall not leave much more in this world than I shall take out of it ; but I happen to have a miniature of a bright-faced boy, with a curling head, and an open shirt-frill waving down his bosom (my mother had it taken for me, but I can't believe that it was ever like), which will be worth nothing to sell, and which I shall beg may be given to Frank. I have written my dear boy a little letter with it, in which I have told him that I felt very sorry to part from him, though bound to confess that I knew no reason why I should remain here. I have given him some short advice, the best in my power, to take warning of the consequences of being nobody's enemy but his own ; and I have endeavoured to comfort him for what I fear he will consider a bereavement, by pointing out to him that I was only a superfluous something to every one but him ; and that having by some means failed to find a place in this great assembly, I am better out of it.

Such (said the poor relation, clearing his throat and beginning to speak a little louder) is the general impression about me. Now, it is a remarkable circumstance, which forms the aim and purpose of my story, that this is all wrong. This is not my life, and these are not my habits. I do not even live in the Clapham Road. Comparatively speaking, I am very seldom there. I reside, mostly, in a—I am almost ashamed to say the word, it sounds so full of pretension—in a Castle. I do not mean that it is an old baronial habitation, but still it is a building always known to every one by the name of a Castle. In it I preserve the particulars of my history; they run thus:

It was when I first took John Spatter (who had been my clerk) into partnership, and when I was still a young man of not more than five-and-twenty, residing in the house of my uncle Chill, from whom I had considerable expectations, that I ventured to propose to Christiana. I had loved Christiana a long time. She was very beautiful, and very winning in all respects. I rather mistrusted her widowed mother, who I feared was of a plotting and mercenary turn of mind; but I thought as well of her as I could, for Christiana's sake. I never had loved any one but Christiana, and she had been all the world, and oh far more than all the world, to me, from our childhood!

Christiana accepted me with her mother's consent, and I was rendered very happy indeed. My life at my uncle Chill's was of a spare dull kind, and my garret chamber was as dull, and bare, and cold as an upper prison room in some stern northern fortress. But, having Christiana's love, I wanted nothing upon earth. I would not have changed my lot with any human being.

Avarice was, unhappily, my uncle Chill's master-vice. Though he was rich, he pinched, and scraped, and clutched, and lived miserably. As Christiana had no fortune, I was for some time a little fearful of confessing our engagement to him; but at length I wrote him a letter, saying how it all truly was. I put it into his hand one night, on going to bed.

As I came downstairs next morning, shivering in the cold December air—colder in my uncle's unwarmed house than in the street, where the winter sun did sometimes shine, and which was at all events enlivened by cheerful faces and voices passing along—I carried a heavy heart towards the long, low breakfast-room in which my uncle sat. It was a large room with a small fire, and there was a great bay window in it which the rain had marked in the night as if with the tears of houseless people. It stared upon a raw yard, with a cracked stone pavement, and some rusted iron railings half uprooted, whence an ugly out-building that had once been a dissecting-room (in the time of the great surgeon who had mortgaged the house to my uncle) stared at it.

We rose so early always that at that time of the year we breakfasted by candle-light. When I went into the room my uncle was so contracted by the cold, and so huddled together in his chair behind the one dim candle, that I did not see him until I was close to the table.

As I held out my hand to him, he caught up his stick (being infirm, he always walked about the house with a stick), and made a blow at me, and said, " You fool ! "

" Uncle," I returned, " I didn't expect you to be so angry as this." Nor had I expected it, though he was a hard and angry old man.

" You didn't expect ! " said he ; " when did you ever expect ? When did you ever calculate, or look forward, you contemptible dog ? "

" These are hard words, uncle ! "

" Hard words ? Feathers, to pelt such an idiot as you with," said he. " Here ! Betsy Snap ! Look at him ! "

Betsy Snap was a withered, hard-favoured, yellow old woman—our only domestic—always employed, at this time of the morning, in rubbing my uncle's legs. As my uncle adjured her to look at me, he put his lean grip on the crown of her head, she kneeling beside him, and turned her face towards me. An involuntary thought connecting them both with the dissecting-room, as it must often have been in the surgeon's time, passed across my mind in the midst of my anxiety.

" Look at the snivelling milksop ! " said my uncle. " Look at the baby ! This is the gentleman who, people say, is nobody's enemy but his own. This is the gentleman who can't say no. This is the gentleman who was making such large profits in his business that he must needs take a partner, t'other day. This is the gentleman who is going to marry a wife without a penny, and who falls into the hands of Jezebels who are speculating on my death ! "

I knew, now, how great my uncle's rage was ; for nothing short of his being almost beside himself would have induced him to utter that concluding word, which he held in such repugnance that it was never spoken or hinted at before him on any account.

" On my death," he repeated, as if he were defying me by defying his own abhorrence of the word. " On my death—death—Death ! But I'll spoil the speculation. Eat your last under this roof, you feeble wretch, and may it choke you ! "

You may suppose that I had not much appetite for the breakfast to which I was bidden in these terms ; but I took my accustomed seat. I saw that I was repudiated henceforth by my uncle ; still I could bear that very well, possessing Christiana's heart.

He emptied his basin of bread and milk as usual, only that he took it on his knees with his chair turned away from the table where I sat. When he had done, he carefully snuffed out the candle ; and the cold, slate-coloured, miserable day looked in upon us.

" Now, Mr. Michael," said he, " before we part, I should like to have a word with these ladies in your presence."

"As you will, sir," I returned; "but you deceive yourself, and wrong us cruelly, if you suppose that there is any feeling at stake in this contract but pure, disinterested, faithful love."

To this, he only replied, "You lie!" and not one other word.

We went, through half-thawed snow and half-frozen rain, to the house where Christiana and her mother lived. My uncle knew them very well. They were sitting at their breakfast, and were surprised to see us at that hour.

"Your servant, ma'am," said my uncle to the mother. "You divine the purpose of my visit, I dare say, ma'am. I understand there is a world of pure, disinterested, faithful love cooped up here. I am happy to bring it all it wants, to make it complete. I bring you your son-in-law, ma'am—and you, your husband, miss. The gentleman is a perfect stranger to me, but I wish him joy of his wise bargain."

He snarled at me as he went out, and I never saw him again.

It is altogether a mistake (continued the poor relation) to suppose that my dear Christiana, over-persuaded and influenced by her mother, married a rich man, the dirt from whose carriage-wheels is often, in these changed times, thrown upon me as she rides by. No, no. She married me.

The way we came to be married rather sooner than we intended was this. I took a frugal lodging and was saving and planning for her sake, when, one day, she spoke to me with great earnestness, and said:

"My dear Michael, I have given you my heart. I have said that I loved you, and I have pledged myself to be your wife. I am as much yours through all changes of good and evil as if we had been married on the day when such words passed between us. I know you well, and know that if we should be separated and our union broken off, your whole life would be shadowed, and all that might, even now, be stronger in your character for the conflict with the world would then be weakened to the shadow of what it is!"

"God help me, Christiana!" said I. "You speak the truth."

"Michael!" said she, putting her hand in mine, in all maidenly devotion, "let us keep apart no longer. It is but for me to say that I can live content upon such means as you have, and I well know you are happy. I say so from my heart. Strive no more alone; let us strive together. My dear Michael, it is not right that I should keep secret from you what you do not suspect, but what distresses my whole life. My mother—without considering that what you have lost, you have lost for me, and on the assurance of my faith—sets her heart on riches, and urges another suit upon me, to my misery. I cannot bear this, for to bear it is to be untrue to you. I would rather share your struggles than look on. I want no better home than you can give me. I know that you will aspire and labour with a higher courage if I am wholly yours, and let it be so when you will!"

I was blest indeed, that day, and a new world opened to me. We were married in a very little while, and I took my wife to our happy home. That was the beginning of the residence I have spoken of; the Castle we have ever since inhabited together dates from that time. All our children have been born in it. Our first child—now married—was a little girl, whom we called Christiana. Her son is so like Little Frank that I hardly know which is which.

The current impression as to my partner's dealings with me is also quite erroneous. He did not begin to treat me coldly, as a poor simpleton, when my uncle and I so fatally quarrelled; nor did he afterwards gradually possess himself of our business and edge me out. On the contrary, he behaved to me with the utmost good faith and honour.

Matters between us took this turn:—On the day of my separation from my uncle, and even before the arrival at our counting-house of my trunks (which he sent after me, *not* carriage paid), I went down to our room of business, on our little wharf, overlooking the river; and there I told John Spatter what had happened. John did not say, in reply, that rich old relatives were palpable facts, and that love and sentiment were moonshine and fiction. He addressed me thus:

"Michael," said John, "we were at school together, and I generally had the knack of getting on better than you, and making a higher reputation."

"You had, John," I returned.

"Although," said John, "I borrowed your books and lost them; borrowed your pocket-money, and never repaid it; got you to buy my damaged knives at a higher price than I had given for them new; and to own to the windows that I had broken."

"All not worth mentioning, John Spatter," said I, "but certainly true."

"When you were first established in this infant business, which promises to thrive so well," pursued John, "I came to you, in my search for almost any employment, and you made me your clerk."

"Still not worth mentioning, my dear John Spatter," said I; "still, equally true."

"And finding that I had a good head for business, and that I was really useful *to* the business, you did not like to retain me in that capacity, and thought it an act of justice soon to make me your partner."

"Still less worth mentioning than any of those other little circumstances you have recalled, John Spatter," said I; "for I was, and am, sensible of your merits and my deficiencies."

"Now, my good friend," said John, drawing my arm through his, as he had had a habit of doing at school; while two vessels outside the windows of our counting-house—which were shaped like the stern windows of a ship—went lightly down the river with the tide, as John and I might then be sailing away in company, and in trust and confidence, on our voyage of life; "let there, under these friendly circumstances, be a right understanding between us. You are too easy, Michael. You are nobody's enemy but your own. If I were to give you that damaging character among our connection, with a shrug, and a shake of the head, and a sigh; and if I were further to abuse the trust you place in me——"

"But you never will abuse it at all, John," I observed.

"Never!" said he; "but I am putting a case—I say, and if I were further to abuse that trust by keeping this piece of our common affairs in the dark, and this other piece in the light, and again this other piece in the twilight, and so on, I should strengthen my strength, and weaken your weakness, day by day, until at last I found myself on the high road to fortune, and you left behind on some bare common, a hopeless number of miles out of the way."

"Exactly so," said I.

"To prevent this, Michael," said John Spatter, "or the remotest chance of this, there must be perfect openness between us. Nothing must be concealed, and we must have but one interest."

"My dear John Spatter," I assured him, "that is precisely what I mean."

"And when you are too easy," pursued John, his face glowing with friendship, "you must allow me to prevent that imperfection in your nature from being taken advantage of by any one; you must not expect me to humour it——"

"My dear John Spatter," I interrupted, "I *don't* expect you to humour it. I want to correct it."

"And I, too," said John.

"Exactly so!" cried I. "We both have the same end in view; and, honourably seeking it, and fully trusting one another, and having but one interest, ours will be a prosperous and happy partnership."

"I am sure of it!" returned John Spatter. And we shook hands most affectionately.

I took John home to my Castle, and we had a very happy day. Our partnership throve well. My friend and partner supplied what I wanted, as I had foreseen that he would; and by improving both the business and myself, amply acknowledged any little rise in life to which I had helped him.

I am not (said the poor relation, looking at the fire as he slowly rubbed his hands) very rich, for I never cared to be that ; but I have enough, and am above all moderate wants and anxieties. My Castle is not a splendid place, but it is very comfortable, and it has a warm and cheerful air, and is quite a picture of Home.

Our eldest girl, who is very like her mother, married John Spatter's eldest son. Our two families are closely united in other ties of attachment. It is very pleasant of an evening, when we are all assembled together—which frequently happens—and when John and I talk over old times, and the one interest there has always been between us.

I really do not know, in my Castle, what loneliness is. Some of our children or grandchildren are always about it, and the young voices of my descendants are delightful—oh, how delightful!—to me to hear. My dearest and most devoted wife, ever faithful, ever loving, ever helpful and sustaining and consoling, is the priceless blessing of my house ; from whom all its other blessings spring. We are rather a musical family, and when Christiana sees me, at any time, a little weary or depressed, she steals to the piano and sings a gentle air she used to sing when we were first betrothed. So weak a man am I that I cannot bear to hear it from any other source. They played it once at the Theatre when I was there with Little Frank ; and the child said, wondering, " Cousin Michael, whose hot tears are these that have fallen on my hand ? "

Such is my Castle, and such are the real particulars of my life therein preserved. I often take Little Frank home there. He is very welcome to my grandchildren, and they play together. At this time of the year—the Christmas and New Year time—I am seldom out of my Castle. For the associations of the season seem to hold me there, and the precepts of the season seem to teach me that it is well to be there.

" And the Castle is——" observed a grave, kind voice among the company.

" Yes. My Castle," said the poor relation, shaking his head as he still looked at the fire, " is in the Air. John our esteemed host suggests its situation accurately. My Castle is in the Air ! I have done. Will you be so good as to pass the story ! "

CHARLES DICKENS

THE STORY OF RICHARD DOUBLEDICK

In the year one thousand seven hundred and ninety-nine a relative of mine came limping down, on foot, to this town of Chatham. I call it this town, because if anybody present knows to a nicety where Rochester ends and Chatham begins, it is more than I do. He was a poor traveller, with not a farthing in his pocket. He sat by the fire in this very room, and he slept one night in a bed that will be occupied to-night by some one here.

My relative came down to Chatham to enlist in a cavalry regiment, if a cavalry regiment would have him; if not, to take King George's shilling from any corporal or sergeant who would put a bunch of ribbons in his hat. His object was to get shot; but he thought he might as well ride to death as be at the trouble of walking.

My relative's Christian name was Richard, but he was better known as Dick. He dropped his own surname on the road down, and took up that of Doubledick. He was passed as Richard Doubledick; age, twenty-two; height, five foot ten; native place, Exmouth, which he had never been near in his life. There was no cavalry in Chatham when he limped over the bridge here with half a shoe to his dusty feet, so he enlisted into a regiment of the line, and was glad to get drunk and forget all about it.

You are to know that this relative of mine had gone wrong, and run wild. His heart was in the right place, but it was sealed up. He had been betrothed to a good and beautiful girl, whom he had loved better than she—or perhaps even he—believed; but in an evil hour he had given her cause to say to him solemnly, "Richard, I will never marry another man. I will live single for your sake, but Mary Marshall's lips"—her name was Mary Marshall—"never address another word to you on earth. Go, Richard! Heaven forgive you!" This finished him. This brought him down to Chatham. This made him Private Richard Doubledick, with a determination to be shot.

There was not a more dissipated and reckless soldier in Chatham barracks, in the year one thousand seven hundred and ninety-nine, than Private Richard Doubledick. He associated with the dregs of every regiment ; he was as seldom sober as he could be, and was constantly under punishment. It became clear to the whole barracks that Private Richard Doubledick would very soon be flogged.

Now the Captain of Richard Doubledick's company was a young gentleman not above five years his senior, whose eyes had an expression in them which affected Private Richard Doubledick in a very remarkable way. They were bright, handsome, dark eyes—what are called laughing eyes generally, and, when serious, rather steady than severe—but they were the only eyes now left in his narrowed world that Private Richard Doubledick could not stand. Unabashed by evil report and punishment, defiant of everything else and everybody else, he had but to know that those eyes looked at him for a moment, and he felt ashamed. He could not so much as salute Captain Taunton in the street like any other officer. He was reproached and confused—troubled by the mere possibility of the Captain's looking at him. In his worst moments he would rather turn back, and go any distance out of his way, than encounter those two handsome, dark, bright eyes.

One day, when Private Richard Doubledick came out of the Black hole, where he had been passing the last eight-and-forty hours, and in which retreat he spent a good deal of his time, he was ordered to betake himself to Captain Taunton's quarters. In the stale and squalid state of a man just out of the Black hole he had less fancy than ever for being seen by the Captain ; but he was not so mad yet as to disobey orders, and consequently went up to the terrace overlooking the parade-ground, where the officers' quarters were, twisting and breaking in his hands, as he went along, a bit of the straw that had formed the decorative furniture of the Black hole.

" Come in ! " cried the Captain, when he knocked with his knuckles at the door. Private Richard Doubledick pulled off his cap, took a stride forward, and felt very conscious that he stood in the light of the dark, bright eyes. There was a silent pause. Private Richard Doubledick had put the straw in his mouth, and was gradually doubling it up into his windpipe and choking himself.

" Doubledick," said the Captain, " do you know where you are going to ? "

" To the devil, sir ? " faltered Doubledick.

" Yes," returned the Captain. " And very fast."

Private Richard Doubledick turned the straw of the Black hole in his mouth, and made a miserable salute of acquiescence.

" Doubledick," said the Captain, " since I entered His Majesty's service, a boy of seventeen, I have been pained to see many men of promise going that road ; but I have never been so pained to see a man determined to make the shameful journey as I have been, ever since you joined the regiment, to see you."

Private Richard Doubledick began to find a film stealing over the floor at which he looked; also to find the legs of the Captain's breakfast-table turning crooked, as if he saw them through water.

"I am only a common soldier, sir," said he. "It signifies very little what such a poor brute comes to."

"You are a man," returned the Captain, with grave indignation, "of education and superior advantages; and if you say that, meaning what you say, you have sunk lower than I had believed. How low that must be, I leave you to consider, knowing what I know of your disgrace, and seeing what I see."

"I hope to get shot soon, sir," said Private Richard Doubledick; "and then the regiment and the world together will be rid of me."

The legs of the table were becoming very crooked. Doubledick, looking up to steady his vision, met the eyes that had so strong an influence over him. He put his hand before his own eyes, and the breast of his disgrace-jacket swelled as if it would fly asunder.

"I would rather," said the young Captain, "see this in you, Doubledick, than I would see five thousand guineas counted out upon this table for a gift to my good mother. Have you a mother?"

"I am thankful to say she is dead, sir."

"If your praises," returned the Captain, "were sounded from mouth to mouth through the whole regiment, through the whole army, through the whole country, you would wish she had lived to say, with pride and joy, 'He is my son!'"

"Spare me, sir," said Doubledick; "she would never have heard any good of me. She would never have had any pride and joy in owning herself my mother. Love and compassion she might have had, and would have always had, I know; but not—Spare me, sir! I am a broken wretch, quite at your mercy!" And he turned his face to the wall, and stretched out his imploring hand.

"My friend——" began the Captain.

"God bless you, sir!" sobbed Private Richard Doubledick.

"You are at the crisis of your fate. Hold your course unchanged a little longer, and you know what must happen. *I* know even better than you can imagine, that, after that has happened, you are lost. No man who could shed those tears could bear those marks."

"I fully believe it, sir," in a low, shivering voice, said Private Richard Doubledick.

"But a man in any station can do his duty," said the young Captain, "and, in doing it, can earn his own respect, even if his case should be so very unfortunate and so very rare that he can earn no other man's. A common soldier, poor brute though you called him just now, has this advantage in the stormy times we live in, that he always does his duty before a host of sympathising witnesses. Do you doubt that he may so do it as to be extolled through a whole regiment, through a whole army, through a whole country ? Turn while you may yet retrieve the past, and try."

" I will ! I will ask for only one witness, sir," cried Richard, with a bursting heart.

" I understand you. I will be a watchful and a faithful one."

I have heard from Private Richard Doubledick's own lips that he dropped down upon his knee, kissed that officer's hand, arose and went out of the light of the dark, bright eyes, an altered man.

In that year, one thousand seven hundred and ninety-nine, the French were in Egypt, in Italy, in Germany, where not ? Napoleon Bonaparte had likewise begun to stir against us in India, and most men could read the signs of the great troubles that were coming on. In the very next year, when we formed an alliance with Austria against him, Captain Taunton's regiment was on service in India. And there was not a finer non-commissioned officer in it—no, nor in the whole line—than Corporal Richard Doubledick.

In eighteen hundred and one the Indian army were on the coast of Egypt. Next year was the year of the proclamation of the short peace, and they were recalled. It had then become well known to thousands of men that wherever Captain Taunton, with the dark, bright eyes, led, there, close to him, ever at his side, firm as a rock, true as the sun, and brave as Mars, would be certain to be found, while life beat in their hearts, that famous soldier, Sergeant Richard Doubledick.

Eighteen hundred and five, besides being the great year of Trafalgar, was a year of hard fighting in India. That year saw such wonders done by a Sergeant-Major, who cut his way single-handed through a solid mass of men, recovered the colours of his regiment, which had been seized from the hand of a poor boy shot through the heart, and rescued his wounded Captain, who was down, and in a very jungle of horses' hoofs and sabres—saw such wonders done, I say, by this brave Sergeant-Major, that he was specially made the bearer of the colours he had won ; and Ensign Richard Doubledick had risen from the ranks.

Sorely cut up in every battle, but always reinforced by the bravest of men—for the fame of following the old colours, shot through and through, which Ensign Richard Doubledick had saved, inspired all breasts—this regiment fought its way through the Peninsular War, up to the investment of Badajos in eighteen hundred and twelve. Again and again it had been cheered through the British ranks until the tears had sprung into men's eyes at the mere hearing of the mighty British voice, so exultant in their valour ; and there was not a drummer-boy but knew the legend, that wherever the two friends, Major Taunton, with the dark, bright eyes, and Ensign Richard Doubledick, who was devoted to him, were seen to go, there the boldest spirits in the English army became wild to follow.

One day, at Badajos—not in the great storming, but in repelling a hot sally of the besieged upon our men at work in the trenches, who had given way—the two officers found themselves hurrying forward face to face against a party of French infantry, who made a stand. There was an officer at their head, encouraging his men—a courageous, handsome, gallant officer, of five-and-thirty, whom Doubledick saw hurriedly, almost momentarily, but saw well. He particularly noticed this officer waving his sword, and rallying his men with an eager and excited cry, when they fired in obedience to his gesture, and Major Taunton dropped. It was over in ten minutes more, and Doubledick returned to the spot where he had laid the best friend man ever had on a coat spread upon the wet clay. Major Taunton's uniform was opened at the breast, and on his shirt were three little spots of blood.

"Dear Doubledick," said he, "I am dying."

"For the love of Heaven, no!" exclaimed the other, kneeling down beside him, and passing his arm round his neck to raise his head. "Taunton! My preserver, my guardian angel, my witness! Dearest, truest, kindest of human beings! Taunton! For God's sake!"

The bright, dark eyes—so very, very dark now, in the pale face—smiled upon him; and the hand he had kissed thirteen years ago laid itself fondly on his breast.

"Write to my mother. You will see Home again. Tell her how we became friends. It will comfort her, as it comforts me."

He spoke no more, but faintly signed for a moment towards his hair as it fluttered in the wind. The Ensign understood him. He smiled again when he saw that, and, gently turning his face over on the supporting arm as if for rest, died, with his hand upon the breast in which he had revived a soul.

No dry eye looked on Ensign Richard Doubledick that melancholy day. He buried his friend on the field, and became a lone, bereaved man. Beyond his duty he appeared to have but two remaining cares in life—one, to preserve the little packet of hair he was to give to Taunton's mother; the other, to encounter that French officer who had rallied the men under whose fire Taunton fell. A new legend now began to circulate among our troops; and it was, that when he and the French officer came face to face once more, there would be weeping in France. The war went on—and through it went the exact picture of the French officer on the one side, and the bodily reality upon the other—until the battle of Toulouse was fought. In the returns sent home appeared these words: "Severely wounded, but not dangerously, Lieutenant Richard Doubledick."

At midsummer-time, in the year eighteen hundred and fourteen, Lieutenant Richard Doubledick, now a browned soldier, seven-and-thirty years of age, came home to England invalided. He brought the hair with him, near his heart. Many a French officer had he seen since that day; many a dreadful night, in searching with men and lanterns for his wounded, had he relieved French officers lying disabled; but the mental picture and the reality had never come together.

Though he was weak and suffered pain, he lost not an hour in getting down to Frome in Somersetshire, where Taunton's mother lived. In the sweet compassionate words that naturally present themselves to the mind to-night, "he was the only son of his mother, and she was a widow." It was a Sunday evening, and the lady sat at her quiet garden-window reading the Bible; reading to herself, in a trembling voice, that very passage in it, as I have heard him tell. He heard the words: "Young man, I say unto thee, arise!"

He had to pass the window; and the bright, dark eyes of his debased time seemed to look at him. Her heart told her who he was; she came to the door quickly, and fell upon his neck.

"He saved me from ruin, made me a human creature, won me from infamy and shame. O God for ever bless him! As He will, He will."

"He will!" the lady answered. "I know he is in Heaven!" Then she piteously cried, "But oh, my darling boy, my darling boy!"

Never from the hour when Private Richard Doubledick enlisted at Chatham had the Private, Corporal, Sergeant, Sergeant-Major, Ensign or Lieutenant breathed his right name, or the name of Mary Marshall, or a word of the story of his life, into any ear except his reclaimer's. That previous scene in his existence was closed. He had firmly resolved that his expiation should be to live unknown; to disturb no more the peace that had long grown over his old offences; to let it be revealed, when he was dead, that he had striven and suffered, and had never forgotten; and then, if they could forgive him and believe him—well, it would be time enough—time enough!

But that night, remembering the words he had cherished for two years, "Tell her how we became friends. It will comfort her, as it comforts me," he related everything. It gradually seemed to him as if in his maturity he had recovered a mother; it gradually seemed to her as if in her bereavement she had found a son. During his stay in England, the quiet garden into which he had slowly and painfully crept, a stranger, became the boundary of his home ; when he was able to rejoin his regiment in the spring, he left the garden, thinking this was indeed the first time he had ever turned his face towards the old colours with a woman's blessing !

He followed them—so ragged, so scarred and pierced now, that they would scarcely hold together—to Quatre Bras and Ligny. He stood beside them, in an awful stillness of many men, shadowy through the mist and drizzle of a wet June forenoon, on the field of Waterloo. And down to that hour the picture in his mind of the French officer had never been compared with the reality.

The famous regiment was in action early in the battle, and received its first check in many an eventful year, when he was seen to fall. But it swept on to avenge him, and left behind it no such creature in the world of consciousness as Lieutenant Richard Doubledick.

Through pits of mire, and pools of rain ; along deep ditches, once roads, that were pounded and ploughed to pieces by artillery, heavy waggons, tramp of men and horses, and the struggle of every wheeled thing that could carry wounded soldiers ; jolted among the dying and the dead, so disfigured by blood and mud as to be hardly recognisable for humanity ; undisturbed by the moaning of men and the shrieking of horses, which, newly taken from the peaceful pursuits of life, could not endure the sight of the stragglers lying by the wayside, never to resume their toilsome journey ; dead, as to any sentient life that was in it, and yet alive—the form that had been Lieutenant Richard Doubledick, with whose praises England rang, was conveyed to Brussels. There it was tenderly laid down in hospital ; and there it lay, week after week, through the long bright summer days, until the harvest, spared by war, had ripened and was gathered in.

Over and over again the sun rose and set upon the crowded city ; over and over again the moonlight nights were quiet on the plains of Waterloo ; and all that time was a blank to what had been Lieutenant Richard Doubledick. Rejoicing troops marched into Brussels, and marched out ; brothers and fathers, sisters, mothers and wives, came thronging thither, drew their lots of joy and agony, and departed ; so many times a day the bells rang : so many times the shadows of the great buildings changed ; so many lights sprang up at dusk ; so many feet passed here and there upon the pavements ; so many hours of sleep and cooler air of night succeeded : indifferent to all, a marble face lay on a bed, like the face of a recumbent statue on the tomb of Lieutenant Richard Doubledick.

Slowly labouring, at last, through a long heavy dream of confused time and place, presenting faint glimpses of army surgeons whom he knew, and of faces that had been familiar to his youth—dearest and kindest among them, Mary Marshall's, with a solicitude upon it more like reality than anything he could discern—Lieutenant Richard Doubledick came back to life. To the beautiful life of a calm autumn evening sunset, to the peaceful life of a fresh quiet room with a large window standing open; a balcony beyond, in which were moving leaves and sweet-smelling flowers; beyond, again, the clear sky, with the sun full in his sight, pouring its golden radiance on his bed. It was so tranquil and so lovely that he thought he had passed into another world. And he said in a faint voice, "Taunton, are you near me?"

A face bent over him. Not his, his mother's.

"I came to nurse you. We have nursed you many weeks. You were moved here long ago. Do you remember nothing?"

"Nothing."

The lady kissed his cheek, and held his hand, soothing him.

"Where is the regiment? What has happened? Let me call you mother. What has happened, mother?"

"A great victory, dear. The war is over, and the regiment was the bravest in the field."

His eyes kindled, his lips trembled, he sobbed, and the tears ran down his face. He was very weak, too weak to move his hand.

"Was it dark just now?" he asked presently.

"No."

"It was only dark to me. Something passed away, like a black shadow. But as it went, and the sun—oh the blessed sun, how beautiful it is!—touched my face, I thought I saw a light white cloud pass out at the door. Was there nothing that went out?"

She shook her head, and in a little while he fell asleep, she still holding his hand, and soothing him.

From that time he recovered. Slowly, for he had been desperately wounded in the head, and had been shot in the body, but making some little advance every day. When he had gained sufficient strength to converse as he lay in bed, he soon began to remark that Mrs. Taunton always brought him back to his own history. Then he recalled his preserver's dying words, and thought, "It comforts her."

One day he awoke out of a sleep, refreshed, and asked her to read to him. But the curtain of the bed, softening the light, which she always drew back when he awoke, that she might see him from her table at the bedside where she sat at work, was held undrawn; and a woman's voice spoke, which was not hers.

"Can you bear to see a stranger?" it said softly. "Will you like to see a stranger?"

"Stranger!" he repeated. The voice awoke old memories, before the days of Private Richard Doubledick.

" A stranger now, but not a stranger once," it said in tones that thrilled him. " Richard, dear Richard, lost through so many years, my name——"

He cried out her name, " Mary," and she held him in her arms, and his head lay on her bosom.

" I am not breaking a rash vow, Richard. These are not Mary Marshall's lips that speak. I have another name."

She was married.

" I have another name, Richard. Did you ever hear it ? "

" Never ! "

He looked into her face, so pensively beautiful, and wondered at the smile upon it through her tears.

" Think again, Richard. Are you sure you never heard my altered name ?"

" Never ! "

" Don't move your head to look at me, dear Richard. Let it lie here, while I tell my story. I loved a generous, noble man ; loved him with my whole heart ; loved him for years and years ; loved him faithfully, devotedly ; loved him with no hope of return ; loved him, knowing nothing of his highest qualities—not even knowing that he was alive. He was a brave soldier. He was honoured and beloved by thousands of thousands, when the mother of his dear friend found me, and showed me that in all his triumphs he had never forgotten me. He was wounded in a great battle. He was brought, dying, here, into Brussels. I came to watch and tend him, as I would have joyfully gone, with such a purpose, to the dreariest ends of the earth. When he knew no one else, he knew me. When he suffered most, he bore his sufferings barely murmuring, content to rest his head where yours rests now. When he lay at the point of death he married me, that he might call me Wife before he died. And the name, my dear love, that I took on that forgotten night——"

" I know it now ! " he sobbed. " The shadowy remembrance strengthens. It is come back. I thank Heaven that my mind is quite restored ! My Mary, kiss me ; lull this weary head to rest, or I shall die of gratitude. His parting words were fulfilled. I see Home again ! " Well ! They were happy. It was a long recovery but they were happy through it all. The snow had melted on the ground, and the birds were singing in the leafless thickets of the early spring, when those three were first able to ride out together, and when people flocked about the open carriage to cheer and congratulate Captain Richard Doubledick.

But even then it became necessary for the Captain, instead of returning to England, to complete his recovery in the climate of Southern France. They found a spot upon the Rhône, within a ride of the old town of Avignon, and within view of its broken bridge, which was all they could desire; they lived there, together, six months; then returned to England. Mrs. Taunton, growing old after three years—though not so old as that her bright, dark eyes were dimmed—and remembering that her strength had been benefited by the change, resolved to go back for a year to those parts. So she went with a faithful servant, who had often carried her son in his arms; and she was to be rejoined and escorted home, at the year's end, by Captain Richard Doubledick.

She wrote regularly to her children (as she called them now), and they to her. She went to the neighbourhood of Aix; and there, in their own château near the farmer's house she rented, she grew into intimacy with a family belonging to that part of France. The intimacy began in her often meeting among the vineyards a pretty child, a girl with a most compassionate heart, who was never tired of listening to the solitary English lady's stories of her poor son and the cruel wars. The family were as gentle as the child, and at length she came to know them so well that she accepted their invitation to pass the last month of her residence abroad under their roof. All this intelligence she wrote home, piecemeal as it came about, from time to time; and at last enclosed a polite note, from the head of the château, soliciting, on the occasion of his approaching mission to that neighbourhood, the honour of the company of cet homme si justement célèbre, Monsieur le Capitaine Richard Doubledick.

Captain Doubledick, now a hardy, handsome man in the full vigour of life, broader across the chest and shoulders than he had ever been before, dispatched a courteous reply, and followed it in person. Travelling through all that extent of country after three years of Peace, he blessed the better days on which the world had fallen. The corn was golden, not drenched in unnatural red; was bound in sheaves for food, not trodden under foot by men in mortal fight. The smoke rose up from peaceful hearths, not blazing ruins. The carts were laden with the fair fruits of the earth, not with wounds and death. To him who had so often seen the terrible reverse, these things were beautiful indeed; and they brought him in a softened spirit to the old château near Aix upon a deep blue evening.

It was a large château of the genuine old ghostly kind, with round towers and extinguishers, and a high leaden roof, and more windows than Aladdin's Palace. The lattice blinds were all thrown open after the heat of the day, and there were glimpses of rambling walls and corridors within. Then there were immense out-buildings fallen into partial decay, masses of dark trees, terrace-gardens, balustrades; tanks of water, too weak to play and too dirty to work; statues, weeds, and thickets of iron railing that seemed to have overgrown themselves like the shrubberies, and to have branched out in all manner of wild shapes. The entrance doors stood open, as doors often do in that country when the heat of the day is past; and the Captain saw no bell or knocker, and walked in.

He walked into a lofty stone hall refreshingly cool and gloomy after the glare of a Southern day's travel. Extending along the four sides of this hall was a gallery, leading to suites of rooms; and it was lighted from the top. Still no bell was to be seen.

"Faith," said the Captain, halting, ashamed of the clanking of his boots, "this is a ghostly beginning!"

He started back, and felt his face turn white. In the gallery, looking down at him, stood the French officer—the officer whose picture he had carried in his mind so long and so far. Compared with the original, at last—in every lineament how like it was!

He moved, and disappeared, and Captain Richard Doubledick heard his steps coming quickly down into the hall. He entered through an archway. There was a bright, sudden look upon his face, much such a look as it had worn in that fatal moment.

"Monsieur le Capitaine Richard Doubledick? Enchanted to receive him! A thousand apologies! The servants were all out in the air. There was a little fête among them in the garden. In effect, it was the fête day of my daughter, the little cherished and protected of Madame Taunton."

He was so gracious and so frank that Monsieur le Capitaine Richard Doubledick could not withhold his hand. "It is the hand of a brave Englishman," said the French officer, retaining it while he spoke. "I could respect a brave Englishman, even as my foe, how much more as my friend! I also am a soldier."

"He has not remembered me, as I have remembered him; he did not take such note of my face, that day, as I took of his," thought Captain Richard Doubledick. "How shall I tell him?"

The French officer conducted his guest into a garden and presented him to his wife, an engaging and beautiful woman, sitting with Mrs. Taunton in a whimsical old-fashioned pavilion. His daughter, her fair young face beaming with joy, came running to embrace him; and there was a boy-baby to tumble down among the orange trees on the broad steps, in making for his father's legs. A multitude of children visitors were dancing to sprightly music; and all the servants and peasants about the château were dancing too. It was a scene of innocent happiness that might have been invented for the climax of the scenes of peace which had soothed the Captain's journey.

He looked on, greatly troubled in his mind, until a resounding bell rang, and the French officer begged to show him his rooms. They went upstairs into the gallery from which the officer had looked down; and Monsieur le Capitaine Richard Doubledick was cordially welcomed to a grand outer chamber, and a smaller one within, all clocks and draperies, and hearths, and brazen dogs, and tiles, and cool devices, and elegance, and vastness.

"You were at Waterloo," said the French officer.

"I was," said Captain Richard Doubledick. "And at Badajos."

Left alone with the sound of his own stern voice in his ears, he sat down to consider, What shall I do, and how shall I tell him? At that time, unhappily, many deplorable duels had been fought between English and French officers, arising out of the recent war; and these duels, and how to avoid this officer's hospitality, were the uppermost thought in Captain Richard Doubledick's mind.

He was thinking, and letting the time run out in which he should have dressed for dinner, when Mrs. Taunton spoke to him outside the door, asking if he could give her the letter he had brought from Mary. "His mother, above all," the Captain thought. "How shall I tell *her*?"

"You will form a friendship with your host, I hope," said Mrs. Taunton, whom he hurriedly admitted, "that will last for life. He is so true-hearted and so generous, Richard, that you can hardly fail to esteem one another. If He had been spared," she kissed (not without tears) the locket in which she wore his hair, "he would have appreciated him with his own magnanimity, and would have been truly happy that the evil days were past which made such a man his enemy."

She left the room; and the Captain walked, first to one window, whence he could see the dancing in the garden, then to another window, whence he could see the smiling prospect and the peaceful vineyards.

"Spirit of my departed friend," said he, "is it through thee these better thoughts are rising in my mind? Is it thou who hast shown me, all the way I have been drawn to meet this man, the blessings of the altered time? Is it thou who hast sent thy stricken mother to me, to stay my angry hand? Is it from thee the whisper comes, that this man did his duty as thou didst,—and as I did, through thy guidance, which has wholly saved me here on earth,—and that he did no more?"

He sat down, with his head buried in his hands, and, when he rose up, made the second strong resolution of his life,—that neither to the French officer, nor to the mother of his departed friend, nor to any soul, while either of the two was living, would he breathe what only he knew. And when he touched that French officer's glass with his own, that day at dinner, he secretly forgave him in the name of the Divine Forgiver of injuries.

CHARLES DICKENS

BOOTS AT THE HOLLY-TREE

WHERE had he been in his time? he repeated, when I asked him the question. Lord, he had been everywhere! And what had he been? Bless you, he had been everything you could mention a'most!

Seen a good deal? Why, of course he had. I should say so, he could assure me, if I only knew about a twentieth part of what had come in *his* way. Why, it would be easier for him, he expected, to tell what he hadn't seen than what he had. Ah! A deal, it would.

What was the curiousest thing he had seen? Well! He didn't know. He couldn't momently name what was the curiousest thing he had seen,—unless it was a Unicorn,—and he see *him* once at a Fair. But supposing a young gentleman not eight year old was to run away with a fine young woman of seven, might I think *that* a queer start? Certain. Then that was a start as he himself had had his blessed eyes on, and he had cleaned the shoes they run away in—and they was so little that he couldn't get his hand into 'em.

Master Harry Walmers's father, you see, he lived at the Elmses, down away by Shooter's Hill there, six or seven miles from Lunnon. He was a gentleman of spirit, and good-looking, and held his head up when he walked, and had what you may call Fire about him. He wrote poetry, and he rode, and he ran, and he cricketed, and he danced, and he acted, and he done it all equally beautiful. He was uncommon proud of Master Harry as was his only child; but he didn't spoil him neither. He was a gentleman that had a will of his own and a eye of his own, and that would be minded. Consequently, though he made quite a companion of the fine bright boy, and was delighted to see him so fond of reading his fairy books, and was never tired of hearing him say my name is Norval, or hearing him sing his songs about Young May Moons is beaming love, and When he as adores thee has left but the name, and that; still he kept the command over the child, and the child *was* a child, and it's to be wished more of 'em was!

How did Boots happen to know all this? Why, through being under-gardener. Of course he couldn't be under-gardener, and be always about, in the summer-time, near the windows on the lawn, a mowing, and sweeping, and weeding, and pruning, and this and that, without getting acquainted with the ways of the family. Even supposing Master Harry hadn't come to him one morning early, and said, "Cobbs, how should you spell Norah, if you was asked?" and then began cutting it in print all over the fence.

He couldn't say he had taken particular notice of children before that; but really it was pretty to see them two mites a going about the place together, deep in love. And the courage of the boy! Bless your soul, he'd have throwed off his little hat, and tucked up his little sleeves, and gone in at a Lion, he would, if they had happened to meet one, and she had been frightened of him. One day he stops, along with her, where Boots was hoeing weeds in the gravel, and says, speaking up, "Cobbs," he says, "I like *you*." "Do you, sir? I'm proud to hear it." "Yes, I do, Cobbs. Why do I like you, do you think, Cobbs?" "Don't know, Master Harry, I am sure." "Because Norah likes you, Cobbs." "Indeed—sir? That's very gratifying." "Gratifying, Cobbs? It's better than millions of the brightest diamonds to be liked by Norah." "Certainly, sir." "You're going away, ain't you, Cobbs?" "Yes, sir." "Would you like another situation, Cobbs?" "Well, sir, I shouldn't object, if it was a good 'un." "Then, Cobbs," says he, "you shall be our Head Gardener when we are married." And he tucks her, in her little sky-blue mantle, under his arm, and walks away.

Boots could assure me that it was better than a picter, and equal to a play, to see them babies, with their long, bright, curling hair, their sparkling eyes, and their beautiful light tread, a rambling about the garden, deep in love. Boots was of opinion that the birds believed they was birds, and kept up with 'em, singing to please 'em. Sometimes they would creep under the Tulip-tree, and would sit there with their arms round one another's necks, and their soft cheeks touching, a reading about the Prince and the Dragon, and the good and bad enchanters, and the king's fair daughter. Sometimes he would hear them planning about having a house in a forest, keeping bees and a cow, and living entirely on milk and honey. Once he came upon them by the pond, and heard Master Harry say, "Adorable Norah, kiss me, and say you love me to distraction, or I'll jump in head-foremost." And Boots made no question he would have done it if she hadn't complied. On the whole, Boots said it had a tendency to make him feel as if he was in love himself—only he didn't exactly know who with.

"Cobbs," said Master Harry, one evening, when Cobbs was watering the flowers, "I am going on a visit, this present Midsummer, to my grandmamma's at York."

"Are you indeed, sir? I hope you'll have a pleasant time. I am going into Yorkshire, myself, when I leave here."

"Are you going to your grandmamma's, Cobbs?"

"No, sir. I haven't got such a thing."

"Not as a grandmamma, Cobbs?"

"No, sir."

The boy looked on at the watering of the flowers for a little while, and then said, "I shall be very glad indeed to go, Cobbs,—Norah's going."

"You'll be all right then, sir," says Cobbs, "with your beautiful sweetheart by your side."

"Cobbs," returned the boy, flushing, "I never let anybody joke about it, when I can prevent them."

"It wasn't a joke, sir," says Cobbs, with humility,—"wasn't so meant."

"I am glad of that, Cobbs, because I like you, you know, and you're going to live with us.—Cobbs!"

"Sir."

"What do you think my grandmamma gives me when I go down there?"

"I couldn't so much as make a guess, sir."

"A Bank of England five-pound note, Cobbs."

"Whew!" says Cobbs, "that's a spanking sum of money, Master Harry."

"A person could do a good deal with such a sum of money as that, —couldn't a person, Cobbs?"

"I believe you, sir!"

"Cobbs," said the boy, "I'll tell you a secret. At Norah's house, they have been joking her about me, and pretending to laugh at our being engaged,—pretending to make game of it, Cobbs!"

"Such, sir," says Cobbs, "is the depravity of human natur."

The boy, looking exactly like his father, stood for a few minutes with his glowing face towards the sunset, and then departed with, "Good-night, Cobbs. I'm going in."

If I was to ask Boots how it happened that he was a going to leave that place just at that present time, well, he couldn't rightly answer me. He did suppose he might have stayed there till now if he had been anyways inclined. But, you see, he was younger then, and he wanted change. That's what he wanted,—change. Mr. Walmers, he said to him when he gave him notice of his intentions to leave, "Cobbs," he says, "have you anythink to complain of? I make the inquiry because if I find that any of my people really has anythink to complain of, I wish to make it right if I can." "No, sir," says Cobbs; "thanking you, sir, I find myself as well sitiwated here as I could hope to be anywheres. The truth is, sir, that I'm a-going to seek my fortun'." "Oh, indeed, Cobbs!" he says; "I hope you may find it." And Boots could assure me—which he did, touching his hair with his boot-jack, as a salute in the way of his present calling—that he hadn't found it yet.

Well, sir! Boots left the Elmses when his time was up, and Master Harry, he went down to the old lady's at York, which old lady would have given that child the teeth out of her head (if she had had any), she was so wrapped up in him. What does that Infant do,—for Infant you may call him and be within the mark,—but cut away from that old lady's with his Norah, on a expedition to go to Gretna Green and be married!

Sir, Boots was at this identical Holly-Tree Inn (having left it several times since to better himself, but always come back through one thing or another), when, one summer afternoon, the coach drives up, and out of the coach gets them two children. The Guard says to our Governor, "I don't quite make out these little passengers, but the young gentleman's words was, that they was to be brought here." The young gentleman gets out; hands his lady out; gives the Guard something for himself; says to our Governor, "We're to stop here to-night, please. Sitting-room and two bedrooms will be required. Chops and cherry-pudding for two!" and tucks her, in her little sky-blue mantle, under his arm, and walks into the house much bolder than Brass.

Boots leaves me to judge what the amazement of that establishment was, when these two tiny creatures all alone by themselves was marched into the Angel,—much more so, when he, who had seen them without their seeing him, give the Governor his views of the expedition they was upon. "Cobbs," says the Governor, "if this is so, I must set off myself to York, and quiet their friends' minds. In which case you must keep your eye upon 'em, till I come back. But before I take these measures, Cobbs, I should wish you to find from themselves whether your opinion is correct." "Sir, to you," says Cobbs, "that shall be done directly."

So Boots goes upstairs to the Angel, and there he finds Master Harry on a e-normous sofa,—immense at any time, but looking like the Great Bed of Ware, compared with him,—a drying the eyes of Miss Norah with his pocket-hankecher. Their little legs was entirely off the ground, of course, and it really is not possible for Boots to express to me how small them children looked.

"It's Cobbs! It's Cobbs!" cried Master Harry, and comes running to him, and catching hold of his hand. Miss Norah comes running to him on t'other side and catching hold of his t'other hand, and they both jump for joy.

"I see you a getting out, sir," says Cobbs. "I thought it was you. I thought I couldn't be mistaken in your height and figure. What's the object of your journey, sir?—Matrimonial?"

"We are going to be married, Cobbs, at Gretna Green," returned the boy. "We have run away on purpose. Norah has been in rather low spirits, Cobbs; but she'll be happy, now we have found you to be our friend."

"Thank you, sir, and thank *you*, miss," says Cobbs, "for your good opinion. *Did* you bring any luggage with you, sir?"

If I will believe Boots when he gives me his word and honour upon it, the lady had got a parasol, a smelling-bottle, a round and a half of cold buttered toast, eight peppermint drops, and a hair-brush,—seemingly a doll's. The gentleman had got about half a dozen yards of string, a knife, three or four sheets of writing-paper folded up surprising small, a orange, and a Chaney mug with his name upon it.

"What may be the exact natur of your plans, sir?" says Cobbs.

"To go on," replied the boy,—which the courage of that boy was something wonderful!—"in the morning, and be married to-morrow."

"Just so, sir," says Cobbs. "Would it meet your views, sir, if I was to accompany you?"

When Cobbs said this, they both jumped for joy again, and cried out, "Oh, yes, yes, Cobbs! Yes!"

"Well, sir," says Cobbs. "If you will excuse my having the freedom to give an opinion, what I should recommend would be this. I'm acquainted with a pony, sir, which, put in a pheayton that I could borrow, would take you and Mrs. Harry Walmers, Junior (myself driving, if you approved), to the end of your journey in a very short space of time. I am not altogether sure, sir, that this pony will be at liberty to-morrow, but even if you had to wait over to-morrow for him, it might be worth your while. As to the small account here, sir, in case you was to find yourself running at all short, that don't signify; because I'm a part proprietor of this inn, and it could stand over."

Boots assures me that when they clapped their hands, and jumped for joy again, and called him "Good Cobbs!" and "Dear Cobbs!" and bent across him to kiss one another in the delight of their confiding hearts, he felt himself the meanest rascal for deceiving 'em that ever was born.

"Is there anything you want just at present, sir?" says Cobbs, mortally ashamed of himself.

"We should like some cakes after dinner," answered Master Harry, folding his arms, putting out one leg, and looking straight at him, "and two apples,—and jam. With dinner we should like to have toast-and-water. But Norah has always been accustomed to half a glass of currant wine at dessert. And so have I."

"It shall be ordered at the bar, sir," says Cobbs; and away he went.

Boots has the feeling as fresh upon him at this minute of speaking as he had then, that he would far rather have had it out in half-a-dozen rounds with the Governor than have combined with him; and that he wished with all his heart there was any impossible place where those two babies could make an impossible marriage, and live impossibly happy ever afterwards. However, as it couldn't be, he went into the Governor's plans, and the Governor set off for York in half an hour.

The way in which the women of that house—without exception—every one of 'em—married *and* single—took to that boy when they heard the story, Boots considers surprising. It was as much as he could do to keep 'em from dashing into the room and kissing him. They climbed up all sorts of places, at the risk of their lives, to look at him through a pane of glass. They was seven deep at the keyhole. They was out of their minds about him and his bold spirit.

In the evening, Boots went into the room to see how the runaway couple was getting on. The gentleman was on the window-seat, supporting the lady in his arms. She had tears upon her face, and was lying, very tired and half asleep, with her head upon his shoulder.

"Mrs. Harry Walmers, Junior, fatigued, sir?" says Cobbs.

"Yes, she is tired, Cobbs; but she is not used to be away from home, and she has been in low spirits again. Cobbs, do you think you could bring a biffin please?"

"I ask your pardon, sir," says Cobbs. "What was it you——?"

"I think a Norfolk biffin would rouse her, Cobbs. She is very fond of them."

Boots withdrew in search of the required restorative, and, when he brought it in, the gentleman handed it to the lady, and fed her with a spoon, and took a little himself; the lady being heavy with sleep, and rather cross. "What should you think, sir," says Cobbs, "of a chamber candlestick?" The gentleman approved; the chambermaid went first, up the great staircase; the lady, in her sky-blue mantle, followed, gallantly escorted by the gentleman; the gentleman embrace. her at her door, and retired to his own apartment, where Boots softly locked him up.

Boots couldn't but feel with increased acuteness what a base deceiver he was, when they consulted him at breakfast (they had ordered sweet milk-and-water, and toast and currant jelly, overnight) about the pony. It really was as much as he could do, he don't mind confessing to me, to look them two young things in the face, and think what a wicked old father of lies he had grown up to be. Howsomever, he went on a lying like a Trojan about the pony. He told 'em that it did so unfort'nately happen that the pony was half clipped, you see, and that he couldn't be taken out in that state, for fear it should strike to his inside. But that he'd be finished clipping in the course of the day, and that to-morrow morning at eight o'clock the pheayton would be ready. Boots's view of the whole case, looking back on it in my room, is, that Mrs. Harry Walmers, Junior, was beginning to give in. She hadn't had her hair curled when she went to bed, and she didn't seem quite up to brushing it herself, and its getting in her eyes put her out. But nothing put out Master Harry. He sat behind his breakfast-cup, a tearing away at the jelly, as if he had been his own father.

After breakfast, Boots is inclined to consider that they drawed soldiers,—at least, he knows that many such was found in the fireplace, all on horseback. In the course of the morning, Master Harry rang the bell,—it was surprising how that there boy did carry on,—and said, in a sprightly way, " Cobbs, is there any good walks in this neighbourhood ? "

" Yes, sir," says Cobbs. " There's Love-lane."

" Get out with you, Cobbs ! "—that was that there boy's expression,—" you're joking."

" Begging your pardon, sir," says Cobbs, " there really is Love-lane. And a pleasant walk it is, and proud shall I be to show it to yourself and Mrs. Harry Walmers, Junior."

" Norah, dear," said Master Harry, " this is curious. We really ought to see Love-lane. Put on your bonnet, my sweetest darling, and we will go there with Cobbs."

Boots leaves me to judge what a Beast he felt himself to be, when that young pair told him, as they all three jogged along together, that they had made up their minds to give him two thousand guineas a year as head-gardener, on accounts of his being so true a friend to 'em. Boots could have wished at the moment that the earth would have opened and swallowed him up, he felt so mean, with their beaming eyes a looking at him, and believing him. Well, sir, he turned the conversation as well as he could, and he took 'em down Love-lane to the water-meadows, and there Master Harry would have drowned himself in half a moment more, a getting out a water-lily for her,—but nothing daunted that boy. Well, sir, they was tired out. All being so new and strange to 'em, they was tired as tired could be. And they laid down on a bank of daisies. like the children in the wood, leastways meadows, and fell asleep.

Boots don't know—perhaps I do,—but never mind, it don't signify either way—why it made a man fit to make a fool of himself to see them two pretty babies a lying there in the clear still sunny day, not dreaming half so hard when they was asleep as they done when they was awake. But, lord ! when you come to think of yourself, you know, and what a game you have been up to ever since you was in your own cradle, and what a poor sort of a chap you are, and how it's always either Yesterday with you, or else To-morrow, and never To-day, that's where it is!

Well, sir, they woke up at last, and then one thing was getting pretty clear to Boots, namely, that Mrs. Harry Walmerses, Junior's temper was on the move. When Master Harry took her round the waist, she said he "teased her so"; and when he says, "Norah, my young May Moon, your Harry tease you?" she tells him, "Yes; and I want to go home!"

A biled fowl, and baked bread-and-butter pudding, brought Mrs. Walmers up a little; but Boots could have wished, he must privately own to me, to have seen her more sensible of the woice of love, and less abandoning of herself to currants. However, Master Harry, he kept up, and his noble heart was as fond as ever. Mrs. Walmers turned very sleepy about dusk, and began to cry. Therefore, Mrs. Walmers went off to bed as per yesterday; and Master Harry ditto repeated.

About eleven or twelve at night comes back the Governor in a chaise, along with Mr. Walmers and a elderly lady. Mr. Walmers looks amused and very serious, both at once, and says to our missis, "We are much indebted to you, ma'am, for your kind care of our little children, which we can never sufficiently acknowledge. Pray, ma'am, where is my boy?" Our missis says, "Cobbs has the dear child in charge, sir. Cobbs, show Forty!" Then he says to Cobbs, "Ah, Cobbs, I am glad to see *you*! I understood you was here!" And Cobbs says, "Yes, sir. Your most obedient, sir."

I may be surprised to hear Boots say it, perhaps; but Boots assures me that his heart beat like a hammer, going upstairs. "I beg your pardon, sir," says he, while unlocking the door; "I hope you are not angry with Master Harry. For Master Harry is a fine boy, sir, and will do you credit and honour." And Boots signifies to me, that, if the fine boy's father had contradicted him in the daring state of mind in which he then was, he thinks he should have "fetched him a crack," and taken the consequences.

But Mr. Walmers only says, "No, Cobbs. No, my good fellow. Thank you!" And, the door being opened, goes in.

Boots goes in too, holding the light, and he sees Mr. Walmers go up to the bedside, bend gently down, and kiss the little sleeping face. Then he stands looking at it for a moment, looking wonderfully like it (they do say he ran away with Mrs. Walmers); and then he gently shakes the little shoulder.

"Harry, my dear boy! Harry!"

Master Harry starts up and looks at him. Looks at Cobbs too. Such is the honour of that mite, that he looks at Cobbs, to see whether he has brought him into trouble.

"I am not angry, my child. I only want you to dress yourself and come home."

"Yes, pa."

Master Harry dresses himself quickly. His breast begins to swell when he has nearly finished, and it swells more and more as he stands, at last, a looking at his father: his father standing a looking at him, the quiet image of him.

"Please may I"—the spirit of that little creatur, and the way he kept his rising tears down!—"please, dear pa—may I—kiss Norah before I go?"

"You may, my child."

So he takes Master Harry in his hand, and Boots leads the way with the candle, and they come to that other bedroom, where the elderly lady is seated by the bed, and poor little Mrs. Harry Walmers, Junior, is fast asleep. There the father lifts the child up to the pillow, and he lays his little face down for an instant by the little warm face of poor unconscious little Mrs. Harry Walmers, Junior, and gently draws it to him,—a sight so touching to the chambermaids who are peeping through the door, that one of them calls out, "It's a shame to part 'em!" But this chambermaid was always, as Boots informs me, a soft-hearted one. Not that there was any harm in that girl. Far from it.

Finally, Boots says, that's all about it. Mr. Walmers drove away in the chaise, having hold of Master Harry's hand. The elderly lady and Mrs. Harry Walmers, Junior, that was never to be (she married a Captain long afterwards, and died in India), went off next day. In conclusion, Boots put it to me whether I hold with him in two opinions: firstly, that there are not many couples on their way to be married who are half as innocent of guile as those two children; secondly, that it would be a jolly good thing for a great many couples on their way to be married, if they could only be stopped in time, and brought back separately.

CHARLES DICKENS

DR. MANETTE'S MS.

I, Alexandre Manette, unfortunate physician, native of Beauvais, and afterwards resident in Paris, write this melancholy paper in my doleful cell in the Bastille, during the last month of the year 1767. I write it at stolen intervals, under every difficulty. I design to secrete it in the wall of the chimney, where I have slowly and laboriously made a place of concealment for it. Some pitying hand may find it there, when I and my sorrows are dust.

These words are formed by the rusty iron point with which I write with difficulty in scrapings of soot and charcoal from the chimney, mixed with blood, in the last month of the tenth year of my captivity. Hope has quite departed from my breast. I know from terrible warnings I have noted in myself that my reason will not long remain unimpaired, but I solemnly declare that I am at this time in the possession of my right mind—that my memory is exact and circumstantial—and that I write the truth as I shall answer for these my last recorded words, whether they be ever read by men or not, at the Eternal Judgment-seat.

One cloudy moonlight night, in the third week of December (I think the twenty-second of the month) in the year 1757, I was walking on a retired part of the quay by the Seine for the refreshment of the frosty air, at an hour's distance from my place of residence in the Street of the School of Medicine, when a carriage came along behind me, driven very fast. As I stood aside to let that carriage pass, apprehensive that it might otherwise run me down, a head was put out at the window, and a voice called to the driver to stop.

The carriage stopped as soon as the driver could rein in his horses, and the same voice called to me by my name. I answered. The carriage was then so far in advance of me that two gentlemen had time to open the door and alight before I came up with it. I observed that they were both wrapped in cloaks, and appeared to conceal themselves. As they stood side by side near the carriage door, I also observed that they both looked of about my own age, or rather younger, and that they were greatly alike, in stature, manner, voice, and (as far as I could see) face too.

" You are Doctor Manette ? " said one.

" I am."

" Doctor Manette, formerly of Beauvais," said the other ; " the young physician, originally an expert surgeon, who within the last year or two has made a rising reputation in Paris ? "

" Gentlemen," I returned, " I am that Doctor Manette of whom you speak so graciously."

" We have been to your residence," said the first, " and not being so fortunate as to find you there, and being informed that you were probably walking in this direction, we followed, in the hope of overtaking you. Will you please to enter the carriage ? "

The manner of both was imperious, and they both moved, as these words were spoken, so as to place me between themselves and the carriage door. They were armed. I was not.

" Gentlemen," said I, " pardon me ; but I usually inquire who does me the honour to seek my assistance, and what is the nature of the case to which I am summoned."

The reply to this was made by him who had spoken second. " Doctor, your clients are people of condition. As to the nature of the case, our confidence in your skill assures us that you will ascertain it for yourself better than we can describe it. Enough. Will you please to enter the carriage ? "

I could do nothing but comply, and I entered it in silence. They both entered after me—the last springing in, after putting up the steps. The carriage turned about, and drove on at its former speed.

I repeat this conversation exactly as it occurred. I have no doubt that it is, word for word, the same. I describe everything exactly as it took place, constraining my mind not to wander from the task. Where I make the broken marks that follow here, I leave off for the time, and put my paper in its hiding-place. * * * *

The carriage left the streets behind, passed the North Barrier, and emerged upon the country road. At two-thirds of a league from the Barrier—I did not estimate the distance at that time, but afterwards when I traversed it—it struck out of the main avenue, and presently stopped at a solitary house. We all three alighted, and walked, by a damp soft footpath in a garden where a neglected fountain had overflowed, to the door of the house. It was not opened immediately, in answer to the ringing of the bell, and one of my two conductors struck the man who opened it, with his heavy riding-glove, across the face.

There was nothing in this action to attract my particular attention, for I had seen common people struck more commonly than dogs. But the other of the two, being angry likewise, struck the man in like manner with his arm ; the look and bearing of the brothers were then so exactly alike, that I then first perceived them to be twin brothers.

From the time of our alighting at the outer gate (which we found locked, and which one of the brothers had opened to admit us, and had re-locked), I had heard cries proceeding from an upper chamber. I was conducted to this chamber straight, the cries growing louder as we ascended the stairs, and I found a patient in a high fever of the brain, lying on a bed.

The patient was a woman of great beauty, and young ; assuredly not much past twenty. Her hair was torn and ragged, and her arms were bound to her sides with sashes and handkerchiefs. I noticed that these bonds were all portions of a gentleman's dress. On one of them, which was a fringed scarf for a dress of ceremony, I saw the armorial bearings of a Noble, and the letter E.

I saw this, within the first minute of my contemplation of the patient ; for in her restless strivings she had turned over on her face on the edge of the bed, had drawn the end of the scarf into her mouth and was in danger of suffocation. My first act was to put out my hand to relieve her breathing ; and in moving the scarf aside, the embroidery in the corner caught my sight.

I turned her gently over, placed my hands upon her breast to calm her and keep her down, and looked into her face. Her eyes were dilated and wild, and she constantly uttered piercing shrieks, and repeated the words, " My husband, my father, and my brother ! " and then counted up to twelve, and said, " Hush ! " For an instant, and no more, she would pause to listen, and then the piercing shrieks would begin again, and she would repeat the cry, " My husband, my father, and my brother ! " and would count up to twelve, and say " Hush ! " There was no variation in the order, or the manner. There was no cessation, but the regular moment's pause, in the utterance of these sounds.

" How long," I asked, " has this lasted ? "

To distinguish the brothers, I will call them the elder and the younger ; by the elder, I mean him who exercised the most authority. It was the elder who replied, " Since about this hour last night."

" She has a husband, a father, and a brother ? "

" A brother."

" I do not address her brother ? "

He answered with great contempt, " No."

" She has some recent association with the number twelve ? "

The younger brother impatiently rejoined, " With twelve o'clock ? "

" See, gentlemen," said I, still keeping my hands upon her breast, " how useless I am, as you have brought me ! If I had known what

I was coming to see, I could have come provided. As it is, time must be lost. There are no medicines to be obtained in this lonely place."

The elder brother looked to the younger, who said haughtily, "There is a case of medicines here"; and brought it from a closet, and put it on the table. * * * *

I opened some of the bottles, smelt them, and put the stoppers to my lips. If I had wanted to use anything save narcotic medicines that were poisons in themselves, I would not have administered any of those.

"Do you doubt them?" asked the younger brother.

"You see, monsieur, I am going to use them," I replied, and said no more.

I made the patient swallow, with great difficulty, and after many efforts, the dose that I desired to give. As I intended to repeat it after a while, and as it was necessary to watch its influence, I then sat down by the side of the bed. There was a timid and suppressed woman in attendance (wife of the man downstairs), who had retreated into a corner. The house was damp and decayed, indifferently furnished—evidently, recently occupied and temporarily used. Some thick old hangings had been nailed up before the windows to deaden the sound of the shrieks. They continued to be uttered in their regular succession with the cry, "My husband, my father, and my brother!" the counting up to twelve, and "Hush!" The frenzy was so violent that I had not unfastened the bandages restraining the arms; but I had looked to them to see that they were not painful. The only spark of encouragement in the case was, that my hand upon the sufferer's breast had this much soothing influence, that for minutes at a time it tranquillised the figure. It had no effect upon the cries; no pendulum could be more regular.

For the reason that my hand had this effect (I assume), I had sat by the side of the bed for half an hour, with the two brothers looking on, before the elder said:

"There is another patient."

I was startled, and asked, "Is it a pressing case?"

"You had better see," he carelessly answered; and took up a light. * * * *

The other patient lay in a back room across a second staircase, which was a species of loft over a stable. There was a low plastered ceiling to a part of it; the rest was open to the ridge of the tiled roof, and there were beams across. Hay and straw were stored in that portion of the place, fagots for firing, and a heap of apples in sand. I had to pass through that part to get at the other. My memory is circumstantial and unshaken. I try it with these details and I see them all, in this my cell in the Bastille, near the close of the tenth year of my captivity, as I saw them all that night.

On some hay on the ground, with a cushion thrown under his head, lay a handsome peasant boy—a boy of not more than seventeen at the most. He lay on his back, with his teeth set, his right hand clenched on his breast, and his glaring eyes looking straight upward. I could not see where his wound was, as I kneeled on one knee over him ; but I could see that he was dying of a wound from a sharp point.

" I am a doctor, my poor fellow," said I. " Let me examine it."

" I do not want it examined," he answered ; " let it be."

It was under his hand, and I soothed him to let me move his hand away. The wound was a sword-thrust, received from twenty to twenty-four hours before, but no skill could have saved him if it had been looked to without delay. He was then dying fast. As I turned my cycs to the elder brother I saw him looking down at this handsome boy whose life was ebbing out, as if he were a wounded bird, or hare, or rabbit ; not at all as if he were a fellow-creature.

" How has this been done, monsieur ? " said I.

" A crazed young common dog ! A serf ! Forced my brother to draw upon him, and has fallen by my brother's sword—like a gentleman."

There was no touch of pity, sorrow, or kindred humanity in this answer. The speaker seemed to acknowledge that it was inconvenient to have that different order of creature dying there, and that it would have been better if he had died in the usual obscure routine of his vermin kind. He was quite incapable of any compassionate feeling about the boy, or about his fate.

The boy's eyes had slowly moved to him as he had spoken, and they now slowly moved to me.

" Doctor, they are very proud, these Nobles ; but we common dogs are proud too, sometimes. They plunder us, outrage us, beat us, kill us ; but we have a little pride left, sometimes. She—have you seen her, Doctor ? "

The shrieks and the cries were audible there, though subdued by the distance. He referred to them as if she were lying in our presence.

I said, " I have seen her."

" She is my sister, Doctor. They have had their shameful rights, these Nobles, in the modesty and virtue of our sisters, many years, but we have had good girls among us. I know it, and have heard my father say so. She was a good girl. She was betrothed to a good young man, too : a tenant of his. We were all tenants of his—that man's who stands there. The other is his brother the worst of a bad race."

It was with the greatest difficulty that the boy gathered bodily force to speak ; but his spirit spoke with a dreadful emphasis.

"We were so robbed by that man who stands there, as all we common dogs are by those superior Beings—taxed by him without mercy, obliged to work for him without pay, obliged to grind our corn at his mill, obliged to feed scores of his tame birds on our wretched crops, and forbidden for our lives to keep a single tame bird of our own, pillaged and plundered to that degree that when we chanced to have a bit of meat we ate it in fear, with the door barred, and the shutters closed, that his people should not see it and take it from us—I say, we were so robbed, and hunted, and were made so poor, that our father told us it was a dreadful thing to bring a child into the world, and that what we should most pray for was that our women might be barren and our miserable race die out!"

I had never before seen the sense of being oppressed, bursting forth like a fire. I had supposed that it must be latent in the people somewhere; but I had never seen it break out until I saw it in the dying boy.

"Nevertheless, Doctor, my sister married. He was ailing at that time, poor fellow, and she married her lover, that she might tend and comfort him in our cottage—our dog hut, as that man would call it. She had not been married many weeks, when that man's brother saw her and admired her, and asked that man to lend her to him—for what are husbands among us! He was willing enough, but my sister was good and virtuous, and hated his brother with a hatred as strong as mine. What did the two then, to persuade her husband to use his influence with her, to make her willing?"

The boy's eyes, which had been fixed on mine, slowly turned to the looker-on, and I saw in the two faces that all he said was true. The two opposing kinds of pride confronting one another, I can see, even in this Bastille; the gentleman's, all negligent indifference; the peasant's, all trodden-down sentiment and passionate revenge.

"You know, Doctor, that it is among the Rights of these Nobles to harness us common dogs to carts and drive us. They so harnessed him and drove him. You know that it is among their Rights to keep us in their grounds all night, quieting the frogs, in order that their noble sleep may not be disturbed. They kept him out in the unwholesome mists at night, and ordered him back into his harness in the day. But he was not persuaded. No! Taken out of harness one day at noon, to feed—if he could find food—he sobbed twelve times, once for every stroke of the bell, and died on her bosom."

Nothing human could have held life in the boy but his determination to tell all his wrong. He forced back the gathering shadows of death, as he forced his clenched right hand to remain clenched and to cover his wound.

"Then, with that man's permission and even with his aid, his brother took her away; in spite of what I know she must have told his brother—and what that is, will not be long unknown to you, Doctor, if it is now—his brother took her away—for his pleasure and diversion, for a little while. I saw her pass me on the road. When I took the tidings home, our father's heart burst; he never spoke one of the words that filled it. I took my young sister (for I have another to a place beyond the reach of this man, and where, at least, she will never be *his* vassal. Then I tracked the brother here, and last night) climbed in—a common dog, but sword in hand.—Where is the loft window? It was somewhere here?"

The room was darkening to his sight; the world was narrowing around him. I glanced about me, and saw that the hay and straw were trampled over the floor, as if there had been a struggle.

"She heard me, and ran in. I told her not to come near us till he was dead. He came in and first tossed me some pieces of money; then struck at me with a whip. But I, though a common dog, so struck at him as to make him draw. Let him break into as many pieces as he will the sword that he stained with my common blood; he drew to defend himself—thrust at me with all his skill for his life."

My glance had fallen, but a few moments before, on the fragments of a broken sword lying among the hay. That weapon was a gentleman's. In another place lay an old sword that seemed to have been a soldier's.

"Now, lift me up, Doctor; lift me up. Where is he?"

"He is not here," I said, supporting the boy, and thinking that he referred to the brother.

"He! Proud as these Nobles are, he is afraid to see me. Where is the man who was here? Turn my face to him."

I did so, raising the boy's head against my knee. But, invested for the moment with extraordinary power, he raised himself completely: obliging me to rise too, or I could not have still supported him.

"Marquis," said the boy, turned to him with his eyes opened wide, and his right hand raised, "in the days when all these things are to be answered for, I summon you and yours, to the last of your bad race, to answer for them. I mark this cross of blood upon you, as a sign that I do it. In the days when all these things are to be answered for, I summon your brother, the worst of the bad race to answer for them separately. I mark this cross of blood upon him, as a sign that I do it."

Twice he put his hand to the wound in his breast, and with his forefinger drew a cross in the air. He stood for an instant with the finger yet raised, and, as it dropped, he dropped with it, and I laid him down dead. * * * *

When I returned to the bedside of the young woman I found her raving in precisely the same order and continuity. I knew that this might last for many hours, and that it would probably end in the silence of the grave.

I repeated the medicines I had given her, and I sat at the side of the bed until the night was far advanced. She never abated the piercing quality of her shrieks, never stumbled in the distinctness or the order of her words. They were always "My husband, my father, and my brother! One, two, three, four, five, six, seven, eight, nine, ten, eleven, twelve. Hush!"

This lasted twenty-six hours from the time when I first saw her. I had come and gone twice, and was again sitting by her when she began to falter. I did what little could be done to assist that opportunity, and by-and-by she sank into a lethargy and lay like the dead.

It was as if the wind and rain had lulled at last after a long and fearful storm. I released her arms, and called the woman to assist me to compose her figure and the dress she had torn. It was then that I knew her condition to be that of one in whom the first expectations of being a mother had arisen; and it was then that I lost the little hope I had had of her.

"Is she dead?" asked the Marquis, whom I will still describe as the elder brother, coming booted into the room from his horse.

"Not dead," said I, "but like to die."

"What strength there is in these common bodies!" he said, looking down at her with some curiosity.

"There is prodigious strength," I answered him, "in sorrow and despair."

He first laughed at my words, and then frowned at them. He moved a chair with his foot near to mine, ordered the woman away, and said in a subdued voice:

"Doctor, finding my brother in this difficulty with these hinds, I recommended that your aid should be invited. Your reputation is high, and, as a young man with your fortune to make, you are probably mindful of your interest. The things that you see here are things to be seen and not spoken of."

I listened to the patient's breathing, and avoided answering.

"Do you honour me with your attention, Doctor?"

"Monsieur," said I, "in my profession the communications of patients are always received in confidence." I was guarded in my answer, for I was troubled in my mind with what I had heard and seen.

Her breathing was so difficult to trace, that I carefully tried the pulse and the heart. There was life and no more. Looking round as I resumed my seat, I found both the brothers intent upon me.* * * *

I write with so much difficulty, the cold is so severe, I am so fearful of being detected and consigned to an underground cell and total darkness, that I must abridge this narrative. There is no confusion or failure in my memory ; it can recall, and could detail, every word that was ever spoken between me and those brothers.

She lingered for a week. Towards the last, I could understand some few syllables that she said to me, by placing my ear close to her lips. She asked me where she was, and I told her ; who I was, and I told her. It was in vain that I asked her for her family name. She faintly shook her head upon the pillow, and kept her secret, as the boy had done.

I had no opportunity of asking her any question until I had told the brothers she was sinking fast and could not live another day. Until then, though no one was ever presented to her consciousness save the woman and myself, one or other of them had always jealously sat behind the curtain at the head of the bed when I was there. But when it came to that, they seemed careless what communication I might hold with her ; as if—the thought passed through my mind—I were dying too.

I always observed that their pride bitterly resented the younger brother's (as I call him) having crossed swords with a peasant, and that peasant a boy. The only consideration that appeared to affect the mind of either of them was the consideration that this was highly degrading to the family, and was ridiculous. As often as I caught the younger brother's eyes, their expression reminded me that he disliked me deeply for knowing what I knew from the boy. He was smoother and more polite to me than the elder ; but I saw this. I also saw that I was an incumbrance in the mind of the elder, too.

My patient died two hours before midnight—at a time, by my watch, answering almost to the minute when I had first seen her. I was alone with her when her forlorn young head drooped gently on one side, and all her earthly wrongs and sorrows ended.

The brothers were waiting in a room downstairs, impatient to ride away. I heard them, alone at the bedside, striking their boots with their riding-whips, and loitering up and down.

" At last she is dead ? " said the elder, when I went in.

" She is dead," said I.

" I congratulate you, my brother," were his words as he turned round.

He had before offered me money, which I had postponed taking. He now gave me a rouleau of gold. I took it from his hand, but laid it on the table. I had considered the question, and had resolved to accept nothing.

" Pray excuse me," said I. " Under the circumstances, no."

They exchanged looks, but bent their heads to me as I bent mine to them, and we parted without another word on either side. * * * *

I am weary, weary, weary—worn down by misery. I cannot read what I have written with this gaunt hand.

Early in the morning, the rouleau of gold was left at my door in a little box, with my name on the outside. From the first, I had anxiously considered what I ought to do. I decided, that day, to write privately to the Minister, stating the nature of the two cases to which I had been summoned, and the place to which I had gone: in effect, stating all the circumstances. I knew what Court influence was, and what the immunities of the Nobles were, and I expected that the matter would never be heard of; but I wished to relieve my own mind. I had kept the matter a profound secret, even from my wife; and this, too, I resolved to state in my letter. I had no apprehension whatever of my real danger; but I was conscious that there might be danger for others, if others were compromised by possessing the knowledge that I possessed.

I was much engaged that day, and could not complete my letter that night. I rose long before my usual time next morning to finish it. It was the last day of the year. The letter was lying before me just completed when I was told that a lady waited who wished to see me. * * * *

I am growing more and more unequal to the task I have set myself. It is so cold, so dark, my senses are so benumbed, and the gloom upon me is so dreadful.

The lady was young, engaging, and handsome, but not marked for long life. She was in great agitation. She presented herself to me as the wife of the Marquis St. Evrémonde. I connected the title by which the boy had addressed the elder brother with the initial letter embroidered on the scarf, and had no difficulty in arriving at the conclusion that I had seen that nobleman very lately.

My memory is still accurate, but I cannot write the words of our conversation. I suspect that I am watched more closely than I was, and I know not at what times I may be watched. She had in part suspected, and in part discovered, the main facts of the cruel story, of her husband's share in it, and my being resorted to. She did not know that the girl was dead. Her hope had been, she said in great distress, to show her, in secret, a woman's sympathy. Her hope had been to avert the wrath of Heaven from a House that had long been hateful to the suffering many.

She had reason for believing that there was a young sister living, and her greatest desire was to help that sister. I could tell her nothing but that there was such a sister; beyond that I knew nothing. Her inducement to come to me, relying on my confidence, had been the hope that I could tell her the name and place of abode. Whereas to this wretched hour I am ignorant of both. * * * *

These scraps of paper fail me. One was taken from me, with a warning, yesterday. I must finish my record to-day.

She was a good, compassionate lady, and not happy in her marriage. How could she be! The brother distrusted and disliked her, and his influence was all opposed to her; she stood in dread of him, and in dread of her husband too. When I handed her down to the door, there was a child, a pretty boy from two to three years old, in her carriage.

"For his sake, Doctor," she said, pointing to him in tears, "I would do all I can to make what poor amends I can. He will never prosper in his inheritance otherwise. I have a presentiment that if no other innocent atonement is made for this, it will one day be required of him. What I have left to call my own—it is little beyond the worth of a few jewels—I will make it the first charge of his life to bestow, with the compassion and lamenting of his dead mother, on this injured family, if the sister can be discovered."

She kissed the boy, and said, caressing him, "It is for thine own dear sake. Thou wilt be faithful, little Charles?" The child answered her bravely, "Yes!" I kissed her hand, and she took him in her arms, and went away caressing him. I never saw her more.

As she had mentioned her husband's name in the faith that I knew it, I added no mention of it to my letter. I sealed my letter, and, not trusting it out of my own hands, delivered it myself that day.

That night, the last night of the year, towards nine o'clock, a man in a black dress rang at my gate, demanded to see me, and softly followed my servant, Ernest Defarge, a youth, upstairs. When my servant came into the room where I sat with my wife—oh, my wife, beloved of my heart! My fair young English wife!—we saw the man, who was supposed to be at the gate, standing silent behind him.

An urgent case in the Rue St. Honoré, he said. It would not detain me, he had a coach in waiting.

It brought me here, it brought me to my grave. When I was clear of the house a black muffler was drawn tightly over my mouth from behind, and my arms were pinioned. The two brothers crossed the road from a dark corner, and identified me with a single gesture. The Marquis took from his pocket the letter I had written, showed it me, burnt it in the light of a lantern that was held, and extinguished the ashes with his foot. Not a word was spoken. I was brought here, I was brought to my living grave.

If it had pleased God to put it in the hard heart of either of the brothers, in all these frightful years, to grant me any tidings of my dearest wife—so much as to let me know by a word whether alive or dead—I might have thought that He had not quite abandoned them. But, now I believe that the mark of the red cross is fatal to them, and that they have no part in His mercies. And them and their descendants, to the last of their race, I, Alexandre Manette, unhappy prisoner, do this last night of the year 1767, in my unbearable agony, denounce to the times when all these things shall be answered for. I denounce them to Heaven and to earth.

CHARLES DICKENS

TO BE TAKEN WITH A GRAIN OF SALT

I HAVE always noticed a prevalent want of courage, even among persons of superior intelligence and culture, as to imparting their own psychological experiences when those have been of a strange sort. Almost all men are afraid that what they could relate in such wise would find no parallel or response in a listener's internal life, and might be suspected or laughed at. A truthful traveller, who should have seen some extraordinary creature in the likeness of a sea-serpent, would have no fear of mentioning it ; but the same traveller, having had some singular presentiment, impulse, vagary of thought, vision (so called), dream, or other remarkable mental impression, would hesitate considerably before he would own to it. To this reticence I attribute much of the obscurity in which such subjects are involved. We do not habitually communicate our experiences of these subjective things as we do our experiences of objective creation. The consequence is, that the general stock of experience in this regard appears exceptional, and really is so, in respect of being miserably imperfect.

In what I am going to relate, I have no intention of setting up, opposing, or supporting any theory whatever. I know the history of the Bookseller of Berlin, I have studied the case of the wife of a late Astronomer-Royal as related by Sir David Brewster, and I have followed the minutest details of a much more remarkable case of Spectral Illusion occurring within my private circle of friends. It may be necessary to state as to this last, that the sufferer (a lady) was in no degree, however distant, related to me. A mistaken assumption on that head might suggest an explanation of a part of my own case,—but only a part,—which would be wholly without foundation. It cannot be referred to my inheritance of any developed peculiarity, nor had I ever before any at all similar experience, nor have I ever had any at all similar experience since.

It does not signify how many years ago, or how few, a certain murder was committed in England, which attracted great attention. We hear more than enough of murderers as they rise in succession to their atrocious eminence, and I would bury the memory of this particular brute, if I could, as his body was buried, in Newgate Jail. I purposely abstain from giving any direct clue to the criminal's individuality. When the murder was first discovered, no suspicion fell—or I ought rather to say, for I cannot be too precise in my facts, it was nowhere publicly hinted that any suspicion fell—on the man who was afterwards brought to trial. As no reference was at that time made to him in the newspapers, it is obviously impossible that any description of him can at that time have been given in the newspapers. It is essential that this fact be remembered.

Unfolding at breakfast my morning paper, containing the account of that first discovery, I found it to be deeply interesting, and I read it with close attention. I read it twice, if not three times. The discovery had been made in a bedroom, and, when I laid down the paper, I was aware of a flash—rush—flow—I do not know what to call it,—no word I can find is satisfactorily descriptive,—in which I seemed to see that bedroom passing through my room, like a picture impossibly painted on a running river. Though almost instantaneous in its passing, it was perfectly clear; so clear that I distinctly, and with a sense of relief, observed the absence of the dead body from the bed.

It was in no romantic place that I had this curious sensation, but in chambers in Piccadilly, very near to the corner of St. James's Street. It was entirely new to me. I was in my easy-chair at the moment, and the sensation was accompanied with a peculiar shiver which started the chair from its position. (But it is to be noted that the chair ran easily on castors.) I went to one of the windows (there are two in the room, and the room is on the second floor) to refresh my eyes with the moving objects down in Piccadilly. It was a bright autumn morning, and the street was sparkling and cheerful. The wind was high. As I looked out, it brought down from the Park a quantity of fallen leaves, which a gust took, and whirled into a spiral pillar. As the pillar fell and the leaves dispersed, I saw two men on the opposite side of the way, going from west to east. They were one behind the other. The foremost man often looked back over his shoulder. The second man followed him, at a distance of some thirty paces, with his right hand menacingly raised. First, the singularity and steadiness of this threatening gesture in so public a thoroughfare attracted my attention; and next, the more remarkable circumstance that nobody heeded it. Both men threaded their way among the other passengers with a smoothness hardly consistent even with the action of walking on a pavement; and no single creature, that I could see, gave them place, touched them, or looked after them. In passing before my windows, they both stared up at me. I saw their two faces very distinctly, and I knew that I could recognise them anywhere. Not that I had consciously noticed anything very remarkable in either face, except that the man who went first had an unusually lowering appearance, and that the face of the man who followed him was of the colour of impure wax.

I am a bachelor, and my valet and his wife constitute my whole establishment. My occupation is in a certain Branch Bank, and I wish that my duties as head of a Department were as light as they are popularly supposed to be. They kept me in town that autumn, when I stood in need of change. I was not ill, but I was not well. My reader is to make the most that can be reasonably made of my feeling jaded, having a depressing sense upon me of a monotonous life, and being "slightly dyspeptic." I am assured by my renowned doctor that my real state of health at that time justified no stronger description, and I quote his own from his written answer to my request for it. As the circumstances of the murder, gradually unravelling, took stronger and stronger possession of the public mind, I kept them away from mine by knowing as little about them as was possible in the midst of the universal excitement. But I knew that a verdict of Wilful Murder had been found against the suspected murderer, and that he had been committed to Newgate for trial. I also knew that his trial had been postponed over one Sessions of the Central Criminal Court, on the ground of general prejudice and want of time for the preparation of the defence. I may further have known, but I believe I did not, when, or about when, the Sessions to which his trial stood postponed would come on.

My sitting-room, bedroom, and dressing-room are all on one floor. With the last there is no communication but through the bedroom. True, there is a door in it, once communicating with the staircase; but a part of the fitting of my bath has been—and had been then for some years—fixed across it. At the same period, and as a part of the same arrangement, the door had been nailed up and canvased over.

I was standing in my bedroom late one night, giving some directions to my servant before he went to bed. My face was towards the only available door of communication with the dressing-room, and it was closed. My servant's back was towards that door. While I was speaking to him, I saw it open, and a man look in, who very earnestly and mysteriously beckoned to me. That man was the man who had gone second of the two along Piccadilly, and whose face was the colour of impure wax. The figure, having beckoned, drew back, and closed the door. With no longer pause than was made by my crossing the bedroom, I opened the dressing-room door and looked in. I had a lighted candle already in my hand. I felt no inward expectation of seeing the figure in the dressing-room, and I did not see it there.

Conscious that my servant stood amazed, I turned round to him, and said: "Derrick, could you believe that in my cool senses I fancied I saw a——" As I there laid my hand upon his breast, with a sudden start he trembled violently, and said, "O Lord, yes, Sir! A dead man beckoning!"

Now I do not believe that this John Derrick, my trusty and attached servant for more than twenty years, had any impression whatever of having seen any such figure, until I touched him. The change in him was so startling, when I touched him, that I fully believe he derived his impression in some occult manner from me at that instant.

I bade John Derrick bring some brandy, and I gave him a dram, and was glad to take one myself. Of what had preceded that night's phenomenon I told him not a single word. Reflecting on it, I was absolutely certain that I had never seen that face before, except on the one occasion in Piccadilly. Comparing its expression when beckoning at the door with its expression when it had stared up at me as I stood at my window, I came to the conclusion that on the first occasion it had sought to fasten itself upon my memory, and that on the second occasion it had made sure of being immediately remembered.

I was not very comfortable that night, though I felt a certainty, difficult to explain, that the figure would not return. At daylight I fell into heavy sleep, from which I was awakened by John Derrick's coming to my bedside with a paper in his hand.

This paper, it appeared, had been the subject of an altercation at the door between its bearer and my servant. It was a summons to me to serve upon a Jury at the forthcoming Sessions of the Central Criminal Court at the Old Bailey. I had never before been summoned on such a Jury, as John Derrick well knew. He believed—I am not certain at this hour whether with reason or otherwise—that that class of Jurors were customarily chosen on a lower qualification than mine, and he had at first refused to accept the summons. The man who served it had taken the matter very coolly. He had said that my attendance or non-attendance was nothing to him; there the summons was; and I should deal with it at my own peril, and not at his.

For a day or two I was undecided whether to respond to this call, or take no notice of it. I was not conscious of the slightest mysterious bias, influence, or attraction, one way or other. Of that I am as strictly sure as of every other statement that I make here. Ultimately I decided, as a break in the monotony of my life, that I would go.

The appointed morning was a raw morning in the month of November. There was a dense brown fog in Piccadilly, and it became positively black and in the last degree oppressive east of Temple Bar. I found the passages and staircases of the Court House flaringly lighted with gas, and the Court itself similarly illuminated. I *think* that, until I was conducted by officers into the Old Court and saw its crowded state, I did not know that the Murderer was to be tried that day. I *think* that, until I was so helped into the Old Court with considerable difficulty, I did not know into which of the two Courts sitting my summons would take me. But this must not be received as a positive assertion, for I am not completely satisfied in my mind on either point. I took my seat in the place appropriated to Jurors in waiting, and I looked about the Court as well as I could through the cloud of fog and breath that was heavy in it. I noticed the black vapour hanging like a murky curtain outside the great windows, and I noticed the stifled sound of wheels on the straw or tan that was littered in the street; also, the hum of the people gathered there, which a shrill whistle, or a louder song or hail than the rest, occasionally pierced. Soon afterwards the Judges, two in number, entered, and took their seats. The buzz in the Court was awfully hushed. The direction was given to put the Murderer to the bar. He appeared there. And in that same instant I recognised in him the first of the two men who had gone down Piccadilly.

If my name had been called then, I doubt if I could have answered to it audibly. But it was called about sixth or eighth in the panel, and I was by that time able to say "Here!" Now, observe. As I stepped into the box, the prisoner, who had been looking on attentively, but with no sign of concern, became violently agitated, and beckoned to his attorney. The prisoner's wish to challenge me was so manifest, that it occasioned a pause, during which the attorney, with his hand upon the dock, whispered with his client, and shook his head. I afterwards had it from that gentleman, that the prisoner's first affrighted words to him were, "*At all hazards, challenge that man!*" But that, as he would give no reason for it, and admitted that he had not even known my name until he heard it called and I appeared, it was not done.

Both on the ground already explained, that I wish to avoid reviving the unwholesome memory of that Murderer, and also because a detailed account of his long trial is by no means indispensable to my narrative, I shall confine myself closely to such incidents in the ten days and nights during which we, the Jury, were kept together, as directly bear on my own curious personal experience. It is in that, and not in the Murderer, that I seek to interest my reader. It is to that, and not to a page of the Newgate Calendar, that I beg attention.

I was chosen Foreman of the Jury. On the second morning of the trial, after evidence had been taken for two hours (I heard the church clocks strike), happening to cast my eyes over my brother-jurymen, I found an inexplicable difficulty in counting them. I counted them several times, yet always with the same difficulty. In short, I made them one too many.

I touched the brother-juryman whose place was next me, and I whispered to him, " Oblige me by counting us." He looked surprised by the request, but turned his head and counted. " Why," says he, suddenly, " we are Thirt——but no, it's not possible. No. We are twelve." According to my counting that day, we were always right in detail, but in the gross we were always one too many. There was no appearance—no figure—to account for it ; but I had now an inward foreshadowing of the figure that was surely coming.

The Jury were housed at the London Tavern. We all slept in one large room on separate tables, and we were constantly in the charge and under the eye of the officer sworn to hold us in safe-keeping. I see no reason for suppressing the real name of that officer. He was intelligent, highly polite, and obliging, and (I was glad to hear) much respected in the City. He had an agreeable presence, good eyes, enviable black whiskers, and a fine sonorous voice. His name was Mr. Harker.

When we turned into our twelve beds at night, Mr. Harker's bed was drawn across the door. On the night of the second day, not being disposed to lie down, and seeing Mr. Harker sitting on his bed, I went and sat beside him, and offered him a pinch of snuff. As Mr. Harker's hand touched mine in taking it from my box, a peculiar shiver crossed him, and he said, " Who is this ? "

Following Mr. Harker's eyes, and looking along the room, I saw again the figure I expected,—the second of the two men who had gone down Piccadilly. I rose, and advanced a few steps ; then stopped, and looked round at Mr. Harker. He was quite unconcerned, laughed, and said in a pleasant way, " I thought for a moment we had a thirteenth juryman, without a bed. But I see it is the moonlight."

Making no revelation to Mr. Harker, but inviting him to take a walk with me to the end of the room, I watched what the figure did. It stood for a few moments by the bedside of each of my eleven brother jurymen, close to the pillow. It always went to the right-hand side of the bed, and always passed out crossing the foot of the next bed. It seemed, from the action of the head, merely to look down pensively at each recumbent figure. It took no notice of me, or of my bed, which was that nearest to Mr. Harker's. It seemed to go out where the moonlight came in, through a high window, as by an aerial flight of stairs.

Next morning at breakfast, it appeared that everybody present had dreamed of the murdered man last night except myself and Mr. Harker.

I now felt as convinced that the second man who had gone down Piccadilly was the murdered man (so to speak), as if it had been borne into my comprehension by his immediate testimony. But even this took place, and in a manner for which I was not at all prepared.

On the fifth day of the trial, when the case for the prosecution was drawing to a close, a miniature of the murdered man, missing from his bedroom upon the discovery of the deed, and afterwards found in a hiding-place where the murderer had been seen digging, was put in evidence. Having been identified by the witness under examination, it was handed up to the Bench, and thence handed down to be inspected by the Jury. As an officer in a black gown was making his way with it across to me, the figure of the second man who had gone down Piccadilly impetuously started from the crowd, caught the miniature from the officer, and gave it to me with his own hands, at the same time saying, in a low and hollow tone,—before I saw the miniature, which was in a locket,—"*I was younger then, and my face was not then drained of blood.*" It also came between me and the brother juryman to whom I would have given the miniature, and between him and the brother juryman to whom he would have given it, and so passed it on through the whole of our number, and back into my possession. Not one of them, however, detected this.

At table, and generally when we were shut up together in Mr. Harker's custody, we had from the first naturally discussed the day's proceedings a good deal. On that fifth day, the case for the prosecution being closed, and we having that side of the question in a completed shape before us, our discussion was more animated and serious. Among our number was a vestryman,—the densest idiot I have ever seen at large,—who met the plainest evidence with the most preposterous objections, and who was sided with by two flabby parochial parasites ; all the three impanelled from a district so delivered over to fever that they ought to have been upon their own trial for five hundred murders. When these mischievous blockheads were at their loudest, which was towards midnight, while some of us were already preparing for bed, I again saw the murdered man. He stood grimly behind them, beckoning to me. On my going towards them, and striking into the conversation, he immediately retired. This was the beginning of a separate series of appearances, confined to that long room in which *we* were confined. Whenever a knot of my brother jurymen laid their heads together, I saw the head of the murdered man among theirs. Whenever their comparison of notes was going against him, he would solemnly and irresistibly beckon to me.

It will be borne in mind that down to the production of the miniature, on the fifth day of the trial, I had never seen the Appearance in Court. Three changes occurred now that we entered on the case for the defence. Two of them I will mention together, first. The figure was now in Court continually, and it never there addressed itself to me, but always to the person who was speaking at the time. For instance: the throat of the murdered man had been cut straight across. In the opening speech for the defence it was suggested that the deceased might have cut his own throat. At that very moment, the figure, with its throat in the dreadful condition referred to (this it had concealed before), stood at the speaker's elbow, motioning across and across its windpipe, now with the right hand, now with the left, vigorously suggesting to the speaker himself the impossibility of such a wound having been self-inflicted by either hand. For another instance: a witness to character, a woman, deposed to the prisoner's being the most amiable of mankind. The figure at that instant stood on the floor before her, looking her full in the face, and pointing out the prisoner's evil countenance with an extended arm and an outstretched finger.

The third change now to be added impressed me strongly as the most marked and striking of all. I do not theorise upon it; I accurately state it, and there leave it. Although the Appearance was not itself perceived by those whom it addressed, its coming close to such persons was invariably attended by some trepidation or disturbance on their part. It seemed to me as if it were prevented, by laws to which I was not amenable, from fully revealing itself to others, and yet as if it could invisibly, dumbly, and darkly overshadow their minds. When the leading counsel for the defence suggested that hypothesis of suicide, and the figure stood at the learned gentleman's elbow, frightfully sawing at its severed throat, it is undeniable that the counsel faltered in his speech, lost for a few seconds the thread of his ingenious discourse, wiped his forehead with his handkerchief, and turned extremely pale. When the witness to character was confronted by the Appearance, her eyes most certainly did follow the direction of its pointed finger, and rest in great hesitation and trouble upon the prisoner's face. Two additional illustrations will suffice. On the eighth day of the trial, after the pause which was every day made early in the afternoon for a few minutes' rest and refreshment, I came back into Court with the rest of the Jury some little time before the return of the Judges. Standing up in the box and looking about me, I thought the figure was not there, until, chancing to raise my eyes to the gallery, I saw it bending forward, and leaning ever a very decent woman, as if to assure itself whether the Judges had resumed their seats or not. Immediately afterwards that woman screamed, fainted and was carried out. So with the venerable, sagacious, and patient Judge who conducted the trial. When the case was over, and he settled himself and his papers to sum up, the murdered man, entering by the Judges' door, advanced to his Lordship's desk, and looked eagerly over his shoulder at the pages of his notes which he was turning. A change came over his Lordship's face ; his hand stopped ; the peculiar shiver, that I knew so well, passed over him ; he faltered, " Excuse me, gentlemen, for a few moments. I am somewhat oppressed by the vitiated air " ; and did not recover until he had drunk a glass of water.

Through all the monotony of six of those interminable ten days,—the same Judges and others on the bench, the same murderer in the dock, the same lawyers at the table, the same tones of question and answer rising to the roof of the Court, the same scratching of the Judge's pen, the same ushers going in and out, the same lights kindled at the same hour when there had been any natural light of day, the same foggy curtain outside the great windows when it was foggy, the same rain pattering and dripping when it was rainy, the same footmarks of turnkeys and prisoner day after day on the same sawdust, the same keys locking and unlocking the same heavy doors,—through all the wearisome monotony which made me feel as if I had been Foreman of the Jury for a vast period of time, and Piccadilly had flourished coevally with Babylon, the murdered man never lost one trace of his distinctness in my eyes, nor was he at any moment less distinct than anybody else. I must not omit, as a matter of fact, that I never once saw the Appearance which I call by the name of the murdered man look at the murderer. Again and again I wondered, " Why does he not ? " But he never did.

Nor did he look at me, after the production of the miniature, until the last closing minutes of the trial arrived. We retired to consider at seven minutes before ten at night. The idiotic vestryman and his two parochial parasites gave us so much trouble that we twice returned into Court to beg to have certain extracts from the Judge's notes re-read. Nine of us had not the smallest doubt about those passages, neither, I believe, had any one in the Court ; the dunder-headed triumvirate, however, having no idea but obstruction, disputed them for that very reason. At length we prevailed, and finally the Jury returned into Court at ten minutes past twelve.

The murdered man at that time stood directly opposite the Jury-box, on the other side of the Court. As I took my place, his eyes rested on me with great attention ; he seemed satisfied, and slowly shook a great grey veil, which he carried on his arm for the first time, over his head and whole form. As I gave in our verdict, " Guilty," the veil collapsed, all was gone, and his place was empty.

The murderer, being asked by the Judge, according to usage whether he had anything to say before sentence of death should be passed upon him, indistinctly muttered something which was described in the leading newspapers of the following day as " a few rambling, incoherent, and half-audible words, in which he was understood to complain that he had not had a fair trial, because the Foreman of the Jury was prepossessed against him." The remarkable declaration that he really made was this: " *My Lord, I knew I was a doomed man, when the Foreman of the Jury came into the box. My Lord, I knew he would never let me off, because before I was taken, he somehow got to my bedside in the night, woke me, and put a rope round my neck.*"

CHARLES DICKENS

NO. 1 BRANCH LINE: THE SIGNALMAN

"HALLOA! Below there!"

When he heard a voice thus calling to him, he was standing at the door of his box, with a flag in his hand, furled round its short pole. One would have thought, considering the nature of the ground, that he could not have doubted from what quarter the voice came; but instead of looking up to where I stood on the top of the steep cutting nearly over his head, he turned himself about, and looked down the Line. There was something remarkable in his manner of doing so, though I could not have said for my life what. But I know it was remarkable enough to attract my notice, even though his figure was foreshortened and shadowed, down in the deep trench, and mine was high above him, so steeped in the glow of an angry sunset that I had shaded my eyes with my hand before I saw him at all.

"Halloa! Below!"

From looking down the Line, he turned himself about again, and, raising his eyes, saw my figure high above him.

"Is there any path by which I can come down and speak to you?"

He looked up at me without replying, and I looked down at him without pressing him too soon with a repetition of my idle question. Just then there came a vague vibration in the earth and air, quickly changing into a violent pulsation, and an oncoming rush that caused me to start back, as though it had force to draw me down. When such vapour as rose to my height from this rapid train had passed me, and was skimming away over the landscape, I looked down again, and saw him refurling the flag he had shown while the train went by.

I repeated my inquiry. After a pause, during which he seemed to regard me with fixed attention, he motioned with his rolled-up flag towards a point on my level, some two or three hundred yards distant. I called down to him, "All right!" and made for that point. There, by dint of looking closely about me, I found a rough zigzag descending path notched out, which I followed.

The cutting was extremely deep, and unusually precipitate. It was made through a clammy stone, that became oozier and wetter as I went down. For these reasons, I found the way long enough to give me time to recall a singular air of reluctance or compulsion with which he had pointed out the path.

When I came down low enough upon the zigzag descent to see him again, I saw that he was standing between the rails on the way by which the train had lately passed, in an attitude as if he were waiting for me to appear. He had his left hand at his chin, and that left elbow rested on his right hand, crossed over his breast. His attitude was one of such expectation and watchfulness that I stopped a moment, wondering at it.

I resumed my downward way, and stepping out upon the level of the railroad, and drawing nearer to him, saw that he was a dark sallow man, with a dark beard and rather heavy eyebrows. His post was in as solitary and dismal a place as ever I saw. On either side, a dripping-wet wall of jagged stone, excluding all view but a strip of sky ; the perspective one way only a crooked prolongation of this great dungeon ; the shorter perspective in the other direction terminating in a gloomy red light, and the gloomier entrance to a black tunnel, in whose massive architecture there was a barbarous, depressing, and forbidding air. So little sunlight ever found its way to this spot, that it had an earthy, deadly smell ; and so much cold wind rushed through it, that it struck chill to me, as if I had left the natural world.

Before he stirred, I was near enough to him to have touched him. Not even then removing his eyes from mine, he stepped back one step, and lifted his hand.

This was a lonesome post to occupy (I said), and it had riveted my attention when I looked down from up yonder. A visitor was a rarity, I should suppose ; not an unwelcome rarity, I hoped ? In me, he merely saw a man who had been shut up within narrow limits all his life, and who, being at last set free, had a newly-awakened interest in these great works. To such purpose I spoke to him ; but I am far from sure of the terms I used ; for, besides that I am not happy in opening any conversation, there was something in the man that daunted me.

He directed a most curious look towards the red light near the tunnel's mouth, and looked all about it, as if something were missing from it, and then looked at me.

That light was part of his charge ? Was it not ?

He answered in a low voice, " Don't you know it is ? "

The monstrous thought came into my mind, as I perused the fixed eyes and the saturnine face, that this was a spirit, not a man. I have speculated since, whether there may have been infection in his mind.

In my turn I stepped back. But in making the action, I detected in his eyes some latent fear of me. This put the monstrous thought to flight.

" You look at me," I said, forcing a smile, " as if you had a dread of me."

" I was doubtful," he returned, " whether I had seen you before."

" Where ? "

He pointed to the red light he had looked at.

" There ? " I said.

Intently watchful of me, he replied (but without sound), " Yes."

" My good fellow, what should I do there ? However, be that as it may, I never was there, you may swear."

" I think I may," he rejoined. " Yes ; I am sure I may."

His manner cleared, like my own. He replied to my remarks with readiness, and in well-chosen words. Had he much to do there ? Yes ; that was to say, he had enough responsibility to bear ; but exactness and watchfulness were what was required of him, and of actual work—manual labour—he had next to none. To change that signal, to trim those lights, and to turn this iron handle now and then, was all he had to under that head. Regarding those many long and lonely hours of which I seemed to make so much, he could only say that the routine of his life had shaped itself into that form, and he had grown used to it. He had taught himself a language down here,—if only to know it by sight, and to have formed his own crude ideas of its pronunciation, could be called learning it. He had also worked at fractions and decimals, and tried a little algebra ; but he was, and had been as a boy, a poor hand at figures. Was it necessary for him when on duty always to remain in that channel of damp air, and could he never rise into the sunshine from between those high stone walls ? Why, that depended upon times and circumstances. Under some conditions there would be less upon the Line than under others, and the same held good as to certain hours of the day and night. In bright weather, he did choose occasions for getting a little above those lower shadows ; but, being at all times liable to be called by his electric bell, and at such times listening for it with redoubled anxiety, the relief was less than I would suppose.

He took me into his box, where there was a fire, a desk for an official book in which he had to make certain entries, a telegraphic instrument with its dial, face, and needles, and the little bell of which he had spoken. On my trusting that he would excuse the remark that he had been well educated, and (I hoped I might say without offence) perhaps educated above that station, he observed that instances of slight incongruity in such wise would rarely be found wanting among large bodies of men ; that he had heard it was so in workhouses, in the police force, even in that last desperate resource, the army; and that he knew it was so, more or less, in any great railway staff. He had been, when young (if I could believe it, sitting in that hut,—he scarcely could), a student of natural philosophy, and had attended lectures; but he had run wild, misused his opportunities, gone down, and never risen again. He had no complaint to offer about that. He had made his bed, and he lay upon it. It was far too late to make another.

All that I have here condensed he said in a quiet manner, with his grave dark regards divided between me and the fire. He threw in the word "Sir" from time to time, and especially when he referred to his youth,—as though to request me to understand that he claimed to be nothing but what I found him. He was several times interrupted by the little bell, and had to read off messages and send replies. Once he had to stand without the door, and display a flag as a train passed, and make some verbal communication to the driver. In the discharge of his duties, I observed him to be remarkably exact and vigilant, breaking off his discourse at a syllable, and remaining silent until what he had to do was done.

In a word, I should have set this man down as one of the safest of men to be employed in that capacity, but for the circumstance that while he was speaking to me he twice broke off with a fallen colour, turned his face towards the little bell when it did NOT ring, opened the door of the hut (which was kept shut to exclude the unhealthy damp), and looked out towards the red light near the mouth of the tunnel. On both of those occasions he came back to the fire with the inexplicable air upon him which I had remarked, without being able to define, when we were so far asunder.

Said I, when I rose to leave him, "You almost make me think that I have met with a contented man."

(I am afraid I must acknowledge that I said it to lead him on.)

"I believe I used to be so," he rejoined, in the low voice in which he had first spoken; "but I am troubled, sir, I am troubled."

He would have recalled the words if he could. He had said them, however, and I took them up quickly.

"With what? What is your trouble?"

"It is very difficult to impart, sir. It is very, very difficult to speak of. If ever you make me another visit, I will try to tell you."

"But I expressly intend to make you another visit. Say, when shall it be?"

"I go off early in the morning, and I shall be on again at ten to-morrow night, sir."

"I will come at eleven."

He thanked me, and went out at the door with me. "I'll show my white light, sir," he said, in his peculiar low voice, "till you have found the way up. When you have found it, don't call out ! And when you are at the top, don't call out ! "

His manner seemed to make the place strike colder to me, but I said no more than " Very well."

" And when you come down to-morrow night, don't call out! Let me ask you a parting question. What made you cry, ' Halloa ! Below there ! ' to-night ? "

" Heaven knows," said I, " I cried something to that effect——"

" Not to that effect, sir. Those were the very words. I know them well."

" Admit those were the very words. I said them, no doubt, because I saw you below."

" For no other reason ? "

" What other reason could I possibly have ? "

" You have no feeling that they were conveyed to you in any supernatural way ? "

" No."

He wished me good-night, and held up his light. I walked by the side of the down Line of rails (with a very disagreeable sensation of a train coming behind me) until I found the path. It was easier to mount than to descend, and I got back to my inn without any adventure.

Punctual to my appointment, I placed my foot on the first notch of the zigzag next night as the distant clocks were striking eleven. He was waiting for me at the bottom, with his white light on. " I have not called out," I said, when we came close together ; " may I speak now ? " " By all means, sir." " Good-night, then, and here's my hand." " Good-night, sir, and here's mine." With that we walked side by side to his box, entered it, closed the door, and sat down by the fire.

" I have made up my mind, sir," he began bending forward as soon as we were seated, and speaking in a tone but a little above a whisper, " that you shall not have to ask me twice what troubles me. I took you for some one else yesterday evening. That troubles me."

" That mistake ? "

" No. That some one else."

" Who is it ? "

" I don't know."

" Like me ? "

" I don't know. I never saw the face. The left arm is across the face, and the right arm is waved—violently waved. This way."

I followed his action with my eyes, and it was the action of an arm gesticulating, with the utmost passion and vehemence, " For God's sake, clear the way ! "

"One moonlight night," said the man, "I was sitting here, when I heard a voice cry, 'Halloa! Below there!' I started up, looked from that door, and saw this some one else standing by the red light near the tunnel, waving as I just now showed you. The voice seemed hoarse with shouting, and it cried, 'Look out! Look out!' And then again, 'Halloa! Below there! Look out!' I caught up my lamp, turned it on red, and ran towards the figure, calling, 'What's wrong? What has happened? Where?' It stood just outside the blackness of the tunnel. I advanced so close upon it that I wondered at its keeping the sleeve across its eyes. I ran right up at it, and had my hand stretched out to pull the sleeve away, when it was gone."

"Into the tunnel?" said I.

"No. I ran on into the tunnel, five hundred yards. I stopped, and held my lamp above my head, and saw the figures of the measured distance, and saw the wet stains stealing down the walls and trickling through the arch. I ran out again faster than I had run in (for I had a mortal abhorrence of the place upon me), and I looked all round the red light with my own red light, and I went up the iron ladder to the gallery atop of it, and I came down again, and ran back here. I telegraphed both ways. 'An alarm has been given. Is anything wrong?' The answer came back, both ways, 'All well.'"

Resisting the slow touch of a frozen finger tracing out my spine, I showed him how that this figure must be a deception of his sense of sight; and how that figures, originating in disease of the delicate nerves that minister to the functions of the eye, were known to have often troubled patients, some of whom had become conscious of the nature of their affliction, and had even proved it by experiments upon themselves. "As to an imaginary cry," said I, "do but listen for a moment to the wind in this unnatural valley while we speak so low, and to the wild harp it makes of the telegraph wires."

That was all very well, he returned, after we had sat listening for a while, and he ought to know something of the wind and the wires,—he who so often passed long winter nights there, alone and watching. But he would beg to remark that he had not finished.

I asked his pardon, and he slowly added these words, touching my arm:

"Within six hours after the Appearance, the memorable accident on this Line happened, and within ten hours the dead and wounded were brought along through the tunnel over the spot where the figure had stood."

A disagreeable shudder crept over me, but I did my best against it. It was not to be denied, I rejoined, that this was a remarkable coincidence, calculated deeply to impress his mind. But it was unquestionable that remarkable coincidences did continually occur, and they must be taken into account in dealing with such a subject. Though to be sure I must admit, I added (for I thought I saw that he was going to bring the objecton to bear upon me), men of common sense did not allow much for coincidences in making the ordinary calculations of life.

He again begged to remark that he had not finished.

I again begged his pardon for being betrayed into interruptions.

" This," he said, again laying his hand upon my arm, and glancing over his shoulder with hollow eyes, " was just a year ago. Six or seven months passed, and I had recovered from the surprise and shock, when one morning, as the day was breaking, I, standing at the door, looked towards the red light, and saw the spectre again." He stopped, with a fixed look at me.

" Did it cry out ? "

" No. It was silent."

" Did it wave its arm ? "

" No. It leaned against the shaft of the light with both hands before the face. Like this."

Once more I followed his action with my eyes. It was an action of mourning. I have seen such an attitude on stone figures on tombs.

" Did you go up to it ? "

" I came in and sat down, partly to collect my thoughts, partly because it had turned me faint. When I went to the door again, daylight was above me, and the ghost was gone."

" But nothing followed ? Nothing came of this ? "

He touched me on the arm with his forefinger twice or thrice, giving a ghastly nod each time :

" That very day, as a train came out of the tunnel, I noticed, at a carriage window on my side, what looked like a confusion of hands and heads, and something waved. I saw it just in time to signal the driver, Stop ! He shut off, and put his brake on, but the train drifted past here a hundred and fifty yards or more. I ran after it, and, as I went along, heard terrible screams and cries. A beautiful young lady had died instantaneously in one of the compartments, and was brought in here, and laid down on this floor between us."

Involuntarily I pushed my chair back, as I looked from the boards at which he pointed to himself.

" True, sir. True. Precisely as it happened, so I tell it you."

I could think of nothing to say, to any purpose, and my mouth was very dry. The wind and the wires took up the story with a long lamenting wail.

He resumed, " Now, sir, mark this, and judge how my mind is troubled. The spectre came back a week ago. Ever since, it has been there, now and again, by fits and starts."

"At the light?"

"At the Danger-light."

"What does it seem to do?"

He repeated, if possible with increased passion and vehemence, that former gesticulation of "For God's sake, clear the way!"

Then he went on. "I have no peace or rest for it. It calls to me, for many minutes together, in an agonised manner, 'Below there! Look out! Look out!' It stands waving to me. It rings my little bell——"

I caught at that. "Did it ring your bell yesterday evening when I was here, and you went to the door?"

"Twice."

"Why, see," said I, "how your imagination misleads you. My eyes were on the bell, and my ears were open to the bell, and if I am a living man, it did NOT ring at those times. No, nor at any other time, except when it was rung in the natural course of physical things by the station communicating with you."

He shook his head. "I have never made a mistake as to that yet, sir. I have never confused the spectre's ring with the man's. The ghost's ring is a strange vibration in the bell that it derives from nothing else, and I have not asserted that the bell stirs to the eye. I don't wonder that you failed to hear it. But *I* heard it."

"And did the spectre seem to be there when you looked out?"

"It WAS there."

"Both times?"

He repeated firmly: "Both times."

"Will you come to the door with me, and look for it now?"

He bit his under lip as though he were somewhat unwilling, but arose. I opened the door, and stood on the step, while he stood in the doorway. There was the Danger-light. There was the dismal mouth of the tunnel. There were the high, wet stone walls of the cutting. There were the stars above them.

"Do you see it?" I asked him, taking particular note of his face. His eyes were prominent and strained, but not very much more so, perhaps, than my own had been when I had directed them earnestly towards the same spot.

"No," he answered. "It is not there."

"Agreed," said I.

We went in again, shut the door, and resumed our seats. I was thinking how best to improve this advantage, if it might be called one, when he took up the conversation in such a matter-of-course way, so assuming that there could be no serious question of fact between us, that I felt myself placed in the weakest of positions.

"By this time you will fully understand, sir," he said, "that what troubles me so dreadfully is the question, What does the spectre mean ? "

I was not sure, I told him, that I did fully understand.

" What is its warning against ? " he said, ruminating, with his eyes on the fire, and only by times turning them on me. " What is the danger ? Where is the danger ? There is danger overhanging somewhere on the Line. Some dreadful calamity will happen. It is not to be doubted this third time, after what has gone before. But surely this is a cruel haunting of *me*. What can I do ? "

He pulled out his handkerchief, and wiped the drops from his heated forehead.

" If I telegraph Danger on either side of me, or on both, I can give no reason for it," he went on, wiping the palms of his hands. " I should get into trouble and do no good. They would think I was mad. This is the way it would work,—Message : ' Danger ! Take care ! ' Answer : ' What Danger ? Where ? ' Message : ' Don't know. But for God's sake, take care !' They would displace me. What else could they do ? "

His pain of mind was most pitiable to see. It was the mental torture of a conscientious man, oppressed beyond endurance by an unintelligible responsibility involving life.

" When it first stood under the Danger-light," he went on, putting his dark hair back from his head, and drawing his hands outward across and across his temples in an extremity of feverish distress, " why not tell me where that accident was to happen,—if it must happen ? Why not tell me how it could be averted,—if it could have been averted ? When on its second coming it hid its face, why not tell me, instead, ' She is going to die. Let them keep her at home ' ? If it came, on those two occasions, only to show me that its warnings were true, and so to prepare me for the third, why not warn me plainly now ? And I, Lord help me ! A mere poor signalman on this solitary station ! Why not go to somebody with credit to be believed, and power to act ? "

When I saw him in this state, I saw that for the poor man's sake, as well as for the public safety, what I had to do for the time was to compose his mind. Therefore, setting aside all question of reality or unreality between us, I represented to him that whoever thoroughly discharged his duty must do well, and that at least it was his comfort that he understood his duty, though he did not understand these confounding Appearances. In this effort I succeeded far better than in the attempt to reason him out of his conviction. He became calm ; the occupations incidental to his post as the night advanced began to make larger demands on his attention : and I left him at two in the morning. I had offered to stay through the night, but he would not hear of it.

That I more than once looked back at the red light as I ascended the pathway, that I did not like the red light, and that I should have slept but poorly if my bed had been under it, I see no reason to conceal. Nor did I like the two sequences of the accident and the dead girl. I see no reason to conceal that either.

But what ran most in my thoughts was the consideration how ought I to act, having become the recipient of this disclosure ? I had proved the man to be intelligent, vigilant, painstaking, and exact ; but how long might he remain so, in his state of mind ? Though in a subordinate position, still he held a most important trust, and would I (for instance) like to stake my own life on the chances of his continuing to execute it with precision ?

Unable to overcome a feeling that there would be something treacherous in my communicating what he had told me to his superiors in the Company, without first being plain with himself and proposing a middle course to him, I ultimately resolved to offer to accompany him (otherwise keeping his secret for the present) to the wisest medical practitioner we could hear of in those parts, and to take his opinion. A change in his time of duty would come round next night, he had apprised me, and he would be off an hour or two after sunrise, and on again soon after sunset. I had appointed to return accordingly.

Next evening was a lovely evening, and I walked out early to enjoy it. The sun was not yet quite down when I traversed the field-path near the top of the deep cutting. I would extend my walk for an hour, I said to myself, half an hour on and half an hour back, and it would then be time to go to my signalman's box.

Before pursuing my stroll, I stepped to the brink, and mechanically looked down, from the point from which I had first seen him. I cannot describe the thrill that seized upon me, when, close at the mouth of the tunnel, I saw the appearance of a man, with his left sleeve across his eyes, passionately waving his right arm.

The nameless horror that oppressed me passed in a moment, for in a moment I saw that this appearance of a man was a man indeed, and that there was a little group of other men standing at a short distance, to whom he seemed to be rehearsing the gesture he made. The Danger-light was not yet lighted. Against its shaft a little low hut entirely new to me, had been made of some wooden supports and tarpaulin. It looked no bigger than a bed.

With an irresistible sense that something was wrong—with a flashing self-reproachful fear that fatal mischief had come of my leaving the man there, and causing no one to be sent to overlook or correct what he did,—I descended the notched path with all the speed I could make.

" What is the matter ? " I asked the men.

" Signalman killed this morning, sir."

" Not the man belonging to that box ? "

" Yes, sir."

" Not the man I know ? "

" You will recognise him, sir, if you knew him," said the man who spoke for the others, solemnly uncovering his own head, and raising an end of the tarpaulin, " for his face is quite composed."

" Oh, how did this happen, how did this happen ? " I asked, turning from one to another as the hut closed in again.

" He was cut down by an engine, sir. No man in England knew his work better. But somehow he was not clear of the outer rail. It was just at broad day. He had struck the light, and had the lamp in his hand. As the engine came out of the tunnel, his back was towards her, and she cut him down. That man drove her, and was showing how it happened. Show the gentleman, Tom."

The man who wore a rough dark dress, stepped back to his former place at the mouth of the tunnel.

" Coming round the curve in the tunnel, sir," he said, " I saw him at the end, like as if I saw him down a perspective-glass. There was no time to check speed, and I knew him to be very careful. As he didn't seem to take heed of the whistle, I shut it off when we were running down upon him, and called to him as loud as I could call."

" What did you say ? "

" I said, ' Below there ! Look out ! Look out ! For God's sake, clear the way ! "

I started.

" Ah ! it was a dreadful time, sir. I never left off calling to him. I put this arm before my eyes not to see, and I waved this arm to the last ; but it was no use."

Without prolonging the narrative to dwell on any one of its curious circumstances more than on any other, I may, in closing it, point out the coincidence that the warning of the engine-driver included, not only the words which the unfortunate signalman had repeated to me as haunting him, but also the words which I myself—not he—had attached, and that only in my own mind, to the gesticulation he had imitated.

VIII
ENGLISH

THE

Masterpiece Library of Short Stories

The Thousand Best Complete Tales of all Times and all Countries

Selected by

AN INTERNATIONAL BOARD OF EMINENT CRITICS

Sir William Robertson Nicoll, LL.D.

Sir Arthur Quiller-Couch	Sir Frederick Wedmore
Clement Shorter	Sir Edmund Gosse, C.B., LL.D.
George Saintsbury, LL.D.	W. P. Trent, LL.D.
Richard le Gallienne	Carl Van Doren
Brander Matthews, Litt.D.	Thomas Seccombe

Edited by

Sir J. A. Hammerton

VIII. ENGLISH

LONDON
THE EDUCATIONAL BOOK COMPANY LIMITED

Contents of Volume VIII

THE ENGLISH STORY-TELLERS

From Charles Reade to Conan Doyle

In the period covered by the present volume the English reading public increased enormously. The writing of fiction ceased to be a pursuit or pastime of the few. It became the definite calling of a large class of professional authors. Fiction formed a regular feature of daily as well as weekly newspapers. Magazines sprang into existence that were wholly or mainly devoted to it. The three-volume novel faded from view, and its one-volume successor, at a fifth of the old price, achieved circulations that outranged completely those of the older form of publication.

The popular serial had to be written so that each instalment was almost a short story; and while the novel proper, attaining a standard of interest and technique never approached before except at the hands of the greater writers, tended more and more to become a reflection of the problems of the new social order—to be a vehicle of ideas—the short story proper, hitherto comparatively halting in interest and crude in form, appearing fitfully in keepsakes and magazines as a stop-gap between, or a relief from, more substantial work, developed a perfection comparable to that of the sonnet or lyric contrasted with larger works in verse.

Pictorial, impressionist, suggestive, achieving its purpose by means of dialogue, or hitting off in outline a personality or a mystery, a medium for the expression of comedy, tragedy, or farce, the short story touched every note in the gamut of human emotion. Of the stories, thirty-five in number, by twenty-nine authors, selected for inclusion in this volume, the scenes of sixteen are laid in England. Taken together they give a good conspectus of the progress of the art of the short story during the later decades of the nineteenth century.

CHARLES READE

Charles Reade (1814–1884), the author of "The Box Tunnel," took the vocation of writer seriously. "I propose," he said in a notable phrase, "never to guess where I can know." He built up all his books, many of which were written with a definite purpose, on documentary evidence. He wrote nearly a score of novels and between thirty and forty plays; but his reputation is based mainly on his historical romance of the fifteenth century, *The Cloister and the Hearth.*

Seriously as he took himself, he possessed a real gift of humour, as "The Box Tunnel," the story of an unconventional courtship, by which he is represented in our pages, amply testifies. It was written in 1857, four years after his first novel. At that time the Great Western main line ran through the tunnel after which the story is named. "The Box Tunnel" is an admirable bit of work, slender in theme but masterly in construction, contains no word not necessary to the progress of the miniature plot, and winds up with a surprise in keeping with the atmosphere of the entire narrative.

ANTHONY TROLLOPE

Another methodical writer, with gifts rather cavalierly dismissed in his autobiography, was Anthony Trollope (1815–1882), whose "Malachi's Cove" tells not of Barsetshire, the shire that had no existence save in his imagination, but of love and adventure on the rugged northern coast of Cornwall. For its depth of feeling, delicacy of thought, strength of characterisation, and quality of construction, "Malachi's Cove" well merits preservation. The background and the knowledge displayed of local life and customs are reproduced and utilised as carefully as the character of the unconventional heroine Mahala is portrayed. The story offers a striking companion study to the Rev. Sabine Baring-Gould's "Genefer," to which we shall refer later.

JOHN RUSKIN

"The King of the Golden River" is the only attempt made at this kind of composition by John Ruskin (1819–1900), in whom a keen sense of the romantic and the beautiful accompanied high critical powers and a burning desire for social reform. The story, a fairy tale with a purpose, that purpose being to draw a contrast between natural charity of soul and innate avarice, and to point the reward that waits for the one and the doom reserved for the other, was written in 1841, at a couple of sittings, in answer to a challenge by the lady who later became Mrs. Ruskin. It is easily one of the more popular of the author's minor works, and is characterised by the magic of words as well as of ideas. Although touching the extreme limit of length allowed to the selections for this work, the editors felt that so delicate and charming a work of imagination could not well be excluded.

WILKIE AND CHARLES COLLINS

"A Terribly Strange Bed" is frank, thrilling adventure, told by a master of plot-construction and a pioneer of the detective tale, William Wilkie Collins (1824–1889). Its picture of a low type of Parisian gambling-hell is photographic, and the experiences of the victim are described with a minuteness of detail the equivalent of which it would be difficult to find elsewhere except in the pages of Daniel Defoe or Edgar Allan Poe. The reader is kept in alert suspense from first to last.

Charles Allston Collins (1828–1873), painter and Pre-Raphaelite, had perhaps a finer sense of literature than his elder brother Wilkie possessed. "The Tête Noir," the scene of which is laid in France, while it has much in common with "A Terribly Strange Bed," and the somewhat conventional theme of an adventure in a lonely inn, is distinguished by a greater breadth of treatment. The two stories, read side by side, compel an interest quite independent of their fascinating narrative values.

GEORGE WALTER THORNBURY

Another able writer, associated, as were the brothers Collins, with Charles Dickens, was George Walter Thornbury (1828–1876), who is best remembered by his popular topographical and historical works, especially *Old and New London.* Dickens spoke of him as one of the most valuable contributors to *Household Words* and *All the Year Round.* His two stories, "To be Taken in Water" and "Mons. Cassecruche's Inspiration," both deal with personal adventure. The first is seasoned with the spice of peril and flavoured with rapid sequence of incident ; the second is well garnished with humour, the richness of which comes to the reader as a sort of grateful after-taste.

LEOPOLD LEWIS

Leopold David Lewis (1828–1890) was a man rather spoiled by one success, his stage adaptation from Erckmann-Chatrian's *Le Juif*

Polonais,—*The Bells*, in which Sir Henry Irving scored so signal a success at the old Lyceum Theatre. " A Dreadful Bell " displays his ability to handle a very commonplace incident and turn it into a screaming farce, leaving the reader more or less mystified till the *dénouement* is reached. It was Leopold Lewis who conceived the idea of a competition in the Reading Room of the British Museum in which each claimant to literary originality should be locked in a transparent glass case and denied access to either books or notes. Lewis said he would back himself, in such circumstances, to turn out more original copy in a given time than any other man in town.

JAMES PAYN

There follow three stories from the once famous periodical *Once a Week*, two of them anonymous and one by a writer whose name, John Harwood, is possibly a pseudonym. The eeriness of " The Alibi," the naturalness and carefully contrived surprise of " The Revenue Officer's Story," and the vividness of " The Centurion's Escape " can hardly have been the work of any 'prentice hand. There is a *soupçon* of acidity as well as playfulness in the amusing skit at the expense of certain University professors in " How Jones got the English Verse Medal," by James Payn (1830–1898), the once popular novelist who was sometime editor first of *Chambers's Journal* and then of *The Cornhill Magazine*.

MARK RUTHERFORD

In the next story, " Mr. Whittaker's Retirement," by Mark Rutherford, whose real name was William Hale White (1830–1913), we are brought into close touch with the tragedy of commercial competition in a great city. The leading character is a man who suddenly finds himself lagging superfluous on the stage, and whose personal importance vanished with the position that imparted it. Here is a real transcript from life, with the essential melancholy softened by the keen sympathy of the writer, and the manner in which the narrative is brought to a close. " Mr. Whittaker's Retirement " represents an author remarkable for his skilful handling of the trivial and the sad, for searching realism, and for the understanding that informed his satirical contempt for tinsel and sham.

AMELIA B. EDWARDS—MANVILLE FENN

" Picking up Terrible Company," by Amelia B. Edwards (1831–1892), manifestly owes much to the author's studies of French life and character. One may question whether Victor Hugo, in *Les Misérables*, which appeared in the following year, excites more sympathy for his Jean Valjean than Miss Edwards compels—without declamation, but with wonderful narrative skill—for her François Thierry. From the purgatory of the chained gangs of Toulon, and the dizzy perils of the lamplighters of St. Peter's at Eastertide, we come, in "My Fare," by George Manville Fenn (1831–1909), to a Hampstead idyll—the story of a cabman, a widow lady, and her dying daughter. It is a slight sketch, distinguished by much insight and power of characterisation.

WILLIAM MORRIS

In William Morris (1834–1896), scholar, poet, Pre-Raphaelite artist, master-craftsman, and socialist, the spirit of mediaevalism was incarnate. When in the study he lived in a kind of thirteenth-century dream-world, and his love of mediaeval architecture finds eloquent expression in the mystical "The Story of the Unknown Church," from *The Oxford and Cambridge Magazine*, which he helped to found. The picture of the master-mason dying with his chisel in his hand, underneath the last lily of the tomb he had so lovingly carved, is typical of the best of William Morris's teaching.

BARING-GOULD

Few novelists have been more versatile and prolific than the Rev. Sabine Baring-Gould (1834–1924). Comparative religion, old-world customs, folk-lore, topography, ethnology, biography, and hymn-writing were among the subjects he handled with more than common ability. As a novelist and short-story writer, taking the portrayal of rustic life in the west of England for his province, he achieved marked success, his gifts of characterisation and scenic word-painting being specially notable. In "Genefer" these qualities are in the ascendant. The sunny-natured Cornish farm-girl, with her inherent honesty of heart, her practical grip of essentials, and her resourcefulness, forms a delightful companion portrait to Anthony Trollope's Mahala.

RICHARD GARNETT

Richard Garnett (1835–1906) was an accomplished critic, especially of poetry, well equipped in scholarship, and with a feeling for the old world that is beautifully expressed in "The Dumb Oracle." The legend on which this story is based goes back to the days of the *Gesta Romanorum*. Dr. Garnett transfers it to classical times. The young priest's disillusionment, his travels, his return, the miracle, the rebuke of Apollo, "If the Oracle of Dorylaeum was an imposture, hadst thou no oracle in thine own bosom?" and the dedication of Eubulides to the service of humanity are features in a story which, old as it is in essentials, can never lose its intrinsic charm. The theme had been worked by Longfellow and Browning, but Dr. Garnett's setting has a grace all its own. As an example of a scholar's recreation it may be compared with Ruskin's incursion into fairyland.

F. C. BURNAND

"Mr. Lorquison's Story," though essentially "Victorian," is an amusing little travesty of London suburban life, seen through the quizzical eyes of a born humorist, Sir Francis Cowley Burnand (1836–1917), in his time a favourite writer of burlesque and comedy, and from 1880 to 1906 editor of *Punch*. "F. C. B." wrote one long romance, *My Time and What I've Done With It,* which more than suggested the possible novelist of distinction. "Mr. Lorquison's Story" hits off without malice the limitations of a city alderman who has an elementary but self-satisfied sense of humour, and is the unconscious victim of a peculiarly ridiculous form of practical joke, the perpetration of which, while it turns the tables on him so absurdly, leaves him in a simple state of wonderment that is described in most diverting fashion.

JOSEPH HATTON

Joseph Hatton (1840–1907) was an accomplished journalist who made a great hit with a novel of Russian life, *By Order of the Czar*. His sense of the actual, and his power of introducing the reader to some quite ordinary scene and then showing how near allied is the prosaic to the abnormal, are seen to advantage in "Uncle Hartlebury's Romance." His titular character is an elderly Recorder, met as he stands watching his wife and family bathing at Boulogne, but at the back of whose mind are strange memories of adventure in youth. He is made to tell one of thrilling interest. The way in which the author, while touching the notes of deep tragedy, preserves the relief of the conversational form calls for appreciative remark.

THOMAS HARDY

Thomas Hardy (1840–1928), one of the most honoured names in English letters, was master alike of novel and short story, and a poet of distinction. We give two examples of his Wessex tales. He did not invent the name of Wessex, he revived it, but it will always be associated with his name. First used by him in *Far from the Madding Crowd* (1874), it connotes that part of south-western England which includes the shires of Dorset, the scene of the majority of his novels, Somerset,

Devon, Wilts, and Berks. He recreates the scenery—his feeling for nature in all her moods was deep and sure—his characters have that vitality which belongs only to the creations of the great novelists, and he makes them live partly by his use of an intimate knowledge of the past history of the localities in which his scenes are set.

Perhaps his mastery of plot-construction was due in some measure to his ten years' study as an architect. " The Melancholy Hussar of the German Legion " is from one of his three volumes of short stories, *Life's Little Ironies.* The scene is Bincombe, near Weymouth, in the days of one of the Four Georges, and the incidents are matters of local history, extracted from the burial register of the parish. The facts, however, form only the dry bones of the tale, which, in the impression it creates of brooding fate overshadowing the unhappy lives of the lonely Phyllis Grove and the exiled Matthäus Tina, represents that vein of sober realism in Thomas Hardy's work that has caused many to speak of him as a pessimist, when they should rather pay tribute to his masterly understanding of the forces of environment. " The Melancholy Hussar " may be ranked as one of the more striking short stories if not actually the best by a modern English author. " Absent-mindedness in a Parish Choir," an extract from the legends of Puddlehinton and Puddletrenthide, near Puddletown, displays the author's gift for humorous narrative. Short as it is, it leaves a lasting impress on the memory and it is not without its shaft of irony.

OUIDA

Mlle. Louise de la Ramée, better known by her pen-name of Ouida (1840–1908), though she lived for the greater part of her life in Italy, was born in England, at Bury St. Edmunds. While the bulk of her more ambitious work is hardly likely to survive the flux of time, her short stories include a number of little masterpieces ; and of these " The Marriage Plate " is probably the best. In it is displayed Ouida's passionate sympathy with an insight into the obscure heroism of humble lives, and her more than passionate love of animals. Fuello and his sheep-dog Pastore will not readily be forgotten by any reader of this finely told and moving Florentine tale, which has the virtue of a happy ending.

CLARK RUSSELL—FLORA ANNIE STEEL

In " The Adventures of Three Sailors," by W. Clark Russell (1844–1911), who was himself at sea when sail was yielding to steam and timber to iron, and did much for the merchant sailor, is a picture of seafaring experience that would have delighted the heart of Captain

Marryat. It possesses humour as well as actuality. Of women novelists who have brought the East nearer to the West, and taken to the task an appreciation of more than externals, Flora Annie Steel (1847–1929) is easily first. "In the Permanent Way" is the most remarkable and most haunting of her short stories. The yellow-headed Saxon, Nathaniel James Craddock, who couldn't keep off the drink, and the jogi who couldn't keep off the permanent way, have an abiding place in Anglo-Indian literature.

GRANT ALLEN

Than "The Reverend John Creedy," by Charles Grant Blairfindie Allen (1848–1899), who gave to fiction and journalism what was meant for science, no more powerful story of a mixed marriage has been written. The relapse of the Oxford educated son of a Gold Coast chief, when he returned to his native land, the horror that gradually encompasses his English wife, the catastrophe, the lie with which he makes his final effort at redemption in the eyes of the dying woman, the passionate digging of her grave, and the ultimate surrender to inborn instincts are finely imagined. The story progresses with steadily gathering strength to its end.

ROBERT BARR

A short sociological work of slighter texture but far from negligible is "An Alpine Divorce," by Robert Barr (1850–1912), whose sense of the dramatic is shown in his "Gentlemen; The King!" the climax to which is as cleverly conceived as it is admirably led up to. Robert Barr was a typical writer of his time. Though a Scotsman by birth, only his childhood was spent in his native land. He was educated in Canada, and after being a school teacher there, became a member of the staff of the *Detroit Free Press*, his contributions to which made his pen-name of Luke Sharp familiar all over the world. Coming to England in 1881, he joined forces with Jerome K. Jerome, and the two, gathering together a bright staff of kindred spirits, founded the *Idler* magazine, which, under their control, added not a little to the gaiety of London journalism. He began novel-writing about the time the *Idler* was started, and he is represented in this volume as a compromise between the possible claims of Scotland, Canada, and the United States; and after all, his best work was done in England.

WEYMAN—F. ANSTEY

"The Clockmaker of Poissy," by Stanley John Weyman (1855–1928), is a romantic episode of love and Court intrigue in that period of French history which the author had made peculiarly his own. Weyman, an Oxford man, educated at Christ Church, was called to the Bar in 1881, and practised until 1889. A contributor of short stories to the *Cornhill Magazine*, then under the editorship of James Payn, he was induced by Payn to try his hand at novel-writing. His reputation as a novelist was established by the publication in 1893 of *A Gentleman of France*, a work that has been translated into several languages. There followed at fairly regular intervals other popular favourites, including *Memoirs of a Minister of France*, from which "The Clockmaker of Poissy" is taken. He was largely influenced by Scott and Stevenson, and his popularity has been gained by his delightful excursions into the byways of French history. His dialogue sparkles with ready wit and humour, qualities that also brilliantly distinguish "A Canine Ishmael," by Thomas Anstey Guthrie (b. 1856), familiar to readers of *Punch* as F. Anstey. In this little dinner-table story, a woman's conversational powers are set off against a man's slower understanding, the key to his mystification, so cleverly imagined, being reserved for the last line.

MORLEY ROBERTS

Morley Roberts (b. 1857) is represented by "The Miracle of the Black Cañon," a grimly realistic and powerful tale of the days of the gold fever in British Columbia; and "The Young Man who stroked Cats," a romance of the telephone, remarkable for genuine humour and unforced sentiment. Morley Roberts, one of the most voluminous of writers, could draw for his material upon a life of extraordinary variety and adventure. A fellow-student with George Gissing at Owens College, Manchester, he worked as a labourer on Australian railroads, as a cattleman in the Australian bush, served before the mast in the mercantile marine, spent some time in the War Office and India Office in London, and then "roughed it" for several years in the wild and woolly west, the South Seas, South Africa, and other parts of the world. His first book, *The Western Avernus*, came out in 1887. "The Miracle of the Black Cañon" is from the volume characteristically entitled *The Great Jester*, 1896.

EGERTON CASTLE

For the background of his story of the time when malefactors were hung in chains, Egerton Castle (1858–1920) has gone to a part of what is now known as the Hardy country—the downland in the vicinity of the Shaftesbury road. "Moon's Gibbet" is a sort of paternal parallel in prose to Tennyson's "Rizpah." Egerton Castle, who was a member of a family of newspaper proprietors, won distinction in natural science at

Trinity College, Cambridge, studied law at the Inner Temple, and was for a time in the army. Of his numerous novels several have been dramatised, and most were written in collaboration with his wife, a gifted Irishwoman. They are marked usually with a fine feeling for romance —notably *Young April*, 1899; and the title chosen for his collection of short stories is *The House of Romance*, 1901. They contain some of the best descriptions of sword play in modern fiction, Egerton Castle having been an expert swordsman and the author of a standard work on schools and masters of fence.

CONAN DOYLE

The two contrasting tales which close the volume are the work of Sir Arthur Conan Doyle (1859–1930), novelist, historian, short-story writer, and creator of Sherlock Holmes. "A Straggler of '15" was turned by its author into a one-act play for Sir Henry Irving, whose impersonation of Corporal David Brewster proved one of the more outstanding of his minor character-parts. This unique study of a Waterloo veteran's last days at Woolwich, told with fine sympathy and discretion, is representative of Sir Arthur Conan Doyle's art at its best; and "The Last Galley," a transcript, with a moral, from the second century B.C., when Carthage fought and lost her last battle for sea-power against the rising might of Rome, displays his high quality of historical vision and his fine gift of graphic narrative, so characteristic of the more important part of his literary work.

W. F. A.

CHARLES READE
1814–1884

THE BOX TUNNEL

THE 10.15 train glided from Paddington, May 7, 1847. In the left compartment of a certain first-class carriage were four passengers; of these two were worth description. The lady had a smooth, white, delicate brow, strongly marked eyebrows, long lashes, eyes that seemed to change colour, and a good-sized delicious mouth, with teeth as white as milk. A man could not see her nose for her eyes and mouth; her own sex could and would have told us some nonsense about it. She wore an unpretending greyish dress buttoned to the throat with lozenge-shaped buttons, and a Scottish shawl that agreeably evaded colour. She was like a duck, so tight her plain feathers fitted her, and there she sat, smooth, snug, and delicious, with a book in her hand, and the soupçon of her wrist just visible as she held it. Her opposite neighbour was what I call a good style of man—the more to his credit, since he belonged to a corporation that frequently turns out the worst imaginable style of young men. He was a cavalry officer, aged twenty-five. He had a moustache, but not a very repulsive one; not one of those subnasal pigtails on which soup is suspended like dew on a shrub; it was short, thick, and black as a coal. His teeth had not yet been turned by tobacco smoke to the colour of juice, his clothes did not stick to nor hang to him, he had an engaging smile, and, what I liked the dog for, his vanity, which was inordinate, was in its proper place, his heart, not in his face, jostling mine and other people's who have none; in a word, he was what one oftener hears of than meets—a young gentleman.

He was conversing in an animated whisper with a companion, a fellow-officer; they were talking about what it is far better not to—women. Our friend clearly did not wish to be overheard; for he cast ever and anon a furtive glance at his fair *vis-à-vis* and lowered his voice. She seemed completely absorbed in her book, and that reassured him.

At last the two soldiers came down to a whisper (the truth must be told); the one who got down at Slough, and was lost to posterity, bet ten pounds to three that he who was going down with us to Bath and immortality would not kiss either of the ladies opposite upon the road. " Done, done ! "

Now I am sorry a man I have hitherto praised should have lent himself, even in a whisper, to such a speculation ; " but nobody is wise at all hours," not even when the clock is striking five-and twenty ; and you are to consider his profession, his good looks, and the temptation—ten to three.

After Slough the party was reduced to three ; at Twyford one lady dropped her handkerchief ; Captain Dolignan fell on it like a lamb ; two or three words were interchanged on this occasion.

At Reading the Marlborough of our tale made one of the safe investments of that day, he bought a *Times* and *Punch* ; the latter full of steel-pen thrusts and wood-cuts. Valour and beauty deigned to laugh at some inflamed humbug or other punctured by *Punch.* Now laughing together thaws our human ice ; long before Swindon it was a talking match—at Swindon who so devoted as Captain Dolignan ?—he handed them out—he souped them—he tough-chickened them—he brandied and cochinealed one, and brandied and burnt-sugared the other ; on their return to the carriage, one lady passed into the inner compartment to inspect a certain gentleman's seat on that side of the line.

Reader, had it been you or I, the beauty would have been the deserter, the average one would have stayed with us till all was blue, ourselves included ; not more surely does our slice of bread and butter, when it escapes from our hand, revolve it ever so often, alight face downward on the carpet.

But this was a bit of a fop, Adonis, dragoon—so Venus remained *tête-à-tête* with him. You have seen a dog meet an unknown female of the species ; how handsome, how *impressé,* how expressive he becomes ; such was Dolignan after Swindon, and to do the dog justice, he got handsomer and handsomer ; and you have seen a cat conscious of approaching cream—such was Miss Haythorn ; she became demurer and demurer ; presently our captain looked out of the window and laughed ; this elicited an inquiring look from Miss Haythorn.

" We are only a mile from the Box Tunnel."

" Do you always laugh a mile from the Box Tunnel ? " said the lady.

" Invariably."

" What for ? "

" Why, hem ! it is a gentleman's joke."

Captain Dolignan then recounted to Miss Haythorn the following :

" A lady and her husband sat together going through the Box Tunnel—there was one gentleman opposite ; it was pitch dark ; after the tunnel the lady said, 'George, how absurd of you to salute me going through the tunnel.' 'I did no such thing.' 'You didn't?' 'No! Why?' 'Because somehow I thought you did!'"

Here Captain Dolignan laughed and endeavoured to lead his companion to laugh, but it was not to be done. The train entered the tunnel.

Miss Haythorn. Ah!

Dolignan. What is the matter?

Miss Haythorn. I am frightened.

Dolignan (moving to her side). Pray do not be alarmed; I am near you.

Miss Haythorn. You are near me—very near me, indeed, Captain Dolignan.

Dolignan. You know my name?

Miss Haythorn. I heard you mention it. I wish we were out of this dark place.

Dolignan. I could be content to spend hours here, reassuring you, my dear lady.

Miss Haythorn. Nonsense!

Dolignan. Pweep! (Grave reader, do not put your lips to the next pretty creature you meet or you will understand what this means.)

Miss Haythorn. Eh! Eh!

Friend. What is the matter?

Miss Haythorn. Open the door! Open the door!

There was a sound of hurried whispers, the door was shut and the blind pulled down with hostile sharpness.

If any critic falls on me for putting inarticulate sounds in a dialogue as above, I answer with all the insolence I can command at present, "Hit boys as big as yourself"; bigger perhaps, such as Sophocles, Euripides, and Aristophanes; they began it, and I learned it of them, sore against my will.

Miss Haythorn's scream lost most of its effect because the engine whistled forty thousand murders at the same moment; and fictitious grief makes itself heard when real cannot.

Between the tunnel and Bath our young friend had time to ask himself whether his conduct had been marked by that delicate reserve which is supposed to distinguish the perfect gentleman.

With a long face, real or feigned, he held open the door; his late friends attempted to escape on the other side—impossible! they must pass him. She whom he had insulted (Latin for kissed) deposited somewhere at his feet a look of gentle, blushing reproach; the other, whom he had not insulted, darted red-hot daggers at him from her eyes; and so they parted.

It was perhaps fortunate for Dolignan that he had the grace to be a friend of Major Hoskyns of his regiment, a veteran laughed at by the youngsters, for the major was too apt to look coldly upon billiard-balls and cigars ; he had seen cannon-balls and linstocks. He had also, to tell the truth, swallowed a good bit of the mess-room poker, which made it impossible for Major Hoskyns to descend to an ungentlemanlike word or action as to brush his own trousers below the knee.

Captain Dolignan told this gentleman his story in gleeful accents ; but Major Hoskyns heard him coldly, and as coldly answered that he had known a man to lose his life for the same thing.

" That is nothing," continued the major, " but unfortunately he deserved to lose it."

At this blood mounted to the younger man's temples ; and his senior added, " I mean to say he was thirty-five ; you, I presume, are twenty-one ! "

" Twenty-five."

" That is much the same thing ; will you be advised by me ? "

" If you will advise me."

" Speak to no one of this, and send White the £3, that he may think you have lost the bet."

" That is hard, when I won it."

" Do it for all that, sir."

Let the disbelievers in human perfectibility know that this dragoon capable of a blush did this virtuous action, albeit with violent reluctance ; and this was his first damper. A week after these events he was at a ball. He was in that state of factious discontent which belongs to us amiable English. He was looking in vain for a lady, equal in personal attraction to the idea he had formed of George Dolignan as a man, when suddenly there glided past him a most delightful vision ! a lady whose beauty and symmetry took him by the eyes—another look : " It can't be ! Yes, it is ! " Miss Haythorn ! (not that he knew her name !) but what an apotheosis !

The duck had become a peahen—radiant, dazzling, she looked twice as beautiful and almost twice as large as before. He lost sight of her. He found her again. She was so lovely she made him ill—and he, alone, must not dance with her, speak to her. If he had been content to begin her acquaintance the usual way, it might have ended in kissing ; it must end in nothing.

As she danced, sparks of beauty fell from her on all around, but him—she did not see him ; it was clear she never would see him—one gentleman was particularly assiduous ; she smiled on his assiduity ; he was ugly, but she smiled on him. Dolignan was surprised at his success, his ill taste, his ugliness, his impertinence. Dolignan at last found himself injured : " Who was this man ? and what right had he to go on so ? He never kissed her, I suppose," said Dolle.

Dolignan could not prove it, but he felt that somehow the rights of property were invaded.

He went home and dreamed of Miss Haythorn, and hated all the ugly successful. He spent a fortnight trying to find out who his beauty was—he never could encounter her again. At last he heard of her in this way: A lawyer's clerk paid him a little visit and commenced a little action against him in the name of Miss Haythorn, for insulting her in a railway train.

The young gentleman was shocked; endeavoured to soften the lawyer's clerk; that machine did not thoroughly comprehend the meaning of the term. The lady's name, however, was at last revealed by this untoward incident; from her name to her address was but a short step; and the same day our crest-fallen hero lay in wait at her door, and many a succeeding day, without effect.

But one fine afternoon she issued forth quite naturally, as if she did it every day, and walked briskly on the parade. Dolignan did the same, met and passed her many times on the parade, and searched for pity in her eyes, but found neither look nor recognition, nor any other sentiment; for all this she walked and walked; till all the other promenaders were tired and gone—then her culprit summoned resolution, and taking off his hat, with a voice for the first time tremulous, besought permission to address her.

She stopped, blushed, and neither acknowledged nor disowned his acquaintance. He blushed, stammered out how ashamed he was, how he deserved to be punished, how he was punished, how little she knew how unhappy he was, and concluded by begging her not to let all the world know the disgrace of a man who was already mortified enough by the loss of her acquaintance.

She asked an explanation; he told her of the action that had been commenced in her name; she gently shrugged her shoulders and said, "How stupid they are!" Emboldened by this, he begged to know whether or not a life of distant unpretending devotion would, after a lapse of years, erase the memory of his madness—his crime!

"She did not know!"

"She must now bid him adieu, as she had preparations to make for a ball in the Crescent, where everybody was to be."

They parted, and Dolignan determined to be at the ball, where everybody was to be. He was there, and after some time he obtained an introduction to Miss Haythorn, and he danced with her. Her manner was gracious. With the wonderful tact of her sex, she seemed to have commenced the acquaintance that evening.

That night, for the first time, Dolignan was in love. I will spare the reader all a lover's arts, by which he succeeded in dining where she dined, in dancing where she danced, in overtaking her by accident when she rode. His devotion followed her to church, where the dragoon was rewarded by learning there is a world where they neither polk nor smoke—the two capital abominations of this one.

He made an acquaintance with her uncle, who liked him, and he saw at last with joy that her eye loved to dwell upon him, when she thought he did not observe her. It was three months after the Box Tunnel that Captain Dolignan called one day upon Captain Haythorn, R.N., whom he had met twice in his life, and slightly propitiated by violently listening to a cutting-out expedition ; he called, and in the usual way asked permission to pay his addresses to his daughter.

The worthy captain straightway began doing quarter-deck, when suddenly he was summoned from the apartment by a mysterious message. On his return he announced, with a total change of voice, that " It was all right, and his visitor might run alongside as soon as he chose." My reader has divined the truth ; this nautical commander was in complete and happy subjugation to his daughter, our heroine.

As he was taking leave, Dolignan saw his divinity glide into the drawing-room. He followed her, observed a sweet consciousness deepen into confusion—she tried to laugh and cried instead, and then she smiled again ; when he kissed her hand at the door it was " George " and " Marian " instead of " Captain " this and " Miss " the other.

A reasonable time after this (for my tale is merciful and skips formalities and torturing delays), these two were very happy ; they were once more upon the railroad, going to enjoy their honeymoon all by themselves. Marian Dolignan was dressed just as before—ducklike and delicious ; all bright except her clothes ; but George sat beside her this time instead of opposite ; and she drank him in gently from her long eyelashes.

" Marian," said George, " married people should tell each other all. Will you ever forgive me if I own to you ; no——"

" Yes ! yes ! "

" Well, then, you remember the Box Tunnel." (This was the first allusion he had ventured to it.) " I am ashamed to say I had £3 to £10 with White I would kiss one of you two ladies," and George, pathetic externally, chuckled within.

" I know that, George ; I overheard you," was the demure reply.

" Oh ! you overheard me ! impossible."

" And did you not hear me whisper to my companion ? I made a bet with her."

" You made a bet ! how singular ! What was it ? "

" Only a pair of gloves, George."

" Yes, I know ; but what about it ? "

"That if you did you should be my husband, dearest."

"Oh! but stay; then you could not have been so very angry with me, love. Why, dearest, then you brought that action against me."

Mrs. Dolignan looked down.

"I was afraid you were forgetting me! George, you will never forgive me!"

"Angel! why, here is the Box Tunnel!"

Now, reader—fie! no! no such thing! you can't expect to be indulged in this way every time we come to a dark place. Besides, it is not the thing. Consider, two sensible married people. No such phenomenon, I assure you, took place. No scream in hopeless rivalry of the engine—this time!

ANTHONY TROLLOPE
1815–1882

MALACHI'S COVE

On the northern coast of Cornwall, between Tintagel and Bossiney, down on the very margin of the sea, there lived not long since an old man who got his living by saving seaweed from the waves, and selling it for manure. The cliffs there are bold and fine, and the sea beats in upon them from the north with a grand violence. I doubt whether it be not the finest morsel of cliff scenery in England, though it is beaten by many portions of the west coast of Ireland, and perhaps also by spots in Wales and Scotland. Cliffs should be nearly precipitous, they should be broken in their outlines, and should barely admit here and there of an insecure passage from their summit to the sand at their feet. The sea should come, if not up to them, at least very near to them, and then, above all things, the water below them should be blue, and not of that dead leaden colour which is so familiar to us in England. At Tintagel all these requisites are there, except that bright blue colour which is so lovely. But the cliffs themselves are bold and well broken, and the margin of sand at high water is very narrow—so narrow that at spring-tides there is barely a footing there.

Close upon this margin was the cottage or hovel of Malachi Trenglos, the old man of whom I have spoken. But Malachi, or old Glos, as he was commonly called by the people around him, had not built his house absolutely upon the sand. There was a fissure in the rock so great that at the top it formed a narrow ravine, and so complete from the summit to the base that it afforded an opening for a steep and rugged track from the top of the rock to the bottom. This fissure was so wide at the bottom that it had afforded space for Trenglos to fix his habitation on a foundation of rock, and here he had lived for many years. It was told of him that in the early days of his trade he had always carried the weed in a basket on his back to the top, but latterly he had been possessed of a donkey which had been trained to go up and down the steep track with a single pannier over his loins, for the rocks would not admit of panniers hanging by his side; and for this assistant he had built a shed adjoining his own, and almost as large as that in which he himself resided.

But, as years went on, old Glos procured other assistance than that of the donkey, or, as I should rather say, Providence supplied him with other help ; and, indeed, had it not been so, the old man must have given up his cabin and his independence and gone into the workhouse at Camelford. For rheumatism had afflicted him, old age had bowed him till he was nearly double, and by degrees he became unable to attend the donkey on its upward passage to the world above, or even to assist in rescuing the coveted weed from the waves.

At the time to which our story refers Trenglos had not been up the cliff for twelve months, and for the last six months he had done nothing towards the furtherance of his trade, except to take the money and keep it, if any of it was kept, and occasionally to shake down a bundle of fodder for the donkey. The real work of the business was done altogether by Mahala Trenglos, his grand-daughter.

Mally Trenglos was known to all the farmers round the coast, and to all the small tradespeople in Camelford. She was a wild-looking, almost unearthly creature, with wild-flowing, black, uncombed hair, small in stature, with small hands and bright black eyes ; but people said that she was very strong, and the children around declared that she worked day and night, and knew nothing of fatigue. As to her age there were many doubts. Some said she was ten, and others five-and-twenty, but the reader may be allowed to know that at this time she had in truth passed her twentieth birthday. The old people spoke well of Mally, because she was so good to her grandfather ; and it was said of her that though she carried to him a little gin and tobacco almost daily, she bought nothing for herself ; and as to the gin, no one who looked at her would accuse her of meddling with that. But she had no friends, and but few acquaintances among people of her own age. They said that she was fierce and ill-natured, that she had not a good word for any one, and that she was, complete at all points, a thorough little vixen. The young men did not care for her ; for, as regarded dress, all days were alike with her. She never made herself smart on Sundays. She was generally without stockings, and seemed to care not at all to exercise any of those feminine attractions which might have been hers had she studied to attain them. All days were the same to her in regard to dress ; and, indeed, till lately, all days had, I fear, been the same to her in other respects. Old Malachi had never been seen inside a place of worship since he had taken to live under the cliff.

But within the last two years Mally had submitted herself to the teaching of the clergyman at Tintagel, and had appeared at church on Sundays, if not absolutely with punctuality, at any rate so often that no one who knew the peculiarity of her residence was disposed to quarrel with her on that subject. But she made no difference in her dress on these occasions. She took her place on a low stone seat just inside the church door, clothed as usual in her thick red serge petticoat and loose brown serge jacket, such being the apparel which she had found to be best adapted for her hard and perilous work among the waters. She had pleaded to the clergyman when he attacked her on the subject of church attendance with vigour that she had got no church-going clothes. He had explained to her that she would be received there without distinction to her clothing. Mally had taken him at his word, and had gone, with a courage which certainly deserved admiration, though I doubt whether there was not mingled with it an obstinacy which was less admirable.

For people said that old Glos was rich, and that Mally might have proper clothes if she chose to buy them. Mr. Polwarth, the clergyman, who, as the old man could not come to him, went down the rocks to the old man, did make some hint on the matter in Mally's absence. But old Glos, who had been patient with him on other matters, turned upon him so angrily when he made an allusion to money, that Mr. Polwarth found himself obliged to give that matter up, and Mally continued to sit upon the stone bench in her short serge petticoat, with her long hair streaming down her face. She did so far sacrifice to decency as on such occasions to tie up her back hair with an old shoe-string. So tied it would remain through the Monday and Tuesday, but by Wednesday afternoon Mally's hair had generally managed to escape.

As to Mally's indefatigable industry there could be no manner of doubt, for the quantity of seaweed which she and the donkey amassed between them was very surprising. Old Glos, it was declared, had never collected half what Mally gathered together; but then the article was becoming cheaper, and it was necessary that the exertion should be greater. So Mally and the donkey toiled and toiled, and the seaweed came up in heaps which surprised those who looked at her little hands and light form. Was there not some one who helped her at nights, some fairy, or demon, or the like? Mally was so snappish in her answers to people that she had no right to be surprised if ill-natured things were said of her.

No one ever heard Mally Trenglos complain of her work, but about this time she was heard to make great and loud complaints of the treatment she received from some of her neighbours. It was known that she went with her plaints to Mr. Polwarth; and when he could not help her, or did not give her such instant help as she needed, she went—ah, so foolishly! to the office of a certain attorney at

Camelford, who was not likely to prove himself a better friend than Mr. Polwarth.

Now the nature of her injury was as follows. The place in which she collected her seaweed was a little cove ; the people had come to call it Malachi's Cove from the name of the old man who lived there ; —which was so formed, that the margin of the sea therein could only be reached by the passage from the top down to Trenglos's hut. The breadth of the cove when the sea was out might perhaps be two hundred yards, and on each side the rocks ran out in such a way that both from north and south the domain of Trenglos was guarded from intruders. And this locality had been well chosen for its intended purpose.

There was a rush of the sea into the cove, which carried there large, drifting masses of seaweed, leaving them among the rocks when the tide was out. During the equinoctial winds of the spring and autumn the supply would never fail ; and even when the sea was calm, the long, soft, salt-bedewed, trailing masses of the weed could be gathered there when they could not be found elsewhere for miles along the coast. The task of getting the weed from the breakers was often difficult and dangerous, so difficult that much of it was left to be carried away by the next incoming tide.

Mally doubtless did not gather half the crop that was there at her feet. What was taken by the returning waves she did not regret ; but when interlopers came upon her cove, and gathered her wealth—her grandfather's wealth, beneath her eyes, then her heart was broken. It was this interloping, this intrusion, that drove poor Mally to the Camelford attorney. But, alas, though the Camelford attorney took Mally's money, he could do nothing for her, and her heart was broken !

She had an idea, in which no doubt her grandfather shared, that the path to the cove was, at any rate, their property. When she was told that the cove, and sea running into the cove, were not the freeholds of her grandfather, she understood that the statement might be true. But what then as to the use of the path ? Who had made the path what it was ? Had she not painfully, wearily, with exceeding toil, carried up bits of rock with her own little hands, that her grandfather's donkey might have footing for his feet ? Had she not scraped together crumbs of earth along the face of the cliff that she might make easier to the animal the track of that rugged way ? And now, when she saw big farmers' lads coming down with other donkeys—and, indeed, there was one who came with a pony ; no boy, but a young man, old enough to know better than rob a poor old man and a young girl—she reviled the whole human race, and swore that the Camelford attorney was a fool.

Any attempt to explain to her that there was still weed enough for her was worse than useless. Was it not all hers and his, or, at any rate, was not the sole way to it his and hers? And was not her trade stopped and impeded? Had she not been forced to back her laden donkey down, twenty yards she said, but it had, in truth, been five, because Farmer Gunliffe's son had been in the way with his thieving pony? Farmer Gunliffe had wanted to buy her weed at his own price, and because she had refused he had set on his thieving son to destroy her in this wicked way.

"I'll hamstring the beast the next time as he's down here!" said Mally to old Glos, while the angry fire literally streamed from her eyes.

Farmer Gunliffe's small homestead—he held about fifty acres of land—was close by the village of Tintagel, and not a mile from the cliff. The sea-wrack, as they call it, was pretty well the only manure within his reach, and no doubt he thought it hard that he should be kept from using it by Mally Trenglos and her obstinacy.

"There's heaps of other coves, Barty," said Mally to Barty Gunliffe, the farmer's son.

"But none so nigh, Mally, nor yet none that fills 'emselves as this place."

Then he explained to her that he would not take the weed that came up close to hand. He was bigger than she was, and stronger, and would get it from the outer rocks, with which she never meddled. Then, with scorn in her eye, she swore that she could get it where he durst not venture, and repeated her threat of hamstringing the pony. Barty laughed at her wrath, jeered her because of her wild hair, and called her a mermaid.

"I'll mermaid you!" she cried. "Mermaid, indeed! I wouldn't be a man to come and rob a poor girl and an old cripple. But you're no man, Barty Gunliffe! You're not half a man."

Nevertheless, Bartholomew Gunliffe was a very fine young fellow, as far as the eye went. He was about five feet eight inches high, with strong arms and legs, with light curly brown hair and blue eyes. His father was but in a small way as a farmer, but, nevertheless, Barty Gunliffe was well thought of among the girls around. Everybody liked Barty—excepting only Mally Trenglos, and she hated him like poison.

Barty, when he was asked why so good-natured a lad as he persecuted a poor girl and an old man, threw himself upon the justice of the thing. It wouldn't do at all, according to his view, that any single person should take upon himself to own that which God Almighty sent as the common property of all. He would do Mally no harm, and so he had told her. But Mally was a vixen, a wicked little vixen; and she must be taught to have a civil tongue in her head. When once Mally would speak him civil as he went for weed, he would get his father to pay the old man some sort of toll for the use of the path.

"Speak him civil?" said Mally. "Never; not while I have a tongue in my mouth!" And I fear old Glos encouraged her rather than otherwise in her view of the matter.

But her grandfather did not encourage her to hamstring the pony. Hamstringing a pony would be a serious thing, and old Glos thought it might be very awkward for both of them if Mally were put into prison. He suggested, therefore, that all manner of impediments should be put in the way of the pony's feet, surmising that the well-trained donkey might be able to work in spite of them. And Barty Gunliffe, on his next descent, did find the passage very awkward when he came near to Malachi's hut, but he made his way down, and poor Mally saw the lumps of rock at which she had laboured so hard pushed on one side or rolled out of the way with a steady persistency of injury towards herself that almost drove her frantic.

"Well, Barty, you're a nice boy," said old Glos, sitting in the doorway of the hut, as he watched the intruder.

"I ain't a-doing no harm to none as doesn't harm me," said Barty. "The sea's free to all, Malachi."

"And the sky's free to all, but I mustn't get up on the top of your big barn to look at it," said Mally, who was standing among the rocks with a long hook in her hand. The long hook was the tool with which she worked in dragging the weed from the waves. "But you ain't got no justice nor yet no sperrit, or you wouldn't come here to vex an old man like he."

"I didn't want to vex him, nor yet to vex you, Mally. You let me be for a while and we'll be friends yet."

"Friends!" exclaimed Mally. "Who'd have the likes of you for a friend? What are you moving them stones for? Them stones belongs to grandfather." And in her wrath she made a movement as though she were going to fly at him.

"Let him be, Mally," said the old man; "let him be. He'll get his punishment. He'll come to be drowned some day if he comes down here when the wind is inshore."

"That he may be drowned then!" said Mally, in her anger. "If he was in the big hole there among the rocks, and the sea running in at half tide, I wouldn't lift a hand to help him out."

"Yes, you would, Mally; you'd fish me up with your hook like a big stick of seaweed."

She turned from him with scorn as he said this, and went into the hut. It was time for her to get ready for her work, and one of the great injuries done her lay in this, that such a one as Barty

Gunliffe should come and look at her during her toil among the breakers.

It was an afternoon in April, and the hour was something after four o'clock. There had been a heavy wind from the north-west all the morning, with gusts of rain, and the sea-gulls had been in and out of the cove all the day, which was a sure sign to Mally that the incoming tide would cover the rocks with weed.

The quick waves were now returning with wonderful celerity over the low reefs, and the time had come at which the treasure must be seized, if it was to be garnered on that day. By seven o'clock it would be growing dark, at nine it would be high water, and before daylight the crop would be carried out again if not collected. All this Mally understood very well, and some of this Barty was beginning to understand also.

As Mally came down with her bare feet, bearing her long hook in her hand, she saw Barty's pony standing patiently on the sand, and in her heart she longed to attack the brute. Barty at this moment, with a common three-pronged fork in his hand, was standing down on a large rock, gazing forth towards the waters. He had declared that he would gather the weed only at places which were inaccessible to Mally, and he was looking out that he might settle where he would begin.

" Let 'un be, let 'un be," shouted the old man to Mally, as he saw her take a step towards the beast, which she hated almost as much as she hated the man.

Hearing her grandfather's voice through the wind, she desisted from her purpose, if any purpose she had had, and went forth to her work. As she passed down the cove, and scrambled in among the rocks, she saw Barty still standing on his perch ; out beyond, the white-curling waves were cresting and breaking themselves with violence, and the wind was howling among the caverns and abutments of the cliff.

Every now and then there came a squall of rain, and though there was sufficient light, the heavens were black with clouds. A scene more beautiful might hardly be found by those who love the glories of the coast. The light for such objects was perfect. Nothing could exceed the grandeur of the colours—the blue of the open sea, the white of the breaking waves, the yellow sands, or the streaks of red and brown which gave such richness to the cliff.

But neither Mally nor Barty was thinking of such things as these. Indeed they were hardly thinking of their trade after its ordinary forms. Barty was meditating how he might best accomplish his purpose of working beyond the reach of Mally's feminine powers, and Mally was resolving that wherever Barty went she would go farther.

And, in many respects, Mally had the advantage. She knew

every rock in the spot, and was sure of those which gave a good foothold, and sure also of those which did not. And then her activity had been made perfect by practice for the purpose to which it was to be devoted. Barty, no doubt, was stronger than she, and quite as active. But Barty could not jump among the waves from one stone to another as she could do, nor was he as yet able to get aid in his work from the very force of the water as she could get it. She had been hunting seaweed in that cove since she had been an urchin of six years old, and she knew every hole and corner and every spot of vantage. The waves were her friends, and she could use them. She could measure their strength, and knew when and where it would cease.

Mally was great down in the salt pools of her own cove—great, and very fearless. As she watched Barty make his way forward from rock to rock, she told herself, gleefully, that he was going astray. The curl of the wind as it blew into the cove would not carry the weed up to the northern buttresses of the cove ; and then there was the great hole just there—the great hole of which she had spoken when she wished him evil.

And now she went to work, hooking up the dishevelled hairs of the ocean, and landing many a cargo on the extreme margin of the sand, whence she would be able in the evening to drag it back before the invading waters would return to reclaim the spoil.

And on his side also Barty made his heap up against the northern buttresses of which I have spoken. Barty's heap became big and still bigger, so that he knew, let the pony work as he might, he could not take it all up that evening. But still it was not as large as Mally's heap. Mally's hook was better than his fork, and Mally's skill was better than his strength. And when he failed in some haul Mally would jeer him with a wild, weird laughter, and shriek to him through the wind that he was not half a man. At first he answered her with laughing words, but before long, as she boasted of her success and pointed to his failure, he became angry, and then he answered her no more. He became angry with himself, in that he missed so much of the plunder before him.

The broken sea was full of the long straggling growth which the waves had torn up from the bottom of the ocean, but the masses were carried past him, away from him—nay, once or twice over him ; and then Mally's weird voice would sound in his ear, jeering him. The gloom among the rocks was now becoming thicker and thicker, the tide was beating in with increased strength, and the gusts of wind came with quicker and greater violence. But still he worked on. While Mally worked he would work, and he would work for some time after she was driven in. He would not be beaten by a girl.

The great hole was now full of water, but of water which seemed to be boiling as though in a pot. And the pot was full of floating masses—large treasures of seaweed which were thrown to and fro upon its surface, but lying there so thick that one would seem almost able to rest upon it without sinking.

Mally knew well how useless it was to attempt to rescue aught from the fury of that boiling cauldron. The hole went in under the rocks, and the side of it towards the shore lay high, slippery, and steep. The hole, even at low water, was never empty; and Mally believed that there was no bottom to it. Fish thrown in there could escape out to the ocean, miles away—so Mally in her softer moods would tell the visitors to the cove. She knew the hole well. Poulnadioul she was accustomed to call it; which was supposed, when translated, to mean that this was the hole of the Evil One. Never did Mally attempt to make her own of weed which had found its way into that pot.

But Barty Gunliffe knew no better, and she watched him as he endeavoured to steady himself on the treacherously slippery edge of the pool. He fixed himself there and made a haul, with some small success. How he managed it she hardly knew, but she stood still for a while watching him anxiously, and then she saw him slip. He slipped, and recovered himself; slipped again, and again recovered himself.

"Barty, you fool!" she screamed; "if you get yourself pitched in there, you'll never come out no more."

Whether she simply wished to frighten him, or whether her heart relented and she had thought of his danger with dismay, who shall say? She could not have told herself. She hated him as much as ever, but she could hardly have wished to see him drowned before her eyes.

"You go on, and don't mind me," said he, speaking in a hoarse, angry tone.

"Mind you!—who minds you?" retorted the girl. And then she again prepared herself for her work.

But as she went down over the rocks with her long hook balanced in her hands, she suddenly heard a splash, and, turning quickly round, saw the body of her enemy tumbling amidst the eddying waves in the pool. The tide had now come up so far that every succeeding wave washed into it and over it from the side nearest to the sea, and then ran down again back from the rocks, as the rolling wave receded, with a noise like the fall of a cataract. And then, when the surplus water had retreated for a moment, the surface of the pool would be partly calm, though the fretting bubbles would still boil up and down, and there was ever a simmer on the surface, as though, in truth, the cauldron were heated. But this time of comparative rest was but a moment, for the succeeding breaker would come up almost as soon as the foam of the preceding one had gone, and then again the waters would be dashed upon the rocks, and the sides would echo with the roar of the angry wave.

Instantly Mally hurried across to the edge of the pool, crouching down upon her hands and knees for security as she did so. As a wave receded, Barty's head and face was carried round near to her, and she could see that his forehead was covered with blood. Whether he were alive or dead she did not know. She had seen nothing but his blood, and the light-coloured hair of his head lying amidst the foam. Then his body was drawn along by the suction of the retreating wave ; but the mass of water that escaped was not on this occasion large enough to carry the man out with it.

Instantly Mally was at work with her hook, and getting it fixed into his coat, dragged him towards the spot on which she was kneeling. During the half-minute of repose she got him so close that she could touch his shoulder. Straining herself down, laying herself over the long bending handle of the hook, she strove to grasp him with her right hand. But she could not do it ; she could only touch him.

Then came the next breaker, forcing itself on with a roar, looking to Mally as though it must certainly knock her from her resting-place, and destroy them both. But she had nothing for it but to kneel, and hold by her hook.

What prayer passed through her mind at that moment for herself or for him, or for that old man who was sitting unconsciously up at the cabin, who can say ? The great wave came and rushed over her as she lay almost prostrate, and when the water was gone from her eyes, and the tumult of the foam, and the violence of the roaring breaker had passed by her, she found herself at her length upon the rock, while his body had been lifted up, free from her hook, and was lying upon the slippery ledge, half in the water and half out of it. As she looked at him, in that instant, she could see that his eyes were open and that he was struggling with his hands.

"Hold by the hook, Barty," she cried, pushing the stick of it before him, while she seized the collar of his coat in her hands.

Had he been her brother, her lover, her father, she could not have clung to him with more of the energy of despair. He did contrive to hold by the stick which she had given him, and when the succeeding wave had passed by, he was still on the ledge. In the next moment she was seated a yard or two above the hole, in comparative safety, while Barty lay upon the rocks with his still bleeding head resting upon her lap.

What could she do now ? She could not carry him ; and in fifteen minutes the sea would be up where she was sitting. He was quite insensible and very pale, and the blood was coming slowly—

very slowly—from the wound on his forehead. Ever so gently she put her hand upon his hair to move it back from his face ; and then she bent over his mouth to see if he breathed, and as she looked at him she knew that he was beautiful.

What would she not give that he might live ? Nothing now was so precious to her as his life—as this life which she had so far rescued from the waters. But what could she do ? Her grandfather could scarcely get himself down over the rocks, if indeed he could succeed in doing so much as that. Could she drag the wounded man backwards, if it were only a few feet, so that he might lie above the reach of the waves till further assistance could be procured ?

She set herself to work and she moved him, almost lifting him. As she did so she wondered at her own strength, but she was very strong at that moment. Slowly, tenderly, falling on the rocks herself so that he might fall on her, she got him back to the margin of the sand, to a spot which the waters would not reach for the next two hours.

Here her grandfather met them, having seen at last what had happened from the door.

" Dada," she said, " he fell into the pool yonder, and was battered against the rocks. See there at his forehead."

" Mally, I'm thinking that he's dead already," said old Glos, peering down over the body.

" No, dada ; he is not dead ; but mayhap he's dying. But I'll go at once up to the farm."

" Mally," said the old man, " look at his head. They'll say we murdered him."

" Who'll say so ? Who'll lie like that ? Didn't I pull him out of the hole ? "

" What matters that ? His father'll say we killed him."

It was manifest to Mally that whatever any one might say hereafter, her present course was plain before her. She must run up the path to Gunliffe's farm and get necessary assistance. If the world were as bad as her grandfather said, it would be so bad that she would not care to live longer in it. But be that as it might, there was no doubt as to what she must do now.

So away she went as fast as her naked feet could carry her up the cliff. When at the top she looked round to see if any person might be within ken, but she saw no one. So she ran with all her speed along the headland of the corn-field which led in the direction of old Gunliffe's house, and as she drew near to the homestead she saw that Barty's mother was leaning on the gate. As she approached, she attempted to call, but her breath failed her for any purpose of loud speech, so she ran on till she was able to grasp Mrs. Gunliffe by the arm.

"Where's himself?" she said, holding her hand upon her beating heart that she might husband her breath.

"Who is it you mean?" said Mrs. Gunliffe, who participated in the family feud against Trenglos and his grand-daughter. "What does the girl clutch me for in that way?"

"He's dying, then, that's all."

"Who is dying? Is it old Malachi? If the old man's bad, we'll send some one down."

"It ain't dada, it's Barty! Where's himself? where's the master?" But by this time Mrs. Gunliffe was in an agony of despair, and was calling out for assistance lustily. Happily Gunliffe, the father, was at hand, and with him a man from the neighbouring village.

"Will you not send for the doctor?" said Mally. "Oh, man, you should send for the doctor!"

Whether any orders were given for the doctor she did not know, but in a very few minutes she was hurrying across the field again towards the path to the cove, and Gunliffe with the other man and his wife were following her.

As Mally went along she recovered her voice, for their step was not so quick as hers, and that which to them was a hurried movement, allowed her to get her breath again. And as she went she tried to explain to the father what had happened, saying but little, however, of her own doings in the matter. The wife hung behind listening, exclaiming every now and again that her boy was killed, and then asking wild questions as to his being yet alive. The father, as he went, said little. He was known as a silent, sober man, well spoken of for diligence and general conduct, but supposed to be stern and very hard when angered.

As they drew near to the top of the path, the other man whispered something to him, and then he turned round upon Mally and stopped her.

"If he has come by his death between you, your blood shall be taken for his," said he.

Then the wife shrieked out that her child had been murdered, and Mally, looking round into the faces of the three, saw that her grandfather's words had come true. They suspected her of having taken the life, in saving which she had nearly lost her own.

She looked round at them with awe in her face, and then, without saying a word, preceded them down the path. What had she to answer when such a charge as that was made against her? If they chose to say that she pushed him into the pool, and hit him with her hook as he lay amidst the waters, how could she show that it was not so?

Poor Mally knew little of the law of evidence, and it seemed to her that she was in their hands. But as she went down the steep track with a hurried step—a step so quick that they could not keep up with her—her heart was very full, very full and very high. She had striven for the man's life as though he had been her brother. The blood was yet not dry on her own legs and arms, where she had torn them in his service. At one moment she had felt sure that she would die with him in that pool. And now they said that she had murdered him! It might be that he was not dead, and what would he say if ever he should speak again? Then she thought of that moment when his eyes had opened, and he had seemed to see her. She had no fear for herself, for her heart was very high. But it was full also—full of scorn, disdain, and wrath.

When she had reached the bottom, she stood close to the door of the hut waiting for them, so that they might precede her to the other group, which was there in front of them, at a little distance on the sand.

"He is there, and dada is with him. Go and look at him," said Mally.

The father and mother ran on, stumbling over the stones, but Mally remained behind by the door of the hut.

Barty Gunliffe was lying on the sand where Mally had left him, and old Malachi Trenglos was standing over him, resting himself with difficulty upon a stick.

"Not a move he's moved since she left him," said he, "not a move. I put his head on the old rug as you see, and I tried 'un with a drop of gin, but he wouldn't take it—he wouldn't take it."

"Oh, my boy! my boy!" said the mother, throwing herself beside her son upon the sand.

"Haud your tongue, woman," said the father, kneeling down slowly by the lad's head, "whimpering that way will do 'un no good."

Then having gazed for a minute or two upon the pale face beneath him, he looked up sternly into that of Malachi Trenglos.

The old man hardly knew how to bear this terrible inquisition.

"He would come," said Malachi; "he brought it all upon hisself."

"Who was it struck him?" said the father.

"Sure he struck hisself, as he fell among the breakers."

"Liar!" said the father, looking up at the old man.

"They have murdered him!—they have murdered him!" shrieked the mother.

"Haud your peace, woman!" said the husband again. "They shall give us blood for blood."

Mally, leaning against the corner of the hovel, heard it all, but did not stir. They might say what they liked. They might make it out to be murder. They might drag her and her grandfather to

Camelford gaol, and then to Bodmin, and the gallows; but they could not take from her the conscious feeling that was her own. She had done her best to save him—her very best. And she had saved him!

She remembered her threat to him before they had gone down on the rocks together, and her evil wish. Those words had been very wicked; but since that she had risked her life to save his. They might say what they pleased of her, and do what they pleased. She knew what she knew.

Then the father raised his son's head and shoulders in his arms, and called on the others to assist him in carrying Barty towards the path. They raised him between them carefully and tenderly, and lifted their burden on towards the spot at which Mally was standing. She never moved, but watched them at their work; and the old man followed them, hobbling after them with his crutch.

When they had reached the end of the hut she looked upon Barty's face, and saw that it was very pale. There was no longer blood upon the forehead, but the great gash was to be seen there plainly, with its jagged cut, and the skin livid and blue round the orifice. His light brown hair was hanging back, as she had made it to hang when she had gathered it with her hand after the big wave had passed over them. Ah, how beautiful he was in Mally's eyes with that pale face, and the sad scar upon his brow! She turned her face away, that they might not see her tears; but she did not move, nor did she speak.

But now, when they had passed the end of the hut, shuffling along with their burden, she heard a sound which stirred her. She roused herself quickly from her leaning posture, and stretched forth her head as though to listen; then she moved to follow them. Yes, they had stopped at the bottom of the path, and had again laid the body on the rocks. She heard that sound again, as of a long, long sigh, and then, regardless of any of them, she ran to the wounded man's head.

"He is not dead," she said. "There; he is not dead."

As she spoke Barty's eyes opened, and he looked about him.

"Barty, my boy, speak to me," said the mother.

Barty turned his face upon his mother, smiled, and then stared about him wildly.

"How is it with thee, lad?" said his father. Then Barty turned his face again to the latter voice, and as he did so his eyes fell upon Mally.

"Mally!" he said, "Mally!"

It could have wanted nothing further to any of those present to teach them that, according to Barty's own view of the case, Mally had not been his enemy; and, in truth, Mally herself wanted no further triumph. That word had vindicated her, and she withdrew back to the hut.

" Dada," she said, " Barty is not dead, and I'm thinking they won't say anything more about our hurting him."

Old Glos shook his head. He was glad the lad hadn't met his death there ; he didn't want the young man's blood, but he knew what folk would say. The poorer he was, the more sure the world would be to trample on him. Mally said what she could to comfort him, being full of comfort herself.

She would have crept up to the farm if she dared, to ask how Barty was. But her courage failed her when she thought of that, so she went to work again, dragging back the weed she had saved to the spot at which on the morrow she would load the donkey. As she did this she saw Barty's pony still standing patiently under the rock, so she got a lock of fodder and threw it down before the beast.

It had become dark down in the cove, but she was still dragging back the seaweed, when she saw the glimmer of a lantern coming down the pathway. It was a most unusual sight, for lanterns were not common down in Malachi's Cove. Down came the lantern rather slowly, much more slowly than she was in the habit of descending, and then through the gloom she saw the figure of a man standing at the bottom of the path. She went up to him, and saw that it was Mr. Gunliffe, the father.

" Is that Mally ? " said Gunliffe.

" Yes, it is Mally ; and how is Barty, Mr. Gunliffe ? "

" You must come to 'un yourself, now at once," said the farmer. " He won't sleep a wink till he's seed you. You must not say but you'll come."

" Sure I'll come if I'm wanted," said Mally.

Gunliffe waited a moment, thinking that Mally might have to prepare herself, but Mally needed no preparation. She was dripping with salt water from the weed which she had been dragging, and her elfin locks were streaming wildly from her head ; but, such as she was, she was ready.

" Dad's in bed," she said, " and I can go now if you please."

Then Gunliffe turned round and followed her up the path, wondering at the life which this girl led so far away from all her sex. It was now dark night, and he had found her working at the very edge of the rolling waves by herself, in the darkness, while the only human being who might seem to be her protector had already gone to his bed.

When they were at the top of the cliff, Gunliffe took her by her hand, and led her along. She did not comprehend this, but she made no attempt to take her hand from his. Something he said about falling on the cliffs, but it was muttered so lowly that Mally hardly understood him. But, in truth, the man knew that she had saved his boy's life, and that he had injured her instead of thanking her. He was now taking her to his heart, and as words were wanting to him, he was showing his love after this silent fashion. He held her by the hand as though she were a child, and Mally tripped along at his side asking him no questions.

When they were at the farm-yard gate, he stopped there for a moment.

" Mally, my girl," he said, " he'll not be content till he sees thee, but thou must not stay long wi' him, lass. Doctor says he's weak like, and wants sleep badly."

Mally merely nodded her head, and then they entered the house. Mally had never been within it before, and looked about with wondering eyes at the furniture of the big kitchen. Did any idea of her future destiny flash upon her then, I wonder ? But she did not pause here a moment, but was led up to the bedroom above stairs, where Barty was lying on his mother's bed.

" Is it Mally herself ? " said the voice of the weak youth.

" It's Mally herself," said the mother, " so now you can say what you please."

" Mally," said he, " Mally, it's along of you that I'm alive this moment."

" I'll not forget it on her," said the father, with his eyes turned away from her. " I'll never forget it on her."

" We hadn't a one but only him," said the mother, with her apron up to her face.

" Mally, you'll be friends with me now ? " said Barty.

To have been made lady of the manor of the cove for ever, Mally couldn't have spoken a word now. It was not only that the words and presence of the people there cowed her and made her speechless, but the big bed, and the looking-glass, and the unheard-of wonders of the chamber, made her feel her own insignificance. But she crept up to Barty's side, and put her hand upon his.

" I'll come and get the weed, Mally ; but it shall all be for you," said Barty.

" Indeed, you won't then, Barty dear," said the mother ; " you'll never go near the awesome place again. What would we do if you were took from us ? "

" He mustn't go near the hole if he does," said Mally, speaking at last in a solemn voice, and imparting the knowledge which she had kept to herself while Barty was her enemy ; " 'specially not if the wind's any way from the nor'ard."

" She'd better go down now," said the father.

Barty kissed the hand which he held, and Mally, looking at him as he did so, thought that he was like an angel.

" You'll come and see us to-morrow, Mally," said he.

To this she made no answer, but followed Mrs. Gunliffe out of the room. When they were down in the kitchen, the mother had tea for her, and thick milk, and a hot cake—all the delicacies which the farm could afford. I don't know that Mally cared much for the eating and drinking that night, but she began to think that the Gunliffes were good people, very good people. It was better thus, at any rate, than being accused of murder and carried off to Camelford prison.

" I'll never forget it on her—never," the father had said.

Those words stuck to her from that moment, and seemed to sound in her ears all the night. How glad she was that Barty had come down to the cove—oh yes, how glad! There was no question of his dying now, and as for the blow on his forehead, what harm was that to a lad like him?

" But father shall go with you," said Mrs. Gunliffe, when Mally prepared to start for the cove by herself. Mally, however, would not hear of this. She could find her way to the cove whether it was light or dark.

" Mally, thou art my child now, and I shall think of thee so," said the mother, as the girl went off by herself.

Mally thought of this too as she walked home. How could she become Mrs. Gunliffe's child; ah, how?

I need not, I think, tell the tale any further. That Mally did become Mrs. Gunliffe's child, and how she became so the reader will understand; and in process of time the big kitchen and all the wonders of the farm-house were her own. The people said that Barty Gunliffe had married a mermaid out of the sea; but when it was said in Mally's hearing I doubt whether she liked it; and when Barty himself would call her a mermaid she would frown at him, and throw about her black hair, and pretend to cuff him with her little hand.

Old Glos was brought up to the top of the cliff, and lived his few remaining days under the roof of Mr. Gunliffe's house; and as for the cove and the right of seaweed, from that time forth all that has been supposed to attach itself to Gunliffe's farm, and I do not know that any of the neighbours are prepared to dispute the right.

JOHN RUSKIN
1819–1900

THE KING OF THE GOLDEN RIVER, OR THE BLACK BROTHERS

I

In a secluded and mountainous part of Stiria there was, in old time, a valley of the most surprising and luxuriant fertility. It was surrounded on all sides by steep and rocky mountains, rising into peaks, which were always covered with snow, and from which a number of torrents descended in constant cataracts. One of these fell westward, over the face of a crag so high, that, when the sun had set to everything else, and all below was darkness, his beams still shone full upon this waterfall, so that it looked like a shower of gold. It was therefore called by the people of the neighbourhood the Golden River. It was strange that none of these streams fell into the valley itself. They all descended on the other side of the mountains, and wound away through broad plains and by populous cities. But the clouds were drawn so constantly to the snowy hills, and rested so softly in the circular hollow, that in time of drought and heat, when all the country round was burnt up, there was still rain in the little valley; and its crops were so heavy, and its hay so high, and its apples so red, and its grapes so blue, and its wine so rich, and its honey so sweet, that it was a marvel to every one who beheld it, and was commonly called the Treasure Valley. The whole of this little valley belonged to three brothers, called Schwartz, Hans, and Gluck. Schwartz and Hans, the two elder brothers, were very ugly men, with overhanging eyebrows and small dull eyes, which were always half shut, so that you couldn't see into *them*, and always fancied they saw very far into *you*. They lived by farming the Treasure Valley, and very good farmers they were. They killed everything that did not pay for its eating. They shot the blackbirds, because they pecked the fruit; and killed the hedgehogs, lest they should suck the cows; they poisoned the crickets for eating the crumbs in the kitchen, and smothered the cicadas, which used to sing all summer in the lime trees. They worked their servants without any wages, till they would not work any more, and then quarrelled with them, and turned them out of doors without paying them. It would have been very odd if with such a farm, and such a system of farming, they hadn't got very rich; and very rich they *did* get. They generally contrived to keep their corn by them till it was very dear, and then sell it for twice its value; they had heaps of gold lying about on their floors, yet it was never known that they had given so much as a penny or a crust in charity; they never went to mass; grumbled perpetually at paying tithes; and were, in a word, of so cruel and grinding a temper as to receive from all those with whom they had any dealings the nick-name of the "Black Brothers." The youngest brother, Gluck, was as completely opposed, in both appearance and character, to his seniors as could possibly be imagined or desired. He was not above twelve years old, fair, blue-eyed, and kind in temper to every living thing. He did not, of course, agree particularly well with his brothers, or rather they did not agree with *him*. He was usually appointed to the honourable office of turnspit, when there was anything to roast, which was not often; for, to do the brothers justice, they were hardly less sparing upon themselves than upon other people. At other times he used to clean the shoes, floors, and sometimes the plates, occasionally getting what was left on them by way of encouragement, and a wholesome quantity of dry blows by way of education.

Things went on in this manner for a long time. At last came a very wet summer, and everything went wrong in the country round. The hay had hardly been got in, when the haystacks were floated bodily down to the sea by an inundation; the vines were cut to pieces with the hail; the corn was all killed by a black blight; only in the Treasure Valley, as usual, all was safe. As it had rain when there was rain nowhere else, so it had sun when there was sun nowhere else. Everybody came to buy corn at the farm, and went away pouring maledictions on the Black Brothers. They asked what they liked, and got it, except from the poor people, who could only beg, and several of whom were starved at their very door, without the slightest regard or notice.

It was drawing towards winter, and very cold weather, when one day the two elder brothers had gone out, with their usual warning to little Gluck, who was left to mind the roast, that he was to let nobody in and give nothing out. Gluck sat down quite close to the fire, for it was raining very hard, and the kitchen walls were by no means dry or comfortable looking. He turned and turned, and the roast got nice and brown. "What a pity," thought Gluck, "my brothers never ask anybody to dinner. I'm sure when they've got such a nice piece of mutton as this, and nobody else has got so much as a piece of dry bread, it would do their hearts good to have somebody to eat it with them."

Just as he spoke there came a double knock at the house door, yet heavy and dull, as though the knocker had been tied up—more like a puff than a knock. "It must be the wind," said Gluck; "nobody else would venture to knock double knocks at our door." No, it wasn't the wind; there it came again very hard, and what was particularly astounding, the knocker seemed to be in a hurry, and not to be in the least afraid of the consequences. Gluck went to the window, opened it, and put his head out to see who it was. It was the most extraordinary looking little gentleman he had ever seen in his life. He had a very long nose, slightly brass-coloured, and expanding towards its termination into a development not unlike the lower extremity of a key bugle. His cheeks were very round and very red, and might have warranted a supposition that he had been blowing a refractory fire for the last eight-and-forty hours. His eyes twinkled merrily through long silky eyelashes, his moustaches curled twice round like a corkscrew on each side of his mouth, and his hair, of a curious mixed pepper and salt colour, descended far over his shoulders. He was about four feet six in height, and wore a conical pointed cap of nearly the same altitude, decorated with a black feather some three feet long. His doublet was prolonged behind into something resembling a violent exaggeration of what is now termed a "swallow-tail," but was much obscured by the swelling folds of an enormous black, glossy-looking cloak, which must have been very much too long in calm weather, as the wind, whistling round the old house, carried it clear out from the wearer's shoulders to about four times his own length.

Gluck was so perfectly paralysed by the singular appearance of his visitor that he remained fixed without uttering a word, until the old gentleman, having performed another and a more energetic concerto on the knocker, turned round to look after his fly-away cloak. In so doing he caught sight of Gluck's little yellow head jammed in the window, with its mouth and eyes very wide open indeed.

"Hollo!" said the little gentleman, "that's not the way to answer the door: I'm wet, let me in."

To do the little gentleman justice, he *was* wet. His feather hung down between his legs like a beaten puppy's tail, dripping like an umbrella, and from the ends of his moustaches the water was running into his waistcoat pockets and out again like a mill stream.

"I beg pardon, sir," said Gluck, "I'm very sorry, but I really can't."

"Can't what?" said the old gentleman.

"I can't let you in, sir—I can't indeed; my brothers would beat me to death, sir, if I thought of such a thing. What do you want, sir?"

"Want?" said the old gentleman petulantly. "I want fire and shelter; and there's your great fire there blazing, crackling, and dancing on the walls, with nobody to feel it. Let me in, I say; I only want to warm myself."

Gluck had had his head, by this time, so long out of the window, that he began to feel it was really unpleasantly cold, and when he turned and saw the beautiful fire rustling and roaring, and throwing long bright tongues up the chimney, as if it were licking its chops at the savoury smell of the leg of mutton, his heart melted within him that it should be burning away for nothing. "He does look *very* wet," said little Gluck; "I'll just let him in for a quarter of an hour." Round he went to the door and opened it; and as the little gentleman walked in, there came a gust of wind through the house that made the old chimneys totter.

"That's a good boy," said the little gentleman. "Never mind your brothers. I'll talk to them."

"Pray, sir, don't do any such thing," said Gluck. "I can't let you stay till they come; they'd be the death of me."

"Dear me," said the old gentleman, "I'm very sorry to hear that. How long may I stay?"

"Only till the mutton's done, sir," replied Gluck, "and it's very brown."

Then the old gentleman walked into the kitchen and sat himself down on the hob, with the top of his cap accommodated up the chimney, for it was a great deal too high for the roof.

"You'll soon dry there, sir," said Gluck, and sat down again to turn the mutton. But the old gentleman did *not* dry there, but went on drip, drip, dripping among the cinders, and the fire fizzed and sputtered, and began to look very black and uncomfortable; never was such a cloak; every fold in it ran like a gutter.

"I beg pardon, sir," said Gluck at length, after watching the water spreading in long, quicksilver-like streams over the floor for a quarter of an hour; "mayn't I take your cloak?"

"No, thank you," said the old gentleman.

"Your cap, sir?"

"I am all right, thank you," said the old gentleman rather gruffly.

"But,—sir,—I'm very sorry," said Gluck, hesitatingly; "but—really, sir,—you're—putting the fire out."

"It'll take longer to do the mutton, then," replied his visitor drily.

Gluck was very much puzzled by the behaviour of his guest; it was such a strange mixture of coolness and humility. He turned away at the string meditatively for another five minutes.

"That mutton looks very nice," said the old gentleman at length. "Can't you give me a little bit?"

"Impossible, sir," said Gluck.

"I'm very hungry," continued the old gentleman. "I've had nothing to eat yesterday, nor to-day. They surely couldn't miss a bit from the knuckle!"

He spoke in so very melancholy a tone, that it quite melted Gluck's heart. "They promised me one slice to-day, sir," said he. "I can give you that, but not a bit more."

"That's a good boy," said the old gentleman again.

Then Gluck warmed a plate, and sharpened a knife. "I don't care if I do get beaten for it," thought he. Just as he had cut a large slice out of the mutton, there came a tremendous rap at the door. The old gentleman jumped off the hob, as if it had suddenly become inconveniently warm. Gluck fitted the slice into the mutton again, with desperate efforts at exactitude, and ran to open the door.

"What did you keep us waiting in the rain for?" said Schwartz, as he walked in, throwing his umbrella in Gluck's face. "Ay! what for, indeed, you little vagabond?" said Hans, administering an educational box on the ear, as he followed his brother into the kitchen.

"Bless my soul!" said Schwartz when he opened the door.

"Amen," said the little gentleman, who had taken his cap off, and was standing in the middle of the kitchen, bowing with the utmost possible velocity.

"Who's that?" said Schwartz, catching up a rolling-pin, and turning to Gluck with a fierce frown.

"I don't know, indeed, brother," said Gluck in great terror.

"How did he get in?" roared Schwartz.

"My dear brother," said Gluck deprecatingly, "he was so *very* wet!"

The rolling-pin was descending on Gluck's head; but, at the instant, the old gentleman interposed his conical cap, on which it crashed with a shock that shook the water out of it all over the room. What was very odd, the rolling-pin no sooner touched the cap than it flew out of Schwartz's hand, spinning like a straw in a high wind, and fell into the corner at the farther end of the room.

"Who are you, sir?" demanded Schwartz, turning upon him.

"What's your business?" snarled Hans.

"I'm a poor old man, sir," the little gentleman began very modestly, "and I saw your fire through the window, and begged shelter for a quarter of an hour."

"Have the goodness to walk out again, then," said Schwartz. "We've quite enough water in our kitchen without making it a drying-house."

"It is a cold day to turn an old man out in, sir; look at my grey hairs." They hung down to his shoulders, as I told you before.

"Ay!" said Hans, "there are enough of them to keep you warm. Walk!"

"I'm very, very hungry, sir; couldn't you spare me a bit of bread before I go?"

"Bread, indeed!" said Schwartz; "do you suppose we've nothing to do with our bread but to give it to such red-nosed fellows as you?"

"Why don't you sell your feather?" said Hans sneeringly. "Out with you."

"A little bit," said the old gentleman.

"Be off!" said Schwartz.

"Pray, gentlemen."

"Off, and be hanged!" cried Hans, seizing him by the collar. But he had no sooner touched the old gentleman's collar, than away he went after the rolling-pin, spinning round and round, till he fell into the corner on the top of it. Then Schwartz was very angry, and ran at the old gentleman to turn him out; but he also had hardly touched him, when away he went after Hans and the rolling-pin, and hit his head against the wall as he tumbled into the corner. And so there they lay, all three.

Then the old gentleman spun himself round with velocity in the opposite direction; continued to spin until his long cloak was all wound neatly about him; clapped his cap on his head, very much on one side (for it could not stand upright without going through the ceiling), gave an additional twist to his cork-screw moustaches, and replied with perfect coolness, "Gentlemen, I wish you a very good morning. At twelve o'clock to-night, I'll call again; after such a refusal of hospitality as I have just experienced, you will not be surprised if that visit is the last I ever pay you."

"If ever I catch you here again," muttered Schwartz, coming half-frightened out of the corner—but before he could finish his sentence the old gentleman had shut the house door behind him with a great bang: and there drove past the window, at the same instant, a wreath of ragged cloud, that whirled and rolled away down the valley in all manner of shapes, turning over and over in the air, and melting away at last in a gush of rain.

"A very pretty business, indeed, Mr. Gluck!" said Schwartz. "Dish the mutton, sir. If ever I catch you at such a trick again—bless me, why the mutton's been cut!"

"You promised me one slice, brother, you know," said Gluck.

"Oh! and you were cutting it hot, I suppose, and going to catch all the gravy. It'll be long before I promise you such a thing again. Leave the room, sir; and have the kindness to wait in the coal-cellar till I call you."

Gluck left the room, melancholy enough. The brothers ate as

much mutton as they could, locked the rest in the cupboard, and proceeded to get very drunk after dinner.

Such a night as it was! Howling wind, and rushing rain, without intermission. The brothers had just sense enough left to put up all the shutters, and double bar the door, before they went to bed. They usually slept in the same room. As the clock struck twelve, they were both awakened by a tremendous crash. Their door burst open with a violence that shook the house from top to bottom.

"What's that?" cried Schwartz, starting up in his bed.

"Only I," said the little gentleman.

The two brothers sat up on their bolster, and stared into the darkness. The room was full of water, and by a misty moonbeam, which found its way through a hole in the shutter, they could see in the midst of it an enormous foam globe, spinning round, and bobbing up and down like a cork, on which, as on a most luxurious cushion, reclined the little old gentleman, cap and all. There was plenty of room for it now, for the roof was off.

"Sorry to incommode you," said their visitor ironically. "I'm afraid your beds are dampish; perhaps you had better go to your brother's room; I've left the ceiling on there."

They required no second admonition, but rushed into Gluck's room, wet through, and in an agony of terror.

"You'll find my card on the kitchen table," the old gentleman called after them. "Remember, the *last* visit."

"Pray Heaven it may!" said Schwartz, shuddering. And the foam globe disappeared.

Dawn came at last, and the two brothers looked out of Gluck's little window in the morning. The Treasure Valley was one mass of ruin and desolation. The inundation had swept away trees, crops, and cattle, and left, in their stead, a waste of red sand and grey mud. The two brothers crept shivering and horror-struck into the kitchen. The water had gutted the whole first floor; corn, money, almost every movable thing had been swept away, and there was left only a small white card on the kitchen table. On it, in large, breezy, long-legged letters were engraved the words:

II

South West Wind, Esquire, was as good as his word. After the momentous visit above related, he entered the Treasure Valley no more; and, what was worse, he had so much influence with his relations, the West Winds in general, and used it so effectually, that they all adopted a similar line of conduct. So no rain fell in the valley from one year's end to another. Though everything remained green and flourishing in the plains below, the inheritance of the Three Brothers was a desert. What had once been the richest soil in the kingdom became a shifting heap of red sand; and the brothers, unable longer to contend with the adverse skies, abandoned their valueless patrimony in despair, to seek some means of gaining a livelihood among the cities and people of the plains. All their money was gone, and they had nothing left but some curious old-fashioned pieces of gold plate, the last remnants of their ill-gotten wealth.

"Suppose we turn goldsmiths?" said Schwartz to Hans, as they entered the large city. "It is a good knave's trade; we can put a great deal of copper into the gold without any one's finding it out."

The thought was agreed to be a very good one; they hired a furnace, and turned goldsmiths. But two slight circumstances affected their trade: the first, that people did not approve of the coppered gold; the second, that the two elder brothers, whenever they had sold anything, used to leave little Gluck to mind the furnace, and go and drink out the money in the ale-house next door. So they melted all their gold, without making money enough to buy more, and were at last reduced to one large drinking-mug, which an uncle of his had given to little Gluck, and which he was very fond of, and would not have parted with for the world, though he never drank anything out of it but milk and water. The mug was a very odd mug to look at. The handle was formed of two wreaths of flowing golden hair, so finely spun that it looked more like silk than metal, and these wreaths descended into and mixed with a beard and whiskers of the same exquisite workmanship, which surrounded and decorated a very fierce little face, of the reddest gold imaginable, right in the front of the mug, with a pair of eyes in it which seemed to command its whole circumference. It was impossible to drink out of the mug without being subjected to an intense gaze out of the side of these eyes; and Schwartz positively averred that once, after emptying it, full of Rhenish, seventeen times, he had seen them wink! When it came to the mug's turn to be made into spoons, it half broke poor little Gluck's heart; but the brothers only laughed at him, tossed the mug into the melting-pot, and staggered out to the ale-house, leaving him, as usual, to pour the gold into bars when it was all ready.

When they were gone, Gluck took a farewell look at his old friend in the melting-pot. The flowing hair was all gone ; nothing remained but the red nose, and the sparkling eyes, which looked more malicious than ever. " And no wonder," thought Gluck, " after being treated in that way." He sauntered disconsolately to the window, and sat himself down to catch the fresh evening air and escape the hot breath of the furnace. Now this window commanded a direct view of the range of mountains, which, as I told you before, overhung the Treasure Valley, and more especially of the peak from which fell the Golden River. It was just at the close of the day, and, when Gluck sat down at the window, he saw the rocks of the mountain tops, all crimson and purple with the sunset ; and there were bright tongues of fiery cloud burning and quivering about them ; and the river, brighter than all, fell, in a waving column of pure gold, from precipice to precipice, with the double arch of a broad purple rainbow stretched across it, flushing and fading alternately in the wreaths of spray.

" Ah ! " said Gluck aloud, after he had looked at it for a little while, " if that river were really all gold, what a nice thing it would be."

" No, it wouldn't, Gluck," said a clear metallic voice close at his ear.

" Bless me, what's that ? " exclaimed Gluck, jumping up. There was nobody there. He looked round the room, and under the table, and a great many times behind him, but there was certainly nobody there, and he sat down again at the window. This time he didn't speak, but he couldn't help thinking again that it would be very convenient if the river were really all gold.

" Not at all, my boy," said the same voice, louder than before.

" Bless me ! " said Gluck again, " what *is* that ? " He looked again into all the corners and cupboards, and then began turning round and round as fast as he could in the middle of the room, thinking there was somebody behind him, when the same voice struck again on his ear. It was singing now very merrily, " Lala-lira-la " ; no words, only a soft running effervescent melody, something like that of a kettle on the boil. Gluck looked out of the window. No, it was certainly in the house. Upstairs and downstairs. No, it was certainly in that very room, coming in quicker time and clearer notes every moment. " Lala-lira-la." All at once it struck Gluck that it sounded louder near the furnace. He ran to the opening and looked in : yes, he saw right, it seemed to be coming, not only out of the furnace, but out of the pot. He uncovered it, and ran back in a great fright, for the pot was certainly singing ! He stood in the farthest corner of the room, with his hand up and his mouth open, for a minute or two, when the singing stopped, and the voice became clear and pronunciative.

"Hollo!" said the voice.

Gluck made no answer.

"Hollo! Gluck, my boy," said the pot again.

Gluck summoned all his energies, walked straight up to the crucible, drew it out of the furnace, and looked in. The gold was all melted, and its surface as smooth and polished as a river; but instead of reflecting little Gluck's head as he looked in, he saw meeting his glance, from beneath the gold, the red nose and sharp eyes of his old friend of the mug, a thousand times redder and sharper than ever he had seen them in his life.

"Come, Gluck, my boy," said the voice out of the pot again, "I'm all right; pour me out."

But Gluck was too much astonished to do anything of the kind.

"Pour me out, I say," said the voice rather gruffly.

Still Gluck couldn't move.

"*Will* you pour me out?" said the voice passionately, "I'm too hot."

By a violent effort Gluck recovered the use of his limbs, took hold of the crucible, and sloped it, so as to pour out the gold. But instead of a liquid stream there came out first a pair of pretty little yellow legs, then some coat-tails, then a pair of arms stuck akimbo, and, finally, the well-known head of his friend the mug; all which articles, uniting as they rolled out, stood up energetically on the floor, in the shape of a little golden dwarf, about a foot and a half high.

"That's right!" said the dwarf, stretching out first his legs and then his arms, and then shaking his head up and down and as far round as it would go for five minutes without stopping, apparently with the view of ascertaining if he were quite correctly put together, while Gluck stood contemplating him in speechless amazement. He was dressed in slashed doublet of spun gold, so fine in its texture that the prismatic colours gleamed over it as if on a surface of mother of pearl; and over this brilliant doublet his hair and beard fell full half-way to the ground in waving curls, so exquisitely delicate that Gluck could hardly tell where they ended; they seemed to melt into air. The features of the face, however, were by no means finished with the same delicacy; they were rather coarse, slightly inclining to coppery in complexion, and indicative in expression of a very pertinacious and intractable disposition in their small proprietor. When the dwarf had finished his self-examination he turned his small sharp eyes full on Gluck, and stared at him deliberately for a minute or two. "No, it wouldn't, Gluck, my boy," said the little man.

This was certainly rather an abrupt and unconnected mode of

commencing conversation. It might indeed be supposed to refer to the course of Gluck's thoughts, which had first produced the dwarf's observations out of the pot; but whatever it referred to Gluck had no inclination to dispute the dictum.

"Wouldn't it, sir?" said Gluck very mildly and submissively indeed.

"No," said the dwarf conclusively. "No, it wouldn't." And with that the dwarf pulled his cap hard over his brows, and took two turns of three feet long up and down the room, lifting his legs up very high and setting them down very hard. This pause gave time for Gluck to collect his thoughts a little; and, seeing no great reason to view his diminutive visitor with dread, and feeling his curiosity overcome his amazement, he ventured on a question of peculiar delicacy.

"Pray, sir," said Gluck rather hesitatingly, "were you my mug?"

On which the little man turned sharp round, walked straight up to Gluck, and drew himself up to his full height. "I," said the little man, "am the King of the Golden River." Whereupon he turned about again, and took two more turns, some six feet long, in order to allow time for the consternation which this announcement produced in his auditor to evaporate. After which he again walked up to Gluck and stood still, as if expecting some comment on his communication.

Gluck determined to say something at all events. "I hope your majesty is very well," said Gluck.

"Listen!" said the little man, deigning no reply to this polite inquiry. "I am the King of what you mortals call the Golden River. The shape you saw me in was owing to the malice of a stronger kind, from whose enchantments you have this instant freed me. What I have seen of you and your conduct to your wicked brothers renders me willing to serve you, therefore attend to what I tell you. Whoever shall climb to the top of that mountain from which you see the Golden River issue, and shall cast into the stream at its source three drops of holy water, for him, and for him only, the river shall turn to gold. But no one failing in his first can succeed in a second attempt; and if anyone shall cast unholy water into the river it will overwhelm him, and he will become a black stone." So saying, the King of the Golden River turned away and deliberately walked into the centre of the hottest flame of the furnace. His figure became red, white, transparent, dazzling—a blaze of intense light—rose, trembled, and disappeared. The King of the Golden River had evaporated.

"Oh!" cried poor Gluck, running to look up the chimney after him; "oh dear, dear, dear me! My mug! my mug! my mug!"

III

The King of the Golden River had hardly made the extraordinary exit related in the last chapter before Hans and Schwartz came roaring into the house, very savagely drunk. The discovery of the total loss of their last piece of plate had the effect of sobering them just enough to enable them to stand over Gluck, beating him very steadily for a quarter of an hour ; at the expiration of which period they dropped into a couple of chairs, and requested to know what he had got to say for himself. Gluck told them his story, of which of course they did not believe a word. They beat him again till their arms were tired, and staggered to bed. In the morning, however, the steadiness with which he adhered to his story obtained him some degree of credence, the immediate consequence of which was, that the two brothers, after wrangling a long time on the knotty question, which of them should try his fortune first, drew their swords, and began fighting. The noise of the fray alarmed the neighbours, who, finding they could not pacify the combatants, sent for the constable.

Hans, on hearing this, contrived to escape, and hid himself ; but Schwartz was taken before the magistrate, fined for breaking the peace, and, having drunk out his last penny the evening before, was thrown into prison till he should pay.

When Hans heard this, he was much delighted, and determined to set out immediately for the Golden River. How to get the holy water was the question. He went to the priest, but the priest could not give any holy water to so abandoned a character, so Hans went to vespers in the evening for the first time in his life, and, under pretence of crossing himself, stole a cupful, and returned home in triumph.

Next morning he got up before the sun rose, put the holy water into a strong flask, and two bottles of wine and some meat in a basket, slung them over his back, took his alpine staff in his hands, and set off for the mountains.

On his way out of the town he had to pass the prison, and as he looked in at the windows, whom should he see but Schwartz himself peeping out of the bars, and looking very disconsolate.

" Good morning, brother," said Hans ; " have you any message for the King of the Golden River ? "

Schwartz gnashed his teeth with rage, and shook the bars with all his strength ; but Hans only laughed at him, and, advising him to make himself comfortable till he came back again, shouldered his basket, shook the bottle of holy water in Schwartz's face till it frothed again, and marched off in the highest spirits in the world.

It was indeed a morning that might have made any one happy, even with no Golden River to seek for. Level lines of dewy mist lay stretched along the valley, out of which rose the massy mountains—

their lower cliffs in pale grey shadow, hardly distinguishable from the floating vapour, but gradually ascending till they caught the sunlight, which ran in sharp touches of ruddy colour along the angular crags, and pierced, in long level rays, through their fringes of spear-like pine. Far above shot up red splintered masses of castellated rock, jagged and shivered into myriads of fantastic forms, with here and there a streak of sunlit snow, traced down their chasms like a line of forked lightning; and, far beyond, and far above all these, fainter than the morning cloud, but purer and changeless, slept, in the blue sky, the utmost peaks of the eternal snow.

The Golden River, which sprang from one of the lower and snowless elevations, was now nearly in shadow; all but the uppermost jets of spray, which rose like slow smoke above the undulating line of the cataract, and floated away in feeble wreaths upon the morning wind.

On this object, and on this alone, Hans' eyes and thoughts were fixed; forgetting the distance he had to traverse, he set off at an imprudent rate of walking, which greatly exhausted him before he had scaled the first range of the green and low hills. He was, moreover, surprised on surmounting them to find that a large glacier, of whose existence, notwithstanding his previous knowledge of the mountains, he had been absolutely ignorant, lay between him and the source of the Golden River. He entered on it with the boldness of a practised mountaineer; yet he thought he had never traversed so strange or so dangerous a glacier in his life. The ice was excessively slippery, and out of all its chasms came wild sounds of gushing water; not monotonous or low, but changeful and loud, rising occasionally into drifting passages of wild melody, then breaking off into short, melancholy tones or sudden shrieks, resembling those of human voices in distress or pain. The ice was broken into thousands of confused shapes, but none, Hans thought, like the ordinary forms of splintered ice. There seemed a curious *expression* about all their outlines—a perpetual resemblance to living features, distorted and scornful. Myriads of deceitful shadows and lurid lights played and floated about and through the pale blue pinnacles, dazzling and confusing the sight of the traveller; while his ears grew dull and his head giddy with the constant gush and roar of the concealed waters. These painful circumstances increased upon him as he advanced; the ice crashed and yawned into fresh chasms at his feet, tottering spires nodded around him, and fell thundering across his path; and though he had repeatedly faced these dangers on the most terrific glaciers and in the wildest weather, it was with a new and oppressive feeling of panic terror that he leaped the last chasm, and flung himself, exhausted and shuddering, on the firm turf of the mountain.

He had been compelled to abandon his basket of food, which

became a perilous incumbrance, on the glacier, and had now no means of refreshing himself but by breaking off and eating some of the pieces of ice. This, however, relieved his thirst; an hour's repose recruited his hardy frame, and, with the indomitable spirit of avarice, he resumed his laborious journey. His way now lay straight up a ridge of bare red rocks, without a blade of grass to ease the foot or a protecting angle to afford an inch of shade from the south sun. It was past noon, and the rays beat intensely upon the steep path, while the whole atmosphere was motionless and penetrated with heat. Intense thirst was soon added to the bodily fatigue with which Hans was now afflicted; glance after glance he cast on the flask of water which hung at his belt. "Three drops are enough," at last thought he; "I may, at least, cool my lips with it."

He opened the flask, and was raising it to his lips when his eye fell on an object lying on the rock beside him; he thought it moved. It was a small dog, apparently in the last agony of death from thirst. Its tongue was out, its jaws dry, its limbs extended lifeless, and a swarm of black ants were crawling about its lips and throat. Its eye moved to the bottle which Hans held in his hand. He raised it, drank, spurned the animal with his foot, and passed on. And he did not know how it was, but he thought that a strange shadow had suddenly come across the blue sky.

The path became steeper and more rugged every moment; and the high hill air, instead of refreshing him, seemed to throw his blood into a fever. The noise of the hill cataracts sounded like mockery in his ears: they were all distant, and his thirst increased every moment. Another hour passed, and he again looked down to the flask at his side; it was half empty, but there was much more than three drops in it. He stopped to open it, and again, as he did so, something moved in the path above him. It was a fair child, stretched nearly lifeless on the rock, its breast heaving with thirst, its eyes closed, and its lips parched and burning. Hans eyed it deliberately, drank, and passed on. And a dark grey cloud came over the sun, and long, snake-like shadows crept up along the mountain sides. Hans struggled on. The sun was sinking, but its descent seemed to bring no coolness; the leaden weight of the dead air pressed upon his brow and heart, but the goal was near. He saw the cataract of the Golden River springing from the hill-side, scarcely five hundred feet above him. He paused for a moment to breathe, and sprang on to complete his task. At this instant a faint cry fell on his ear. He turned, and saw a grey-haired old man extended on the rocks. His eyes were sunk, his features deadly pale, and gathered into an expression of despair. "Water!" he stretched his arms to Hans, and cried feebly, "Water! I am dying."

"I have none," replied Hans; "thou hast had thy share of life."

He strode over the prostrate body, and darted on. And a flash of blue lightning rose out of the East, shaped like a sword ; it shook thrice over the whole heaven, and left it dark with one heavy, impenetrable shade. The sun was setting ; it plunged towards the horizon like a red-hot ball.

The roar of the Golden River rose on Hans' ear. He stood at the brink of the chasm through which it ran. Its waves were filled with the red glory of the sunset ; they shook their crests like tongues of fire, and flashes of bloody light gleamed along their foam. Their sound came mightier and mightier on his senses ; his brain grew giddy with the prolonged thunder. Shuddering, he drew the flask from his girdle, and hurled it into the centre of the torrent. As he did so, an icy chill shot through his limbs ; he staggered, shrieked, and fell. The waters closed over his cry. And the moaning of the river rose wildly into the night as it gushed over

THE BLACK STONE.

IV

Poor little Gluck waited very anxiously alone in the house for Hans' return. Finding he did not come back, he was terribly frightened, and went and told Schwartz in the prison all that had happened. Then Schwartz was very much pleased, and said that Hans must certainly have been turned into a black stone, and he should have all the gold to himself. But Gluck was very sorry, and cried all night. When he got up in the morning there was no bread in the house nor any money ; so Gluck went and hired himself to another goldsmith, and he worked so hard and so neatly, and so long every day, that he soon got money enough together to pay his brother's fine, and he went and gave it all to Schwartz, and Schwartz got out of prison. Then Schwartz was quite pleased, and said he should have some of the gold of the river. But Gluck only begged he would go and see what had become of Hans.

Now when Schwartz had heard that Hans had stolen the holy water, he thought to himself that such a proceeding might not be considered altogether correct by the King of the Golden River, and determined to manage matters better. So he took some more of Gluck's money, and went to a bad priest, who gave him some holy water very readily for it. Then Schwartz was sure it was all quite right. So Schwartz got up early in the morning before the sun rose, and took some bread and wine in a basket, and put his holy water in a flask, and set off for the mountains. Like his brother, he was much surprised at the sight of the glacier, and had great difficulty in crossing it, even after leaving his basket behind him. The day was cloudless, but not bright; there was a heavy purple haze hanging over the sky, and the hills looked lowering and gloomy. And as Schwartz climbed the steep rock path the thirst came upon him, as it had upon his brother, until he lifted his flask to his lips to drink. Then he saw the fair child lying near him on the rocks, and it cried to him, and moaned for water.

"Water, indeed!" said Schwartz; "I haven't half enough for myself," and passed on. And as he went he thought the sunbeams grew more dim, and he saw a low bank of black cloud rising out of the West; and, when he had climbed for another hour, the thirst overcame him again, and he would have drunk. Then he saw the old man lying before him on the path, and heard him cry out for water. "Water, indeed!" said Schwartz, "I haven't half enough for myself," and on he went. Then again the light seemed to fade from before his eyes, and he looked up, and, behold, a mist, of the colour of blood, had come over the sun; and the bank of black cloud had risen very high, and its edges were tossing and tumbling like the waves of the angry sea. And they cast long shadows, which flickered over Schwartz's path.

Then Schwartz climbed for another hour, and again his thirst returned; and as he lifted his flask to his lips he thought he saw his brother Hans lying exhausted on the path before him, and, as he gazed, the figure stretched its arms to him and cried for water. "Ha, ha," laughed Schwartz, "are you there? Remember the prison bars, my boy. Water, indeed! do you suppose I carried it all the way up here for *you*?" And he strode over the figure; yet, as he passed, he thought he saw a strange expression of mockery about its lips. And when he had gone a few yards farther he looked back, but the figure was not there.

And a sudden horror came over Schwartz, he knew not why; but the thirst for gold prevailed over his fear, and he rushed on. And the bank of black cloud rose to the zenith, and out of it came bursts of spiry lightning, and waves of darkness seemed to heave and float, between their flashes, over the whole heavens. And the sky where the sun was setting was all level and like a lake of blood; and a strong wind came out of that sky, tearing its crimson clouds into fragments, and scattering them far into the darkness. And when Schwartz stood by the brink of the Golden River its waves were black, like thunderclouds, but their foam was like fire; and the roar of the waters below and the thunder above met as he cast the flask into the stream. And as he did so the lightning glared in his eyes, and the earth gave way beneath him, and the waters closed over his cry. And the moaning of the river rose wildly into the night as it gushed over the

TWO BLACK STONES

V

When Gluck found that Schwartz did not come back he was very sorry, and did not know what to do. He had no money, and was obliged to go and hire himself again to the goldsmith, who worked him very hard and gave him very little money. So, after a month or two, Gluck grew tired, and made up his mind to go and try his fortune with the Golden River. " The little king looked very kind," thought he. " I don't think he will turn me into a black stone." So he went to the priest, and the priest gave him some holy water as soon as he asked for it. Then Gluck took some bread in his basket and the bottle of water, and set off very early for the mountains.

If the glacier had occasioned a great deal of fatigue to his brothers, it was twenty times worse for him, who was neither so strong nor so practised on the mountains. He had several very bad falls, lost his basket and bread, and was very much frightened at the strange noises under the ice. He lay a long time to rest on the grass after he had got over, and began to climb the hill just in the hottest part of the day. When he had climbed for an hour he got dreadfully thirsty, and was going to drink like his brothers, when he saw an old man coming down the path above him, looking very feeble, and leaning on a staff. " My son," said the old man, " I am faint with thirst, give me some of that water." Then Gluck looked at him, and when he saw that he was pale and weary he gave him the water : " Only pray don't drink it all," said Gluck. But the old man drank a great deal, and gave him back the bottle two-thirds empty. Then he bade him good speed, and Gluck went on again merrily. And the path became easier to his feet, and two or three blades of grass appeared upon it, and some grasshoppers began singing on the bank beside it ; and Gluck thought he had never heard such merry singing.

Then he went on for another hour, and the thirst increased on him so that he thought he should be forced to drink. But as he raised the flask he saw a little child lying panting by the roadside, and it cried out piteously for water. Then Gluck struggled with himself, and determined to bear the thirst a little longer ; and he put the bottle to the child's lips, and it drank it all but a few drops. Then it smiled on him, and got up and ran down the hill ; and Gluck looked after it, till it became as small as a little star, and then turned and began climbing again. And then there were all kinds of sweet flowers growing on the rocks, bright green moss, with pale pink starry flowers and soft belled gentians, more blue than the sky at its deepest, and pure white transparent lilies. And crimson and purple butterflies darted hither and thither, and the sky sent down such pure light, that Gluck had never felt so happy in his life.

Yet, when he had climbed for another hour, his thirst became intolerable again; and when he looked at his bottle he saw that there were only five or six drops left in it, and he could not venture to drink. And as he was hanging the flask to his belt again he saw a little dog lying on the rocks, gasping for breath—just as Hans had seen it on the day of his ascent. And Gluck stopped and looked at it, and then at the Golden River, not five hundred yards above him; and he thought of the dwarf's words, "that no one could succeed except in their first attempt"; and he tried to pass the dog, but it whined piteously, and Gluck stopped again. "Poor beastie," said Gluck, "it'll be dead when I come down again if I don't help it." Then he looked closer and closer at it, and its eye turned on him so mournfully that he could not stand it. "Confound the King, and his gold too," said Gluck, and he opened the flask and poured all the water into the dog's mouth. The dog sprang up and stood on its hind legs. Its tail disappeared, its ears became long, longer, silky, golden; its nose became very red, its eyes became very twinkling; in three seconds the dog was gone, and before Gluck stood his old acquaintance, the King of the Golden River.

"Thank you," said the monarch; "but don't be frightened, it's all right," for Gluck showed manifest symptoms of consternation at this unlooked-for reply to his last observation. "Why didn't you come before," continued the dwarf, "instead of sending me those rascally brothers of yours for me to have the trouble of turning into stones? Very hard stones they make too."

"Oh, dear me!" said Gluck, "have you really been so cruel?"

"Cruel!" said the dwarf; "they poured unholy water into my stream: do you suppose I'm going to allow that?"

"Why," said Gluck, "I am sure, sir—your Majesty, I mean—they got the water out of the church font."

"Very probably," replied the dwarf; "but," and his countenance grew stern as he spoke, "the water which has been refused to the cry of the weary and dying is unholy, though it had been blessed by every saint in heaven; and the water which is found in the vessel of mercy is holy, though it had been defiled with corpses."

So saying, the dwarf stooped and plucked a lily that grew at his feet. On its white leaves there hung three drops of clear dew. And the dwarf shook them into the flask which Gluck held in his hand. "Cast these into the river," he said, "and descend on the other side of the mountains into the Treasure Valley. And so good speed."

As he spoke the figure of the dwarf became indistinct. The playing colours of his robe formed themselves into a prismatic mist of dewy light; he stood for an instant veiled with them as with the belt of a broad rainbow. The colours grew faint, the mist rose into the air; the monarch had evaporated.

And Gluck climbed to the brink of the Golden River, and its waves were as clear as crystal and as brilliant as the sun. And when he cast the three drops of dew into the stream there opened where they fell a small circular whirlpool, into which the waters descended with a musical noise. Gluck stood watching it for some time very much disappointed, because not only the river was not turned into gold, but its waters seemed much diminished in quantity. Yet he obeyed his friend the dwarf, and descended the other side of the mountains, towards the Treasure Valley ; and as he went he thought he heard the noise of water working its way under the ground. And when he came in sight of the Treasure Valley, behold, a river, like the Golden River, was springing from a new cleft of the rocks above it, and was flowing in innumerable streams among the dry heaps of red sand. And as Gluck gazed, fresh grass sprang beside the new streams, and creeping plants grew and climbed among the moistening soil. Young flowers opened suddenly along the river-sides, as stars leap out when twilight is deepening, and thickets of myrtle and tendrils of vine cast lengthening shadows over the valley as they grew. And thus the Treasure Valley became a garden again, and the inheritance which had been lost by cruelty was regained by love. And Gluck went and dwelt in the valley, and the poor were never driven from his door, so that his barns became full of corn and his house of treasure. And for him the river had, according to the dwarf's promise, become a River of Gold. And to this day the inhabitants of the valley point out the place where the three drops of holy dew were cast into the stream, and trace the course of the Golden River under the ground, until it emerges in the Treasure Valley. And at the top of the cataract of the Golden River are still to be seen two BLACK STONES, round which the waters howl mournfully every day at sunset, and these stones are still called by the people of the valley

THE BLACK BROTHERS.

WILLIAM WILKIE COLLINS
1824–1889

A TERRIBLY STRANGE BED

SHORTLY after my education at college was finished I happened to be staying at Paris with an English friend. We were both young men then, and lived, I am afraid, rather a wild life in the delightful city of our sojourn. One night we were idling about the neighbourhood of the Palais Royal, doubtful to what amusement we should next betake ourselves. My friend proposed a visit to Frascati's; but his suggestion was not to my taste. I knew Frascati's, as the French saying is, by heart; had lost and won plenty of five-franc pieces there, merely for amusement's sake, until it was amusement no longer, and was thoroughly tired, in fact, of all the ghastly respectabilities of such a social anomaly as a respectable gambling-house. "For Heaven's sake," said I to my friend, "let us go somewhere where we can see a little genuine, blackguard, poverty-stricken gaming, with no false gingerbread glitter thrown over it at all. Let us get away from fashionable Frascati's, to a house where they don't mind letting in a man with a ragged coat, or a man with no coat, ragged or otherwise." "Very well," said my friend, "we needn't go out of the Palais Royal to find the sort of company you want. Here's the place just before us, as blackguard a place, by all report, as you could possibly wish to see." In another minute we arrived at the door and entered the house.

When we got upstairs, and had left our hats and sticks with the doorkeeper, we were admitted into the chief gambling-room. We did not find many people assembled there. But, few as the men were who looked up at us on our entrance, they were all types—lamentably true types—of their respective classes.

We had come to see blackguards; but these men were something worse. There is a comic side, more or less appreciable, in all blackguardism—here there was nothing but tragedy—mute, weird tragedy. The quiet in the room was horrible. The thin, haggard, long-haired young man, whose sunken eyes fiercely watched the turning up of the cards, never spoke; the flabby, fat-faced, pimply player, who pricked his piece of pasteboard perseveringly to register how often black won and how often red—never spoke ; the dirty, wrinkled old man, with the vulture eyes and the darned greatcoat, who had lost his last *sou*, and still looked on desperately after he could play no longer—never spoke. Even the voice of the croupier sounded as if it were strangely dulled and thickened in the atmosphere of the room. I had entered the place to laugh, but the spectacle before me was something to weep over. I soon found it necessary to take refuge in excitement from the depression of spirits which was fast stealing on me. Unfortunately I sought the nearest excitement by going to the table and beginning to play. Still more unfortunately, as the event will show, I won—won prodigiously, won incredibly ; won at such a rate that the regular players at the table crowded round me ; and, staring at my stakes with hungry, superstitious eyes, whispered to one another that the English stranger was going to break the bank.

The game was *Rouge et Noir*. I had played at it in every city in Europe, without, however, the care or the wish to study the Theory of Chances—that philosopher's stone of all gamblers ! And a gambler, in the strict sense of the word, I had never been. I was heart-whole from the corroding passion for play. My gaming was a mere idle amusement. I never resorted to it by necessity, because I never knew what it was to want money. I never practised it so incessantly as to lose more than I could afford, or to gain more than I could coolly pocket without being thrown off my balance by my good luck. In short, I had hitherto frequented gaming-tables—just as I frequented ball-rooms and opera-houses—because they amused me, and because I had nothing better to do with my leisure hours.

But on this occasion it was very different—now, for the first time in my life I felt what the passion for play really was. My success first bewildered, and then, in the most literal meaning of the word, intoxicated me. Incredible as it may appear, it is nevertheless true, that I only lost when I attempted to estimate chances, and played according to previous calculation. If I left everything to luck, and staked without any care or consideration, I was sure to win—to win in the face of every recognised probability in favour of the bank. At first, some of the men present ventured their money safely enough on my colour ; but I speedily increased my stakes to sums which they dared not risk. One after another they left off playing, and breathlessly looked on at my game.

Still, time after time, I staked higher and higher, and still won. The excitement in the room rose to fever pitch. The silence was interrupted by a deep-muttered chorus of oaths and exclamations in different languages every time the gold was shovelled across to my side of the table—even the imperturbable croupier dashed his rake on the floor in a (French) fury of astonishment at my success. But one man present preserved his self-possession, and that man was my friend. He came to my side, and, whispering in English, begged me to leave the place, satisfied with what I had already gained. I must do him the justice to say that he repeated his warnings and entreaties several times, and only left me and went away after I had rejected his advice (I was to all intents and purposes gambling-drunk) in terms which rendered it impossible for him to address me again that night.

Shortly after he had gone a hoarse voice behind me cried, "Permit me, my dear sir!—permit me to restore to their proper place two Napoleons which you have dropped. Wonderful luck, sir! I pledge you my word of honour, as an old soldier, in the course of my long experience in this sort of thing, I never saw such luck as yours! —never! Go on, sir—*Sacré mille bombes!* Go on boldly, and break the bank!"

I turned round and saw, nodding and smiling at me with inveterate civility, a tall man, dressed in a frogged and braided surtout.

If I had been in my senses I should have considered him, personally, as being rather a suspicious specimen of an old soldier. He had goggling blood-shot eyes, mangy mustachios, and a broken nose. His voice betrayed a barrack-room intonation of the worst order, and he had the dirtiest pair of hands I ever saw—even in France. These little personal peculiarities exercised, however, no repelling influence on me. In the mad excitement, the reckless triumph of that moment, I was ready to "fraternise" with anybody who encouraged me in my game. I accepted the old soldier's offered pinch of snuff, clapped him on the back, and swore he was the honestest fellow in the world, the most glorious relic of the Grand Army that I had ever met with. "Go on!" cried my military friend, snapping his fingers in ecstasy. "Go on, and win! Break the bank—*Mille tonnerres!* my gallant English comrade, break the bank!"

And I *did* go on—went on at such a rate, that in another quarter of an hour the croupier called out, "Gentlemen! the bank has discontinued for to-night." All the notes and all the gold in that "bank" now lay in a heap under my hands; the whole floating capital of the gambling-house was waiting to pour into my pockets!

"Tie up the money in your pocket-handkerchief, my worthy sir," said the old soldier, as I wildly plunged my hands into my heap of gold. "Tie it up, as we used to tie up a bit of dinner in the Grand Army; your winnings are too heavy for any breeches pockets that ever were sewed. There? that's it! Shovel them in, notes and all! *Crediè!* what luck!—Stop! another Napoleon on the floor! *Ah! sacré petit polisson de Napoleon!* have I found thee at last?

Now then, sir—two tight double knots each way with your honourable permission, and the money's safe. Feel it! feel it, fortunate sir! hard and round as a cannon ball—*Ah, bah!* if they had only fired such cannon balls at us at Austerlitz—*nom d'une pipe!* if they only had! And now, as an ancient grenadier, as an ex-brave of the French army, what remains for me to do? I ask what? Simply this: to entreat my valued English friend to drink a bottle of champagne with me, and toast the goddess Fortune in foaming goblets before we part!"

Excellent ex-brave! Convivial ancient grenadier! Champagne by all means! An English cheer for an old soldier! Hurrah! hurrah! Another English cheer for the goddess Fortune! Hurrah! hurrah! hurrah!

"Bravo! the Englishman; the amiable, gracious Englishman, in whose veins circulates the vivacious blood of France! Another glass? *Ah, bah!*—the bottle is empty! Never mind! *Vive le vin!* I, the old soldier, order another bottle—and half a pound of *bon-bons* with it!"

"No, no, ex-brave; never—ancient grenadier! *Your* bottle last time, *my* bottle this. Behold it! Toast away! The French Army!—the great Napoleon!—the present company! the croupier! the honest croupier's wife and daughters—if he has any! the ladies generally! Everybody in the world!"

By this time the second bottle of champagne was emptied. I felt as if I had been drinking liquid fire—my brain seemed all aflame. No excess in wine had ever had this effect on me before in my life. Was it the result of a stimulant acting upon my system when I was in a highly excited state? Was my stomach in a particularly disordered condition? Or was the champagne amazingly strong?

"Ex-brave of the French Army!" cried I, in a mad state of exhilaration, "*I* am on fire! how are *you*? You have set me on fire! Do you hear, my hero of Austerlitz? Let us have a third bottle of champagne to put the flame out!"

The old soldier wagged his head, rolled his goggle eyes, until I expected to see them slip out of their sockets; placed his dirty forefinger by the side of his broken nose, solemnly ejaculated, "Coffee!" and immediately ran off into an inner room.

The word pronounced by the eccentric veteran seemed to have a magical effect on the rest of the company present. With one accord they all rose to depart. Probably they had expected to profit by my intoxication; but finding that my new friend was benevolently bent on preventing me from getting dead drunk, had now abandoned all hope of thriving pleasantly on my winnings. Whatever their motive might be, at any rate they went away in a body. When the old soldier returned and sat down again opposite to me at the table, we had the room to ourselves. I could see the croupier, in a sort of vestibule which opened out of it, eating his supper in solitude. The silence was now deeper than ever.

A sudden change, too, had come over the "ex-brave." He assumed a portentously solemn look, and when he spoke to me again his speech was ornamented by no oaths, enforced by no finger-snapping, enlivened by no apostrophes or exclamations.

"Listen, my dear sir," said he, in mysteriously confidential tones, —"listen to an old soldier's advice. I have been to the mistress of the house (a very charming woman, with a genius for cookery!) to impress on her the necessity of making us some particularly strong and good coffee. You must drink this coffee in order to get rid of your little amiable exaltation of spirits before you think of going home—you *must*, my good and gracious friend! With all that money to take home to-night, it is a sacred duty to yourself to have your wits about you. You are known to be a winner to an enormous extent by several gentlemen present to-night, who, in a certain point of view, are very worthy and excellent fellows; but they are mortal men, my dear sir, and they have their amiable weaknesses! Need I say more? Ah, no, no! you understand me! Now, this is what you must do. Send for a cabriolet when you feel quite well again, draw up all the windows when you get into it, and tell the driver to take you home only through the large and well-lighted thoroughfares. Do this, and you and your money will be safe. Do this, and to-morrow you will thank an old soldier for giving you a word of honest advice."

Just as the ex-brave ended his oration in very lachrymose tones, the coffee came in, ready poured out in two cups. My attentive friend handed me one of the cups with a bow. I was parched with thirst, and drank it off at a draught. Almost instantly afterwards I was seized with a fit of giddiness, and felt more completely intoxicated than ever. The room whirled round and round furiously; the old soldier seemed to be regularly bobbing up and down before me like the piston of a steam-engine. I was half deafened by a violent singing in my ears; a feeling of utter bewilderment, helplessness, idiocy overcame me. I rose from my chair, holding on by the table to keep my balance, and stammered out that I felt dreadfully unwell, so unwell that I did not know how I was to get home.

"My dear friend," answered the old soldier—and even his voice seemed to be bobbing up and down as he spoke—"my dear friend, it would be madness to go home in *your* state; you would be sure to lose your money; you might be robbed and murdered with the greatest ease. *I* am going to sleep here: do *you* sleep here, too—they make up capital beds in this house—take one; sleep off the effects of the wine, and go home safely with your winnings to-morrow—to-morrow, in broad daylight."

I had but two ideas left: one, that I must never let go hold of my handkerchief full of money; the other, that I must lie down somewhere immediately and fall off into a comfortable sleep. So I agreed to the proposal about the bed, and took the offered arm of the old soldier, carrying my money with my disengaged hand. Preceded by the croupier, we passed along some passages and up a flight of stairs into the bedroom which I was to occupy. The ex-brave shook me warmly by the hand, proposed that we should breakfast together, and then, followed by the croupier, left me for the night.

I ran to the wash-hand stand, drank some of the water in my jug, poured the rest out, and plunged my face into it, then sat down in a chair and tried to compose myself. I soon felt better. The change for my lungs from the fetid atmosphere of the gambling-room to the cool air of the apartment I now occupied; the almost equally refreshing change for my eyes from the glaring gas-lights of the "Salon" to the dim, quiet flicker of one bedroom candle, aided wonderfully the restorative effects of cold water. The giddiness left me, and I began to feel a little like a reasonable being again. My first thought was of the risk of sleeping all night in a gambling-house; my second, of the still greater risk of trying to get out after the house was closed, and of going home alone at night, through the streets of Paris, with a large sum of money about me. I had slept in worse places than this on my travels; so I determined to lock, bolt, and barricade my door and take my chance till the next morning.

Accordingly, I secured myself against all intrusion, looked under the bed and into the cupboard, tried the fastening of the window, and then, satisfied that I had taken every proper precaution, pulled off my upper clothing, put my light, which was a dim one, on the hearth among a feathery litter of wood ashes, and got into bed, with the handkerchief full of money under my pillow.

I soon felt not only that I could not go to sleep, but that I could not even close my eyes. I was wide awake, and in a high fever. Every nerve in my body trembled—every one of my senses seemed to be preternaturally sharpened. I tossed and rolled, and tried every kind of position, and perseveringly sought out the old corners of the bed, and all to no purpose. Now, I thrust my arms over the clothes; now, I poked them under the clothes; now, I violently shot my legs straight out down to the bottom of the bed; now, I convulsively coiled them up as near my chin as they would go; now, I shook out my crumpled pillow, changed it to the cool side, patted it flat, and lay down quietly on my back; now, I fiercely doubled it in two, set it up on end, thrust it against the board of the bed, and tried a sitting posture. Every effort was in vain; I groaned with vexation, as I felt that I was in for a sleepless night.

What could I do? I had no book to read. And yet, unless I found out some method of diverting my mind, I felt certain that I was in the condition to imagine all sorts of horrors; to rack my brain with forebodings of every possible and impossible danger; in short, to pass the night in suffering all conceivable varieties of nervous terror.

I raised myself on my elbow, and looked about the room, which was brightened by a lovely moonlight pouring straight through the window—to see if it contained any pictures or ornaments that I could at all clearly distinguish. While my eyes wandered from wall to wall, a remembrance of Le Maistre's delightful little book, *Voyage autour de ma Chambre*, occurred to me. I resolved to imitate the French author, and find occupation and amusement enough to relieve the tedium of my wakefulness by making a mental inventory of every article of furniture I could see, and by following up to their sources the multitude of associations which even a chair, a table, or a wash-hand stand may be made to call forth.

In the nervous unsettled state of my mind at that moment I found it much easier to make my inventory than to make my reflections, and thereupon soon gave up all hope of thinking in Le Maistre's fanciful track—or, indeed, of thinking at all. I looked about the room at the different articles of furniture, and did nothing more.

There was, first, the bed I was lying in; a four-post bed, of all things in the world to meet with in Paris!—yes, a thorough clumsy British four-poster, with the regular top lined with chintz—the regular fringed valance all round—the regular stifling unwholesome curtains, which I remembered having mechanically drawn back against the posts without particularly noticing the bed when I first got into the room. Then there was the marble-topped wash-hand stand, from which the water I had spilt, in my hurry to pour it out, was still dripping, slowly and more slowly, on to the brick floor. Then two small chairs, with my coat, waistcoat, and trousers flung on them. Then a large elbow-chair covered with dirty-white dimity, with my cravat and shirt-collar thrown over the back. Then a chest of drawers with two of the brass handles off, and a tawdry, broken china inkstand placed on it by way of ornament for the top. Then the dressing-table, adorned by a very small looking-glass, and a very large pincushion. Then the window—an unusually large window. Then a dark old picture, which the feeble candle dimly showed me. It was the picture of a fellow in a high Spanish hat, crowned with a plume of towering feathers. A swarthy, sinister ruffian, looking upward, shading his eyes with his hand, and looking intently upward—it might be at some tall gallows at which he was going to be hanged. At any rate, he had the appearance of thoroughly deserving it.

This picture put a kind of constraint upon me to look upward too—at the top of the bed. It was a gloomy and not an interesting object, and I looked back at the picture. I counted the feathers in the man's hat—they stood out in relief—three white, two green. I observed the crown of his hat, which was of a conical shape, according to the fashion supposed to have been favoured by Guido Fawkes. I wondered what he was looking up at. It couldn't be at the stars; such a desperado was neither astrologer nor astronomer. It must be at the high gallows, and he was going to be hanged presently. Would the executioner come into possession of his conical-crowned hat and plume of feathers? I counted the feathers again—three white, two green.

While I still lingered over this very improving and intellectual employment, my thoughts insensibly began to wander. The moonlight shining into the room reminded me of a certain moonlight night in England—the night after a picnic party in a Welsh valley. Every incident of the drive homeward, through lovely scenery, which the moonlight made lovelier than ever, came back to my remembrance, though I had never given the picnic a thought for years; though, if I had *tried* to recollect it, I could certainly have recalled little or nothing of that scene long past. Of all the wonderful faculties that help to tell us we are immortal, which speaks the sublime truth more eloquently than memory? Here was I, in a strange house of the most suspicious character, in a situation of uncertainty and even of peril, which might seem to make the cool exercise of my recollection almost out of the question; nevertheless, remembering, quite involuntarily, places, people, conversations minute circumstances of every kind, which I had thought forgotten for ever, which I could not possibly have recalled at will, even under the most favourable auspices. And what cause had produced in a moment the whole of this strange, complicated, mysterious effect? Nothing but some rays of moonlight shining in at my bedroom window. I was still thinking of the picnic—of our merriment on the drive home—of the sentimental young lady who *would* quote *Childe Harold* because it was moonlight. I was absorbed by these past scenes and past amusements, when, in an instant, the thread on which my memories hung snapped asunder: my attention immediately came back to present things more vividly than ever, and I found myself, I neither knew why nor wherefore, looking hard at the picture again.

Looking for what?

Good God! the man had pulled his hat down on his brows!—No!—the hat itself was gone! Where was the conical crown?

Where the feathers—three white, two green ? Not there ! In place of the hat and feathers, what dusky object was it that now hid his forehead, his eyes, his shading hand ?

Was the bed moving ?

I turned on my back and looked up. Was I mad ? drunk ? dreaming ? giddy again ? or was the top of the bed really moving down—sinking slowly, regularly, silently, horribly right down throughout the whole of its length and breadth—right down upon me as I lay underneath ?

My blood seemed to stand still. A deadly paralysing coldness stole all over me as I turned my head round on the pillow and determined to test whether the bed-top was really moving or not by keeping my eye on the man in the picture.

The next look in that direction was enough. The dull, black, frowsy outline of the valance above me was within an inch of being parallel with his waist. I still looked breathlessly. And steadily, and slowly—very slowly—I saw the figure, and the line of frame below the figure, vanish as the valance moved down before it.

I am, constitutionally, anything but timid. I have been on more than one occasion in peril of my life, and have not lost my self-possession for an instant ; but when the conviction first settled on my mind that the bed-top was really moving, was steadily and continuously sinking down upon me, I looked up shuddering, helpless, panic-stricken, beneath the hideous machinery for murder, which was advancing closer and closer to suffocate me where I lay.

I looked up, motionless, speechless, breathless. The candle, fully spent, went out ; but the moonlight still brightened the room. Down and down, without pausing and without sounding, came the bed-top, and still my panic-terror seemed to bind me faster and faster to the mattress on which I lay—down and down it sank, till the dusty odour from the lining of the canopy came stealing into my nostrils.

At that final moment the instinct of self-preservation startled me out of my trance and I moved at last. There was just room for me to roll myself sideways off the bed. As I dropped noiselessly to the floor the edge of the murderous canopy touched me on the shoulder.

Without stopping to draw my breath, without wiping the cold sweat from my face, I rose instantly on my knees to watch the bed-top. I was literally spell-bound by it. If I had heard footsteps behind me, I could not have turned round ; if a means of escape had been miraculously provided for me, I could not have moved to take advantage of it. The whole life in me was, at that moment, concentrated in my eyes.

It descended—the whole canopy, with the fringe round it, came down—down—close down, so close that there was not room now to squeeze my finger between the bed-top and the bed. I felt at the sides, and discovered that what had appeared to me from beneath to be the ordinary light canopy of a four-post bed was in reality a thick, broad mattress, the substance of which was concealed by the valance and its fringe. I looked up and saw the four posts rising hideously bare. In the middle of the bed-top was a huge wooden screw that had evidently worked it down through a hole in the ceiling, just as ordinary presses are worked down on the substance selected for compression. The frightful apparatus moved without making the faintest noise. There had been no creaking as it came down; there was now not the faintest sound from the room above. Amid a dead and awful silence I beheld before me—in the nineteenth century, and in the civilised capital of France—such a machine for secret murder by suffocation as might have existed in the worst days of the Inquisition, in the lonely inns among the Hartz Mountains, in the mysterious tribunals of Westphalia! Still, as I looked on it I could not move, I could hardly breathe, but I began to recover the power of thinking, and in a moment I discovered the murderous conspiracy framed against me in all its horror. My cup of coffee had been drugged, and drugged too strongly. I had been saved from being smothered by having taken an overdose of some narcotic. How I had chafed and fretted at the fever-fit which had preserved my life by keeping me awake! How recklessly I had confided myself to the two wretches who had led me into this room, determined, for the sake of my winnings, to kill me in my sleep by the surest and most horrible contrivance for secretly accomplishing my destruction! How many men, winners like me, had slept, as I had proposed to sleep, in that bed and had never been seen or heard of more! I shuddered at the bare idea of it.

But ere long all thought was again suspended by the sight of the murderous canopy moving once more. After it had remained on the bed—as nearly as I could guess—about ten minutes, it began to move up again. The villains who worked it from above evidently believed that their purpose was now accomplished. Slowly and silently, as it had descended, that horrible bed-top rose towards its former place. When it reached the upper extremities of the four posts, it reached the ceiling too. Neither hole nor screw could be seen; the bed became in appearance an ordinary bed again—the canopy an ordinary canopy—even to the most suspicious eyes.

Now, for the first time, I was able to move—to rise from my knees—to dress myself in my upper clothing—and to consider of how I should escape. If I betrayed, by the smallest noise, that the attempt to suffocate me had failed, I was certain to be murdered. Had I made any noise already? I listened intently, looking towards the door.

No! no footsteps in the passage outside—no sound of a tread, light or heavy, in the room above—absolute silence everywhere. Besides locking and bolting my door I had moved an old wooden chest against it, which I had found under the bed. To remove this chest (my blood ran cold as I thought of what its contents *might* be!) without making some disturbance was impossible; and, moreover, to think of escaping through the house, now barred up for the night, was sheer insanity. Only one chance was left me—the window. I stole to it on tiptoe.

My bedroom was on the first floor, above an *entresol*, and looked into the back street. I raised my hand to open the window, knowing that on that action hung, by the merest hair's-breadth, my chance of safety. They keep vigilant watch in a House of Murder. If any part of the frame cracked, if the hinge creaked, I was a lost man! It must have occupied me at least five minutes, reckoning by time—five *hours*, reckoning by suspense—to open that window. I succeeded in doing it silently—in doing it with all the dexterity of a housebreaker—and then looked down into the street. To leap the distance beneath me would be almost certain destruction! Next, I looked round at the sides of the house. Down the left side ran the thick water-pipe—it passed close by the outer edge of the window. The moment I saw the pipe I knew I was saved. My breath came and went freely for the first time since I had seen the canopy of the bed moving down upon me!

To some men the means of escape which I had discovered might have seemed difficult and dangerous enough—to *me* the prospect of slipping down the pipe into the street did not suggest even a thought of peril. I had always been accustomed, by the practice of gymnastics, to keep up my school-boy powers as a daring and expert climber, and knew that my head, hands, and feet would serve me faithfully in any hazards of ascent or descent. I had already got one leg over the window-sill when I remembered the handkerchief filled with money under my pillow. I could well have afforded to leave it behind me, but I was revengefully determined that the miscreants of the gambling-house should miss their plunder as well as their victim. So I went back to the bed and tied the heavy handkerchief at my back by my cravat. Just as I had made it tight and fixed it in a comfortable place, I thought I heard a sound of breathing outside the door. The chill feeling of horror ran through me again as I listened. No! dead silence still in the passage—I had only heard the night-air blowing softly into the room. The next moment I was on the window-sill—and the next I had a firm grip on the water-pipe with my hands and knees.

I slid down into the street easily and quietly, as I thought I should, and immediately set off at the top of my speed to a branch "Prefecture" of Police, which I knew was situated in the immediate neighbourhood. A " Sub-prefect " and several picked men among his subordinates happened to be up, maturing, I believe, some scheme for discovering the perpetrator of a mysterious murder which all Paris was talking of just then. When I began my story, in a breathless hurry and in very bad French, I could see that the Sub-prefect suspected me of being a drunken Englishman who had robbed somebody ; but he soon altered his opinion as I went on, and before I had anything like concluded, he shoved all the papers before him into a drawer, put on his hat, supplied me with another (for I was bare-headed), ordered a file of soldiers, desired his expert followers to get ready all sorts of tools for breaking open doors and ripping up brick-flooring, and took my arm in the most friendly and familiar manner possible to lead me with him out of the house. I will venture to say that when the Sub-prefect was a little boy, and was taken for the first time to the play, he was not half as much pleased as he was now at the job in prospect for him at the gambling-house !

Away we went through the streets, the Sub-prefect cross-examining and congratulating me in the same breath as we marched at the head of our formidable *posse comitatus*. Sentinels were placed at the back and front of the house the moment we got to it ; a tremendous battery of knocks was directed against the door ; a light appeared at a window ; I was told to conceal myself behind the police—then came more knocks, and a cry of " Open in the name of the law ! " At that terrible summons bolts and locks gave way before an invisible hand, and the moment after the Sub-prefect was in the passage, confronting a waiter half-dressed and ghastly pale. This was the short dialogue which immediately took place :

" We want to see the Englishman who is sleeping in this house."

" He went away hours ago."

" He did no such thing. His friend went away ; *he* remained. Show us to his bedroom ! "

" I swear to you, Monsieur le Sous-prefect, he is not here ! he——"

" I swear to you, Monsieur le Garçon, he is. He slept here—he didn't find your bed comfortable—he came to us to complain of it—here he is among my men—and here am I ready to look for a flea or two in his bedstead. Renaudin ! (calling to one of the subordinates and pointing to the waiter) collar that man and tie his hands behind him. Now, then, gentlemen, let us walk upstairs ! "

Every man and woman in the house was secured—the " Old Soldier " the first. Then I identified the bed in which I had slept, and then we went into the room above.

No object that was at all extraordinary appeared in any part of it. The Sub-prefect looked round the place, commanded everybody to be silent, stamped twice on the floor, called for a candle, looked attentively at the spot he had stamped on, and ordered the flooring there to be carefully taken up. This was done in no time. Lights were produced, and we saw a deep raftered cavity between the floor of this room and the ceiling of the room beneath. Through this cavity there ran perpendicularly a sort of case of iron thickly greased, and inside the case appeared the screw which communicated with the bed-top below. Extra lengths of screw, freshly oiled; levers covered with felt; all the complete upper works of a heavy press—constructed with infernal ingenuity so as to join the fixtures below, and when taken to pieces again to go into the smallest possible compass—were next discovered and pulled out on the floor. After some little difficulty the Sub-prefect succeeded in putting the machinery together, and, leaving his men to work it, descended with me to the bedroom. The smothering canopy was then lowered, but not so noiselessly as I had seen it lowered. When I mentioned this to the Sub-prefect, his answer, simple as it was, had a terrible significance. "My men," said he, "are working down the bed-top for the first time—the men whose money you won were in better practice."

We left the house in the sole possession of two police agents—every one of the inmates being removed to prison on the spot. The Sub-prefect, after taking down my "*procès-verbal*" in his office, returned with me to my hotel to get my passport. "Do you think," I asked as I gave it to him, "that any men have really been smothered in that bed as they tried to smother *me*?"

"I have seen dozens of drowned men laid out at the Morgue," answered the Sub-prefect, "in whose pocket-books were found letters stating that they had committed suicide in the Seine, because they had lost everything at the gaming-table. Do I know how many of those men entered the same gambling-house that *you* entered? won as *you* won? took that bed as *you* took it? slept in it? were smothered in it? and were privately thrown into the river with a letter of explanation written by the murderers and placed in their pocket-books? No man can say how many or how few have suffered the fate from which you have escaped. The people of the gambling-house kept their bedstead machinery a secret from *us*—even from the police! The dead kept the rest of the secret for them. Good-night, or rather good-morning, Monsieur Faulkner! Be at my office again at nine o'clock—in the meantime, *au revoir*!"

The rest of my story is soon told. I was examined and re-examined; the gambling-house was strictly searched all through from top to bottom; the prisoners were separately interrogated, and two of the less guilty among them made a confession. *I* discovered that the Old Soldier was the master of the gambling-house—*justice* discovered that he had been drummed out of the army as a vagabond years ago; that he had been guilty of all sorts of villainies since;

that he was in possession of stolen property, which the owners identified; and that he, the croupier, another accomplice, and the woman who had made my cup of coffee were all in the secret of the bedstead. There appeared some reason to doubt whether the inferior persons attached to the house knew anything of the suffocating machinery, and they received the benefit of that doubt by being treated simply as thieves and vagabonds. As for the Old Soldier and his two head-myrmidons, they went to the galleys; the woman who had drugged my coffee was imprisoned for I forget how many years; the regular attendants at the gambling-house were considered "suspicious" and placed under "surveillance"; and I became, for one whole week (which is a long time), the head "lion" in Parisian society. My adventure was dramatised by three illustrious playmakers, but never saw theatrical daylight, for the censorship forbade the introduction on the stage of a correct copy of the gambling-house bedstead.

One good result was produced by my adventure which any censorship must have approved: it cured me of ever again trying *Rouge et Noir* as an amusement. The sight of a green cloth, with packs of cards and heaps of money on it, will henceforth be for ever associated in my mind with the sight of a bed-canopy descending to suffocate me in the silence and darkness of the night.

CHARLES ALLSTON COLLINS
1828–1873

THE TÊTE NOIRE

It happened that at one period of my life the path of my destiny lay along the highways and byways of France, and that I had occasion to make frequent stoppages at common French roadside cabarets—that kind of tavern which has a very bad name in French books and French plays. I had engaged myself in an undertaking which rendered such journeys necessary. A very old friend of mine had recently established himself at Paris in a wholesale commercial enterprise, into the nature of which it is not necessary for our present purpose to enter. He had proposed to me a certain share in the undertaking, and one of the duties of my post was to involve occasional journeys among the smaller towns and villages of France with the view of establishing agencies and opening connections. My friend had applied to me to undertake this function rather than to a native, feeling that he could trust me better than a stranger. He knew also that, in consequence of my having been half my life at school in France, my knowledge of the language would be sufficient for every purpose that could be required.

I accepted my friend's proposal, and entered with such energy as I could command upon my new mode of life. Sometimes my journeyings from place to place were accomplished by means of the railroad or other public conveyance ; but there were other occasions, and these I liked the best, when it was necessary I should go to out-of-the-way places, and by such cross-roads as rendered it more convenient for me to travel with a carriage and horse of my own. My carriage was a kind of phaeton without a coach-box, with a leather hood that would put up and down ; and there was plenty of room at the back for such specimens or samples of goods as it was necessary that I should carry with me. For my horse—it was absolutely indispensable that it should be an animal of some value, as no horse but a very good one would be capable of performing the long courses day after day which my mode of travelling rendered necessary. It cost me two thousand francs, and was anything but dear at the price.

Many were the journeys we performed together over the broad acres of beautiful France. Many were the hotels, many the *auberges*, many the bad dinners, many the damp beds, and many the fleas which I encountered *en route*. Many were the dull old fortified towns over whose drawbridges I rolled ; many the still more dull old towns without fortifications and without drawbridges, at which my avocations made it necessary for me to halt.

I don't know how it was that on the morning when I was to start from the town of Doulaise, with the intention of sleeping at Francy-le-Grand, I was an hour later in commencing my journey than I ought to have been. I have said I don't know how it was, but this is scarcely true. I do know how it was. It was because on that morning, to use a popular expression, everything went wrong. So it was an hour later than it ought to have been, gentlemen, when I drew up the sheep-skin lining of my carriage apron over my legs, and establishing my little dog comfortably on the seat beside me, set off on my journey. In all my expeditions I was accompanied by a favourite terrier of mine, which I had brought with me from England. I never travelled without her, and found her a companion.

It was a miserable day in the month of October. A perfectly grey sky, with white gleams about the horizon, gave unmistakable evidence that the small drizzle which was falling would continue for four-and-twenty hours at least. It was cold and cheerless weather, and on the deserted road I was pursuing there was scarcely a human being (unless it was an occasional cantonnier, or road-mender) to break the solitude. A deserted way indeed, with poplars on each side of it, which had turned yellow in the autumn, and had shed their leaves in abundance all across the road, so that my mare's footsteps had quite a muffled sound as she trampled them under her hoofs. Widely extending flats spread out on either side till the view was lost in an inconceivably melancholy scene, and the road itself was so perfectly straight that you could see something like ten miles of it diminishing to a point in front of you, while a similar view was visible through the little window at the back of the carriage.

In the hurry of the morning's departure I had omitted to inquire, as I generally did in travelling an unknown road, at what village it would be best for me to stop, about noon, to bait, and what was the name of the most respectable house of public entertainment in my way ; so that when I arrived between twelve and one o'clock at a certain place where four roads met, and when at one of the corners formed by their union I saw a great bare-looking inn, with the sign of the Tête Noire swinging in front, I had nothing for it but to put up there, without knowing anything of the character of the house.

The look of the place did not please me. It was a great bare uninhabited-looking house, which seemed much larger than was necessary, and presented a black and dirty appearance, which, considering the distance from any town, it was difficult to account for. All the doors and all the windows were shut, there was no sign of any living creature about the place, and niched into the wall above the principal entrance was a grim and ghastly looking life-size figure of a Saint. For a moment I hesitated whether I should turn into the open gates of the stable-yard or go farther in search of some more attractive halting-place. But my mare was tired, I was more than half-way on my road, and this would be the best division of the journey. Besides, gentlemen, why *not* put up here? If I was only going to stop at such places of entertainment as completely satisfied me, externally as well as internally, I had better give up travelling altogether.

There were no more signs of life in the interior of the yard than were presented by the external aspect of the house, as it fronted the road. Everything seemed shut up. All the stables and outhouses were characterised by closed doors, without so much as a straw clinging to their thresholds to indicate that these buildings were sometimes put to a practical use. I saw no manure strewed about the place, and no living creature: no pigs, no ducks, no fowls. It was perfectly still and quiet, and, as it was one of those days when a fine small rain descends quite straight, without a breath of air to drive it one way or other, the silence was complete and distressing. I gave a loud shout, and began undoing the harness while my summons was taking effect.

The first person whom the sound of my voice appeared to have reached was a small but precocious boy, who opened a door in the back of the house, and, descending the flight of steps which led to it, approached to aid me in my task. I was just undoing the final buckle on my side of the harness when, happening to turn round, I discovered, standing close behind me, a personage who had approached so quietly that it would have been a confusing thing to find him so near even if there had been nothing in his appearance which was calculated to startle one. He was the most ill-looking man, gentlemen, that it was ever my fortune to behold. Nearer fifty than any other age I could give him, his dry spare nature had kept him as light and active as a restless boy. An absence of flesh, however, was not the only want I felt to exist in the personal appearance of the landlord of the Tête Noire. There was a much more serious defect in him than this—a want of any hint of mercy, or conscience, or any accessible approach to the better side (if there was a better side) of the man's nature. When first I looked at his eyes, as he stood behind me in the open court, and as they rapidly glanced over the comely points of my horse, and thence to the packages inside my carriage and the portmanteau strapped on in front of it—at that time, the colour of his eyes appeared to me to be of an almost orange tinge; but when, a minute afterwards, we stood together in the dark stable, I noted that a kind of blue phosphorescence gleamed upon their surface, veiling their real hue, and imparting to them a tigerish lustre. The moment when I remarked this, by the by, was when the organs I have been describing were fixed upon the very large gold ring which I had not ceased to wear when I adopted my adventurous life, and which you may see upon my finger now. There were two other things about this man that struck me. These were, a bald red projecting lump of flesh at the back of his head, and a deep scar, which a scrap of frouzy whisker on his cheek wholly declined to conceal.

"A nasty day for a journey of pleasure," said the landlord, looking at me with a satirical smile.

"Perhaps it is *not* a journey of pleasure," I answered dryly.

"We have few such travellers on the road now," said the evil-faced man. "The railroads make the country a desert, and the roads are as wild as they were three hundred years ago."

"They are well enough," I answered carelessly, "for those who are obliged to travel by them. Nobody else, I should think, would be likely to make use of them."

"Will you come into the house?" said the landlord abruptly, looking me full in the face.

I never felt a stronger repugnance than I entertained towards the idea of entering this man's doors. Yet what other course was open to me? My mare was already half through the first instalment of her oats, so there was no more excuse for remaining in the stable. To take a walk in the drenching rain was out of the question, and to remain sitting in my *calèche* would have been a worse indication of suspicion and mistrust. Besides, I had had nothing since the morning's coffee, and I wanted something to eat and drink. There was nothing to be done, then, but to accept my ill-looking friend's offer. He led the way up the flight of steps which gave access to the interior of the building.

The room in which I found myself on passing through the door at the top of these steps was one of those rooms which an excess of light not only fails to enliven, but seems even to invest with an additional degree of gloom. There is *sometimes* this character about light, and I have seen before now a workhouse ward, and a barren school-room, which have owed a good share of their melancholy to an immoderate amount of cold grey daylight. This room, then, into which I was shown, was one of those which, on a wet day, seemed several degrees lighter than the open air. Of course it could not be really lighter than the thing that lit it, but it seemed so. It also appeared larger than the whole outdoor world; and this, certainly, could not be either, but seemed so. Vast as it was, there appeared through two glass doors in one of the walls another apartment of similar dimensions. It was not a square room, nor an oblong room, but was smaller at one end than at the other: a phenomenon which, as you have very likely observed, gentlemen, has always an unpleasant effect. The billiard-table, which stood in the middle of the apartment, though really of the usual size, looked quite a trifling piece of furniture; and as to the other tables, which were planted sparingly here and there for purposes of refreshment, they were quite lost in the immensity of space about them. A cupboard, a rack of billiard cues, a marking-board, and a print of the murder of the Archbishop of Paris in a black frame, alone broke the uniformity of wall. The ceiling, as far as one could judge of anything at that altitude, appeared to be traversed by an enormous beam with rings fastened into it adapted for suicidal purposes, and splashed with the whitewash with which the ceiling itself and the walls had just been decorated. Even my little terrier, whom I had been obliged to take up in my arms on account of the disposition she had manifested to fly at the shins of our detested landlord, looked round the room with a gaze of horror as I set her down, and trembled and shivered as if she would come out of her skin.

"And so you don't like him, Nelly, and your little beads of eyes, that look up at me from under that hairy penthouse, with nothing but love in them, are all ablaze with fury when they are turned upon his sinister face? And how did he get that scar, Nelly? Did he get it when he slaughtered his last traveller? And what do you think of his eyes, Nelly? And what do you think of the back of his head, my dog? What do you think he's about now, eh? What mischief do you think he's hatching? Don't you wish you were sitting by my side in the *calèche*, and that we were out on the free road again?"

To all these questions and remarks my little companion responded very intelligibly by faint thumpings of the ground with her tail, and by certain flutterings of her ears, which, from long habits of intercourse, I understood very well to mean that whatever my opinion might be, she coincided in it.

I had ordered an omelette and some wine when I first entered the house, and, as I now sat waiting for it, I observed that my landlord would every now and then leave what he was about in the other room—where I concluded that he was engaged preparing my meal—and would come and peer at me furtively through the glass doors which connected the room I was in with that in which he was. Once, too, I heard him go out, and I felt sure that he had retired to the stables to examine more minutely the value of my horse and carriage.

I took it into my head that my landlord was a desperate rogue; that his business was not sufficient to support him; that he had remarked that I was in possession of a very valuable horse, a carriage which would fetch something, and a quantity of luggage in which there were probably articles of price. I had other things of worth about my person, including a sum of money, without which I could not be travelling about, as he saw me, from place to place.

While my mind was amusing itself with these cheerful reflections, a little girl of about twelve years old entered the room through the glass doors, and, after honouring me with a long stare, went to the cupboard at the other end of the apartment, and, opening it with a bunch of keys which she brought with her in her hand, took out a small white paper packet about four inches square, and retired with it by the way by which she had entered, still staring at me so diligently that, from want of proper attention to where she was going, she got (I am happy to state) a severe bump against the door as she passed through it. She was a horrid little girl this, with eyes that, in shirking the necessity of looking straight at anybody or anything, had got at last to look only at her nose—finding it, probably, as bad a nose as could be met with, and therefore a congenial companion. She had, moreover, frizzy and fluey hair, was excessively dirty, and had a slow crab-like way of going along without looking at what she was about, which was very noisome and detestable.

It was not long before this young lady reappeared, bearing in her hand a plate containing the omelette, which she placed upon the table without going through the previous form of laying a cloth. She next cut an immense piece of bread from a loaf shaped like a ring, and having clapped this also down upon the dirtiest part of the table, and having further favoured me with a wiped knife and fork, disappeared once more. She disappeared to fetch the wine. When this had been brought, and some water, the preparations for my feast were considered complete, and I was left to enjoy it alone.

I must not omit to mention that the horrid waiting-maid appeared to excite as strong an antipathy in the breast of my little dog as that which my landlord himself had stirred up; and, I am happy to say, that as the child left the room I was obliged to interfere to prevent Nelly from harassing her retreating calves.

Gentlemen, an experienced traveller soon learns that he must eat to support nature, closing his eyes, nose, and ears to all suggestions. I set to work, then, at the omelette with energy, and at the tough sour bread with good will, and had swallowed half a tumbler of wine and water when a thought suddenly occurred to me which caused me to set the glass down upon the table. I had no sooner done this than I raised it again to my lips, took a fresh sip, rolled the liquid about in my mouth two or three times, and spat it out upon the floor. But I uttered, as I did so, in an audible tone, the monosyllable " Pooh ! "

" Pooh ! Nelly," I said, looking down at my dog, who was watching me intensely with her head on one side—" pooh ! Nelly," I repeated, " what frantic and inconceivable nonsense ! "

And what was it that I thus stigmatised ? What was it that had given me pause in the middle of my draught ? What thought was it that caused me to set down my glass with half its contents remaining in it ? It was a suspicion, driven straight and swift as an arrow into the innermost recesses of my soul, that the wine I had just been drinking, and which, contrary to my custom, I had mingled with water, was drugged !

There are some thoughts which, like noxious insects, come buzzing back into one's mind as often as we repulse them. We confute them in argument, prove them illogical, leave them not a leg to stand upon, and yet there they are the next moment as brisk as bees, and stronger on their pins than ever. It was just such a thought as this with which I had now to deal. It was well to say " Pooh ! " it was well to remind myself that this was the nineteenth century, that I was not acting a part in a French melodrama, that such things as I was thinking of were only known in romances ; it was well to argue that to set a respectable man down as a murderer, because he had peculiar coloured eyes and a scar upon his cheek, were ridiculous things to do. There seemed to be two separate parties within me : one possessed of great powers of argument and a cool judgment ; the other, an irrational or opposition party, whose chief force consisted in a system of dogged assertion, which all the arguments of the rational party were insufficient to put down.

It was not long before an additional force was imparted to the tactics of the irrational party by certain symptoms which began to develop themselves in my internal organisation, and which seemed favourable to the view of the case I was so anxious to refute. In spite of all my efforts to the contrary, I could not help feeling that some very remarkable sensations were slowly and gradually stealing over me. First of all, I began to find that I was a little at fault in my system of calculating distances ; so that when I took up any object and attempted to replace it on the table, I either brought it into contact with that article of furniture with a crash, in consequence of conceiving it to be lower than it was ; or else, imagining that the table was several inches nearer to the ceiling than was the case, I abandoned whatever I held in my hand sooner than I should, and found that I was confiding it to space. Then, again, my head felt light upon my shoulders, there was a slight tingling in my hands, and a sense that they, as well as my feet (which were very cold), were swelling to gigantic size, and were also surrounded with numerous rapidly revolving wheels of a light structure, like Catherine-wheels previous to ignition. It also appeared to me that when I spoke to my dog my voice had a curious sound, and my words were very imperfectly articulated.

It would happen, too, that when I looked towards the glass doors my landlord was there, peering at me through the muslin curtains; or the horrid little girl would enter, with no obvious intention, and having loitered for a little time about the room, would leave it again. At length the landlord himself came in, and coolly walking up to the table at which I was seated, glanced at the hardly tasted wine before me.

"It would appear that the wine of the country is not to your taste," he said.

"It is good enough," I answered as carelessly as I could, the words sounding to me as if they were uttered inside the cupola of St. Paul's, and were conveyed by iron tubes to the place I occupied.

I was in a strange state—perfectly conscious, but imperfectly able to control my thoughts, my words, my actions. I believe my landlord stood staring down at me as I sat staring up at him, and watching the Catherine-wheels as they revolved round his eyes and nose and chin—gentlemen, they seemed absolutely to *fizz* when they got to the scar on his cheek.

At this time a noisy party entered the main room of the auberge, which I have described as being visible through the glass doors, and the landlord had to leave me for a time to go and attend to them. I think I must have fallen into a slight and strongly resisted doze, and that when I started out of it, it was in consequence of the violent barking of my terrier. The landlord was in the room; he was just unlocking the cupboard from which the little girl had taken the paper parcel. He took out just such another paper parcel, and returned again through the doors. As he did so I remember stupidly wondering what had become of the little girl. Presently his evil face appeared again at the door.

"I am going to prepare the coffee," said the landlord; "perhaps monsieur will like it better than the wine."

As the man disappeared I started suddenly and violently upon my feet. I could deceive myself no longer. My thoughts were like lightning. "The wine, having been taken in so small a quantity and so profusely mixed with water, has done its work (as this man can see) but imperfectly. The coffee will finish that work. He is now preparing it. The cupboard, the little parcel—there can be no doubt. I will leave this place while I yet can. Now or never; if those men whose voices I hear in the other room leave the house it will be too late. With so many witnesses no attempt can be made to prevent my departure. I *will* not sleep—I *will* act—I *will* force my muscles to their work, and get away from this place."

Gentlemen, in compensation for a set of nerves of distressing sensitiveness I have received from nature a remarkable power of controlling my nerves for a time. I staggered to the door, closing it after me more violently than I had intended, and descended—the fresh air making me feel very giddy—into the yard.

As I went down the steps I saw the truculent little girl of whom I have already spoken entering the yard, followed by a blacksmith, carrying a hammer and some other implements of his trade. Catching sight of me, the little girl spoke quickly to the blacksmith, and in an instant they both changed their course, which was directed towards the stable, and entered an outhouse on the other side of the yard. The thought entered my head that this man had been sent for to drive a nail into my horse's foot, so that in the event of the drugged wine failing I might still be unable to proceed. This horrible idea added new force to my exertions. I seized the shafts of my carriage and commenced dragging it out of the yard and round to the front of the house: feeling that if it was once in the highway there would be less possibility of offering any impediment to my starting. I am conscious of having fallen twice to the ground, in my struggles to get the carriage out of the yard. Next, I hastened to the stable. My mare was still harnessed, with the exception of the headstall. I managed to get the bit into her mouth, and dragged her to the place where I had left the carriage. After I know not how many efforts to place the docile beast in the shafts—for I was as incapable of calculating distances as a drunken man—I recollect, but how I know not, securing the assistance of the boy I had seen. I was making a final effort to fasten the trace to its little pin, when a voice behind me said:

"Are you going away without drinking your coffee?"

I turned round and saw my landlord standing close beside me. He was watching my bungling efforts to secure the harness, but he made no movement to assist me.

"I do not want any coffee," I answered.

"No coffee, and no wine! It would appear that the gentleman is not a great drinker. You have not given your horse much of a rest," he added, presently.

"I am in haste. What have I to pay?"

"You will take something else," said the landlord; "a glass of brandy before starting in the wet?"

"No, nothing more. What have I to pay?"

"You will at least come in for an instant, and warm your feet at the stove."

"No. Tell me at once how much I am to pay."

Baffled in all his efforts to get me again into the house, my detested landlord had nothing for it but to answer my demand.

"Four litres of oats," he muttered, "a half-truss of hay, breakfast, wine, coffee"—he emphasised the last two words with a malignant grin—"seven francs fifty centimes."

My mare was by this time somehow or other buckled into the shafts, and now I had to get out my purse to pay this demand. My hands were cold, my head was giddy, my sight was dim, and, as I brought out my purse (which was a *porte-monnaie*, opening with a hinge), I managed while paying the bill to turn the purse over and to drop some gold pieces.

"Gold!" cried the boy who had been helping me to harness the horse, speaking as if by an irresistible impulse.

The landlord made a sudden dart at it, but instantly checked himself.

"People want plenty of gold," he said, "when they make a journey of pleasure."

I felt myself getting worse. I could not pick up the gold pieces as they lay on the ground. I fell on my knees, and my head bowed forward. I could not hit the place where a coin lay; I could see it but I could not guide my fingers to it. Still I did not yield. I got some of the money up, and the stable-boy, who was very officious in assisting me, gave me one or two pieces—to this day, I don't know how many he kept. I cast a hasty glance around, and, seeing no more gold on the ground, raised myself by a desperate effort and scrambled to my place in the carriage. I shook the reins instinctively and the mare began to move.

The well-trained beast was beginning to trot away as cleverly as usual, when a thought suddenly flashed into my brain, as will sometimes happen when we are just going to sleep—a thought which woke me up like a pistol-shot, and caused me to spring forward and gather up the reins so violently as almost to bring the mare back upon her haunches.

"My dog, my dear little Nelly!" I had left her behind!

To abandon my little favourite was a thing that never entered my head. "No, I must return. I must go back to the horrible place I have just escaped from. He has seen my gold, too, now," I said to myself, as I turned my horse's head with many clumsy efforts; "the men who were drinking in the *auberge* are gone; and, what is worse than all, I feel more under the influence of the drugs I have swallowed."

As I approached the *auberge* once more, I remember noticing that its walls looked blacker than ever, that the rain was falling more heavily, that the landlord and the stable-boy were on the steps of the inn, evidently on the look-out for me. One thing more I noticed;—on the road a small speck, as of some vehicle nearing the place.

"I have come back for my dog," said I.

"I know nothing of your dog."

"It is false! I left her shut up in the inner room."

"Go there and find her, then," retorted the man, throwing off all disguise.

"I will," was my answer.

I knew it was a trap to get me into the house; I knew I was lost if I entered it; but I did not care. I descended from the carriage, I clambered up the steps with the aid of the banisters, I heard the barking of my little Nelly as I passed through the outer room and approached the glass doors, steadying myself as I went by the articles of furniture in the room. I burst the doors open, and my favourite bounded into my arms.

And now I felt that it was too late. As I approached the door that opened to the road I saw my carriage being led round to the back of the house, and the form of the landlord appeared in the doorway blocking up the passage. I made an effort to push past him, but it was useless. My little Nelly fell out of my arms on the steps outside; the landlord slammed the door heavily; and I fell, without sense or knowledge, at his feet.

. . . .

It was dark, gentlemen—dark and very cold. The little patch of sky I was looking up at had in it a marvellous number of stars, which would have looked bright but for a blazing planet which seemed to eclipse, in the absence of the moon, all the other luminaries round about it. To lie thus was, in spite of the cold, quite a luxurious sensation. As I turned my head to ease it a little (for it seemed to have been in this position some time), I felt stiff and weak. At this moment, too, I feel a stirring close beside me, and first a cold nose touching my hand, and then a hot tongue licking it. As to my other sensations, I was aware of a gentle rumbling sound, and I could feel that I was being carried slowly along, and that every now and then there was a slight jolt; one of which, perhaps, more marked than the rest, might be the cause of my being awake at all.

Presently, other matters began to dawn upon my mind through the medium of my senses. I could see the regular movement of a horse's ears walking in front of me; surely I saw, too, part of the figure of a man—a pair of sturdy shoulders, the hood of a coat, and a head with a wideawake hat upon it. I could hear the occasional sounds of encouragement which seemed to emanate from this figure, and which were addressed to the horse. I could hear the tinkling of bells upon the animal's neck. Surely, too, I heard a rumbling sound behind us, and the tread of a horse's feet—just as if there were another vehicle following close upon us. Was there anything more? Yes, in the distance I was able to detect the twinkling of a light or two, as if a town were not far off.

Now, gentlemen, as I lay and observed all these things there was such a languor shed over my spirits, such a sense of utter but not unpleasant weakness, that I hardly cared to ask myself what it all meant, or to inquire where I was, or how I came there. A conviction that all was well with me, lay like an anodyne upon my heart, and it was only slowly and gradually that any curiosity as to how I came to be so, developed itself in my brain. I daresay we had been jogging along for a quarter of an hour during which I had been perfectly conscious, before I struggled up into a sitting posture, and recognised the hooded back of the man at the horse's head.

"Dufay?"

The man with the hooded coat who was walking by the side of the horse, suddenly cried out, "Wo!" in a sturdy voice; then ran to the back of the carriage and cried out, "Wo!" again; and then we came to a standstill. In another moment he had mounted on the step of the carriage and had taken me cordially by the hand.

"What," he said, "awake at last? Thank Heaven! I had almost begun to despair of you."

"My dear friend, what does all this mean? Where am I? Where did you come from? This is not my *calèche*, that is not my horse."

"Both are safe behind," said Dufay heartily; "and having told you so much, I will not utter another word till you are safe and warm at the Lion d'Or. See! There are the lights of the town. Now, not another word." And pulling the horsecloth under which I was lying, more closely over me, my friend dismounted from the step; started the vehicle with the customary cry of "Allons donc!" and a crack of the whip, and we were soon once more in motion.

Castaing Dufay was a man into whose company circumstances had thrown me very often, and with whom I had become intimate from choice. Of the numerous class to which he belonged, those men whose sturdy vehicles and sturdier horses are to be seen standing in the yards and stables of all the inns in provincial France—the class of the commis-voyageurs, or French commercial travellers—Castaing Dufay was more than a favourable specimen. I was very fond of him. In the course of our intimacy I had been fortunate enough to have the opportunity of being useful to him in matters of some importance. I think, gentlemen, we like those we have served quite as well as they like us.

The town lights were, indeed, close by, and it was not long

before we turned into the yard of the Lion d'Or and found ourselves in the midst of warmth and brightness, and surrounded by faces which, after the dangers I had passed through, looked perfectly angelic.

I had no idea, till I attempted to move, how weak and dazed I was. I was too far gone for dinner. A bed and a fire were the only things I coveted, and I was soon in possession of both.

I was no sooner snugly ensconced with my head on the pillow, watching the crackling logs as they sparkled—my little Nelly lying outside the counterpane—than my friend seated himself beside me and volunteered to relieve my curiosity as to the circumstances of my escape from the Tête Noire. It was now my turn to refuse to listen, as it had been his before, to refuse to speak.

" Not one word," I said, " till you have had a good dinner, after which you will come up and sit beside me, and tell me all I am longing to know. And stay—you will do one thing more for me, I know ; when you come up you will bring a plateful of bones for Nelly ; she will not leave me to-night, I swear, to save herself from starving."

" She deserves some dinner," said Dufay, as he left the room, " for I think it is through her instrumentality that you are alive at this moment."

The bliss in which I lay after Dufay had left the room is known only to those who have passed through some great danger, or who, at least, are newly relieved from some condition of severe and protracted suffering. It was a state of perfect repose and happiness.

When my friend came back, he brought, not only a plate of fowl-bones for Nelly, but a basin of soup for me. When I had finished lapping it up, and while Nelly was still crunching the bones, Dufay spoke as follows :

" I said just now that it was to your little dog you owe the preservation of your life, and I must now tell you how it was. You remember that you left Doulaise this morning——"

" It seems a week ago," I interrupted.

—" This morning," continued Dufay. " Well ! You were hardly out of the inn-yard before I drove into it, having made a small stage before breakfast. I heard where you were gone, and, as I was going that way too, I determined to give my horse a rest of a couple of hours, while I breakfasted and transacted some business in the town, and then to set off after you. 'Have you any idea,' I said, as I left the inn at Doulaise, 'whether monsieur meant to stop *en route*, and if so, where ? ' The garçon did not know. 'Let me see,' I said, ' the Tête Noire at Mauconseil would be a likely place, wouldn't it ? ' 'No,' said the boy ; ' the house does not enjoy a good character, and no one from here ever stops there.' ' Well,' said I, thinking no more of what he said, ' I shall be sure to find him. I will inquire after him as I go along.'

" The afternoon was getting on, when I came within sight of the inn of the Tête Noire. As you know, I am a little near-sighted, but I saw, as I drew near the *auberge*, that a conveyance of some kind was being taken round to the yard at the back of the house. This circumstance, however, I should have paid no attention to, had not my attention been suddenly caught by the violent barking of a dog, which seemed to be trying to gain admittance at the closed door of the inn. At a second glance I knew the dog to be yours. Pulling up my horse, I got down and ascended the steps of the *auberge*. One sniff at my shins was enough to convince Nelly that a friend was at hand, and her excitement as I approached the door was frantic.

" On my entering the house I did not at first see you, but on looking in the direction towards which your dog had hastened as soon as the door was opened, I saw a dark wooden staircase, which led out of one corner of the apartment I was standing in. I saw also, that you, my friend, were being dragged up the stairs in the arms of a very ill-looking man, assisted by (if possible) a still more ill-looking little girl, who had charge of your legs. At sight of me the man deposited you upon the stairs and advanced to meet me.

" ' What are you doing with that gentleman ? ' I asked.

" ' He is unwell,' replied the ill-looking man, ' and I am helping him upstairs to bed.'

" ' That gentleman is a friend of mine. What is the meaning of his being in this state ? '

" ' How should I know ? ' was his answer ; ' I am not the guardian of the gentleman's health.'

" ' Well, then, I *am*,' said I, approaching the place where you were lying ; ' and I prescribe, to begin with, that he shall leave this place at once.'

" I must own," continued Dufay, " that you were looking horribly ill, and, as I bent over, and felt your hardly fluttering pulse, I felt for a moment doubtful whether it was safe to move you. However, I determined to risk it.

" ' Will you help me,' I said, ' to move this gentleman to his carriage ? '

" ' No,' replied the ruffian, ' he is not fit to travel. Besides, what right have you over him ? '

" ' The right of being his friend.'

" ' How do I know that ? '

" ' Because I tell you so. See, his dog knows me.'

" ' And suppose I decline to accept that as evidence, and refuse to let this gentleman leave my house in his present state of health ? '

" ' You dare not do it.'

" ' Why ? '

" ' Because,' I answered slowly, ' I should go to the Gendarmerie in the village, and mention under what suspicious circumstances I found my friend here, and because your house has not the best of characters.'

" The man was silent for a moment, as if a little baffled. He seemed, however, determined to try once more.

" ' And suppose I close my doors, and decline to let either of you go ; what is to prevent me ? '

" ' In the first place,' I answered, ' *I* will effectually prevent your detaining me single-handed. If you have assistance near, I am expected to-night at Francy, and if I do not arrive there I shall soon be sought out. It was known that I left Doulaise this morning, and most people are aware that there is an *auberge* on the road which does not bear the best of reputations, and that its name is La Tête Noire. *Now*, will you help me ? '

" ' No,' replied the savage. ' I will have nothing to do with the affair.'

" It was not an easy task to drag you without assistance from the place where you were lying, out into the open air, down the steps, and to put you into my conveyance which was standing outside ; but I managed to do it. The next thing I had to accomplish was the feat of driving two carriages and two horses single-handed. I could see only one way of managing this. I led my own horse round to the gate of the stable-yard, where I could keep my eye upon him, while I went in search of your horse and carriage, which I had to get right without assistance. It was done at last. I fastened your horse's head by a halter to the back of my carriage, and then leading my own beast by the bridle I managed to start the procession. And so (though only at a foot pace) we turned our backs upon the Tête Noire. And now you know everything."

" I feel, Castaing, as if I should never be able to think of this adventure, or to speak of it again. It wears, somehow or other, such a ghastly aspect, that I sicken at the mere memory of it."

" Not a bit of it," said Dufay cheerily ; " you will live to tell it as a stirring tale some winter night, take my word for it."

Gentlemen, the prediction is verified.

GEORGE WALTER THORNBURY
1828–1876

TO BE TAKEN IN WATER

MINNIE, my blessed little wife, and I had been just one month married. We had returned only two days from our honeymoon tour at Killarney. I was a junior partner in the firm of Schwarzmoor and Laddock, Bankers, Lombard Street (I must conceal real names), and I had four days more of my leave of absence still to enjoy. I was supremely happy in my bright new cottage south-west of London, and was revelling in delicious idleness on that bright October day, watching the great yellow leaves fall in the sunshine. Minnie sat by me under the hawthorn-tree ; otherwise I should *not* have been supremely happy.

Little Betsy, Minnie's maid, came fluttering down the garden with an ominous-looking telegram in her hand.

It was a telegram from Mr. Schwarzmoor. It contained only these words :

" We want you to start to the Continent directly with specie. Neapolitan loan. No delay. Transactions of great importance since you left. Sorry to break up holiday. Be at office by 6.30. Start from London Bridge by 9.15 and catch Dover night boat."

" Is the boy gone ? "

" Boy did not leave it, sir. Elderly gentleman, going to Dawson's, brought it. The office boy was out, and the gentleman happened to be coming past our house."

" Herbert dear, you won't go, you mustn't go," said Minnie, leaning on my shoulder and bending down her face. " Don't go."

" I must, my dearest. The firm has no one to trust to but me in such a case. It is but a week's absence. I must start in ten minutes and catch the 4.20 on its way up."

" That was a very important telegram," I said sharply to the station-master, " and you ought not to have sent it by any unknown and unauthorised person. Who *was* this old gentleman, pray ? "

" Who was it, Harvey ? " said the station-master rather sulkily to the porter.

"Old gent, sir, very respectable, as comes to the Dawsons', the training-stables. Has horses there."

"Do not let that sort of thing occur again, Mr. Jennings," I said, "or I shall be obliged to report it. I wouldn't have had that telegram mislaid for a hundred pounds."

Mr. Jennings, the station-master, grumbled something and then boxed the telegraph boy's ears, which seemed to do him (Mr. Jennings) good.

"We were getting very anxious," said Mr. Schwarzmoor as I entered the bank parlour, only three minutes late. "Very anxious, weren't we, Goldrick?"

"Very anxious," said the little neat head clerk. "Very anxious."

Mr. Schwarzmoor was a full-faced man of about sixty, with thick white eyebrows and a red face—a combination which gave him an expression of choleric old age. He was a shrewd severe man of business: a little impetuous and fond of rule, but polite, kind, and considerate.

"I hope your charming wife is quite well. Sorry, indeed, to break up your holiday; but no help for it, my dear fellow. There is the specie in those two iron boxes, enclosed in leather to look like samples. They are fastened with letter-locks and contain a quarter of a million in gold. The Neapolitan king apprehends a rebellion." (It was three years before Garibaldi's victories.) "You will take the money to Messrs. Pagliavicini and Rossi, No. 172 Toledo, Naples. The names that open the locks are, on the one with the white star on the cover, Masinisa; on the one with the black star, Cotopaxo. Of course you will not forget the talismanic words. Open the boxes at Lyons to make sure that all is safe. Talk to no one. Make no friends on the road. Your commission is of vast importance."

"I shall pass," said I, "for a commercial traveller."

"Pardon me for my repeated cautions, Blamyre, but I am an older man than you and know the danger of travelling with specie. If your purpose was known to-night in Paris, your road to Marseilles would be as dangerous as if all the galley-slaves at Toulon had been let loose in special chase of you. I do not doubt your discretion: I only want you to be careful. Of course, you go armed?"

I opened my coat, and showed a belt under my waistcoat with a revolver in it, at which war-like spectacle the old clerk drew back in alarm.

"Good!" said Mr. Schwarzmoor. "But one grain of prudence is worth five times the five bullets in those five barrels. You will stop in Paris to-morrow to transact business with Lefebre and Desjeans, and you will go on by the 12.15 (night) to Marseilles, catching the boat on Friday. We will telegraph to you at Marseilles. Are the letters for Paris ready, Mr. Hargrave ? "

" Yes, sir, nearly ready. Mr. Wilkins is hard at them."

I reached Dover by midnight, and instantly engaged four porters to carry my specie chests down the stone steps leading from the pier to the Calais boat. The first was taken on board quite safely ; but while the second was being carried down, one of the men slipped, and would certainly have fallen into the water had he not been caught in the arms of a burly old Indian officer who, laden with various traps, and urging forward his good-natured but rather vulgar wife, was preceding me.

" Steady there, my lad," he said. " Why, what have you got there ? Hardware ? "

" Don't know, sir ; I only know it's heavy enough to break any man's back," was the rough answer as the man thanked his questioner in his blunt way.

" These steps, sir, are very troublesome for bringing down heavy goods," said an obliging voice behind me. " I presume, sir, from your luggage that we are of the same profession ? "

I looked round as we just then stepped on board. The person who addressed me was a tall thin man, with a long and rather Jewish nose and a narrow elongated face. He wore a greatcoat too short for him, a flowered waistcoat, tight trousers, a high shirt collar, and a light sprigged stiff neckcloth.

I replied that I *had* the honour to be a commercial traveller, and that I thought we were going to have a rough night of it.

" Decidedly dirty night," he replied ; " and I advise you, sir, to secure a berth at once. The boat, I see, is very crowded."

I went straight to my berth and lay down for an hour ; at the end of that time I got up and looked around me. At one of the small tables sat half-a-dozen of the passengers, including the old Indian and my old-fashioned interrogator. They were drinking bottled porter and appeared very sociable. I rose and joined them, and we exchanged some remarks not complimentary to night travelling.

" By Jove, sir, it is simply unbearable ! " said the jovial Major Baxter (for he soon told us his name) ; " it is as stifling as Peshawah when the hot Tinsang wind is blowing ; suppose we three go on deck and take a little air ? My wife suffers in these crossings ; she's invisible, I know, till the boat stops. Steward, bring up some more bottled porter."

When we got on deck, I saw, to my extreme surprise, made conspicuous by their black and white stars, four other cases exactly similar to mine, except that they had no painted brand upon them.

I could hardly believe my eyes; but there they were; leather covers, letter-locks, and all.

"Those are mine, sir," remarked Mr. Levison (I knew my fellow-commercial's name from the captain's having addressed him by it). "I am travelling for the house of Mackintosh. Those cases contain waterproof paletots, the best made. Our house has used such cases for forty years. It is sometimes inconvenient, this accidental resemblance of luggage—leads to mistakes. Your goods are much heavier than my goods, as I judge? Gas improvements, railway chairs, cutlery, or something else in iron?"

I was silent, or I made some vague reply.

"Sir," said Levison, "I augur well of your future; trade secrets should be kept inviolate. Don't you think so, sir?"

The major thus appealed to replied, "Sir, by Jove, you're right! One cannot be too careful in these days. Egad, sir, the world is a mass of deceit."

"There's Calais light!" cried some one at that moment; and there it was, straight ahead, casting sparkles of comfort over the dark water.

I thought no more of my travelling companions. We parted at Paris: I went my way and they went their way. The major was going to pay a visit at Dromont, near Lyons; thence he would go to Marseilles en route for Alexandria. Mr. Levison was bound for Marseilles, like myself and the major, but not by my train—at least he feared not—as he had much to do in Paris.

I had transacted my business in the French capital, and was on my way to the Palais Royal with M. Lefebre fils, a great friend of mine. It was about six o'clock, and we were crossing the Rue St. Honoré when there passed us a tall Jewish-looking person in a huge white mackintosh whom I recognised as Mr. Levison. He was in a hired open carriage and his four boxes were by his side. I bowed to him, but he did not seem to notice me.

"Eh bien! That drôle, who is that?" said my friend with true Parisian superciliousness.

I replied that it was only a fellow-passenger, who had crossed with me the night before.

In the very same street I ran up against the major and his wife, on their way to the railway station.

"Infernal city this," said the major; "smells so of onion. I should like, if it was mine, to wash it out, house by house; 'tain't wholesome, 'pon my soul 'tain't wholesome. Julia, my dear, this is my pleasant travelling companion of last night. By the bye, just saw that commercial traveller! Sharp business man that: no sight-seeing about *him*. Bourse and bank all day—senior partner some day."

" And how many more ? " said my friend Lefebre when we shook hands and parted with the jolly major. " That is a good boy—he superabounds—he overflows—but he is one of your epicurean lazy officers, I am sure. Your army, it must be reformed, or India will slip from you like a handful of sand—vous verrez, mon cher."

Midnight came, and I was standing at the terminus, watching the transport of my luggage, when a cab drove up, and an Englishman leaping out asked the driver in excellent French for change for a five-franc piece. It was Levison; but I saw no more of him, for the crowd just then pushed me forward.

I took my seat with only two other persons in the carriage—two masses of travelling cloak and capote—two bears for all I could see to the contrary.

Once away from the lights of Paris and in the pitch dark country, I fell asleep and dreamed of my dear little wife and our dear little home. Then a feeling of anxiety ran across my mind. I dreamed that I had forgotten the words with which to open the letter-locks. I ransacked mythology, history, science, in vain. Then I was in the banking parlour at No. 172 Toledo, Naples, threatened with instant death by a file of soldiers if I did not reveal the words or explain where the boxes had been hid; for I had hidden them for some inscrutable no reason. At that moment an earthquake shook the city, a flood of fire rolled past beneath the window, Vesuvius had broken loose and was upon us. I cried in my agony—" Gracious Heaven, reveal to me those words ! " when I awoke.

" Dromont ! Dromont ! Dix minutes d'arrête, messieurs."

Half-blinded with the sudden light, I stumbled to the buffet and asked for a cup of coffee, when three or four noisy young English tourists came hurrying in, surrounding a quiet, imperturbable, elderly commercial traveller. It was actually Levison again ! They led him along in triumph and called for champagne.

" Yes ! yes ! " the leader said. " You must have some, old fellow. We have won three games, you know, and you held such cards, too. Come along, look alive, you fellow with the nightcap—Cliquot—gilt top, you duffer. You shall have your revenge before we get to Lyons, old chap."

Levison chattered good-humouredly about the last game and took the wine. In a few minutes the young men had drunk their champagne and had gone out to smoke. In another moment Levison caught my eye.

" Why, good gracious," he said, " who'd have thought of this ! Well, I am glad to see you. Now, my dear sir, you must have some champagne with me. Here, another bottle, monsieur, if you please. I hope, long before we get to Lyons, to join you, my dear sir. I am tired of the noise of those youngsters. Besides, I object to high stakes, on principle."

The moment the waiter brought the champagne Levison took the bottle.

"No," he said, "I never allow any one to open wine for me." He turned his back from me to remove the wire; removed it, and was filling my glass, when up dashed a burly hearty man to shake hands with me—so awkward in his heartiness that he broke the champagne bottle. Not a drop of the wine was saved. It was the major—hot as usual and in a tremendous bustle.

"By Jove, sir; dooced sorry. Let me order another bottle. How are you, gentlemen? Lucky, indeed, to meet you both again. Julia's with the luggage. We can be very cozy together. More champagne here. What's bottle in French? Most shameful thing! Those French friends of Julia's were gone off to Biarritz, pretending to have forgotten that we were coming—after six weeks with us in London, too! Precious shabby, not to put too fine a point upon it. By Jove, sir, there's the bell. We'll all go in the same carriage. They will not bring that champagne."

Levison looked rather annoyed. "I shall not see you," he said, "for a station or two. I must join those boys and let them give me my revenge. Cleared me out of twenty guineas! I have not been so imprudent since I was first on the road. Good-bye, Major Baxter—good-bye, Mr. Blamyre!"

I wondered how this respectable old fellow, who so keenly relished his game at whist, had got hold of my name; but I remembered in a moment that he must have seen the direction on my luggage.

Flashes of crimson and green lights, a shout from some pointsman, glimpse of rows of poplars and lines of suburban houses, and we once more plunged into the yielding darkness.

I found the major very droll and pleasant, but evidently ruled by his fussy, good-natured, managing, masculine wife. He was full of stories of bungalows, compounds, and the hills; in all of which narrations he was perpetually interrupted by Mrs. Baxter.

"By Jove, sir!" he said, "I wish I could sell out and go into your line of business. I am almost sick of India—it deranges one's liver so infernally."

"Now, John, how can you go on so! You know you never had a day's illness in all your life, except that week when you smoked out a whole box of Captain Mason's cheroots."

"Well, I pulled through it, Julia," said the major, striking himself a tremendous blow on the chest; "but I've been an unlucky devil as to promotion—always bad luck in everything. If I bought a horse, it made a point of going lame next day; never went in a train but it broke down."

"Now don't, John; pray don't go on so," said Mrs. Baxter, "or I shall really be very angry. Such nonsense! You'll get your step in time. Be patient like me, major; take things more quietly. I hope you put a direction on that hat-box of yours? Where is the sword-case? If it wasn't for me, major, you'd get to Suez with nothing but the coat on your back."

Just then the train stopped at Charmont, and in tripped Levison, with his white mackintosh over his arm, and his bundle of umbrellas and sticks.

"No more sovereign points for me!" he said, producing a pack of cards. "But if you and the major and Mrs. Baxter would like a rubber—shilling points—I'm for you. Cut for partners."

We assented with pleasure. We cut for partners. I and Mrs. Baxter against the major and Levison. We won nearly every game. Levison played too cautiously, and the major laughed, talked, and always forgot what cards were out.

Still it killed the time; the red and black turned up, changed, and ran into remarkable sequences; and the major's flukes and extraordinary luck in holding (not in playing) cards amused us, we laughed at Levison's punctilious care and at Mrs. Baxter's avarice for tricks, and were as pleasant a party as the dim lamp of a night-train ever shone on. I could think of little, nevertheless, but my precious boxes.

There we were rushing through France, seeing nothing, heeding nothing, and having as little to do with our means of transit as if we had been four Arabian princes seated on a flying enchanted carpet.

The game gradually grew more intermittent, the conversation more incessant. Levison, stiff of neckcloth as ever, and imperturbable and punctilious as ever, became chatty. He grew communicative about his business.

"I have at last," he said in his precise and measured voice, "after years of attention to the subject, discovered the great secret which the waterproofers have so long coveted; how to let out the heated air of the body and yet at the same time to exclude the rain. On my return to London, I offer this secret to the Mackintosh firm for ten thousand pounds; if they refuse the offer, I at once open a shop in Paris, call the new fabric Magentosh, in honour of the Emperor's great Italian victory, and sit down and quietly realise a cool million—that's my way!"

"That's the real business tone," said the major admiringly.

"Ah, major," cried his wife, ever ready to improve a subject, "if you had only had a little of Mr. Levison's prudence and energy, then, indeed, you'd have been colonel of your regiment before this."

Mr. Levison then turned the conversation to the subject of locks.

"I always use the letter-lock myself," he said. "My two talismanic words are TURLURETTE and PAPAGAYO—two names I once heard in an old French farce—who could guess them? It would take the adroitest thief seven hours to decipher even one. You find letter-locks safe, sir?" (He turned to me.)

I replied dryly that I did, and asked what time our train was due at Lyons.

"We are due at Lyons at 4.30," said the major; "it is now five to four. I don't know how it is, but I have a sort of presentiment to-night of some breakdown. I am always in for it. When I went tiger-hunting, it was always my elephant that the beast pinned. If some of us were ordered up to an unhealthy out-of-the-way fort, it was always my company. It may be superstitious, I own, but I feel we shall have a breakdown before we get to Marseilles. How fast we're going! Only see how the carriage rocks!"

I unconsciously grew nervous, but I concealed it. Could the major be a rogue, planning some scheme against me? But no: his red bluff face and his clear, good-natured, guileless eyes refuted the suspicion.

"Nonsense, be quiet, major; that's the way you always make a journey disagreeable," said his wife, arranging herself for sleep. Then Levison began talking about his early life, and how in George the Fourth's time he was travelling for a cravat house in Bond Street. He grew eloquent in favour of the old costume.

"Low Radical fellows," he said, "run down the first gentleman in Europe, as he was justly called. I respect his memory. He was a wit and the friend of wits; he was lavishly generous and disdained poor pitiful economy. He dressed well, sir; he looked well, sir; he was a gentleman of perfect manners. Sir, this is a slovenly and shabby age. When I was young, no gentleman ever travelled without at least two dozen cravats, four whalebone stiffeners, and an iron to smooth the tie and produce a thin equal edge to the muslin. There were no less, sir, than eighteen modes of putting on the cravat; there was the cravate à la Diane, the cravate à l'Anglaise, the cravate au nœud Gordien, the cravate——"

The train jolted, moved on, slackened, stopped.

The major thrust his head out of window and shouted to a passing guard:

"Where are we?"

"Twenty miles from Lyons—Fort Rouge, monsieur."

"What is the matter? Anything the matter?"

An English voice answered from the next window:

"A wheel broken, they tell us. We shall have to wait two hours and transfer the luggage."

"Good Heaven!" I could not help exclaiming.

Levison put his head out of window. "It is but too true," he said, drawing it in again; "two hours' delay, the man says. Tiresome, very—but such things will happen on the road; take it coolly. We'll have some coffee and another rubber. We must each look to our own luggage; or, if Mr. Blamyre goes in and orders supper, I'll see to it all. But, good gracious, what is that shining out there by the station lamps? Hei, monsieur!" (to a passing gendarme whom the major had hailed), "what is going on at the station?"

"Monsieur," said the gendarme, saluting, "those are soldiers of the First Chasseurs; they happened to be at the station on their way to Châlons; the station-master has sent them to surround the luggage-van, and see to the transfer of the luggage. No passenger is to go near it, as there are Government stores of value in the train."

Levison spat on the ground and muttered execrations to himself—I supposed at French railways.

"By Jove, sir, did you ever see such clumsy carts?" said Major Baxter, pointing to two country carts, each with four strong horses, that were drawn up under a hedge close to the station, for we had struggled on as far as the first turn-table, some hundred yards from the first houses of the village of Fort Rouge.

Levison and I tried very hard to get near our luggage, but the soldiers sternly refused our approach. It gave me some comfort, however, to see my chests transferred carefully, with many curses on their weight. I saw no sign of Government stores, and I told the major so.

"Oh, they're sharp," he replied, "dooced sharp. Maybe the empress's jewels—one little package only, perhaps; but still not difficult to steal in a night confusion."

Just then there was a shrill piercing whistle, as if a signal. The horses in the two carts tore into a gallop, and flew out of sight.

"Savages, sir; mere barbarians still," exclaimed the major; "unable to use railways even now we've given them to them."

"Major!" said his wife, in a voice of awful reproof, "spare the feelings of these foreigners, and remember your position as an officer and a gentleman."

The major rubbed his hands, and laughed uproariously.

"A pack of infernal idiots," cried Levison; "they can do nothing without soldiers; soldiers here, soldiers there, soldiers everywhere."

"Well, these precautions are sometimes useful, sir," said Mrs. B.; "France is a place full of queer characters. The gentleman next you any day at a table d'hôte may be a returned convict. Major, you remember that case at Cairo three years ago?"

"Cairo, Julia, my dear, is not in France."

"I know that, major, I hope. But the house was a French hotel, and that's the same thing." Mrs. B. spoke sharply.

"I shall have a nap, gentlemen. For my part, I'm tired," said the major, as we took our place in the Marseilles train, after three hours' tedious delay. "The next thing will be the boat breaking down, I suppose."

"Major, you wicked man, don't fly out against Providence," said his wife.

Levison grew eloquent again about the Prince Regent, his diamond epaulettes, and his inimitable cravats; but Levison's words seemed to lengthen, and gradully became inaudible to me, until I heard only a soothing murmur, and the rattle and jar of the wheels.

Again my dreams were nervous and uneasy. I imagined I was in Cairo, threading narrow dim streets, where the camels jostled me and the black slaves threatened me, and the air was heavy with musk, and veiled faces watched me from latticed casements above. Suddenly a rose fell at my feet. I looked up, and a face like my Minnie's, only with large liquid dark eyes like an antelope's, glanced forth from behind a water-vase and smiled. At that moment, four Mamelukes appeared, riding down the street at full gallop, and came upon me with their sabres flashing. I dreamed I had only one hope, and that was to repeat the talismanic words of my letter-locks. Already I was under the hoofs of the Mamelukes' horses. I cried out with great difficulty, "Cotopaxo! Cotopaxo!" A rough shake awoke me. It was the major, looking bluff but stern.

"Why, you're talking in your sleep!" he said; "why the devil do you talk in your sleep? Bad habit. Here we are at the breakfast place."

"What was I talking about?" I asked, with ill-concealed alarm.

"Some foreign gibberish," returned the major.

"Greek, I think," said Levison; "but I was just off too."

We reached Marseilles. I rejoiced to see its almond-trees and its white villas. I should feel safer when I was on board ship, and my treasure with me. I was not of a suspicious temperament, but I had thought it remarkable that during that long journey from Lyons to the seaboard I had never fallen asleep without waking and finding an eye upon me—either the major's or his wife's. Levison had slept during the last four hours incessantly. Latterly, we had all of us grown silent, and even rather sullen. Now we brightened up.

"Hôtel de Londres! Hôtel de l'Univers! Hôtel Impérial!" cried the touts, as we stood round our luggage, agreeing to keep together.

"Hôtel Impérial, of course," said the major; "best house."

A one-eyed saturnine half-caste tout shrunk up to us.

"Hôtel Impérial, sare. I am Hôtel Impérial; all full; not a bed; no—pas de tout—no use, sare!"

"Hang it! the steamer will be the next thing to fail."

"Steamer, sare—accident with boiler; won't start till minuit et vingt minutes—half-past midnight, sare."

"Where shall we go?" said I, turning round and smiling at the three blank faces of my companions. "Our journey seems doomed to be unlucky. Let us redeem it by a parting supper. My telegraphing done, I am free till half-past eleven."

"I will take you," said Levison, "to a small but very decent hotel down by the harbour. The Hôtel des Étrangers."

"Cursed low nasty crib—gambling place!" said the major, lighting a cheroot, as he got into an open fly.

Mr. Levison drew himself up in his punctilious way. "Sir," he said, "the place is in new hands, or I would not have recommended the house, you may rely upon it."

"Sir," said the major, lifting his broad-brimmed white hat, "I offer you my apologies. I was not aware of that."

"My dear sir, never mention the affair again."

"Major, you're a hot-headed simpleton," were Mrs. B.'s last words, as we drove off together.

As we entered a bare-looking salon with a dinner-table in the middle and a dingy billiard-table at one end, the major said to me, "I shall go and wash and dress for the theatre, and then take a stroll while you do your telegraphing. Go up first, Julia, and see the rooms."

"What slaves we poor women are!" said Mrs. B., as she sailed out.

"And I," said Levison, laying down his railway rug, "shall go out and try and do some business before the shops shut. We have agents here in the Canabière."

"Only two double-bedded rooms, sare," said the one-eyed tout, who stood over the luggage.

"That will do," said Levison, promptly, and with natural irritation at our annoyances. "My friend goes by the boat to-night; he does not sleep here. His luggage can be put in my room, and he can take the key, in case he comes in first."

"Then now we are all right," said the major. "So far, so good!"

When I got to the telegraph-office, I found a telegram from London awaiting me. To my surprise and horror, it contained only these words:

"You are in great danger. Do not wait a moment on shore. There is a plot against you. Apply to the prefect for a guard."

It must be the major, and I was in his hands! That rough hearty manner of his was all a trick. Even now he might be carrying off the chests. I telegraphed back:

"Safe at Marseilles. All right up to this."

Thinking of the utter ruin of our house if I were robbed, and of dear Minnie, I flew back to the hotel, which was situated in a dirty, narrow street near the harbour. As I turned down the street, a man darted from a doorway and seized my arm. It was one of the waiters. He said hurriedly in French: "Quick, quick, monsieur; Major Baxter is anxious to see you, instantly, in the salon. There is no time to lose."

I ran to the hotel and darted into the salon. There was the major pacing up and down in extraordinary excitement; his wife was looking anxiously out of window. The manner of both was entirely changed. The major ran up and seized me by the hand. "I am a detective officer, and my name is Arnott," he said. "That man Levison is a notorious thief. He is at this moment in his room, opening one of your specie chests. You must help me to nab him. I knew his little game, and have checkmated him. But I wanted to catch him in the act. Julia, finish that brandy-and-water while Mr. Blamyre and myself transact our business. Have you got a revolver, Mr. Blamyre, in case he shows fight? I prefer this." (He pulled out a staff.)

"I have left my revolver in the bedroom," I breathlessly exclaimed.

"That's bad; never mind, he is not likely to hit us in the flurry. He may not even think of it. You must rush at the door at the same moment as I do. These foreign locks are never any good. It's No. 15. Gently!"

We came to the door. We listened a moment. We could hear the sound of money clinking in a bag. Then a low dry laugh, as Levison chuckled over the word he had heard me utter in my sleep. "Cotopaxo—ha! ha!"

The major gave the word, and we both rushed at the door. It shook, splintered, was driven in. Levison, revolver in hand, stood over the open box, ankle deep in gold. He had already filled a huge digger's belt that was round his waist, and a courier's bag that hung at his side. A carpet bag, half full, lay at his feet, and, as he let it fall to open the window bolt, it gushed forth a perfect torrent of gold. He did not utter a word. There were ropes at the window, as if he had been lowering, or preparing to lower, bags into the side alley. He gave a whistle, and some vehicle could be heard to drive furiously off.

"Surrender, you gallows-bird! I know you," cried the major. "Surrender! I've got you now, old boy."

Levison's only reply was to pull the trigger of the revolver; fortunately, there was no discharge. I had forgotten to cap it.

"The infernal thing is not capped. One for you, Bobby," he said quietly. Then hurling it at the major with a sudden fury, he threw open the window and leaped out.

I leaped after him—it was a ground-floor room—raising a hue-and cry. Arnott remained to guard the money.

A moment more and a wild rabble of soldiers, sailors, mongrel idlers, and porters were pursuing the flying wretch with screams and hoots, as in the dim light (the lamps were just beginning to be kindled) we tore after him, doubling and twisting like a hare, among the obstacles that crowded the quay. Hundreds of blows were aimed at him; hundreds of hands were stretched to seize him; he wrested himself from one; he felled another; he leaped over a third; a Zouave's clutch was all but on him, when suddenly his foot caught in a mooring ring, and he fell headlong into the harbour. There was a shout as he splashed and disappeared in the dark water, near which the light of only one lamp moved and glittered. I ran down the nearest steps and waited while the gendarmes took a boat and stolidly dragged with hooks for the body.

"They are foxes, these old thieves. I remember this man here at Toulon. I saw him branded. I knew his face again in a moment. He has dived under the shipping, got into some barge, and hid. You'll never see him again," said the old grey gendarme who had taken me into the boat.

"Yes we shall, for here he is!" cried a second, stooping down and lifting a body out of the water by the hair.

"Oh, he *was* an artful file," said a man from a boat behind us. It was Arnott. "Just came to see how you were getting on, sir. It's all right with the money; Julia's minding it. I often said that fellow would catch it some day; now he's got it. He all but had you, Mr. Blamyre. He'd have cut your throat when you were asleep, rather than miss the money. But I was on his track. He didn't know me. This was my first cruise for some time against this sort of rogue. Well, his name is off the books; that's one good thing. Come, comrades, bring that body to land. We must strip him of the money he has upon him, which at least did one good thing while in his possession—it sent the scoundrel to the bottom."

Even in death, the long face looked craftily respectable when we turned it to the lamp-light.

Arnott told me all, in his jovial way, on my return to the hotel, where I loaded him and Mrs. B. (another officer) with thanks. On the night I started he had received orders from the London head office to follow me and watch Levison. He had not had time to communicate with my partners. The driver of our train had been bribed to make the engine break down at Fort Rouge, where Levison's accomplices were waiting with carts to carry off the luggage in the confusion and darkness, or even during a sham riot and fight. This plan Arnott had frustrated by getting the police to telegraph from Paris for soldiers to be sent from Lyons, and be kept in readiness at the station. The champagne he spilt had been drugged. Levison, defeated in his first attempt, had then resolved to try other means. My unlucky disclosure of the mystery of the letter-lock had furnished him with the power of opening that one chest. The breakdown of the steamer, which was accidental (as far as could ever be ascertained), gave him a last opportunity.

That night, thanks to Arnott, I left Marseilles with not one single piece of money lost. The journey was prosperous. The loan was effected on very profitable terms. Our house has flourished ever since, and Minnie and I have flourished likewise—and increased.

GEORGE WALTER THORNBURY

MONS. CASSECRUCHE'S INSPIRATION

MONSIEUR ÆNEAS EGLANTINE CASSECRUCHE, Auquatrième, No. 23, Bolshoi Moskoi, St. Petersburg, was at the end of his Latin—or, to use a thoroughly English idiom, he had not a penny to bless himself with.

The gentleman in question was the solitary member left of a company of French actors that had come to Russia in 1840. The rest had returned to France, leaving their gay companion like a piece of light drift that has washed up beyond reach of the return tide; like a butterfly that had ventured out too late in the autumn, and got nipped with the frost.

M. Cassecruche had tried to draw teeth, but had failed to earn enough to keep his own grinders going. He had tried to teach drawing, but his advertisements had drawn no one; he had ventured at scene-painting, and the manager had kicked him out of the theatre. He had speculated on the turf, but betting with no capital leads to inadequate results. He had taught Italian, but as he knew no Russian and could not pronounce Italian, his pupils made scarcely sufficient progress. He went on the Moscow stage, and the theatre instantly closed, as if in sheer spite. He had thought the Russians rich fools! and easily cheated, but he had found them sharp rogues, neglectful of all true talent. So, now, in his vexation he wished to go back to France, as his creditors grew daily more pressing, and the horrible Russian winter was rapidly setting in.

It was the thirtieth day of October, and the city of St. Peter was entirely intent on checkmating the coming winter. There were men everywhere putting up double window-sashes, filling up the intermediate spaces with salt or sand, and pasting paper over every chink. Doors were being hammered into place; the great white porcelain stoves, reaching from ceiling to floor, were being scraped out and overhauled, and their flues and pipes caulked and soldered for the winter campaign. It was quite alarming, to a needy thin-clad stranger, to see the mountains of white-barked birch-logs piled up in the courtyards, or being tossed out of the enormous wood-barges on the Neva. In the suburbs the servants were drawing out the sledges, examining their steel runners, and gossiping about the fun of the snow time. The great iron fireplaces for the coachmen outside the Winter Palace and the Opera House now assumed a look of terrible significance. People were talking of the bridges being soon removed. All the tailors in St. Petersburg were busily preparing and altering fur coats for officers and civilians. There was a hard time coming, and M. Cassecruche knew it.

But how to get away from thirty-two hungry creditors, with a suspicious Government watching him, and only three sous in his pocket was the difficulty. Thirteen Napoleons to Paris, through Poland and Prussia. Half as much by Yorkshire steamer to Perfidious Albion. " Hein ? "

One miserable October day M. Cassecruche sat in his dreary apartment and pondered over his difficulties. It was a doleful wet day. A wind from Siberia had blown over the marshes, and given an acidity to the rain that drenched the streets, and frothed down from every spout. M. Cassecruche sat at his table, drew on the back of a letter countless ballet-dancers, and finished off with a gigantic head of the Emperor Nicholas. M. Cassecruche arose and lighted a cigarette ; the smoke curled up in sharp-cut blue circles ; it was incense offered to his Good Genius.

" Ha ! ma belle France, how I grieve for thee ; how I regard thee, a poor exile from thy paradise ! " exclaimed M. Cassecruche, rhapsodising aloud. " Ma foi, how I am hungry. Pon ! pon ! there goes a champagne cork at the execrable next door. Ha ! now I smell the stew. Gracious Heavens ! what torment to smell a stew which is not by one's self to be eaten. Oh, what veritable agony for the poor exile from beautiful France ! But stop. I raise my gun. I bring down an idea—a magnificent, a majestic idea. My good genius has returned to me—to me, rising from the vapour of a stew. M. Cassecruche, I congratulate you. Courage, courage, my friend. You shall still return to la belle France. There is but one step from misery to hope. Good angel of Hope, permit me now to take that step ! "

A change had come over M. Cassecruche. He sang, he danced, finally he washed his face in a tumbler, adjusted his hair in the glass of his snuff-box, brushed his coat, blackened his too obvious toes with ink, so that they might look like part of his boots, lighted another cigarette, drew a sketch of a ballet-dancer, and then proceeded downstairs to the shop of M. Brisenoy, a military tailor, and his landlord, on the first floor.

Humming an air from the last opera, M. Cassecruche knocked boldly at the door.

The door opened, and M. Louis Brisenoy presented himself without his coat or waistcoat, in slippers, and with hanks of red thread strung round his neck. In one hand he held a heavy pressing-iron, in the other a pair of scarlet trousers. M. Cassecruche, in spite of severely burning himself with the flat-iron, shook his landlord by both hands.

"Congratulate me, congratulate me, my friend," he said, "fortune smiles upon me. I am appointed Professor of French at the University of Karkoff; hundreds of roubles a year."

"Glad of it," said Brisenoy, "for I was just coming up to ask for my three months' rent."

"Three months! Six months' rent would not be sufficient to repay you for your unwearied kindness, and the confidence you have ever placed in me. Come, my dear friend, at once, and dine with me at the great restaurant in the Nevsky."

"But your clothes?" suggested Brisenoy.

"True," sighed Cassecruche, looking down at his coat; "and the rest of my wardrobe is——"

"No better. Well, we are all pinched one way or the other. I can lend you a suit of clothes for one night. Do you prefer evening dress, or military?"

"I could not wear anything but evening dress," replied M. Cassecruche, with injured dignity. "Remember, I am a professor now, and a Government servant."

"True. Eh, bien! We shall have a pleasant evening. What do you say to the opera afterwards?"

"By all means. I adore the opera," replied the tailor's agreeable friend.

M. Cassecruche, arrayed in brand-new close-fitting black, with white neckcloth and a cloak with a sable collar two feet deep, looked a veritable Amphitryon as he stepped forth with M. Brisenoy from a drosky at the door of the great restaurant in the Nevsky Prospekt, with the grand air of a general about to commence a campaign.

M. Cassecruche, in his plated spectacles, was not merely grand; he was tremendous; he took off his hat and hung it on a peg with the air of a prince. With the dignified endurance of a monarch he resigned himself to the bowing waiters, who ran to remove his heavy furred cloak. M. Brisenoy was a mere bourgeois shadow beside this great type of office. The groups of officers round the various tables looked up for a moment with a certain knowing look, as much as to say, "Here comes a celebrated foreign professor, who is going to dine with M. Brisenoy, the fashionable military tailor of the Bolshoi Moskoi."

M. Cassecruche called for the carte. He ran it down with a haughty and supercilious air—an air half epicurean, half contemptuous. He seemed to imply, "Gracious Heaven! here is another day's dinner, and so horribly like the last ! Half my annual salary to any one who will discover me a new dish. I am weary of the luxuries of the Emperor Alexander's time."

" What shall we begin with ? " said the generous host, tossing the carte almost contemptuously to M. Brisenoy.

" Oh, shtshee [cabbage soup], they make it well here," replied the guest timidly, for he was dazzled by the magnificence of his tenant's new manner.

(Now, a true Russian cannot dine without cabbage soup ; there is, indeed, a proverb that the three deities of Russia are " Tshin, Tshai, and Shtshee "—official rank, tea, and cabbage.)

" It is poor stuff," said the professor, " but I suppose we must begin with it." There is but one way of beginning a Russian dinner. You begin by eating a small section of pickled fish and drinking a gilt egg-cup full of raw spirits.

M. Cassecruche ate a whole sardine, but with strong protest—the waiter watched him with awe and respect because he grumbled, made faces, and complained. But when it came to the spirits, he drew back like a pointer when it comes upon a covey of partridges. He sipped, he sniffed to show his hatred, contempt, and disgust.

" Is this what you call Maraschino ? "

" Yes, sir."

" The Maraschino of Zara ? "

" Of Sarah ? "

" Of Zara, blockhead."

" No, sir, it is not."

" Not of Zara ! How dare you then bring a French gentleman any Maraschino, ass, fool, but that of Zara ? Take the trash away."

M. Cassecruche uttered these complaints in a loud and angry voice. The major looked round, the two colonels smiled, the ensigns applauded audibly. " This is some great inostranez " [foreigner], thought the waiter. " He is not accustomed to our rough Russian ways. They do things differently on the other side."

The soup came—cabbages, barley-meal, beans, butter, salt, mutton, and cream constitute what is called by the Russians shtshee.

M. Cassecruche dipped in his spoon and lifted out a great yellow heap of macerated cabbages. There was a fatal streak of green on the outside leaf. He splashed it down with abhorrence.

" Away with it ! Away with it, ape, fool. Keep such stuff for your poor merchants. Order some batvinya instead, and do you hear, fool ? Quick."

M. Brisenoy was impressed, but he was also sorry ; for he was hungry, and the steam of the cabbage soup made his mouth water.

" Bring a bottle of the best Cliquot," cried M. Cassecruche the inexorable, " to pass the time till your detestable cook prepares the batvinya."

" Isn't it rather late in the year for batvinya ? " suggested M. Brisenoy timidly.

" It is late ; but what can we do in this infamous hole ? "

Infamous hole ! The first restaurant in the first city of the Russian empire ; the restaurant where all the officers of the Imperial Body Guard dined. Could M. Brisenoy believe his own ears ? Could this be Æneas Cassecruche, his once humble—abjectly humble and impecunious lodger ? The batvinya came. Such a mess ! Beer, raw herbs, red berries, chopped cucumbers, square lumps of salmon, slices of lemon, toasted black bread cut small, and jostling lumps of ice.

Horrible mélange ! Chaos of indigestion ! Yet custom has made this dish palatable to forty millions of Russians.

To the batvinya succeeded cutlets à la Marengo and other savoury morceaux. M. Cassecruche grew complacent and more satisfied. Then followed reptschiks, the delicious tree-partridge and quails, each little quail recumbent on a little cushion of bacon.

The champagne corks exploded around the heads of the two friends. The wine of Veuve Cliquot rose, beading up with tipsy haste in the tall tapering glasses. M. Cassecruche grew extravagantly merry, his eyes sparkled, he talked louder and faster. He proposed toasts, he hummed tunes of the most heterodox character.

The pastry coming in stopped his vivacious mouth. Jellies, golden and transparent, melted before him ; strange sweetmeats and iced fruits thawed and vanished at his approach. Then came little glasses of Dantzic golden water, the volatile sparks of gold-leaf floating in luscious and spirituous oil.

The tables were cleared, the coffee was brought in thick white porcelain cups. M. Cassecruche called for cognac, put some in his saucer, set fire to it, and then lighted his cigarette at the blue flame with consummate nonchalance. The two friends were enraptured with one another. They chinked their glasses together, and swore eternal friendship : an interesting ceremony, but perhaps injudicious when done loudly and noisily in a public room, and among ceremonious and choleric strangers.

More silver-topped bottles came at M. Cassecruche's call ; out flew their bulgy corks, released from the slavery of the wire ; the transparent golden wine bubbled up in perpetual fountains of joy and mirth. The white cream froth, fragrant and exhilarating, might have crested the very nectar of the gods, or Homer's care-dispelling nepenthe. Jokes and droll sayings flew from M. Cassecruche's mouth like detonations from a cracker or fire from a squib. He grew so loud that M. Brisenoy, in a humble deprecating voice, glanced at the two captains and the scowling major, and suggested moderation.

M. Cassecruche tossed off two more glasses of wine in angry succession, and then exploded like a powder magazine in a series of fierce vituperations, uttered at the pitch of his voice.

"Moderation? Voice? Mon Dieu! no talk? Ten million thousand curses on the land of the knout and the serf—the land where liberty freezes in prison, and tyranny rejoices in splendour! Down with the timid bourgeois who would crouch to such gilded infamy—no, let Russia manacle the Pole, and squeeze out the heart's blood of her slaves, but let her not set one finger——"

Here an irrepressible colonel laid his hand on the imprudent orator's collar. M. Brisenoy already saw himself hobnobbing with a bear in a Siberian log-hut. But M. Cassecruche was desperate. He wrenched himself from the grasp of the irrepressible colonel, and, snatching up an empty champagne bottle, deliberately ran to a bust of the Emperor Nicholas, and beat off its august nose with a shout of demoniacal and republican laughter. Everybody started on his legs, and M. Brisenoy fainted. "Kill the Republican conspirator!" cried the ensigns.

"Send for a guard to arrest him!" shouted the irrepressible colonel.

"Beat him!" cried every one. But this the colonel would not allow. M. Cassecruche, struggling like a frog in a stork's claws, kept shouting, "Vive la République!" and making frantic faces at the noseless and disconsolate marble emperor.

The guard arrived with fixed bayonets, a crowd of chattering and indignant officers, waiters, cooks, and scullions stood around M. Cassecruche. All at once a man pushed through the crowd, waving a yard of white paper covered with memoranda and figures.

"Search the wretch's pocket!" he cried—it was the proprietor of the restaurant. "He owes me thirty roubles for his dinner and champagne. He must have plenty of money—all these conspirators have."

Six waiters leaped simultaneously like hungry wolves on M. Cassecruche, and searched his pockets. They contained a stump of a cigar, a dirty ace of spades, and three sous. The six waiters were furious; they would have torn his very hair off in search for concealed money, but the colonel beat them away with the flat of his sword.

"Dogs," he said, "begone! This is an important political offender. Whether he has paid for his dinner or not is of no possible consequence. Soldiers, remove your prisoner. Follow me! M. the Captain, adieu; friends must separate when duty calls. We'll play out our billiard match to-morrow."

"There is the man who must pay then," said the proprietor to the band of excited waiters, and he pointed to the half-paralysed M.

Brisenoy. They leaped upon him, and squeezed from him many curses, some tears, hundreds of groans, and thirty roubles.

Next day, M. Æneas Eglantine Cassecruche, sober but not penitent, was comfortably sitting in a warm first-class railway carriage, on his way to the Prussian frontier, banished for ever from Russia as a dangerous alien, an outrageous republican, a subversive democratic emperor's nose-breaking socialist, not to be discharged until safely carted out and turned loose in the wilds of Paris. So M. Cassecruche journeyed rejoicing, chuckling at his *ruse de guerre*, and his timely escape from herds of enraged and hungry creditors ; rejoicing at his gratuitous dinner, at his vexatious landlord's discomfiture, and at his cheap and luxurious journey from St. Petersburg to Paris.

LEOPOLD LEWIS
1828–1890

A DREADFUL BELL

I

OUT OF DOORS

It was one of those large and important hotels that seem to swoop down and take possession of little villages. The first object that caught the eye of the traveller as he approached the hamlet over the neighbouring hill was the new Grand Hotel, with its white staring walls and numberless windows, and the letters of its name in black paint running across it. It had scattered the little houses to the right and left of it. It had fixed itself in the best possible situation in front of the sea, and had swallowed up in its erection all the most time-honoured and distinguished characteristics of the locality. In short, instead of the hotel being considered as belonging to the village, the village was now looked upon as an appurtenance to the hotel. The cause of this change was that the little fishing hamlet being prettily situated on the sea-coast in North Wales, " the Faculty " had passed its opinion in favour of the place, and the hotel had in consequence sprung up like magic—" The Montmorency Hotel," with plate-glass windows and a grand portico, hundreds of bedrooms and sitting-rooms, bathing-machines, hot and vapour baths, invalid chairs, and various other conveniences.

How I came to be stopping at " The Montmorency " was in this wise: my old college chum, Tom Marlowe, had just got married to his Julia, and having spent their honeymoon abroad, they took it into their heads that a little repose and a little peaceful enjoyment of each other's society would not be an inappropriate change. Accordingly they had taken apartments in one of the houses in Montmorency Terrace. Tom had heard that I was going to Ireland for my vacation, and had written to ask me to stop and see him on my way.

I accepted the invitation, and put up at the hotel, as there was no vacant room in Tom's house, and I intended to make only a flying visit.

On an evening when the village was undergoing one of its very heartiest squalls, and the wind and the rain and the sea were all roaring together, I had enjoyed a pleasant dinner with Tom and his Julia. The storm without had made the windows rattle rather noisily in their frames: and the street door would persist in flying open suddenly, and when once open, banging itself; the chimneys, too, were altogether uncomfortable, and grumbled incessantly, and the whole establishment had exhibited decided symptoms of a general shakiness of constitution peculiar to mansions that are rapidly "run up" in rising localities. But we were so merry, and had so much to talk about—Tom was in such good spirits, and his Julia was emphatically what he had so often described her to me to be, "a born angel"—that I believe if the house itself had been carried away bodily out to sea, it would have been a matter of indifference to them, provided they had gone with it, in each other's society. The time had passed so pleasantly and quickly that I was quite startled when a clock struck eleven; and, as I knew they were early people at "The Montmorency," I rose to take my leave.

"By Jove! what a night!" said Tom, as he opened the street door to let me out. "Will you have a rug to put round you, or my top-coat?"

"No, thank you."

"Well, get home as fast as you can. How it does come down, and as dark as pitch. Come round in the morning, there's a good fellow."

"All right. Good-night, old boy."

"Good-night."

"The Montmorency" was only about five hundred yards distant. I ran as fast as I could, and soon reached the portico, but the whole of the hotel was in darkness. Everybody had evidently gone to bed.

"They are early people with a vengeance," I muttered, as I seized the bell and rang vigorously.

"They will think that rather a strong pull, but one can't wait out long in such a night as this."

And it was a night! The portico afforded no protection. The wind howled round its columns, and the rain dashed through it. There was not a soul about. The sky and the sea were both as black as ink.

"Confound it," I said, after I had waited some considerable time; "I wonder when they're going to open the door. I'll wait two minutes more and then I'll ring again."

The two minutes seemed to be twenty, and no one came.

Surely it was not intentional to keep me out in the rain, to give me the street for shelter, because I was not in before the door was shut. It certainly was an hotel where such an arrangement might have been adopted as a " Rule," but the mere thought of such an absurdity gave me new vigour, and I rang the bell violently for several minutes, and only desisted from sheer exhaustion. I had just commenced to consider whether in the circumstances I should not be justified in throwing a few stones and smashing one or two of the upstairs windows, when, through the pane of glass at the side of the door I saw to my great relief a faint glimmer of light thrown into the hall. This gradually became brighter and brighter, as if some one were slowly coming down the principal staircase, which was at right angles with the door, bearing a light. It proved to be so, for the next moment I saw, standing on the last step of the stairs, an old gentleman of about sixty, with perfectly white hair, habited in a dressing-gown, and carrying high above his head a lighted bedroom candle.

" Some one I have awakened at last by my ringing," thought I. " One of the visitors, no doubt. I shall apologise to him when he has opened the door, and the early hour at which I commenced to ring, and the state of the night will surely be a sufficient excuse."

I steadily fixed my eyes on the old gentleman, and got nearer to the door ready for the chain to be dropped and the bolts to be drawn, for I was becoming more bitterly cold every minute. The old gentleman advanced cautiously into the hall and crossed it, without however once looking towards the door. When he had reached the side of the hall farthest from the stairs he looked up, as if contemplating something fearfully high upon the wall, and as he did so I saw that his arm which held the candle trembled violently.

" You shall hear me at any rate," thought I, and I rang again.

To my utter astonishment immediately I had done this, the old gentleman, still without looking towards the door, gave a start, and appeared to shake from head to foot. By his profile, which was towards me, I could see that the expression of his face was one of intense alarm. I heard him utter a shout of horror, and then with a bound he turned on his heel, dashed up the stairs he had so lately descended, and the hall was once more plunged in darkness.

I had scarcely time to question myself as to what could possibly be the meaning of these strange proceedings, before my attention was attracted by a great noise in the upper part of the hotel. It sounded to me as if a number of people were running about. Then doors banged violently. Then there was a succession of crashes. Then shouts of men and screams of women. Nobody, however, appeared in the hall. I rushed into the road and looked up at the hotel. Gracious Heavens ! What was the matter ? Nearly all the windows, before so black, were now illumined with a bright light. Dark outlines of the human form passed hurriedly backwards and forwards upon the blinds looking like struggling and excited phantoms. Still not a window opened. The noise continued with unabated fury ; then, as gradually as it had commenced, the shouting ceased and became murmurs, the doors banged off one by one, until there seemed no more to bang, the lights went out like specks of fire upon a burnt paper, and then all was again in darkness and silence. What could it mean ? In vain I asked myself the question, and no one came to the door to enlighten me upon the subject, or to give me admittance. " I'll try once more," I exclaimed, " and this shall be the last time." I rang feebly and despairingly. Instantly bells seemed to ring all over the house and passages. Big bells and little bells, near bells and distant bells, upstairs bells and downstairs bells, burst out together in one long continuous angry jangle. The last little bell was still tinkling away somewhere upin the garrets, when a light once again appeared, and this time as if it were coming up a trap in the floor of the hall. I saw it was borne by the head-waiter. He was only partly dressed, and he wore a nightcap made out of a red handkerchief. He looked for an instant towards where I stood, and then shambled in his slippers to the door, let down the chain, half opened the door, put his nose through the opening, and breathed out a ghostly, inflamed, husky whisper, " Who is it ? "

" It's me," I said somewhat petulantly, " open the door."

He rubbed his eyes, held up the light, looked intensely hard at the wick of the candle, said " Oh !" and opened the door.

" Well, you have kept me a pretty time outside," I said as I entered. " I have been ringing the bell since eleven, and by George, there goes one o'clock. I'm wet to the skin and nearly dead with cold."

The head-waiter was putting the chain up in a fumbling uncertain sort of gaoler fashion. He didn't seem to be altogether quite awake yet, and from the fumes of rum and the smell of tobacco smoke that pervaded him, and the very fishy and winking condition of his eyes, I concluded that Bacchus had assisted Morpheus in the task of lulling him to sleep. In reply to my observation he simply breathed out another rum-and-water " Oh !" and hoisted his apparel about his waist in a dreamy way.

" Has anything been the matter ? " I continued, as I lighted a bedroom candle. " What a terrible row there was in the house at about half-past twelve."

" Was there, though ? " he said, with a yawn, a hiccup, and a lurch. " Now, was there, though ? Well, you knows best, I've no doubt."

And without another word he shuffled away, with his two long braces dragging behind him and bumping their buckles on the floor, looking like a drunken old bashaw, whilst I went off to bed.

II

IN-DOORS

I never slept so sound in my life as I did that night. It was eleven o'clock before I came downstairs and entered the coffee-room to order breakfast. There was only one gentleman in the room, and he was seated at a table at the extreme end having breakfast, with a newspaper balancing against the coffee biggin, and simultaneously devouring the news and the buttered toast in the heartiest manner possible. He was a small, middle-aged gentleman, and was evidently suffering from severe nervousness, for he made a great clatter with the cups and spoons, knocking them together loudly; and I noticed that his hands and head shook so continuously that he had the greatest difficulty in carrying anything in a direct line to his mouth. His hair, which was short and black, stood up very straight and stiff, and he wore a large pair of gold eye-glasses. As I entered and took my seat at a table near the window, he fixed his glasses with greater steadiness upon his nose, and directed at me a long and anxious gaze. Apparently, however, finding that I was a stranger, he turned the newspaper with much gesticulation, and went on with his breakfast.

It was not a rude look. It was only the stare of a short-sighted man; but still it made me think of three trifling incidents that had occurred to me on my passage downstairs from my bedroom to the coffee-room. On the first landing I had met the chambermaid. Immediately she had seen me she had backed into a corner, and had stared at me with mingled curiosity and terror until I had passed. On a lower floor I had encountered the Boots. On seeing me, he had instantly dropped a bootjack, two chamber-candlesticks, three pairs of slippers, and a warming-pan, with a terrible clatter, and then wagged his head reprovingly at me as if I had done it. Finally, in crossing the hall, the second waiter—a limp wretch in a perpetual perspiration—on meeting me, turned on his heel, and, with a half-smothered cry, fled up a passage. The head-waiter here entered the room. He had resumed his usual dignified appearance; his white cravat was stiff and spotless, and his black wig was curled and oiled into quite a lustrous condition. He made a complete circuit of the room, walking in a solemn manner, and looking at me gravely the while; and, having done this, he approached my table, leant over it on the knuckles of his hands, and contemplated me sternly and inquiringly.

"Breakfast, waiter, if you please."

"Oh! breakfast?" he repeated, without altering his position. "Well now, sir, did you order breakfast?"

"Yes," I answered; "and I should like it as quick as possible."

" Ah ! " said the waiter, heaving a deep sigh, and still in a contemplative condition. " Should you ? Mind, I don't say you shouldn't. Only it may be difficult—and then, again, it's rather unnatural—that's all." And then, before I could express my surprise at this extraordinary conduct on his part, he bent his head near to mine, and whispered in my ear : " You've done it."

" Done it ! Done what ? What do you mean ? " I said, instinctively adopting a whispered tone.

" Horful ! " gasped the waiter in the same horrid whisper, and throwing his head and eyes up. " No one could have believed it. I am not a bad sort, sir ; but I am a family man, sir ; I have a wife and three small children, one of 'em, sir, now in arms and cutting its teeth, sir ; and when a family man has been examined in the way I have been ; when it's been extricated out of me by threats—threats of the most horrid natur—when a hunder waiter has been threatened to be put over my head—a hunder waiter so ignorant of 'rithmetic that he don't know plated spoons from silver ones—how could I help it ? "

" Help what ? " I said. " What are you talking about ? I don't understand a word of what you are saying. Am I to have any breakfast or not ? "

At this last question the head-waiter drew himself up to his full height, and in a perfectly serious—indeed, solemn—manner, said : " Well, sir, if you ask me as a matter of opinion, I should say that you are *not* to have any breakfast. Mind, it is a matter of opinion on my part. Howiver, no one have ever accused me of possessing the feelings of a wolf, and so I will go and make the inquiry."

Either the waiter was mad, or he had not entirely recovered from his last night's libations. I ordered him again to bring the breakfast, and threatened to speak to the proprietor of the hotel if he any longer delayed doing so.

" Well ! " he said, looking at me curiously. " Well, I always said philosophy were a wonderful invention, but if ever I see such a go as this—skewer me ! You knows what I mean, and what you've done—you knows you did ! " And then, with a look full of meaning and reproach, he whispered, " F.D. ! " and slid gravely out of the room.

I was still lost in astonishment at the waiter's conduct, when, happening to look round, I perceived that the little gentleman at the other end of the room, having by this time clattered through his breakfast and finished with the newspaper, was now steadily observing me. He had certainly not been able to overhear my whispered conversation with the waiter, but he had evidently noticed that what had taken place had been the cause of exciting my anger, for he now said :

"Stupid fellow that!" I experienced quite a feeling of gratitude towards the stranger for his sympathy.

"I cannot think what is the matter with him," I said, as I passed down the room to a table nearer to the little gentleman. "He don't seem in condition to take an order for breakfast."

"Oh!" said the stranger, fidgeting in his chair, and nervously endeavouring to fix the cruets in their stand. "Ah, it's very extraordinary! I can't make him out either. He has been bringing me wrong things all the morning. I ordered fish, and he brought me cutlets. I don't like cutlets. Then he brought me a fish-slice to cut the butter with. Ridiculous! And, look at these cruets, not one of them will go into the stand. As an excuse, he says he has been greatly agitated. So have I been agitated! So has every one been agitated after the disgraceful proceedings of last night."

"Indeed?" said I. "I heard something, but I was unable to distinguish what it was." The little gentleman stared hard at me.

"You must be a sound sleeper, young man—a very sound sleeper; but perhaps it did not happen to you. Did it?"

Not having the remotest idea as to what the question referred, I answered in the negative.

"Perhaps," said the little gentleman, "you do not even know what did happen—eh?" "No."

"Very extraordinary," said the little gentleman, and then he went on nervously: "I never went through such a night—never. A man of my weak nerves, too. My doctor sent me down here for quiet and repose. 'Go down, Bamby,' he said, 'no railway station within three miles, no organs, no yelling black men, no Punches and Judies, in fact, a Paradise of peace and comfort.' So I came. I arrived yesterday in the midst of the most terrible storm I ever saw. I went to bed about half-past ten, and, contrary to my usual custom, soon dropped off to sleep. I am a bad sleeper, young man. About half-past twelve o'clock I was awoke by some one knocking violently at my door. I had bolted it before getting into bed. Judge of my alarm at such a proceeding at such an hour. The knocking continued in violence, then a heavy body seemed to be thrown against the door, which, after repeated shocks, burst open, and a man fell head foremost into my room;—a tall, powerful man, in a coloured gown and Wellington boots, with a pair of trousers tied round his throat. Before I had time to utter a word, he had started to his feet and assumed a threatening attitude. 'Help! murder! fire! thieves!' I shouted out at the top of my voice. 'I'll help you,' he cried, dancing wildly round me, 'come out of this!' And in a moment he had seized the bedclothes and had dragged off the counterpane and blankets. 'Come out of this!' he again cried, and again pounced upon me, this time clutching me by the ankle of my left leg and commencing to drag me—a man of my weak nerves—bodily off the bed. Maddened with terror, I clung to the head of the bedstead, and shouted still louder for assistance. The more I shouted the more the villain tugged at my leg. The struggle was fearful. Chairs, table, drawers, looking-glasses and fire-irons all seemed to be tumbling and crashing about the room indiscriminately. The very bedstead, with myself still madly clinging to it, seemed to be whirled round and round in the fury of the conflict. At length my assailant appeared to weaken in his efforts, and summoning all my remaining strength with my disengaged leg, I gave him one terrible kick full in the chest that sent him staggering back on to the wash-hand stand, in his fall knocking it down, smashing the jugs and basins into atoms, and deluging the room with water. Just fancy the situation to a man of my weak nerves!"

"Did you capture him?"

"No; before I could recover myself he was on his legs again,—had rushed out of the room and was gone. Winding the remains of the bedclothes round me, I dashed out after him, shouting, 'Stop thief!' To my astonishment I found the whole house in an uproar. Ladies and gentlemen, in the most extraordinary state of deshabille I ever saw, were running about with lights, asking each other what it was, and where it was, and who had done it, and what it meant? Everybody seemed to have been served in the way I had been. The mistress of the hotel appeased us by saying that the matter should have full inquiry in the morning, and eventually we retired to rest again. You must admit, young man, you were a very sound sleeper not to have been awakened by these proceedings."

I was considerably astonished at this recital. This, then, accounted for the excitement in the hotel whilst I was ringing at the door.

"And what was the explanation of this extraordinary affair?" I inquired.

"The explanation," continued Mr. Bamby, "as far as I have heard it, is more mysterious to me than the affair itself. The landlady, in answer to my inquiries this morning, informed me it was the F.D., and everybody I have asked has answered me in the same way; but who the F.D. is, or what the F.D. is, or why the deuce the F.D. pulled everybody out of bed, last night, by the leg, is a problem I mean to have unravelled before I leave this place."

I gave quite a start of astonishment. The head-waiter had whispered these mysterious letters into my ear. For a moment a thought flashed through my mind that I might be suspected of being the perpetrator of the outrages described by Mr. Bamby; but then I was not in the hotel at the time they occurred, and no one knew this better than the head-waiter, who had opened the door to me.

"Do you think you would know your aggressor again," I said, "if you saw him?"

"I don't know," said Mr. Bamby. "It was so dark at the time, and I was so bewildered; but dear me, how very late it is. What a thing it is to have one's rest disturbed. It loses one's whole day. I should like to catch my friend the F.D. or the Funny Devil, or whatever he is, I'd show him some fun, although I am a man of weak nerves. Good morning."

And Mr. Bamby took up his hat and umbrella, and trotted out of the room. As he went out the head-waiter came in. I looked hungrily towards him, but he only carried an empty plate in one hand, and advanced with great solemnity, bearing it before him like a churchwarden going round after a charity sermon. He presented it to me. I looked at him and then at the plate.

"What's this? Where is the breakfast, fellow? What in the name of heaven is the meaning of all this? What's that plate for?"

Without a movement of his face he still advanced the plate before me. I really think I was about to take it out of his hand and hurl it through the window, when I caught sight of a paper lying upon it. I took it up and looked at it. It was my bill!

"What's this?" I demanded fiercely.

"What is that, sir?" said the head-waiter. "That is the bill, sir. We have *not* charged for breakfast. We have *not*, I believe, charged for a bed to-night; but the attendance is included."

"I will see the proprietor at once," I cried, "and have this affair explained. A pretty hotel this seems to be. I am kept waiting half the night ringing at the bell. Breakfast is refused me, and my bill is thrust upon me without my asking for it. What do you take me for? Eh?"

I advanced upon the head-waiter; he retreated in terror.

"Don't, sir, don't. I am a family man, and not a bad sort: but hotels is hotels, sir, and can't afford to be ruined. Whole families turning out—families from the Philippine Islands—two Nabobs, and one a general—ain't they nothing? Then, to see the deluges—the breakages—the spiled linen—oh! to see it——"

It was clear I was taken for the author of the last night's proceedings—the mysterious F.D. referred to by Mr. Bamby. I heard no more. I rushed out of the room, intending at once to have an interview with the proprietor of the hotel and explain matters. In the hall there were groups of servants, all talking anxiously. As I made my appearance there was a general movement of excitement amongst them; all eyes were directed towards me, and I again heard the mention of the mysterious letters in an undertone, clearly, in reference to myself.

" Can I see the proprietor ? " I addressed a young woman in the bar of the hotel.

" Walk this way," she answered, in a sharp, snappish tone.

I passed through the bar and into a back room. Here was seated the landlady, with a large book before her. As I entered, and she saw who it was, she started up, took off her spectacles, and confronted me with a glare of terrible indignation.

" So, Number 24," she said, before I could open my mouth, " I hope you are satisfied with the mischief of which you have been the cause. The affair of last night may be my ruin, and I have to thank you for it. (She pointed to the book.) I am now making out the bill of Number 4, a gentleman suffering from the gout. How can he be expected to remain in a hotel where he is pulled out of bed in the middle of the night, and dragged about his room by the leg ? Here is the family in Number 18, who have been in hysterics ever since, and who threaten me with an action for the loss of wigs and teeth and all sorts of valuable property. And here is the Indian General in Number 82, who declares he will have your life, and there will be murder on the premises in the height of the season. It's shameful of you. It is disgraceful."

" Madam," I interrupted, " I assure you I am perfectly innocent of the outrages which I have heard were committed last night in this hotel."

" How dare you, Number 24," cried the landlady, " utter such wilful falsehoods ? Is it not enough what you have done ? I have perfect confidence in the statement made to me by Mr. Loverock, our head-waiter."

" If Mr. Loverock," I urged, " has made a charge against me of being the author of this affair, he is a villain, since he knows that such a charge is false."

" He is no villain," said the landlady, now in a towering passion. " He is no villain ; and he is not false. He was not at first willing to divulge you ; and it was only when I threatened to remove him from his situation that he made the statement he did. He is no villain, Number 24. It is you, and you alone, who are the villain. You, who have been the cause of all this misery and ruin."

The matter was becoming to me momentarily more inexplicable. I was about to make further reply to the landlady, when I was startled by a loud noise outside the bar, and I heard a man's voice exclaiming :

" Where is he ? Where is he ? Where is the ruffian ? Let me reach him. Let me grasp his throat. Let me revenge my wife. Let me revenge my three daughters. Out of the way ! "

" It is the General ! " shrieked the landlady ; and at the same moment a gentleman in a furious rage bounded into the room. He carried a bootjack in one hand, which he waved wildly over his head, and he was advancing to seize me, when another gentleman jumped into the room after him, threw his arms round his waist, and held him as if he were in a vice.

"Let me go," shouted the first gentleman, struggling to get free.

"I shan't," shouted the second gentleman. "What do you want to do?"

I knew the voice. It was Tom Marlowe.

"Tom," I cried, "what is all this about? I am charged with the most extraordinary conduct. Speak for me, old fellow."

"Why—what——" exclaimed Tom, putting his head round the General's body without relaxing his hold. "Good gracious! is it you? If this gentleman would only have the kindness to leave off struggling, and abandon his bloodthirsty intentions, I could discuss the matter with him. There is some mistake."

"There's not!" roared the General.

"There is!" I shouted.

"You had better retire, sir," interposed the landlady, addressing me. "Your presence only serves to excite the General's frenzy. I am willing to explain matters to Mr. Marlowe."

"Go into the next room, will you," said Tom, again putting his head round the General's body, "and lock the door on him, ma'am. I won't let go of this gentleman unless you do."

"Go, sir!" exclaimed the landlady to me, and pointing to an inner room in a Lady Macbeth attitude.

I entered. The door was immediately closed and locked upon me. It was quite an hour before Tom made his appearance. Directly he came in he fell into a chair, and burst into a fit of laughter. When he had partially recovered himself, he said:

"Excuse me, my dear fellow, laughing in this wild manner; but for the last hour I have been dying with suppressed emotion. I have been wanting to laugh, and have not dared."

"What is it all about?"

"Well, my dear boy," said Tom, "it seems it was you who did it after all."

"Impossible! I wasn't in the hotel."

"Just listen for one moment. I have been making inquiries all over the house, and have had interviews with the parties concerned. I think I have found it all out, and if I know anything of the laws of cause and effect, it was you who did it. However, don't make yourself uneasy. I have cleared up the matter now, and appeased the landlady, and they have determined to forgive you."

"Forgive me—but what for? What have I done?"

"It seems," said Tom, "that there is an elderly gentleman from America stopping in the house with his family. He is of very nervous temperament, and from having some short time ago severely suffered from the effects of a fire upon his premises, exists in a perpetual state of alarm as to one breaking out wherever he may be. In fact, he is almost a monomaniac upon the subject. Now, it appears that it was you who rang the bell last night. Loverock, the waiter, who sleeps downstairs, says he opened the street door to you at one o'clock. You left me at eleven, so that you were at it about two hours."

"That's true," I said. "They wouldn't open the door. What was I to do ?"

"Precisely," continued Tom. "At about half-past twelve o'clock it further appears that the fire-fearing gentleman having listened to a violent and almost continuous ringing of a bell for an hour and a half, at length took it into his head to travel out of his bedroom to discover the cause. On reaching the hall——"

"Yes, I saw him through the door-window."

"On reaching the hall, he examined all the bells upon the wall, and seeing a particularly large one madly ringing came to the conclusion it was the fire-bell. The alarm of fire always drives him out of his senses, and the instinct of preserving his fellow-creatures at such a time is so strong upon him that it becomes a madness. It was this feeling that drove him through the house shouting for help, bursting open doors, pulling the furniture out of the rooms and the people out of their beds—in fact, acting as if a fire were actually raging in the hotel."

"But why should he have thought it was the fire-bell ?"

"Come and see," said Tom.

We passed into the hall.

In the midst of a cluster of bells hanging upon the wall, each of which had its number, was one bell of an unusually large size, and underneath this, painted in red, were the mysterious letters, "F.D."

"That's the bell you rung," said Tom. "The American gentleman, in his excitement, not unnaturally concluded it gave the alarm of fire."

"And what, in the name of Heaven, do those initials stand for ?"

"Front Door !"

ANONYMOUS
PUB. 1861

THE ALIBI

I WHOLLY disbelieve in spirit-rapping, table-turning, and all supernatural eccentricities of that nature. I refuse credence to the best authenticated ghost story (mind you, *ghost* story *pur et simple*).

I can sleep in the gloomiest haunted room in the gloomiest haunted house without the slightest fear of a nocturnal visit from the other world.

But, although I scoff at white ladies, bleeding nuns, *et hoc genus omne*, there is a species of supernatural occurrence in which I am, I confess, an unwilling and hesitating believer.

The circumstances I am about to relate are of this nature, and were told me by an intimate friend of mine, as having lately occurred to a relation of his own.

I give the story as he gave it to me, namely, in the words as nearly as possible of the principal actor in it.

Two years ago, towards the end of the London season, weary of the noise and bustle that for the last three months had been ceaselessly going on around me, I determined upon seeking a few days' rest and quiet in the country. The next evening saw me comfortably installed in a pretty farm-house about two miles from the cathedral town of X——. The little cottage in which I had taken up my quarters belonged to an old servant of my father's, and had long been a favourite resort of mine when wishing for quiet and fresh air.

The evening of the second day after my arrival was unusually close and sultry, even for the time of year. Weary with the heat, and somewhat sated with the two days' experience I had enjoyed of a quiet country life, I went up to my bedroom about half-past ten, with the intention of taking refuge from the *ennui* which was growing on me in a good long night's sleep. Finding, however, the heat an insuperable obstacle to closing my eyes, I got up, put on my dressing-gown, and, lighting a cigar, sat down at the open window, and dreamily gazed out on the garden in front of the cottage. Before me several low, flat meadows stretched down to the river, which separated us from the town. In the distance the massive towers of the cathedral appeared in strong and bright relief against the sky. The whole landscape, indeed, was bathed in a flood of light from the clear summer moon.

I was gradually getting sleepy, and beginning to think of turning in, when I heard a soft, clear voice, proceeding apparently from some one just beneath my window, saying :

" George, George, be quick ! You are wanted in the town."

I immediately looked from the window, and although the moon still shone most brilliantly, somewhat to my surprise I could see no one. Thinking, however, that it was some friend of my landlord's who was begging him to come into the town upon business, I turned from the window, and, getting into bed, in a few minutes was fast asleep.

I must have slept about three hours, when I awoke with a sudden start, and with a shivering " gooseskin " feeling all over me. Fancying that this was caused by the morning air from the open window, I was getting out of bed to close it, when I heard the same voice proceeding from the very window itself.

" George, be quick ! You are wanted in the town."

These words produced an indescribable effect upon me. I trembled from head to foot, and, with a curious creeping about the roots of the hair, stood and listened. Hearing nothing more, I walked quickly to the window, and looked out. As before, nothing was to be seen. I stood in the shade of the curtain for some minutes, watching for the speaker to show himself, and then, laughing at my own nervousness, closed the window and returned to bed.

The grey morning light was now gradually overspreading the heavens, and daylight is antagonistic to all those fears which under cover of the darkness will steal at times over the boldest. In spite of this, I could not shake off the uncomfortable feeling produced by that voice. Vainly I tried to close my eyes. Eyes remained obstinately open ; ears sensitively alive to the smallest sound.

Some half-hour had elapsed, when again I felt the same chill stealing over me. With the perspiration standing on my forehead, I started up in bed, and listened with all my might. An instant of dead silence, and the mysterious voice followed :

" George, be quick ! You *must* go into the town."

The voice was in the room—nay, more, by my very bedside. The miserable fear that came over me I cannot attempt to describe. I felt that the words were addressed to me, and that by no human mouth.

Hearing nothing more, I slowly got out of bed, and by every

means in my power convinced myself that I was wide awake and not dreaming. Looking at myself in the glass on the dressing-table, I was at first shocked, and then, in spite of myself, somewhat amused by the pallid hue and scared expression of my countenance.

I grinned a ghastly grin at myself, whistled a bit of a polka, and got into bed again.

I had a horrible sort of notion that some one was looking at me, and that it would never do to let them see that I was the least uneasy.

I soon found out, however, that bed, in the circumstances, was a mistake, and I determined to get up and calm my nerves in the fresh morning air.

I dressed hurriedly, with many a look over my shoulder, keeping as much as possible to one corner of the room, where nobody could get behind me. The grass in front of my window was glistening with the heavy morning dew, on which no foot could press without leaving a visible trace.

I searched the whole garden thoroughly, but no sign could I see of any person having been there.

Pondering over the events of the night, which, in spite of broad daylight and common sense, persisted in assuming a somewhat supernatural aspect, I wandered across the meadows towards the river by a footpath which led to the ferry. As I drew near to the boatman's cottage I saw him standing at his door, looking up the path by which I was approaching. As soon as he saw me, he turned and walked down to his boat, where he waited my arrival. "You are early on foot, my friend, this morning," said I, as I joined him.

"Early, sir," answered he, in a somewhat grumbling tone ; "yes, it is early, sir, and I have been waiting here for you this two hours or more."

"Waiting for me, my friend—how so ?"

"Yes, sir, I have ; for they seemed so very anxious that you should not be kept waiting ; they have been down from the farm twice this blessed night telling me that you would want to cross the ferry very early this morning."

I answered the man not a word, and, getting into his boat, was quickly put across the water. As I walked rapidly up towards the town, I endeavoured to persuade myself that somebody was endeavouring to play a silly hoax upon me. At last, stopping at a gate through which I had to pass, I determined upon proceeding no further. As I turned to retrace my steps, suddenly the same shivering sensation passed over me—I can only describe it as a cold damp blast of air meeting me in the face, and then, stealing round and behind me, enveloping me in its icy folds.

I distinctly heard the words, " George, George," uttered in my very ear, in a somewhat plaintive and entreating tone.

I shuddered with a craven fear, and, turning hastily round, hurried on towards the town.

A few minutes' walking brought me into the market-place. It was evidently market day, for, in spite of the early hour, there was already a considerable bustle going on. Shops were being opened, and the country people were exposing their butter, poultry, and eggs for sale, and for about two hours I wandered amongst the busy and constantly increasing crowd, listening to every scrap of conversation that reached my ear, and vainly endeavouring to connect them with the strange summons that had roused me from my bed, and led me *nolens volens* to the town.

I could hear nothing that interested me in any way, and, feeling tired and hungry, I decided on breakfasting at the hotel, which overlooked the market-place, and then taking myself back to the cottage, in spite of the mysterious voice.

The cheerful and noisy bustle of the market had indeed partly dissipated the morbid turn which my fancies had taken.

After I had breakfasted I lit my cigar, and strolled into the bar, where I talked for ten minutes with the landlord without elucidating anything of greater moment than that it was his (the landlord's) opinion that things were bad—very; that Squire Thornbury was going to give a great ball on the occasion of his daughter's approaching marriage, and that Mr. Weston's ox was certain to carry off the prize at the next Agricultural Meeting.

I bade him good-morning, and turned my steps homeward. I was checked on my way down the High Street by a considerable crowd, and upon inquiring what was the matter, was informed that the Assizes were being held and that an " interesting murder case " was going on. My curiosity was roused, I turned into the court-house, and, meeting an acquaintance who fortunately happened to be a man in authority, was introduced into the court, and accommodated with a seat.

The prisoner at the bar, who was accused of robbing and murdering a poor country girl, was a man of low, slight stature, with a coarse, brutal cast of features, rendered peculiarly striking by their strangely sinister expression.

As his small bright eyes wandered furtively round the court they met mine, and for an instant rested upon me. I shrank involuntarily from his gaze, as I would from that of some loathsome reptile, and kept my eyes steadily averted from him till the end of the trial, which had been nearly concluded the previous evening. The evidence, as summed up by the judge, was principally circumstantial, though apparently overwhelming in its nature. In spite of his counsel's really excellent defence, the jury unhesitatingly found him "guilty."

The judge, before passing sentence, asked the prisoner, as usual, if he had anything further to urge why sentence of death should not be passed upon him.

The unfortunate man, in an eager, excited manner, emphatically denied his guilt—declared that he was an honest, hard-working, travelling glazier, that he was at Bristol, many miles from the scene of the murder on the day of its commission, and that he knew no more about it than a babe unborn. When asked why he had not brought forward this line of defence during the trial, he declared that he had wished it, but that the gentleman who had conducted his defence had refused to do so.

His counsel, in a few words of explanation, stated that, although he had every reason to believe the story told by the prisoner, he had been forced to confine his endeavours in his behalf to breaking down the circumstantial evidence for the prosecution—that most minute and searching inquiries had been made at Bristol, but that from the short time the prisoner had passed in that town (some three or four hours), and from the lengthened period which had elapsed since the murder, he had been unable to find witnesses who could satisfactorily have proved an *alibi*, and had therefore been forced to rely upon the weakness of the evidence produced by the prosecution. Sentence of death was passed upon the prisoner, who was removed from the bar loudly and persistently declaring his innocence.

I left the court painfully impressed with the conviction that he was innocent. The passionate earnestness with which he had pleaded his own cause, the fearless, haughty expression that crossed his ill-omened features, when, finding his assertions entirely valueless, he exclaimed with an imprecation, "Well, then, do your worst, but I *am* innocent. I never saw the poor girl in my life, much less murdered her," caused the whole court, at least the unprofessional part of it, to feel that there was some doubt about the case, and that circumstantial evidence, however strong, should rarely be permitted to carry a verdict of "guilty." I am sure that the fervent though unsupported assertions made by the prisoner affected the jury far more than the florid defence made for him by his counsel.

The painful scene that I had just witnessed entirely put the events of the morning out of my head, and I walked home with my thoughts fully occupied with the trial.

The earnest protestations of the unfortunate man rang in my ears, and his face, distorted with anxiety and passion, rose ever before me.

I passed the afternoon writing answers to several business letters, which had found me out in my retreat, and soon after dinner retired to my room, weary with want of sleep the previous night and with the excitement of the day.

It had been my habit for many years to make every night short notes of the events of the day, and this evening, as usual, I sat down to write my journal. I had hardly opened the book when, to my horror, the deadly chill that I had experienced in the morning again crept round me.

I listened eagerly for the voice that had hitherto followed, but this time in vain ; not a sound could I hear but the ticking of my watch upon the table, and, I fear I must add, the beating of my own coward heart.

I got up and walked about, endeavouring to shake off my fears. The cold shadow, however, followed me about, impeding, as it seemed, my very respiration. I hesitated for a moment at the door, longing to call up the servant upon some pretext, but, checking myself, I turned to the table, and resolutely sitting down, again opened my journal.

As I turned over the leaves of the book, the word Bristol caught my eye. One glance at the page, and in an instant the following circumstances flashed across my memory.

I had been in Bristol on that very day—the day on which this dreadful murder had been committed!

On my way to a friend's house I had missed at Bristol the train I had expected to catch, and having a couple of hours to spare, wandered into the town, and entering the first hotel I came to, called for some luncheon. The annoyance I felt at having some hours to wait was aggravated by the noise a workman was making in replacing a pane of glass in one of the coffee-room windows. I spoke to him once or twice, and finding my remonstrances of no avail, walked to the window and, with the assistance of the waiter, forced the man to discontinue his work.

In an instant I recalled the features of the workman. It was the very man I had seen in the felons' dock that morning. There was no doubt about it. That hideous face as it peered through the broken pane had fixed itself indelibly in my memory, and now identified itself beyond the possibility of doubt with the sinister countenance that had impressed me so painfully in the morning.

I have little more to add. I immediately hurried back to the town and laid these facts before the judge. On communicating with the landlady of the hotel at Bristol, she was able to prove the payment of a small sum on that day to a travelling glazier. She came down to X——, and from among a crowd of felons unhesitatingly picked out the convicted man as the person to whom she had paid the money.

The poor fellow being a stranger at Bristol, and having only passed two or three hours there, was utterly unable to remember at what houses he had been employed. I myself had forgotten the fact of my having ever been in that town.

A week later the man was at liberty. Some matter-of-fact people may endeavour to divest these circumstances of their, to me, mysterious nature by ascribing them to a disordered imagination and the fortuitous recognition of a prisoner condemned to die.

Nothing will ever efface from my mind the conviction that Providence in this case chose to work out its ends by extraordinary and supernatural means.

Here ended his story. I give it you without addition or embellishment as he told it to me. It is second-hand, I confess, but hitherto I have never been fortunate enough to hear a story with aught of supernatural in it that was not open to the same objection.

JOHN HARWOOD
PUB. 1861

THE REVENUE OFFICER'S STORY

THIRTY years ago, when I was an officer of His Majesty's Customs, the maritime counties of England were in a very different condition from that in which we now observe them. The contraband trade was still flourishing; high duties and large prices tempted the smuggler to constant exertions, and there was by no means the same uniform vigilance on the part of Government officials which characterises the present day. Although I am an old man, and feel a natural fondness for bygone times when I was young and vigorous, I cannot but own that the Preventive Service of Queen Victoria's reign keeps the coasts in much better order and security than was the case under those of her grandfather and her uncles. How, indeed, could it be otherwise! We were appointed by private favour, quite without respect to merit; we were scarcely looked after by our superiors, and had a hundred reasons for our remissness. Some of us were lazy, others were timid, and not a few were bribed to hear and see nothing. Then the instruments we had to work with were not of first-rate quality. Those seaports which returned members to Parliament had their own revenue boats, manned by freemen, who drew snug salaries, and were chosen for their votes, not for their powers as oarsmen. I have known the crew of one boat quite unable to row, that of another to be found drunk and helpless at a corporation supper when wanted for a call of duty; and yet these were the assistants on whom we were compelled to rely. Our own men were not much more efficient; the Revenue gang, as it was called, consisted of dissolute scamps, seldom sober, and not seldom in league with the smugglers themselves. At the very best they were disorderly and unprincipled to an extent hardly to be believed by those who are only accustomed to the steady, well disciplined Coastguard of the present day.

In these circumstances it is not wonderful that so many prizes slipped through our fingers. The real wonder is that we made as many captures as we did. But we were not all drones in the hive. Some of us were as zealous as it is possible to be, and to this number in the year 1827 I belonged. I was then a young man, but I had been for some years in the Customs, and having recently been promoted to the rank of a riding officer, had attained to a sufficient salary to permit me to marry. My station was on the Kentish coast, near the town of D——, and it was one that gave me ample opportunities of showing my activity and zeal for the King's interest. In those days Kent and Sussex were the headquarters of what was called the Fair Trade, and a colossal traffic it was. Most of the sailors along the coast were concerned in the smuggling; almost all the traders of the towns had capital embarked in it; and even the farmers for miles inland had at least an annual share in some contraband venture. Many and many an old house is still in existence, under which are all manner of secret cellars and crypts, wherein the tea and brandy and other goods were stored when first landed; thence they were transferred to the barns of farmhouses a few miles from the coast, to disused kilns and quarries, to caves and woods and other places of concealment until they could be escorted to London.

There were great magazines of smuggled wares inland, the existence of which we vaguely knew of, but which we never even attempted to meddle with, however such a statement may provoke the incredulity of a generation accustomed to regard the law as omnipotent. But the truth is that we dared not go too far in repression of these illicit practices. If we had acted up to the full measure of our duty, we should have brought the whole hornets' nest about our ears, and that was not a risk to be made light of.

To capture a vessel and cargo did not much provoke the smugglers: their well-known calculation was that one venture successfully brought to market paid for the loss of two freights, so great were the profits in those times of a repressive tariff. But if we—the Philistines, as they called us—interfered with any of their haunts and hiding-places on shore, they regarded such an aggression as a breach of fair play, and resented it accordingly.

More than once I had received well-meant warnings from reputable townsmen or farmers that I was "too keen" in the exercise of my calling, that I should "do myself no good" if I persisted in my active career, and that I had better take pattern by old Mr. Peabody of D——, who had for forty years looked with purblind eyes after the rights of the Crown, to the great satisfaction of the fair traders. But I was too young and hot-blooded—I hope I may add, too honest—to follow this kindly advice. To be a dumb, toothless watchdog like old Lieutenant Peabody, neither barking nor biting, but eating the King's bread on false pretences, had something in it unconquerably repulsive to me. I liked to do my duty, to receive the praise of my chiefs, the Assistant Commissioners, who had already begun to talk of my future promotion. I even took a sort of pleasure in remembering that my name was known and my vigilance feared by the hardiest desperadoes of the coast, and that my exploits had even found a niche in a corner of the county newspaper.

But I had yet another and more solid reason for trying in every way to win advancement by merit superior to that of my colleagues. I was married, as I have said, and to one born in a rank of life rather above my own—the orphan daughter of a clergyman. Cheerfully and smilingly had Lucy shared my poverty, but still I longed to be able to provide her with the comforts that had surrounded her in her youth, and it was mostly for her sake that I aspired to rise in my profession. Let no one laugh that a gauger should be ambitious. There are callings more popular and exalted, ay, and more agreeable, but no trade deserves to be utterly despised in which a man can do his work honourably and keep his hands clean from knavish practices.

The autumn of the year I have named had been a rough one, with strong, blustering weather. Such weather as that we had had is that which smugglers love. Bright nights and moonlit seas are less to their fancy than the dark and dirty weather that hides their operations from hostile eyes. In spite of the revenue officers, then, the "runs" had been many and profitable. The Government cutters had made few captures; the guard on shore had been baffled in almost every instance. In only one case had a large seizure been effected, and I thought myself the most fortunate of mankind in being the cause of it. Little did I dream, however, when in my lonely rides across the downs I came upon that solitary hiding-place and detected its secrets, that it was my own destruction I was toiling to effect! Little did I imagine what was to follow, and what dire vengeance I was thoughtlessly provoking, when I made that ill-omened discovery. The hiding-place was in itself very curious and ingenious. Near a lone farmhouse on the high chalk downs, four miles from the sea, was a well, an old, deep well, with buckets, chain, windlass, and wooden cover, not in the least differing from a thousand other wells in the south of England. But forty feet below the surface there was a cave, or tunnelled passage, excavated in the side of this well wide enough to admit two men, and it led to a large grotto scooped out of the solid chalk, and which made a dry and roomy storehouse for the kegs and bales that filled it. Any one might have peeped down the well and suspected nothing; nor should I had I not happened to ride up just as two men, toiling at the windlass, had drawn to the light of day a bucket containing, not water, but a man in a pea-jacket and red cap, with a keg on his knee suspiciously suggestive of Hollands. This was enough for me as I reined up my horse in the shadow of the peach-wall of the garden and peered cautiously at the scene. Quietly, as a huntsman who marks the fox steal out of covert, I made my way homewards across the springy turf, but not unseen, for when I returned with a strong force in two hours' time, the lace and silks had been removed from the well, and nothing but the bulky spirits, claret, and tea remained at the disposal of His Majesty's servants. Still, this capture made a great noise. The Assistant Commissioner, Sir John Buckram, came to D—— on purpose to report upon it, praised me at the corporation feast, and in private promised me both reward and advancement on the very next occasion when the Minister should ask him to dinner, and thus afford him an opportunity of urging my claims.

Elated by all this, I cared little for the melancholy way in which some of those townsmen who were supposed to have the best means of knowing the opinions of the smugglers shook their heads at me when we met, and heeded even less the threatening letters which now began to arrive at my house. Ugly documents they were these latter; misspelt and scrawled in villainous caligraphy as if the authors wrote with a bayonet dipped in moistened gunpowder; but their contents many a time made Lucy's bright eyes grow dim and blanched her blooming cheek. I almost wish I had kept one or two that I might favour the public with a facsimile; but it can easily be imagined what sort of menaces would suggest themselves to rude, untutored beings, as wild as the waves on which they pursued their illegal and dangerous calling. I paid no heed to these threats, however, but pursued the same course as before.

One dark December afternoon—the fifth of the month it was, for I have cause to remember the date—a letter of a different stamp arrived at my dwelling. It bore the signature of the superintendent, my immediate superior, and was dated from F——, a neighbouring town, where I knew that officer resided. The letter informed me that, according to intelligence received from private sources, a great cargo was on that very night to be landed on the coast between D—— and F——. I was instructed to repair at eleven o'clock precisely to a particular part of the cliff, where I should find the superintendent and his men, who were desirous to avail themselves of my local knowledge and well-known activity in effecting this most important capture. The letter was addressed in red ink as usual, bearing the talismanic "On His Majesty's service," and was sealed with the huge red seal commonly decorating such documents. One portion of the letter I have forgotten to mention. The superintendent strictly enjoined me to come alone, and on no account to speak of his communication or the rendezvous to any person at D——, whether connected with the service or not.

All that evening while I was preparing for my nocturnal expedition Lucy was sad and out of spirits, and I continually found her eyes fixed upon me with a mournful tenderness that struck a chill to my heart in spite of myself. I, on the contrary, was rather disposed to be gay and hopeful, for here was a capital opportunity of again signalising my zeal for the King's interests and of earning the good-will of my chiefs and perhaps that promotion which had been so lately promised me.

But Lucy was not happy ; her wistful glance followed me as I moved about the little humble parlour, oiling and loading my pistols, getting ready my sword and belts, my waterproof cloak and high boots, and laying everything in the place where I could most readily snatch it up when after supper it should be time to start. Many a night had Lucy seen me busied with the self-same preparations, but never before had her heart been so heavy or her blue eyes so tearful. She was always recurring in a restless manner to the letter of the superintendent, asking to see it again and again, reading it over slowly, weighing every syllable as a scholar cons some rare manuscript in a half-forgotten language, and questioning me as to the writer's purport and meaning, in a way that would have been provoking in any one else.

" Was I *quite* sure," she asked, " that the letter was really in the superintendent's handwriting, and had I any of his former epistles in the house with which I could compare it ? "

I laughed at her ; but she persisted, and then I was obliged to own that I did not know the official's penmanship in the least. He had been newly appointed and was personally a stranger in those parts ; and though I thought I had seen documents in his writing at the Custom-house, I had never paid any attention to the caligraphy and should not know it again.

Next, Lucy fell to examining the seal, as I have seen antiquaries poring over some half-effaced medal or coin in a museum. But this, she was forced to confess, was exactly as usual, the same lion and unicorn, the same royal arms, and the identical motto ; even the prodigality with which the sealing-wax had been used and the smears and blotches of it that had fallen on the envelope had an official character that defied dispute. Then Lucy must proceed to ask questions about the contents of the document, and to wonder especially why the superintendent should have desired me so peremptorily to bring no one with me from D—— and to observe strict silence as to the orders received ?

To this I could only answer, firstly, that my business was to obey my superiors, not to interrogate their motives ; and, secondly, that no doubt the superintendent was aware that some of our hired men were allies of the smugglers and in their pay, and that others were drunken rascals, who would be certain in their cups to divulge the whole affair in some water-side public-house. In fact, there were very few, in those days before the Reform Bill, on whom reliance could be placed, especially in a borough like D——, where the freemen who were in Government employ, on account of their votes, were frequently near relations of the very smugglers whom they were set to watch.

Now the superintendent, whom I had heard described as an energetic officer, had brought down with him a party of trusty subordinates, who had no local ties or likings to interfere with their utility. It was natural that he should prefer relying on his own people, and no less natural that he should desire to benefit by the minute acquaintance with the various gullies and coves of the coast for which I had acquired some credit.

My young wife listened to all this, and was silenced, but not satisfied.

Supper was a melancholy meal that night, in spite of the cheerfulness I sought to impart by dwelling upon the bright prospects in store for us. I talked of the certainty of my speedy promotion to the place which it was daily expected would be resigned by the superannuated Lieutenant Peabody ; and then I made a mental leap over the next two or three years and saw myself a superintendent and on the high-road to a still snugger berth in London itself in the head Custom-house. And I talked of a nice cottage at Islington, with garden and coach-house, and of the best of schooling for little Alfred, who was to grow up a gentleman and be in the Church like his grandfather, and in fact I built a score of those castles in the air which Lucy, in common with many young mothers, dearly loved. But though my wife tried to smile and prattle in her customary style, it was to no purpose ; and whenever she thought I did not observe her, her eyes would fix on me in a frightened sort of way, as if she saw a peril that was invisible to others.

From one mood to another the transition is often very abrupt, and perhaps it is hardly wonderful that, having failed to cheer up Lucy, I should next have grown irritable and morose. I looked at my watch, took an extra glass of grog, and, pushing aside my plate, rose from the table and began to get on my accoutrements in silence. As I buckled the broad leathern belt around me and stuck my pistols in it Lucy shuddered perceptibly. Often had she seen me go forth before on nights as dark and on errands as full of danger, but without any tremor, outwardly, at least. I took no notice ; I finished equipping myself, linking my sword close up to my left side lest it should rattle, and throwing my thick rough greggoe over all. But then Lucy came nestling to my side and passed her soft arm around my neck and spoke and looked so tenderly and graciously that I must have been made of crabbed stuff indeed had not my ill-temper vanished before the true eyes and the fond smile. And then nothing would serve her but she must bring baby out of his little cot to kiss papa before he went away; and the child cried, of course, at being disturbed out of his slumber and because he did not know me in the huge cloak and oilskin hat, and Lucy hushed him in that marvellous way she had—a power of coaxing that the most stubborn urchin could never have resisted. But there was something solemn in this outburst of Lucy's tenderness; the terrors, vague and shapeless, had not quite died out of her dear blue eyes and her voice trembled as she made baby join his little pink hands and murmur his little prayer for papa. I had heard her do so before, but never with such a depth of troubled expression, and I could tell that she was ill at ease. However, I pressed my lips on Lucy's soft cheek and then on the child's little rosy face and hurried out of the room.

I had got but a short way down the cobble-stoned pavement of the narrow street, dark and silent as the tomb, before I heard my name called.

"Alfred! Alfred! *One* word, dearest!"

I came back and found Lucy standing in the doorway, peering out into the night.

"Well! What is this wonderful word?" asked I. "Be quick, love, or I shall get a scolding for not being punctual."

"Alfred, dear!" said my wife hesitatingly, "something weighs on my mind to-night. Are you quite, *quite* sure about that letter?"

"Sure of what?" asked I perhaps a little peevishly.

"Sure that it really came from F—— ? that the superintendent really wrote it?"

I laughed, stopped her mouth with a kiss, telling her she was a little goose, not fit to be a sailor's wife, and strode fast down the street again. At the corner I looked back half involuntarily, and there was the door still ajar and a streak of yellow light falling across the pavement, and Lucy on the threshold, watching my retreating steps. I waved my hand, turned the corner, and plunged into the still and sombre town.

I had a long way to walk through the roughly paved, mean streets of the little seaport, dimly lighted as they were by the miserable oil-lamps that swung in the boisterous wind. The shutters were up everywhere, though now and then a gush of light would stream from between their chinks and I could hear voices chatting over the cozy fires and supper-tables. The public-houses that I passed were not empty, for there was a crimson glow visible through their red curtains and voices were heard singing or disputing in sea slang.

I got clear of the town at last and took my lonely way up the white chalk road that led to the lofty cliffs. It was a wild night. The wind dragged and tore at my cloak, and but for the ribbon I wore I should have lost my hat before I had got twenty yards beyond the lee of the last house. Above there was a tempestuous sky, where the black clouds were rolled along in masses before the gale and the moon peeped out very seldom—a faint new moon, like a little white crescent—while it was very dark and cheerless. In spite of my efforts I could not keep a light heart in my breast: all nature seemed to menace and frown, and do what I would Lucy's mournful mood, the shadow of coming evil, weighed down my usually elastic spirits. Her last question, idle as I had deemed it, kept recurring to my memory: "Was I *quite* sure that the superintendent wrote the letter?" In vain I dismissed the question; in vain I called it silly, trivial, the mere suggestion of fancy; it rang in my ears again and again as I battled my way onwards against the powerful wind.

I was off the chalk road by this time and my feet were treading the crisp herbage of the downs. I was now obliged to advance with precaution for the ground was irregular and I had to climb up a steep slope of turf to reach the place of rendezvous. I came to it at last: I knew it well; a giant cliff beetling proudly above the chafing sea and in shape resembling a monstrous wheel placed edgewise on its tire. A well-known landmark was that cliff over many a league of sea; beacon fires had blazed on it in old times; a mighty poet had described its towering steep in words as grandly simple as itself, and throughout the length and breadth of England the precipice was known by the poet's name. For a moment I lingered on the brow of the grim sea rampart and looked out into the pall of darkness, through which the waves murmured with a mysterious sound, unseen as they were. Far away over the waters I could catch, through a break in the phalanx of clouds, the red glare of a light to warn ships from a place of peril. A moment and the dark sky swallowed it up. No trace of man or his works was now visible. A shudder ran through me; an impulse seemed to urge me to fly, to hurry away homewards, to shun—what? Pshaw! What a pitiful coward I should grow were I often thus! Was I a child to fear a dark night and a high wind! I pushed on, sneering at my own qualms. In a couple of minutes I could make out a clump of black objects specking the hillside and standing within a few feet of the verge itself. Bushes or men? Men, for I hear the muttering of their voices. The superintendent and his party, no doubt. I hastened up to them.

"Good night, gentlemen!"

They answered never a word. In silence they opened their ranks to receive me; my practised eye made out, as I passed in among them, that they numbered eighteen or twenty. A whistle, sharp and shrill, a roar of triumph, and I was seized and grappled with by a dozen strong hands at once. So sudden was the attack, so complete the surprise, that, although neither a feeble nor a timid man, before I could strike a blow or draw a pistol I was pinioned, disarmed, and borne down. The smugglers! Quick as lightning itself the terrible thought flashed upon me that I had fallen into a cunningly devised snare and was at the mercy of those lawless men, who had most cause to hate me.

"A rat in a trap!—a rat in trap!" cried several hoarse voices at once; "we've got the gauger at last!" And then followed a storm of abusive epithets and coarse taunts mingled with still feller curses.

"Murder the scoundrel!" "Blow his brains out without more palaver!" "Cut him into bait for eels!" "Pitch the land-shark over the cliffs!" Such were a few of the savage proposals of those who crowded round me.

"Stop!" called out a voice in tones of authority; "drag the fellow up; help him to his feet, some of you; and you, Bill, flash the glim on his face to make sure he's the right devil's chicken for us."

I was dragged to my feet; my hands were by this time securely bound with a lanyard and all resistance was impossible. Involuntarily I closed my eyes as the red bull's-eye of a dark-lantern was flashed full on my face.

"Our bird! We've netted the villain himself!" was the unanimous acclaim. I opened my eyes, and by the partial glare of the lantern, dazzled as I was, I could see that I was in the grasp of several stoutly made men in sailor garb, but much muffled and disguised. They were armed, for I could see the brass hilts of cutlasses and the brass-bound stocks of pistols peep here and there from under a peacoat or an oilskin wraprascal, but every man wore a crape mask or else had his face so besmeared with soot and gunpowder as to present the aspect of a negro and baffled recognition. He who seemed their chief was taller and more slender of build than the rest, though clad and armed in the same way, and he wore a loose crape before his face that fluttered with the action of his breath. I could see only his eyes looking out from the slits in the veil; his voice was less gruff than the voices of his comrades; I felt assured that he, alone, was a man of education and that on his fiat hung my doom.

"The same," said the leader after a pause, "Alfred Harvey."

There was another roar.

"Kill him!" "Drown the gauger as you'd drown a mangy kitten!" "Pitch him over!" "Shoot him!" and other pleasant propositions were bellowed forth on every hand. Nor were the marks of ill-will entirely verbal. I was roughly shaken and struck by my captors, and nothing but the crowd that pressed around saved me from the more lethal strokes of clubs and cutlasses which were aimed at my defenceless head by some of the more excited of my foes.

" Who boarded the *Blue Bell*," growled one husky voice, " and grabbed twenty puncheons of as good Hollands as——? "

" Who stopped the waggon by the ninth mile-stone and seized the goods that would have given a merry Christmas to half Lingham parish ? " interrupted a second fellow.

" Who made me a poor man along of tobacco ? " fiercely demanded a scowling mariner, whose face I vainly scanned, so completely was it disguised by its swart colouring.

" This be he," snarled a fourth accuser, " that, when we'd made the D—— boat's crew as drunk as the Baltic ocean, must needs go and bring down the cursed revenue cutter upon our craft, by token of which I had three years in a man-o'-war till I gave leg-bail, and sha'n't I have my revenge now ? "

" Think of the Well ! " bawled a fifth, and then the rage of the ruffians became overpowering. I was buffeted, overthrown, and thought I should have been trampled to death. Then I was on my feet again, bruised and dizzy, and I felt something like a cold metal ring pressing my forehead, and I knew it was the muzzle of a pistol. I shut my eyes mechanically, breathed an inward prayer to heaven, and resigned myself to my fate.

" Fire, Jack ! " exclaimed several of the gang.

" Hold ! " cried the voice of the leader of this infernal crew, " hold ! Would you cheat the gallows of its due ? The eaves-dropping rogue does not deserve to go out of the world in so gentlemanly a fashion."

" That's true," was the rejoinder, and then followed some fresh comments.

" Shootin's too easy a death for such as he ! "

" Captain's right ! "

" Hang the land-shark ! " " Over the cliff !—over the cliff ! "

And the pistol was withdrawn. I was almost sorry. Death had only left me for a moment to return in some more hideous shape.

" No hurry, boys," said the superior ruffian ; " let us hear if he's anything to say in his own defence." There was a murmur, but the man had evidently much influence, and I was accordingly drawn before him and bidden to " speak up." I never shall forget that scene. The stormy night, the wild cliff, the lantern flashing upon the grim circle of blackened faces, the figure of the self-constituted judge, tall and shadowy, with only his eyes gleaming through the fluttering veil—all these were the features rather of a nightmare than of anything belonging to the real world. The whole was like some shocking dream, but it had a ghastly truth in it.

" Alfred Harvey," said the chief, and for all his soft tones I felt more fear of him than of all the rest of the howling pack, " Alfred Harvey, if you have anything to plead—speak."

I spoke, but with despair at my heart. I declared that I had done nothing but my duty to the King without fear or favour—that I had borne no grudge to any man—had never been unnecessarily severe or harsh, and had merely behaved as any honest officer in my position would have done. But my plea failed of its effect. Those rugged jurors were too prejudiced to give me a hearing. They drowned my words with oaths and violent clamour.

" Silence the sea-lawyer ! " was the cry, and I bitterly felt that hope was at an end.

" Alfred Harvey," said the leader, " listen, and you, men, hearken to the sentence. This gauger is not one of the common run of Philistines for whom some mild punishment, such as the slitting of nose and ears, or keelhauling, or even flogging and pickling, might have been enough. I declare that if it were not for that Well business I should be for some such light infliction, but, unhappily, my duty is a sterner one. Gauger, your sentence is—death ! Tie him neck and heels and pitch him to the fishes."

" Tide's out ! " remarked a fellow who held me by the shoulder.

" Our friend will not, then, fall so soft as I thought," said the smuggler-captain.

A hoarse laugh hailed the brutal pleasantry. I made a violent effort to break the cord on my wrists, but though I loosened I could not snap the bonds ; and though I struggled hard I was completely helpless in so many muscular hands. I pleaded no more. I scorned to ask for mercy, but, alas ! my entreaties would have been idle. They led me, unresisting, to the edge of the tall cliff, beneath which boomed the sea. The moon, by this, had broken through the clouds a little, and by her wan white light I could just see, at an awful depth below me, the narrow strip of beach, the narrower strip of sand beyond, spotted with chalk boulders, and the line of foamy breakers boiling on the shore.

" Now, lads, take a good grip of the gauger," cried the chief. " One, two, three, and away ! " I was drawn back a pace or two and lifted from the ground by several strong arms.

" I give the word," said the chief. " One ! "

I was silent in my agony ; I bit my lips lest a cry for mercy should escape ; I grudged my tormentors that triumph.

" Two ! " called out the leader.

There was a pause. I was swinging half off the cliff and my

captors were preparing to launch me into the abyss. "Three!" already trembled on the lips of the smuggler-captain.

"Poor Lucy! God guard my wife and child!" broke from my lips half unconsciously as I was on the point of being hurled over the precipice into the blackness of the night. There was a murmur and a movement among the men who held me. Those last words of mine, not addressed to them, had produced an effect which no oratory could have done. My entreaties they would have mocked; but after all, rugged and fierce as they were, they had wives and children of their own that they loved, and my outspoken prayer had touched a chord in their wild hearts that made them pause.

"Three!" said the leader, but no response followed. They set me down and stood hesitating, muttering to one another in low tones.

"I'll have no hand in it," said one, the very fellow who had put the pistol to my brow.

"Jem says he's seen her," grumbled another voice.

"Ay!" answered Jem, "a pretty little blue-eyed lass she be; kind to the poor, too, my old mother said."

"Sink me if I like it!" said another.

"Are ye chicken-hearted, you tender-conscienced, go-to-meeting dunces?" sneered the captain.

But the rough hearts of the men were touched, and they got round their leader, muttering what I could not hear. A long discussion followed. I stood, meanwhile, dazed and stupefied, quivering, as it were, on the threshold betwixt death and life. The debate, of which I did not catch a word, ended with a guffaw of boisterous laughter that went roaring away on the wind. Then the captain spoke.

"Gauger," said he, "we are going to give you a chance. Instead of pitching you to the crabs, we mean to hang you over the edge of the cliff, like a limpet on a rock, and leave you clinging. If you hold on till morning some shepherd will save you for the gallows. If you drop—good night!" Before I could reply, I was seized again, a gag was thrust into my mouth, I was closely blindfolded, and led along the cliff to its highest point. As far as I could judge I thus traversed above a hundred yards. Then the wretches lifted me over the edge and lowered me until my chin just rested on the turf, while my hands, still tied together by the rope, were placed on the edge, so as to take a firm hold of the earth and tufted grass.

"Hold fast, gauger!" were the last words I heard, and they were almost drowned by the yells of laughter, wild, unfeeling laughter, of the ruffians who thus sported with my anguish. I could hear their retiring steps. Their voices grew feebler and more faint; they had left me to perish. "Cruel, indeed, are the tender mercies of the wicked." I was spared merely as a cat spares a half-dead mouse; my agonies were prolonged. But for the gag I would have called to beg that a bullet might end my sufferings. But they were gone, and I remained, blindfolded, and suspended by my hands over the stony beach and the roaring sea. Like the fabled coffin of Mahomet, I hung between heaven and earth in mid-air. Death—a death cruel and imminent was before me. On the other hand, but a few feet of the perpendicular chalk wall divided me from life and liberty. But I was powerless to lift myself out of that nether abyss over which I swung as the strong wind rocked me sideways on my dangerous perch. For the first few minutes there was a humming in my ears like the noise of bees murmuring among the flowers in the pleasant summertime. Then this sensation, which must have been caused by a rush of blood to the head, faded away and my thoughts became endowed with almost supernatural activity. Dangling thus over my yawning grave, I seemed to take in at one eagle glance my whole past life, things long forgotten, the joys and sorrows of infancy, lessons learned at my mother's knee, childish quarrels and frowardness, and reconciliations; how I played truant at school, how I won the prize, how I was punished for some boyish fault. These and many other scenes of early life passed before my blinded eyes as if painted on the slides of a magic lantern. Then I was a man and already in my profession; my first capture, my first encounter with smugglers came before me with startling vividness, and in fancy I felt the boat bound over the phosphorescent sea, all aglow with its blue sparkles, and as we neared the prize, and the firing and shouting began, I imagined myself once more in the old wild excitement, cheering the rowers, and with my heart bounding to every stroke of the flashing oars that carried us up to the doomed lugger. And next I was a young lover, walking at Lucy's side among the white and pink blossoms of a Devonshire orchard, and I was whispering in her ear as she blushed and faltered a rosier, fairer bloom than aught else the summer could show on the day I asked her to be mine. Then I saw little Alfred's childish face and wondering eyes, very near to mine, it seemed, and wonderfully clear and distinct, and I heard the lisping of the innocent baby's voice as he prayed for me. And then I laughed, or seemed to laugh, a horrid mad laugh, that shook and tortured me, but the gag was fast between my teeth and no sound came forth. Next I grew half delirious and my thoughts were fantastic and quaint. I was a spider swinging by a thread from a wall; I was a bat hanging by its claws in a church tower; I was a sea-mew poised on white wings over a seething sea. And then pain and cold brought back my senses. The wind was bitter, and my teeth seemed to chatter, and my feet were cold as stones and heavy as lead. Already I had hung for some time over the rock, and my hands were aching, and there were sharp cramps racking my overstrained joints, and my neck was half-dislocated. Still for dear life I clung on. My mind was active. My thoughts flew off to Lucy and her child, to her terrors and grief, to the cold, bare poverty in store for her and hers, now the bread-winner was gone. For I deemed myself already dead. Hope was a mockery now. No mortal strength could maintain that despairing grip until the morning, and even were dawn at hand aid might not come for hours. No, for me all was over. My fancy pictured Lucy, in black, pale and poor, plying her needle in some garret, far off in some dismal quarter of a great city, where alone could scanty bread be earned for herself and her pining child. And then the clock on the belfry tower of St. James's Church in D—— struck the hour, and the wind bore the sound to my ears. Twelve! every metallic chime clear and plain! Twelve! Eight more hours of darkness. No man's strength could endure a tithe of the trial. Poor Lucy! I prayed inwardly, not for life, that seemed gone, save a miracle should pluck me back from the grave, but for pardon of my sins, for mercy to those I left, that the wind might not visit too harshly those poor lone lambs. The gale slackened and a cold rain fell, lashing my face as I clung. The cramped position of my limbs gave me much pain, gradually increasing to unbearable torture. I was tempted to loosen my grasp, and to drop at once into the depths below. Still, I held on. Blindfolded as I was I vividly pictured the beach below, the pebbly bank of shingle, the yellow sand, the fragments of chalk that lay as they had fallen, the waves beating on the shore. If I fell on the beach while the tide was still out I should be dashed to pieces, surely. Would such a death be very painful? I imagined the rush through the air, the sense of falling through space, the breathless rapidity of the descent, the crash upon the hard beach. Should I feel it? Was it possible that I should lie for hours, like a crushed worm, with broken bones and spine, longing for death, but lingering on? Better be drowned than this. Ah, if I could but hold on till the tide makes, the sea will give me a comparatively painless ending. This new sad hope made me tighten my clutch: I could not live, but drowning, I had heard, was an easier death than such a fall as that before me. But why die at all if I could keep my grasp till the sea washed the cliff's foot? I could swim well. I might escape. Never, never, the cruel cord that tied my galled wrists would prevent my buffeting the waves. Should I end the suspense and spring out to meet my doom half-way? No, no! I heard the waves howling nearer; I would wait, wait. Cramped, racked with pains, I could hardly hold on. But for the support my chin afforded I must have succumbed before. I had driven my stiffening fingers into the short turf, and held it in a death-grip. But my powers were going fast ; I was sick, dizzy, worn out. Ha ! I may as well die like a man, in a struggle for life. I remembered that by a great effort I might climb to the top of the cliff and be saved. True, the exertion would be exhausting to my last remains of strength ; true, there were heavy odds against it, bound as I was, but in a few moments it would be too late to try. I nerved myself for the trial, and manfully tried to lift myself, like a gymnast, by my hands, above the beetling cliff. For a moment I rose ; I was poised in mid-air ? I was succeeding, but the cord restrained me, my tortured arms gave way ; I sank, my chin slipped off the edge of the precipice, and I now dangled, swaying at the full extent of my arms. This could not last. The pain was great ; my strength was gone ; in a minute I must let go and fall to die. And then a wild notion seized me that perhaps the smugglers, less utterly barbarous than I thought, were at hand, watching me, ready to save me at the last. Surely, surely, it must be so. I strove to cry to them for help, to scream that in a second it would be too late. I was gagged. No word could I utter. The bitterness of death came upon me. *I let go my hold.* But no rush, no swift dart into mid-air followed. My feet sank but a few inches and then touched the ground, the firm, solid ground ! It was no dream ! Was I snatched from destruction by a miracle ? I fainted, and fell to the earth. When I came to myself it was morning ; I was lying, soaked and chilled, on the wet ground ; two men, shepherds, were beside me, and one of them was trying to force gin from a pocket-flash between my teeth, while the other was loosening my cravat. The bandage had been removed from the eyes, and the cord cut that tied my wrists. I looked up, wondering whether I were in this world or the next.

" I'm mortal glad, master, you're come round at last," said one of the shepherds, " though how you comed here nobody could guess."

I looked wildly about. I was not on the beach ; no cliff towered overhead. I was lying in a sort of scoop or bowl in the chalk downs, not uncommon on the cliffs of the Kentish coast. And I may as well at once explain as well as I can the cruel trick of which I had been the victim. I have no doubt whatever that the smugglers, when they ensnared me by means of the forged letter, meant to have my life, which at the last moment they spared by one of those wayward impulses of generosity which sometimes sway even the most abandoned men. They had abstained from spilling my blood, not for my sake, but for the sake of my innocent wife and child, the only plea which could have moved them. But they had not been willing to let me altogether escape punishment for my over-zeal, and accordingly they had placed me in a position where I was sure to feel all the bitterness of death save the final pang. They had left me suspended, blindfold, over the edge of a shallow pit in the chalk, less than nine feet in depth, but with the full conviction that I was actually dangling over the giddy edge of the giant cliff, with a terrible death creeping upon me by slow degrees. The bottom was never above a yard from my feet, and when I fell to the full extent of my arms, being a man six feet in height, I was within some six inches of the ground. But I died a thousand deaths in one during the awful hour I spent upon Poet's Cliff.

. . . .

I resigned my situation. The illness brought on by that dreadful night aged and enfeebled me much, and I was glad to accept a clerk's place in a London institution, which my pitying friends procured for me. I have thriven in another walk of life. Lucy is still by my side, my stay and comfort, and my children are all I could wish. But I have never quite recovered the hideous anguish of that grim ordeal.

ANONYMOUS
PUB. 1863

THE CENTURION'S ESCAPE

A TALE OF THE EGYPTIAN PRIESTHOOD[1]

" How cursedly hot it is," muttered the Centurion Septimius to his lieutenant, grave old Lepidus, as he lay half stripped in the shade of his tent, longing for the Northern wind.

And he might well say so. The place was Syene, the time the month of August, and the almost vertical sun was pouring down his rays with a fierceness such as the Roman officer had never felt before.

Septimius and his cohort had been marched up to Syene to hold in check the inhabitants of the neighbourhood, who, servile in general, and little recking then as now who was their master, provided the taxes were not too heavy, had been stirred up by the priests to a state of most unwonted agitation, in consequence of some insult offered by the Roman soldiery to the sacred animals of the district.

The palm-trees were standing motionless, not a breath stirring their long pendent branches ; the broad, swollen Nile was glittering like molten metal as he rolled majestically to the sea. In the background the steep sandy ridges and black crags were baking in the sun, and the only sound that broke the silence was the roar of the distant cataract.

[1] The plot of the following tale first suggested itself to the writer while examining the wonderful remains of secret passages, dungeons, etc., in the Island of Philæ, at the southern extremity of Egypt. The story has *no foundation in fact* ; but, so far as passages, escapes, etc., are concerned, *might possibly* have happened. Somewhere similar machinery has been employed in the early portion of Moore's *Epicurean*. The only *unexplained mystery*, the visions which were seen by Lepidus, might have been managed by the help of a magic-lantern ; and his subsequent fainting fit is easily explained, by the use of the fumes of Indian hemp or some similar narcotic. The whole magic in the story is *trickery*. How far the Egyptians, particularly in the olden time, may have been acquainted with mesmerism, clairvoyance, second sight, or similar phenomena is a difficult, perhaps an unanswerable, question. That, in later times, they adopted mere mechanical and chemical jugglery there can be no doubt.

"Curse these Egyptians and their gods," muttered poor melting Septimius. "I only wish I had the bull Apis here to-day, or that lumbering brute Basis which pretty Cleopatra used to worship at Hermonthis, and I would see how *he* could stand this weather. I say, Lepidus, a steak cut out of Apis would be a blessed change for us from those eternal scraggy fowls that they feed us on. How snug the fat brute looked in his temple at Memphis. I only wish the Emperor's Centurions were put up half as luxuriously."

"Hush, hush, Septimius," answered Lepidus, his second in command, "you shouldn't ventilate those free-thinking opinions of yours so openly. Whatever you *think*, keep a check on your tongue, for the old priesthood is jealous and powerful even yet, and strange stories are told of their secret doings."

"A fig for the priesthood!" quoth Septimius. "What care I for Apis or Osiris either? I am a Roman citizen and a Roman soldier. I fear no man but my superior officer, and I know no god but the Emperor."

"Mark my words," was the reply. "Antony was a greater than you, Septimius, and *he* bowed the knee to Apis and Osiris too; why, they say he was consecrated himself, and stood high in the priestly ranks, and yet he crouched like a beaten hound to old Petamon, the priest of Isis, and obeyed his very nod. I have heard strange things of that Petamon; men say he knew the old Egyptian secrets, and could raise the very dead from their long sleep to answer him. And his grandson and successor is a mightier enchanter than his sire. It was he that stirred up these poor Egyptian slaves almost to rebellion not ten days ago, because one of the legionaries broke the head of a dirty ape that he caught stealing the stores. They say he is at Philæ just now concocting some new plot; so, my good fellow, *do* keep your eyes open and your mouth shut—if you can."

Septimius laughed, half good-naturedly, half contemptuously; and, humming a stave of Horace, turned in to take a nap, while Lepidus went round the sentries to see that none were sleeping on their posts.

It was evening, the sun had set some half-hour before; and the sky, after melting through all the hues of the rainbow had merged in one delicious violet, in which the pure clear moon and the planet Venus were shining with a glorious light such as they never attain in duller climes, and throwing long, quivering, silver reflections across the dark water; the soldiery were preparing for their night's rest, and the simple inhabitants of the country had already forgotten all their cares in sleep. The silence was broken only by the baying of a few dogs and the howl of a distant jackal when Septimius, shaking off his drowsiness, left his tent to saunter through the village and see how his troop were faring.

The beauty and stillness of the night tempted him to extend his ramble. The purlieus of the town were soon passed, the few dogs he met shrank cowering from before his tall form and the clank of the good sword at his side, and in a few moments he was alone in the desert. He had more than once followed the same track towards the now silent quarries, where the old Egyptians once hewed those blocks of granite which are a wonder to all succeeding ages. It was the *same* scene, yet how different! When he had marched over the ground once before at the head of his legionaries to check an incursion of one of the marauding desert tribes, the sky seemed brass, the earth iron, the sun was blazing overhead like a ball of molten metal, and scorching all colour and life out of the landscape; the heat, reflected from the black basalt and red syenite rocks, had beaten on his armour almost beyond endurance, while his stout soldiers could barely struggle on through the heavy sand, sighing and groaning for one drop of water where none was to be had.

How different it was now; the moon, hanging low in the heavens, threw the long black shadows of the craggy rocks over the silvered sand; and the air was deliciously cool and fresh after the extreme heat of the day.

So he wandered on till he reached a huge boulder, on which some old Pharaoh, now forgotten, had carved the record of his marches and victories. The figures of gods and kings were half obliterated, but the Centurion stood trying to follow the mouldering lines in idle curiosity.

"Be their gods true or false," muttered he, "they were great men, these Egyptians, and their works are mighty—surely 'there were giants in those days.'"

As he turned round a huge crag behind him was shaped out by the uncertain moonlight into the figure of a colossus seated on a throne, such as he had seen at Thebes, on his way to Syene, and that so distinctly that he was for a moment fairly startled. Ere long the light changed and the colossus faded away again into an ordinary rock.

Suddenly from behind the boulder an old man advanced to him, and bowing low, with the cringing servility to which the lower classes of the Egyptians had been reduced by long ages of tyranny, prostrated himself at the feet of the Centurion, and in broken Greek craved a hearing. Septimius was good-natured and at a loss for occupation: he therefore gladly welcomed the interruption, and as he was, like all well-educated men of his time, as well or better acquainted with Greek than with his native tongue, in a few kindly words bade the old man speak on.

" My lord Centurion," said the beggar, " I have followed your steps for days in the hope of obtaining a hearing. My tongue is Greek, but my heart is true. You have heard of the Egyptian priesthood and their wiles ; not long ago one of your nation, a Centurion like yourself, fell into their hands, and they hold him captive in the neighbourhood. If you would deliver him come here to-morrow night, and come alone ; I will tell you *then* what must be done, but I cannot now—meanwhile farewell."

And ere the Centurion could utter a word he had vanished behind the rocks.

" By Castor and Pollux," muttered Septimius, " was ever a decent fellow—*not* that I *am* a particularly decent fellow—in such a fix before ? It *may* be a trap set for me ; yet surely they *dare* not touch a soldier of the Emperor's—a Centurion too," he said. " Ay, poor Claudius vanished a month ago ; they said it was a crocodile, but none saw it—yes, it must be Claudius ; go I will, let Lepidus say what he likes ; but stay, if I tell Lepidus he will have my steps dogged, or some such nonsense. I'll keep my own counsel ; I'll go, and go alone." With a brisk step he turned on his heel and wended his way back to his quarters.

The beggar stood behind the rock, his keen black eyes glittering with the light of triumph ; his long white beard fell off, and the rags dropped from his shoulders as he joined his companion who was lying perdue behind the rock. He drew himself up to his full stature, and his haughty step and proud port marked Petamon, the son of Osorkon, and grandson of Petamon, the High Priest of Isis at Philæ.

" Hey, Sheshonk," he laughed to his subordinate, with a snort of scorn, " I have baited the trap for my eagle right daintily, and the noble bird shall have his wings clipped ere long. *He* mocks the divine Apis, does he, and blasphemes the Ape of Thoth ! *He* thinks to come here and lord it over us all with his licentious soldiery and his cursed Roman pride. We have been slaves before, but we have never been slaves for long ; and, as the Shepherds and the Persians have passed away to nothingness and *we* remain, so these Romans shall have their day and perish too. The vengeance of Heaven fell heavily on Cambyses for the blood of the murdered Apis, and shall this son of the Italian wolf escape ? By Him that sleeps in Philæ he shall bow the knee to the gods, and swear to betray his country and his Emperor, or die ! " And his pale face, in which, worn though it was with care, and distorted by passion, might still be traced the majestic lineaments of the great Rameses himself, spoke his unchangeable resolve.

" Well done, Petamon," quoth Sheshonk, the assistant-priest, whose low forehead, heavy brow, and sensual lips were in strange contrast to his companion's face, "what a pity there is nobody here to listen to you, and that such eloquence should be thrown away upon me, who know, as well as you do yourself, if the truth were told, that Apis is only a bull after all, and Thoth's ape is a very dirty troublesome ape; at least the one I had charge of at Hermopolis was."

"Peace, fool," replied Petamon, with an angry glare of his eye, "the beasts are but beasts, that *I* know as well as you: but the beast is only the type of the divinity, whom the vulgar may not know. Enough."

The rest of their conversation was lost in the distance as they slowly wended their way to the south.

Next day Septimius was somewhat thoughtful; he retired early to his tent on the pretence of weariness, and when all was still he stole out of the town as before. The hour was the same, but how different this night was from the last. A tornado had been blowing from the south all day, raising the sand in huge clouds, which obscured everything and nearly choked man and beast with a penetrating and impalpable dust. Even now the air was hot and depressing, the sand felt heavy under foot, and the Centurion's heart was so full of foreboding that more than once he had almost turned back.

At last he reached the granite boulder, and, crouching in its shade as before, sat the beggar. He rose as the Centurion approached, and beckoned him silently to proceed. Somewhat puzzled, Septimius obeyed and followed in silence, plodding wearily through the deep sand. At last the beggar turned.

"Sir Centurion," he said, "the night is hot and the way heavy; let me ease you of your sword"; and before Septimius could remonstrate or resist, his nimble hands had unstrapped the belt, and slung the sword over his own shoulder. "What men you Romans are!" he continued, slightly raising his voice as they passed along a narrow track between high rocks on either side. "You fear nothing in heaven or on earth. I verily believe you would *make beef-steaks of the Divine Apis*"; and he halted full in the way and seemed absolutely to grow before the Centurion's eyes, he loomed so large and majestic in the moonlight, while his eyes glared like blazing coals with hatred and revenge.

The Centurion recoiled, and at the same moment two from each side, four strange white figures, each with the head of a hawk, surmounted by the disk of the sun, glided forth and laid hands on him. Septimius struggled like a snared lion, but it was of no avail; he threatened them with the wrath of the Emperor, and they answered with a low mocking laugh. He made one furious rush at the *ci-devant* beggar who had betrayed him, and clutched him by the robe. Petamon quietly threw the sword far away over the sand and crossed his arms, while his ghostly allies advanced to the rescue. In another moment the prisoner was torn away, but not before he had rent off a fragment of the priest's robes, which fell upon the sand. His good sword was gone far beyond his reach, and after a few frantic plunges he was bound hand and foot and lashed to a rude litter which was brought from behind the rock. The four mysterious phantoms silently raised the litter and bore it swiftly across the sands, while Petamon, with a vigour remarkable in one so far advanced in years, led the way.

They had advanced along the sandy tract for some distance when suddenly the eye of Septimius, who could just raise his head and look forward by straining painfully against his bonds, caught the glimmer of the moonlight on the water, and before him rose perhaps the most unearthly, most beautiful scene that can meet the eyes of man.

Ruined as it now is, with its broken columns and shattered piers, marked at every turn by the hand of the destroyer, Philæ, and Philæ by moonlight, is wondrously lovely; what must it have been then?

In the midst of a quiet lagoon lay the Sacred Island, girt in by hills, on whose rugged sides the black basaltic rocks were piled in the most magnificent confusion—a green spot in the midst of a desert of stone—and, amid the Grove of Palms upon its shore, rose the roofs of temples and the tops of huge pyramidal gateways, while the solemn moonlight poured over all. A boat, manned by four more of the strange hawk-headed beings, was anchored at the shore. Silently the priest embarked, silently Septimius was lifted on board, silently the rowers bent to their oars, and in a few minutes they were passing along under the massy wall which rises sheer out of the water on the western side.

Suddenly the boat stopped and the Priest struck the wall thrice, repeating each time, "In the name of Him who sleeps at Philæ." Silently a portion of the apparently massy wall swung back and disclosed a narrow stair, up which they carried the Centurion; and by a side door entered the outer court. Before them rose the huge gateway, on each of whose towers was carved the giant semblance of a conqueror grasping with his left hand a group of captives by the hair, while he lifts the right to strike the death-blow. They hurried on through the great Hall of Pillars up a narrow stair, and, opening a small aperture, more like a window than a door, thrust in the Centurion, and left him, bound hand and foot, to his own reflections. These, you may imagine, were not of the most cheerful description, and might be put in words as follows: "Well, I *have* made a fool of myself pretty effectually this time; what a laugh honest Lepidus will have at me when I get back, if I *do* get back at all, of which there does not seem to be much prospect at present. I wonder what the fellows mean to do with me; and what, in the name of Pluto and Proserpine, were those hawk-heads that fell upon me—were they men or demons? I remember there were some pictures of things very like them at Thebes; and who can the old fox be that trapped me so cleverly? Lepidus was talking of their Egyptian guile. It *must* be Petamon himself, or perhaps the Ape of Thoth; it was a most apish trick he played me. And if they *do* put an end to me, what next? Will that be the finish, or is there a world beyond? If there *be* I hope it is something different from this, for it would be somewhat fatiguing to be a Centurion for ever and hear every day that eternal story of Domitian's, of how to boil a turbot, for ten years on end." And here Septimius, who was young and cheery, began to hum a tune, and ere long fell fast asleep.

Next morning Lepidus was early astir, and, after going his rounds, entered the tent of Septimius. It was empty, the bed had not been slept on, and there were no signs whatever of the tenant. "Mad boy," muttered Lepidus; "off on some frolic as usual. I must hush it up, or Septimius, great though his family interest be, will get but a rough welcome from the General on our return. I must say he is sick, or tired, or busy. He gives me more trouble than the whole cohort put together, and yet I love the lad for his merry face and his kindly smile more than I love anything on earth": and for a moment the soldier's rough face was mellowed by a smile of wondrous softness.

Noonday and evening came and went, and still Septimius was absent; and next morning, Lepidus, blaming himself much for having delayed so long, gave the alarm that the Centurion had vanished or been spirited away, and instituted a regular inquiry. Little information could be elicited. One of the sentries had noticed Septimius wandering away towards the desert, but he was too much accustomed to his officer's little vagaries to take much note of the fact. Doubt and gloom hung over all, for the Centurion, rash as he was, was a brave leader and a kindly, cheerful man. Parties were detached to search the neighbourhood in every direction, and Lepidus could only sit and wait for information, chafing inwardly at every moment's delay.

Towards evening one of the sergeants craved an audience of him, and when they were alone together produced the Centurion's sword and a piece of a heavy golden fringe. He had struck into the desert, come upon a spot where there were evident marks of a struggle, and picked up the sword and torn fringe lying on the ground. Sergeant and officer looked at each other, and the same fear clouded the faces of both.

"Petamon is at Philæ?" inquired Lepidus.

"He is, sir."

"Then may Jove the Preserver help the poor boy, for he will need all his help. I see it now: his foolish scoffs at the gods have reached the ears of the crafty priest, who has hated us Romans bitterly for long, and he has kidnapped the lad. We may be too late to *save* him, not too late for *revenge*. Muster the men at once and let us to Philæ—*quick!*"

In half an hour the cohort were tramping through the sand under the still moonlight, and an hour more brought them to the banks of the quiet river. There was no boat, and they had to halt till morning broke.

At sunrise a boat was brought from the neighbouring village, and Lepidus, embarking with a portion of his troop, was rowed over to the Sacred Island. He landed at a flight of steps on the northern side, and mounting them, halted for an instant, giving the quick imperative, "In the name of the Emperor." Ere many minutes elapsed a band of priests, headed by Petamon himself, appeared at the great gateway, and the Centurion, advancing briefly demanded to speak with their High Priest.

Petamon, with the rising sun flashing on his leopard-skin cloak and the golden fringe of his girdle, with his head and beard close shaven, in his pure linen garments and papyrus sandals, stepped forward.

"I am Petamon, the grandson of Petamon, High Priest of Isis. Roman soldier, speak on."

"I seek," commenced Lepidus; but he stopped abruptly. His eye had caught the glitter of the golden fringe, and he saw that at one side a piece had been torn away. He sprung forward like a tiger and grasped the priest's throat. "Petamon, Priest of Isis, I arrest you on the charge of kidnapping a Roman citizen. In the name of Cæsar Domitian; Soldiers, secure him!"

Priests and soldiers stood for a moment transfixed with amazement while Lepidus slowly released his grasp on the priest's throat, and they stood face to face till the Roman almost quailed before the fierce glare of the Egyptian's eye. The other priests began to press forward with threatening gestures; they outnumbered the Romans three times, and, though the strength and discipline of the latter would doubtless have proved victorious in the end, might have offered a stout resistance; but Petamon motioned them back. "Fear not, children," he said, speaking in the Greek tongue, so that both parties might understand him, "the gods can protect their own, and *you*, Sir Roman, that have laid hands on the servant of Isis, *tremble* ! " He walked forward and surrendered himself to two of the soldiers.

" Rather him than me," muttered Sheshonk. " The gods are all very well to fool the people with, but I doubt if Isis herself will save him under the Roman rods."

Petamon raised his eyes and met those of Sheshonk. A few words in the Egyptian tongue and a few secret signals passed between them, and Sheshonk, with a deep obeisance, retired into the temple and disappeared.

The soldiers were despatched to search the Island, and poor Septimius heard them several times pass the very door of his prison, but his gaolers had had time to thrust a gag into his mouth, so he could give no alarm. He lay there sick at heart, for he was stiff and weary, and even his cheerful spirits felt nearly broken.

The search was fruitless, as Lepidus had fully expected ; and he commanded Petamon again to be brought before him. " Sir Priest," he said, " I seek Septimius the Centurion, who is or was in your hands ; unless he is restored before to-morrow's sun sinks in the west you die the death."

" It is well," said the priest, while the mock submission of his attitude was belied by the sinister fire of his eye ; " the gods can protect their own."

Towards evening Petamon requested an audience of Lepidus, and when they were again together addressed him with more civility than he had hitherto condescended to use. He explained that it was the practice that the High Priest should, at certain seasons, sleep in the sacred recesses of the temple, and have the decrees of the goddess revealed to him in visions ; he humbly craved permission to perform this sacred duty, it might be for the last time. Lepidus mused for a moment and then gave orders that the priest, chained between two soldiers, should have leave to sleep where he would.

The night closed in ; the shrine of the goddess was illuminated ; and the blaze of a hundred lamps flashed on the rich colours and quaint designs on the walls of the shrine. One picture specially, behind the altar, attracted the eye of Lepidus. It represented King Ptolemy trampling down an enemy, while Isis stood by his side, with her hand raised in blessing, and Osiris held out a huge blue falchion as if to bid him complete his task. Before the altar stood Sheshonk burning incense, while Petamon, chained between his guards, bowed for a time in prayer. By midnight the ceremony was over ; Petamon, chained to a soldier on each side, lay down before the altar ; the lights, all but one, were extinguished ; the great door of the sacred chamber was closed. Lepidus lay down across it with his drawn sword in his hand, and, wearied with anxiety and care, soon fell fast asleep.

The sun was rising when he awoke, and, hastily rising, gave orders to change the guard upon the prisoner, and himself entered the chamber to see that the fetters were properly secured. The lamp was burning dimly, and there lay the two soldiers: but *where* was the prisoner? He was gone—utterly gone. The fetters were there, but Petamon had vanished. Half mad with vexation Lepidus gave one of his soldiers an angry kick; the man neither stirred nor groaned; he snatched up the lamp and threw its rays upon the soldier's face. It was white and still, and a small stream of blood, which had flowed from a wound over the heart, told too plain a tale. It was the same with the other; the soldiers' last battle was fought, and they had gone to their long home.

Terrified and perplexed beyond measure Lepidus rushed out into the court, and hastily roused the cohort. It was some minutes ere he could get them to comprehend what had happened; and even then the men followed him most unwillingly as he snatched up a torch and hurried back. To his amazement the corpses of the soldiers were gone, and in their place lay two rams, newly slaughtered, and bound with palm ropes; the fetters had also vanished. He raised his eyes and now noticed what he had not seen before—the picture of Osiris and Isis was behind the altar still, but the blade of the falchion of the god was dyed red, and dripping with newly-shed gore. Shuddering and horror-stricken, he left the chamber, followed by the soldiers; and, as he passed out of the temple, met Sheshonk in his priestly robes going in to perform the morning services.

A panic seized the soldiery, in which Lepidus more than half concurred. They were men, they said; why fight against the gods? In half an hour they had left Philæ and were marching through the desert to Syene, with dropping heads and weary steps, under the already scorching sun.

Terrified though he was at this awful tragedy, Lepidus was too honest and true to abandon the quest. The soldiers positively refused to assist further in the search, and he was left almost to his own resources. After much thought he published a proclamation in Egyptian and Greek offering a thousand pieces of gold for the Centurion, if alive; five hundred for the conviction of his murderers, if dead; and five hundred more for the head of the priest Petamon; and threatening the last penalty of the law on all men detaining the Roman a prisoner or sheltering his murderers.

His hopes were faint, but he could do no more; and having despatched a full report of the whole case to the Roman General at Alexandria, he waited, impatiently enough, his heart sickened with alternate hopes and fears.

During the next few days he was much disturbed by the sentiments of disaffection which he heard being muttered among the soldiers. Like all ignorant men they were superstitious, the events which had occurred at Philæ had produced a deep impression on their minds, and they murmured almost openly at Lepidus for having taken them to such a fearful place, and even now for halting in so ill-omened a neighbourhood.

This feeling was much increased by an old beggar-man who constantly haunted the camp. He had attracted the attention of the soldiers by some ordinary tricks of magic, and was constantly telling fortunes and reciting prophecies, all foreboding evil to the cohort if it stayed in the neighbourhood; and, indeed, foretelling the speedy and utter downfall of the Roman power.

Much grieved and perplexed, Lepidus ordered the beggar to be brought before him, and when he came taxed him with attempting to incite the soldiers to mutiny, and sternly reminded him that the punishment for such an attempt was death. The old man listened quietly and calmly, crossing his arms and fixing his glittering eye, which seemed strangely familiar to Lepidus, on the Roman officer.

After a pause he spoke—"My lord," and again the tone struck Lepidus as strangely familiar to his ear, "I serve the gods, and you the Emperor: let us both serve our masters truly. You would have news of Septimius the Centurion? It may be that the gods will permit you to see a vision: shall it be so?"

A slight curl of contempt was on the Roman's lips as he answered:

"You know the proclamation. I am prepared to fulfil its terms."

The old man shook himself like an awakening lion, and again the gesture struck Lepidus as familiar.

"I seek not gold," he said; "give me your attention, and keep the gold for those that need it."

"It is well," said Lepidus; "proceed."

A small stove was burning in the tent; the old man cast upon the charcoal some drugs that raised a dense smoke, and filled the tent with a heavy perfumed smell.

"Look!" said the old man, pointing to the smoke; and retiring behind Lepidus he crouched upon the ground.

A circle of light formed itself clearly and well defined among the smoke, and in its midst Lepidus suddenly saw the image of the bull Apis, as he had seen him once before at Memphis, with all his gorgeous scarlet and gold trappings, and the golden disk between his horns. A moment, and the image suddenly grew smaller and smaller, and vanished from the eyes of the wondering Roman.

Again the circle of light formed and he saw Osiris seated on his judgment throne, and the human soul being tried before him.

There was the child Horus seated on a lotus flower, with his finger at his lips. There was the dog of the infernal regions, panting to devour the wicked; and there was the Ape of Thoth, watching the turn of the balance. Again the vision faded.

"These are our gods," said the beggar. "Now behold thine own."

The circle formed again, and he saw the Emperor Domitian, his features bloated with intemperance, revelling among the degenerate senators and trembling patricians. The soldier sighed and the vision faded again.

Again the circle formed, and this time he saw the Centurion Septimius sitting at his tent door, as when we first saw him, and, stranger still, he saw himself in converse with him.

But suddenly, whether it was the perfumes or the excitement that overcame him he never knew, but the circle of light, the old man, the tent spun round and round, and he sank fainting to the ground.

When he awoke from his swoon the stove was burnt out, the old man was gone, and he hardly knew whether he had been dreaming or not. He felt dull and heavy and could scarcely rise. His servant entered with a light. He glanced at his finger, on which he wore his signet-ring, with which all important despatches must be sealed, and which marked their authenticity—it was gone. He felt in his bosom for the secret orders which the general had entrusted to him rather than to the headlong Septimius—they were gone too. His head still swum round; he could not think, he fell upon his bed, and sank into a long heavy dreamless slumber.

We must now return to Philæ—on the fifth day after Lepidus so hurriedly left it.

Septimius was still alive. A scanty allowance of bread and water was daily furnished him and his bonds had been somewhat loosed, but he had not seen the light of day since his capture, and his heart sank within him in hopeless despondency. Release seemed impossible, rescue hopeless; he could see no way out of his calamities but by death. He had never seen or spoken to any one since his capture; invisible were the hands that had relaxed his bonds, and invisible the attendants who supplied his daily food.

Petamon had been stirring here, there, and everywhere, rousing priests and people, reminding them of old wrongs and old memories, and urging them to join in one strong effort, and expel the Roman despots.

The news of Lepidus' proclamation had just reached the Island of Philæ. It was the turn of Sheshonk to officiate at the altar of Isis, and, while the incense was burning, he stood for a few moments wrapped in deep thought.

"Petamon is crafty and wise," so his meditations ran; "but Rome is strong, and we can never resist her. Better swim with the flood of the river and release that poor Centurion—and the gold, ay, the gold!—and the wrath of the gods, what of that? I have helped the trickery here for so many years that I hardly know whether there be gods at all. Petamon believes in them; but I am not Petamon. The gold is my god. I will save the youngster yet."

He mused for a few moments longer and then proceeded briskly about his accustomed duties.

The evening closed, the night was half spent, and Petamon, who had been away all day—on what errand the reader may easily guess—had not returned, when Sheshonk stole silently up the stair with a bundle under his arm, and, touching the spring, entered the dungeon of Septimius. The weary-worn Centurion inquired in a languid voice who it was.

"A friend," whispered Sheshonk. "Hush, Sir Centurion, and hearken. Lepidus, your second in command, has offered a thousand pieces of gold for your safe return; do you confirm the offer?"

"Ay, and add a thousand to it," answered the Centurion. "I have an old father in Rome, who values his son at that sum ten times told, spendthrift youngster though he be."

"Good," said the priest. "Petamon seeks your life, and in a few days will take it; you cannot be worse than you are, therefore, you can lose nothing by trusting me—will you do so?"

"I will," said the Centurion.

A knife was drawn gently across the cords which bound him, and he stretched his limbs here and there with a delicious sense of recovered freedom. Cautiously the priest struck a light with flint and steel and lighted a small lantern, after which he produced from his bundle a pair of huge hawk's heads, surmounted by the disk of the sun, with great glass eyes, and a pair of white disguises, such as the original captors of Septimius had worn. The Centurion eyed them with an amused smile, and muttered to himself, "So much for the hawk demons," proceeded to array himself in the disguise, while Sheshonk did the same. This accomplished, the priest opened the door and they cautiously descended the stair. They met a young priest, but at a whispered word from Sheshonk he bowed and passed them by. They entered a small chamber on the west side; the priest touched a mark on the floor, and a trap-door opened at their feet, showing a long dark stair. Down this they slowly made their way, the priest stopping for a moment to draw a heavy bolt on the under side of the trap-door to impede pursuit. After some time the Centurion heard a rushing of water above him, the passage grew damper and damper, and the priest in a whisper explained that they

89*

were passing under the bed of the river. In a little while they again ascended a high flight of steps, another trap-door opened at the touch of Sheshonk, and they emerged in a small temple on the island of Snem, now called Biggeh. The priest silently opened the door, and they stole out. The fresh breeze was blowing from the north, and Septimius, raising for a moment the choking weight of the hawk's head, let the air play about his temples, and then, at a warning sign from his companion, replaced the mask.

The moon had set and the night was almost dark. Cautiously picking their steps they crossed the island, and found at the other side a small skiff lying at anchor, and two swarthy Nubian rowers in attendance; a few words passed between them and Sheshonk.

"We must wait," he said, "till the day breaks; they dare not pass the cataract by night. Sleep if you can, and I will watch."

Septimius was too glad of the permission; he had slept but ill in his dungeon, and, taking off the heavy mask, he buried his head in his garments and fell fast asleep.

In a few hours the morning broke, and ere the sun was risen Sheshonk and Septimius were on board the boat. The rowers pulled stoutly at their oars, and they soon neared the cataract, whose roar became louder as they advanced. Before them lay a stretch of the river, fenced in on either hand with desolate rocky hills; here, there, everywhere, in the course of the stream jutted out the heads of cruel black rocks, round which the water foamed and raced like the stream of a mill dam. On sped the boat. The Centurion shut his eyes and held his breath; the current caught them; they were hurried helplessly along for a moment, stern foremost, and were on the point of being dashed upon a rock, when a dexterous stroke of one of the oars righted them: a rush—a tumult of waters—dashing spray and the roar of the current for a moment, then the boat floated again in calm water and the danger was past.

In a few moments they reached the Roman encampment. The Nubians, at a word from Sheshonk, pulled away up the stream, while the two hawk-headed ones hurried through the camp, to the no small wonderment of several drowsy sentries.

Lepidus was just awakening with the weary disheartened feelings of one who dreads impending misfortune, when the flap of his tent-door was thrown back, and the sleepy officer fancied he must still be dreaming when he saw a strange hawk-headed phantom rush into the room.

It was no phantom, as he found to his cost, for it hugged him close in his arms, while its huge beak left a dent on his face that he bore till his dying day, and a voice—the voice of Septimius—issued forth, hollow sounding, from the depths of the mask:

"Dear, dear, old Lepidus. I never thought to see your sulky face again."

There was little time for greeting and congratulations. Sheshonk was urgent on them to complete their work, and ere long the legionaries, their fears dispelled by the reappearance of the gay young Centurion, hastened again across the desert to Philæ, burning so hotly to wipe out the insult that had been offered to the Roman name that they never felt the sun.

Several boats were lying at the shore, and while Lepidus with the main body of the men made for the stairs upon the northern side, Septimius and a few chosen followers, under the guidance of Sheshonk, crept along under the western wall in a small boat and reached the secret door. It opened, obedient to the touch of the priest, and silently they mounted the stair—they met the other party in the great Hall of Columns; the island seemed deserted—no living thing was to be seen.

Sheshonk's eye twinkled.

"Five hundred golden pieces for Petamon's head!"

"Ay, and five hundred more," said Septimius.

The priest beckoned them on. They entered the sacred chamber where Petamon had kept his vigil on that memorable night, and Lepidus half shuddered as he looked round at the familiar paintings on the wall. The altar was prepared and the fire burning on it. The priest advanced and set his foot heavily on one side of the step in front. Suddenly altar and step, solid though they seemed, rolled away noiselessly to one side, disclosing a dark passage beneath. In a moment the Romans leapt down, Lepidus hastily lighting a torch at the altar fire as they did so. The passage led them to a small room in the thickness of the wall, and throwing in the light of his torch, he saw the arms and accoutrements of the two murdered soldiers, and the fetters that had bound Petamon lying in a corner. Here the passage apparently terminated abruptly, but the priest raised a stone in the roof with his hand, and they crept up through the narrow aperture thus opened. A strongly barred wooden door was on their left. They shot back the bolts and the door opened, revealing a small cell hewn out of one solid stone, with no aperture save the door for the admission of air; the light of day never has penetrated those gloomy recesses. The cell was untenanted, but a heap of human bones at one corner told of the uses to which it had been applied.

Shuddering they closed the door, and upon Sheshonk touching another spring, a square aperture opened, through which they glided, serpentwise, into another of the sacred chambers, and gladly hailed the light of day as it glimmered faintly through the door.

They searched the whole temple, but in vain; secret chambers they found more than one; even the dungeon of Septimius was opened, but nothing was discovered, and even the bloodhound sagacity of Sheshonk seemed for a moment at fault.

But his eye soon brightened, and muttering to himself, "five hundred pieces of gold," he led them through the court under the high painted pillars, and opening a door in one of the sides of the pyramidal gateway, proceeded up a long narrow stair. Suddenly a rustle of garments was heard above them, and they caught sight of the robes of Petamon, his leopard-skin cloak and his golden fringe, as he fled before them. The two Romans dashed after him like greyhounds on a hare, but as they reached the top of the staircase Septimius stumbled and fell, and so checked the pursuit for an instant. In a moment he recovered himself, but in that instant Petamon, casting back on his pursuers a glance of baffled malignity, sprang from the tower, and in another moment lay, dashed upon the pavement of the hall, a shapeless mass, while his blood and brains were splashed over the gay painting of the pillars.

The soldiers and Sheshonk, horror-struck, hastened down, and were standing beside the body—Lepidus had just recovered from the finger of the priest the signet-ring that he had lost, and was in the act of drawing the roll of secret orders from his bosom—Sheshonk had raised his head-dress and was wiping the perspiration from his brow, when suddenly, from aloft—it almost seemed from heaven—a sharp dagger was hurled with unerring aim. It cleft the bald skull of the traitor, and he fell, with scarcely a groan, on the top of Petamon's corpse.

The Romans looked up: no one was to be seen. With a party of soldiers they searched the huge gateway towers, but without a guide such a quest was hopeless, and they never traced the hand from which the dagger came.

Their main object was accomplished. Petamon was dead, and with him expired all chances of a revolutionary outbreak. Sheshonk was dead too; but, as Lepidus said, *that* saved the good gold pieces.

The same evening they returned to Syene, and next day the camp was broken up, and the cohort embanked on the river and floated down to rejoin the garrison at Memphis.

Little more need be said. In six months Septimius and Lepidus left Egypt for good, and when they were fairly out of sight of land they seemed to breathe more freely.

"I owe you many a good turn, Lepidus, old boy," said the Centurion; "but I'll never admit, to the end of time, that Apis would not have made splendid beefsteaks."

"Whoever said he wouldn't?" retorted the other, his grim features relaxing into a smile; "only I think it would need a braver man than either you or I to eat them under the nose of old Petamon."

No doubt a good deal more interesting conversation would have followed, but the wind at this point freshened, the sea began to rise, and the two Romans became deplorably sick.

JAMES PAYN
1830–1898

HOW JONES GOT THE ENGLISH VERSE MEDAL

My name is Herbert Brown, and my calling and profession is that of a maker of poems ; however incredible it may appear to mere money-spinners and prosaic persons of all sorts, I am perfectly convinced that I was born for that express end and object, and any attempt at persuading me to the contrary will be thrown away. I don't flatter myself that I am a bit of a poet ; I don't consider that I have a very pretty talent for making verses ; I don't amuse myself in my leisure hours with culling a chaplet for my brows from Olympus' top, and wooing the bashful muse ; I cannot find words to express my contempt for any such practices ; of all idiots the sentimental idiot being to me the most abhorrent.

I am accustomed to drink vast quantities of bitter beer during composition, and my favourite supper is toasted cheese with onions. I think Shakespeare was the greatest stunner who ever breathed, and I am happy to believe that when he met the late Mr. Bowdler in Hades he punched the head of him for presuming to meddle with his original text ; that he gave him one for his nob for each impertinent and unnecessary elimination. I think it would have done Mr. Wordsworth all the good in the world to have got what Burns calls fou at least once in every three weeks of his poetic career. I go in for nature and high spirits. The thoughts which I think I am used to express as well as I am able, instead of employing every artifice to conceal them, and of playing a sort of graceful hide-and-seek with the unhappy reader. Do not suppose, when I say that I despise the metaphysical and spasmodic poets, that I admire Byron ; because I don't at all. But for his frightful vice, he seems to me as *whine-and-watery*, and complainingly egotistic, as any of them, and if he had chanced to have been born an actor instead of a lord, we should never have heard the last of that smell of the footlights which pervades him. I go in for sunshine and fresh air. However, in spite of his bad grammar, one discovers easily enough what Byron means.

This is also the case with the poetry of Herbert Brown, or I am much mistaken. I go in for Saxon and sense, and clearness of thought, and that is why I lost the Chancellor's Medal for English Verse at the university; or rather, Jones, with all his glittering verbiage, is obscure and afflicts the reader with vertigo, and that—as you shall hear—is why he gained it.

There is always a great competition for the English verse prize. The classical men write for it, after the same style in which they do their Greek and Latin verses, with pretty good metre, but with a great insufficiency of ideas. The mathematical men, too, are excited in no small numbers, by the unnatural ambition; but most of them are stopped by the first couplet, and subside into blank verse, which is looked upon by the examiners with great disfavour. All the idle literary and fast intellectual men are also candidates for the laurel, and they gain it, as may be expected, at least as often as any other class. It is almost the only university distinction which can be attained, as the classic phrase runs, without "sweating" for it, and your gin-punch-and-Shelley undergraduate is, to say truth, not much inclined to laborious application. Though there are, perhaps, in reality more competitors for this prize than any other, in appearance there are very few; scarcely any, where all must fail save one, will own to writing for it; and many are downright ashamed of the imputation of making poems (although they secretly pride themselves upon the fancied gift beyond measure), and so deny the soft impeachment, as being too soft to be confessed. I never denied it. As soon as the subject—The Aurora Borealis—was given out, I immediately announced my intention of becoming a candidate; and my friends (I say it to their credit), who believed in me almost as much as I believed in myself, disseminated the information. Jones, too, to do him justice, was not wanting in self-confidence, although he pusillanimously declined to take my five dozen of bottled porter to two, which I had offered upon my chance against his.

It was curious to remark how the Aurora Borealis pervaded university talk during that term; how the north pole thrust itself into general conversation, and the Esquimaux obtained a social footing in undergraduate circles. Tangent of John's, a man who was spoken of as embryo Smith's prizeman, but who was not a good hand at rhyming, went about complaining to his friends that he could not get anything to chime with walrus; his poem, he said, was perfect, except in this one particular, which was, however, of the greatest importance, because he had caused his hero to be attacked by that Arctic monster. I supplied him with this couplet:

Storm and iceberg, bear and walrus,
Combined to make his prospects dol'rous;

for which he thanked me heartily, and stuck it amongst his heroic verses, just as it was.

Now the examiners for the English verse prize were three.

One: The vice-chancellor of that year, who was not thought very highly of as an intellectual person, but who made up in obstinacy for what he wanted in wits, and was, therefore, highly respected and seldom opposed.

Two: A mathematical professor, who was accustomed to amuse himself in leisure moments with making artificial suns as good, and almost as large, as the real one; and whose modesty was such as to have once caused him to observe that he was not a conceited man by any means, but still that he knew everything (if he were not mistaken) except how to play on the violin.

Three: A classical professor, who had passed five-and-thirty years of his life in the study of the Greek particles, and who maintained with pride that he had not mastered their astonishing subtlety of meaning even yet.

The vice was not only incompetent to write what was worth reading (although he had written a good deal in his time), but also what could be read at all. His handwriting was the wanderings of a centipede who had just escaped from the ink-pot, and had crawled and sprawled over the paper. It was, therefore, arranged that he, who had the privilege of reading the poems first, should signify his approbation or disapproval by one simple letter *g* for good, or *b* for bad, and not venture upon giving a written opinion. He then impressed upon his two coadjutors the necessity of their being impartial, and quite independent of his opinion, in such a manner that they both retired from the presence secretly determined to agree with his high mightiness at all hazards.

This may seem a little hard upon the two professors; but, if I spoke of them as strictly honest, it must be at the expense of their wisdom—and where are the professors who would not rather be accounted wise than held immaculate? It is also impossible for me to forget that it was these two misguided men who did in fact award the chancellor's medal to Jones.

All the manuscripts arrived at the appointed time at the vice-chancellor's, neatly folded up and sealed, each with its motto, as though it were a pastrycook's kiss: three-and-forty Palmam-qui-meruit-ferats, and thirteen quotations culled from the Latin grammar, besides all the beautifully appropriate superscriptions of the classical men, whose poetic merits upon these occasions are a good deal concentrated in the mottoes. The vice-chancellor must have had a very fearful time of it for the next three nights, if he really did read those various effusions; they do say he got his butler to help him; but the thing occurred long since, and it is well to let bygones be bygones. If he really did read them, I repeat, it is a wonder he did not die of Aurora Borealis. However, he finished his work at last somehow or other, and sent the terrible epics on (by cart) to No. Two.

Now, the mathematical professor was a mistaken man in being so convinced that he knew everything except how to play on the violin. He knew nothing whatever of poetry. To him, as to a certain brother professor before him, it was all assertion without one word of proof. When he came to the manuscript marked *g* he opened it, with his mind half made up already. Although the dazzling no-meaningness of the author greatly puzzled him—and how that Aurora Borealis did flash about Jones's poem!—yet, seeing within as without, the *g g g* occurring where the verses were, to him, even more incomprehensible than elsewhere, he quietly put his *g g g* opposite to the same place, deeming that the things, perhaps, were what people called poetic ideas, although with scorn in his mind.

There were no *g*'s, I am truly happy to say, about Herbert Brown's manuscript.

No. Three, on getting the cartful of epics in his turn, divorced his mind with pain from the Greek particles to give them his best attention, which, in the circumstances, was very good; and, coming upon the vice-chancellor's *g*'s, endorsed with the *g*'s of No. Two, he at once concluded that Jones must needs be the man for the chancellor's medal; while his own inability to understand him he set down to the same cause which rendered himself incapable of grappling with anything else—the particles; his *g* was accordingly inscribed opposite to the others, making an array of approbation triply strong for the fortunate Jones. That spasmodic and slightly incoherent young man, therefore, obtained the medal, and recited in the senate-house to a brilliant audience of wondering but fashionably attired ladies his panegyric upon the Northern Lights, and Herbert Brown was nowhere.

When, however, the three examiners met at some social entertainment shortly afrerwards, and the bonds of official reserve had got relaxed, the following conversation arose:

"Why," said the vice-chancellor to No. Three, "did you and your brother professor there put a *g* opposite to that insane epic of Mr. Jones's?"

No. Three, who was as usual among the particles, had to disentangle himself before he could reply; so No. Two anticipated him.

"Why, you put a *g* yourself, Mr. Vice-Chancellor, you know you did."

"A *g*, sir? Pooh, sir," responded that dignitary in a contemptuous tone. "I thought it sheer madness. I put a *q*, sir—a *q* for query; meaning that I could not for the life of me understand what the young man meant."

And that was how Jones got the English verse medal.

MARK RUTHERFORD (WILLIAM HALE WHITE) 1830–1913

MR. WHITTAKER'S RETIREMENT

I HAD been a partner in the house of Whittaker, Johnson, & Marsh, in the wholesale drug trade, for twenty-five years, and for the last ten years senior partner. For the first nine years of my seniority I was not only nominally, but practically, the head of the firm. I had ceased to occupy myself with details, but nothing of importance was concluded without consulting me: I was the pivot on which the management turned. In the tenth year, after a long illness, my wife died: I was very ill myself, and for months not a paper was sent to me. When I returned to work I found that the junior partners, who were pushing men, had distributed between them what I was accustomed to do, and that some changes which they thought to be indispensable had been made. I resumed my duties as well as I could, but it was difficult to pick up the dropped threads, and I was dependent for explanation upon my subordinates. Many transactions too, from a desire to avoid worrying me, were carried through without my knowledge, although formerly, as a matter of course, they would have been submitted to me. Strangers, when they called, asked to see Johnson or Marsh. I directed the messenger that they were to be shown into my room if I was disengaged. This was a failure, for when they came I was obliged to ask for help, which was not given very generously. Sometimes I sent for the papers, but it took a long time to read them, and my visitors became impatient. During one of these interviews I remember that I was sorely perplexed, but I had managed to say something loosely with no particular meaning. Johnson came in and at once took up the case, argued for ten minutes while I sat silent and helpless, and an arrangement was concluded in which I really had no voice whatever. Now and then I strove to assert myself by disapproval of suggestions offered to me, but in the end was generally forced to admit I was wrong. We had a very large order for which we were obliged to make special arrangements with manufacturers. Both Johnson and Marsh were of opinion that a particular firm which had often supplied us was not to be trusted, as our dealings with them during my absence had been unsatisfactory. I was inclined foolishly, but naturally, to attach little importance to anything which had been done entirely without me, ridiculed their objections, and forced my decision upon them. The firm broke down, our contract with them was cancelled, another had to be made under pressure, and we lost about five hundred pounds. Although I was not reminded of my responsibility in so many words, I knew that I was solely to blame; I became more than ever convinced I was useless, and I was much dejected. At last I made up my mind to retire. I was urged to remain, but not, as I imagined, with any great earnestness, and on December 31, 1856, I left the office in Eastcheap never to enter it again.

For the first two or three weeks I enjoyed my freedom, but when they had passed I had had enough of it. *I had nothing to do!* Every day at the hours when business was at its height I thought of the hurry, of the inquiries, of the people waiting in the anteroom, of the ringing of bells, of the rapid instructions to clerks, of the consultations after the letters were opened, of our anxious deliberations, of the journeys to Scotland at an hour's notice, and of the interviews with customers. I pictured to myself that all this still went on, but went on without me, while I had no better occupation than to unpack a parcel, pick the knots out of the string, and put it in a string-box. I saw my happy neighbours drive off in the morning and return in the evening. I envied them the haste, which I had so often cursed, over breakfast. I envied them, while I took an hour over lunch, the chop devoured in ten minutes; I envied them the weariness with which they dragged themselves along their gravel-paths, half an hour late for dinner. I was thrown almost entirely amongst women. I had no children, but a niece thirty-five years old, devoted to evangelical church affairs, kept house for me, and she had a multitude of female acquaintances, two or three of whom called every afternoon. Sometimes, to relieve my loneliness, I took afternoon tea, and almost invariably saw the curate. I was the only man present. It was just as if, being strong, healthy, and blessed with a good set of teeth, I were being fed on water-gruel. The bird-wittedness, the absence of resistance and of difficulty were intolerable. The curate, and occasionally the rector, tried to engage me, as I was a good subscriber, in discussion on church affairs, but there seemed to me to be nothing in these which required the force which was necessary for the commonest day in the City. Mrs. Coleman and the rector were once talking together most earnestly when I entered the room, and I instinctively sat down beside them, but I found that the subject of their eager debate was the allotment of stalls at a bazaar. They were really excited—stirred, I fully admit, to their depths. I believe they were more absorbed and anxious than I was on that never-to-be-forgotten morning when Mortons and Nicholsons both failed, and for two hours it was just a toss-up whether we should not go too.

I went with my niece one day to St. Paul's Churchyard to choose a gown, but it was too much for me to be in a draper's shop when the brokers' drug sales were just beginning. I left my niece, walked round the Churchyard as fast as I could, trying to make people believe I was busy, and just as I came to Doctors Commons I stumbled against Larkins, who used to travel for Jackman & Larkins.

"Hullo, Whittaker!" said he, "haven't seen you since you left. Lucky dog! Wish I could do the same. Ta-ta; can't stop."

A year ago Mr. Larkins, with the most pressing engagement in front of him, would have spared me just as much time as I liked to give him.

Formerly I woke up (sometimes, it is true, after a restless night) with the feeling that before me lay a day of adventure. I did not know what was in my letters, nor what might happen. Now, when I rose I had nothing to anticipate but fifteen hours of monotony varied only by my meals. My niece proposed that I should belong to a club, but the members of clubs were not of my caste. I had taken a pride in my garden, and determined I would attend to it more myself. I bought gardening books, but the gardener knew far more than I could ever hope to know, and I could not displace him. I had been in the habit of looking through a microscope in the evening, although I did not understand any science in which the microscope is useful, and my slides were bought ready-made. I brought it out now in the daytime, but I was soon weary of it and sold it. We went to Worthing for a month. We had what were called comfortable lodgings and the weather was fine, but if I had been left to myself I should have gone back to Stockwell directly my boxes were unpacked. We drove eastwards as far as we could and then westward, and after that there was nothing more to be done except to do the same thing over again. At the end of the first week I could stand it no longer, and we returned. I fancied my liver was out of order and consulted a physician. He gave me some medicine and urged me to "cultivate cheerful society," and to take more exercise. I therefore tried long walks, and often extended them beyond Croydon, and once as far as Reigate, but I had never been accustomed to walking by myself, and as I knew the names of scarcely half-a-dozen birds or trees, my excursions gave me no pleasure. I have stood on Banstead Downs in the blaze of sunlight on a still October morning, and when I saw the smoke-cloud black as night hang over the horizon northwards, I have longed with the yearning of an imprisoned convict to be the meanest of the blessed souls enveloped in it.

I determined at last to break up my household at Stockwell, to move far away into the country; to breed fowls—an occupation which I was assured was very profitable and very entertaining; dismiss my niece and marry again. I began to consider which lady of those whom I knew would suit me best, and I found one who was exactly the person I wanted. She was about thirty-five years old, was cheerful, fond of going out (I never was), a good housekeeper, played the piano fairly well, and, as the daughter of a retired major in the Army, had a certain air and manner which distinguished her from the wives and daughters of our set and would secure for me an acquaintance with the country gentlefolk, from which, without her, I should probably be debarred. She had also told me when I mentioned my project to her, but saying nothing about marriage, that she doted on fowls—they had such pretty ways. As it was obviously prudent not to engage myself until I knew more of her, I instigated my niece in a careless way to invite her to stay a fortnight with us. She came, and once or twice I was on the verge of saying something decisive to her, but I could not. A strange terror of change in my way of life took hold of me. I should now have to be more at home, and although I might occupy myself with the fowls during the morning and afternoon, the evening must be spent in company, and I could not endure for more than half an hour a drawing-room after dinner. There was another reason for hesitation. I could see the lady would accept me if I proposed to her, but I was not quite sure why. She would in all probability survive me, and I fancied that her hope of survival might be her main reason for consenting. I gave her up, but no sooner had she left us than I found myself impelled to make an offer to a handsome girl of eight-and-twenty who I was ass enough to dream might love me. I was happily saved by an accident not worth relating, and although I afterwards dwelt upon the charms of two or three other ladies and settled with myself I would take one of them, nothing came of my resolution. I was greatly distressed by this growing indecision. It began to haunt me. If I made up my mind to-day that I would do this or that, I always had on the morrow twenty reasons for not doing it. I was never troubled with this malady in Eastcheap. I was told that decay in the power of willing was one of the symptoms of softening of the brain, and this then was what was really the matter with me! It might last for years! Wretched creature! my life was to be nothing better than that of the horse in Bewick's terrible picture. I was "waiting for death."

Part of my income was derived from interest on money lent to a cousin. Without any warning I had a letter to say that he was bankrupt, and that his estate would probably not pay eighteeenpence in the pound. It was quite clear that I must economise, and what to do and whither to go was an insoluble problem to me. By chance I met an old City acquaintance who told me of a " good thing " in Spanish bonds which, when information was disclosed which he possessed, were certain to rise 20 per cent. If what he said was true—and I had no reason to doubt him—I could easily get back without much risk about two-thirds of the money I had lost. Had I been in full work, I do not believe I should have wasted a shilling on the speculation, but the excitement attracted me, and I ventured a considerable sum. In about a fortnight there was a sudden jump of 2 per cent. in my securities, and I was so much elated that I determined to go further. I doubled my stake ; in three weeks another rise was announced ; I again increased the investment, and now I watched the market with feverish eagerness. One day I was downstairs a quarter of an hour earlier than usual waiting for the boy who brought the paper. I tore it open, and to my horror saw that there was a panic on the stock Exchange ; my bonds were worthless, and I was ruined.

I had always secretly feared that this would happen, and that I should be so distracted as to lose my reason. To my surprise, I was never more self-possessed, and I was not so miserable as might have been expected. I at once gave notice of discharge to my servants, sold nearly all my furniture, and let my house. I was offered help, but declined it. I moved into a little villa in one of the new roads then being made at Brixton, and found that I possessed a capital which, placed in Consols—for I would not trust anything but the public funds—brought me one hundred and twenty-five pounds a year. This was not enough for my niece, myself, and a maid, and I was forced to consider whether I could not obtain some employment. To return to Eastcheap was clearly out of the question, but there was a possibility, although I was fifty-six, that my experience might make me useful elsewhere. I therefore called on Jackman & Larkins at twelve o'clock, the hour at which I knew there was a chance of finding them able to see me. During my prosperity I always walked straight into their room marked " private," but now I went into the clerk's office, took off my hat, and modestly inquired if either Mr. Jackman or Mr. Larkins could spare me a minute. I was not asked to sit down—I, to whom these very clerks a little over a twelvemonth ago would have risen when I entered ; but my message was taken, and I was told in reply that both Mr. Jackman and Mr. Larkins were engaged. I was bold enough to send in another message, and was informed I might call in two hours' time. I went out, crossed London Bridge, and seeing the doors of St. Saviour's, Southwark, open, rested there awhile. When I returned at the end of two hours I had to wait another ten minutes until a luncheon tray came out. A bell then rang, which a clerk answered, and in about five minutes, with a "come this way," I was ushered into the presence of Jackman, who was reading the newspaper with a decanter and a glass of sherry by his side.

"Well, Whittaker, what brings you here? Ought to be looking after your grapes at Stockwell—but I forgot; heard you'd given up grape-growing. Ah! odd thing, a man never retires but he gets into some mess; marries or dabbles on the Stock Exchange. I've known lots of cases like yours. What can we do for you? Times are horribly bad." Jackman evidently thought I was going to borrow some money of him, and his tone altered when he found I did not come on that errand.

"I was very sorrry—really I was, my dear fellow—to hear of your loss, but it was a damned foolish thing to do, excuse me."

"Mr. Jackman," said I, "I have not lost all my property, but I cannot quite live on what is left. Can you give me some work? My connection and knowledge of your business may be of some service." I had put hundreds of pounds in this man's pocket, but forbore to urge this claim upon him.

"Delighted, I am sure, if it were possible, but we have no vacancy, and, to be quite plain with you, you are much too old. We could get more out of a boy at ten shillings a week than we could out of you."

Mr. Jackman drank another glass of sherry.

"But, sir"—(sir! that I should ever call Tom Jackman "sir," but I did)—"as I just said, my experience and connection might be valuable."

"Oh, as to experience, me and Larkins supply all that, and the clerks do as they are told. Never keep a clerk more than two years: he then begins to think he knows too much and wants more pay. As to connection, pardon me—mean nothing, of course—but your recommendation now wouldn't bring much."

At this moment the door opened and Larkins entered in haste. "I say, Jackman——" then turning and seeing me,—"Hullo, Whittaker, what the devil are you doing here? Jackman, I've just heard——"

"Good-bye, Whittaker," said Jackman, "sorry can't help you."

Neither of them offered to shake hands, and I passed out into the street. The chop-houses were crammed; waiters were rushing hither and thither; I looked up at the first floor of that very superior house, used solely by principals, where I often had my lunch, and again crossed London Bridge on my way back. London Bridge at half-past one ! I do not suppose I had ever been there at half-past one in my life. I saw a crowd still passing both southwards and northwards. At half-past nine it all went one way and at half-past six another. It was the morning and evening crowd which was the people to me. These half-past one o'clock creatures were strange to me, loafers, nondescripts. I was faint and sick when I reached home, for I walked all the way, and after vainly trying to eat something, went straight to bed. But the next post brought me a note saying that Jackman & Larkins were willing to engage me at a salary of £100 a year—much more, it was added, than they would have paid for more efficient service, but conceded as a recognition of the past. The truth was, as I afterwards found out, that Larkins persuaded Jackman that it would increase their reputation to take old Whittaker. Larkins too had become a little tired of soliciting orders, and I could act as his substitute. I was known to nearly all the houses with which they did business, and very likely should gain admittance where a stranger would be denied. My hours would be long, from nine till seven, and must be observed rigidly. Instead of my three-and-sixpenny lunch I should now have to take in my pocket whatever I wanted in the middle of the day. For dinner I must substitute a supper—a meal which did not suit me. I should have to associate with clerks, to meet as a humble subordinate those with whom I was formerly intimate as an equal ; but all this was overlooked, and I was happy, happy as I had not been for months.

It was on a Wednesday when I received my appointment, and on Monday I was to begin. I said my prayers more fervently that night than I had said them for years, and determined that, please God, I would always go to church every Sunday morning no matter how fine it might be. There were only three clear week-days, Thursday, Friday, and Saturday, to be got through. I imagined them to be holidays, although I had never before taken three consecutive holidays, save in those wretched Augusts or Septembers, when pride annually forced me away to the seaside. At last Monday came : our breakfast hour was henceforth fixed at half-past seven, and at eight o'clock I started to walk to Kennington, and thence to ride by an omnibus to King William's statue. Oh ! with what joy did I shut the little garden gate and march down the road, once more somebody ! I looked round, saw other little front gates open, each by-street contributed, so that in the Kennington Road there was almost a procession moving steadily and uniformly Citywards, and *I* was in it. I was still a part of the great world ; something depended on me. Fifty-six ? Yes, but what was that ? Many men are at their best at fifty-six. So exhilarated was I, that just before I mounted the omnibus—it was a cold morning, but I would not ride inside—I treated myself to a twopenny cigar. My excitement soon wore off.

I could not so far forget myself as not to make suggestions now and then, and Jackman took a delight in snubbing me. It was a trial to me also to sit with the clerks. We had never set ourselves up as grand people at Stockwell, but I had all my life been accustomed to delicate food properly cooked, and now that my appetite was declining with my years, I would almost at any time have gone without a meal rather than eat anything that was coarse or dirtily served. My colleagues ridiculed my "Stockwell manners," as they called them, and were very witty, so they thought, in their inquiries when I produced my sandwich wrapped up in a clean napkin, how much it cost for my washing. They were a very cheap set, had black finger-nails, and stuck their pens behind their ears. One of them always brought a black-varnished canvas bag with him, not respectably stiff like leather—a puckered, dejected-looking bag. It was deposited in the washing place to be out of the way of the sun. At one o'clock it was brought out and emptied of its contents, which were usually a cold chop and a piece of bread. A plate, knife and fork, and some pepper and salt were produced from the desk, and after the meat, which could be cut off from the chop, was devoured, the bone was gnawed, wrapped up in paper, and put back in the bag. The plate, knife, and fork were washed in the wash-hand basin and wiped with the office jack-towel. It was hard when old business friends called and I had to knock at the inner door and say, "Mr. —— wants to see you, sir," the object of the visit not being entrusted to me. A few of them behaved politely to me, but to others it seemed to be a pleasure to humble me. On that very first Monday, Bullock, the junior in Wiggens, Moggs, & Bullock, burst into the room. He knew me very well, but took no notice of me, although I was alone, except to ask—

"Is Mr. Jackman in?"

"No, sir, can I do anything for you?"

He did not deign to say a word, but went out, slamming the door behind him.

Nevertheless I kept up my spirits, or rather they kept themselves up. At five o'clock, when the scramble to get the letters signed began, I thought of our street at home, so dull at that hour, of the milkman, and the muffin-boy, of the curate, and of my niece's companions, and reflected, thank God, that I was in the City, a man amongst men. When seven o'clock came and the gas was put out, there was the anticipation also of the fight for a place in the omnibus, especially if it was a wet night, and the certainty that I should meet with one or two neighbours who would recognise me. No more putting up window-blinds, pulling up weeds in the back garden, sticking in seeds which never grew, or errands to suburban shops at midday. How I used in my retirement to detest the sight of those little shopkeepers when the doors of Glyn's Bank were swinging to and fro! I came home dead-beaten now, it is true, but it was a luxury to be dead-beaten, and I slept more soundly than I had ever slept in my life. In about six months my position improved a little. Jackman's love for sherry grew upon him, and once or twice, to Larkins's disgust, his partner was not quite as fit to appear in public as he ought to have been. Very often he was absent, sick. Two of the cheap clerks also left in order to better themselves. I never shall forget the afternoon—I felt as if I could have danced for joy—when Larkins said to me, "Whittaker, Mr. Jackman hasn't very good health, and if he's not here when I am out, you must answer anybody who calls, but don't commit yourself—and—let me see—I was going to tell you you'll have ten pounds a year more, beginning next quarter—and there was something else—Oh! I recollect, if anybody should want to see Mr. Jackman when he happens to be unwell here, and I am not with him, send for me if you know where I am. If you don't know, you must do the best you can." My office coat had hitherto been an old shiny, ragged thing, and I had always taken off my shirt-cuffs when I began work, because they soon became dirty. I rammed the old coat that night into the fire; brought my second-best coat in a brown paper parcel the next morning, and wore my shirt-cuffs all day long. Continually I had to think—only fancy, to *think*—once more; in a very small way, it is true, but still to think and to act upon my thought, and when Larkins came in and inquired if anybody had called, he now and then said "all right" when I told him what I had done. A clerk from my old office swaggered in and did not remove his hat. I descended from my stool and put on my own hat. The next time he came he was more polite. I have now had two years of it, and have not been absent for a day. I hope I may go on till I drop. My father died in a fit; his father died in a fit; and I myself often feel giddy, and things go round for a few seconds. I should not care to have a fit here, because there would be a fuss and a muddle, but I should like, just when everything was *quite* straight, to be able to get home safely and then go off. To lie in bed for weeks and worry about my work is what I could not endure.

AMELIA B. EDWARDS
1831–1892

PICKING UP TERRIBLE COMPANY

I AM a Frenchman by birth, and my name is François Thierry. I need not weary you with my early history. Enough, that I committed a political offence—that I was sent to the galleys for it—that I am an exile for it to this day. The brand was not abolished in my time. If I chose, I could show you the fiery letters on my shoulder.

I was arrested, tried, and sentenced, in Paris. I went out of the court with my condemnation ringing in my ears. The rumbling wheels of the prison-van repeated it all the way from Paris to Bicêtre that evening, and all the next day, and the next, and the next, along the weary road from Bicêtre to Toulon. When I look back upon that time, I think I must have been stupefied by the unexpected severity of my sentence ; for I remember nothing of the journey, nor of the places where we stopped—nothing but the eternal repetition of " travaux forcés—travaux forcés—travaux forcés à perpétuité," over and over, and over again. Late in the afternoon of the third day, the van stopped, the door was thrown open, and I was conducted across a stone yard, through a stone corridor, into a huge stone hall, dimly lighted from above. Here I was interrogated by a military superintendent, and entered by name in a ponderous ledger bound and clasped with iron, like a book in fetters.

" Number Two Hundred and Seven," said the superintendent. " Green."

They took me into an adjoining room, searched, stripped, and plunged me into a cold bath. When I came out of the bath, I put on the livery of the galleys—a coarse canvas shirt, trousers of tawny serge, a red serge blouse, and heavy shoes clamped with iron. Last of all, a green woollen cap. On each leg of the trousers, and on the breast and back of the blouse, were printed the fatal letters " T. F." On a brass label in the front of the cap were engraved the figures " 207." From that moment I lost my individuality. I was no longer François Thierry. I was Number Two Hundred and Seven. The superintendent stood by and looked on.

" Come, be quick," said he, twirling his long moustache between his thumb and forefinger. " It grows late, and you must be married before supper."

" Married ! " I repeated.

The superintendent laughed, and lighted a cigar, and his laugh was echoed by the guards and jailers.

Down another stone corridor, across another yard, into another gloomy hall, the very counterpart of the last, but filled with squalid figures, noisy with the clank of fetters, and pierced at each end with a circular opening, through which a cannon's mouth showed grimly.

" Bring Number Two Hundred and Six," said the superintendent, " and call the priest."

Number Two Hundred and Six came from a farther corner of the hall, dragging a heavy chain, and along with him a blacksmith, bare-armed and leather-aproned.

" Lie down," said the blacksmith, with an insulting spurn of the foot.

I lay down. A heavy iron ring attached to a chain of eighteen links was then fitted to my ankle, and riveted with a single stroke of the hammer. A second ring next received the disengaged ends of my companion's chain and mine, and was secured in the same manner. The echo of each blow resounded through the vaulted roof like a hollow laugh.

" Good," said the superintendent, drawing a small red book from his pocket. " Number Two Hundred and Seven, attend to the prison code. If you attempt to escape without succeeding, you will be bastinadoed. If you succeed in getting beyond the port, and are then taken, you will receive three years in double-chaining. As soon as you are missed, three cannon shots will be fired, and alarm flags will be hoisted on every bastion. Signals will be telegraphed to the maritime guards, and to the police of the ten neighbouring districts. A price will be set upon your head. Placards will be posted upon the gates of Toulon, and sent to every town throughout the empire. It will be lawful to fire upon you, if you cannot be captured alive."

Having read this with grim complacency, the superintendent resumed his cigar, replaced the book in his pocket, and walked away.

All was over now—all the incredulous wonder, the dreamy dulness, the smouldering hope, of the past three days. I was a felon, and (slavery, in slavery !) chained to a fellow-felon. I looked up, and found his eyes upon me. He was a swart, heavy-browed, sullen-jawed man of about forty ; not much taller than myself, but of immensely powerful build.

" So," said he, " you're for life, are you ? So am I."

" How do you know I am for life ? " I asked, wearily.

" By that." And he touched my cap roughly with the back of his hand. " Green, for life. Red, for a term of years. What are you in for ? "

" I conspired against the Government."

He shrugged his shoulders contemptuously.

" Devil's mass ! Then you're a gentleman-convict, I suppose ! Pity you've not a berth to yourself—we poor forçats hate such fine company."

" Are there many political prisoners ? " I asked, after a moment's pause.

" None, in this department."

Then, as if detecting my unspoken thought, " I am no innocent," he added with an oath. " This is the fourth time I have been here. Did you ever hear of Gasparo ? "

" Gasparo the forger ? "

He nodded.

" Who escaped three or four months since, and——"

" And flung the sentinel over the ramparts, just as he was going to give the alarm. I'm the man."

I had heard of him, as a man, who, early in his career, had been sentenced to a long solitary imprisonment in a gloomy cell, and who had come forth from his solitude hardened into an absolute wild beast. I shuddered, and, as I shuddered, found his evil eye taking vindictive note of me. From that moment he hated me. From that moment I loathed him.

A bell rang, and a detachment of convicts came in from labour. They were immediately searched by the guard, and chained up, two and two, to a sloping wooden platform that reached all down the centre of the hall. Our afternoon meal was then served out consisting of a mess of beans, an allowance of bread and ship-biscuit, and a measure of thin wine. I drank the wine ; but I could eat nothing. Gasparo took what he chose from my untouched allowance, and those who were nearest scrambled for the rest. The supper over, a shrill whistle echoed down the hall, each man took his narrow mattress from under the platform which made our common bedstead, rolled himself in a piece of seaweed matting, and lay down for the night. In less than five minutes, all was profoundly silent. Now and then I heard the blacksmith going round with his hammer, testing the gratings, and trying the locks, in all the corridors. Now and then, the guard stalked past with his musket on his shoulder. Sometimes, a convict moaned, or shook his fetters in his sleep. Thus the weary hours went by. My companion slept heavily, and even I lost consciousness at last.

I was sentenced to hard labour. At Toulon the hard labour is of various kinds: such as quarrying, mining, pumping in the docks, lading and unlading vessels, transporting ammunition, and so forth. Gasparo and I were employed with about two hundred other convicts in a quarry a little beyond the port. Day after day, week after week, from seven in the morning until seven at night, the rocks echoed with our blows. At every blow, our chains rang and rebounded on the stony soil. In that fierce climate, terrible tempests and tropical droughts succeed each other throughout the summer and autumn. Often and often, after toiling for hours under a burning sky, have I gone back to prison and to my pallet, drenched to the skin. Thus the last days of the dreary spring ebbed slowly past; and then the more dreary summer, and then the autumn-time, came round.

My fellow-convict was a Piedmontese. He had been a burglar, a forger, an incendiary. In his last escape he had committed manslaughter. Heaven alone knows how my sufferings were multiplied by that abhorred companionship—how I shrank from the touch of his hand—how I sickened if his breath came over me as we lay side by side at night. I strove to disguise my loathing; but in vain. He knew it as well as I knew it, and he revenged himself upon me by every means that a vindictive nature could devise. That he should tyrannise over me was not wonderful; for his physical strength was gigantic, and he was looked upon as an authorised despot throughout the port; but simple tyranny was the least part of what I had to endure. I had been fastidiously nurtured; he purposely and continually offended my sense of delicacy. I was unaccustomed to bodily labour; he imposed on me the largest share of our daily work. When I needed rest, he would insist on walking. When my limbs were cramped, he would lie down obstinately, and refuse to stir. He delighted to sing blasphemous songs, and related hideous stories of what he had thought and resolved on in his solitude. He would even twist the chain in such wise that it should gall me at every step. I was at that time just twenty-two years of age, and had been sickly from boyhood. To retaliate, or to defend myself, would have been alike impossible. To complain to the superintendent would only have been to provoke my tyrant to greater cruelty.

There came a day, at length, when his hatred seemed to abate. He allowed me to rest when our hour of repose came round. He abstained from singing the songs I abhorred, and fell into long fits of abstraction. The next morning, shortly after we had begun work, he drew near enough to speak to me in a whisper.

"François, have you a mind to escape?"

I felt the blood rush to my face. I clasped my hands. I could not speak.

"Can you keep a secret?"

"To the death."

"Listen, then. To-morrow, a renowned marshal will visit the port. He will inspect the docks, the prisons, the quarries. There will be plenty of cannonading from the forts and the shipping, and if two convicts escape, a volley more or less will attract no attention round about Toulon. Do you understand?"

"You mean that no one will recognise the signals?"

"Not even the sentries at the town-gates—not even the guards in the next quarry. Devil's mass! What can be easier than to strike off each other's fetters with the pickaxe when the superintendent is not looking, and the salutes are firing? Will you venture?"

"With my life!"

"A bargain. Shake hands on it."

I had never touched his hand in fellowship before, and I felt as if my own were blood-stained by the contact. I knew by the sullen fire in his glance that he interpreted my faltering touch aright.

We were roused an hour earlier than usual the following morning, and went through a general inspection in the prison-yard. Before going to work, we were served with a double allowance of wine. At one o'clock we heard the first far-off salutes from the ships of war in the harbour. The sound ran through me like a galvanic shock. One by one, the forts took up the signal. It was repeated by the gun-boats closer in shore. Discharge followed discharge, all along the batteries on both sides of the port, and the air grew thick with smoke.

"As the first shot is fired yonder," whispered Gasparo, pointing to the barracks behind the prison, "strike at the first link of my chain, close to the ankle."

A rapid suspicion flashed across me.

"If I do, how can I be sure that you will free me afterwards? No, Gasparo; you must deal the first blow."

"As you please," he replied, with a laugh and an imprecation.

At the same instant came a flash from the battlements of the barrack close by, and then thunderous reverberation, multiplied again and again by the rocks around. As the roar burst over our heads, I saw him strike, and felt the fetters fall. Scarcely had the echo of the first gun died away, when the second was fired. It was now Gasparo's turn to be free. I struck; but less skilfully, and had twice to repeat the blow before breaking the stubborn link. We then went on, apparently, with our work, standing somewhat close together, with the chain huddled up beween us. No one had observed us, and no one, at first sight, could have detected what we had done. At the third shot, a party of officers and gentlemen made their appearance at the bend of the road leading up to the quarry.

In an instant, every head was turned in their direction ; every felon paused in his work ; every guard presented arms. At that moment we flung away our caps and pickaxes, scaled the rugged bit of cliff on which we had been toiling, dropped into the ravine below, and made for the mountain passes that lead into the valley. Encumbered still with the iron anklets to which our chains had been fastened, we could not run very swiftly. To add to our difficulties, the road was uneven, strewn with flints and blocks of fallen granite, and tortuous as the windings of a snake. Suddenly on turning a sharp angle of projecting cliff, we came upon a little guard-house and a couple of sentries. To retreat was impossible. The soldiers were within a few yards of us. They presented their pieces, and called to us to surrender. Gasparo turned upon me like a wolf at bay.

" Curse you ! " said he, dealing me a tremendous blow, " stay and be taken ! I have always hated you ! "

I fell as if struck by a sledge-hammer, and, as I fell, saw him dash one soldier to the ground, dart past the other, heard a shot, and then . . . all became dark, and I knew no more.

When I next opened my eyes, I found myself lying on the floor of a small unfurnished room, dimly lighted by a tiny window close against the ceiling. It seemed as if weeks had gone by since I lost consciousness. I had scarcely strength to rise, and, having risen, kept my feet with difficulty. Where my head had lain, the floor was wet with blood. Giddy and perplexed, I leaned against the wall, and tried to think.

In the first place, where was I ? Evidently in no part of the prison from which I had escaped. There, all was solid stone and iron grating ; here, was only whitewashed lath and plaster. I must be in a chamber of the little guard-house : probably in an upper chamber. Where, then, were the soldiers ? Where was Gasparo ? Had I strength to clamber up to that window, and if so, in what direction did that window look out ? I stole to the door, and found it locked. I listened, breathlessly, but could hear no sound either below or above. Creeping back again, I saw that the little window was at least four feet above my head. The smooth plaster offered no projections by which I could raise myself, and there was not even a fireplace in the room from which I could have wrenched a bar to dig out holes in the wall for my feet and hands. Stay ! There was my leather belt, and on the belt the iron hook which used to sustain my chain when I was not at work. I tore off the hook, picked away the lath and plaster in three or four places, climbed up, opened the window, and gazed out eagerly. Before me, at a distance of not more than thirty-five or forty feet, rose the rugged cliff under whose shelter the guard-house was built ; at my feet lay a little kitchen-garden, divided from the base of the rock by a muddy ditch which seemed to run through the ravine ; to the right and left, as well as I could judge, lay the rocky path along which our course had been directed. My decision was taken at once. To stay was certain capture ; to venture, at all hazards, would make matters no worse. Again I listened, and again all was quiet. I drew myself through the little casement, dropped as gently as I could upon the moist earth, and, crouching against the wall, asked myself what I should do next. To climb the cliff would be to offer myself as a target to the first soldier who saw me. To venture along the ravine would be, perhaps, to encounter Gasparo and his captors face to face. Besides, it was getting dusk, and, under cover of the night, if I could only conceal myself till then, I might yet escape. But where was that concealment to be found ? Heaven be thanked for the thought ! There was the ditch.

Only two windows looked out upon the garden from the back of the guard-house. From one of those windows I had just now let myself down, and the other was partly shuttered up. I did not dare, however, openly to cross the garden. I dropped upon my face, and crawled in the furrows between the rows of vegetables, until I came to the ditch. Here, the water rose nearly to my waist, but the banks on either side were considerably higher, and, by stooping, I found that I could walk without bringing my head to the level of the road. I thus followed the course of the ditch for some two or three hundred yards in the direction of Toulon, thinking that my pursuers would be less likely to suspect me of doubling back towards prison than of pushing forward towards the country. Half lying, half crouching under the rank grasses that fringed the bank above, I then watched the gathering shadows. By-and-by I heard the evening gun, and a moment after, something like a distant sound of voices. Hark ! was that a shout ? Unable to endure the agony of suspense, I lifted my head, and peeped cautiously out. There were lights moving in the windows of the guard-house—there were dark figures in the garden—there were hasty tramplings of feet upon the road above ! Presently a light flashed over the water only a few yards from my hiding-place ! I slid gently down at full length, and suffered the foul ooze to close noiselessly over me. Lying thus, I held my breath till the very beatings of my heart seemed to suffocate me, and the veins in my temples were almost bursting. I could bear it no longer—I rose to the surface—I breathed again—I looked —I listened. All was darkness and silence. My pursuers were gone by !

I suffered an hour to go by, too, before I ventured to move again. By that time it was intensely dark, and had begun to rain heavily. The water in the ditch became a brawling torrent, through which I waded, unheard, past the very windows of the guard-house.

After toiling through the water for a mile or more, I ventured out upon the road again ; and so, with the rain and wind beating in my face, and the scattered boulders tripping me up continually, I made my way through the whole length of the winding pass, and came out upon the more open country about midnight. With no other guide than the wind, which was blowing from the north-east, and without even a star to help me, I then struck off to the right, following what seemed to be a rough by-road, lying through a valley. By-and-by the rain abated, and I discerned the dark outlines of a chain of hills extending all along to the left of the road. These, I concluded must be the Maures. All was well, so far. I had taken the right direction, and was on the way to Italy.

Excepting to sit down now and then for a few minutes by the wayside, I never paused in my flight the whole night through. Fatigue and want of food prevented me, it is true, from walking very fast ; but the love of liberty was strong within me, and by keeping steadily on, I succeeded in placing about eighteen miles between myself and Toulon. At five o'clock, just as the day began to dawn, I heard a peal of chimes, and found that I was approachng a large town. In order to avoid this town, I was forced to turn back for some distance, and take to the heights. The sun had now risen, and I dared go no farther ; so, having pulled some turnips in a field as I went along, I took refuge in a little lonely copse in a hollow among the hills, and there lay all day in safety. When night again closed in, I resumed my journey, keeping always among the mountains, and coming now and then on grand glimpses of moonlit bays, and tranquil islands lying off the shore ; now and then on pastoral hamlets nestled up among the palmy heights ; or on promontories overgrown with the cactus and the aloe. I rested all the second day in a ruined shed at the bottom of a deserted sand-pit, and, in the evening, feeling that I could no longer sustain life without some fitting nourishment, made my way down towards a tiny fishing village on the coast below. It was quite dark by the time I reached the level ground. I walked boldly past the cottages of the fishermen, meeting only an old woman and a little child on the way, and knocked at the curé's door. He opened it himself. I told my story in half-a-dozen words. The good man believed and pitied me. He gave me food and wine, an old handkerchief to wrap about my head, an old coat to replace my convict's jacket, and two or three francs to help me on my way. I parted from him with tears.

I walked all that night again, and all the next, keeping somewhat close upon the coast, and hiding among the cliffs during the day time. On the fifth morning, having left Antibes behind me during the night's march, I came to the banks of the Var ; crossed the torrent about half a mile below the wooden bridge ; plunged into the pine-woods on the Sardinian side of the frontier ; and lay down to rest on Italian ground at last !

How, though comparatively safe, I still pursued my journey by the least frequented ways—how I bought a file at the first hamlet to which I came, and freed myself from the iron anklet—how, having lurked about Nice till my hair and beard had grown, I begged my way on to Genoa—how, at Genoa, I hung about the port earning a scanty livelihood by any chance work that I could get, and so struggled, somehow, through the inclement winter—how, towards the early spring, I worked my passage on board a small trader from Genoa to Fiumicino, touching at all the ports along the coast—and how, coming slowly up the Tiber in a barge laden with oil and wine, I landed one evening in March on the Ripetta quay, in Rome ;—how all these things happened, and what physical hardships I endured in the meanwhile I have no time here to relate in detail. My object had been to get to Rome, and that object was at last attained. In so large a city, and at so great a distance from the scene of my imprisonment, I was personally safe. I might hope to turn my talents and education to account. I might even find friends among the strangers who would flock thither to the Easter festivals. Full of hope, therefore, I sought a humble lodging in the neighbourhood of the quay, gave up a day or two to the enjoyment of my liberty and of the sights of Rome and then set myself to find some regular employment.

Regular employment, or, indeed, employment of any kind, was not, however, so easily to be obtained. It was a season of distress. The previous harvest had been a failure, and the winter unusually severe. There had also been disturbances in Naples, and the travellers this spring were fewer by some thousands than the ordinary average. So dull a carnival had not been known for years. The artists had sold no paintings, and the sculptors no statues. The cameo-cutters and mosaicists were starving. The tradesmen, the hotel-keepers, the professional ciceroni, were all complaining bitterly. Day by day, my hopes faded and my prospects darkened. Day by day, the few scudi I had scraped together on the passage melted away. I had thought to obtain a clerkship, or a secretaryship, or a situation in some public library. Before three weeks were over, I would gladly have swept a studio. At length there came a day when I saw nothing before me but starvation ; when my last bajocco was expended ; when my padrone (or landlord) shut the door in my face, and I knew not where to turn for a meal or a shelter. All that afternoon, I wandered hopelessly about the streets. It was Good Friday, of all days in the year. The churches were hung with black ; the bells were tolling ; and thoroughfares were crowded with people in mourning. I went into the little church of Santa Martina. They were chanting a miserere, probably with no great skill, but with a pathos that seemed to open up all the sources of my despair.

Outcast that I was, I slept that night under a dark arch near the theatre of Marcellus. The morning dawned upon a glorious day, and I crept out, shivering, into the sunshine. Lying crouched against a bit of warm wall, I caught myself wondering more than once how long it would be worth while to endure the agonies of hunger, and whether the brown waters of the Tiber were deep enough to drown a man. It seemed hard to die so young. My future might have been so pleasant, so honourable. The rough life that I had been leading of late, too, had strengthened me in every way, physically and mentally. I had grown taller. My muscles were more developed. I was twice as active, as energetic, as resolute as I had been a year before. And of what use were these things to me? I must die, and they could only serve to make me die the harder.

I got up and wandered about the streets, as I had wandered the day before. Once I asked for alms, and was repulsed. I followed mechanically in the stream of carriages and foot passengers, and found myself, by-and-by, in the midst of the crowd that ebbs and flows continually about Saint Peter's during Easter week. Stupefied and weary, I turned aside into the vestibule of the Sagrestia, and cowered down in the shelter of a doorway. Two gentlemen were reading a printed paper wafered against a pillar close by.

"Good Heavens!" said one to the other, "that a man should risk his neck for a few pauls!"

"Ay, and with the knowledge that out of eighty workmen, six or eight are dashed to pieces every time," added his companion.

"Shocking! Why, that is an average of ten per cent!"

"No less. It is a desperate service."

"But a fine sight," said the first speaker, philosophically; and with this they walked away.

I sprang to my feet and read the placard with avidity. It was headed "Illumination of Saint Peter's," and announced that, eighty workmen being required for the lighting of the dome and cupola, and three hundred for the cornices, pillars, colonnade, and so forth, the amministratore was empowered, etc. etc. In conclusion, it stated that every workman employed on the dome and cupola should receive in payment a dinner and twenty-four pauls, the wages of the rest being less than a third of that sum.

A desperate service, it was true; but I was a desperate man. After all, I could but die, and I might as well die after a good dinner as from starvation. I went at once to the amministratore, was entered in his list, received a couple of pauls as earnest of the contract, and engaged to present myself punctually at eleven o'clock on the following morning. That evening I supped at a street stall, and, for a few bajocchi, obtained leave to sleep on some straw, in a loft over a stable at the back of the Via del Arco.

At eleven o'clock on the morning of Easter Sunday, April 16, I found myself, accordingly, in the midst of a crowd of poor fellows, most of whom, I dare say, were as wretched as myself, waiting at the door of the administrator's office. The piazza in front of the cathedral was like a moving mosaic of life and colour. The sun was shining, the fountains were playing, the flags were flying over Saint Angelo. It was a glorious sight; but I saw it for only a few moments. As the clocks struck the hour, the folding-doors were thrown open, and we passed, in a crowd, into a hall, where two long tables were laid for our accommodation. A couple of sentinels stood at the door; an usher marshalled us, standing, round the tables; and a priest read grace.

As he began to read, a strange sensation came upon me. I felt impelled to look across to the opposite table, and there . . . yes, by Heaven! there I saw Gasparo.

He was looking full at me, but his eyes dropped on meeting mine. I saw him turn lividly white. The recollection of all he had made me suffer, and of the dastardly blow that he had dealt me on the day of our flight, overpowered for the moment even my surprise at seeing him in this place. Oh that I might live to meet him yet, under the free sky, where no priest was praying, and no guards were by!

The grace over, we sat down, and fell to. Not even anger had power to blunt the edge of my appetite just then. I ate like a famishing wolf, and so did most of the others. We were allowed no wine, and the doors were locked upon us, that we might not procure any elsewhere. It was a wise regulation, considering the task we had to perform; but it made us none the less noisy. In certain circumstances danger intoxicates like wine; and on this Easter Sunday, we eighty sanpietrini, any one of whom might have his brains dashed about the leads before supper-time, ate, talked, jested, and laughed, with a wild gaiety that had in it something appalling.

The dinner lasted long, and when no one seemed disposed to eat more, the tables were cleared. Most of the men threw themselves on the floor and benches, and went to sleep; Gasparo among the number. Seeing this, I could refrain no longer. I went over, and stirred him roughly with my foot.

"Gasparo! You know me?"

He looked up, sullenly.

"Devil's mass! I thought you were at Toulon."

"It is not your fault that I am not at Toulon! Listen to me.

If you and I survive this night, you shall answer to me for your treachery!"

He glared at me from under his deep brows, and, without replying, turned over on his face again, as if to sleep.

"Ecco un maladetto!" (There's an accursed fellow!) said one of the others, with a significant shrug, as I came away.

"Do you know anything of him!" I asked, eagerly.

"Cospetto! I know nothing of him; but that solitude is said to have made him a Wolf."

I could learn no more, so I also stretched myself upon the floor, as far as possible from my enemy, and fell profoundly asleep.

At seven, the guards roused those who still slept, and served each man with a small mug of thin wine. We were then formed into a double file, marched round by the back of the cathedral, and conducted up an inclined plane to the roof below the dome. From this point, a long series of staircases and winding passages carried us up between the double walls of the dome; and, to different stages in the ascent, a certain number of us were detached and posted ready for work. I was detached about half-way up, and I saw Gasparo going higher still. When we were all posted, the superintendents came round and gave us our instructions. At a given signal, every man was to pass out through the loophole or window before which he was placed, and seat himself astride upon a narrow shelf of wood hanging to a strong rope just below. This rope came through the window, was wound round a roller, and secured from within. At the next signal, a lighted torch would be put into his right hand, and he was to grasp the rope firmly with his left. At the third signal the rope was to be unwound from within by an assistant placed there for the purpose, he was to be allowed to slide rapidly down, over the curve of the dome, and, while thus sliding, was to apply his torch to every lamp he passed in his downward progress.

Having received these instructions, we waited, each man at his window, until the first signal should be given.

It was fast getting dark, and the silver illumination had been lighted since seven. All the great ribs of the dome, as far as I could see; all the cornices and friezes of the façade below; all the columns and parapets of the great colonnade surrounding the piazza four hundred feet below, were traced out in lines of paper lanterns, the light from which, subdued by the paper, gleamed with a silvery fire which had a magical and wondrous look. Between and among these lanternoni were placed, at different intervals all over the cathedral on the side facing the piazza, iron cups called padelle, ready filled with tallow and turpentine. To light those on the dome and cupola was the perilous task of the sanpietrini; when they were all lighted the golden illumination would be effected.

A few moments of intense suspense elapsed. At every second the evening grew darker, the lanternoni burned brighter, the surging hum of thousands in the piazza and streets below rose louder to our ears. I felt the quickening breath of the assistant at my shoulder—I could almost hear the beating of my heart. Suddenly, like the passing of an electric current, the first signal flew from lip to lip. I got out, and crossed my legs firmly round the board ; with the second signal I seized the blazing torch ; with the third, I felt myself launched, and, lighting every cup as I glided past, saw all the mountainous dome above and below me spring into lines of leaping flame. The clock was now striking eight, and when the last stroke sounded the whole cathedral was glowing in outlines of fire. A roar, like the roar of a great ocean, rose up from the multitude below, and seemed to shake the very dome against which I was clinging. I could even see the light upon the gazing faces, the crowd upon the bridge of Saint Angelo, and the boats swarming along the Tiber.

Having dropped safely to the full length of my rope, and lighted my allotted share of lamps, I was now sitting in secure enjoyment of this amazing scene. All at once I felt the rope vibrate. I looked up, saw a man clinging by one hand to the iron rod supporting the padelle, and with the other . . . Merciful Heaven ! It was the Piedmontese firing the rope above me with his torch !

I had no time for thought—I acted upon instinct. It was done in one fearful moment. I clambered up like a cat, dashed my torch full in the solitary felon's face, and grasped the rope an inch or two above the spot where it was burning ! Blinded and baffled, he uttered a terrible cry, and dropped like a stone. Through all the roar of the living ocean below I could hear the dull crash with which he came down upon the leaded roof—resounding through all the years that have gone by since that night, I hear it now !

I had scarcely drawn breath when I found myself being hauled up. The assistance came not a moment too soon, for I was sick and giddy with horror, and fainted as soon as I was safe in the corridor. The next day I waited on the amministratore, and told him all that had happened. My statement was corroborated by the vacant rope from which Gasparo had descended and the burnt fragment by which I had been drawn up. The amministratore repeated my story to a prelate high in office ; and while none, even of the sanpietrini, suspected that my enemy had come by his death in any unusual manner, the truth was whispered from palace to palace until it reached the Vatican. I received much sympathy, and such pecuniary assistance as enabled me to confront the future without fear. Since that time my fortunes have been various, and I have lived in many countries.

GEORGE MANVILLE FENN

1831–1909

MY FARE

DON'T you make a mistake now, and think I'm not a working-man, because I am. Don't you run away with the idea that because I go of a morning and find my horse and cab waiting ready cleaned for me, and I jumps up and drives off, as I don't work as hard as any mechanic, because I do ; and I used to work harder, for it used to be Sunday and week-days, till the missus and me laid our heads together, and said if we couldn't live on six days' work a week at cabbing, we'd try something else ; so now I am only a six-days' man—Hansom cab, V.R., licensed to carry two persons.

None o' your poor broken-kneed knackers for me. I takes my money in to the governor regular, and told him flat that if I couldn't have a decent horse I wouldn't drive ; and I spoke a bit sharp, having worked for him ten years.

" Take your chice, Steve Wilkins," he says ; and I took it, and drove Kangaroo, the wall-eyed horse with a rat tail.

I had a call one day off the stand by the Foundling, and has to go into New Ormond Street, close by ; and I takes up an old widow lady and her daughter—as beautiful a girl of seventeen or eighteen as ever I set eyes on, but so weak that I had to go and help her down to the cab, when she thanked me so sweetly that I couldn't help looking again and again, for it was a thing I wasn't used to.

" Drive out towards the country, cabman, the nearest way," says the old lady, " and when we want to turn back, I'll speak."

" Poor gal ! " I says ; " she's an invalid. She's just such a one as my Fan would have been if she'd lived " ; and I says this to myself as I gets on to my box, feeling quite soft, for though I knew my gal wouldn't have been handsome, what did that matter ? I didn't like to lose her.

" Let's see," I says again, " she wants fresh air. We'll go up the hill and through Hampstead " ; and I touches Kangaroo on the flank, and away we goes, and I picks out all the nicest bits I could, and when I comes across a pretty bit of view I pulls up, and pretends as there's a strap wanted tightening, or a hoof picking, or a fresh knot at the end of the whip, and so on. Then I goes pretty quickly along the streety bits, and walks very slowly along the green lanes; and so we goes on for a good hour, when the old lady pushes the lid open with her parasol, and tells me to turn back.

"All right, mum," I says, and takes 'em back another way, allers following the same plan; and at last pulls up at the house where I supposed they was lodgers, for that's a rare place for lodgings about there.

I has the young lady leaning on my arm when she gets out, and when she was at the door she says "Thank you" again so sweetly and sadly that it almost upset me. But the old lady directly after asked me the fare, and I tells her, and she gives me sixpence too much, and though I wanted to pocket it, I wouldn't, but hands it back.

"Thank you, cabman," she says, "that's for being so kind and attentive to my poor child."

"God bless her, mum," I says, "I don't want paying for that."

Then she smiles quite pleasant, and asks me if it would be worth my while to call again the next afternoon if it was fine, and I says it would; and next day, just in the same way, I goes right off past Primrose Hill, and seeing as what they wanted was the fresh air, I makes the best o' my way right out, and then, when we was amongst the green trees, Kangaroo and me takes it easy, and just saunters along. Going uphill I walks by his head, and picks at the hedges, while them two, seeing as I took no notice of 'em, took no notice o' me. I mean, you know, treated me as if we was old friends, and asked me questions about the different places we passed, and so on.

Bimeby I drives 'em back, and the old lady again wanted to give me something extra for what she called my kind consideration; but "No, Stevey," I says to myself, "if you can't do a bit o' kindness without being paid for it, you'd better put up the shutters, and take to some other trade."

So I wouldn't have it, and the old lady thought I was offended; but I laughed, and told her as the young lady had paid me; and so she had with one of her sad smiles, and I said I'd be there again nex' day if it was fine.

And so I was; and so we went on day after day, and week after week; and I could see that, though the sight of the country and the fresh air brightened the poor girl up a bit, yet she was getting weaker and weaker, so that at last I half carried her to the cab, and back again after the ride. One day while I was waiting the servant tells me that they wouldn't stay in town, only on account of a great doctor, as they went to see at first, but who came to them now; and last of all, when I went to the house I used always to be in a fidget for fear the poor gal should be too ill to come out. But no, month after month she kep' on, and when I helped her, used to smile so sweetly and talk so about the trouble she gave me, that one day, feeling a bit low, I turned quite silly ; and, happening to look at her poor mother a-standing there with the tears in her eyes, I had to hurry her in, and get up on to my seat as quick as I could, to keep from breaking down myself.

Poor gal ! always so loving and kind to all about her—always thanking one so sweetly, and looking all the while so much like what one would think an angel would look—it did seem so pitiful to feel her get lighter and lighter week by week—so feeble, that at last I used to go upstairs to fetch her, and always carried her down like a child.

Then she used to laugh, and say, " Don't let me fall, Stephen "—for they got to call me by my name, and to know the missus, by her coming in to help a bit ; for the old lady asked me to recommend 'em an honest woman, and I knowed none honester than my wife. And so it was with everybody—it didn't matter who it was—they all loved the poor gal ; and I've had the wife come home and sit and talk about her, and about our Fanny as died, till she's been that upset she's cried terribly.

Autumn came in werry wet and cold, and there was an end to my jobs there. Winter was werry severe, but I kep' on hearing from the missus how the poor gal was—sometimes better, sometimes worse ; and the missus allus shook her head werry sadly when she talked about her.

Jennywerry and Feberwerry went by terribly cold, and then March came in quite warm and fine, so that things got so forrard, you could buy radishes wonderful cheap in April ; and one night the wife comes home and tells me that if it was as fine nex' day as it had been I was to call and take the old lady and her daughter out.

Nex' day was splendid. It was as fine a spring day as ever I did see, and I sticks a daffydowndilly in on each side of Kangaroo's head, and then spends twopence in a couple o' bunches o' wilets, and pins 'em in on the side where the poor gal used to sit, puts clean straw in the boot, and then drives to the place with the top lid open, so as to sweeten the inside, because swells had been smoking there that morning.

" Jest run yer sponge and leather over the apron a bit, Buddy," I says to our waterman afore I left the stand.

" Got a wedding on ? " he says, seeing how pertickler I was.

" There, look alive ! " I says quite snappish, for I didn't feel in a humour to joke ; and then when I'd got all as I thought right, I drives up, keeping the lid open, as I said afore.

When I draws up I puts the nose-bag on the old horse, for him to amuse himself with, and so as I could leave him, for he wouldn't stir an inch with that bag on to please all the pleacemen in London.

Then I rings and waits, and at last gets my orders to go and help the young lady down.

I takes off my hat, wipes my shoes well, and goes up, and there she was waiting, and smiled so pleasantly again, and held out her hand to me, as though I'd been a friend instead of a rough, weather-battered street cabman. And do you know what I did as I went in there, with my eyes all dim at seeing her so, so changed? Why, I felt as if I ought to do it, and I knelt down and took her beautiful white hand in mine and kissed it, and left a big tear on it; for something seemed to say so plainly that she'd soon be where I hoped my own poor gal was, whom I always say we lost, but my wife says, "No, not lost, for she is ours still."

She was so light now that I carried her down in a minute; and when she was in the cab and saw the wilets, she took 'em down, and held 'em in her hand, and nodded and smiled again at me as though she thanked me for them.

"Go the same way as you went first time, Stephen," she says.

And I pushed over all the quieter bits, and took her out beyond Hampstead; and there, in the greenest and prettiest spot I could find, I pulls up, and sits there listening to the soft whispers of her voice, and feeling somehow that it was for the last time.

After a bit I goes gently on again, more and more towards the country, where the hedges were turning beautiful and green, and all looked so bright and gay.

Bimeby I stops again, for there was a pretty view, and you could see miles away. Of course I didn't look at them if I could help it, for the real secret of people enjoying a ride is being with a driver who seems no more to 'em than the horse—a man, you see, who knows his place. But I couldn't help just stealing one or two looks at the inside where that poor gal lay back in the corner, looking out at the bright spring-time, and holding them two bunches o' wilets close to her face. I was walking backwards and forwards then, patting the horse and straightening his harness, when I just catches the old lady's eye, and saw she looked rather frightened, and she leans over to her daughter and calls her by name quickly; but the poor girl did not move, only stared straight out at the blue sky, and smiled so softly and sweetly.

I didn't want no telling what to do, for I was in my seat and the old horse flying amost before you could have counted ten; and away we went, full pace, till I come up to a doctor's, dragged at the bell, and had him up to the cab in no time; and then he rode on the footboard of the cab, in front of the apron, with the shutters let down, and he whispered to me to drive back softly, and I did.

. . . .

The old lady has lodged with us ever since, for I took a better place on purpose, and my missus always attends on her. She's werry fond o' talking with my wife about their two gals who have gone before ; but though I often take her for a drive over the old spots, she never says a word to me about such things ; while soon after the funeral she told Sarah to tell me as the wilets were not taken from the poor gal's hand, same time sending me a fi-pun note to buy a suit o' mourning.

Of course I couldn't wear that every day, but there was a bit o' rusty crape on my old shiny hat not such a werry long time ago ; and I never buy wilets now, for as they lie in the baskets in spring-time, sprinkled with the drops o' bright water, they seem to me to have tears upon 'em, and make me feel sad and upset, for they start me off thinking about " My Fare."

WILLIAM MORRIS
1834–1896

THE STORY OF THE UNKNOWN CHURCH

I WAS the master-mason of a church that was built more than six hundred years ago ; it is now two hundred years since that church vanished from the face of the earth ; it was destroyed utterly—no fragment of it was left ; not even the great pillars that bore up the tower at the cross, where the choir used to join the nave. No one knows now even where it stood, only in this very autumn-tide, if you knew the place, you would see the heaps made by the earth-covered ruins heaving the yellow corn into glorious waves, so that the place where my church used to be is as beautiful now as when it stood in all its splendour. I do not remember very much about the land where my church was ; I have quite forgotten the name of it, but I know it was very beautiful, and even now, while I am thinking of it, comes a flood of old memories, and I almost seem to see it again —that old beautiful land ! only dimly do I see it in spring and summer and winter, but I see it in autumn-tide clearly now ; yes, clearer, clearer, oh ! so bright and glorious ! yet it was beautiful too in spring, when the brown earth began to grow green : beautiful in summer, when the blue sky looked so much bluer, if you could hem a piece of it in between the new white carving ; beautiful in the solemn starry nights, so solemn that it almost reached agony—the awe and joy one had in their great beauty. But of all these beautiful times I remember the whole only of autumn-tide ; the others come in bits to me ; I can think only of parts of them, but all of autumn ; and of all days and nights in autumn I remember one more particularly. That autumn day the church was nearly finished, and the monks, for whom we were building the church, and the people, who lived in the town hard by, crowded round us oftentimes to watch us carving.

Now the great church, and the buildings of the Abbey where the monks lived, were about three miles from the town, and the town stood on a hill overlooking the rich autumn country : it was girt about with great walls that had overhanging battlements, and towers at certain places all along the walls, and often we could see from the churchyard or the Abbey garden the flash of helmets and spears, and the dim shadowy waving of banners, as the knights and lords and men-at-arms passed to and fro along the battlements; and we could see too in the town the three spires of the three churches; and the spire of the Cathedral, which was the tallest of the three, was gilt all over with gold, and always at night-time a great lamp shone from it that hung in the spire midway between the roof of the church and the cross at the top of the spire. The Abbey where we built the church was not girt by stone walls, but by a circle of poplar trees, and whenever a wind passed over them, were it ever so little a breath, it set them all a-ripple; and when the wind was high they bowed and swayed very low, and the wind, as it lifted the leaves and showed their silvery white sides, or as again in the lulls of it, it let them drop, kept on changing the trees from green to white, and white to green; moreover, through the boughs and trunks of the poplars, we caught glimpses of the great golden corn sea, waving, waving, waving for leagues and leagues; and among the corn grew burning scarlet poppies and blue cornflowers; and the cornflowers were so blue that they gleamed, and seemed to burn with a steady light, as they grew beside the poppies among the gold of the wheat. Through the corn sea ran a blue river, and always green meadows and lines of tall poplars followed its windings. The old church had been burned, and that was the reason why the monks caused me to build the new one; the buildings of the Abbey were built at the same time as the burned-down church, more than a hundred years before I was born, and they were on the north side of the church, and joined to it by a cloister of round arches, and in the midst of the cloister was a lawn, and in the midst of that lawn a fountain of marble, carved round about with flowers and strange beasts; and at the edge of the lawn, near the round arches, were a great many sunflowers that were all in blossom on that autumn day; and up many of the pillars of the cloister crept passion-flowers and roses. Then farther from the church, and past the cloister and its buildings, were many detached buildings, and a great garden round them, all within the circle of the poplar trees; in the garden were trellises covered over with roses and convolvulus and the great-leaved fiery nasturtium; and specially all along by the poplar trees were there trellises, but on these grew nothing but deep crimson roses; the hollyhocks too were all out in blossom at that time, great spires of pink, and orange, and red, and white, with their soft downy leaves. I said that nothing grew on the trellises by the poplars but crimson roses, but I was not quite right, for in many places the wild flowers had crept into the garden from without; lush green briony, with green-white blossoms, that grows so fast, one could almost think that we see it grow, and deadly nightshade, La bella donna, Oh! so beautiful; red berry, and purple, yellow-spiked flower, and deadly, cruel-looking, dark green leaf, all growing together in the glorious days of early autumn. And in the midst of the great garden was a conduit, with its sides carved with histories from the Bible, and there was on it too, as on the fountain in the cloister, much carving of flowers and strange beasts. Now the church itself was surrounded on every side but the north by the cemetery, and there were many graves there, both of monks and of laymen, and often the friends of those, whose bodies lay there, had planted flowers about the graves of those they loved. I remember one such particularly, for at the head of it was a cross of carved wood, and at the foot of it, facing the cross, three tall sunflowers; then in the midst of the cemetery was a cross of stone, carved on one side with the Crucifixion of our Lord Jesus Christ, and on the other with Our Lady holding the Divine Child. So that day that I specially remember in autumn-tide, when the church was nearly finished, I was carving in the central porch of the west front (for I carved all those bas-reliefs in the west front with my own hand); beneath me my sister Margaret was carving at the flower-work, and the little quatrefoils that carry the signs of the zodiac and emblems of the months: now my sister Margaret was rather more than twenty years old at that time, and she was very beautiful, with dark brown hair and deep calm violet eyes. I had lived with her all my life, lived with her almost alone latterly, for our father and mother died when she was quite young, and I loved her very much, though I was not thinking of her just then, as she stood beneath me carving. Now the central porch was carved with a bas-relief of the Last Judgment, and it was divided into three parts by horizontal bands of deep flower-work. In the lowest division, just over the doors, was carved The Rising of the Dead; above were angels blowing long trumpets, and Michael the Archangel weighing the souls, and the blessed led into heaven by angels, and the lost into hell by the devil; and in the topmost division was the Judge of the world.

All the figures in the porch were finished except one, and I remember when I woke that morning my exultation at the thought of my church being so nearly finished. I remember, too, how a kind of misgiving mingled with the exultation, which, try all I could, I was unable to shake off; I thought then it was a rebuke for my pride; well, perhaps it was. The figure I had to carve was Abraham, sitting with a blossoming tree on each side of him, holding in his two hands the corners of his great robe, so that it made a mighty fold, wherein, with their hands crossed over their breasts, were the souls of the faithful, of whom he was called Father: I stood on the scaffolding for some time, while Margaret's chisel worked on bravely down below. I took mine in my hand, and stood so, listening to the noise of the masons inside, and two monks of the Abbey came and stood below me, and a knight, holding his little daughter by the hand, who every now and then looked up at him, and asked him strange questions. I did not think of these long, but began to think of Abraham, yet I could not think of him sitting there, quiet and solemn, while the Judgment-Trumpet was being blown; I rather thought of him as he looked when he chased those kings so far; riding far ahead of any of his company, with his mailhood off his head, and lying in grim folds down his back, with the strong west wind blowing his wild black hair far out behind him, with the wind rippling the long scarlet pennon of his lance; riding there amid the rocks and the sands alone; with the last gleam of the armour of the beaten kings disappearing behind the winding of the pass; with his company a long, long way behind, quite out of sight, though their trumpets sounded faintly among the clefts of the rocks; and so I thought I saw him, till on his fierce chase he leapt, horse and man, into a deep river, quiet, swift, and smooth; and there was something in the moving of the water-lilies as the breast of the horse swept them aside, that suddenly took away the thought of Abraham and brought a strange dream of lands I had never seen; and the first was of a place where I was quite alone, standing by the side of a river, and there was the sound of singing a very long way off, but no living thing of any kind could be seen, and the land was quite flat, quite without hills, and quite without trees too, and the river wound very much, making all kinds of quaint curves, and on the side where I stood there grew nothing but long grass, but on the other side grew, quite on to the horizon, a great sea of red corn-poppies, only paths of white lilies wound all among them, with here and there a great golden sunflower. So I looked down at the river by my feet, and saw how blue it was, and how, as the stream went swiftly by, it swayed to and fro the long green weeds, and I stood and looked at the river for long, till at last I felt some one touch me on the shoulder, and. looking round, I saw standing by me my friend Amyot, whom I love better than any one else in the world, but I thought in my dream that I was frightened when I saw him, for his face had changed so, it was so bright and almost transparent, and his eyes gleamed and shone as I had never seen them do before. Oh! he was so wondrously beautiful, so fearfully beautiful! and as I looked at him the distant music swelled, and seemed to come close up to me, and then swept by us, and fainted away, at last died off entirely; and then I felt sick at heart, and faint, and parched, and I stooped to drink of the water of the river, and as soon as the water touched my lips, lo! the river vanished, and the flat country with its poppies and lilies, and I dreamed that I was in a boat by myself again, floating in an almost land-locked bay of the northern sea, under a cliff of dark basalt. I was lying on my back in the boat, looking up at the intensely blue sky, and a long low swell from the outer sea lifted the boat up and let it fall again and carried it gradually nearer and nearer towards the dark cliff; and as I moved on, I saw at last, on the top of the cliff, a castle, with many towers, and on the highest tower of the castle there was a great white banner floating, with a red chevron on it, and three golden stars on the chevron; presently L saw too on one of the towers, growing in a cranny of the worn stones, a great bunch of golden and blood-red wallflowers, and I watched the wallflowers and banner for long; when suddenly I heard a trumpet blow from the castle, and saw a rush of armed men on to the battlements, and there was a fierce fight, till at last it was ended, and one went to the banner and pulled it down, and cast it over the cliff into the sea, and it came down in long sweeps, with the wind making little ripples in it;—slowly, slowly it came, till at last it fell over me and covered me from my feet till over my breast, and I let it stay there and looked again at the castle, and then I saw that there was an amber-coloured banner floating over the castle in place of the red chevron, and it was much larger than the other: also now, a man stood on the battlements, looking towards me; he had a tilting helmet on, with the visor down, and an amber-coloured surcoat over his armour; his right hand was ungauntleted, and he held it high above his head, and in his hand was the bunch of wallflowers that I had seen growing on the wall; and his hand was white and small, like a woman's, for in my dream I could see even very far-off things much clearer than we see real material things on the earth: presently he threw the wallflowers over the cliff, and they fell in the boat just behind my head, and then I saw, looking down from the battlements of the castle, Amyot. He looked down towards me very sorrowfully, I thought, but, even as in the other dream, said nothing; so I thought in my dream that I wept for very pity, and for love of him, for he looked as a man just risen from a long illness, and who will carry till he dies a dull pain about with him. He was very thin, and his long black hair drooped all about his face as he leaned over the battlements looking at me; he was quite pale, and his cheeks were hollow, but his eyes large, and soft, and sad. So I reached out my arms to him, and suddenly I was walking with him in a lovely garden, and we said nothing, for the music which I had heard at first was sounding close to us now, and there were many birds in the boughs of the trees; oh, such birds! gold and ruby, and emerald, but they sung not at all, but were quite silent, as though they too were listening to the music. Now all this time Amyot and I had been looking at each other, but just then I turned my head away from him, and as soon as I did so, the music ended with a long wail, and when I turned again Amyot was gone; then I felt even more sad and sick at heart than I had before when I was by the river, and I leaned against a tree, and put my hands before my eyes. When I looked again the garden was gone, and I knew not where I was, and presently all my dreams were gone. The chips were flying bravely from the stone under my chisel at last, and all my thoughts now were in my carving, when I heard my name, "Walter," called, and when I looked down I saw one standing below me, whom I had seen in my dreams just before—Amyot. I had no hopes of seeing him for a long time, perhaps I might never see him again, I thought, for he was away (as I thought) fighting in the holy wars, and it made me almost beside myself to see him standing close by me in the flesh. I got down from my scaffolding as soon as I could, and all thoughts else were soon drowned in the joy of having him by me; Margaret, too, how glad she must have been, for she had been betrothed to him for some time before he went to the wars and he had been five years away; five years! and how we had thought of him through those many weary days! how often his face had come before me! his brave, honest face, the most beautiful among all the faces of men and women I have ever seen. Yes, I remember how five years ago I held his hand as we came together out of the cathedral of that great, far-off city, whose name I forget now; and then I remember the stamping of the horses' feet; I remember how his hand left mine at last, and then, some one looking back at me earnestly as they all rode on together—looking back, with his hand on the saddle behind him, while the trumpets sang in long solemn peals as they all rode on together, with the glimmer of arms and the fluttering of banners, and the clinking of the rings of the mail, that sounded like the falling of many drops of water into the deep, still waters of some pool that the rocks nearly meet over; and the gleam and flash of the swords, and the glimmer of the lance-heads and the flutter of the rippled banners, that streamed out from them, swept past me and were gone, and they seemed like a pageant in a dream, whose meaning we know not; and those sounds too, the trumpets, and the clink of the mail, and the thunder of the horse-hoofs, they seemed dream-like too—and it was all like a dream that he should leave me, for we had said that we should always be together; but he went away, and now he is come back again.

We were by his bedside, Margaret and I; I stood and leaned over him, and my hair fell sideways over my face and touched his face; Margaret kneeled beside me, quivering in every limb, not with pain, I think, but rather shaken by a passion of earnest prayer. After some time (I know not how long) I looked up from his face to the window underneath which he lay; I do not know what time of the day it was, but I know that it was a glorious autumn day, a day soft with melting, golden haze: a vine and a rose grew together, and trailed half across the window, so that I could not see much of the beautiful blue sky, and nothing of town or country beyond; the vine leaves were touched with red here and there, and three over-blown roses, light pink roses, hung amongst them. I remember dwelling on the strange lines the autumn had made in red on one of the gold-green vine leaves, and watching one leaf of one of the over-blown roses, expecting it to fall every minute; but as I gazed, and felt disappointed that the rose leaf had not fallen yet, I felt my pain suddenly shoot through me, and I remembered what I had lost; and then came bitter, bitter dreams—dreams which had once made me happy—dreams of the things I had hoped would be, of the things that would never be now; they came between the fair vine leaves and rose blossoms and that which lay before the window; they came as before, perfect in colour and form, sweet sounds and shapes. But now in every one was something unutterably miser-able; they would not go away, they put out the steady glow of the golden haze, the sweet light of the sun through the vine leaves, the soft leaning of the full-blown roses. I wandered in them for a long time; at last I felt a hand put me aside gently, for I was standing at the head of—of the bed; then some one kissed my forehead, and words were spoken—I know not what words. The bitter dreams left me for the bitterer reality at last; for I had found him that morning lying dead, only the morning after I had seen him when he had come back from his long absence—I had found him lying dead, with his hands crossed downwards, with his eyes closed, as though the angels had done that for him; and now when I looked at him he still lay there, and Margaret knelt by him with her face touching his: she was not quivering now, her lips moved not at all as they had done just before; and so, suddenly those words came to my mind which she had spoken when she kissed me, and which at the time I had only heard with my outward hearing, for she had said, "Walter, farewell, and Christ keep you; but for me, I must be with him, for so I promised him last night that I would never leave him any more, and God will let me go." And verily Margaret and Amyot did go, and left me very lonely and sad.

It was just beneath the westernmost arch of the nave, there I carved their tomb: I was a long time carving it; I did not think I should be so long at first, and I said, "I shall die when I have finished carving it," thinking that would be a very short time. But so it happened after I had carved those two whom I loved, lying with clasped hands like husband and wife above their tomb, that I could not yet leave carving it; and so that I might be near them I became a monk, and used to sit in the choir and sing, thinking of the time when we should be all together again. And as I had time I used to go to the westernmost arch of the nave and work at the tomb that was there under the great, sweeping arch ; and in process of time I raised a marble canopy that reached quite up to the top of the arch, and I painted it too as fair as I could, and carved it all about with many flowers and histories, and in them I carved the faces of those I had known on earth (for I was not as one on earth now, but seemed quite away out of the world). And as I carved sometimes the monks and other people too would come and gaze, and watch how the flowers grew ; and sometimes too as they gazed, they would weep for pity, knowing how all had been. So my life passed, and I lived in that abbey for twenty years after he died, till one morning, quite early, when they came into the church for matins, they found me lying dead, with my chisel in my hand, underneath the last lily of the tomb.

S. BARING-GOULD
1834–1924

GENEFER

I

In a field of young corn paced Genefer, stooping and plucking the charlock. The yellow mustard flowers formed a sheaf on her left arm, partly wrapped about with a grey-blue apron.

So was it, hour by hour, with Genefer.

Through a gap in the sandhills showed a tract of the Atlantic, dark blue and glancing like a peacock's neck. Over all was the turquoise sky without a cloud.

A church path traversed the cornfield from one stone stile to another. Over that leading from the village stepped a young man, Joe Legassick, son of the farmer at Tregothnan. He was in holiday suit, and had a bunch of faded pansies in his buttonhole.

" Hulloo, Genefer ! Why are you not at the Revel ? " He halted half-way through the wheatfield, and the wind from the sea passed in ripples over the young green corn. It might have been his breath, for he was panting, and his breath was as strong as the wind.

"For the best of reasons, Joe," answered the girl, rising and throwing the gamboge bundle over her shoulder. Her face glowed like a red robin in the hedge, for the day was warm, and she had been working hard. Her large lustrous dark eyes looked as deep as the Atlantic, and like it, now as undisturbed, and smiling.

" What do you call the best of reasons ? "

" Can't," answered the girl. " Find a better reason if you may." Then, again stooping, she continued the charlock gathering.

" Leave that," said the young man, " and answer me more sensibly. Why can't you be at the Revel ? "

" You see, Joe," replied the girl, again rising, " I have my work set me. I cannot afford to loiter. The wheatfield must be cleared by some one."

" Could you not spare a day for amusement ? "

" No—I must gather while the sun shines. It is drashy, dirty work when the corn is wet. Then my petticoats drag me down."

" What does father pay you for weeding this field of his ? "

" Eighteenpence."

" Why, that is not a ha'penny per row. I wouldn't give up my holiday for that sum."

" You've no need for so doing."

Joe considered a moment. " Hang me ! " said he ; " I've chucked away double that sum on nothing at all at the Revel. Here, I'll pay you another eighteenpence for the job."

" I won't take it. I agreed with your father as to the price."

" Then, here goes ! " Joe cast off his coat. " I'll help you myself."

Thereupon he began and continued working vigorously. He began at the opposite extremity of the field to that at which Genefer was engaged, and as the two young people weeded they drew near each other, till at last they were face to face.

" This is hot work," said the young man. " I'm nigh melted and run into the furrow."

" You are not accustomed to this sort of work," said the girl.

" I say, Genefer. Take a whisk of the charlock and fan my face with it."

The girl laughed, and a twinkle as of sun on wavelets came into her eyes as she complied with his request. Joe stood stock-still whilst she wafted the air, scented with wild mustard, over his heated countenance.

" Now you may wipe my face with your apron," said he.

" You'll soon tire of weeding," laughed Genefer, as she plucked off her blue apron and drew it across his brow and cheeks.

" Not so long as I have you to speak to at every turn," said he ; " with the prospect in the weeding "—but he muttered this to himself—" of dropping an E and picking up a D."

At last the field was cleared. Not a yellow flower remained.

" There now, Genefer," said the farmer's son, " I've done half the job. You must give me a cup of tea. I am that dry I'm like to be blown away like a dust heap."

" And a moment ago you were melting into the furrows," said the girl, and the dimples formed on her blooming cheeks, like those in wild rose petals. " Come to the Willis."

The cottage inhabited by Genefer and her grandmother lay in a dip, with a sandhill at the back rising rapidly from it. To the front was a bank with thorn bushes, sprinkled over with ash-grey scabious, In the hollow was a spring, locally termed a *Willis*. The cottage was low, thatched, faced the sun, and was buzzed about by bees, and green-backed flies basked on the walls and preened their wings.

The grandmother was feeble, deaf, cross, and an inveterate scold. No sooner did Genefer enter than the old woman gave rein to her tongue and poured forth a torrent of abuse, regardless of the visitor. Joe listened with ill-suppressed indignation, and wondered at the patience and sweetness with which the girl bore the old creature's humour. He looked round the cottage and admired its scrupulous neatness. A mug with sweet-peas stood in the window. The brass candlesticks and a copper skillet on the chimney shelf were burnished. Everything in the room was clean and in order. After Joe had refreshed himself with a cup of weak tea *sans* milk, he departed, and walked meditatively towards Tregothnan. He had not resumed his coat. He was still warm. Presently, on issuing from the lane, he lighted on his father, who was engaged in walling up a gap in a hedge.

"Joe," said the farmer, "all the workmen be gone to the Revel, so I've just turned to myself. I can't abide having this bit o' fallen wall, and the cattle breaking out may lame themselves. Lend a hand with those big stones. I can't heave 'em myself since I were took wi' rheumatics in the shoulder."

The young man complied, but there was something constrained in his manner, so that old Legassick noticed it, stopped his work, and said, "Why, what ails the boy?"

"Father," answered Joe, turning crimson and looking down, "you and mother have often been at me to get married and settled. Well I've thought about it, and have got the right one at last."

"And who is that?"

"Genefer."

"What, down to the Willis?"

"Yes—I couldn't do better."

The farmer paused before offering a remark. But presently he said, "I haven't a word to say against the maid herself; yet I'm not so sure she is the right one. It's true her father was a farmer, but he died early, and they lost all they had, and she has got nothing at all."

"She is diligent, honest, and good-looking."

"Ah! it's the looks you think of, Joe! Your mother will never give consent. I'm above such considerations, but she is not. Though I am her husband and she is your mother, I must say it—that she's close in money matters as a Jew. There is the butter money and what she gets by poultry and eggs. It is five-and-thirty years that we have been married, and yet I have never seen the colour of a sixpence she has made by them yet. She hoards; it is her one satisfaction. No, Joe; put this thought out of your heart. The old woman is fanciful, and she'd worry herself to fiddle-strings to think that her only child and dear boy—who's the apple of her eye—was throwing himself away on a penniless girl. No. Take my word for it, it won't do."

Somewhat later in the same afternoon Joe had an opportunity of speaking to his mother. She was hot, with her sleeves rolled up and her skirt tucked into her girdle.

" With this weather," said she, " there is no doing anything with the butter. I gave it up in the morning as a bad job ; it's worse now ; and it has been standing in the butter-well all day. Then—what's wrong, Joe ? You look strangely."

" Mother," answered he, " you and father have often said that you'd like to see me settled, that you might retire and have a little rest in your old age. Now I'm going to take a wife."

" Who is she ? " asked Mrs. Legassick, becoming cool at once in spite of the heat.

" Mother, I thought of Genefer, down to the Willis."

Mrs. Legassick let down her skirt and rolled her sleeves over her arms before she spoke. Then she said slowly and unsympathetically : " Joe, I've nothing to say against Genefer. Nobody has. She is thoughtful, clean, careful and considerate of her grandmother, who is a teasy old toad. But your father will never consent. His whole mind is set on money-making. He denies himself many a comfort and never allows himself a holiday, just because he can't bear the thought of spending what has been hard-earned. I know your father's mind better than can any one else, and I am quite sure of this that rather than see you marry a penniless girl he'd see you in your coffin. Take my word for it—if you are obstinate and persist, you'll break the old man's heart and bring his grey hairs with sorrow to the grave. Avarice is a great vice, but it is the only one your father has."

That evening when Mr. and Mrs. Legassick were together alone, said she to her spouse : " This will never do. We must send for Polly Penfound ; I'm a sort of aunt of hers in a roundabout fashion ; but I've not seen her since she was a child. She was a lively little morsel then, and her uncle has died and left her five hundred pounds."

" With five hundred pounds something might be done," said the farmer.

" It would serve to line the nest," said the wife.

II

Polly Penfound arrived.

Invited ostensibly that she might be given change of air and scene after the strain caused by nursing a sick uncle and the sorrow occasioned by his death, she perfectly understood that she was asked to Tregothnan with the idea of a match being made between her and Joe Legassick. The damsel had heard a good report of Joe as well-built, good-humoured, and pleasant-featured. His parents were reputed to be " warm " people. So she said to her mother before she left, " I can take him if I like ; if not, I will lump him."

When Polly arrived, everyone in Tregothnan became aware that she was a person of consequence, who thought a good deal of herself and her five hundred pounds. She was well-favoured, had a pair of dark eyes, which she rolled a good deal, and a pair of red lips ever given to pouting.

In a farmhouse a visitor is expected to lend an occasional hand in the domestic work, at least to reduce to a minimum the additional burden her presence lays on the servants. But Polly did not put out her little finger to assist the hard-worked Mrs. Legassick, and she made confusion and strewed with litter every room she invaded. She had come to Tregothnan to be amused and not to work. She expected her cousin to dance attendance on her, and therefore she drew him away from the farm.

She was a rattle. She talked incessantly, but always of herself. For whatever did not concern herself, nor conduce to her glorification, was devoid of interest to her.

Joe Legassick was shrewd enough to perceive the object his father and mother had in view in inviting Mary Penfound to the farm. Lest he should not perceive it, each threw out observations on her being the happy possessor of five hundred pounds, and Mrs. Legassick remarked, " Five hundred pounds brought into the farm would warm the cockles of your father's heart." The farmer also said, " Half a thousand brought into the family would make your mother grow green again."

Joe made no reply to either.

Three days after the arrival of Polly Penfound one of the cows fell ill, and had to be attended by night as well as by day. Usually Joe was ready to assist his father in an emergency, but now he was taken up with attendance on the visitor, who expected to be driven about to see the sights during the day, and who yawned and complained unless there were a concert or a show to be visited in the evening, and who found that neither was inconsistent with her condition of mourning.

It was not possible for Joe to do two things at once, to attend to the cow and also to Polly. Mrs. Legassick, moreover, was tied to home because her one maid was in a condition of simmering mutiny. Consequently the amusement of Polly devolved on Joe.

On the fourth day the rebellion in the kitchen broke out. The maid forfeited her month's wage and took herself off without warning.

Joe was in the parlour with Polly Penfound. The parlour was an apartment maintained for display and not intended for use. Each chair-back was provided with an antimacassar; the table was strewn with little wool and bead mats; every picture frame was draped with muslin. The room smelt of carpet and curtain and soot. The blinds were invariably drawn. This apartment had been taken possession of by Miss Polly, who would not sit in the kitchen, and Mrs. Legassick's heart and nerves were kept in a quiver of apprehension and distress for the new carpet over which Polly tramped with muddy boots; for the table-cover on which she spilled water when inadvertently knocking over the flower-glasses; for the china ornaments when she whisked about her parasol; for the stiff woolly piano, never used, till Polly strummed waltzes and polkas on it.

"Oh, my dear life!" exclaimed Miss Penfound, looking at herself in the glass, "this sea air has tanned me and made of me a perfect fright."

"That," said Joe gallantly, "is more than even the tooth of time could effect."

"You are polite. Where shall we go to-day?"

"There is a flower show at Wade Bridge, but we shall see nothing there half so lovely as yourself."

In bounced Mrs. Legassick.

"Joe!" she exclaimed. "What is to be done? Susan has taken herself off in a tantrum, and all the butter has to be packed and weighed and sent off by the coach. Then there is no one to do the cooking, and father wants a bran-mash for the cow. I wonder whether, Polly, you will help me a mite to-day? I really don't know how I shall get through all the work."

"Polly and I are going to the flower show at Wade Bridge," said the young man.

"And aunt, dear," said the girl, "I haven't the remotest notion how to make butter, tidy a room, or cook even a potato."

"That Susan," said Mrs. Legassick bitterly, "says that she didn't come here to wait on visitors who unpick seams and strew the floor with bits of thread. Run down, Joe, to the Willis and get Genefer to come up. She can ask a neighbour to look in during the day on the old woman."

"I am sorry, mother, but I really have not time to go for Genefer. I will send the stable-boy."

About an hour after the departure of Polly with Joe, Mrs. Legassick, finding herself alone with her husband, said grimly, "Will you believe it? It is that girl, who is my sort of half-niece, who causes all the worry here, and has driven away Susan, that is a useful girl, but has a temper. I asked Polly to lend a hand, and she wouldn't help me for all I begged her. She has strewn her bedroom floor with threads, and the new carpet in the parlour with bits of butter-scotch she had dropped and trodden in, and that have ruined it. I wonder how long she intends to stay with us?"

"Wife," said Mr. Legassick, "she has twisted Joe round her

finger, and will soon make him as bad as herself. Here am I in this hot weather worked till I am fit to drop, and suffering terrible from my rheumatics, and the cow is sick, and not half an hour's help can I get out of Joe. He is off all day gallivanting with that witch. We shall be thrown back in everything, as there will be no getting things in train again this side Michaelmas. You have Genefer to help you, and she is a host in herself. I—I have no one."

Genefer, however, could not be every day and all day at the farm. She had duties to perform to her grandmother and in the cottage that must be personally discharged. One morning she ran up to Tregothnan, her face bathed in tears, to announce that during the night the old woman had been struck with palsy, that she was speechless, consequently Mrs. Legassick would be obliged to shift without help from Genefer.

"Dear Didums!" gasped Mrs. Legassick, "whatever shall I do? Look here, Genefer, I'll make a push, when I have a moment free, to run down to the Willis and see if there is anything your grandmother requires that I can supply. You've been a good girl, and I'll do anything in my power for you."

That same evening, when the farmer and his wife were alone together, said he to her: "This can't go on. That young female is spoiling Joe wholly, she's reg'lar demoralising him and making him forget his duty to his father and mother—which is the first commandment, with promise."

"I shall go off my head," retorted Mrs. Legassick. "If she stays here much longer the carpet in the parlour will have lost all its colour. She never thinks to draw down the blind, though the sun be streaming in. Whatever made you bring here here?"

"That's fine! You recommended her to be brought. It's my firm conviction that she'd be a dear bargain for all her five hundred pounds. She'd just be the ruin of any farm into which she were put. I only wish——"

He did not finish the sentence. His wife broke in with: "I don't know about a farm only, but any house she were in she'd put all at sixes and sevens. Why, five hundred pounds wouldn't keep her in her extravagant ideas. I only wish——"

Neither did she conclude her sentence.

"It is my candid opinion," continued the old lady, after a pause, "that when this young woman gets Joe, she'll not rest till she has kicked us both out. Rather than that——"

"It is my unalterable resolution," said the farmer, "that she shall never settle in here to have the chance of kicking either of us. If Joe be that besotted as to take her, then let him find a home for her elsewhere. Rather—a thousand times——"

He walked off whistling a minor air.

III

"Genefer," said Mrs. Legassick, in her peremptory though kindly manner, "you've been moping over your grandmother in the house long enough. Be off on to the cliffs and get your lungs full of fresh air. I'll bide by the old woman a while."

"Oh, ma'am, you're so busy."

"That is my affair, not yours. Do as you are bid. Yet, stay. First answer me this. Has my son been here?"

"Mr. Joe!—No, ma'am."

"Not been to inquire after the old lady?"

"No, ma'am."

"And stay, Genefer. When you were up at Tregothnan, did he have any words with you?"

"Words—what sort of words, ma'am?"

"Well, not a quarrel exactly, but t'other thing."

"He asked to have his boots better blacked than had been done by Susan, as Miss Penfound had found fault with their being so dull."

"Nothing else?"

"No, ma'am, nothing."

Mrs. Legassick did not appear to be over-gratified to hear this. She did not mistrust the girl, for Genefer's word was always to be relied on, and in character she was clear and transparent as Atlantic water. The farmer's wife thought that Joe was mightily easily turned from a purpose. She had not given him credit for such pliability of disposition and submissiveness to her opinion.

"Genefer!" said Mrs. Legassick, after some consideration and pursing up of her lips, "I'd have you go up to Tregothnan. You'll find on the side-table in the kitchen a cornflour pudding I have made for your grandmother, and have turned a pie-dish over it against the cats, and there's a medicine bottle, too, of best sherry wine. I did not bring them myself because I wished to give you the run. I'll attend to your patient whilst you are away."

For three-quarters of an hour Mrs. Legassick was in the sick woman's room. She observed the old grandmother attentively, and saw that she was so seriously affected by the stroke that she could neither recognise anyone nor speak. It was eminently doubtful whether she would rally, but possibly she might linger on for some weeks.

When Genefer returned, with a glow in her cheeks from running, she found Mrs. Legassick in a sort of nervous flutter, and impatient to be off. This was easily explicable, circumstanced as the farmer's wife was. Mrs. Legassick departed, but as she left the house, and shut the door, at the same time she closed her eyes and chuckled.

An hour later a rap sounded at the cottage door. Mr. Legassick entered without waiting to be admitted, and inquired after the old woman.

Genefer gave him the desired information, and expected that he would at once leave. But instead of doing so, he asked if he might take a chair.

"I reckon, Genefer, the old lady be gone quite tottle (dazed)."

"She does not know me, nor understand when I speak to her."

"I reckon you are prepared for the worst."

The girl did not answer, but her bosom swelled, and she dropped her head.

"I didn't say it to pain you, maiden," said the farmer, "but because it is ever well to be ready against what may hap. Now, you do as I tell you. Go into her chamber, and tell her that I've come to ask after her; and just inquire as well whether she has any commands for me."

"I do not think she will understand, and she cannot speak."

"Never mind. Do as you are bid. It is a matter of conscience with me. Repeat what I have told you three, or even four times, and put it in various ways, so as to make her understand, if there is a pinch of understanding left in her."

The girl obeyed, and left the kitchen.

No sooner was she gone than Mr. Legassick hastily drew something from his pocket, sought out a little empty jam-pot, stowed away in a nook, put what he had extracted from his pocket into it, and then, kneeling at the hearth, thrust his arm up the chimney till he found a hole, and then introduced it, leaving the jam-pot out of sight above.

By the time the questions had been put to the paralysed woman, and Genefer had waited sufficiently for a response which never came, Mr. Legassick had resumed his chair. Nevertheless, when the girl re-entered the kitchen there were marks of flurry in his face and chalk on his knees, for he had knelt on the whitened hearth-stones.

"She did not understand what I told her, sir, and she made me no answer," said Genefer.

"Then, my dear," said he, "it is my duty to inform you that on your father's death and your leaving the farm at Nantclose, everything was not lost. Your grandmother had managed to save something—how much I cannot say, as she never told me. But this she confided to me one day, against the evil time when such might befall her as has—that she put her little hoard up the chimney, and there you will find it. As I say—I don't pretend to say how much it is, but such as there is, it is yours."

"Grandmother never said a word of this, she always declared she had nothing."

"That was lest you should suspect and look for her savings.

Well, I have done my duty. Now I must leave—the case is terrible bad."

Then Mr. Legassick whisked out of the cottage, but as soon as he shut the door behind him, he screwed up his eyes, tapped his nose with his forefinger, and broke into a cackle.

Nothing that had been done in the parish within the memory of man caused so much speculation and provoked so much talk as did the rumour that suddenly sounded and spread like rings in water when a stone has been thrown in—the rumour to wit, that the old woman at the Willis had been hoarding money, and that her granddaughter had accidentally lighted on her hoard. Genefer had found a hundred pounds in the pillow under the old creature's head. Next she had discovered another hundred in gold in a jam-pot up the chimney. Imagination flickered about these finds, magnified and multiplied them. The mattress of the paralysed woman, it was next reported, was stuffed with bank-notes. Then it was told that stockings filled with guineas were discovered hanging among the cobwebs to the rafters; then that an old kettle brimming with sovereigns was drawn out of the ashpit. Whence had all this come? How long had the old woman been saving it? Why had she made Genefer drudge like a slave when she was rich enough to buy up all in the parish? But the aged woman lay like a log, blinking her dull eyes, and uttered unintelligible sounds. She could answer no questions, she could not even understand the questions put to her.

Farmer Legassick heard the reports and was puzzled at first, then he came to believe everything that was told in its most exaggerated and extravagant form. He hastened to find his son, and, laying hold of the lappet of his coat, said eagerly, "Joe! you remember telling me something about Genefer, and that you had a mind for her. I had no objection whatever at the time; I rather wished it, but I was sore afraid that your mother would set her face against it. And when she takes against a thing, you know——" Farmer Legassick shook his head. "She is a close woman about money. Now, however, that great difficulty is at an end. Genefer's grandmother had laid by money when they left Nantclose. There was a hundred pounds found in a jam-pot up the chimney. That I can understand. A hundred pounds is not so very large a sum after a farm sale. But there was another hundred in the pillow, and folk say bank-notes by the scores in the mattress, and—; but there, you're restless to be off. I see your legs quivering. Run as hard as you can to the Willis and settle matters with Genefer. I'll take it on me mother don't object any longer. Get along before other suitors come, and the lovers will be swarming there directly, like flies about a treacle barrel."

Hardly had Joe left his father before he stumbled on his mother, who gripped him by both shoulders, and said, "Joe, the dearest wish of my heart is about to come to pass. Run down to the Willis and ask Genefer to be your wife. I have always desired it, but was afraid what your father would say—he's that deadly avaricious. Now he'll jump and dance, for Genefer has come in for a lot of money. There was a hundred pound in the pillow. That I can account for. The old woman might have saved so much, but as for the hundred in the jam-pot, that beats me; and the bank-notes in the mattress, and the stockings for six legs all stuffed with guineas, and—— But, bless me! I mustn't detain you. Run along."

Then Mrs. Legassick looked into the parlour, and seeing Polly Penfound there, entered, and said blandly, "My dear niece, I am so very sorry. I really am ashamed to mention it, but we cannot possibly keep you here after to-morrow. You see, Joe is going to be married when the banns have been called—that is in three weeks."

Then Mr. Legassick's head appeared at the door. "*Next* week, my dear, next week, as soon as the lashings (licence) has arrived."

So Polly Penfound had to depart, without having been given the chance of refusing Joe; worse than all, eclipsed, outblazed by the heiress at the Willis.

. . . . . .

Years passed. Mrs. Legassick never found out how the jam-pot got up the chimney, nor Mr. Legassick how the money got into the pillow. Moreover, both persisted in believing that there was some truth in the story of the mattress stuffed with bank-notes, and the stockings with guineas, and the kettle with sovereigns.

When the land in the parish was sold, then Joe Legassick purchased Tregothnan. Folks said, "We always expected it, after marrying Genefer. That cottage at the Willis was just about chokeful of money. But, apart from all that Genefer got of the old woman's hoard, she's a mighty saving person, thrifty and hard-working. Well! anyhow, that was a lucky day when Joe took Genefer."

RICHARD GARNETT
1835–1906

THE DUMB ORACLE

Many the Bacchi that brandish the rod :
Few that be filled with the fire of the God.

I

In the days of King Attalus, before oracles had lost their credit, one of peculiar reputation, inspired, as was believed, by Apollo, existed in the city of Dorylaeum, in Phrygia. Contrary to usage, its revelations were imparted through the medium of a male priest. It was rarely left unthronged by devout questioners, whose inquiries were resolved in writing, agreeably to the method delivered by the pious Lucian in his work *Concerning False Prophecy*. Sometimes, on extraordinary occasions, a voice, evidently that of the deity, was heard declaring the response from the innermost recesses of the shrine. The treasure-house of the sanctuary was stored with tripods and goblets, in general wrought from the precious metals ; its coffers were loaded with coins and ingots ; the sacrifices of wealthy suppliants, and the copious offerings in kind of the country people, provided super-abundantly for the daily maintenance of the temple servitors ; while a rich endowment in land maintained the dignity of its guardians, and of the officiating priest. The latter reverend personage was no less eminent for prudence than for piety; on which account the Gods had rewarded him with extreme obesity. At length he died, whether of excess in meat or in drink is not agreed among historians.

The guardians of the temple met to choose a successor, and, naturally desirous that the sanctity of the oracle should suffer no abatement, elected a young priest of goodly presence and ascetic life ; the humblest, purest, most fervent, and most ingenuous of the sons of men. So rare a choice might well be expected to be accompanied by some extraordinary manifestation, and, in fact, a prodigy took place which filled the sacred authorities with dismay. The responses of the oracle ceased suddenly and altogether. No revelation was vouchsafed to the pontiff in his slumbers ; no access of prophetic fury constrained him to disclose the secrets of the future ; no voice rang from the shrine ; and the unanswered epistles of the suppliants lay a hopeless encumbrance on the great altar. As a natural consequence they speedily ceased to arrive ; the influx of offerings into the treasury terminated along with them ; the temple-courts were bare of worshippers ; and the only victims whose blood smoked within them were those slain by the priest himself, in the hope of appeasing the displeasure of Apollo. The modest hierophant took all the blame upon his own shoulders ; he did not doubt that he had excited the Deity's wrath by some mysterious but heinous pollution ; and was confirmed in this opinion by the unanimous verdict of all whom he approached.

One day as he sat sadly in the temple, absorbed in painful meditation, and pondering how he might best relieve himself of his sacred functions, he was startled by the now unwonted sound of a footstep, and, looking up, espied an ancient woman. Her appearance was rather venerable than prepossessing. He recognized her as one of the inferior ministers of the temple.

" Reverend mother," he addressed her, " doubtless thou comest to mingle with mine thy supplications to the Deity, that it may please him to indicate the cause, and the remedy of his wrath."

" No, son," returned the venerable personage, " I propose to occasion no such needless trouble to Apollo, or any other Divinity. I hold within mine own hand the power of reviving the splendour of this forsaken sanctuary, and for such consideration as thou wilt thyself pronounce equitable, I am minded to impart the same unto thee." And as the astonished priest made no answer, she continued—

" My price is one hundred pieces of gold."

" Wretch ! " exclaimed the priest indignantly, " thy mercenary demand alone proves the vanity of thy pretence of being initiated into the secrets of the Gods. Depart my presence this moment ! "

The old woman retired without a syllable of remonstrance, and the incident soon passed from the mind of the afflicted priest. But on the following day, at the same hour, the aged woman again stood before him, and said, " My price is *two* hundred pieces of gold."

Again she was commanded to depart, and again obeyed without a murmur. But the adventure now occasioned the priest much serious reflection. To his excited fancy, the patient persistency of the crone began to assume something of a supernatural character. He considered that the ways of the Gods are not as our ways, and that it is rather the rule than the exception with them to accomplish their designs in the most circuitous manner, and by the most likely instruments. He also reflected upon the history of the Sibyl and her books, and shuddered to think that unseasonable obstinacy might in the end cost the temple the whole of its revenues. The result of his cogitations was a resolution, if the old woman should present herself on the following day, to receive her in a different manner.

Punctual to the hour she made her appearance, and croaked out, "My price is *three* hundred pieces of gold."

"Venerable ambassador of Heaven," said the priest, "thy boon is granted thee. Relieve the anguish of my bosom as speedily as thou mayest." The old woman's reply was brief and expressive. It consisted in extending her open and hollow palm, into which the priest counted the three hundred pieces of gold with as much expedition as was compatible with the frequent interruptions necessitated by the crone's depositing each successive handful in a leather pouch; and the scrutiny, divided between jealousy and affection, which she bestowed on each individual coin.

"And now," said the priest, when the operation was at length completed, "fulfil thy share of the compact."

"The cause of the oracle's silence," returned the old woman, "is the unworthiness of the minister."

"Alas! 'tis even as I feared," sighed the priest. "Declare now, wherein consists my sin?"

"It consists in this," replied the old woman, "that the beard of thy understanding is not yet grown; and that the egg-shell of thy inexperience is still sticking to the head of thy simplicity; and that thy brains bear no adequate proportion to the skull enveloping them; and in fine, lest I seem to speak overmuch in parables, or to employ a superfluity of epithets, that thou art an egregious nincompoop."

And as the amazed priest preserved silence, she pursued:

"Can aught be more shameful in a religious man than ignorance of the very nature of religion? Not to know that the term, being rendered into the language of truth, doth therein signify deception practised by the few wise upon the many foolish, for the benefit of both, but more particularly the former? O silly as the crowds who hitherto have brought their folly here, but now carry it elsewhere to the profit of wiser men than thou! O fool! to deem that oracles were rendered by Apollo! How should this be, seeing that there is no such person? Needs there, peradventure, any greater miracle for the decipherment of these epistles than a hot needle? As for the supernatural voice, it doth in truth proceed from a respectable, and in some sense a sacred personage, being mine own when I am concealed within a certain recess prepared for me by thy lamented predecessor, whose mistress I was in youth, and whose coadjutor I have been in age. I am now ready to minister to thee in the latter capacity. Be ruled by me; exchange thy abject superstition for common sense; thy childish simplicity for discreet policy; thy unbecoming spareness for a majestic portliness; thy present ridiculous and uncomfortable situation for the repute of sanctity, and the veneration of men. Thou wilt own that this is cheap at three hundred pieces." The young priest had hearkened to the crone's discourse with an expression of the most exquisite distress. When she had finished, he arose, and, disregarding his repulsive companion's efforts to detain him, departed hastily from the temple.

II

It was the young priest's purpose, as soon as he became capable of forming one, to place the greatest possible distance between himself and the city of Dorylaeum. The love of roaming insensibly grew upon him, and ere long his active limbs had borne him over a considerable portion of Asia. His simple wants were easily supplied by the wild productions of the country, supplemented when needful by the proceeds of light manual labour. By degrees, the self-contempt which had originally stung him to desperation took the form of an ironical compassion for the folly of mankind, and the restlessness which had at first impelled him to seek relief in a change of scene gave place to a spirit of curiosity and observation. He learned to mix freely with all orders of men, save one, and rejoiced to find the narrow mysticism which he had imbibed from his previous education gradually yielding to contact with the great world. From one class of men, indeed, he learned nothing—the priests, whose society he eschewed with scrupulous vigilance, nor did he ever enter the temples of the Gods. Diviners, augurs, all that made any pretension whatever to a supernatural character, he held in utter abhorrence, and his ultimate return in the direction of his native country is attributed to his inability to persevere further in the path he was following without danger of encountering Chaldean soothsayers, or Persian magi, or Indian gymnosophists.

He cherished, however, no intention of returning to Phrygia, and was still at a considerable distance from that region, when one night, as he was sitting in the inn of a small country town, his ear caught a phrase which arrested his attention.

"As true as the oracle of Dorylaeum." The speaker was a countryman, who appeared to have been asseverating something regarded by the rest of the company as greatly in need of confirmation. The sudden start and stifled cry of the ex-priest drew all eyes to him, and he felt constrained to ask, with the most indifferent air he could assume:

"Is the oracle of Dorylaeum, then, so exceedingly renowned for veracity?" "Whence comest thou to be ignorant of that?"

demanded the countryman, with some disdain. " Hast thou never heard of the priest Eubulides ? "

" Eubulides ! " exclaimed the young traveller, " that is my own name ! "

" Thou mayest well rejoice, then," observed another of the guests, " to bear the name of one so holy and pure, and so eminently favoured by the happy Gods. So handsome and dignified, moreover, as I may well assert who have often beheld him discharging his sacred functions. And truly, now that I scan thee more closely, the resemblance is marvellous. Only that thy namesake bears with him a certain air of divinity, not equally conspicuous in thee."

" Divinity ! " exclaimed another. " Aye, if Phoebus himself ministered at his own shrine, he could wear no more majestic semblance than Eubulides."

" Or predict the future more accurately," added a priest.

" Or deliver his oracles in more exquisite verse," subjoined a poet.

" Yet is it not marvellous," remarked another speaker, " that for some considerable time after his installation the good Eubulides was unable to deliver a single oracle ? "

" Aye, and that the first he rendered should have foretold the death of an aged woman, one of the ministers of the temple."

" Ha ! " exclaimed Eubulides, " how was that ? "

" He prognosticated her decease on the following day, which accordingly came to pass, from her being choked with a piece of gold, not lawfully appertaining to herself, which she was endeavouring to conceal under the root of her tongue."

" The Gods be praised for that ! " ejaculated Eubulides, under his breath. " Pshaw ! as if there were Gods ! If they existed would they tolerate this vile mockery ? To keep up the juggle—well, I know it must be so ; but to purloin my name ! to counterfeit my person ! By all the Gods that are not, I will expose the cheat, or perish in the endeavour."

He arose early on the following morning and took his way towards the city of Dorylaeum. The further he progressed in this direction, the louder became the bruit of the oracle of Apollo, and the more emphatic the testimonies to the piety, prophetic endowments, and personal attractions of the priest Eubulides, his own resemblance to whom was the theme of continual remark. On approaching the city he found the roads swarming with throngs hastening to the temple, about to take part in a great religious ceremony to be held therein. The seriousness of worship blended delightfully with the glee of the festival, and Eubulides, who at first regarded the gathering with bitter scorn, found his moroseness insensibly yielding to the poetic charm of the scene. He could not but acknowledge that the imposture he panted to expose was at least the source of much innocent happiness, and almost wished that the importance of religion, considered as an engine of policy, had been offered to his contemplation from this point of view, instead of the sordid and revolting aspect in which it had been exhibited by the old woman.

In this ambiguous frame of mind he entered the temple. Before the high altar stood the officiating priest, a young man, the image, yet not the image, of himself. Lineament for lineament, the resemblance was exact, but over the stranger's whole figure was diffused an air of majesty, of absolute serenity and infinite superiority, which excluded every idea of deceit, and so awed the young priest that his purpose of rushing forward to denounce the impostor and drag him from the shrine was immediately and involuntarily relinquished. As he stood confounded and irresolute, the melodious voice of the hierophant rang through the temple: "Let the priest Eubulides stand forth."

This summons naturally created the greatest astonishment in every one but Eubulides, who emerged as swiftly as he could from the swaying and murmuring crowd, and confronted his namesake at the altar. A cry of amazement broke from the multitude as they beheld the pair, whose main distinction in the eyes of most was their garb. But, as they gazed, the form of the officiating priest assumed colossal proportions; a circle of beams, dimming sunlight, broke forth around his head; hyacinthine locks clustered on his shoulders, his eyes sparkled with supernatural radiance; a quiver depended at his back; an unstrung bow occupied his hand; the majesty and benignity of his presence alike seemed augmented tenfold. Eubulides and the crowd sank simultaneously on their knees, for all recognised Apollo.

All was silence for a space. It was at length broken by Phoebus.

"Well, Eubulides," inquired he, with the bland raillery of an Immortal, "has it at length occurred to thee that I may have been long enough away from Parnassus, filling thy place here while thou hast been disporting thyself amid heretics and barbarians?"

The abashed Eubulides made no response. The Deity continued: "Deem not that thou hast in aught excited the displeasure of the Gods. In deserting their altars for Truth's sake, thou didst render them the most acceptable of sacrifices, the only one, it may be, by which they set much store. But, Eubulides, take heed how thou again sufferest the unworthiness of men to overcome the instincts of thine own nature. Thy holiest sentiments should not have been at the mercy of a knave. If the oracle of Dorylaeum was an imposture, hadst thou no oracle in thine own bosom? If the voice of Religion was no longer breathed from the tripod, were the winds and waters silent, or had aught quenched the everlasting stars? If there was no power to impose its mandates from without, couldst thou be unconscious of a power within ? If thou hadst nothing to reveal unto men, mightest thou not have found somewhat to prepound unto them ? Know this, that thou hast never experienced a more truly religious emotion than that which led thee to form the design of overthrowing this my temple, the abode, as thou didst deem it, of fraud and superstition."

" But now, Phoebus," Eubulides ventured to reply, " shall I not return to the shrine purified by thy presence, and again officiate as thy unworthy minister ? " " No, Eubulides," returned Phoebus, with a smile ; " silver is good, but not for ploughshares. Thy strange experience, thy long wanderings, thy lonely meditations, and varied intercourse with men, have spoiled thee for a priest, while, as I would fain hope, qualifying thee for a sage. Some worthy person may easily be found to preside over this temple ; and by the aid of such inspiration as I may from time to time see meet to vouchsafe him, administer its affairs indifferently well. Do thou, Eubulides, consecrate thy powers to a more august service than Apollo's, to one that shall endure when Delphi and Delos know *his* no more."

" To whose service, Phoebus ? " inquired Eubulides.

" To the service of Humanity, my son," responded Apollo.

SIR FRANCIS COWLEY BURNAND
1836–1917

MR. LORQUISON'S STORY

THE account of a story-telling party in *Once a Week* wound up by saying that "*Mr. Lorquison excused himself from any recital because he knew not one.*" This gentleman (generally full of anecdotes, but which on this occasion he seems to have kept to himself) called upon me two days after the merry meeting by the inn fire, and I at once showed him the passage, and taxed him with the decline of his conversational powers. After some little hesitation he told me that I ought to have paid more attention to the final part of that paragraph, the commencement of which I have already quoted. On referring, I find it speaks of the quality of the punch.

"Just so," said Mr. Lorquison, with a queer twinkle, "that accounts for my silence."

The puzzled look on my face caused him to proceed.

"Why, you see, I *do* know a great many stories—good 'uns, too, and I had got up one in particular, ready for 'em on that night—only it wasn't about unpleasant nights and that sort of thing—but whether 'twas the heat of the room, the turn of the stories, or the lateness of the hour, somehow or other my good story went clean out of my head. Mr. Selby told me afterwards that I had greatly amused the company—in what way I can't distinctly recollect; all I know is that the next morning I awoke with a splitting headache."

My curiosity was roused. Did I know the story?

"Well," said he, "I may have told you at some time or other; but I'll give it you now if you like; only mind, if you've heard it before, interrupt me."

I gave him the required promise, and he thus began:

"I think you're something of a gardener, are you not?" I admitted horticultural propensities in a small degree, and he continued, "Then you'll enjoy my story all the more. Well, my father was a great florist, an amateur, and used to take immense pleasure in the cultivation of a moderate-sized garden attached to our suburban cottage at Islington. You seem surprised at my mentioning such a site for a cottage and garden, but I allude to the Islington as I knew it thirty years ago, when Newington ' Green Lanes ' was a dangerous place after dark, and an inhabitant of Upper or Lower Clapton was considered a rustic.

" Numerous little cottages, with their neatly trimmed flower-beds, were to be seen at Islington at the time of which I speak, and conspicuous among them all for artistic arrangement and plants of really great value was my father's garden. How well I recollect the look of satisfaction with which he used to regard the work of his hands as, sitting in his easy-chair on a summer's Sunday evening, he would slowly puff his after-dinner pipe (he was a widower), while drawing the attention of some friend to the peculiarities of certain cuttings, and the various beauties of his favourite shrubs.

" His companion on one of these occasions was a Mr. Tibbs, a thorough Cockney, with about as much idea of country life and agricultural pursuits as a fish has of nut-cracking. He was a tradesman in the city, had risen to the rank of alderman, and was now within no very great distance of the mayoralty. This ' achievement of greatness,' though adding somewhat to his natural pomposity, had in no way diminished his innate relish for a joke. His fun certainly was not refined, nor his raillery elegant ; but, as he used to say, ' a joke's a joke,' and undoubtedly Mr. Tibbs's jokes were peculiarly his own, and no one, I'm sure, would ever think of claiming them.

" ' How's Polly Hanthus ? ' was his invariable greeting on entering our house. After the delivery of which facetious allusion to my father, he would indulge in chuckles of some seconds' duration.

" ' Well,' said he, when my father had finished a long disquisition on the merits of a splendid chrysanthemum, ' well, Lorquison, I don't know much about your kissymythumbs, which is Latin or Greek, or—something or other,' he added after a pause, feeling rather out of his element in an etymological question ; ' but I'll send you a seed or two, the like of which you've never come across, my boy.' Here, taking his pipe from his mouth, he wagged his head in a fat and happy manner.

" ' And what may they be ? ' asked my father, with much interest.

" ' Well, they *may* be anything,' replied Tibbs, with an inward chuckle at his own wit ; ' but they happen to be seeds. Lor' bless you, I ain't a-going to tell you what they are. But they're rare—very rare. Such a gardener ' (he pronounced it gardinger) ' as you ought to tell what the plant is when you looks at the seed. For my part, I don't pretend to call 'em any grand name—it's a very short 'un. Will you have 'em ? '

" ' Delighted ! ' answered my father, ' send them as soon as possible, and I don't doubt but we shall be able to get up a curious paper on the subject in the *Gardeners' Magazine.*'

" 'Very good; then mind you take care in planting of 'em, Lorquison, 'cos they've never been sown afore in this country.'

" Here Mr. Tibbs was taken with a violent fit of coughing, which, although he attributed it to the evening air, or the smoke going 'the wrong way,' my young eyes detected as the effect caused by a series of suppressed chuckles. My father, elated with the idea of his new acquisition, did not remark this. 'Here's my coach,' said Tibbs, knocking the ashes out of his pipe.

" 'Don't forget the seeds,' were my father's last words as his guest departed. I believe my father scarcely slept all that night: he was never a sluggard, but on that Monday morning he was up earlier than ever, and working in his garden with a diligence worthy of 'The old Corycian.' He was clearing out a space of ground for the reception of the promised seeds. During breakfast he was in a perpetual state of fidget; the postman was late—stay—would it come by post ?—no, by carrier. At last, however, the postman did arrive, and delivered into my father's hands, ready at the front gate to receive him, a small packet with a letter from Tibbs, containing an apology for having sent only twenty seeds, and pleading their value as his excuse. These twenty little wonders were quite round and very small, being, as it appeared to us, of a dark red colour. My father inspected them, and looked puzzled; smelt them, and said 'humph!' That 'humph' was portentous; even the stolid Tibbs would cease his chuckle at my father's 'humph!'

" Perhaps you know that all gardeners examine with a glass and taste their seeds; my father was now about to go through this double process. He looked at them through his powerful microscope.

" 'Why, surely——' said my father, and took another survey. Something was wrong. 'I do believe——' he began, and then followed the trial by tasting. He smacked his lips and clicked his tongue against his palate—frowned—spat out the seed—bent down his head to the microscope, and then exclaimed: 'Confound that Tibbs!' I waited anxiously for what was to follow. 'Seeds! *Why, he's sent me the dried roe of a herring!*'

" I recollect how amused I was, as a child, at this practical joke of Tibbs's. My father laughed heartily in spite of his vexation, and, folding up the packet previous to putting it away in his private drawer, said quietly, 'Very well, Mr. Tibbs,' by which I knew that he intended to repay our Cockney friend in his own coin. He wrote, however, thanking Tibbs for his present, and that little gentleman, I have no doubt, retailed the joke to many a friend on 'Change, and began to look upon himself as the Hook of private life.

" But they laugh longest who laugh last. Three weeks after this Tibbs met my father one Saturday afternoon in the City.

" 'How's Polly Hanthus?' inquired Tibbs.

" ' Well, thank you,' replied my father. ' Will you dine with me to-morrow ? ' Tibbs was not the man to refuse a good offer.

" ' By the way,' he slily asked, almost bursting with chuckles, ' how about those seeds, eh ? '

" ' What seeds ? ' asked my father, with an air of utter ignorance.

" ' Oh, that won't do ! ' returned Tibbs. ' I say, are they growing ? 'Twan't bad, was it ? ' My father's serious face prevented a burst of laughter in which his friend was about to indulge.

" ' If you mean those seeds which you sent to me as a curiosity three weeks ago, I can only say that they're getting on capitally.'

" ' Hey ! what ? ' exclaimed the alderman.

" ' Well ! I grant you that it is a *lusus naturae.*'

" ' Oh, indeed ! ' said Tibbs, thinking that this might be the horticultural Latin for a herring.

" ' But come to-morrow and you'll see them yourself. Good-bye ! '

" ' Very curious—very ! ' murmured the bewildered Tibbs to himself as my father hurried off. When my father returned to Islington on that Saturday night he brought with him *twenty red herrings.* Tibbs, according to promise, dined with us on Sunday.

" ' After the post-prandial pipe you shall see how well your seeds are progressing.'

" Tibbs put his hands in his pockets and feebly smiled at my father's words. He had tried during dinner to discover whether real seeds had been sent by some mistake, or the trick had been discovered. But my father began talking about sea anemones, prickly fish, jelly fish, of strange marine inhabitants that had the appearance of vegetables, and so on, till Mr. Tibbs saw but slight difference between a codfish and a fir-tree, and began to think his joke was not so good a one after all.

" Dinner finished, the pipe smoked, my father led the way down the garden-walk. He was enjoying himself immensely. Tibbs began to think of all the persons to whom he had told the excellent story of Lorquison and the herrings, and repented that he had not given more of his time to the study of natural history. On he walked, following my father through rows of geraniums, pinks, bright roses, and marvellous tulips, until at length they arrived at a sequestered part, where, on a fresh dug bed, overshadowed by two fine laburnums, stood twenty inverted flower-pots arranged in four rows. Here my father stopped.

" ' Now,' said he, ' you mustn't be disappointed if they're not so far advanced as you expected ; but I think they're getting on admirably, considering 'tis the first time they've ever been planted in this country.' Tibbs remembered his own words, and mumbled something about ' first time—this country—who'd ha' thought '—and looked very foolish.

" 'There!' said my father, lifting up the first pot. Tibbs caught sight of something beneath it.

" 'Good gracious!' he exclaimed, and put on his spectacles.

" *Sure enough there was the nose of a red herring just visible above the ground.*

" 'Cover it up, Tibbs, the cold air may hurt it,' cried my father, who had been pretending to examine the other pots.

" 'Here's a better one—it has had more sun': he pointed to one which he had just uncovered, whose eyes, just visible above the black earth, were looking up in the most impudent manner.

" Tibbs moved on silently: carefully did he replace the first pot, and, with the gravest face imaginable, examined all the herrings in turn.

" 'They're getting on well,' said my father. ''Tis a curious sight.'

" 'Curious!' echoed Tibbs, regaining his speech. 'It's *wonderful*!! Sir,' said he, taking my father aside in his most impressive manner, 'I thought yesterday 'twas a joke; but I give you my solemn word of honour *that I shouldn't have believed it if I hadn't seen it.*'

" Having given utterance to this remarkable sentence he slowly turned on his heel and walked towards the house, my father following with his handkerchief tightly pressed against his mouth.

" As for me, I stopped behind and pulled up the twenty herrings one after the other, and when I returned to the house Mr. Tibbs had departed.

" Not bad, was it?"

JOSEPH HATTON

1840–1907

UNCLE HARTLEBURY'S ROMANCE

YES, sir, we *have* met before, and I am delighted to see you again. No, you have made no mistake. I am the Recorder of Miningtown, and the portly lady whom you see yonder in the midst of that assembly of romping children, about to bathe after the fashion of this Boulogne, is my wife and these our family. Yes, sir, that is Mrs. Hartlebury. Speak louder, *mon ami,* I am slightly deaf. Yes, I do bathe ; but the exertion of dressing and undressing in this hot weather is too much for one who, like Falstaff, grows fat and hath grey hairs. Have a cigar ? That's right. I know nothing more agreeable than to sit here and watch the sea come rolling in upon those bathers yonder, and especially when you can observe the gambols of your own children, and at the same time let your mind wander out to that wide reach of sea with sails in the distance.

You are a writer, an author. Yes, I saw your last book at the railway station, and bought it. Ah, I knew you would like me all the more for that. Why don't you reply that you had read my lucid and learned judgment in that remarkable forgery case ? Never mind, sir ; I am past that sort of thing. I suppose you are on the look-out for some bits of fresh character and wayside incidents of travel ? No ; you are only here for change and rest ? You have been up to the cathedral, stood once more on the doorstep of Le Sage's house, and refreshed your old memories of the place ? *Ah, oui !*

Old memories ! You would hardly credit me, I suppose, with being afflicted by some strange old memories of personal adventure in this place, or any other, for that matter. You would not take an old gentleman with grey hairs, sitting on the beach at Boulogne whilst his wife and family are bathing, as a fitting subject for the hero of a romance. There are peculiar anomalies in life, you say ? That is evasion, sir. I know what you are thinking well enough. I can only tell you this, my friend, that the story of my first appearance here twenty years ago is far more romantic than half the tales told in your magazines, and thought worthy of wonderful illustrations. I am too old to be vain, and I know something of the lights and shadows of life, something of its untold romances, something of its terrible tragedies.

Ah, my friend, twenty years ago I was as slim and dapper and lady-killing as yourself. You do not aspire to the character of a lady-killer? Don't tell me, sir; all young fellows like to make a favourable impression on the other sex. Why are you so carefully shaved to-day? Why is that bit of showy neckerchief so daintily tied? Why those well-fitting grey trousers, and that smart little cane? Simply because you are accustomed to dress well, and aspire to be regarded as a gentleman.

Very good; and you are anxious to bid at the same time for those feminine glances which are so flattering to youth. There, don't think I imagine you are a fop, and for Heaven's sake don't be annoyed. My criticism is only the result of my own feelings, my own ambition, when I was a young fellow like you. Tell you my story? Yes, if you think it may interest you. It may do for a Christmas paper? Ah, ah! on the look-out for copy, eh?—gathering honey all the day from every opening flower. Well, I feel something of the Ancient Mariner's sensations this morning; it will be a relief to tell the story of that extraordinary creature whose face has haunted me ever since I came here two days ago. You will readily consent to play the wedding-guest to my mariner? Very well, sir; light another cigar and listen: if I bore you, stop me, and we will in to the *Établissement* and read the papers.

It is all bound up in this bit of faded ribbon, my story: this little scrap, you see, which is set in that *petit* rim of gold appended to my watch-seals. I have never worn the trifle since my marriage until this week. My wife has some pardonable womanly notion that I ought not to wear it, and I have humoured her; for, though I say it, she is one of the best women in the world. Above all others, you think, it is I who should say so? You say well, you say well, my young friend. When we were leaving London last week it seemed to me that I could not come even here without this little souvenir of that romance twenty years ago. Twenty years ago! How the time flies!

This is the story. I was engaged to Mrs. Hartlebury; she was a Miss Longford. We had been in the habit of seeing each other from the earliest days of our childhood. I ought to have appreciated her kindly loving disposition all the more on this account; but I did not. It had always been understood that we should be married, and in due course this family understanding bore fruit.

We were engaged, Julia Longford and I, but on this understanding, that if either one or the other saw any other person whom he or she, the said contracting parties, preferred to the before-mentioned parties to this agreement, then either he or she, the said Thomas Hartlebury and Julia Longford, might terminate the previously recited engagement at one day's notice given by post or orally in the presence of witnesses. Yes, I am getting a little involved, I fear, in this semi-legal phraseology ? But you understand the character of that agreement ? Yes, and you think it a very convenient engagement ? And I thought so too, sir, in a very short time after it was made.

That very summer twenty years ago, with the consent and indeed by the advice of my dear old father, I started on a continental tour which was to be inaugurated by a visit to Paris *viâ* Boulogne, and which terminated somewhat suddenly in the French capital. I was quite as much a buck in those days as you are now, not quite so slim as Falstaff boasted himself to be. I was something more than an eagle's talon in the waist, and I could not creep through an alderman's thumb-ring, for I was a strong, well-built young fellow, and not ill-looking—no, sir, not ill-looking. You can readily understand that ? Even though I might play the fat knight with as little padding as Mark Lemon ! It is true, sir, quite true. I can see myself now airing my swell clothes and London manners on the beach here : but there is a sad face rises up beside me, and a figure floating out with the tide yonder which sobers the picture, and makes a shadow upon that sunny water.

Bathing *en famille* was a notion that rather tickled me in those days. You think there is nothing improper in it ? Neither do I, sir, or Mrs. Hartlebury and her daughters would not be enjoying themselves as you see them yonder. The " girl of the period " at ball and opera is much more undressed than the ladies in their pretty bathing costumes ? I quite agree with you ; but my very proper English notions were a little excited at the prospect of a company of lovely mermaidens in a sea-bath. I little thought when I went into the water that I was destined to come out with a pretty girl in my arms. Ah, now I see you are interested. What a subject for a modern magazine picture ! That is what you are thinking, I know. Don't keep you in suspense ? Is that what you said ? I told you I was slightly deaf. Did I come out of the water with a young lady in my arms really ?

Yes, it was in this way. I was swimming about and watching the movements of a most graceful person, floating half-sideways, half on her back, with her arms extended and her head resting on the water ; she was drifting out in the sunshine, the water quite placid, but swelling like her own bosom beneath a thin blue robe ; she was drifting, I say, in the sunshine, like a blessed martyr going out to some better land. I see her now, poor, pretty tender-hearted thing, with the sea rocking her in its great arms, and yet trying all the while to steal away her life.

I watched her at a respectful distance and swam quietly after her; for somehow it occurred to me that she was not quite conscious of the power of that insidious but certain current, which I could feel setting in towards the pier. I had judged aright; by-and-by she turned over, evidently with the intention of swimming home, but she could not accomplish her purpose. She struggled on for a little time, and then to all appearance lost her presence of mind, or was attacked with cramp. She disappeared at all events, and I rapidly quickened my pace towards her, putting my head well to the water and dashing on with that sharp side-stroke, which is so effective in the matter of speed. She rose for the second time as I reached the spot.

In a moment I had seized her by the shoulder, and, supporting her with my left arm, I commenced to swim slowly in the direction of the shore. The young lady's difficulty had been noticed from the beach, and a boat had put off when I dashed after her. It came up by the time I was within easy distance of the shore with my beautiful, half-drowned burden, and I helped to place her in the boat amidst a loud cheer. I got in after her, and was delighted to see signs of rapid recovery in the dear creature. Satisfied with this, and not caring to present myself in my Blondin-like costume to a fashionable and excited throng, I dashed into the water and swam to my machine.

If Mrs. Hartlebury and those girls would do the same it would be just as well. They have been in the water too long already. You don't think so? Mrs. Hartlebury is the best judge of that? I had better proceed with my story; you are getting interested? You want to know what the young lady was like? Like, sir, like no young lady in Boulogne at the present day, or anywhere else that I have seen, for beauty. She was like a poet's dream, sir, or an artist's fancy. Was she a blonde? Not exactly, no; she had brown wavy hair, and such eyes, such a figure! Arms as round and fair as the arms of those women by Rubens in the Louvre—a neck and shoulders in which all the lines of beauty were described. I saw her on that next day after her narrow escape; she found me out, and came to the Hôtel des Bains to thank me.

"I must excuse her," she said, "for calling unattended, she had no friends in Boulogne."

"One at least," I said, taking her hand, and faltering in my speech. She looked up inquiringly at me for a moment with her big dark eyes, and I felt myself gradually becoming powerless in her presence, anxious to say all sorts of gracious things, but unable to do so.

" Good-bye, and believe me I shall never forget your brave action."

She spoke with a pretty musical French accent.

" May I not see you again ? " I asked, and then bolder grown I answered my own question : " I must, indeed I must."

" I am going to Paris in the morning. I have been to London, and am on my way to Paris. I fear I must say good-bye now, monsieur."

" Oh, no," I said, feeling as if I were about to lose everything dear to me in the world. " I love you, mademoiselle ; I love you ; I will make you my wife."

" Oh, monsieur, that can never be," she replied.

" Why not ? " I exclaimed, becoming desperate.

" Do not ask," she said, sadly.

" You could not love me," I said, sitting down and covering my face with my hands.

" There was a time, monsieur, when what you have just said would have awakened a passion of pleasure and gratitude in my heart ; but oh, sir, that time is past ; adieu, *mon très cher ami* ; you will always live in my dearest memory."

She left me, and this only made me more fiercely in love with her. I did not seem to be master of my actions, and I was selfish enough to think that I had a special claim upon her. I rescued her from death, and that ought to make her mine. If she would have had me I would have married her, sir, right off, and should have felt myself blessed. How long would that sentiment have lasted ? Heaven knows.

I followed her, found out her hotel, returned her call, and made her promise to see me in Paris. My next action was to discover by what train she travelled, and on the following day I was on the platform, and constituted myself the lady's *compagnon de voyage.* At first she seemed a little disconcerted at this, but as we journeyed onwards she brightened up, and became chatty and sparkling and lively. Every now and then all this was darkened, like a summer landscape with passing thunder-clouds. Once when the other stupid passengers were asleep I pressed her hand. She returned me a gentle pressure, and with the tears in her eyes she whispered in heartfelt accents that almost brought the tears to mine, " Oh, my dear, dear friend ! "

It seemed like a cry of despair from a breaking heart, and I felt as if a terrible grief was seizing upon me.

You really would not have given me credit for so much romance ? Of course not, it seems ridiculous to you now, looking at the portly recorder and his romping responsibilities yonder. Ah, I am glad the girls are coming out of the water. It does not matter so much about

Frank and Tom and Harry, they are strong fellows, and will have *café noir* and cigars afterwards to keep up the circulation. You object to these interruptions ? These changes from romance to reality, eh ?—from the sublime to the ridiculous.

On our arrival at the Northern Station at Paris, Louise and I, you know her name was Louise, I think I said before, on our arrival a placid, mysterious, light-moustached old German came up to us. He kissed the young lady on the cheek and then looked scowlingly at me. Louise began, therefore, to talk German to him with many gesticulations, explaining the small service I had rendered her. He smiled, I thought, a little sarcastically, and looked incredulously at me ; but mademoiselle stamped her foot angrily at Mein Herr Diable, and he condescended to look civilly upon me.

" We must part here," she said hurriedly to me. " What is your hotel ? "

" The Imperial," I said. " Place Vendôme."

" You must not call on me. I will call upon you to-night. For Heaven's sake be satisfied with this."

I got to my hotel in a dreamy sort of fashion, ordered private rooms, and said I expected a lady to call in the evening ; I should not go out until she came, and they must show her up. It seemed ages that I waited for her ; I waited until they relieved guard at the Napoleon Column and marched by the Rue St. Honoré with their drums and trumpets.

I waited until my heart was sick with fears and doubts, and at last I received a short note, in which the writer said I might see her on the next night at the Arc de l'Étoile at ten o'clock ; but if I really loved her, and wished to cherish the memory of her as something sweet and dear, I ought to see her no more. She offered no apology for keeping me waiting. I kissed her note, and yet smote the table with passion, and stamped about the room with rage. That silent, disgusting German was the cause of all this ! Who was he ? What was he ? I asked myself, but I was never enabled to answer the question. He was a strange unfathomable mystery.

On the following night I was at the Arch of Triumph an hour before the trysting-time, with a longing heart and a brain half-dazed with the glare and glitter of the long rows of gas-lamps and the wandering carriage-lights. The scene was to me then one of such unaccustomed splendour that it seemed as if I had been dropped here by Fate to play a part in some Arabian Night's story.

She came at last, my charmer, muffled up half in disguise, running, I thought, from one who claims her love to one who prays for it as the greatest blessing Heaven or earth can give. We walked to the shadow of an adjacent tree and sat down ; she suffered me to clasp her in my arms. Again I offered her my hand ; talked to her of arrangements for the future ; indicated the sort of letter I would write to my father by the very next post. A mad thing to do ? I must have been off my head ? Ah, so would you have been in presence of that matchless beauty. I never saw so much loveliness in mortal being ; and even after all these years have elapsed I cannot condemn my judgment in that respect.

We wandered about those walks in the Bois de Boulogne, and sat beneath the trees, and talked of a hundred happy things that only lovers' lips can say.

At last she confessed that she loved me with all her heart. " I have never known what love is until now," she said, " my dear, dear friend ; and I understand its sweetness, its purity, when it is too late, too late, my dear monsieur."

" Why too late, Louise ? " I asked ; and then, prepared to learn the worst, I said, " You are not married already ? "

" Oh, no," she said.

" Nor betrothed ? " I asked, hurrying question upon question.

" Cease, cease, I pray you," she exclaimed, in a passion of despair. " Seek to know no more ; I can never be yours : I love you too much."

" You are mine, Louise ; I snatched you from the grave. It was Fate that brought me to your side : Death came between us, and I struck him down. You are mine by all laws human and divine."

She sobbed at this, laid her head on my shoulder, and in a wail of despair said, " Oh, would I were ! Would it might be possible ! Oh, sir, do not tempt me : do not, pray, do not. Your love would end in hate."

" My dear Louise, I am prepared to brave all things."

" I am not prepared to brave your scorn," she said. " Death were bliss to that. Let me go, sir. Farewell ! "

" No, no," I said, detaining her.

" I will raise an alarm," she cried.

" Cruel, cruel," I replied.

" O, mon Dieu, monsieur ! " she exclaimed, and then kissing me on the forehead she said, " You see yon distant lights on the right, and that great cluster in the Champs Élysée ? "

" Yes."

" It is Monsieur Victor's Café Chantant. I will see you once again. Let it be there, to-morrow night, at ten."

" You will not deceive me ? " I said, letting her hand go very reluctantly.

" That is what I will not do for all the world," she replied solemnly and raising her eyes to heaven. " I will *not* deceive you."

" My dear Louise ! " I said. She looked so beautiful in the star-light.

"Better say adieu, now and for ever!" was her response. "But if it must be au revoir! Be it so!"

"Au revoir!" broke from my lips.

She slipped away from me, and disappeared.

The long rows of lights, the distant sounds of music, mocked my despair. I look back now and know what a mad fellow I was; but I do not blame myself, and I learned how heroic woman can be, the most abandoned, when the divine chord of love is really touched by the master hand. Poor lost Louise, she was a martyr for my sake! I can see now, out yonder where the sun is making a long track over the waters, I can see a half-clad figure drifting, drifting, floating away into the darker shade—drifting out into the mist where sea and sky unite and are lost in each other. What creatures of circumstances we are! Ah, there's my wife yonder beckoning to Frank and Harry. The girls are nearly dressed by this time, and yonder are the boys plunging about as if they had only just gone in. There they are, sir, within fifty yards of the spot where I rescued Louise from drowning twenty years ago! All right, my friend; don't be unhappy. My romance will soon be at an end. You think I tell the story well? I am quite eloquent, you say? Ah, it is the eloquence that earnestness gives, I suppose. It does me good to tell you this romance of mine: it has been in my mind at odd times, as if it demanded utterance, for years.

You may be sure I went to that *café* the next night. There was a clear sky and a full moon. The effect of the contending lights of the *café* and the moon among the foliage of the Champs Élysée was weird and magical. It seemed to carry my mind back to a wonderful representation I had seen at a London theatre of *Faust and Marguerite*. Then the woodland scene of *A Midsummer Night's Dream* broke into that memory.

I was not myself, I often think, all through this piece. I know that it shocked me a little when I found myself among a crowd of men and women who were drinking and smoking in this beautiful spot, and applauding an indecent dance; and it shocked me all the more to think that it was here that Louise had selected to meet me, her lover.

Then I thought what a prude I was, and remembered how different were French ideas of these things from ours in England. I would soon coax Louise out of all this semi-barbarous indifference to the proprieties when I had her in England and made her my wife. While I was thinking in this wise, a terrific burst of applause brought my wandering eyes back to the stage. A lady was smiling and bowing her acknowledgments. My heart beat wildly at sight of her. The applause rose again higher and higher.

"Who is this?" I said excitedly to a gentleman who was crowded close up against me.

"Do you not know?" he said in French. "Mademoiselle Victor, it is her first appearance this season; she has just returned from England."

Oh, my friend, I thought I should have lost my breath altogether. There was nothing improper in her bathing dress: she might have walked down Bond Street in it; but the costume in which she now appeared was the wildest kind of ballet dress I had ever seen. She sang with intense vigour in a rich ringing voice, and to the chorus she danced in a voluptuous siren-like fashion that seemed to belong rather to a figure out of one of Etty's pictures than to anything earthly. From this movement she changed her gambols into a mad sort of Mabille dance, in the midst of which she uttered a piercing scream and threw herself upon the floor in the glare and glitter of the footlights. I thought I should go mad. I pushed my way with desperation to the stage to assure myself that I was not the victim of some horrible delusion. They had lifted her up and carried her into the retiring-room. I forced my way in; but I should have been violently ejected had not that old German caught sight of me and snatched me out of the grasp of several yelling rascals who had nearly overpowered me. This mysterious person was evidently in great authority there.

Louise opened her eyes, and seeing me said, "Oh, my God!" and covered her face with her hands. That sneaking German frowned at me, but happily allowed me to remain. In a few minutes mademoiselle had recovered sufficiently for the manager to go out and tell the audience she would reappear shortly. In the midst of the shout of applause which greeted this declaration Louise rose to her feet and called for champagne. She drank the wine greedily, and then turning to me said, "There, monsieur, I told you it could not be: I said I would not deceive you. Adieu! God guard you!"

She took the manager's arm, and he led her once more upon the stage. The old German stood there looking at me like Mephistopheles in the play. I staggered to the door, slipped like a drunkard out into the night, threw myself upon the grass just beyond the enclosure of that painted hell, and wept like a child. .

Bravo, Frank! That was a splendid dive; but I'm glad it is the last; you have certainly had enough of the water for this morning. That's right, my dear boy. Better finish my story before they all come and interrupt us? Is that what you said? *Très bien*, but one requires a little interval now and then to keep down the full rush of the old feeling; mind you, I am enacting all this story over again while I am narrating it to you. And story-telling is warm work in the hottest days of August. You mean to tell it when the weather is cold? Eh? in a Christmas annual? Well, I have no objection, only keep my name out of the story, and don't let me be pointed at as the hero. You believe Mrs. Hartlebury is coming? Well, light another cigar, and we will come to the "Finis."

I passed a miserable night. I lay there on the grass I know not how long, and then I wandered home. I drank a pint of brandy and threw myself upon the bed undressed. I don't think I slept a wink.

Early in the morning that pale, pig's-eyed looking German called upon me, and in a few authoritative words in broken English bade me accompany him on a little visit. He led the way across the Pont St. Michel to the centre of the Marché Neuf, where we entered a small square building.

It was the Morgue! The old Morgue, a much more wretched place than the present edifice. On our left hand there were large windows guarded by a rail, and beyond was the chamber of death. It nearly made me sick to see several dead bodies lying there.

I shuddered and clung to my companion. He looked coldly on, and pointed to a pink dress and some lace that was hanging in the farthest corner; and then, oh mercy! I saw *her* body, cold and white and still. There it lay in awful companionship! I think I must have fainted at sight of the poor lost woman, with her brown hair all damp and clinging to her white round shoulders. I remembered nothing until I found myself on a sofa in a well-furnished room.

My senses were no sooner restored to me than that horrible German with the light moustache and the cold greenish eye came in and, deliberately seizing me by the throat, began to shake and curse me. I felt like a child in his hands, I was so weak and faint, and all the sensations of approaching death came over me. I must have cried out and struggled, I suppose, for a woman rushed into the room and dragged my assailant from me; he left me with an oath, and the woman, a strong, wilful-looking creature, led me into an adjoining room. I could hardly stand, but I was nevertheless strong enough and sensible enough to take the woman's advice and get out of that house.

I stumbled down two pairs of stairs and found my way into the street, where I obtained a cab and went to my hotel. I found a letter, which had been delivered by the post: it was written in French. The words were: "I loved you truly. I was unworthy of you: that is why you will never see your poor Louise again; here is a souvenir of her who blesses you with her last breath."

That souvenir was a small locket fastened to a piece of blue ribbon. I need not tell you how deeply it affected me. During the night which followed these hours of mystery and terror and grief I slept the sleep of one who is at last exhausted in mind and body. I was awakened after midnight by the proprietor of the house, who entered with a candle, and in some little excitement asked me if there was not something wrong. I was out of bed in an instant.

" What is wrong, sir ? " I asked.

" I think your bedroom has been robbed, if I have not disturbed the thief," he replied. " I saw a fellow prowling about before I went to bed, and as soon as I was awakened by the grating of a lock I got up and rang my bell. This was silly ; I ought have gone out and caught the thief. In another minute I heard a door shut ; a stealthy step passed my room, and before I could follow my light was out, his cloak over my head, and Jacques here has come to say that they are after a fellow who leaped from a second-floor window and made off along the Rue St. Honoré." This was the host's story so far as I could make out. We examined the room. My valise had been cut open, sure enough, and there lay beside it a great clasp-knife which had done the business. Louise's little note was gone, her locket had been torn away from the ribbon, and a packet of letters from England had been carried off.

I shall always believe that German was the thief. And it seemed to me at the time that if he had not been disturbed he would have murdered me. He had evidently some mysterious power, or wished to have, over Louise. I stood in his way ; how, I cannot understand ; but it was so. Her liking for me was to him a terrible grievance : he had searched for letters and other tokens of our acquaintanceship.

I told the hotel-keeper I had had a narrow escape : that knife was intended for something more desperate than cutting open a valise. Fancy, if he had murdered me, you would have seen no fat, sentimental recorder on the beach at Boulogne, and that happy-looking regiment of children coming from the machines yonder would not have been in existence. You are very much obliged to that German devil for not cutting my throat ? And I thank my host of the Imperial for disturbing him before he had time to carry out his fell scheme.

Well, sir, to conclude, as the parson says, I put that bit of ribbon, which the thief had left behind him, into my pocket, took the next train to Calais, the next to Dover, returned to my father's house, and married Miss Longford. We are a thoroughly happy pair, as you have already had judgment enough to note. My children are good, contented, and numerous, as you see ; and if that will make a story for Christmas, my friend, you are quite welcome to it, and you can call it Uncle Hartlebury's Romance.

THOMAS HARDY

1840–1928

THE MELANCHOLY HUSSAR OF THE GERMAN LEGION

I

HERE stretch the downs, high and breezy and green, absolutely unchanged since those eventful days. A plough has never disturbed the turf, and the sod that was uppermost then is uppermost now. Here stood the camp; here are distinct traces of the banks thrown up for the horses of the cavalry, and spots where the midden-heaps lay are still to be observed. At night, when I walk across the lonely place, it is impossible to avoid hearing, amid the scourings of the wind over the grass-bents and thistles, the old trumpet and bugle calls, the rattle of the halters; to help seeing rows of spectral tents and the *impedimenta* of the soldiery. From within the canvases come guttural syllables of foreign tongues, and broken songs of the fatherland; for they were mainly regiments of the King's German Legion that slept round the tent-poles hereabout at that time.

It was nearly ninety years ago. The British uniform of the period, with its immense epaulettes, queer cocked-hat, breeches, gaiters, ponderous cartridge-box, buckled shoes, and what not, would look strange and barbarous now. Ideas have changed; invention has followed invention. Soldiers were monumental objects then. A divinity still hedged kings here and there; and war was considered a glorious thing.

Secluded old manor-houses and hamlets lie in the ravines and hollows among these hills, where a stranger had hardly ever been seen till the King chose to take the baths yearly at the seaside watering-place a few miles to the south; as a consequence of which battalions descended in a cloud upon the open country around. Is it necessary to add that the echoes of many characteristic tales, dating from that picturesque time, still linger about here in more or less fragmentary form, to be caught by the attentive ear? Some of them I have repeated; most of them I have forgotten; one I have never repeated, and assuredly can never forget.

Phyllis told me the story with her own lips. She was then an old lady of seventy-five, and her auditor a lad of fifteen. She enjoined silence as to her share in the incident till she should be "dead, buried, and forgotten." Her life was prolonged twelve years after the day of her narration, and she has now been dead nearly twenty. The oblivion which in her modesty and humility she courted for herself has only partially fallen on her, with the unfortunate result of inflicting an injustice upon her memory; since such fragments of her story as got abroad at the time, and have been kept alive ever since, are precisely those which are most unfavourable to her character.

It all began with the arrival of the York Hussars, one of the foreign regiments above alluded to. Before that day scarcely a soul had been seen near her father's house for weeks. When a noise like the brushing skirt of a visitor was heard on the doorstep, it proved to be a scudding leaf; when a carriage seemed to be nearing the door, it was her father grinding his sickle on the stone in the garden for his favourite relaxation of trimming the box-tree borders to the plots. A sound like luggage thrown down from the coach was a gun far away at sea; and what looked like a tall man by the gate at dusk was a yew bush cut into a quaint and attenuated shape. There is no such solitude in country places now as there was in those old days.

Yet all the while King George and his Court were at his favourite seaside resort, not more than five miles off.

The daughter's seclusion was great, but beyond the seclusion of the girl lay the seclusion of the father. If her social condition was twilight, his was darkness. Yet he enjoyed his darkness, while her twilight oppressed her. Dr. Grove had been a professional man whose taste for lonely meditation over metaphysical questions had diminished his practice till it no longer paid him to keep it going; after which he had relinquished it and hired at a nominal rent the small, dilapidated, half farm, half manor-house of this obscure inland nook, to make a sufficiency of an income which in a town would have been inadequate for their maintenance. He stayed in his garden the greater part of the day, growing more and more irritable with the lapse of time, and the increasing perception that he had wasted his life in the pursuit of illusions. He saw his friends less and less frequently. Phyllis became so shy that if she met a stranger anywhere in her short rambles she felt ashamed at his gaze, walked awkwardly, and blushed to her shoulders.

Yet Phyllis was discovered even here by an admirer, and her hand most unexpectedly asked in marriage.

The King, as aforesaid, was at the neighbouring town, where he had taken up his abode at Gloucester Lodge, and his presence in the town naturally brought many county people thither. Among these idlers—many of whom professed to have connections and interests with the Court—was one Humphrey Gould, a bachelor; a personage neither young nor old; neither good-looking nor positively plain. Too steady-going to be " a buck " (as fast and unmarried men were then called), he was an approximately fashionable man of a mild type. This bachelor of thirty found his way to the village on the down: beheld Phyllis; made her father's acquaintance in order to make hers; and by some means or other she sufficiently inflamed his heart to lead him in that direction almost daily; till he became engaged to marry her.

As he was of an old local family, some of whose members were held in respect in the county, Phyllis, in bringing him to her feet, had accomplished what was considered a brilliant move for one in her constrained position. How she had done it was not quite known to Phyllis herself. In those days unequal marriages were regarded rather as a violation of the laws of nature than as a mere infringement of convention, the more modern view, and hence when Phyllis, of the watering-place *bourgeoisie,* was chosen by such a gentlemanly fellow, it was as if she were going to be taken to heaven, though perhaps the uninformed would have seen no great difference in the respective positions of the pair, the said Gould being as poor as a crow.

This pecuniary condition was his excuse—probably a true one—for postponing their union, and as the winter drew nearer and the King departed for the season, Mr. Humphrey Gould set out for Bath, promising to return to Phyllis in a few weeks. The winter arrived, the date of his promise passed, yet Gould postponed his coming, on the ground that he could not very easily leave his father in the city of their sojourn, the elder having no other relative near him. Phyllis, though lonely in the extreme, was content. The man who had asked her in marriage was a desirable husband for her in many ways; her father highly approved of his suit; but this neglect of her was awkward, if not painful, for Phyllis. Love him in the true sense of the word she assured me she never did, but she had a genuine regard for him; admired a certain methodical and dogged way in which he sometimes took his pleasure; valued his knowledge of what the Court was doing, had done, or was about to do; and she was not without a feeling of pride that he had chosen her when he might have exercised a more ambitious choice.

But he did not come; and the spring developed. His letters were regular though formal; and it is not to be wondered that the uncertainty of her position, linked with the fact that there was not much passion in her thoughts of Humphrey, bred an indescribable dreariness in the heart of Phyllis Grove. The spring was soon summer, and the summer brought the King; but still no Humphrey

Gould. All this while the engagement by letter was maintained intact.

At this point of time a golden radiance flashed in upon the lives of people here, and charged all youthful thought with emotional interest. This radiance was the aforesaid York Hussars.

II

The present generation has probably but a very dim notion of the celebrated York Hussars of ninety years ago. They were one of the regiments of the King's German Legion, and (though they somewhat degenerated later on) their brilliant uniform, their splendid horses, and above all, their foreign air and mustachios (rare appendages then), drew crowds of admirers of both sexes wherever they went. These with other regiments had come to encamp on the downs and pastures, because of the presence of the King in the neighbouring town.

The spot was high and airy, and the view extensive, commanding the Isle of Portland in front, and reaching to St. Aldhelm's Head eastward, and almost to the Start on the west.

Phyllis, though not precisely a girl of the village, was as interested as any of them in this military investment. Her father's home stood somewhat apart, and on the highest point of ground to which the lane ascended, so that it was almost level with the top of the church tower in the lower part of the parish. Immediately from the outside of the garden-wall the grass spread away to a great distance, and it was crossed by a path which came close to the wall. Ever since her childhood it had been Phyllis's pleasure to clamber up this fence and sit on the top—a feat not so difficult as it may seem, the walls in this district being built of rubble, without mortar, so that there were plenty of crevices for small toes.

She was sitting up here one day, listlessly surveying the pasture without, when her attention was arrested by a solitary figure walking along the path. It was one of the renowned German Hussars, and he moved onward with his eyes on the ground, and with the manner of one who wished to escape company. His head would probably have been bent like his eyes but for his stiff neck-gear. On nearer view she perceived that his face was marked with deep sadness. Without observing her, he advanced by the footpath till it brought him almost immediately under the wall.

Phyllis was much surprised to see a fine, tall soldier in such a mood as this. Her theory of the military, and of the York Hussars in particular (derived entirely from hearsay, for she had never talked to a soldier in her life), was that their hearts were as gay as their accoutrements.

At this moment the Hussar lifted his eyes and noticed her on her perch, the white muslin neckerchief which covered her shoulders and neck where left bare by her low gown, and her white raiment in general, showing conspicuously in the bright sunlight of this summer day. He blushed a little at the suddenness of the encounter, and without halting a moment from his pace passed on.

All that day the foreigner's face haunted Phyllis; its aspect was so striking, so handsome, and his eyes were so blue and sad and abstracted. It was perhaps only natural that on some following day at the same hour she should look over that wall again, and wait till he had passed a second time. On this occasion he was reading a letter, and at the sight of her his manner was that of one who had half expected or hoped to discover her. He almost stopped, smiled, and made a courteous salute. The end of the meeting was that they exchanged a few words. She asked him what he was reading, and he readily informed her that he was re-perusing letters from his mother in Germany; he did not get them often, he said, and was forced to read the old ones a great many times. This was all that passed at the present interview, but others of the same kind followed.

Phyllis used to say that his English, though not good, was quite intelligible to her, so that their acquaintance was never hindered by difficulties of speech. Whenever the subject became too delicate, subtle, or tender for such words of English as were at his command, the eyes no doubt helped out the tongue, and—though this was later on—the lips helped out the eyes. In short, this acquaintance, unguardedly made, and rash enough on her part, developed and ripened. Like Desdemona, she pitied him, and learnt his history.

His name was Matthäus Tina, and Saarbrück his native town, where his mother was still living. His age was twenty-two, and he had already risen to the grade of corporal, though he had not long been in the army. Phyllis used to assert that no such refined or well-educated young man could have been found in the ranks of the purely English regiments, some of these foreign soldiers having rather the graceful manner and presence of our native officers than of our rank and file.

She by degrees learnt from her foreign friend a circumstance about himself and his comrades which Phyllis would least have expected of the York Hussars. So far from being as gay as its uniform, the regiment was pervaded by a dreadful melancholy, a chronic home-sickness, which depressed many of the men to such an extent that they could hardly attend to their drill. The worst sufferers were the younger soldiers who had not been over here long. They hated England and English life; they took no interest whatever in King George and his island kingdom, and they only wished to be out of it and never to see it any more. Their bodies were here, but their hearts and minds were always far away in their dear fatherland, of which—brave men and stoical as they were in many ways—they would speak with tears in their eyes. One of the worst of the sufferers from this home-woe, as he called it in his own tongue, was Matthäus Tina, whose dreamy musing nature felt the gloom of exile still more intensely from the fact that he had left a lonely mother at home with nobody to cheer her.

Though Phyllis, touched by all this, and interested in his history, did not disdain her soldier's acquaintance, she declined (according to her own account, at least) to permit the young man to overstep the line of mere friendship for a long while—as long, indeed, as she considered herself likely to become the possession of another ; though it is probable that she had lost her heart to Matthäus before she was herself aware. The stone wall of necessity made anything like intimacy difficult ; and he had never ventured to come, or to ask to come, inside the garden, so that all their conversation had been overtly conducted across this boundary.

III

But news reached the village from a friend of Phyllis's father concerning Mr. Humphrey Gould, her remarkably cool and patient betrothed. This gentleman had been heard to say in Bath that he considered his overtures to Miss Phyllis Grove to have reached only the stage of a half-understanding ; and in view of his enforced absence on his father's account, who was too great an invalid now to attend to his affairs, he thought it best that there should be no definite promise as yet on either side. He was not sure, indeed, that he might not cast his eyes elsewhere.

This account—though only a piece of hearsay, and as such entitled to no absolute credit—tallied so well with the infrequency of his letters and their lack of warmth, that Phyllis did not doubt its truth for one moment ; and from that hour she felt herself free to bestow her heart as she should choose. Not so her father ; he declared the whole story to be a fabrication. He had known Mr. Gould's family from his boyhood, and if there was one proverb which expressed the matrimonial aspect of that family well, it was "Love me little, love me long." Humphrey was an honourable man, who would not think of treating his engagement so lightly. "Do you wait in patience," he said ; "all will be right enough in time."

From these words Phyllis at first imagined that her father was in correspondence with Mr. Gould, and her heart sank within her, for in spite of her original intentions, she had been relieved to hear that her engagement had come to nothing. But she presently learnt that her father had heard no more of Humphrey Gould than she herself had done; while he would not write and address her affianced directly on the subject lest it should be deemed an imputation on that bachelor's honour.

"You want an excuse for encouraging one or other of those foreign fellows to flatter you with his unmeaning attentions," her father exclaimed, his mood having of late been a very unkind one towards her. "I see more than I say. Don't you ever set foot outside that garden-fence without my permission. If you want to see the camp I'll take you myself some Sunday afternoon."

Phyllis had not the smallest intention of disobeying him in her actions, but she assumed herself to be independent with respect to her feelings. She no longer checked her fancy for the Hussar, though she was far from regarding him as her lover in the serious sense in which an Englishman might have been regarded as such. The young foreign soldier was almost an ideal being to her, with none of the appurtenances of an ordinary house-dweller; one who had descended she knew not whence, and would disappear she knew not whither; the subject of a fascinating dream—no more.

They met continually now—mostly at dusk—during the brief interval between the going down of the sun and the minute at which the last trumpet-call summoned him to his tent. Perhaps her manner had become less restrained latterly; at any rate that of the Hussar was so; he had grown more tender every day, and at parting after these hurried interviews she reached down her hand from the top of the wall that he might press it. One evening he held it so long that she exclaimed, "The wall is white, and somebody in the field may see your shape against it!"

He lingered so long that night that it was with the greatest difficulty that he could run across the intervening stretch of ground and enter the camp in time. On the next occasion of his awaiting her she did not appear in her usual place at the usual hour. His disappointment was unspeakably keen; he remained staring blankly at the spot, like a man in a trance. The trumpets and tattoo sounded, and still he did not go.

She had been delayed purely by an accident. When she arrived she was anxious because of the lateness of the hour, having heard as well as he the sounds denoting the closing of the camp. She implored him to leave immediately.

"No," he said gloomily. "I shall not go in yet—the moment you come—I have thought of your coming all day."

"But you may be disgraced at being after time."

"I don't mind that. I should have disappearerd from the world some time ago if it had not been for two persons—my beloved here and my mother in Saarbrück. I hate the army. I care more for a minute of your company than for all the promotion in the world."

Thus he stayed and talked to her, and told her interesting details of his native place, and incidents of his childhood, till she was in a simmer of distress at his recklessness in remaining. It was only because she insisted on bidding him good-night and leaving the wall that he returned to his quarters.

The next time that she saw him he was without the stripes that had adorned his sleeve. He had been broken to the level of private for his lateness that night, and as Phyllis considered herself to be the cause of his disgrace her sorrow was great. But the position was now reversed; it was his turn to cheer her.

"Don't grieve, meine Liebliche!" he said. "I have got a remedy for whatever comes. First, even supposing I regain my stripes, would your father allow you to marry a non-commissioned officer in the York Hussars?"

She flushed. This practical step had not been in her mind in relation to such an unrealistic person as he was; and a moment's reflection was enough for it. "My father would not—certainly would not," she answered unflinchingly. "It cannot be thought of! My dear friend, please do forget me: I fear I am ruining you and your prospects!"

"Not at all!" said he. "You are giving this country of yours just sufficient interest to me to make me care to keep alive in it. If my dear land were here also, and my old parent, with you, I could be happy as I am, and would do my best as a soldier. But it is not so. And now listen. This is my plan. That you go with me to my own country, and be my wife there, and live there with my mother and me. I am not a Hanoverian, as you know, though I entered the army as such; my country is by the Saar, and is at peace with France, and if I were once in it I should be free."

"But how get there?" she asked. Phyllis had been rather amazed than shocked at his proposition. Her position in her father's house was growing irksome and painful in the extreme; his parental affection seemed to be quite dried up. She was not a native of the village like all the joyous girls around her; and in some way Matthäus Tina had infected her with his own passionate longing for his country, and mother, and home.

"But how?" she repeated, finding that he did not answer. "Will you buy your discharge?"

"Ah, no," he said. "That's impossible in these times. No; I came here against my will; why should I not escape? Now is the time, as we shall soon be striking camp, and I might see you no more. This is my scheme. I will ask you to meet me on the highway two miles off on some calm night next week that may be appointed.

There will be nothing unbecoming in it, or to cause you shame ; you will not fly alone with me, for I will bring with me my devoted young friend Christoph, an Alsatian, who has lately joined the regiment, and who has agreed to assist in this enterprise. We shall have come from yonder harbour, where we shall have examined the boats, and found one suited to our purpose. Christoph has already a chart of the Channel, and we will then go to the harbour, and at midnight cut the boat from her moorings, and row away round the point out of sight ; and by the next morning we are on the coast of France, near Cherbourg. The rest is easy, for I have saved money for the land journey, and can get a change of clothes. I will write to my mother, who will meet us on the way."

He added details in reply to her inquiries, which left no doubt in Phyllis's mind of the feasibility of the undertaking. But its magnitude almost appalled her, and it is questionable if she would ever have gone further in the wild adventure if, on entering the house that night, her father had not accosted her in the most significant terms.

"How about the York Hussars ?" he said.

"They are still at the camp ; but they are soon going away, I believe."

"It is useless for you to attempt to cloak your actions in that way. You have been meeting one of those fellows ; you have been seen walking with him—foreign barbarians, not much better than the French themselves ! I have made up my mind—don't speak a word till I have done, please !—I have made up my mind that you shall stay here no longer while they are on the spot. You shall go to your aunt's."

It was useless for her to protest that she had never taken a walk with any soldier or man under the sun except himself. Her protestations were feeble, too, for though he was not literally correct in his assertion, he was virtually only half in error.

The house of her father's sister was a prison to Phyllis. She had quite recently undergone experience of its gloom ; and when her father went on to direct her to pack what would be necessary for her to take, her heart died within her. In after years she never attempted to excuse her conduct during this week of agitation ; but the result of her self-communing was that she decided to join in the scheme of her lover and his friend, and fly to the country which he had coloured with such lovely hues in her imagination. She always said that the one feature in his proposal which overcame her hesitation was the obvious purity and straightforwardness of his intentions. He showed himself to be so virtuous and kind ; he treated her with a respect to which she had never before been accustomed, and she was braced to the obvious risks of the voyage by her confidence in him.

IV

It was on a soft, dark evening of the following week that they engaged in the adventure. Tina was to meet her at a point in the highway at which the lane to the village branched off. Christoph was to go ahead of them to the harbour where the boat lay, row it round the Nothe—or Look-out as it was called in those days—and pick them up on the other side of the promontory, which they were to reach by crossing the harbour-bridge on foot, and climbing over the Look-out hill.

As soon as her father had ascended to his room she left the house, and, bundle in hand, proceeded at a trot along the lane. At such an hour not a soul was afoot anywhere in the village, and she reached the junction of the lane with the highway unobserved. Here she took up her position in the obscurity formed by the angle of a fence, whence she could discern every one who approached along the turnpike-road, without being herself seen.

She had not remained thus waiting for her lover longer than a minute—though from the tension of her nerves the lapse of even that short time was trying—when, instead of the expected footsteps, the stage-coach could be heard descending the hill. She knew that Tina would not show himself till the road was clear, and waited impatiently for the coach to pass. Nearing the corner where she was it slackened speed, and, instead of going by as usual, drew up within a few yards of her. A passenger alighted, and she heard his voice. It was Humphrey Gould's.

He had brought a friend with him, and luggage. The luggage was deposited on the grass, and the coach went on its route to the royal watering-place.

"I wonder where that young man is with the horse and trap?" said her former admirer to his companion. "I hope we shan't have to wait here long. I told him half-past nine o'clock precisely."

"Have you got her present safe?"

"Phyllis's? Oh yes. It is in this trunk. I hope it will please her."

"Of course it will. What woman would not be pleased with such a handsome peace-offering?"

"Well—she deserves it. I've treated her rather badly. But she has been in my mind these last two days much more than I should care to confess to everybody. Ah, well; I'll say no more about that. It cannot be that she is so bad as they make out. I am quite sure that a girl of her good wit would know better than to get entangled with any of those Hanoverian soldiers. I won't believe it of her, and there's an end on't."

More words in the same strain were casually dropped as the two men waited, words which revealed to her, as by a sudden illumination, the enormity of her conduct. The conversation was at length cut off by the arrival of the man with the vehicle. The luggage was placed in it, and they mounted, and were driven on in the direction from which she had just come.

Phyllis was so conscience-stricken that she was at first inclined to follow them ; but a moment's reflection led her to feel that it would only be bare justice to Matthäus to wait till he arrived, and explain candidly that she had changed her mind—difficult as the struggle would be when she stood face to face with him. She bitterly reproached herself for having believed reports which represented Humphrey Gould as false to his engagement, when, from what she now heard from his own lips, she gathered that he had been living full of trust in her. But she knew well enough who had won her love. Without him her life seemed a dreary prospect, yet the more she looked at his proposal the more she feared to accept it—so wild as it was, so vague, so venturesome. She had promised Humphrey Gould, and it was only his assumed faithlessness which had led her to treat that promise as nought. His solicitude in bringing her these gifts touched her ; her promise must be kept, and esteem must take the place of love. She would preserve her self-respect. She would stay at home and marry him, and suffer.

Phyllis had thus braced herself to an exceptional fortitude when, a few minutes later, the outline of Matthäus Tina appeared behind a field-gate, over which he lightly leapt as she stepped forward. There was no evading it, he pressed her to his breast.

" It is the first and last time ! " she wildly thought as she stood encircled by his arms.

How Phyllis got through the terrible ordeal of that night she coul never clearly recollect. She always attributed her success in carrying out her resolve to her lover's honour, for as soon as she declare to him in feeble words that she had changed her mind, and fel that she could not, dared not, fly with him, he forbore to urge her grieved as he was at her decision. Unscrupulous pressure on hi part, seeing how romantically she had become attached to him would no doubt have turned the balance in his favour. But he di nothing to tempt her unduly or unfairly.

On her side, fearing for his safety, she begged him to remain This, he declared, could not be. " I cannot break faith with m friend," said he. Had he stood alone he would have abandoned h plan. But Christoph, with the boat and compass and chart, wa waiting on the shore ; the tide would soon turn ; his mother ha been warned of his coming ; go he must.

Many precious minutes were lost while he tarried, unable to te himself away. Phyllis held to her resolve, though it cost her man a bitter pang. At last they parted, and he went down the hill. Before his footsteps had quite died away she felt a desire to behold at least his outline once more, and running noiselessly after him, regained view of his diminishing figure. For one moment she was sufficiently excited to be on the point of rushing forward and linking her fate with his. But she could not. The courage which at the critical instant failed Cleopatra of Egypt could scarcely be expected of Phyllis Grove.

A dark shape, similar to his own, joined him in the highway. It was Christoph, his friend. She could see no more; they had hastened on in the direction of the town and harbour, four miles ahead. With a feeling akin to despair she turned and slowly pursued her way homeward.

Tattoo sounded in the camp; but there was no camp for her now. It was as dead as the camp of the Assyrians after the passage of the Destroying Angel.

She noiselessly entered the house, seeing nobody, and went to bed. Grief, which kept her awake at first, ultimately wrapped her in a heavy sleep. The next morning her father met her at the foot of the stairs.

"Mr. Gould is come!" he said triumphantly.

Humphrey was staying at the inn, and had already called to inquire for her. He had brought her a present of a very handsome looking-glass in a frame of *repoussé* silverwork, which her father held in his hand. He had promised to call again in the course of an hour to ask Phyllis to walk with him.

Pretty mirrors were rarer in country-houses at that day than they are now, and the one before her won Phyllis's admiration. She looked into it, saw how heavy her eyes were, and endeavoured to brighten them. She was in that wretched state of mind which leads a woman to move mechanically onward in what she conceives to be her allotted path. Mr. Humphrey had, in his undemonstrative way, been adhering all along to the old understanding; it was for her to do the same, and to say not a word of her own lapse. She put on her bonnet and tippet, and when he arrived at the hour named she was at the door awaiting him.

V

Phyllis thanked him for his beautiful gift; but the talking was soon entirely on Humphrey's side as they walked along. He told her of the latest movements of the world of fashion—a subject which she willingly discussed to the exclusion of anything more personal—and his measured language helped to still her disquieted heart and brain. Had not her own sadness been what it was she must have observed his embarrassment. At last he abruptly changed the subject.

"I am glad you are pleased with my little present," he said. "The truth is that I brought it to propitiate 'ee, and to get you to help me out of a mighty difficulty."

It was inconceivable to Phyllis that this independent bachelor—whom she admired in some respects—could have a difficulty.

"Phyllis—I'll tell you my secret at once; for I have a monstrous secret to confide before I can ask your counsel. The case is, then, that I am married: yes, I have privately married a dear young belle; and if you knew her, and I hope you will, you would say everything in her praise. But she is not quite the one that my father would have chosen for me—you know the paternal idea as well as I—and I have kept it secret. There will be a terrible noise, no doubt; but I think that with your help I may get over it. If you would only do me this good turn—when I have told my father, I mean—say that you never could have married me, you know, or something of that sort—'pon my life it will help to smooth the way vastly. I am so anxious to win him round to my point of view, and not to cause any estrangement."

What Phyllis replied she scarcely knew, or how she counselled him as to his unexpected situation. Yet the relief that his announcement brought her was perceptible. To have confided her trouble in return was what her aching heart longed to do, and had Humphrey been a woman she would instantly have poured out her tale. But to him she feared to confess; and there was a real reason for silence, till a sufficient time had elapsed to allow her lover and his comrade to get out of harm's way.

As soon as she reached home again she sought a solitary place, and spent the time in half regretting that she had not gone away, and in dreaming over the meetings with Matthäus Tina from their beginning to their end. In his own country, amongst his own countrywomen, he would possibly soon forget her, even to her very name.

Her listlessness was such that she did not go out of the house for several days. There came a morning which broke in fog and mist, behind which the dawn could be discerned in greenish grey, and the outlines of the tents and the rows of horses at the ropes. The smoke from the canteen fires drooped heavily.

The spot at the bottom of the garden where she had been accustomed to climb the wall to meet Matthäus was the only inch of English ground in which she took any interest; and in spite of the disagreeable haze prevailing she walked out there till she reached the well-known corner. Every blade of grass was weighted with little liquid globes, and slugs and snails had crept out upon the plots. She could hear the usual faint noises from the camp, and in the other direction the trot of farmers on the road to the town, for it was market-day. She observed that her frequent visits to this corner had quite trodden down the grass in the angle of the wall, and left marks of garden soil on the stepping-stones by which she had mounted to look over the top. Seldom having gone there till dusk, she had not considered that her traces might be visible by day. Perhaps it was these which had revealed her trysts to her father.

While she paused in melancholy regard, she fancied that the customary sounds from the tents were changing their character. Indifferent as Phyllis was to camp doings now, she mounted by the steps to the old place. What she beheld at first awed and perplexed her, then she stood rigid, her fingers hooked to the wall, her eyes staring out of her head, and her face as if hardened to stone.

On the open green stretching before her all the regiments in the camp were drawn up in line, in the mid-front of which two empty coffins lay on the ground. The unwonted sounds which she had noticed came from an advancing procession. It consisted of the band of the York Hussars playing a Dead March; next two soldiers of that regiment in a mourning coach, guarded on each side, and accompanied by two priests. Behind came a crowd of rustics who had been attracted by the event. The melancholy procession marched along the front of the line, returned to the centre, and halted beside the coffins, where the two condemned men were blindfolded, and each placed kneeling on his coffin; a few minutes' pause was now given while they prayed.

A firing-party of twenty-four men stood ready with levelled carbines. The commanding officer, who had his sword drawn, waved it through some cuts of the sword-exercise till he reached the downward stroke, whereat the firing-party discharged their volley. The two victims fell, one upon his face across his coffin, the other backwards.

As the volley resounded there arose a shriek from the wall of Dr. Grove's garden, and some one fell down inside; but nobody among the spectators without noticed it at the time. The two executed Hussars were Matthäus Tina and his friend Christoph. The soldiers on guard placed the bodies in the coffins almost instantly; but the colonel of the regiment, an Englishman, rode up and exclaimed in a stern voice: "Turn them out—as an example to the men!"

The coffins were lifted endwise, and the dead Germans flung out upon their faces on the grass. Then all the regiments wheeled in sections, and marched past the spot in slow time. When the survey was over the corpses were again coffined, and borne away.

Meanwhile, Dr. Grove, attracted by the noise of the volley, had rushed out into his garden, where he saw his wretched daughter lying motionless against the wall. She was taken indoors, but it was long before she recovered consciousness, and for weeks they despaired of her reason.

It transpired that the luckless deserters from the York Hussars had cut the boat from her moorings in the adjacent harbour, according to their plan, and, with two other comrades who were smarting under ill-treatment from their colonel, had sailed in safety across the Channel. But mistaking their bearings they steered into Jersey, thinking that island the French coast. Here they were perceived to be deserters, and delivered up to the authorities. Matthäus and Christoph interceded for the other two at the court-martial, saying that it was entirely by the former's representations that these were induced to go. Their sentence was accordingly commuted to flogging, the death punishment being reserved for their leaders.

The visitor to the well-known old Georgian watering-place, who may care to ramble to the neighbouring village under the hills and examine the register of burials, will there find two entries in these words:

"*Matth: Tina (Corpl.) in His Majesty's Regmt. of York Hussars, and Shot for Desertion, was Buried June* 30*th,* 1801, *aged* 22 *years. Born in the town of Sarrbruk, Germany.*

"*Christoph Bless, belonging to His Majesty's Regmt. of York Hussars, who was Shot for Desertion, was Buried June* 30*th,* 1801, *aged* 22 *years. Born at Lothaargen, Alsatia.*"

Their graves were dug at the back of the little church, near the wall. There is no memorial to mark the spot, but Phyllis pointed it out to me. While she lived she used to keep their mounds neat; but now they are overgrown with nettles, and sunk nearly flat. The older villagers, however, who know of the episode from their parents, still recollect the place where the soldiers lie. Phyllis lies near.

THOMAS HARDY

ABSENT-MINDEDNESS IN A PARISH CHOIR

"It happened on Sunday after Christmas—the last Sunday ever they played in Longpuddle church gallery, as it turned out, though they didn't know it then. As you may know, sir, the players formed a very good band—almost as good as the Mellstock parish players that were led by the Dewys; and that's saying a great deal. There was Nicholas Puddingcome, the leader, with the first fiddle; there was Timothy Thomas, the bass-viol man; John Biles, the tenor fiddler; Dan'l Hornhead, with the serpent; Robert Dowdle, with the clarionet; and Mr. Nicks, with the oboe—all sound and powerful musicians, and strong-winded men—they that blowed. For that reason they were very much in demand Christmas week for little reels and dancing parties; for they could turn a jig or a hornpipe out of hand as well as ever they could turn out a psalm, and perhaps better, not to speak irreverent. In short, one half-hour they could be playing a Christmas carol in the squire's hall to the ladies and gentlemen, and drinking tay and coffee with 'em as modest as saints; and the next, at The Tinker's Arms, blazing away like wild horses with the 'Dashing White Sergeant' to nine couple of dancers and more, and swallowing rum-and-cider hot as flame.

"Well, this Christmas they'd been out to one rattling randy after another every night, and had got next to no sleep at all. Then came the Sunday after Christmas, their fatal day. 'Twas so mortal cold that year that they could hardly sit in the gallery; for though the congregation down in the body of the church had a stove to keep off the frost, the players in the gallery had nothing at all. So Nicholas sat at morning service, when 'twas freezing an inch an hour, 'Please the Lord I won't stand this numbing weather no longer: this afternoon we'll have something in our insides to make us warm, if it cost a king's ransom.'

"So he brought a gallon of hot brandy and beer, ready mixed, to church with him in the afternoon, and by keeping the jar well wrapped up in Timothy Thomas's bass-viol bag it kept drinkably warm till they wanted it, which was just a thimbleful in the Absolution, and another after the Creed, and the remainder at the beginning o' the sermon. When they'd had the last pull they felt quite comfortable and warm, and as the sermon went on—most unfortunately for 'em it was a long one that afternoon—they fell asleep, every man jack of 'em; and there they slept on as sound as rocks.

"'Twas a very dark afternoon, and by the end of the sermon all you could see of the inside of the church were the pa'son's two candles alongside of him in the pulpit, and his spaking face behind 'em. The sermon being ended at last, the pa'son gie'd out the Evening Hymn. But no choir set about sounding up the tune, and the people began to turn their heads to learn the reason why, and then Levi Limpet, a boy who sat in the gallery, nudged Timothy and Nicholas, and said, 'Begin! begin!'

"'Hey? what?' says Nicholas, starting up; and the church being so dark and his head so muddled he thought he was at the party they had played at all the night before, and away he went, bow and fiddle, at 'The Devil among the Tailors,' the favourite jig of our neighbourhood at that time. The rest of the band, being in the same state of mind and nothing doubting, followed their leader with all their strength, according to custom. They poured out that there tune till the lower bass notes of 'The Devil among the Tailors' made the cobwebs in the roof shiver like ghosts; then Nicholas, seeing nobody moved, shouted out as he scraped (in his usual commanding way at dances when the folk didn't know the figures), 'Top couples cross hands! And when I make the fiddle squeak at the end, every man kiss his pardner under the mistletoe!'

"The boy Levi was so frightened that he bolted down the gallery stairs and out homeward like lightning. The pa'son's hair fairly stood on end when he heard the evil tune raging through the church, and thinking the choir had gone crazy he held up his hand and said: 'Stop, stop, stop! Stop, stop! What's this?' But they didn't hear'n for the noise of their own playing, and the more he called the louder they played.

"Then the folks came out of their pews, wondering down to the ground, and saying: 'What do they mean by such wickedness! We shall be consumed like Sodom and Gomorrah!'

"Then the squire came out of his pew lined wi' green baize, where lots of lords and ladies visiting at the house were worshipping along with him, and went and stood in front of the gallery, and shook his fist in the musicians' faces, saying, 'What! In this reverent edifice! What!'

"And at last they heard'n through their playing, and stopped.

"'Never such an insulting, disgraceful thing—never!' says the squire, who couldn't rule his passion.

" 'Never!' says the pa'son, who had come down and stood beside him.

" 'Not if the Angels of Heaven,' says the squire (he was a wickedish man, the squire was, though now for once he happened to be on the Lord's side)—'not if the Angels of Heaven come down,' he says, 'shall one of you villainous players ever sound a note in this church again; for the insult to me, and my family, and my visitors, and God Almighty, that you've a-perpetrated this afternoon!'

"Then the unfortunate church band came to their senses, and remembered where they were; and 'twas a sight to see Nicholas Puddingcome and Timothy Thomas and John Biles creep down the gallery stairs with their fiddles under their arms, and poor Dan'l Hornhead with his serpent, and Robert Dowdle with his clarionet, all looking as little as ninepins; and out they went. The pa'son might have forgi'ed 'em when he learned the truth o't, but the squire would not. That very week he sent for a barrel-organ that would play two-and-twenty new psalm-tunes, so exact and particular that, however sinful inclined you was, you could play nothing but psalm-tunes whatsomever. He had a really respectable man to turn the winch, as I said, and the old players played no more."

OUIDA (LOUISE DE LA RAMÉE)
1840–1908

THE MARRIAGE PLATE

It was a very old plate—old as the hills ; or so the people thought ; one of those sacred plates, with a circular well in the centre to hold sweetmeats, which were called marriage plates in the old time, and were painted for brave bridal festivities by Maestro Georgio and Orazio Fontane, and all their lesser brother artists in Urbino and Gubbio, Pesaro and Pavia, Castelli and Savona, Faenza and Ferrara, and all the other art towns, where the ceramic painters dwelt in peace amidst the turmoil of tumultuous ages.

It hung, framed in a round worm-eaten bit of wood, on a rusty nail, amongst the dried herbs and the kitchen ware in the house of Giudetta Bernacco, and it was an article of faith with Giudetta and all her kith and kin that it must never be touched or evil would come; dust all round it they might, but touch it never. That it brought good luck hanging there, and would bring evil if removed, they believed as devoutly as they did in their priests and their saints. If asked why, they said because they did so—their fathers had done so before them ; a reason strong enough to satisfy the most sceptical inquiry.

Giudetta would cross herself sometimes when she looked at the plate as if it were a *pietà*.

" It brings good fortune," she would say always.

She was over eighty years of age. She had lost her husband in her youth ; her two sons had been killed—one in battle, the other by lightning. She had known sickness, sorrow, privation, pain of all kinds, summer and winter ; still she thought the plate brought good fortune. " I have lived to bring up Faello," she would say, and think all mercies of Heaven comprised in that phrase.

Faello (Raffaelle) was her grandson, the only male left of her stock, though a tribe of his little sisters had clustered round the soup-pot, and grown up with him ; rosy, vigorous little maidens, strong as donkeys, and useful indoors and out, as Tuscan country girls always are from their infancy. Faello was a youth now, manly and strong, handsome and robust, honest and brave, and the obedient right-hand of his grandmother. Their cottage stood on a wind-swept hill, just underneath the village of Impruneta ; their sole wealth consisted of two mules and a cart, and their means of livelihood came from carrying to and from the city the earthen vases and pots for which Impruneta is famous. Giudetta, when Faello was a baby, and her sons were both dead, had been obliged to keep a lad to drive the mule, and had had many a weary hour, and terrible trouble to keep the soup-pot full for all the tumbling babies, and woollen clothes on their little bodies in the hard winter times ; but now Faello for a space of four years had been old enough to be trusted with this labour, and so the carrying of the pots was now all profit. The little stout maidens plaited straw, fetched water, hoed the plot of ground, gathered firewood in the fir-woods, and cut fodder for the mules. They managed to live, and had a bit of meat sometimes for Sundays and feast days.

" The saints are so good to us," would Giudetta say in all seriousness and content, " and the plate brings fair fortune, you know."

Faello and all his sisters were in great awe and reverence of the Marriage Plate. It was curiously painted in polychrome, like most of these plates, with a scriptural theme—the nuptials of Rebecca and of Isaac ; all the personages were in sixteenth-century garb, and the whole was brilliant with those iridescent hues, those reflections as of mother-of-pearl and of gold, of which these early artists had the mastery. A motto ran round its outer rim in black letters, and the bridegroom offered to his bride a shield emblazoned with many gorgeous quarterings and the coronet of a duke.

They could hardly see it, hung up in the dark over a dresser, as it was, with bundles of dried marjoram and thyme, but now and then they held a lamp up to it and saw the light glow on the colours, and the black letter inscription, which they could not read, and then would tremble as Giudetta told them how it had been always there in her father's father's time, and of how some did say that they themselves came of the great family whose coronet and arms were on it ; not but what that was nonsense, no doubt.

Was it nonsense ? thought Faello ; he did not much care, but he was a proud silent boy, and was called " superbo " by his comrades, because he never was much inclined to drink and play and go trapping birds on Sundays, and chatter at the wineshop doors through summer nights as they did. Faello got up while the east was still dark, harnessed his mule, and walked in with his loads of red lemon-vases and amphoræ for oil and water. He was serious and steady, and loved his grandmother, his young sisters, and his dog Pastore. Perhaps in his heart he put Pastore first. Pastore was one of the many beautiful white sheep dogs of the country ; dogs that would adorn a palace, and might lie on a queen's robes ; dogs that are the very *beau idéal* of their race, brave, gentle, generous, and full of grace, very perfect knights of dogs, such as would become the idols of Fashion were that Lady of Caprice ever to wander up our solitary pine-clad crests and through our high-climbing olive orchards.

Faello and Pastore had passed many a happy year together. On working days, side by side, they walked into the town, their fifteen miles of dust or mud. When Faello went into a place of business Pastore sat outside by the mule's head to guard the cart and the cart's load. At evening they went back again, inside the cart that time; at night Pastore slept in the mule's stable, and guarded mule and master. When there were no vases to be carried, they went higher up into the woods and loaded the cart with the firewood cut there, or the bracken and ling which labourers and brickmakers burn in their ovens, and carried these down into the town for the foresters. At other seasons they would take loads of hay or straw; but whatever the season was, one of the mules and Faello and Pastore went down the long, stony, steep hill every day together, for it was only thus that they could keep the soup-pot full and the wolf from the door. The wolf was terribly near sometimes, especially when the fresh grist tax came, and the hand of the State snatched at the bread of the poorest of the poor. But the wolf never came quite indoors. "It is the blessed Marriage Plate," said Giudetta. "It is the mules and me," thought Faello, and then was afraid that the thought was wicked, for he was a reverential and dutiful lad. A handsome lad too, as Giudetta thought proudly, when she looked at him in his clean saints'-day shirt, with a flower behind his ear, and the sun shining in his large brown eyes and on his gleaming auburn locks.

Girls thought so, too, and cast their glances up at him as they went by with bent heads plaiting their tresses of straw. He did not look in return; these fancies had not touched him; he was always hard at work; he had his sisters for handmaidens, and for companion and friend, Pastore.

"When I am going to mass Pastore never stirs; he looks at my feet and knows that I have my boots on," Faello would say, with pride, of his playfellow. Faello never committed the foolish extravagance of boots except as a mark of respect to the high altar. His firm and shapely feet trod the earth unflinching, but from his boots they flinched very much.

It would seem to the great world a life dreary enough, to go day after day, all the year round, in sunshine and storms, in foul weather and fair, up and down a long hilly road with a mule and its load. But it was not dreary to Faello. He had a sort of soul in him, this boy who could not read or write; the awful rose of dawn, which he saw so well from his hill-side home, was beautiful to him; he loved to hear the deep bells of the monastery as he passed underneath its pile ; he had a vague perception of the loveliness of the flower he put behind his ear, of the canes he cut by the brook-side, of the silence of the pine-woods as he gathered his load. It was not much, but it was enough to make him half sad and half happy ; enough to keep him from guile and from folly ; and then, in time to preserve him from both of these, or at least from the last, at an age when it might have assailed him, old Giudetta died almost suddenly, as the very old do, the life going out like the low flame of a lamp that is spent.

She was sitting on her settle by the fire at Ceppo (Christmastide), and fell back never to rise again.

As Faello caught her, and the terrified children clustered round her, she lifted her trembling finger to the wall, where the Marriage Plate hung.

" Never move it," she muttered. " Never move it. Promise——"

" I promise," murmured Faello, paralysed with the awe of that strange look which he saw on her face, and which yet he did not know was death.

Giudetta nodded her head, and her hands clasped them, and moved feebly about her rosary of wooden beads. Then she opened her eyes with effort, and struggled to speak.

" Unless the dear God were to wish it——" she said.

She was afraid to seem to wish what God did not ; and at that moment, as Faello kissed her, she died ; and thus ended another of the innumerable simple, cleanly, honest, toilsome lives of pain and love, that are swept away like the dead leaves by the winds in autumn.

Faello was just eighteen.

He had been born on Christmas Day.

All night long he sobbed on his rough bed. The next night the body was borne up the hill to its grave, the children bearing torches, that blew about in the chill windy air, and shed their red gleam on the snow.

On the morrow he rose and harnessed the mules. The poor have no time for the luxury of grief.

Without the brave old pious spirit in his house, Faello felt lost. The little there was, he and his sisters inherited. The cottage they rented ; but the things in it, and the cart and the mules, were their own. Candida and Vina, the two elder girls, were old enough to keep domestic matters as they had been ; but to Faello nothing seemed the same. The honest, brown, homely face, withered like a winter apple, had been before him from his birth. Faello, missing it, would go into the stable at supper-time and weep his very heart out, with his arms round the neck of Pastore. Pastore understood him better than his sisters.

The little maidens were good children, and had sorrowed sincerely, yet they were half glad to be alone, to have the dignity of housewives, to have no one to scold them when they lingered at the well, or did their plaiting badly; and Candida put on the brass and glass bead necklace which the pedlar had given her at last autumn's fair, and which her grandmother had forbidden her to wear.

For two weeks and more Faello never noticed it upon her. When he did at last, he went up quietly, unclasped it, and threw it in the well.

"Shall we cease to obey *la Nonna* because she is dead?" he said. "See Pastore," he added, more gently, "he never comes nearer the fire than she allowed him; and, when he is wet, dries himself in the straw before he enters, as she taught him. Shall we think less of her than he thinks?"

The child wept. Pastore got up from his corner, and rubbed his soft white cheek against hers to dry her tears.

Pastore loved them all with that infinite forgiving tenderness of which dogs and a few women are capable. They were good to him. He very often indeed had not enough to eat, but then they themselves had not either. They were very gentle with him, and he lived in the house like one of them; seeing his brethren beaten, kicked, starved, chained, and left out in the bitter snow-storms of the winter nights, Pastore, in his dog's way, thought his home was heaven.

And his young master loved him with a great love. Whenever he had had a holiday in any of the nine years since Pastore first had come to him—a round ball of white wool three months old—Pastore had been his playmate and comrade in preference to any other, and had rambled with him along the chain of hills, covered with oak and sweet chestnut scrub, and with the tall pines spreading their green plumes against the blue sky. Now, Faello had no heart for any holiday; he felt the burden of life on his young shoulders; whilst his grandmother lived he had never known care. Now, night and day he was always thinking: "If I cannot earn enough to keep the children always as she did?" For the little maidens were five in number, and wanted more and more as they grew older and older, and nobody makes much money carrying vases and pots and firewood for other people. The money goes to the potters and the woodsellers.

Moreover, Giudetta had known how to keep the cock and the hens in full health; had known how to fatten a pig; had known how to fill a soup-pot with the mushrooms and sweet herbs of the wild places; had known a hundred ways of saving money; which the little maidens, if they knew, forgot, or else did ill. The hens sickened, or did not lay; the pig remained lean; the soup-pot boiled over, or else cost too much, and once had a mushroom in it that made them all sick; the spiders began to appear, the dust to gather, the chimney to smoke, the cabbages to get the worm. The little girls meant well, but they were very careless, and Candida sulked for her necklace in the well.

The heart of Faello grew very sad.

"You should take a wife, Faello; it would keep your sisters in order," said the neighbours. Faello coloured, for he had never had such a thought put before him; but he answered, quickly and shortly—

"When my sisters are all married, perhaps."

The youngest, Toinetta, was seven years old; the neighbours laughed, and nicknamed him Il Frate, the monk. But Faello did not laugh.

There was a maiden—just this last month or two—who had looked at him as he passed her; not furtively, as did the others, but openly, yet sweetly, with clear blue eyes that made him think of the Madonnas in the King's Galleries down in the city.

He had never spoken to her, nor would have thought of speaking to her. She was the daughter of one of the master potters, whose huge red jars he bore down into Florence, and she had but lately come from a convent where she had been reared and taught delicate handworks. She was as far removed from him as if she had been a noble's daughter, still he loved to think of her—as he thought of the saints. That was all.

Once she had patted Pastore.

Faello had kissed Pastore where her hand had rested, and then had coloured foolishly.

Now in this sweet spring weather—when these sweet blue eyes glanced at him one day, and ever afterwards he saw them in the blue of the sky above and the blue of the myosotis by the brooks—a sore trouble fell upon him. One of his mules died, and a little later the other broke its leg and had to be slain on the road. It was almost as great a loss to Faello as if his own feet had been hewn off; without his mules his power of working was gone. He had no money to buy another. The priest tried to get a trifling sum together to help him, but the people would not give. He was young, they said; there were many wanted more than he, and they all wanted so much themselves. Even the master potters whom he had served would not aid him. He had to hire a mule, but the day's hire almost swallowed up the day's wage. The soup-pot was almost empty, or only simmered with a few herbs and a little parsley in the water. Faello himself only ate bread, and as little of even this as he could, that he might not send Pastore starving to bed.

One day, a saint's day, when he was at home, a man came by, and, asking for a draught of water, said, " I think you have a curious old plate : may I see it ? "

" Surely," said Faello, and pointed at it on the wall.

The man was about to take it down, but Faello stopped him : " You must not do so. We never touch it."

" Never touch it ? " said the man, not comprehending, and got leave to light a lamp-wick and look at it.

" It is odd and old ; I will give you five francs for it," he said, as he blew the light out. Faello answered, " It is not to be sold." " Nonsense," said the man ; " it is of no use hanging there ; say ten." Faello shook his head.

The man slowly bid twenty, twenty-five, thirty, forty, and so on, till, in half an hour's time, he had reached the offer of a sum of one hundred francs. " A hundred francs ! " Faello shivered with longing. It would buy a mule. But he still shook his head and answered, " It is not to be sold." The man flung himself out of the door in a fury and fume.

He was an antiquity-dealer from the city, and had recognised the plate as old Urbin ware of the finest sort and design.

" The wooden-headed young madman ! " said the dealer, with the favourite Tuscan curse. " What can he want with a Marriage Plate on his wall ? May an apoplexy take him ! "

But no apoplexy took Faello, although he went down through the dust in the torrid heats of the summer every day, and only lived on a lump of bread and an onion, and a cupful of bad *mezzo-vino*. Even these he could ill afford, for the previous autumn's vintage had been a bad one, and the best wine was a franc a flask, which means that it is only for the rich.

It was a very curious thing, but after that dealer had gone away in dudgeon several other people came to ask to look at the Marriage Plate, and offered various sums to part with it. It never occurred to Faello that the dealer might have sent them, but he felt the temptation sorely. The mule was but a poor beast which he hired, and the hire of it ran away with nearly all his gains, but he gave them all the same answer, and when he knelt and said his Aves by his grandmother's unmarked grave, in the little white-walled burial-place on the hill, he could say with a clear conscience, " *Nonna mia, ia contenta.*"

The master potter's daughter used to go to the burial-place also, for her mother lay there. Once or twice Faello saw her and lifted his hat to her, she being one of his employer's family ; but he did not dare look at her ; as he did it that once, he felt his heart beat so that he could scarcely breathe. A little later on, he ventured, in her absence, to lay some blue *fleurs de lis* on her mother's grave ; he wondered if she knew who put them there—but how should she know ? The blue lilies had no tongue.

She never spoke to him : she only spoke to Pastore, who, since she had patted him that one day, always ran up to her whenever he saw her near.

" Dea is a pretty girl, and will have a nice nest egg for her dower," Faello heard the neighbours say once in the evening time, when work was done and the stars were out, and those stars of earth, the fireflies, were illuminating hill and dale, and clustering in the corn.

" Ay, she is a pretty girl," said another ; " they do talk of Tista up yonder for her."

Gian Battista was a young Fattore, comely and well-to-do, who rode fine frisking horses, and in winter wore velveteen, and in summer white jean clothes ; he had his home at a grey old tower on a neighbouring hill, and was the dandy and hero of the district.

Faello, listening, felt as if all the light of the stars and the fireflies went out, and left the whole earth grey and dark. Yet what was it to him ? Whether for Gian Battista or not, Dea could never be for himself: Dea, with her soft forget-me-not eyes, and her blonde tresses, and her string of pearls at her throat, and her dower of a good five thousand francs, not to speak of linen.

His fate would always be to see her go by his house—just that and nothing more.

He had to keep the wolf from the door, and the soup-pot full for the five little hungry mouths.

Her father even never noticed him, except to leave him a rough order, or pay him on a Saturday night. Faello was one of the carters —nothing more. Ser Baldassare lived in a house with green blinds and wore a gold watch, and was quite a great man, as greatness is counted up at Impruneta. People said he could fill a dozen of his own big red pots with French banknotes and not be poor ; but perhaps this was exaggeration.

Anyhow, he was a very great man in the eyes of Faello, who humbly carried into the town for him those huge, round-bellied jars, and earthen pots as big as brewers' vats in England, which made so brave a fortune for Dea and her three brothers.

It was a lovely summer time—warm, of course, but refreshed with heavy rains often at nightfall. All the harvests were abundant— wheat, oats, and barley ; hay was cut several times, and the promises of vine and of olive alike were good for the future. But the plenty around did not cross Faello's threshold.

Since Giudetta had died, there seemed no end to the troubles of the poor little household. Candida, the eldest, fell sick almost to death of the ball in the throat (diphtheria), and when, at last, she recovered, was weak and useless, and said that if she had had the necklace that had gone down the well, her throat never would have been bad ; she was not of a very logical brain, and loved a little bit of finery, being pretty and fifteen years old. The pig that had been ill so long at last made its mind up and died; five hens were stolen from the hen-roost one early morning ere Pastore and Faello had got a mile away down the road; little Toinetta broke her ankle climbing up a cherry-tree, and the three middle ones, left under this burden of sickness and work, kept the house but ill, and found the washing of linen, and the cleaning of floors, and the various daily tasks all too much for them. When Faello came home at sunset he had to set to and sweep, and hoe the plot of ground, and even go and wash his own shirts at the women's washing-tank, which more than all made him ashamed, because he felt so ridiculous. The neighbours, indeed, were not unkind, but Giudetta had been always called a proud stomach, as Faello was called after her, and pride, when you are poor, is a thing nobody ever can forgive you—very naturally.

Now and then Faello looked reproachfully up at the Marriage Plate, which was always to bring them fair fortune, and never did so. But to take it down and sell it never occurred to him for an instant. He would as soon have thought of tearing open his granddame's coffin to take the marriage ring off her finger and the linen shroud off her limbs.

Sometimes when he was hoeing, or was washing at the tank in the red glow of evening, he would see Gian Battista go by on his brave grey horse, and would hear people laugh and cry, "Ay, ay, he goes courting to Ser Baldassare; he knows the way to win Dea."

Then Faello's heart would sink as a stone sinks in deep waters, and it would seem to him for a moment as if he never could bear the many burdens of his life. But such moments passed; in the morning he would go to work again; he was brave, and by nature patient.

One day in hot August he rose as usual, and went and got into his cart as the first tinge of rose blushed in the east above the opposite mountain. Pastore jumped on him as they went forth to their labour; hungry, both of them, for they never ate till mid-day, and then not one-half that either needed. Faello went to the potter's yard and found an unusually large load awaiting him there. There had come a great order for flower-pots, large and small, from a nursery garden down in the city. There was also another errand.

The foreman gave him a little packet, sealed.

"It is all notes," he said; "you are to pay them into the bank. The master knows you are honest, so he is not afraid to trust you. Pay them in as soon as you get to the town and have delivered the vases."

Faello coloured with pleasure; it was the first kindly word or recognition of his honesty that Ser Baldassare had ever given him, and the potter was Dea's father. With a lighter heart than he had known for days and months, Faello cracked his whip in the air and started off beside his mule ; Pastore running foremost, as his habit was, a big, snowy, curly form bounding about in the soft light of the daybreak.

Faello felt almost happy. It seemed almost like being nearer Dea, to think that her father would trust him with the money that all Impruneta was aware the potter loved better, as some said, than his very soul itself, and very much better than his daughter.

The sun beamed out in all its glory, and the golden light of it spread itself over all the vastness of Val d'Arno ; the chimes of the Certasa rung for the first mass ; Faello fell on his knees in the dust by a wayside cross, said a prayer, and rose almost happy.

Pastore, pausing as he prayed, leaped on him when he rose. Faello kissed him.

" It is nothing to be honest," said Faello to his dog ; " but oh, dear Pastore, it seems such a great thing when people are so good as to praise you because you are."

Pastore trotted onward, waving the white plume of his tail, perhaps thinking that dogs are always honest, but do not get very much credit or comfort for it from those they serve.

As the day was fully up, they reached the town—empty, silent, full of long shadows, with the fragrance as of a garden in it everywhere, from the bundles of carnations, and roses, and wallflowers placed at all the street corners, waiting for the buyers that would come out a little later.

Faello and Pastore stopped a moment to drink a draught of water at the big bronze trough at the end of the Canto di Borgo San Jaccopo, and then took their cart-load across the city to the place of its destination. By the time the vases were all unloaded it was eleven o'clock ; both dog and youth felt sore pangs of hunger.

" We will pay the money into the bank, and then eat, Pastore," said Faello, and went leisurely with his emptied cart back again through the town to the place of business which he had been bidden to seek. He left Pastore on guard as usual at the head of the mule, and entered the glass doors of the bank.

They made him wait some time up on a second floor, shut up in a close little room ; they were busy, for it was a market-day, and they kept him nigh three-quarters of an hour whilst they wrote out the receipt of the notes he had brought. Faello felt the time very long, it was suffocatingly hot in this room, hotter than in the streets, and he was very hungry, and felt sorry for poor Pastore sitting down on the scorching stones with an empty stomach in the blazing sun. Still he was not uneasy, the cart and mule were safe, for none would touch them with the dog there on guard.

When at last they told him he might go, and gave him his receipt for Ser Baldassare, it was full noon, and an August noon in the streets is good neither for man nor beast.

He hurried lightly down the stairs, and ran out, joyous to be free; but at the threshold he stopped stupidly, and stared up the street and down. Pastore was not there, neither was the mule nor the cart.

He thought he must be dreaming; that the hot air had made him blind and dizzy. Then he put his hand to his mouth, and shouted the dog's name again and again and again.

A shoeblack, who was dozing near in a little niche, under some shade, was wakened by the noise, and came and shook him by the arm.

"Do not yell like that, boy; they will take you up, too. They lassoed your dog half an hour ago."

"What!" said Faello, with a shriek that seemed to him to wrench his very life out with it. The shoeblack nodded.

"They lassoed him. You know the law—no dogs loose in the streets. They came up behind him and—phew! the thing was round his neck, and he throttled and on his back, before you could whistle. They do it always, you know. Don't look like that! He was alive when they hauled him in the barrow."

"And the cart—the mule?" stammered Faello.

"Oh, somebody walked off with them, once the dog was gone. I saw it all, but it was no business of mine. Why, how you look!"

The voice of Faello rang down the emptiness of the street in a pitiless scream.

"Pastore, Pastore! my dog, my friend, my brother! Oh, the fiends!"

"Quiet," said the shoeblack; "if you call names they will arrest you. They took my boy up the other day for wrestling a bit to save his dog. Don't make a noise, but run—they won't have killed him yet, most likely; though he was half strangled as it was, poor brute. Run!"

The man told him where to go, and Faello ran with bare trembling feet on the burning stones. The loss of his mule and his cart he had forgotten. He tore through the city like a madman.

It was the intense dry pitiless heat of the August mid-day, which drives all creatures within doors, and the whole town was as quiet as a graveyard, and all the shutters were closed as for a death. The rays beat on his bare neck, and the pavement blistered his bare feet, but he took no heed. He only thought of his lost friend.

When at length he came to the place which the shoeblack had bidden him seek, he looked like a mad dog himself; his eyes were bloodshot, his tongue clove to his mouth, his lips were covered with thin white foam. He beat on the doors with both hands.

"My dog, my dog! I am come for my dog!"

The doors opened slowly ; an official, angry and stern, looked out and asked how he dared invade their rest like that. A bare-footed boy, dusty and ragged, is never a creature that commends itself to the law.

" You stole my dog—you strangled him ! " cried Faello, fairly beside himself. " They say he is here. I will see him, or I will kill you, everyone ! Let me in—let me in—I am come for my dog ! "

" Get out, fool, or I will give you to the guards," said the jack-in-office, and kicked his foot off the sill and shut the doors again. Faello beat on them with all his might.

" Thieves ! assassins ! stranglers ! Let me in—let me in ! What right have you to touch my dog ? He was doing his duty—he was guarding my cart. You murder him, and the cart is stolen. Listen, listen, listen ! I love him better than myself. He hungers with me, and plays with me, and we are brothers. How dare you touch him ? You lassoed him ! Oh, dear God ! to think of it ! Oh, my dog—my dog ! Listen—I will do any work you like for you if you will just let me see my dog. You shall put me in prison if you will only let me take his place, and will send him home to the children. Will you—will you ? Do you hear ? "

But his cries were only echoed dully back by the closed door and the dead wall, emblems of the human cowardice and the human injustice that make a hell of earth for earth's dumb creatures.

He beat at the wood and the stone, and wept to it, and prayed to it, and cursed it, and then stood dumb and stupid, the sun beating down on his head.

" What shall I do ? " he muttered. " Oh, dear San Rocco, you love dogs—help Pastore, help him ! help him, help him ! "

Then all grew dark, and he fell down, and the vertical rays beating on him seemed to dart like fire through his brain.

When he woke again to the light of day, he had been drawn into the shade of an archway, and the shoeblack was bending over him.

" I thought I would follow you ; I am glad I did," said the shoe-black. " Are you better ? It was the sun. Cover your neck at the back ; you look stupid."

" The dog," muttered Faello between his dry lips, and staggered up on to his feet.

" You should have come and asked humbly, they would have let you in then ; what is the use of calling them names ? They are too strong for us. They are the right side of the door, and we are the wrong. Only that it is noon, and not a guard about, they would have put you in prison for all those words. Oh ! yes, a blacksmith that I know, he is in for three weeks because he helped a fine black dog to slip out of the lasso. He had never set eyes on the beast before, but he felt sorry. Oh ! yes, these are fine times ; this is the freedom, you know, we old fellows fought for ; Lord, the fools we were to fire a shot ! Every bullet then brings us a tax now ! Fine times ! Wait you a bit here—keep in the shade—you look blind still, boy. I know your dog ; I will go see if he be alive."

Faello leaned his back against the archway, and waited ; his brain seemed all on fire, and spinning like a woman's wheel. If he had been shown then the men who had taken his dog, he would have leapt on them and killed them. Petty laws breed great crimes. Few rulers, big or little, remember that.

After moments, that seemed to him years, the shoeblack returned.

" He is alive," he said quickly ; " but he looks bad, and they have muzzled him. They think him dangerous. They will kill him at night if he be not brought back—poor brute ! "

Faello moaned aloud.

" They want five-and-twenty francs for contravention, and five-and-twenty more because he bit them before the rope was quite tight. You will not get him back for less."

" And I have not fifty centimes upon earth ! "

Faello's head fell on his chest, and he sobbed bitterly. The shoeblack shrugged his shoulders, and stood silent.

" It is freedom," he said at last ; " it is what we fought for, we wiseacres."

Faello did not hear him. Every muscle and nerve of his body were quivering.

His dog would die for want of fifty francs !

" Cannot you get the money, since you take it so to heart ? " said the shoeblack. Then he lowered his voice and added, " They want to kill him—that is it—you see he is a fine dog. A surgeon has had his eye on him some time ; the surgeon means to get him and cut him up alive, or burn him to death, after gouging out his eyes. They think to find God in that way, those gentlemen."

Faello gave one shrill weak cry, like a wounded hare's ; then, fleet as the hare, he wrenched himself out of the man's grasp, and tore once more across the wide white waste of the sun-parched streets and squares.

The strength of lions seemed to have flowed back into his veins.

" The devils ! oh, the devils ! " he moaned, as he flew.

He had no clear-shaped thought of what to do, but he said to himself that he would have that fifty francs that day if he seized the silver off a church altar, or dashed his hand through a goldsmith's window. He would try all honest ways first, but if they failed he would go to the galleys himself sooner than let Pastore go to the torture.

Suddenly a hope flashed across him—Would Ser Baldassare lend it ?

He had not touched bit or drop since the previous night; his clothes were wet with sweat as with water; he saw the blinding dust of the road through dizzy eyes; the nerves of his temples were beating like sledge-hammers, but he held on straight along the road, which he knew so well that he could have traversed it blindfold, with that strength of desperation which sustains the panting stag and the jaded fox, as they race before the hunters.

How he returned to the village he never could tell; he ran and walked, ran and walked, alternately, as a sleep-walker might in a dream. But go as fast as he would it was four by the clock when he reached Impruneta, and staggered into the yard of the master potter.

"Could he see Ser Baldassare?"

He had never in all his life asked such a thing before.

"He has lost the money," thought the foreman, and ran and called Ser Baldassare, as he never would have done for any lesser woe.

"You scoundrel! you have lost the money! To the Pretura you shall go!" cried the potter; rushing out with face of purple. Faello put his hand in his belt, and pulled out the banker's receipt. The potter snatched at it suspiciously, read, and, satisfied, grumbled angrily. Why had he been frightened all for nothing?

Faello, with a few gasped words, told his tale, the great tears rolling down his cheeks and stifling his voice, and ended with a piteous prayer to be lent the fifty francs.

"Oh, dear master," he moaned, as he sank on his knees in the dust, "if it were anything for myself I would not dare to pray for it; but it is for Pastore—the innocent soul; the dear, tender, honest, loyal thing that loves me as my sisters never can. Oh, dear master, Pastore is nine years old. All these years he has guarded your vases in the town, summer and winter, waiting for me, and will you let him be tortured to death when you can save him? Oh, master, master, I will work every night, every feast-day, every holy-day, till I have made the money up to you. The saints will not be angry. They will know very well why I do it. Oh, hear me, pray—lend me the money, and I will slave for you, do the mule's work as well as my own—anything, anything, anything! They will torture him to-night if you do not."

He paused suddenly, his great eyes, swimming and agonised, fastened on the face of his employer; hanging breathless on the answer of the mute lips as for his own sentence of life or death.

Ser Baldassare pursed his mouth and was silent; then he smiled a little.

"There are plenty of dogs: you can get another. No; I cannot give a lad like you such a sum."

Faello, without a word, rose to his feet, staggered a little, and went out of the yard.

" A likely story," said the foreman, with a sneer. " The boy has been drinking in Florence."

Faello, staggering still, went out of the gates into the road. The heat had lessened somewhat with the passing of noon, but hot sickly vapours were in the air ; the cloudless sky was of a pallid unnatural hue ; not a leaf moved or a bird sung on the parched trees ; there was only the noisy monotonous hum of the tree-crickets that never ceased, and was like the din of machine-wheels.

Faello stood still, and looked up with his smarting bloodshot eyes at the pale heavens. He was a pious, tender, God-fearing lad, but as he stood there he doubted God. He might have done some desperate thing, for the law, perhaps, makes more criminals than it cures ; but at that moment a hand touched his, and starting and looking down, he saw Dea.

" I have only five francs ; but pray take them," she murmured, as she slid the money towards his fingers. " Tell me, could you not sell that plate they call a Marriage Plate ? "

Faello drew a shuddering sigh. So deep was his musing, so utterly was his heart with his imprisoned and martyred dumb friend, that the presence and touch even of Dea could produce no emotion in him. He was in the desolate abstraction of an overwhelming grief.

" The Marriage Plate ! " he echoed. " But I promised never to move it—I promised."

" But she said—' unless God were to wish it.' Your sisters told me so. God would wish it now," murmured the girl, then, hearing a step, fled away back to her father's house.

Faello stood alone, her little five-franc note curled in the palm of his hand.

God would wish it now.

He muttered the words to himself again and again. Oh, if he could but be sure ! He tried to think and see whether this were but a temptation assailing him, or whether the voice of Dea had been as the voice of an angel.

He prayed in dumb inarticulate fashion, as Pastore himself might have prayed, to have light shed on him to see his path aright. He dropped down a moment on a wayside stone, and covered his face and tried to think.

Yes, surely God would wish it. Surely God would desire him to save the life of an honest innocent living creature from the most hellish torments of man, rather than desire him to keep the mere empty form of a soulless promise ! Surely the dead would wish it too ?

She saw him now—that Faello believed as he believed that the sun shone upon him. She would not be angered ; she would not think it disobedience. She had said, " unless God were to wish it."

And God must wish it now ; God, who had made Pastore, and must have some little love for him—some little heed.

Faello rose to his feet.

His face was as white as the dust beneath him, but his resolve was taken.

" I shall do right ; God must wish it," he said in his heart, and felt in a dull vague way that if God did not, His service had little worth in it and little truth.

Then he went straight to his home, seized the Marriage Plate from the place where it had hung for a century, and carried it with him into the open air. At any other time a terrible fear would have prevented him from touching that sacred thing ; but now all his mind and heart and soul were with his doomed friend. He had room for no other remembrance.

Yet as he passed the threshold he uncovered his head and crossed himself. " *Nonna mia*, you are not angry nor God either ? The saints send me that I be in time ! "

How he reached Florence he never knew. Showing the plate to a man who had a fleet horse, he was taken in by the man and the horse to the town as fast as the wind would have blown, but he had no consciousness of what he did or how he went.

He made his way straight to the dealer, and laid the Marriage Plate down before him.

" Here it is," he muttered ; " give me your hundred francs."

A person standing near stretched his hand out and took the plate before the dealer could.

" I will have it, but it is worth much more, surely. Wait awhile——"

" Not a moment ; the hundred francs ! "

" Is the boy honest ? " murmured the person who all the while held the plate.

" Quite. The plate is his own."

The other drew out a hundred francs in gold, and looked curiously at Faello. Faello snatched them, and flew as a swallow flies, straight through the town to the dog-prison.

Again he beat on the doors and shouted aloud, but this time the doors unclosed and let him enter, for this time he cried, " Let me in : I bring the money ! "

It is the open sesame of the world.

In another moment, weeping and laughing, he held Pastore against his breast, and bathed with his happy tears the dog's wounds.

Faello was carried home by the shoeblack insensible, and Pastore lay on the straw of the cart at his feet and on the pallet of his bed that night.

It was many weeks before the lad was well again; the sun had struck him.

When he could rise at last the great heat had passed; the earth was moist and green, the woods rejoiced, and the vines were heavy with purpling grapes. He stood at his door and held the dog's head against him, and thought how lovely life was.

"We shall have to work very hard, Pastore," he murmured. "The cart is stolen; there is the stolen mule, too, to pay for; the medicines will have cost a great deal, and the children must owe to the baker. Never mind; we are together. I am young, and it will soon be all right again. Oh, my dog, my dear dog!"

And then, with a sudden blush, he thought of Dea. Dea, whose little five-franc note he had unconsciously kept clasped in his hand all the while, so that it had come home with him, and, throughout his illness, could not any way be loosened out of his grasp.

At that moment there approached him the stranger who had bought his Marriage Plate. The stranger greeted him with courtesy and gentleness, and brought the Urbino Plate back with him.

"You sold this for a necessity?"

"Yes."

"Have you any idea of its value?"

"I thought it of none."

The stranger smiled, and turning the back of the plate, showed him four letters placed thus:

V

O F

F

and a date, 1538.

"It is the work of Orazio Fontane, of Castel Durante," he said. "The name tells you nothing. Well, he was a great man; the greatest of all the pottery painters of Urbino in a long past time. The plate is worth fifteen hundred francs. I am not a dealer. I bring you the sum that is just. For the rest, I have heard your story. I am a foreigner; but I am much attached to your country, and I have estates close by here. I will find you a good post; you will live on my lands, and Pastore shall have no need to risk his life in the city."

Faello listened stupefied.

Misfortune he could understand; but this!——

When the truth, in all its ecstasy, broke at last upon him, his face shone like the light of the morning.

"God *did* wish it!" he cried aloud.

Two years later he married Dea, and Pastore headed the wedding procession.

W. CLARK RUSSELL
1844–1911

THE ADVENTURES OF THREE SAILORS

TOLD BY DANIEL SMALL, ONLY MATE

OUR vessel was a little brig, named the *Hindoo Merchant*, and we sailed on a day in March, in the year of our Lord 1857, from Trincomalee bound to Calcutta. The captain, myself, and three sailors were Europeans, the rest of the ship's company natives. Though we were "flying light," as the term is—that is to say, though there was little more in the ship's hold than ballast, and though she had tolerably nimble heels for what one might term a *country wallah*—yet the little ship was so bothered with head winds and light airs, and long days of stagnation, that we had been several weeks afloat before we managed to crawl to the norrad of the Andaman parallels, which yet left a long stretch of waters before us. If this remainder of the ocean was not to be traversed more fleetly than the space we had already measured, then it was certain we should be running short of water many a long while before the Sandheads came within the compass of our horizon; and to provide against the most horrible situation that the crew of a ship can find themselves placed in, we kept a bright look-out for vessels, and within four days managed to speak two; but they had no water to spare, and we pushed on.

But within three days of our speaking the second of the two vessels, we sighted a third—a large barque, who at once backed her topsail to our signals, and hailed us to know what we wanted. My captain, Mr. Roger Blow, stood up in the mizzen-rigging and asked for water. They asked how much we needed. Captain Blow responded that whatever they could spare would be a godsend. On this they sung out: "Send a boat with a cask, and you shall have what we can afford to part with." Captain Blow then told me to put an eighteen-gallon cask in the port-quarter boat, and go away to the barque with it. "They'll not fill it," said he; "but a half'll be better than a quarter, and a quarter'll be good enough; for we stand to pick up more as we go along."

I had called to two of the English sailors, named Mike Jackson and Thomas Fallows, to get into the boat when the cask had been placed in her; and when I had entered her, the darkeys lowered us; we unhooked and shoved off. There was a pleasant breeze of wind blowing; it blew hot, as though it came straight from the inside of an oven, the door of which had been suddenly opened; the sky had the sort of glazed dimness of the human eye in fever; but right overhead it was of a copperish dazzle, where the roasting orb of the sun was. I could not see a speck of cloud anywhere, which rendered what followed the more amazing to my mind for the suddenness of it.

The two vessels at the first of their speaking had been tolerably close together; but some time had been spent in routing up the cask and getting it into the boat, and setting ourselves afloat, so that at the moment of our shoving off—spite of the topsail of each vessel being to the mast—the space had widened between them till, I daresay, it covered pretty nearly a mile. The wind was at west-nor'-west, and the barque bore on the lee-quarter of the *Hindoo Merchant.* The great heat put a languor into the arms of our two seamen, and the oars rose and fell slowly and weakly. Jackson said to me: "I hope," said he, "they'll be able to spare us a bite of ship's bread. Our'n is no better than sawdust, and if it wasn't for the worms in it," said he, "blast me if there'd be any nutriment in it at all. Them Cingalese ought to ha' moored their island off the Chinese coast. They'd have grown rich with teaching the Johnnies more tricks than they're master of at plundering sailors."

"The *Hindoo Merchant's* bread isn't up to much, Fallows," said I, "but this is no atmosphere to talk of bread in. What's aboard will carry us to the Hoogly. It is water we have to fix our minds on."

We drew alongside of the tall barque, and the master, after looking over the rail, asked me to step aboard and drink a glass with him in his cabin, "for," says he, "this is no part of the ocean to be thirsty in"; and he then gave directions for the cask to be got out of the boat, and a drink of rum and water to be handed down to the two seamen.

I stepped into the cabin, and the captain put a bottle of brandy and some cold water on the table. He asked me several questions about the brig, and how long we were out, and where we were from, and the like; and one thing leading to another, he happened to mention the town he was born in, which was my native place too—Ashford in the county of Kent—and here was now a topic to set us yarning, for I knew some of his friends and he knew some of mine;

and the talk seemed to do him so much good, whilst it was so agreeable to me, that neither of us seemed in a hurry to end it. This is the only excuse I can offer for lingering on the barque longer than, as circumstances proved, I ought to have done.

At last I got up and said I must be off, and I thanked him most kindly for the obliging reception of me, and for his goodness in supplying the brig with water, and I gave him Captain Blow's compliments, and desired to know if we could accommodate him in any way in return. He answered, " Nothing, nothing," stepping through the hatch as he said it, and an instant after he set up his throat in a cry.

" You'll have to bear a hand aboard," says he, with a face of astonishment ; " look yonder ! 'Tis rolling down upon your brig like smoke." He pointed to the vessel, and a little way past her I spied a long line of white vapour no higher than Dover cliff as it looked, but as dense as those rocks of chalk too. The sun made steam of it, but already it was putting a likeness of its own blankness into the sky over it, which seemed to be dying out, as the vapour came along, as the light perishes in a looking-glass upon which you breathe. I ran to the side and saw my boat under the gangway and the two men in her. The cask was in the stern of the boat. The master of the barque cried out to me : " Will you not stay till that smother clears ? You may lose your brig in it." I replied : " No, sir ; thank you. I will take my chance. It is more likely I should lose her by remaining here," and with a flourish of the hand I dropped over the side and entered the boat. " Now," cried I, " pull like the devil, men."

They threw their oars over and fell to rowing fiercely ; but the barque was not five cables' length astern of us when the first of the white cliff of vapour smote the *Hindoo Merchant*, and she vanished in it like a star in a cloud. There was a fresh breeze of wind behind that line of sweeping thickness, and in places, at the base of the mass of blankness, it would dart out in swift racings of shadow that made one think of the feelers of some gigantic marine spider, probing under its cobweb as though feeling its way along. In a few minutes the cloud drove down over us with a loud whistling of wind, and the water close to the boat's side ran in short, small seas, every head of it hissing ; but to within the range of a biscuit toss all was flying, glistening obscurity, with occasional bursts of denser thicknesses which almost hid one end of the boat from the other. It was about six o'clock in the afternoon, and there might be yet another hour of sunshine.

" 'Vast rowing ! " says I presently ; " you may keep the oars over, but there's no good of pulling, short of keeping her head to wind. This is too thick to last."

" Ain't so sure of that," says Fallows, taking a slow look round at the smother, " I've been in these here seas for two days running in weather arter this pattern."

" Pity we didn't stay aboard the barque," says Jackson.

" A plague on your pities ! " I cried. " I know my duty, I believe. Suppose we *had* stayed aboard the barque, we stood to be separated from the brig in this breeze and muckiness ; and was her skipper by and by going to sail in search of the *Hindoo Merchant* ? "

" A gun ! " cries Fallows.

" That'll be the brig," says I, catching the dull thud of the explosion of a nine-pounder which the *Hindoo Merchant* carried on her quarter-deck.

" Seems to me as though it sounded from yonder," says Jackson looking away over the starboard beam of the boat.

" What have ye there, men ? " says I, nodding at a bundle of canvas under the amidship thwart.

" Ship's bread," answered Jackson, with a note of sulkiness in his voice. " It was hove to us on my asking for a bite. She was a liberal barque. The cask's more'n three-quarters full."

We hung upon our oars listening and waiting. There was a second gun ten minutes after the first had been fired, and that was the last we heard. The report was thin and distant, but whether ahead or astern I could not have guessed by hearkening. I kept up my own and endeavoured to inspirit the hearts of the others by saying that this fog which had come down in a moment would end in a moment ; that it was all clear sky above, with plenty of moonlight for us in the night if it should happen that the sun went down upon us thus ; that Captain Blow was not going to lose us and his boat and the cask of fresh water if it was in mortal seamanship to hold a vessel in one situation ; but the fellows were not to be cheered, their spirits sank and their faces grew longer as the complexion of the fog told us that the sun was sinking fast ; and I own that when it came at last to his setting, and no break in the flying vapour, and a blackness as of ink stealing into it out of the swift tropic dusk, I myself felt horribly dejected, greatly fearing that we had lost the brig for good.

Just before the last of the twilight faded out of the smoke that shrouded us, we lashed both oars together, and, attaching them to the boat's painter, threw them overboard and rode to them. Our thirst was now extreme, and to appease it—being without a dipper to drop into the cask—we sank a handkerchief through the bung-hole and wrung it out in the half of a cocoa-nut shell that was in the boat as a baler, and by this means procured a drink, each man. Grateful to God indeed was I that we had fresh water with us. I beat the cask, and gathered by the sound that it was more than half full. Heaven was bountiful too in providing us with biscuit. It had been the luckiest of thoughts on Jackson's part, though he desired nothing more than to obtain a relish for his own rations of buffalo hump aboard.

I never remember the like of the pitch darkness of that night. There was a moon, pretty nearly a full one, if I recollect aright; but had she been shining over the other side of the world it would have been all the same. Her delicate silver beam could not pierce the vapour, and never once did I behold the least glistening of her radiance anywhere. There was a constant noise of wind in the dense thickness, and an incessant seething and crackling of waters running nimbly, so that, though we would from time to time bend our ears in the hope of catching the rushing and pouring noise of the sea divided by a ship's stem, we never could hear more than the whistling of the breeze and the lapping of the hurrying little surges. There was a deal of fire in the water, and it came and went in sheets like the reflection of lightning, insomuch that we might have believed ourselves in the heart of an electric storm; but happily the wind never gathered so much weight as to raise a troublesome sea; and though the boat tumbled friskily, she kept dry, and there was nothing in her movements to render me uneasy.

I told the two fellows to lie down in the bottom of the boat, and I kept watch till I reckoned it was drawing on to about one o'clock in the morning. Twice or thrice during that long and wretched vigil there seemed a promise of the weather clearing, and I gazed with the yearning of the shipwrecked; but regularly it thickened and blackened down upon us again in blasts like the belchings of a three-decker's broadside. It was a very watery vapour, and I was early wet to the skin.

At about one o'clock, as I calculated, I awoke Jackson, and bade him keep an eager look-out, and not to spare his ear in putting it against the night, "for," says I, "there's nothing to be done with the eyes; it's all for the hearing at such a time as this, mate, and what you can't watch for you must listen for; and wake me up to any sound you may hear, that our three throats may hail together. O God," says I, "if it would but thin, and show the brig within reach of our shouts!" With that I lay down, and was soon fast asleep, being worn out with excitement and grief; and when I awoke it was daylight, for there's but little dawn off the Andamans; the sun in those seas leaps on to the horizon from the night, as it were, and flashes it into day in a breath.

It was still thick and troubled weather, but clear to about two miles from the side of the boat. There was very little wind, and a long swell of the colour of lead was running from the southward.

The vapour had broken up, and lay in masses round about us—long, white, twisted folds of it, like powder smoke after a great battle ; and to the top of those heaps of thickness the sky sloped in a sort of grey shadow, with a little pencilling here and there of some small livid ring of mist, which looked stirless, as though what air there was blew low. There was nothing in sight ; we strained our gaze into every quarter, but I saw there was nothing to be seen. This smote me to the heart. I had been in my time in several situations of peril at sea, but had never yet experienced the horrors of an open boat amidst a vast waste of waters such as was this Bay of Bengal, with the Andaman Islands some hundreds of miles distant, and a near menace of roasting heat when the wide grey stretch of cloud should have passed away and laid bare the sun's eye of fire. We gazed with melancholy faces one at another.

" What's to be done ? " says Fallows, bringing his bloodshot eyes from the sea to my face. " If we had a sail to set, we might have a chance."

" There are two oars," said I, " for a mast and a yard, and our shirts must furnish a sail."

" But how are we to head ? " says Jackson.

" Right afore the wind, I suppose," says I. " There'll be no ratching with the rags we're going to hoist. Right afore the wind," I says ; " and we must trust to God to keep us in view till something heaves in sight, which is pretty well bound to happen, I suppose, when there comes some wind along."

I opened the canvas parcel, and found a matter of thirty biscuits ; all very sweet, good bread. We took each of us a piece, and followed on with a drink, and then went to work to get our oars in. We all three wore shirts, and we stripped them off our backs and cut them to lie open. I had a little circular cushion of stout pins in my pocket such as a sailor might carry, and with them we brought the squares of the shirts together, and seized the corners to one of the oars by yarns out of an end of painter we cut off, then stepped the other oar, and secured it with another piece of the painter ; and now we had a sort of sail, the mere sight of which, even, was a small satisfaction to us, since the shirts, being white, they must needs make a good mark upon the water—something not to be missed, unless wilfully, by a passing vessel.

The morning passed away, and a little after twelve o'clock the water in the south was darkened by the brushing of a wind, which drove the hovering masses of vapour before it ; and presently they had totally disappeared, leaving a sky with rents and yawns of blue in places, and a clear glass-like circle of horizon, upon which, however, there was nothing to be seen. The boat moved slowly before the wind, which blew hot as a desert breeze. I steered, and Jackson and Fallows sat near me, one or the other from time to time getting on to a thwart to take a view of the ocean, under the sharp of his hand.

In this fashion passed the afternoon. The night came with a deal of fire in the water, and a very clear moon floating in lagoons of velvet softness betwixt the clouds. The weather continued quiet; the long swell made a pleasant cradle of the boat, and the night-wind being full of dew breathed refreshingly upon our hot cheeks; whilst our ears were soothed by the rippling noise of the running waters, which seemed to cool the senses, as the breeze did the body.

It was almost a dead calm, however, at daybreak next morning. The atmosphere was close and heavy, and there was a strange strong smell of seaweed rising off the ocean, which caused me to look narrowly about, with some dim dream of perceiving land, though I should have known there was no land for leagues and leagues.

Whilst we were munching a biscuit, I observed an appearance of steam lifting off the water, at a distance of about half a mile on the starboard side of the boat. The vapour came out of the water in the shape of corkscrews, spirally working, and they melted at a height of perhaps ten or fifteen feet. I counted five of these singular emissions. Jackson said that they were fragments of mist, and we might look out for such another thickness as had lost us the brig. Fallows said: "No: that's no mist, mate; that is as good steam as ever blew out of a kettle. Are there places where the water boils in this here ocean?"

As he said these words, an extraordinary thrill passed through the boat, followed by a sound that seemed more like an intellectual sensation than a real noise. What to compare it to I don't know; it was as though it had thundered under the sea. An instant later, up from the part of the water where the corkscrew appearances were, rose a prodigious body of steam. It soared without a sound from the deep; it was balloon-shaped, but of mountainous proportions.

"A seaquake!" roared Jackson. "Stand by for the rollers!"

But no sea followed. I could witness no commotion whatever in the water; the light, long swell flowed placidly into the base of the mass of whiteness, and there was nothing besides visible on the breast of the sea, save the delicate wrinkling of the weak draught of air. Very quickly the vapour thinned as steam does, and as it melted off the surface, it disclosed to our astonished gaze what at first sight seemed to me the fabric of a great ship, but after viewing it for a moment or two, I distinctly made out the form of an old-fashioned hull, with the half of much such another hull as she alongside, both apparently locked together about the bows; and they seemed to be supported by some huge gleaming black platform; but what it was we could not tell.

The three of us drew a deep breath as we surveyed the floating objects. The steam was gone ; there they lay plain and bare ; it was as though the wand of a magician had touched the white mass and transformed it into the objects we gazed at.

" Down with the sail," says I ; " there's something yonder worth looking at."

We got the oars over, and pulled in the direction of the fabrics. As we approached I could scarce credit the evidence of my own sight. The form of one of the vessels was perfect. She was of an antique build, and belonged to a period that I reckoned was full eighty years dead and gone. The other—the half of her, I should say —showed a much bluffer bow, and had been a vessel of some burthen. But the wonder was the object on which they rested. This was no more nor less than the body of a great dead whale !

We first needed to lose something of our amazement ere we could reasonably speculate upon what we saw ; then how this had happened grew plain to our minds. The two craft, God knows how many long years before, had been in action and foundered in conflict. The smaller vessel—I mean the one that lay whole before us —might have been a privateersman ; she had something of a piratical sheer forward ; there were no signs of a mast aboard either of them. One had grappled the other, to board her I dare say, and they had both gone to the bottom linked. The vessel of which only half remained may have broken her back in settling, and, by and by, the after-part of her drifted away, leaving the dead bows still gripped by the dead enemy alongside. But how came the whale there ? Well, we three men reasoned it thus, and I don't doubt we were right. At the moment of the seaquake the whale was stemming steadily towards the two wrecks resting on the bottom. They were lifted by the explosion, which at the same time killed the whale ; but the impetus of the vast form slided it to under the lifted keels, where it came to a stand. A dead whale floats, as we know. This whale being dead was bound to rise, and the buoyancy of the immense mass brought the two craft up with it, and there they were, poised by the gleaming surface of the whale, which was depressed by their weight, so that no portion of the head, tail, or fluke was visible.

" It's them vessels being connected," says Jackson, " as keeps them afloat. If what holds them together forrard was to part they'd slide off that there slipperiness and sink."

We rode close, the three of us greatly marvelling, as you may suppose, for never had the like of such an incident as this happened at sea within the knowledge of ever a one of us, and Fallows alone was a man of five-and-forty, who had been using the ocean for thirty-three years. It was as scaring as the rising of a corpse out of the depths—as scaring as if that corpse turned to and spoke when his head showed—to see those two vessels lying in the daylight after eighty, ay, and perhaps a hundred, years of the green silence hundreds of fathoms deep, locked in the same posture in which they had gone down, making you almost fancy that you could hear the thunder of their guns, witness the flashing of cutlasses, and the rush of the boarders to the bulwarks amidst a hurricane note of huzzaing and shrieks of the wounded.

They were both of them handsomely crusted with shells, not of the barnacle sort, but such as you would pick up anywhere in Ceylon or the Andaman, some of them finely coloured, many of them white as milk, of a thousand different patterns ; and there was not one of them but what was beautiful.

" Let's board her," says Jackson.

" Ah, but if that whale be alive ! " says Fallows.

" No fear of that," said I ; " if he was alive there'd be some stir in him. The whale's not the danger ; it's the lashing, which may part at any moment. It should be in a fair way of rottenness after so many years of salt water, and if it goes the vessels go."

" I'm for boarding her all the same," says Jackson.

But first of all we pulled round to betwixt the bows of the craft to see what it was that connected them, and we found that they were held together by something stronger than an old grapnel. The bluff of the bows came together like walls cemented by sand and shell, and it was easy by a mere glance to perceive that they would hold together whilst the sea continued tranquil. Betwixt their heels was a hollow which the round of the whale nicely filled ; and there they all three lay, very slowly and solemnly rolling upon the swell in as deep a silence as ever they had risen from.

We hung upon our oars speculating awhile, and then fell to talking ourselves into extravagant notions. Fallows said that if she had been a privateer she might have money in her, or some purchase anyway worth coming at. I was not for ridiculing the fancy, and Jackson gazed at the craft with a yearning eye.

" Let's get aboard," says he.

" Very well," says I, and we agreed that Fallows should keep in the boat ready to pick us up, if the hulk should go down suddenly under us. We easily got aboard. From the gunwale of our boat we could place our hands upon the level of the deck, where the bulwarks were gone, and the shells were like steps to our feet. There was nothing much to be seen, however ; the decks were coated with shells as the sides were, and they went flush from the taffrail to the eyes with never a break, everything being clean gone, saving the line of the hatches, which showed in slightly raised squares under the crust of shells that lay everywhere like armour.

" Lord ! " cried Jackson, " what would I give for a chopper or pick-axe to smash open that there hatch, so as to get inside of her."

"Inside of her?" says I; "why, she'll be full of water!"

"That's to be proved, Mr. Small," says he.

We walked forward into the bows, and clearly made out the shape of a grapnel thick with shells, with its claws upon the bulwark rail of the half-ship alongside, and there was a line stretched between, belayed to what might have been a kevel on a stanchion of the craft we were in. This rope was as lovely as a piece of fancy-work, with tiny shells; but on my touching it to see if it was taut, it parted as if it had been formed of smoke, and each end fell with a little rattle against the side, as though it had been a child's string of beads.

We were gaping about us, almost forgetting our distressed situation in contemplation of these astonishing objects which had risen like ghosts from the mysterious heart of the deep, when we heard Fallows calling, and on our running to the side to learn what he wanted, we saw him standing up in the boat, pointing like a madman into the southward. It was the white canvas of a vessel, clearer to us than to him, who was lower by some feet. The air was still a weak draught, but the sail was rising with a nimbleness that made us know she was bringing a breeze of wind along with her, and in half an hour's time she had risen to the black line of her bulwarks rail, disclosing the fabric of what was apparently a brig or barque, heading almost dead on her end for us.

Jackson and I at once tumbled into the boat, but we were careful to keep her close to the two craft, and the amazing platform they floated on, for they furnished out a show that was not to be missed aboard the approaching vessel, whereas the boat must make little more than a speck, though but half a mile distant.

The breeze the vessel was bringing along with her was all about us presently with a threat of weight in it. We stepped an oar, with the shirts atop, and they blew out bravely and made a good signal.

"Why, see, Mr. Small!" cries Jackson, on a sudden, "ain't she the *Hindoo Merchant*?"

I stood awhile, and then joyfully exclaimed, "Ay, 'tis the old hooker herself, thanks be to God!"

I knew her by her short foretop-gallant mast, by her chequered band, and by other signs clear to a sailor's eye, and the three of us sent up a shout of delight, for it was like stumbling upon one's very home, as it were, after having been all night lost amidst the blackness and snow of the country where one's house stands.

She came along handsomely, with foam to the hawsepipe, thanks to the freshening breeze, and her main-royal and top-gallant sail clewing up as she approached, for our signal had been seen; then drove close alongside with her top-sail aback, and in a few minutes we were aboard, shaking hands with Captain Blow, and all others who extended a fist to us, and spinning our yarn in response to the eager questions put.

"But what have you there, Mr. Small?" said Captain Blow, staring at the two craft and the whale. I explained. "Well," cries he, "call me a missionary if ever I saw such a sight as that afore! Have ye boarded the vessel?" pointing to the one that was whole.

"Yes," said I; "but there's nothing but shells to look at."

"Hatches open?" says he.

"No," says I, "they are as securely cemented with shells as if the stuff had been laid on with a trowel."

Jackson, Fallows, the boatswain, and a few of the darkeys stood near, eagerly catching what we said.

"A wonderful sight truly!" said Captain Blow, surveying the object with a face almost distorted with astonishment and admiration. "How many years will they have been asleep under water, think ye, Mr. Small?"

"All a hundred, sir," said I.

"Ay," says he. "I've seen many prints of old ships, and I'll allow that it's all a hundred, as you say, since she and the likes of she was afloat. Why," cries he with a sort of a nervous laugh, as if half ashamed of what he was about to say, "who's to tell but that there may be a chest or two of treasure stowed away down in her lazerette?"

"That very idea occurred to me, sir," says I.

"By your pardon, capt'n," here interrupted Jackson, knuckling his forehead, "but that may be a question not hard to settle if ye'll send me aboard with a few tools."

The captain looked as if he had had a mind to entertain the idea, then sent a glance to windward.

"She'll be full of water," said I.

"Ay," said the captain, turning to Jackson, "how then?"

"We can but lift a hatch and look out for ourselves, sir," answered the man.

"Right," says the captain; "but you'll have to bear a hand. Get that cask on board. Any water in it?" says he.

"Yes, sir," says I.

"Thank God for the same, then," says he.

But whilst they were manœuvring with the cask the breeze freshened in a sudden squall, and all in a minute, as it seemed, a sort of sloppy sea was set a-running. The captain looked anxious, yet still seemed willing that the boat should go to the wreck. I sent some Lascars aloft to furl the loose canvas, and whilst this was doing the wind freshened yet in another long-drawn blast that swept in a shriek betwixt our masts.

" There's nothing to be done ! " sung out the skipper ; " get that boat under the fall, Jackson ; we must hoist her up."

The darkeys lay aft to the tackles, and Jackson climbed over the rail with a countenance sour and mutinous with disappointment. He had scarcely sprung on to the deck when we heard a loud crash like the report of a small piece of ordnance, and, looking towards the hulks, I was just in time to see them sliding off the back of the whale, one on either side of the greasy, black surface. They vanished in a breath, and the dead carcass, relieved of their weight, seemed to spring, as though it were alive, some ten or twelve feet out of the seething and simmering surface which had been frothed up by the descent of the vessels ; the next moment it turned over and gave us a view of its whole length—a sixty- to seventy-foot whale, if the carcass was an inch, with here and there the black scythe-like dorsal fin of a shark sailing round it.

Jackson hooked a quid out of his mouth and sent it overboard. His face of mutiny left him, and was replaced by an expression of gratitude. Five minutes later the old *Hindoo Merchant* was thrusting through it with her nose heading for the river Hoogly, and the darkeys tying a single reef in the foretop-sail.

FLORA ANNIE STEEL

1847–1929

IN THE PERMANENT WAY

I HEARD this story in a rail-trolly on the Pind-Dadur line, so I always think of it with a running accompaniment—a rhythmic whir of wheels in which, despite its steadiness, you feel the propelling impulse of the unseen coolies behind, then the swift skimming as they set their feet on the trolly for the brief rest which merges at the first hint of lessened speed into the old racing measure. Whir and slide, racing and resting !—while the wheels spin like bobbins and the brick rubble in the permanent way slips under your feet giddily, until you could almost fancy yourself sitting on a stationary engine, engaged in winding up an endless red ribbon—a ribbon edged, as if with tinsel, by steel rails stretching away in ever narrowing lines to the level horizon, stretching straight as a die across a sandy desert, rippled and waved by wrinkled sand-hills into the semblance of a sandy sea.

And that, from its size, must be a seventh wave. I was just thinking this when the buzz of the brake jarred me through to the marrow of my bones.

" What's up ? A train ? " I asked of my companion who was giving me a lift across his section of the desert.

" No ! " he replied laconically. " Now, then ! hurry up, men."

Nothing in the wide world comes to pieces in the hand like a trolly. It was dismembered and off the line in a moment, only, however, much to my surprise, to be replaced upon the rails some half a dozen yards farther along them. I was opening my lips for one question when something I saw at my feet among the brick rubble made me change it for another.

" Hullo ! what the dickens is that ? "

To the carnal eye it was two small squares of smooth stucco, the one with an oval black stone set in it perpendicularly, the other with a round purplish one—curiously ringed with darker circles—set in it horizontally. On the stucco of one were a few dried *tulsi*[1] leaves and grains of rice ; on the other suspicious-looking splashes of dark red.

[1] Marjoram.

" What's what ? " echoed my friend, climbing up to his seat again.

" Why, man, that thing !—that thing in the permanent way," I replied, nettled at his manner.

He gave an odd little laugh, just audible above the first whir of the wheels as we started again.

" That's about it. In the permanent way—considerably." He paused, and I thought he was going to relapse into the silence for which he was famous ; but he suddenly seemed to change his mind.

" Look here," he said, " it's a fifteen-mile run to the first curve, and no trains due, so if you like I'll tell you why we left the track."

And he did.

. . . .

When they were aligning this section I was put on to it—preliminary survey work under an R.E. man who wore boiled shirts in the wilderness, and was great on " Departmental Discipline." He is in Simla now, of course. Well, we were driving a straight line through the whole solar system and planting it out with little red flags, when one afternoon, just behind that big wave of a sand-hill, we came upon something in the way. It was a man. For further description I should say it was a thin man. There is nothing more to be said. He may have been old, he may have been young, he may have been tall, he may have been short, he may have been halt and maimed, he may have been blind, deaf, or dumb, or any or all of these. The only thing I know for certain is that he was thin. The *kalassies* said he was some kind of a Hindu saint, and they fell at his feet promptly. I shall never forget the R.E.'s face as he stood trying to classify the creature according to Wilson's *Hindu Sects*, or his indignation at the *kalassies'* ignorant worship of a man who, for all they knew, might be a follower of *Shiva*, while they were bound to *Vishnu*, or *vice versa*. He was very learned over the *Vaishnavas*, and the *Saivas* ; and all the time that bronze image with its hands on its knees squatted in the sand staring into space perfectly unmoved. Perhaps the man saw us, perhaps he didn't. I don't know ; as I said before, he was thin.

So after a time we stuck a little red flag in the ground close to the small of his back, and went on our way rejoicing until we came to our camp, a mile farther on. It doesn't look like it, but there is a brackish well and a sort of a village away there to the right, and of course we always took advantage of water when we could.

It must have been a week later, just as we came to the edge of the sand-hills, and could see a landmark or two, that I noticed the R.E. come up from his prismatic compass looking rather pale. Then he fussed over to me at the plane table.

" We're out," he said ; " there is a want of Departmental Discipline in this party, and we are out." I forget how many fractions he said, but some infinitesimal curve would have been required to bring us plumb on the next station, and as that would have ruined the R.E.'s professional reputation, we harked back to rectify the error. We found the bronze image still sitting on the sand with its hands on its knees; but apparently it had shifted its position some three feet or so to the right, for the flag was fully that distance to the left of it. That night the R.E. came to my tent with his hands full of maps and his mind of suspicions.

"It seems incredible," he said, "but I am almost convinced that *byragi* or *jogi*, or *gosain* or *sunyasi*, whichever he may be, has had the unparalleled effrontery to move my flag. I can't be sure, but if I were, I would have him arrested on the spot."

I suggested he was that already; but it is sometimes difficult to make an R.E. see a Cooper's Hill joke, especially when he is your superior officer. So we did that bit over again. As it happened, my chief was laid up with sun fever when we came to the bronze image and I had charge of the party. I don't know why, exactly, but it seemed to me rough on the thin man to stick a red flag at the small of his back, as a threat that we meant to annex the only atom of things earthly to which he still clung; time enough for that when the line was actually under construction. So I told the *kalassies* to let him do duty as a survey mark; for, from what I had heard, I knew that once a man of that sort fixes on a place in which to gain immortality by penance, he sticks to it till the mortality, at any rate, comes to an end. And this one, I found out from the villagers, had been there for ten years. Of course, they said he never ate, nor drank, nor moved, but that, equally of course, was absurd.

A year after this I came along again in charge of a construction party, with an overseer called Craddock, a big yellow-headed Saxon who couldn't keep off the drink, and who had in consequence been going down steadily in one department or another for years—as good a fellow as ever stepped when he was sober. Well, we came right on the thin one again, plump in the very middle of the permanent way. We dug round him and levelled up to him for some time, and then one day Craddock gave a nod at me and walked over to where that image squatted, staring into space. I can see the two now, Craddock in his navvy's dress, his blue eyes keen yet kind in the red face shaded by the dirty pith hat, and the thin man without a rag of any sort to hide his bronze anatomy.

"Look here, sonny," said Craddock, stopping over the other, "you're in the way—in the permanent way."

Then he just lifted him right up gently, as if he had been a child, and set him down about four feet to the left. It was to be a metre gauge, so that was enough for safety. There he sat after we had propped him up again with his *byraga*, or cleft stick, under the left arm, as if he were quite satisfied with the change. But next day he was in the old place. It was no use arguing with him. The only thing to be done was to move him out of the way when we wanted it. Of course when the earthwork was finished there was the plate-laying and ballasting and what not to be done, so it came to be part of the big Saxon's regular business to say in his Oxfordshire drawl:

" Sonny, yo're in the waiy—in the permanent waiy."

Craddock, it must be mentioned, was in a peculiarly sober, virtuous mood, owing, no doubt, to the desolation of the desert, in which, by the way, I found him quite a godsend as a companion, for when he was on the talk the quaintness of his ideas was infinitely amusing, and his knowledge of the natives, picked up as a loafer in many a bazaar and *serai*, was surprisingly wide, if appallingly inaccurate.

" There is something, savin' yo're presence, sir, blamed wrong in the whole blamed business," he said to me, with a mild remonstrance in his blue eyes, one evening after he had removed the obstruction to progress. " That pore feller, sir, 'e's a-meditatin' on the word *Hom—Hommi-puddenhome,*[1] it is, sir, I've bin told, an' doin' 'is little level to make the spiritooal man subdoo 'is fleshly hinstinckts. And I, Nathaniel James Craddock, so called in Holy Baptism, I do assure you, a-eatin' and a-drinkin' 'earty, catches 'im right up like a baby, and sets 'im on one side, as if I was born to it. And so I will—'an willin', too—so as to keep 'im from 'arm's way; for 'eathin or Christian, sir, 'e's an eggsample to the spiritooal part of me which, savin' your presence, sir, is most ways drink."

Poor Craddock! He went on the spree hopelessly the day after we returned to civilisation, and it was with the greatest difficulty that I succeeded in getting him a trial as driver to the material train which commenced running up and down the section. The first time I went with it on business I had an inspection carriage tacked on behind the truck-loads of coolies and ballast, so that I could not make out why on earth we let loose a danger whistle and slowed down to full stop in the very middle of the desert until I jumped down and ran forward. Even then I was only in time to see Craddock coming back to his engine with a redder face than ever.

" It's only old Meditations, sir," he said apologetically, as I climbed in beside him. " It don't take a minute; no longer nor a cow, and them's in the reg'lations. You see, sir, I wouldn't 'ave 'arm come to the pore soul afore 'is spiritooal nater 'ad the straight tip hoam. Neither would none of us, sir, coolie nor driver, sir, on

[1] *Om mi pudmi houm.* The Buddhist invocation.

the section. We all likes old *Hommipuddenhome* ; 'e sticks to it so stiddy, that's where it is."

" Do you mean to say that you always have to get out and lift him off the line ? " I asked, wondering rather at the patience required for the task.

" That's so, sir," he replied slowly, in the same apologetic tones. " It don't take no time you see, sir, that's where it is. P'r'aps you may 'ave thought, like as I did first time, that 'e'd save 'is bacon when the engine come along. Lordy ! the cold sweat broke out on me that time. I brought 'er up, sir, with the buffers at the back of 'is 'ed like them things the photographers jimmy you straight with. But 'e ain't that sort, ain't Meditations." Here Craddock asked leave to light his pipe, and in the interval I looked ahead along the narrowing red ribbon with its tinsel edge, thinking how odd it must have been to see it barred by that bronze image.

" No ! that ain't his sort," continued Craddock meditatively, " though wot 'is sort may be, sir, is not my part to say. I've arst, and arst, and arst them pundits, but there ain't one of them can really tell, sir, cos he ain't got any marks about him. You see, sir, it's by their marks, like cattle, as you tell 'em. Some says he worships bloody *Shivers*[1]—'im 'oo's wife you know, sir, they calls *Martha Davy*[2]—a Christian sort 'o name, ain't it, sir, for a 'eathin idol ?—and some says 'e worships *Wishnyou Lucksmi*,[3] an' that lot, an' *Holy*,[4] too, though, savin' your presence, sir, it ain't much holiness I see at them times, but mostly drink. It makes me feel quite 'omesick, I do assure you, sir, more as if they was humans like me, likewise."

" And which belief do you incline to ? " I asked, for the sake of prolonging the conversation.

He drew his rough hand over his corn-coloured beard, and quite a grave look came to the blue eyes. " I inclines to *Shiver*," he said decisively, " and I'll tell you why, sir. *Shiver's* bloody ; but 'e's dead on death. They calls 'im the Destroyer. 'E don't care a damn for the body ; 'e's all for the spiritooal nater, like old Meditations there. Now *Wishnyou Lucksmi* an' that lot is the Preservers. They eats an' drinks 'earty, like me. So it stands to reason, sir, don't it ? that 'e's a *Shiver*, and I'm a *Wishnyou Lucksmi*." He stood up under pretence of giving a wipe round a valve with the oily rag he held, and looked out to the horizon where the sun was setting, like a huge red signal right on the narrowing line. " So," he went on after a pause, " that's why I wouldn't 'ave 'arm come to old Meditations. 'E's a *Shiver*, I'm a *Wishnyou Lucksmi*. That's what *I* am."

[1] *Shiva.*
[2] *Mata devi.*
[3] *Vishnu Lukshmi.*
[4] *Holi*, Indian Saturnalia.

His meaning was quite clear, and I am not ashamed to say that it touched me.

"Look here," I said, "take care you don't run over that old chap some day when you are drunk, that's all."

He bent over another valve, burnishing it. "I hope to God I don't," he said, in a low voice. "That'd about finish me altogether, I expect."

We returned the next morning before daybreak; but I went on the engine, being determined to see how that bronze image looked on the permanent way when you were steaming up to it.

"You ketch sight of 'im clear this side," said Craddock, "a good two mile or more; ef you had a telescope, ten for that matter. It ain't so easy t'other side with the sun a-shining bang inter the eyes. And there ain't no big wave as a signal over there. But Lordy! there ain't no fear of my missin' old Meditations."

Certainly, none that morning. He showed clear, first against the rosy flush of dawn, afterwards like a dark stain on the red ribbon.

"I'll run up close to him to-day, sir," said Craddock, "so as you shall see wot 'e's made of."

The whistle rang shrill over the desert of sand, which lay empty of all save that red with the dark stain upon it; but the stain never moved, never stirred, though the snorting demon from the west came racing up to it full speed.

"Have a care, man! Have a care!" I shouted; but my words were almost lost in the jar of the brake put on to the utmost. Even then I could only crane round the cab with my eyes fixed on that bronze image straight ahead of us. Could we stop in time—would it move? Yes! no! yes! Slower and slower—how many turns of the fly-wheel to so many yards? I felt as if I were working the sum frantically in my head, when, with a little backward shiver, the great circle of steel stopped dead, and Craddock's voice came in cheerful triumph:

"There! didn't I tell you, sir? Ain't 'e stiddy? Ain't 'e a-subdooin' of mortality beautiful?" The next instant he was out, and as he stooped to his task he flung me back a look.

"Now, sonny, you'll 'ave to move. You're in the way—the permanent way, my dear."

That was the last I saw of him for some time, for I fell sick and went home. When I returned to work I found, much to my surprise, that Craddock was in the same appointment; in fact, he had been promoted to drive the solitary passenger train which now ran daily across the desert. He had not been on the spree once, I was told; indeed, the R.E., who was of the Methodist division of that gallant regiment, took great pride in a reformation which, he informed me, was largely due to his religious teaching combined with Departmental Discipline.

"And how is Meditations ?" I asked, when the great rough hand had shaken mine vehemently.

Craddock's face seemed to me to grow redder than ever. "'E's very well, sir, thanking you kindly. There's a native driver on the Goods now. 'E's a *Shiver-Martha-Davy* lot, so I pays 'im five rupee a month to nip out sharp with the stoker an' shovel 'is old saint to one side. I'm gettin' good pay now, you know, sir."

I told him there was no reason to apologise for the fact, and that I hoped it might long continue ; whereat he gave a sheepish kind of laugh, and said he hoped so too.

Christmas came and went uneventfully without an outbreak, and I could not refrain from congratulating Craddock on one temptation safely over.

He smiled broadly.

"Lor' bless you, sir," he said, "you didn't never think, did you, that Nathaniel James Craddock, which his name was given to 'im in Holy Baptism, I do assure you, was going to knuckle down that way to old *Hommipuddenhome* ? 'Twouldn't be fair on Christmas noways, sir, and though I don't set the store 'e does on 'is spiritooal nater, I was born and bred in a Christian country, I do assure you."

I congratulated him warmly on his sentiments, and hoped again that they would last, to which he replied as before that he hoped so too.

And then *Holi*-time came round, and, as luck would have it, the place was full of riff-raff low whites going on to look for work in a further section. I had to drive through the bazaar on my way to the railway station, and it beat anything I had ever seen in various vice. East and West were outbidding each other in iniquity, and to make matters worse, an electrical dust-storm was blowing hard. You never saw such a scene ; it was pandemonium, background and all. I thought I caught a glimpse of a corn-coloured beard and a pair of blue eyes in a wooden balcony among tinkling *sútáras* and jasmin chaplets, but I wasn't sure. However, as I was stepping into the inspection carriage, which, as usual, was the last in the train, I saw Craddock crossing the platform to his engine. His white coat was all splashed with the red dye they had been throwing at each other, *Holi* fashion, in the bazaar ; his walk, to my eyes, had a lilt in it, and finally, the neck of a black bottle showed from one pocket.

Obedient to one of those sudden impulses which come, Heaven knows why, I took my foot off the step and followed him to the engine.

"Comin' aboard, sir," he said quite collectedly. "You'd be

better be'ind to-night, for it's blowin' grit fit to make me a walkin' sandpaper inside and out." And before I could stop him the bottle was at his mouth. This decided me. Perhaps my face showed my thoughts, for as I climbed into the cab he gave an uneasy laugh. "Don't be afraid, sir; it's black as pitch, but I knows where old Meditations comes by instinck, I do assure you. One hour an' seventeen minutes from the distance signal with pressure as it oughter be. Hillo! there's the whistle and the baboo a-waving. Off we goes!"

As we flashed by a red light I looked at my watch.

"Don't you be afraid, sir," he said, again looking at his. "It's ten to ten now, and in one hour an' seventeen minutes on goes the brake. That's the ticket for *Shivers* and *Martha Davy*, though I am a *Wishnyou Lucksmi*." He paused a moment, and as he stood put his hand on a stanchion to steady himself.

"Very much of a *Wishnyou Lucksmi*," he went on, with a shake of the head. "I've 'ad a drop too much, and I know it; but it ain't fair on a fellar like me, 'aving so many names to them, when they're all the same—a eatin' an' drinkin' lot like me. There's *Christen*[1]—you'd 'ave thought he'd 'ave been a decent chap by 'is name, but 'e went on orful with them *Gopis*—that's Hindu for milk-maids, sir. And *Harry*[2]—well, he wasn't no better than some other Harrys I've heard on. And *Canyer*,[3] I expect he could just about. To say nothin' of *Gopi-naughty*[4]; and naughty he were, as no doubt you've heard tell, sir. There's too many on them for a pore fellar who don't set store by 'is spiritooal nater; especially when they mixes themselves up with Angcore whisky an' ginger ale."

His blue eyes had a far-away look in them, and his words were fast losing independence, but I understood what he meant perfectly. In that brief glimpse of the big bazaar I had seen the rows of Western bottles standing cheek by jowl with the bowls of *dolee* dye, the sour curds and sweetmeats of *Holi*-tide.

"You had better sit down, Craddock," I said severely, for I saw that the fresh air was having its usual effect. "Perhaps if you sleep a bit you'll be more fit for work. I'll look out and wake you when you're wanted."

He gave a silly laugh, let go the stanchion, and drew out his watch.

"Don't you be afraid, sir! One hour and seventeen minutes from the distance signal. I'll keep 'im out o' 'arm's way, an' willing, to the end of the chapter."

He gave a lurch forward to the seat, stumbled, and the watch dropped from his hand. For a moment I thought he might go overboard, and I clutched at him frantically; but with another

[1] *Kristna*. [2] *Hari*. [3] *Kaniya*.
[4] *Copi-nath*. These are all names of *Vishnu* in his various avatars.

lurch and an indistinct admonition to me not to be afraid, he sank into the corner of the bench and was asleep in a second. Then I stooped to pick up the watch, and, rather to my surprise, found it uninjured and still going.

Craddock's words, " ten minutes to ten," recurred to me. Then it would be twenty-seven minutes past eleven before he was wanted. I sat down to wait, bidding the native stoker keep up the fire as usual. The wind was simply shrieking round us, and the sand drifted thick on Craddock's still, upturned face. More than once I wiped it off, feeling he might suffocate. It was the noisiest and at the same time the most silent journey I ever undertook. Pandemonium, with seventy times seven of its devils, let loose outside the cab; inside, Craddock asleep, or dead—he might have been the latter from his stillness. It became oppressive after a time, as I remembered that other still figure, miles down the track, which was so strangely bound to this one beside me. The minutes seemed hours, and I felt a distinct relief when the watch, which I had held in my hand most of the time, told me it was seventeen minutes past eleven. Only ten minutes before the brake should be put on; and Craddock would require all that time to get his senses about him.

I might as well have tried to awaken a corpse, and it was three minutes to the twenty-seven when I gave up the idea as hopeless. Not that it mattered, since I could drive an engine as well as he; still the sense of responsibility weighed heavily upon me. My hand on the brake valve trembled visibly as I stood watching the minute-hand of the watch. Thirty seconds before the time I put the brake on hard, determined to be on the safe side. And then when I had taken this precaution a perfectly unreasoning anxiety seized on me. I stepped on to the footboard and craned forward into the darkness which, even without the wind and the driving dust, was blinding. The lights in front shot slantways, showing an angle of red ballast, barred by gleaming steel; beyond that a formless void of sand. But the centre of the permanent way, where that figure would be sitting, was dark as death itself.

What a fool I was, when the great circle of the fly-wheel was slackening, slackening, every second. And yet the fear grew lest I should have been too late, lest I should have made some mistake. To appease my own folly I drew out my watch in confirmation of the time. Great God! a difference of two minutes!—two whole minutes! Yet the watches had been the same at the distance signal?—the fall, of course! the fall!

I seemed unable to do anything but watch that slackening wheel, even though I became conscious of a hand on my shoulder, of some one standing beside me on the footboard. No! not standing—swaying, lurching.

" Don't ! " I cried. " Don't ! it's madness ! " But that some one was out in the darkness. Then I saw a big white figure dash across the angle of light with outspread arms.

" Now then, sonny ! yo're in the way—the permanent way."

. . . .

The inspector paused, and I seemed to come back to the sliding whir of the trolly wheels. In the distance a semaphore was dropping its red arm, and a pointsman, like a speck on the ribbon, was at work shunting us into a siding.

" Well ? " I asked.

" There isn't anything more. When a whole train goes over two men locked in each other's arms it is hard—hard to tell—well, which is *Shivers Martha Davy*, and which is *Wishnyou Lucksmi*. It was right out in the desert in the hot weather, no parsons or people to object ; so I buried them there in the permanent way."

" And those are tombstones, I suppose ? "

He laughed. " No ; altars. The native employés put them up to their saint. The oval black upright stone is *Shiva*, the Destroyer's *lingam* ; those splashes are blood. The flat one, decorated with flowers, is the *salagrama*,[1] sacred to *Vishnu*, the Preserver. You see nobody really knew whether old Meditations was a *Saiva* or a *Vaishnava*, so I suggested this arrangement as the men were making a sectarian quarrel out of the question." He paused again and added :

" You see it does for both of them."

The jar of the points prevented me from replying.

[1] A fossil ammonite.

CHARLES GRANT ALLEN

1848–1899

THE REVEREND JOHN CREEDY

I

"ON Sunday next, the 14th inst., the Reverend John Creedy, B.A., of Magdalen College, Oxford, will preach in Walton Magna Church, on behalf of the Gold Coast Mission." Not a very startling announcement that, and yet, simple as it looks, it stirred Ethel Berry's soul to its inmost depths. For Ethel had been brought up by her Aunt Emily to look upon foreign missions as the one thing on earth worth living for and thinking about, and the Reverend John Creedy, B.A., had a missionary history of his own, strange enough even in these strange days of queer juxtapositions between utter savagery and advanced civilisation.

"Only think," she said to her aunt, as they read the placard on the schoolhouse-board, "he's a real African negro, the vicar says, taken from a slaver on the Gold Coast when he was a child, and brought to England to be educated. He's been to Oxford and got a degree; and now he's going out again to Africa to convert his own people. And he's coming down to the vicar's to stay on Wednesday."

"It's my belief," said old Uncle James, Aunt Emily's brother, the superannuated skipper, "that he'd much better stop in England for ever. I've been a good bit on the Coast myself in my time, after palm oil and such, and my opinion is that a nigger's a nigger anywhere, but he's a sight less of a nigger in England than out yonder in Africa. Take him to England, and you make a gentleman of him: send him home again, and the nigger comes out at once in spite of you."

"Oh, James," Aunt Emily put in, "how can you talk such unchristianlike talk, setting yourself up against missions, when we know that all the nations of the earth are made of one blood?"

"I've always lived a Christian life myself, Emily," answered Uncle James, "though I have cruised a good bit on the Coast, too, which is against it, certainly ; but I take it a nigger's a nigger whatever you do with him. The Ethiopian cannot change his skin, the Scripture says, nor the leopard his spots, and a nigger he'll be to the end of his days ; you mark my words, Emily."

On Wednesday, in due course, the Reverend John Creedy arrived at the vicarage, and much curiosity there was throughout the village of Walton Magna that week to see this curious new thing, a coal-black parson. Next day, Thursday, an almost equally unusual event occurred to Ethel Berry, for, to her great surprise, she got a little note in the morning inviting her up to a tennis party at the vicarage the same afternoon. Now, though the vicar called on Aunt Emily often enough, and accepted her help readily for school feasts and other village festivities of the milder sort, the Berrys were hardly up to that level of society which is commonly invited to the parson's lawn-tennis parties. And the reason why Ethel was asked on this particular Thursday must be traced to a certain pious conspiracy between the vicar and the secretary of the Gold Coast Evangelistic Society. When those two eminent missionary advocates had met a fortnight before at Exeter Hall, the secretary had represented to the vicar the desirability of young John Creedy's taking to himself an English wife before his departure. "It will steady him, and keep him right on the Coast," he said, "and it will give him importance in the eyes of the natives as well." Whereto the vicar responded that he knew exactly the right girl to suit the place in his own parish, and that by a providential conjunction she already took a deep interest in foreign missions. So these two good men conspired in all innocence of heart to sell poor Ethel into African slavery ; and the vicar had asked John Creedy down to Walton Magna on purpose to meet her.

That afternoon Ethel put on her pretty sateen and her witching little white hat, with two natural dog-roses pinned on one side, and went pleased and proud up to the vicarage. The Reverend John Creedy was there, not in full clerical costume, but arrayed in tennis flannels, with only a loose white tie beneath his flap collar to mark his newly acquired spiritual dignity. He was a comely looking negro enough, full-blooded, but not too broad-faced nor painfully African in type ; and when he was playing tennis his athletic quick limbs and his really handsome build took away greatly from the general impression of an inferior race. His voice was of the ordinary Oxford type, open, pleasant, and refined, with a certain easy-going air of natural gentility, hardly marred by just the faintest tinge of the thick negro blur in the broad vowels. When he talked to Ethel—and the vicar's wife took good care that they should talk together a great deal—his conversation was of a sort that she seldom heard at Walton Magna. It was full of London and Oxford, of boat-races at Iffley and cricket-matches at Lord's ; of people and books whose very names Ethel had never heard—one of them was a Mr. Mill, she thought, and another a Mr. Aristotle—but which she felt vaguely to be one step higher in the intellectual scale than her own level. Then his friends, to whom he alluded casually, not like one who airs his grand acquaintances, were such very distinguished people. There was a real live lord, apparently, at the same college with him, and he spoke of a young baronet whose estate lay close by, as plain " Harrington of Christchurch," without any " Sir Arthur "—a thing which even the vicar himself would hardly have ventured to do. She knew that he was learned, too ; as a matter of fact he had taken a fair second class in Greats at Oxford ; and he could talk delightfully of poetry and novels. To say the truth, John Creedy, in spite of his black face, dazzled poor Ethel, for he was more of a scholar and a gentleman than anybody with whom she had ever before had the chance of conversing on equal terms.

When Ethel turned the course of talk to Africa, the young parson was equally eloquent and fascinating. He didn't care about leaving England for many reasons, but he would be glad to do something for his poor brethren. He was enthusiastic about missions ; that was a common interest ; and he was so anxious to raise and improve the condition of his fellow-negroes that Ethel couldn't help feeling what a noble thing it was of him thus to sacrifice himself, cultivated gentleman as he was, in an African jungle, for his heathen countrymen. Altogether, she went home from the tennis-court that afternoon thoroughly overcome by John Creedy's personality. She didn't for a moment think of falling in love with him—a certain indescribable race-instinct set up an impassable barrier against that—but she admired him and was interested in him in a way that she had never yet felt with any other man.

As for John Creedy, he was naturally charmed with Ethel. In the first place, he would have been charmed with any English girl who took so much interest in himself and his plans, for, like all negroes, he was frankly egotistical, and delighted to find a white lady who seemed to treat him as a superior being. But in the second place, Ethel was really a charming, simple English village lassie, with sweet little manners and a delicious blush, who might have impressed a far less susceptible man than the young negro parson. So, whatever Ethel felt, John Creedy felt himself truly in love. And after all, John Creedy was in all essentials an educated English gentleman, with the same chivalrous feelings towards a pretty and attractive girl that every English gentleman ought to have.

On Sunday morning Aunt Emily and Ethel went to the parish church, and the Reverend John Creedy preached the expected sermon. It was almost his first—sounded like a trial trip, Uncle

James muttered—but it was undoubtedly what connoisseurs describe as an admirable discourse. John Creedy was free from any tinge of nervousness—negroes never know what that word means—and he spoke fervently, eloquently, and with much power of manner about the necessity for a Gold Coast Mission. Perhaps there was really nothing very original or striking in what he said, but his way of saying it was impressive and vigorous. The negro, like many other lower races, has the faculty of speech largely developed, and John Creedy had been noted as one of the readiest and most fluent talkers at the Oxford Union debates. When he enlarged upon the need for workers, the need for help, the need for succour and sympathy in the great task of evangelisation, Aunt Emily and Ethel forgot his black hands, stretched out open-palmed towards the people, and felt only their hearts stirred within them by the eloquence and enthusiasm of that appealing gesture.

The end of it all was, that instead of a week John Creedy stopped for two months at Walton Magna, and during all that time he saw a great deal of Ethel. Before the end of the first fortnight he walked out one afternoon along the river-bank with her, and talked earnestly of his expected mission.

" Miss Berry," he said, as they sat to rest awhile on the parapet of the little bridge by the weeping willows, " I don't mind going to Africa, but I can't bear going all alone. I am to have a station entirely by myself up the Ancobra river, where I shall see no other Christian face from year's end to year's end. I wish I could have had some one to accompany me."

" You will be very lonely," Ethel answered. " I wish indeed you could have some companionship."

" Do you really ? " John Creedy went on. " It is not good for man to live alone ; he wants a helpmate. Oh, Miss Ethel, may I venture to hope that perhaps, if I can try to deserve you, you will be mine ? "

Ethel started in dismay. Mr. Creedy had been very attentive, very kind, and she had liked to hear him talk and had encouraged his coming, but she was hardly prepared for this. The nameless something in our blood recoiled at it. The proposal stunned her, and she said nothing but " Oh, Mr. Creedy, how *can* you say such a thing ? "

John Creedy saw the shadow on her face, the unintentional dilatation of her delicate nostrils, the faint puckering at the corner of her lips, and knew with a negro's quick instinct of face-reading what it all meant. " Oh, Miss Ethel," he said, with a touch of genuine bitterness in his tone, " don't you, too, despise us. I won't ask you for any answer now ; I don't want an answer. But I want you to think it over. Do think it over, and consider whether you can ever love me. I won't press the matter on you. I won't insult you by importunity, but I will tell you just this once, and once for all, what I feel. I love you, and I shall always love you, whatever you answer me now. I know it would cost you a wrench to take me, a greater wrench than to take the least and the unworthiest of your own people. But if you can only get over that first wrench, I can promise earnestly and faithfully to love you as well as ever woman yet was loved. Don't say anything now," he went on, as he saw she was going to open her mouth again : " wait and think it over ; pray it over ; and if you can't see your way straight before you when I ask you this day fortnight ' yes or no,' answer me ' no,' and I give you my word of honour as a gentleman I will never speak to you of the matter again. But I shall carry your picture written on my heart to my grave."

And Ethel knew that he was speaking from his very soul.

When she went home, she took Aunt Emily up into her little bedroom, over the porch where the dog-roses grew, and told her all about it. Aunt Emily cried and sobbed as if her heart would break, but she saw only one answer from the first. " It is a gate opened to you, my darling," she said : " I shall break my heart over it, Ethel, but it is a gate opened." And though she felt that all the light would be gone out of her life if Ethel went, she worked with her might from that moment forth to induce Ethel to marry John Creedy and go to Africa. Poor soul, she acted faithfully up to her lights.

As for Uncle James, he looked at the matter very differently. " Her instinct is against it," he said stoutly, " and our instincts wasn't put in our hearts for nothing. They're meant to be a guide and a light to us in these dark questions. No white girl ought to marry a black man, even if he *is* a parson. It ain't natural : our instinct is against it. A white man may marry a black woman if he likes : I don't say anything against him, though I don't say I'd do it myself, not for any money. But a white woman to marry a black man, why, it makes our blood rise, you know, 'specially if you've happened to have cruised worth speaking of along the Coast."

But the vicar and the vicar's wife were charmed with the prospect of success, and spoke seriously to Ethel about it. It was a call, they thought, and Ethel oughtn't to disregard it. They had argued themselves out of those wholesome race instincts that Uncle James so rightly valued, and they were eager to argue Ethel out of them too. What could the poor girl do ? Her aunt and the vicar on the one hand, and John Creedy on the other, were too much between them for her native feelings. At the end of the fortnight John Creedy asked her his simple question " yes or no," and half against her will she answered " yes." John Creedy took her hand delicately in his and fervidly kissed the very tips of her fingers ; something within him told him he must not kiss her lips. She started at the kiss, but she said nothing. John Creedy noticed the start, and said within himself, "I shall so love and cherish her that I will make her love me in spite of my black skin." For with all the faults of his negro nature, John Creedy was at heart an earnest and affectionate man, after his kind.

And Ethel really did, to some extent, love him already. It was such a strange mixture of feeling. From one point of view he was a gentleman by position, a clergyman, a man of learning and of piety; and from this point of view Ethel was not only satisfied, but even proud of him. For the rest, she took him as some good Catholics take the veil, from a sense of the call. And so, before the two months were out, Ethel Berry had married John Creedy, and both started together at once for Southampton, on their way to Axim. Aunt Emily cried, and hoped they might be blessed in their new work, but Uncle James never lost his misgivings about the effect of Africa upon a born African. "Instincts is a great thing," he said, with a shake of his head, as he saw the West Coast mail steam slowly down Southampton Water, "and when he gets among his own people his instincts will surely get the better of him, as safe as my name is James Berry."

II

The little mission bungalow at Butabué, a wooden shed neatly thatched with fan palms, had been built and garnished by the native catechist from Axim and his wife before the arrival of the missionaries, so that Ethel found a habitable dwelling ready for her at the end of her long boat journey up the rapid stream of the Ancobra. There the strangely matched pair settled down quietly enough to their work of teaching and catechising, for the mission had already been started by the native evangelist, and many of the people were fairly ready to hear and accept the new religion. For the first ten or twelve months Ethel's letters home were full of praise and love for dear John. Now that she had come to know him well, she wondered she had ever feared to marry him. No husband was ever so tender, so gentle, so considerate. He nursed her in all her little ailments like a woman; she leaned on him as a wife leans on the strong arm of her husband. And then he was so clever, so wise, so learned. Her only grief was that she feared she was not and would never be good enough for him. Yet it was well for her that they were living so entirely away from all white society at Butabué, for there she had nobody with whom to contrast John but the half-clad savages around them. Judged by the light of that startling contrast, good John Creedy, with his cultivated ways and gentle manners, seemed like an Englishman indeed.

John Creedy, for his part, thought no less well of his Ethel. He was tenderly respectful to her ; more distant, perhaps, than is usual between husband and wife, even in the first months of marriage, but that was due to his innate delicacy of feeling, which made him half unconsciously recognise the depth of the gulf that still divided them. He cherished her like some saintly thing, too sacred for the common world. Yet Ethel was his helper in all his work, so cheerful under the necessary privations of their life, so ready to put up with bananas and cassava balls, so apt at kneading plantain paste, so willing to learn from the negro women all the mysteries of mixing agadey, cankey, and koko pudding. No tropical heat seemed to put her out of temper ; even the horrible country fever itself she bore with such gentle resignation, John Creedy felt in his heart of hearts that he would willingly give up his life for her, and that it would be but a small sacrifice for so sweet a creature.

One day, shortly after their arrival at Butabué, John Creedy began talking in English to the catechist about the best way of setting to work to learn the native language. He had left the country when he was nine years old, he said, and had forgotten all about it. The catechist answered him quickly in a Fantee phrase. John Creedy looked amazed and started.

" What does he say ? " asked Ethel.

" He says that I shall soon learn if only I listen ; but the curious thing is, Ethie, that I understand him."

" It has come back to you, John, that's all. You are so quick at languages, and now you hear it again you remember it."

" Perhaps so," said the missionary slowly, " but I have never recalled a word of it for all these years. I wonder if it will all come back to me."

" Of course it will, dear," said Ethel ; " you know, things come to you so easily in that way. You almost learned Portuguese while we were coming out from hearing those Benguela people."

And so it did come back, sure enough. Before John Creedy had been six weeks at Butabué he could talk Fantee as fluently as any of the natives around him. After all, he was nine years old when he was taken to England, and it was no great wonder that he should recollect the language he had heard in his childhood till that age. Still, he himself noticed rather uneasily that every phrase and word, down to the very heathen charms and prayers of his infancy, came back to him now with startling vividness and without an effort.

Four months after their arrival John saw one day a tall and ugly negro woman, in the scanty native dress, standing near the rude market-place where the Butabué butchers killed and sold their reeking goat-meat. Ethel saw him start again, and with a terrible foreboding in her heart she could not help asking him why he started. " I can't tell you, Ethie," he said piteously ; " for heaven's sake don't press me. I want to spare you." But Ethel would hear. "Is it your mother, John ?" she asked hoarsely.

"No, thank heaven, not my mother, Ethie," he answered her, with something like pallor on his dark cheek, "not my mother ; but I remember the woman."

"A relative ?"

"Oh, Ethie, don't press me. Yes, my mother's sister. I remember her years ago. Let us say no more about it." And Ethel, looking at that gaunt and squalid savage woman, shuddered in her heart and said no more.

Slowly, as time went on, however, Ethel began to notice a strange shade of change coming over John's ideas and remarks about the negroes. At first he had been shocked and distressed at their heathendom and savagery, but the more he saw of it the more he seemed to find it natural enough in their position, and even in a sort of way to sympathise with it or apologise for it. One morning, a month or two later, he spoke to her voluntarily of his father. He had never done so in England. "I can remember," he said, "he was a chief, a great chief. He had many wives, and my mother was one. He was beaten in war by Kola, and I was taken prisoner. But he had a fine palace at Kwantah, and many fan-bearers." Ethel observed with a faint terror that he seemed to speak with pride and complacency of his father's chieftaincy. She shuddered again and wondered. Was the West African instinct getting the upper hand in him over the Christian gentleman ?

When the dries were over, and the koko-harvest gathered, the negroes held a grand feast. John had preached in the open air to some of the market people in the morning, and in the evening he was sitting in the hut with Ethel, waiting till the catechist and his wife should come in to prayers, for they carried out their accustomed ceremony decorously, even there, every night and morning. Suddenly they heard the din of savage music out of doors, and the noise of a great crowd laughing and shouting down the street. John listened, and listened with deepening attention. "Don't you hear it, Ethie ?" he cried. "It's the tom-toms. I know what it means. It's the harvest battle-feast !"

"How hideous !" said Ethel, shrinking back.

"Don't be afraid, dearest," John said, smiling at her. "It means no harm. It's only the people amusing themselves." And he began to keep time to the tom-toms rapidly with the palms of his hands.

The din drew nearer, and John grew more evidently excited at every step. "Don't you hear, Ethie ?" he said again. "It's the Salonga. What inspiriting music ! It's like a drum and fife band ; it's like the bagpipes ; it's like a military march. By jove, it compels one to dance !" And he got up as he spoke, in English clerical dress (for he wore clerical dress even at Butabué), and began capering in a sort of hornpipe round the tiny room.

" Oh, John, don't," cried Ethel. " Suppose the catechist were to come in ! "

But John's blood was up. " Look here," he said excitedly, " it goes like this. Here you hold your matchlock out ; here you fire ; here you charge with cutlasses ; here you hack them down before you ; here you hold up your enemy's head in your hands, and here you kick it off among the women. Oh, it's grand ! " There was a terrible light in his black eyes as he spoke, and a terrible trembling in his clenched black hands.

" John," cried Ethel, in an agony of horror, " it isn't Christian, it isn't human, it isn't worthy of you. I can never, never love you if you do such a thing again."

In a moment John's face changed and his hand fell as if she had stabbed him. " Ethie," he said in a low voice, creeping back to her liked a whipped spaniel, " Ethie, my darling, my own soul, my beloved ; what *have* I done ! Oh, heavens, I will never listen to the accursed thing again. Oh, Ethie, for heaven's sake, for mercy's sake, forgive me ! "

Ethel laid her hand, trembling, on his head. John sank upon his knees before her, and bowed himself down with his head between his arms, like one staggered and penitent. Ethel lifted him gently, and at that moment the catechist and his wife came in. John stood up firmly, took down his Bible and Prayer-book, and read through evening prayer at once in his usual impressive tone. In one moment he had changed back again from the Fantee savage to the decorous Oxford clergyman.

It was only a week later that Ethel, hunting about in the little storeroom, happened to notice a stout wooden box carefully covered up. She opened the lid with some difficulty, for it was fastened down with a native lock, and to her horror she found inside it a surreptitious keg of raw negro rum. She took the keg out, put it conspicuously in the midst of the storeroom, and said nothing. That night she heard John in the jungle behind the yard, and looking out, she saw dimly that he was hacking the keg to pieces vehemently with an axe. After that he was even kinder and tenderer to her than usual for the next week, but Ethel vaguely remembered that once or twice before he had seemed a little odd in his manner, and that it was on those days that she had seen gleams of the savage nature peeping through. Perhaps, she thought, with a shiver, his civilisation was only a veneer, and a glass of raw rum or so was enough to wash it off.

Twelve months after their first arrival, Ethel came home very feverish one evening from her girls' school, and found John gone from the hut. Searching about in the room for the quinine bottle, she came once more upon a rum-keg, and this time it was empty. A nameless terror drove her into the little bedroom. There, on the bed, torn into a hundred shreds, lay John Creedy's black coat and European clothing. The room whirled around her, and though she had never heard of such a thing before, the terrible truth flashed across her bewildered mind like a hideous dream. She went out, alone, at night, as she had never done before since she came to Africa, into the broad lane between the huts which constituted the chief street of Butabué. So far away from home, so utterly solitary among all those black faces, so sick at heart with that burning and devouring horror! She reeled and staggered down the street, not knowing how or where she went, till at the end, beneath the two tall date-palms, she saw lights flashing and heard the noise of shouts and laughter. A group of natives, men and women together, were dancing and howling round a dancing and howling negro. The central figure was dressed in the native fashion, with arms and legs bare, and he was shouting a loud song at the top of his voice in the Fantee language, while he shook a tom-tom. There was a huskiness as of drink in his throat, and his steps were unsteady and doubtful. Great heavens! could that reeling, shrieking black savage be John Creedy?

Yes, instinct had gained the day over civilisation; the savage in John Creedy had broken out; he had torn up his English clothes and, in West African parlance, "had gone Fantee." Ethel gazed at him, white with horror—stood still and gazed, and never cried nor fainted, nor said a word. The crowd of negroes divided to right and left, and John Creedy saw his wife standing there like a marble figure. With one awful cry he came to himself again, and rushed to her side. She did not repel him, as he expected; she did not speak; she was mute and cold like a corpse, not like a living woman. He took her up in his strong arms, laid her head on his shoulder, and carried her home through the long line of thatched huts, erect and steady as when he first walked up the aisle of Walton Magna church. Then he laid her down gently on the bed, and called the wife of the catechist. "She has the fever," he said in Fantee. "Sit by her."

The catechist's wife looked at her, and said, "Yes; the yellow fever."

And so she had. Even before she saw John the fever had been upon her, and that awful revelation had brought it out suddenly in full force. She lay unconscious upon the bed, her eyes open, staring ghastlily, but not a trace of colour in her cheek nor a sign of life upon her face.

John Creedy wrote a few words on a piece of paper, which he folded in his hand, gave a few directions in Fantee to the woman at the bedside, and then hurried out like one on fire into the darkness outside.

III

It was thirty miles through the jungle, by a native trackway, to the nearest mission station at Effuenta. There were two Methodist missionaries stationed there, John Creedy knew, for he had gone round by boat more than once to see them. When he first came to Africa he could no more have found his way across the neck of the river-fork by that tangled jungle-track than he could have flown bodily over the top of the cocoa palms; but now, half naked, barefooted, and inspired with an overpowering emotion, he threaded his path through the darkness among the creepers and lianas of the forest in true African fashion. Stooping here, creeping on all-fours there, running in the open at full speed anon, he never once stopped to draw breath till he had covered the whole thirty miles, and knocked in the early dawn at the door of the mission hut at Effuenta.

One of the missionaries opened the barrel door cautiously. "What do you want?" he asked in Fantee of the bare-legged savage, who stood crouching by the threshold.

"I bring a message from Missionary John Creedy," the bare-legged savage answered, also in Fantee. "He wants European clothes."

"Has he sent a letter?" asked the missionary.

John Creedy took the folded piece of paper from his palm. The missionary read it. It told him in a few words how the Butabué people had pillaged John's hut at night and stolen his clothing, and how he could not go outside his door till he got some European dress again.

"This is strange," said the missionary. "Brother Felton died three days ago of the fever. You can take his clothes to Brother Creedy if you will."

The bare-limbed savage nodded acquiescence. The missionary looked hard at him, and fancied he had seen his face before, but he never even for a moment suspected that he was speaking to John Creedy himself. A bundle was soon made of dead Brother Felton's clothes, and the bare-limbed man took it in his arms and prepared to run back again the whole way to Butabué.

"You have had nothing to eat," said the lonely missionary. "Won't you take something to help you on your way?"

"Give me some plantain paste," answered John Creedy. "I can eat it as I go." And when they gave it him he forgot himself for the moment, and answered, "Thank you" in English. The missionary stared, but thought it was only a single phrase that he had picked up at Butabué, and that he was anxious, negro-fashion, to air his knowledge. Back through the jungle, with the bundle in his arms, John Creedy wormed his way once more, like a snake or a tiger, never pausing or halting on the road till he found himself again in the open space outside the village of Butabué. There he stayed awhile, and behind a clump of wild ginger he opened the bundle and arrayed himself once more from head to foot in English clerical dress. That done, too proud to slink, he walked bold and erect down the main alley, and quietly entered his own hut. It was high noon, the baking high noon of Africa, as he did so.

Ethel lay unconscious still upon the bed. The negro woman crouched, half asleep after her night's watching, at the foot. John Creedy looked at his watch, which stood hard by on the little wooden table. "Sixty miles in fourteen hours," he said aloud. "Better time by a great deal than when we walked from Oxford to the White Horse eighteen months since." And then he sat down silently by Ethel's bedside.

"Has she moved her eyes ?" he asked the negress.

"Never, John Creedy," answered the woman. Till last night she had always called him "Master."

He watched the lifeless face for an hour or two. There was no change in it till about four o'clock ; then Ethel's eyes began to alter their expression. He saw the dilated pupils contract a little, and knew that consciousness was gradually returning.

In a moment more she looked round at him and gave a little cry. "John," she exclaimed, with a sort of awakening hopefulness in her voice, "where on earth did you get those clothes ?"

"These clothes ?" he answered softly. "Why, you must be wandering in your mind, Ethie dearest, to ask such a question now. At Standen's, in the High at Oxford, my darling." And he passed his black hand gently across her loose hair.

Ethel gave a great cry of joy. "Then it was a dream, a horrid dream, John, or a terrible mistake ? Oh, John, say it was a dream !"

John drew his hand across his forehead slowly. "Ethie darling," he said, "you are wandering, I'm afraid. You have a bad fever. I don't know what you mean."

"Then you didn't tear them up, and wear a Fantee dress, and dance with a tom-tom down the street ? Oh, John !"

"Oh, Ethel ! No. What a terrible delirium you must have had !"

"It is all well," she said. "I don't mind if I die now." And she sank back exhausted into a sort of feverish sleep.

"John Creedy," said the black catechist's wife solemnly in Fantee, "you will have to answer for that lie to a dying woman with your soul !"

"*My* soul !" cried John Creedy passionately, smiting both breasts with his clenched fists. "*My* soul ! Do you think, you negro wench, I wouldn't give *my* poor, miserable, black soul to eternal torments a thousand times over, if only I could give her little white heart one moment's forgetfulness before she dies ? "

For five days longer Ethel lingered in the burning fever, sometimes conscious for a minute or two, but for the most part delirious or drowsy all the time. She never said another word to John about her terrible dream, and John never said another word to her. But he sat by her side and tended her like a woman, doing everything that was possible for her in the bare little hut, and devouring his full heart with a horrible gnawing remorse too deep for pen or tongue to probe and fathom. For civilisation with John Creedy was really at bottom far more than a mere veneer ; though the savage instincts might break out with him now and again, such outbursts no more affected his adult and acquired nature than a single bump supper or wine party at college affects the nature of many a gentle-minded English lad. The truest John Creedy of all was the gentle, tender, English clergyman.

As he sat by her bedside sleepless and agonized, night and day for five days together, one prayer only rose to his lips time after time : " Heaven grant she may die ! " He had depth enough in the civilised side of his soul to feel that that was the only way to save her from a life-long shame. " If she gets well," he said to himself, trembling, " I will leave this accursed Africa at once. I will work my way back to England as a common sailor, and send her home by the mail with my remaining money. I will never inflict my presence upon her again, for she cannot be persuaded, if once she recovers, that she did not see me, as she did see me, a bare-limbed heathen Fantee brandishing a devilish tom-tom. But I shall get work in England—not a parson's ; that I can never be again—but clerk's work, labourer's work, navvy's work, anything ! Look at my arms : I rowed five in the Magdalen eight : I could hold a spade as well as any man. I will toil, and slave, and save, and keep her still like a lady, if I starve for it myself, but she shall never see my face again, if once she recovers. Even then it will be a living death for her, poor angel ! There is only one hope—Heaven grant she may die ! " On the fifth day she opened her eyes once. John saw that his prayer was about to be fulfilled. " John," she said feebly—" John, tell me, on your honour, it was only my delirium." And John, raising his hand to heaven, *splendide mendax*, answered in a firm voice, " I swear it." Ethel smiled and shut her eyes. It was for the last time.

Next morning, John Creedy—tearless, but parched and dry in the mouth, like one stunned and unmanned—took a pickaxe and hewed out a rude grave in the loose soil near the river. Then he fashioned a rough coffin from twisted canes with his own hands, and in it he reverently placed the sacred body. He allowed no one to help him or come near him—not even his fellow-Christians, the catechist and his wife : Ethel was too holy a thing for their African hands to touch. Next he put on his white surplice, and for the first and only time in his life he read, without a quaver in his voice, the Church of England burial service over the open grave. And when he had finished he went back to his desolate hut, and cried with a loud voice of utter despair, "The one thing that bound me to civilisation is gone. Henceforth I shall never speak another word of English. I go to my own people." So saying, he solemnly tore up his European clothes once more, bound a cotton loin-cloth round his waist, covered his head with dirt, and sat fasting and wailing piteously, like a broken-hearted child, in his cabin.

Nowadays, the old half-caste Portuguese rum-dealer at Batabué can point out to any English pioneer who comes up the river which one, among a crowd of dilapidated negroes who lie basking in the soft dust outside his hut, was once the Reverend John Creedy, B.A., of Magdalen College, Oxford.

ROBERT BARR
1850–1912

AN ALPINE DIVORCE

In some natures there are no half-tones; nothing but raw primary colours. John Bodman was a man who was always at one extreme or the other. This probably would have mattered little had he not married a wife whose nature was an exact duplicate of his own.

Doubtless there exists in this world precisely the right woman for any given man to marry, and *vice versa*; but when you consider that a human being has the opportunity of being acquainted with only a few hundred people, and out of the few hundred that there are but a dozen or less whom he knows intimately, and, out of the dozen, one or two friends at most, it will easily be seen, when we remember the number of millions who inhabit this world, that probably since the earth was created the right man has never yet met the right woman. The mathematical chances are all against such a meeting, and this is the reason that divorce courts exist. Marriage at best is but a compromise, and if two people happen to be united who are of an uncompromising nature there is trouble.

In the lives of these two young people there was no middle distance. The result was bound to be either love or hate, and in the case of Mr. and Mrs. Bodman it was hate of the most bitter and arrogant kind.

In some parts of the world incompatibility of temper is considered a just cause for obtaining a divorce, but in England no such subtle distinction is made, and so, until the wife became criminal, or the man became both criminal and cruel, these two were linked together by a bond that only death could sever. Nothing can be worse than this state of things, and the matter was only made the more hopeless by the fact that Mrs. Bodman lived a blameless life, and her husband was no worse, but rather better, than the majority of men. Perhaps, however, that statement held only up to a certain point, for John Bodman had reached a state of mind in which he resolved to get rid of his wife at all hazards. If he had been a poor man he would probably have deserted her, but he was rich, and a man cannot freely leave a prospering business because his domestic life happens not to be happy.

When a man's mind dwells too much on any one subject, no one can tell just how far he will go. The mind is a delicate instrument, and even the law recognises that it is easily thrown from its balance. Bodman's friends—for he had friends—claim that his mind was unhinged; but neither his friends nor his enemies suspected the truth of the episode, which turned out to be the most important, as it was the most ominous, event in his life.

Whether John Bodman was sane or insane at the time he made up his mind to murder his wife will never be known, but there was certainly craftiness in the method he devised to make the crime appear the result of an accident. Nevertheless, cunning is often a quality in a mind that has gone wrong.

Mrs. Bodman well knew how much her presence afflicted her husband, but her nature was as relentless as his, and her hatred of him was, if possible, more bitter than his hatred of her. Wherever he went she accompanied him, and perhaps the idea of murder would never have occurred to him if she had not been so persistent in forcing her presence upon him at all times and on all occasions. So, when he announced to her that he intended to spend the month of July in Switzerland, she said nothing, but made her preparations for the journey. On this occasion he did not protest, as was usual with him, and so to Switzerland this silent couple departed.

There is an hotel near the mountain-tops, which stands on a ledge over one of the great glaciers. It is a mile and a half above the level of the sea, and it stands alone, reached by a toilsome road that zigzags up the mountain for six miles. There is a wonderful view of snow-peaks and glaciers from the verandahs of this hotel, and in the neighbourhood are many picturesque walks to points more or less dangerous.

John Bodman knew the hotel well, and in happier days he had been intimately acquainted with the vicinity. Now that the thought of murder arose in his mind, a certain spot two miles distant from this inn continually haunted him. It was a point of view overlooking everything, and its extremity was protected by a low and crumbling wall. He arose one morning at four o'clock, slipped unnoticed out of the hotel, and went to this point, which was locally named the Hanging Outlook. His memory had served him well. It was exactly the spot, he said to himself. The mountain which rose up behind it was wild and precipitous. There were no inhabitants near to overlook the place. The distant hotel was hidden by a shoulder of rock. The mountains on the other side of the valley were too far away to make it possible for any casual tourist or native to see what was going on on the Hanging Outlook. Far down in the valley the only town in view seemed like a collection of little toy houses.

One glance over the crumbling wall at the edge was generally sufficient for a visitor of even the strongest nerves. There was a sheer drop of more than a mile straight down, and at the distant bottom were jagged rocks and stunted trees that looked, in the blue haze, like shrubbery.

"This is the spot," said the man to himself, "and to-morrow morning is the time."

John Bodman had planned his crime as grimly and relentlessly, and as coolly, as ever he had concocted a deal on the Stock Exchange. There was no thought in his mind of mercy for his unconscious victim. His hatred had carried him far.

The next morning, after breakfast, he said to his wife: "I intend to take a walk in the mountains. Do you wish to come with me?"

"Yes," she answered briefly.

"Very well, then," he said; "I shall be ready at nine o'clock."

"I shall be ready at nine o'clock," she repeated after him.

At that hour they left the hotel together, to which he was shortly to return alone. They spoke no word to each other on their way to the Hanging Outlook. The path was practically level, skirting the mountains, for the Hanging Outlook was not much higher above the sea than the hotel.

John Bodman had formed no fixed plan for his procedure when the place was reached. He resolved to be guided by circumstances. Now and then a strange fear arose in his mind that she might cling to him and possibly drag him over the precipice with her. He found himself wondering whether she had any premonition of her fate, and one of his reasons for not speaking was the fear that a tremor in his voice might possibly arouse her suspicions. He resolved that his action should be sharp and sudden, that she might have no choice either to help herself or to drag him with her. Of her screams in that desolate region he had no fear. No one could reach the spot except from the hotel, and no one that morning had left the house, even for an expedition to the glacier—one of the easiest and most popular trips from the place.

Curiously enough, when they came within sight of the Hanging Outlook, Mrs. Bodman stopped and shuddered. Bodman looked at her through the narrow slits of his veiled eyes, and wondered again if she had any suspicion. No one can tell, when two people walk closely together, what unconscious communication one mind may have with another.

"What is the matter?" he asked gruffly. "Are you tired?"

"John," she cried, with a gasp in her voice, calling him by his

Christian name for the first time in years, " don't you think that if you had been kinder to me at first things might have been different ? "

" It seems to me," he answered, not looking at her, " that it is rather late in the day for discussing that question."

" I have much to regret," she said quaveringly. " Have you nothing ? "

" No," he answered.

" Very well," replied his wife, with the usual hardness returning to her voice. " I was merely giving you a chance. Remember that."

Her husband looked at her suspiciously.

" What do you mean ? " he asked, " giving me a chance ? I want no chance nor anything else from you. A man accepts nothing from one he hates. My feeling towards you is, I imagine, no secret to you. We are tied together, and you have done your best to make the bondage insupportable."

" Yes," she answered, with her eyes on the ground, " we are tied together—we are tied together ! "

She repeated these words under her breath as they walked the few remaining steps to the Outlook. Bodman sat down upon the crumbling wall. The woman dropped her alpenstock on the rock, and walked nervously to and fro, clasping and unclasping her hands. Her husband caught his breath as the terrible moment drew near.

" Why do you walk about like a wild animal ? " he cried. " Come here and sit down beside me, and be still."

She faced him with a light he had never before seen in her eyes—a light of insanity and of hatred.

" I walk like a wild animal," she said, " because I am one. You spoke a moment ago of your hatred of me ; but you are a man, and your hatred is nothing to mine. Bad as you are, much as you wish to break the bond which ties us together, there are still things which I know you would not stoop to. I know there is no thought of murder in your heart, but there is in mine. I will show you, John Bodman, how much I hate you."

The man nervously clutched the stone beside him, and gave a guilty start as she mentioned murder.

" Yes," she continued, " I have told all my friends in England that I believed you intended to murder me in Switzerland."

" Good God ! " he cried. " How could you say such a thing ? "

" I say it to show how much I hate you—how much I am prepared to give for revenge. I have warned the people at the hotel, and when we left two men followed us. The proprietor tried to persuade me not to accompany you. In a few moments those two men will come in sight of the Outlook. Tell them, if you think they will believe you, that it was an accident."

The mad woman tore from the front of her dress shreds of lace and scattered them around.

Bodman started up to his feet, crying, " What are you about ? " But before he could move toward her she precipitated herself over the wall, and went shrieking and whirling down the awful abyss.

The next moment two men came hurriedly round the edge of the rock and found the man standing alone. Even in his bewilderment he realised that if he told the truth he would not be believed.

ROBERT BARR

"GENTLEMEN: THE KING!"

THE room was large, but with a low ceiling, and at one end of the lengthy, broad apartment stood a gigantic fireplace, in which was heaped a pile of blazing logs, whose light, rather than that of several lanterns hanging from nails along the timbered walls, illuminated the faces of the twenty men who sat within. Heavy timbers, blackened with age and smoke, formed the ceiling. The long, low, diamond-paned window in the middle of the wall opposite the door had been shuttered as completely as possible, but less care than usual was taken to prevent the light from penetrating into the darkness beyond, for the night was a stormy and tempestuous one, the rain lashing wildly against the hunting châlet, which, in its time, had seen many a merry hunting party gathered under its ample roof.

Every now and then a blast of wind shook the wooden edifice from garret to foundation, causing a puff of smoke to come down the chimney, and the white ashes to scatter in little whirlwinds over the hearth. On the opposite side from the shuttered window was the door, heavily barred. A long oaken table occupied the centre of the room, and round this in groups, seated and standing, were a score of men, all with swords at their sides; bearing, many of them, that air of careless hauteur which is supposed to be a characteristic of noble birth.

Flagons were scattered upon the table, and a barrel of wine stood in a corner of the room farthest from the fireplace, but it was evident that this was no ordinary drinking party, and that the assemblage was brought about by some high purport, of a nature so serious that it stamped anxiety on every brow. No servants were present, and each man who wished a fresh flagon of wine had to take his measure to the barrel in the corner and fill for himself.

The hunting châlet stood in a wilderness, near the confines of the kingdom of Alluria, twelve leagues from the capital, and was the property of Count Staumn, whose tall, gaunt form stood erect at the head of the table as he silently listened to the discussion which every moment was becoming more and more heated, the principal speaking parts being taken by the obstinate, rough-spoken Baron

Brunfels, on the one hand, and the crafty, fox-like ex-Chancellor Steinmetz on the other.

"I tell you," thundered Baron Brunfels, bringing his fist down on the table, "I will not have the King killed. Such a proposal goes beyond what was intended when we banded ourselves together. The King is a fool, so let him escape like a fool. I am a conspirator, but not an assassin."

"It is justice rather than assassination," said the ex-Chancellor suavely, as if his tones were oil and the Baron's boisterous talk were troubled waters.

"Justice!" cried the Baron, with great contempt. "You have learned that cant word in the Cabinet of the King himself before he thrust you out. He eternally prates of justice, yet, much as I loathe him, I have no wish to compass his death, either directly or through gabbling of justice."

"Will you permit me to point out the reason that induces me to believe his continued exemption and State policy will not run together?" replied the advocate of the King's death. "If Rudolph escape, he will take up his abode in a neighbouring territory, and there will inevitably follow plots and counter-plots for his restoration—thus Alluria will be kept in a state of constant turmoil. There will doubtless grow up within the kingdom itself a party sworn to his restoration. We shall thus be involved in difficulties at home and abroad, and all for what? Merely to save the life of a man who is an enemy to each of us. We place thousands of lives in jeopardy, render our own positions insecure, bring continual disquiet upon the State, when all might be avoided by the slitting of one throat, even though that throat belong to the King."

It was evident that the lawyer's persuasive tone brought many to his side, and the conspirators seemed about evenly divided upon the question of life or death to the King. The Baron was about to break out again with some strenuousness in favour of his own view of the matter, when Count Staumn made a proposition that was eagerly accepted by all save Brunfels himself.

"Argument," said Count Staumn, "is ever the enemy of good comradeship. Let us settle the point at once and finally with the dice-box. Baron Brunfels, you are too seasoned a gambler to object to such a mode of terminating a discussion. Steinmetz, the law, of which you are so distinguished a representative, is often compared to a lottery, so you cannot look with disfavour upon a method that is conclusive and as reasonably fair as the average decision of a judge. Let us throw, therefore, for the life of the King. I, as chairman of this meeting, will be umpire. Single throws, and the highest number wins. Baron Brunfels, you will act for the King, and, if you win, may bestow upon the monarch his life. Chancellor Steinmetz stands for the State. If he wins, then is the King's life forfeit. Gentlemen, are you agreed ? "

" Agreed, agreed," cried the conspirators, with practically unanimous voice.

Baron Brunfels grumbled somewhat, but when the dice-horn was brought, and he heard the rattle of the bones within the leathern cylinder, the light of a gambler's love shone in his eyes, and he made no further protest.

The ex-Chancellor took the dice-box in his hand, and was about to shake when there came suddenly upon them three stout raps against the door, given apparently with the hilt of a sword. Many not already standing started to their feet, and nearly all looked one upon another with deep dismay in their glances. The full company of conspirators was present ; exactly a score of men knew of the rendezvous, and now the twenty-first man outside was beating the oaken panels. The knocking was repeated, but now accompanied by the words :

" Open, I beg you."

Count Staumn left the table and, stealthily as a cat, approached the door.

" Who is there ? " he asked.

" A wayfarer, weary and wet, who seeks shelter from the storm."

" My house is already filled," spoke the Count. " I have no room for another."

" Open the door peacefully," cried the outlander, " and do not put me to the necessity of forcing it."

There was a ring of decision in the voice which sent quick pallor to more than one cheek. Ex-Chancellor Steinmetz rose to his feet with chattering teeth and terror in his eyes ; he seemed to recognise the tones of the invisible speaker. Count Staumn looked over his shoulder at the assemblage with an expression that plainly said, " What am I to do ? "

" In the fiend's name," hissed Baron Brunfels, taking the precaution, however, to speak scarce above his breath, " if you are so frightened when it comes to a knock at the door, what will it be when the real knocks are upon you. Open, Count, and let the insistent stranger in. Whether he leave the place alive or no there are twenty men here to answer."

The Count undid the fastenings and threw back the door. There entered a tall man completely enveloped in a dark cloak that was dripping wet. Drawn over his eyes was a hunter's hat of felt, with a drooping, bedraggled feather on it.

The door was immediately closed and barred behind him, and the stranger, pausing a moment when confronted by so many inquiring eyes, flung off his cloak, throwing it over the back of a chair; then he removed his hat with a sweep, sending the raindrops flying. The intriguants gazed at him, speechless, with varying emotions. They saw before them His Majesty, Rudolph, King of Alluria.

If the King had any suspicion of his danger he gave no token of it. On his smooth, lofty forehead there was no trace of frown and no sign of fear. His was a manly figure, rather over, than under, six feet in height; not slim and gaunt like Count Staumn, nor yet stout to excess like Baron Brunfels. The finger of Time had touched with frost the hair at his temples, and there were threads of white in his pointed beard, but his sweeping moustache was still as black as the night from which he came.

His frank, clear, honest eyes swept the company, resting momentarily on each, then he said in a firm voice, without the suspicion of a tremor in it: "Gentlemen, I give you good evening, and although the hospitality of Count Staumn has needed spurring, I lay that not up against him, because I am well aware his apparent reluctance arose through the unexpectedness of my visit; and, if the Count will act as cup-bearer, we will drown all remembrance of a barred door in a flagon of wine, for, to tell truth, gentlemen, I have ridden hard in order to have the pleasure of drinking with you."

As the King spoke these ominous words, he cast a glance of piercing intensity upon the company, and more than one quailed under it. He strode to the fireplace, spurs jingling as he went, and stood with his back to the fire, spreading out his hands to the blaze. Count Staumn left the bolted door, took an empty flagon from the shelf, filled it at the barrel in the corner, and, with a low bow, presented the brimming measure to the King.

Rudolph held aloft his beaker of Burgundy, and, as he did so, spoke in a loud voice that rang to the beams of the ceiling:

"Gentlemen, I give you a suitable toast. May none here gathered encounter a more pitiless storm than that which is raging without!"

With this he drank off the wine, and, inclining his head slightly to the Count, returned the flagon. No one, save the King, had spoken since he entered. Every word he had uttered seemed charged with double meaning, and brought to the suspicious minds of his hearers visions of a trysting-place surrounded by troops, and the King standing there playing with them as a tiger plays with its victims. His easy confidence appalled them.

When first he came in several who were seated remained so, but one by one they rose to their feet, with the exception of Baron Brunfels, although he, when the King gave the toast, also stood. It was clear enough their glances of fear were not directed towards the King but towards Baron Brunfels. Several pairs of eyes beseeched him in silent supplication, but the Baron met none of these glances, for his gaze was fixed upon the King.

Every man present knew the Baron to be reckless of consequences; frankly outspoken, thoroughly a man of the sword, and a despiser of diplomacy. They feared that at any moment he might blurt out the purport of the meeting, and more than one was thankful for the crafty ex-Chancellor's planning, who throughout had insisted there should be no documentary evidence of their designs, either in their houses or on their persons. Some startling rumour must have reached the King's ear to bring him thus unexpectedly upon them.

The anxiety of all was that some one should persuade the King they were merely a storm-besieged hunting party. They trembled in anticipation of Brunfels's open candour, and dreaded the revealing of the real cause of their conference. There was now no chance to warn the Baron, a man who spoke his mind, who never looked an inch beyond his nose, even though his head should roll off in consequence, and if a man does not value his own head, how can he be expected to care for the heads of his neighbours?

"I ask you to be seated," said the King, with a wave of the hand.

Now, what should that stubborn fool of a Baron do but remain standing, when all but Rudolph and himself had seated themselves, thus drawing His Majesty's attention directly towards him, and making a colloquy between them well-nigh inevitable. Those next the ex-Chancellor were nudging him, in God's name, to stand also, and open whatever discussion there must ensue between themselves and His Majesty, so that it might be smoothly carried on, but the Chancellor was ashen grey with fear, and his hand trembled on the table.

"My Lord of Brunfels," said the King, a smile hovering about his lips, "I see that I have interrupted you at your old pleasure of dicing; while requesting you to continue your game as though I had not joined you, may I venture to hope the stakes you play for are not high?"

Every one held his breath, awaiting with deepest concern the reply of the frowning Baron, and when it came growling forth, there was little in it to ease their disquiet.

"Your Majesty," said Baron Brunfels, "the stakes are the highest that a gambler may play for."

"You tempt me, Baron, to guess that the hazard is a man's soul, but I see that your adversary is my worthy ex-Chancellor, and as I should hesitate to impute to him the character of the devil, I am led, therefore, to the conclusion that you play for a human life. Whose life is in the cast, my Lord of Brunfels?"

Before the Baron could reply, ex-Chancellor Steinmetz arose, with some indecision, to his feet. He began in a trembling voice:

"I beg your gracious permission to explain the reason of our gathering——"

"Herr Steinmetz," cried the King sternly, "when I desire your interference I shall call for it; and remember this, Herr Steinmetz, the man who begins a game must play it to the end, even though he finds luck running against him."

The ex-Chancellor sat down again, and drew his hand across his damp forehead.

"Your Majesty," spoke up the Baron, a ring of defiance in his voice, "I speak not for my comrades but for myself. I begin no game that I fear to finish. We were about to dice in order to discover whether Your Majesty should live or die."

A simultaneous moan seemed to rise from the assembled traitors. The smile returned to the King's lips.

"Baron," he said, "I have ever chided myself for loving you, for you were always a bad example to weak and impressionable natures. Even when your overbearing, obstinate intolerance compelled me to dismiss you from the command of my army, I could not but admire your sturdy honesty. Had I been able to graft your love of truth upon some of my councillors, what a valuable group of advisers might I have gathered round me. But we have had enough of comedy and now tragedy sets in. Those who are traitors to their ruler must not be surprised if a double traitor is one of their number. Why am I here? Why do two hundred mounted and armed men surround this doomed châlet? Miserable wretches, what have you to say that judgment be not instantly passed upon you?"

"I have this to say," roared Baron Brunfels, drawing his sword, "that whatever may befall this assemblage, you, at least, shall not live to boast of it."

The King stood unmoved as Baron Brunfels was about to rush upon him, but Count Staumn and others threw themselves between the Baron and his victim, seeing in the King's words some intimation of mercy to be held out to them could but actual assault upon his person be prevented.

"My Lord of Brunfels," said the King calmly, "sheathe your sword. Your ancestors have often drawn it, but always for, and never against, the occupant of the Throne. Now, gentlemen, hear my decision, and abide faithfully by it. Seat yourselves at the table, ten on each side, the dice-box between you. You shall not be disappointed, but shall play out the game of life and death. Each dices with his opposite. He who throws the higher number escapes. He who throws the lower places his weapons on the empty chair, and stands against yonder wall to be executed for the traitor that he is. Thus half of your company shall live, and the other half seek death with such courage as may be granted them. Do you agree, or shall I give the signal ? "

With unanimous voice they agreed, all excepting Baron Brunfels, who spoke not.

" Come, Baron, you and my devoted ex-Chancellor were about to play when I came in. Begin the game."

" Very well," replied the Baron nonchalantly. " Steinmetz, the dice-box is near your hand : throw."

Some one placed the cubes in the leathern cup and handed it to the ex-Chancellor, whose shivering fingers relieved him of the necessity of shaking the box. The dice rolled out on the table ; a three, a four, and a one. Those nearest reported the total.

" Eight ! " cried the King. " Now, Baron."

Baron Brunfels carelessly threw the dice into their receptacle, and a moment after the spotted bones clattered on the table.

" Three sixes ! " cried the Baron. " Lord, if I only had such luck when I played for money ! "

The ex-Chancellor's eyes were starting from his head, wild with fear.

" We have three throws," he screamed.

" Not so," said the King.

" I swear I understood that we were to have three chances," shrieked Steinmetz, springing from his chair. " But it is all illegal, and not to be borne. I will not have my life diced away to please either King or commons."

He drew his sword and placed himself in an attitude of defence.

" Seize him ; disarm him, and bind him," commanded the King. " There are enough gentlemen in this company to see that the rules of the game are adhered to."

Steinmetz, struggling and pleading for mercy, was speedily overpowered and bound ; then his captors placed him against the wall, and resumed their seats at the table. The next man to be doomed was Count Staumn. The Count arose from his chair, bowed first to the King and then to the assembled company ; drew forth his sword, broke it over his knee, and walked to the wall of the condemned.

The remainder of the fearful contest was carried on in silence, but with great celerity, and before a quarter of an hour was past, ten men had their backs to the wall, while the remaining ten were seated at the table, some on one side, and some on the other.

The men ranged against the wall were downcast, for however bravely a soldier may meet death in hostile encounter, it is a different matter to face it bound and helpless at the hands of an executioner.

A shade of sadness seemed to overspread the countenance of the King, who still occupied the position he had taken at the first, with his back towards the fire.

Baron Brunfels shifted uneasily in his seat, and glanced now and then with compassion at his sentenced comrades. He was first to break the silence.

"Your Majesty," he said, "I am always loath to see a coward die. The whimpering of your former Chancellor annoys me; therefore will I gladly take his place, and give to him the life and liberty you perhaps design for me, if, in exchange, I have the privilege of speaking my mind regarding you and your precious Kingship."

"Unbind the valiant Steinmetz," said the King. "Speak your mind freely, Baron Brunfels."

The Baron rose, drew sword from scabbard, and placed it on the table.

"Your Majesty, backed by brute force," he began, "has condemned to death ten of your subjects. You have branded us as traitors, and such we are, and so find no fault with your sentence; merely recognising that you represent, for the time being, the upper hand. You have reminded me that my ancestors fought for yours, and that they never turned their swords against their sovereign. Why, then, have our blades been pointed towards your breast? Because, King Rudolph, you are yourself a traitor. You belong to the ruling class and have turned your back upon your order. You, a king, have made yourself a brother to the demagogue at the street corner, yearning for the cheap applause of the serf. You have shorn nobility of its privileges, and for what?"

"And for what?" echoed the King with rising voice. "For this; that the ploughman on the plain may reap what he has sown; that the shepherd on the the hillside may enjoy the increase which comes to his flock; that taxation may be light, that my nobles shall deal honestly with the people, and not use their position for thievery and depredation; that those whom the State honours by appointing to positions of trust shall content themselves with the recompense lawfully given, and refrain from peculation; that peace and security shall rest on the land; and that bloodthirsty swashbucklers shall not go up and down inciting the people to carnage and rapine under the name of patriotism. This is the task I set myself when I came to the Throne. What fault have you to find with the programme, my Lord Baron?"

"The simple fault that it is the programme of a fool," replied the Baron calmly. "In following it you have gained the resentment of your nobles, and have not even received the thanks of those pitiable hinds, the ploughman in the valley or the shepherd on the hills. You have impoverished us so that the clowns may have a few more coins with which to muddle in drink their already stupid brains. You are hated in cot and castle alike. You would not stand in your place for a moment were not an army behind you. Being a fool, you think the common people love honesty, whereas they only curse that they have not a share in the thieving."

"The people," said the King soberly, "have been misled. Their ear has been abused by calumny and falsehood. Had it been possible for me personally to explain to them the good that must ultimately accrue to a land where honesty rules, I am confident I would have had their undivided support, even though my nobles deserted me."

"Not so, Your Majesty; they would listen to you and cheer you, but when the next orator came among them, promising to divide the moon and give a share to each, they would gather round his banner and hoot you from the kingdom. What care they for rectitude of government? They see no farther than the shining florin that glitters on their palm. When your nobles were rich they came to their castles among the people, and scattered their gold with a lavish hand. Little recked the peasants how it was got so long as they shared it. 'There,' they said, 'the coin comes to us that we have not worked for.'

"But now, with castles deserted, and retainers dismissed, the people have to sweat to wring from traders the reluctant silver, and they cry: 'Thus it was not in times of old, and this king is the cause of it,' and so they spit upon your name, and shrug their shoulders, when your honesty is mentioned. And now, Rudolph of Alluria, I have done, and I go the more jauntily to my death that I have had fair speech with you before the end."

The King looked at the company, his eyes veiled with moisture. "I thought," he said slowly, "until to-night, that I had possessed some qualities at least of a ruler of men. I came here alone among you, and although there are brave men in this assembly, yet I had the ordering of events as I chose to order them, notwithstanding that odds stood a score to one against me. I still venture to think that whatever failures have attended my eight years' rule in Alluria arose from faults of my own, and not through imperfections in the plan or want of appreciation in the people.

"I have now to inform you that if it is disastrous for a king to act without the co-operation of his nobles, it is equally disastrous for them to plot against their leader. I beg to acquaint you with the fact that the insurrection so carefully prepared has broken out prematurely. My capital is in possession of the factions, who are industriously cutting each other's throats to settle which one of two smooth-tongued rascals shall be their President. While you were dicing to settle the fate of an already deposed king, and I was sentencing you to a mythical death, we were all alike being involved in common ruin.

"I have seen to-night more property in flames than all my savings during the last eight years would pay for. I have no horsemen at my back and have stumbled here blindly, a much bedraggled fugitive, having lost my way in every sense of the phrase. And so I beg of the hospitality of Count Staumn another flagon of wine, and either a place of shelter for my patient horse, who has been left too long in the storm without, or else direction towards the frontier, whereupon my horse and I will set out to find it."

"Not towards the frontier!" cried Baron Brunfels, grasping again his sword and holding it aloft, "but towards the capital. We will surround you, and hew for you a way through that fickle mob back to the throne of your ancestors."

Each man sprang to his weapon and brandished it above his head, while a ringing cheer echoed to the timbered ceiling.

"The King! The King!" they cried.

Rudolph smiled and shook his head.

"Not so," he said. "I leave a thankless throne with a joy I find it impossible to express. As I sat on horseback, half-way up the hill above the burning city, and heard the clash of arms, I was filled with amazement to think that men would actually fight for the position of ruler of the people. Whether the insurrection has brought freedom to themselves or not, the future alone can tell, but it has at least brought freedom to me. I now belong to myself. No man may question either my motives or my acts. Gentlemen, drink with me to the new President of Alluria, whoever he may be."

But the King drank alone, none other raising flagon to lip. Then Baron Brunfels cried aloud:

"*Gentlemen: the King!*"

And never in the history of Alluria was a toast so heartily honoured.

STANLEY JOHN WEYMAN
1855–1928

THE CLOCKMAKER OF POISSY

FORESEEING that some who do not love me will be swift to allege that in the preparation of these memoirs I have set down only such things as redound to my credit, and have suppressed the many experiences not so propitious which fall to the lot of the most sagacious while in power, I take this opportunity of refuting that calumny. For the truth stands so far the other way that my respect for the King's person has led me to omit many things creditable to me; and some, it may be, that place me in a higher light than any I have set down. And not only that: but I propose in this very place to narrate the curious details of an adventure wherein I showed to less advantage than usual; and on which I should, were I moved by the petty feelings imputed to me by malice, be absolutely silent.

One day, about a fortnight after the quarrel between the King and the Duchess of Beaufort, which arose, it will be remembered, out of my refusal to pay the christening expenses of her second son on the scale of a child of France, I was sitting in my lodgings at St. Germains when Maignan announced that M. de Perrot desired to see me. Knowing Perrot to be one of the most notorious beggars about the court, with an insatiable maw of his own and an endless train of nephews and nieces, I was at first for being employed; but, reflecting that in the crisis in the King's affairs which I saw approaching—and which must, if he pursued his expressed intention of marrying the Duchess, be fraught with infinite danger to the State and himself—the least help might be of the greatest moment, I bade them admit him; privately determining to throw the odium of any refusal upon the overweening influence of Madame de Sourdis, the Duchess's aunt.

Accordingly I met him with civility, and was not surprised when, with his second speech, he brought out the word *favour*. But I was surprised—for, as I have said, I knew him to be the best practised beggar in the world—to note in his manner some indications of embarrassment and nervousness; which, when I did not immediately assent, increased to a sensible extent.

"It is a very small thing, M. de Rosny," he said, breathing hard.

On that hint I declared my willingness to serve him. "But," I added, shrugging my shoulders and speaking in a confidential tone, "no one knows the Court better than you do, M. de Perrot. You are in all our secrets, and you must be aware that at present—I say nothing of the Duchess, she is a good woman, and devoted to his Majesty—but there are others——"

"I know," he answered, with a flash of malevolence that did not escape me. "But this is a private favour, M. de Rosny. It is nothing that Madame de Sourdis can desire, either for herself or for others."

That aroused my curiosity. Only the week before, Madame de Sourdis had obtained a Hat for her son, and the post of Assistant Deputy Comptroller of Buildings for her Groom of the Chambers. For her niece the Duchess she meditated obtaining nothing less than a crown. I was at pains, therefore, to think of any office, post, or pension that could be beyond the pale of her desires; and in a fit of gaiety I bade M. de Perrot speak out and explain his riddle.

"It is a small thing," he said, with ill-disguised nervousness. "The King hunts to-morrow."

"Yes," I said.

"And very commonly he rides back in your company, M. le Marquis."

"Sometimes," I said; "or with M. d'Epernon. Or, if he is in a mood for scandal, with M. la Varenne or Vitry."

"But with you, if you wish it, and care to contrive it so," he persisted, with a cunning look.

I shrugged my shoulders. "Well?" I said, wondering more and more what he would be at.

"I have a house on the farther side of Poissy," he continued. "And I should take it as a favour, M. de Rosny, if you could induce the King to dismount there to-morrow and take a cup of wine."

"That is a very small thing," I said bluntly, wondering much why he had made so great a parade of the matter, and still more why he seemed so ill at ease. "Yet, after such a prelude, if any but a friend of your tried loyalty asked it, I might expect to find Spanish liquorice in the cup."

"That is out of the question, in my case," he answered with a slight assumption of offence, which he immediately dropped. "And you say it is a small thing; it is the more easily granted, M. de Rosny."

"But the King goes and comes at his pleasure," I replied warily.

"Of course, he might take it into his head to descend at your house. There would be nothing surprising in such a visit. I think that he has paid you one before, M. de Perrot?"

He assented eagerly.

"And he may do so," I said, smiling, "to-morrow. But then, again, he may not. The chase may lead him another way; or he may be late in returning; or—in fine, a hundred things may happen."

I had no mind to go farther than that; and I supposed that it would satisfy him, and that he would thank me and take his leave. To my surprise, however, he stood his ground, and even pressed me more than was polite; while his countenance, when I again eluded him, assumed an expression of chagrin and vexation so much in excess of the occasion as to awaken fresh doubts in my mind. But these only the more confirmed me in my resolution to commit myself no farther, especially as he was not a man I loved or could trust; and in the end he had to retire with such comfort as I had already given him.

In itself, and on the surface, the thing seemed to be a trifle, unworthy of the serious consideration of any man. But in so far as it touched the King's person and movements, I was inclined to view it in another light; and this the more, as I still had fresh in my memory the remarkable manner in which Father Cotton, the Jesuit, had given me a warning by a word about a boxwood fire. After a moment's thought, therefore, I summoned Boisrueil, one of my gentlemen, who had an acknowledged talent for collecting gossip; and I told him in a casual way that M. de Perrot had been with me.

"He has not been at Court for a week," he remarked.

"Indeed?" I said.

"He applied for the post of Assistant Deputy Comptroller of Buildings for his nephew, and took offence when it was given to Madame de Sourdis' Groom of the Chambers."

"Ha!" I said; "a dangerous malcontent."

Boisrueil smiled. "He has lived a week out of the sunshine of his Majesty's countenance, your excellency. After that, all things are possible."

This was my own estimate of the man, whom I took to be one of those smug, pliant self-seekers whom Courts and peace breed up. I could imagine no danger that could threaten the King from such a quarter; while curiosity inclined me to grant his request. As it happened, the deer the next day took us in the direction of Poissy, and the King, who was always itching to discuss with me the question of his projected marriage, and as constantly, since our long talk in the garden at Rennes, avoiding the subject when with me, bade me ride home with him. On coming within half a mile of

Perrot's I let fall his name, and in a very natural way suggested that the King should alight there for a few minutes.

It was one of the things Henry delighted to do, for, endowed with the easiest manners, and able in a moment to exchange the formality of the Louvre for the freedom of the camp, he could give to such cheap favours their full value. He consented on the instant, therefore; and turning our horses into a by-road, we sauntered down it with no greater attendance than a couple of pages.

The sun was near setting, and its rays, which still gilded the tree-tops, left the wood below pensive and melancholy. The house stood in a solitary place on the edge of the forest, half a mile from Poissy; and these two things had their effect on my mind. I began to wish that we had brought with us half a troop of horse, or at least two or three gentlemen; and, startled by the thought of the unknown chances to which, out of mere idle curiosity, I was exposing the King, would gladly have turned back. But without explanation I could not do so; and while I hesitated Henry cried out gaily that we were there.

A short avenue of limes led from the forest road to the door. I looked curiously before us as we rode under the trees, in some fear lest M. de Perrot's preparations should discover my complicity, and apprise the King that he was expected. But so far was this from being the case that no one appeared; the house rose still and silent in the mellow light of sunset, and, for all that we could see, might have been the fabled palace of enchantment.

"'He is Jean de Nivelle's dog; he runs away when you call him,'" the King quoted. "Get down, Rosny. We have reached the palace of the Sleeping Princess. It remains only to sound the horn, and——"

I was in the act of dismounting, with my back to him, when his words came to this sudden stop. I turned to learn what caused it, and saw standing in the aperture of the wicket, which had been silently opened, a girl, a little more than a child, of the most striking beauty. Surprise shone in her eyes, and shyness and alarm had brought the colour to her cheeks; while the level rays of the sun, which forced her to screen her eyes with one small hand, clothed her figure in a robe of lucent glory. I heard the King whistle low. Before I could speak he had flung himself from his horse and, throwing the reins to one of the pages, was bowing before her.

"We were about to sound the horn, Mademoiselle," he said, smiling.

"The horn, Monsieur?" she exclaimed, opening her eyes in wonder, and staring at him with the prettiest face of astonishment.

"Yes, Mademoiselle; to awaken the Sleeping Princess," he rejoined. "But I see that she is already awake."

Through the innocence of her eyes flashed a sudden gleam of archness. "Monsieur flatters himself," she said, with a smile that just revealed the whiteness of her teeth.

It was such an answer as delighted the King; who loved, above all things, a combination of wit and beauty, and never for any long time wore the chains of a woman who did not unite sense to more showy attractions. From the effect which the grace and freshness of the girl had on me, I could judge in a degree of the impression made on him; his next words showed not only its depth, but that he was determined to enjoy the adventure to the full. He presented me to her as M. de Sage, and inquiring affectionately after Perrot, learned in a trice that she was his niece, not long from a convent at Loches; finally, begging to be allowed to rest awhile, he dropped a gallant hint that a cup of wine from her hands would be acceptable.

All this, and her innocent doubt what she ought to do, thus brought face to face with two strange cavaliers, threw the girl into such a state of blushing confusion as redoubled her charms. It appeared that her uncle had been summoned unexpectedly to Marly, and had taken his son with him; and that the household had seized the occasion to go to a village *fête* at Achères. Only an old servant remained in the house; who presently appeared and took her orders. I saw from the man's start of consternation that he knew the King; but a glance from Henry's eyes bidding me keep up the illusion, I followed the fellow and charged him not to betray the King's incognito. When I returned, I found that Mademoiselle had conducted her visitor to a grassy terrace which ran along the south side of the house, and was screened from the forest by an alley of apple trees, and from the east wind by a hedge of yew. Here, where the last rays of the sun threw sinuous shadows on the turf, and Paris seemed a million miles away, they were walking up and down, the sound of their laughter breaking the woodland silence. Mademoiselle had a fan, with which and an air of convent coquetry she occasionally shaded her eyes. The King carried his hat in his hand. It was such an adventure as he loved, with all his heart; and I stood a little way off, smiling, and thinking grimly of M. de Perrot.

On a sudden, hearing a step behind me, I turned, and saw a young man in a riding-dress come quickly through an opening in the yew hedge. As I turned, he stopped; his jaw fell, and he stood rooted to the ground, gazing at the two on the terrace, while his face, which a moment before had worn an air of pleased expectancy, grew on a sudden dark with passion, and put on such a look as made me move towards him. Before I reached him, however, M. de Perrot himself appeared at his side. The young man flashed round on him. "*Mon Dieu*, sir!" he cried, in a voice choked with anger; "I see it all now! I understand why I was carried away to Marly! I—but it shall not be! I swear it shall not!"

Between him and me—for, needless to say, I, too, understood all—M. de Perrot was awkwardly placed. But he showed the presence of mind of the old courtier. "Silence, sir!" he exclaimed imperatively. "Do you not see M. de Rosny? Go to him at once and pay your respects to him, and request him to honour you with his protection. Or—I see that you are overcome by the honour which the King does us. Go, first, and change your dress. Go, boy!"

The lad retired sullenly, and M. de Perrot, free to deal with me alone, approached me, smiling assiduously, and trying hard to hide some consciousness and a little shame under a mask of cordiality. "A thousand pardons, M. de Rosny," he cried with effusion, "for an absence quite unpardonable. But I so little expected to see his Majesty after what you said, and——"

"Are in no hurry to interrupt him now you are here," I replied bluntly, determined that, whoever he deceived, he should not flatter himself he deceived me. "Pooh, man! I am not a fool," I continued.

"What is this?" he cried, with a desperate attempt to keep up the farce. "I don't understand you!"

"No, the shoe is on the other foot—I understand you," I replied drily. "Chut, man!" I continued, "you don't make a catspaw of me. I see the game. You are for sitting in Madame de Sourdis' seat, and giving your son a Hat, and your groom a Comptrollership, and your niece a——"

"Hush, hush, M. de Rosny," he muttered, turning white and red, and wiping his brow with his kerchief. "*Mon Dieu!* your words might——"

"If overheard, make things very unpleasant for M. de Perrot," I said.

"And M. de Rosny?"

I shrugged my shoulders contemptuously. "Tush, man!" I said. "Do you think that I sit in no safer seat than that?"

"Ah! But when Madame de Beaufort is Queen?" he said slily.

"If she ever is," I replied, affecting greater confidence than I at that time felt.

"Well, to be sure," he said slowly, "if she ever is." And he looked towards the King and his companion, who were still chatting gaily. Then he stole a crafty glance at me. "Do you wish her to be?" he muttered.

"Queen?" I said. "God forbid!"

"It would be a disgrace to France?" he whispered; and he laid his hand on my arm, and looked eagerly into my face.

"Yes," I said.

" A blot on his fame ? "

I nodded.

" A—a slur on a score of noble families ? "

I could not deny it.

" Then—is it not worth while to avoid all that ? " he murmured, his face pale, and his small eyes glued to mine. " Is it not worth a little—sacrifice, M. de Rosny ? "

" And risk ? " I said. " Possibly."

While the words were still on my lips something stirred close to us, behind the yew hedge beside which we were standing. Perrot darted in a moment to the opening, and I after him. We were just in time to catch a glimpse of a figure disappearing round the corner of the house. " Well," I said grimly, " what about being overheard now ? "

M. de Perrot wiped his face. " Thank heaven ! " he said, " it was only my son. Now let me explain to you——"

But our hasty movement had caught the King's eye, and he came towards us, covering himself as he approached. I had now an opportunity of learning whether the girl was, in fact, as innocent as she seemed, and as every particular of our reception had declared her ; and I watched her closely when Perrot's mode of address betrayed the King's identity. Suffice it that the vivid blush which on the instant suffused her face, and the lively emotion which almost overcame her, left me in no doubt. With a charming air of bashfulness, and just so much timid awkwardness as rendered her doubly bewitching, she tried to kneel and kiss the King's hand. He would not permit this, however, but saluted her cheek.

" It seems that you were right, sire," she murmured, curtseying in a pretty confusion, " the princess was not awake."

Henry laughed gaily. " Come now ; tell me frankly, Mademoiselle," he said. " For whom did you take me ? "

" Not for the King, sire," she answered, with a gleam of roguishness. " You told me that the King was a good man, whose benevolent impulses were constantly checked——"

" Ah ! "

" By M. de Rosny, his Minister."

The outburst of laughter which greeted this apprised her that she was again at fault ; and Henry, who liked nothing better than such mystifications, introducing me by my proper name, we diverted ourselves for some minutes with her alarm and excuses. After that it was time to take leave, if we would sup at home and the King would not be missed ; and accordingly, but not without some further badinage, in which Mademoiselle de Brut displayed wit equal to her beauty, and an agreeable refinement not always found with either, we departed.

It should be clearly understood at this point that, notwithstanding all I have set down, I was fully determined (in accordance with a rule I have constantly followed, and would enjoin on all who do not desire to find themselves one day saddled with an ugly name) to have no part in the affair ; and this though the advantage of altering the King's intentions towards Madame de Beaufort was never more vividly present to my mind. As we rode, indeed, he put several questions concerning the Baron, and his family, and connections ; and, falling into a reverie, and smiling a good deal at his thoughts, left me in no doubt as to the impression made upon him. But being engaged at the time with the Spanish treaty, and resolved, as I have said, to steer a course uninfluenced by such intrigues, I did not let my mind dwell upon the matter ; nor gave it, indeed, a second thought until the next afternoon, when, sitting at an open window of my lodging, I heard a voice in the street ask where the Duchess de Beaufort had her apartment.

The voice struck a chord in my memory, and I looked out. The man who had put the question, and who was now being directed on his way—by Maignan, my equerry, as it chanced—had his back to me, and I could see only that he was young, shabbily dressed, and with the air of a workman carried a small frail of tools on his shoulder. But presently, in the act of thanking Maignan, he turned so that I saw his face, and with that it flashed upon me in a moment who he was.

Accustomed to follow a train of thought quickly, and to act on its conclusion with energy, I had Maignan called and furnished with his instructions before the man had gone twenty paces ; and within the minute I had the satisfaction of seeing the two return together. As they passed under the window I heard my servant explaining with the utmost naturalness that he had misunderstood the stranger, and that *this* was Madame de Beaufort's ; after which scarce a minute elapsed before the door of my room opened, and he appeared ushering in young Perrot !

Or so it seemed to me ; and the start of surprise and consternation which escaped the stranger when he first saw me confirmed me in the impression. But a moment later I doubted ; so natural was the posture into which the man fell, and so stupid the look of inquiry which he turned first on me and then on Maignan. As he stood before me, shifting his feet and staring about him in vacant wonder, I began to think that I had made a mistake ; and, clearly, either I had done so or this young man was possessed of talents and a power of controlling his features beyond the ordinary. He unslung his tools, and saluting me abjectly waited in silence. After a moment's thought, I asked him peremptorily what was his errand with the Duchess de Beaufort.

"To show her a watch, your excellency," he stammered, his mouth open, his eyes staring. I could detect no flaw in his acting.

"What are you, then?" I said.

"A clockmaker, my lord."

"Has Madame sent for you?"

"No, my lord," he stuttered, trembling.

"Do you want to sell her the watch?"

He muttered that he did; and that he meant no harm by it.

"Show it to me, then," I said curtly.

He grew red at that, and seemed for an instant not to understand. But on my repeating the order he thrust his hand into his breast, and producing a parcel began to unfasten it. This he did so slowly that I was soon for thinking that there was no watch in it; but in the end he found one and handed it to me.

"You did not make this," I said, opening it.

"No, my lord," he answered; "it is German, and old."

I saw that it was of excellent workmanship, and I was about to hand it back to him, almost persuaded that I had made a mistake, when in a second my doubts were solved. Engraved on the thick end of the egg, and partly erased by wear, was a dog's head, which I knew to be the crest of the Perrots.

"So," I said, preparing to return it to him, "you are a clockmaker?"

"Yes, your excellency," he muttered. And I thought that I caught the sound of a sigh of relief.

I gave the watch to Maignan to hand to him. "Very well," I said. "I have need of one. The clock in the next room—a gift from his Majesty—is out of order, and at a standstill. You can go and attend to it; and see that you do so skilfully. And do you, Maignan," I continued with meaning, "go with him. When he has made the clock go, let him go; and not before, or you answer for it. You understand, sirrah?"

Maignan saluted obsequiously, and in a moment hurried young Perrot from the room; leaving me to congratulate myself on the strange and fortuitous circumstance that had thrown him in my way, and enabled me to guard against a *rencontre* that might have had the most embarrassing consequences.

It required no great sagacity to foresee the next move; and I was not surprised when, about an hour later, I heard a clatter of hoofs outside, and a voice inquiring hurriedly for the Marquis de Rosny. One of my people announced M. de Perrot, and I bade them admit him. In a twinkling he came up, pale with heat, and covered with dust, his eyes almost starting from his head, and his cheeks trembling with agitation. Almost before the door shut, he cried out that we were undone.

I was willing to divert myself with him for a time, and I pretended to know nothing. " What ? " I said, rising. " Has the King met with an accident ? "

" Worse ! worse ! " he cried, waving his hat with a gesture of despair. " My son—you saw my son yesterday ? "

" Yes," I said.

" He overheard us ! "

" Not us," I said drily. " You. But what then, M. de Perrot ? You are master in your own house."

" But he is not in my house," he wailed. " He has gone ! Fled ! Decamped ! I had words with him this morning, you understand."

" About your niece ? "

M. de Perrot's face took a delicate shade of red, and he nodded ; he could not speak. He seemed for an instant in danger of some kind of fit. Then he found his voice again. " The fool prated of love ! Of love ! " he said with such a look—like that of a dying fowl—that I could have laughed aloud. " And when I bade him remember his duty he threatened me. He, that unnatural boy, threatened to betray me, to ruin me, to go to Madame de Beaufort and tell her all—all, you understand. And I doing so much, and making such sacrifices for him ! "

" Yes," I said, " I see that. And what did you do ? "

" I broke my cane on his back," M. de Perrot answered with unction, " and locked him in his room. But what is the use ? The boy has no natural feelings ! "

" He got out through the window ? "

Perrot nodded ; and being at leisure, now that he had explained his woes, to feel their full depth, shed actual tears of rage and terror ; now moaning that Madame would never forgive him, and that if he escaped the Bastille he would lose all his employments and be the laughing-stock of the Court ; and now striving to show that his peril was mine, and that it was to my interest to help him.

I allowed him to go on in this strain for some time, and then, having sufficiently diverted myself with his forebodings, I bade him in an altered voice to take courage. " For I think I know," I said, " where your son is."

" At Madame's ? " he groaned.

" No ; here," I said.

" *Mon Dieu !* Where ? " he cried. And he sprang up, startled out of his lamentations.

" Here ; in my lodging," I answered.

" My son is here ? " he said.

" In the next room," I replied, smiling indulgently at his astonishment, which was only less amusing than his terror. " I have but to touch this bell, and Maignan will bring him to you."

Full of wonder and admiration, he implored me to ring and have him brought immediately; since until he had set eyes on him he could not feel safe. Accordingly I rang my hand-bell, and Maignan opened the door. "The clockmaker," I said, nodding.

He looked at me stupidly. "The clockmaker, your excellency?"

"Yes; bring him in," I said.

"But—he has gone!" he exclaimed.

"Gone?" I cried, scarcely able to believe my ears. "Gone, sirrah! and I told you to detain him!"

"Until he had mended the clock, my lord," Maignan stammered, quite out of countenance. "But he set it going half an hour ago; and I let him go, according to your order."

It is in the face of such *contretemps* as these that the low-bred man betrays himself. Yet such was my chagrin on this occasion, and so sudden the shock, that it was all I could do to maintain my *sang-froid*, and, dismissing Maignan with a look, be content to punish M. de Perrot with a sneer. "I did not know that your son was a tradesman," I said.

He wrung his hands. "He has low tastes," he cried. "He always had. He has amused himself that way. And now by this time he is with Madame de Beaufort and we are undone!"

"Not we," I answered curtly; "speak for yourself, M. de Perrot."

But though, having no mind to appear in his eyes dependent on Madame's favour or caprice, I thus checked his familiarity, I am free to confess that my calmness was partly assumed; and that, though I knew my position to be unassailable—based as it was on solid services rendered to the King, my master, and on the familiar affection with which he honoured me through so many years—I could not view the prospect of a fresh collision with Madame without some misgiving. Having gained the mastery in the two quarrels we had had, I was the less inclined to excite her to fresh intrigues; and as unwilling to give the King reason to think that we could not live at peace. Accordingly, after a moment's consideration, I told Perrot that, rather than he should suffer, I would go to Madame de Beaufort myself, and give such explanations as would place another complexion on the matter.

He overwhelmed me with thanks, and, besides, to show his gratitude—for he was still on thorns, picturing her wrath and resentment—he insisted on accompanying me to the Cloître de St. Germain, where Madame had her apartment. By the way, he asked me what I should say to her.

"Whatever will get you out of the scrape," I answered curtly.

"Then anything!" he cried with fervour. "Anything, my dear friend. Oh, that unnatural boy!"

"I suppose that the girl is as big a fool?" I said.

"Bigger! bigger!" he answered. "I don't know where she learned such things!"

"She prated of love, too, then?"

"To be sure," he groaned, "and without a sou of *dot!*"

"Well, well," I said, "here we are. I will do what I can."

Fortunately the King was not there, and Madame would receive me. I thought, indeed, that her doors flew open with suspicious speed, and that way was made for me more easily than usual; and I soon found that I was not wrong in the inference I drew from these facts. For when I entered her chamber that remarkable woman, who, whatever her enemies may say, combined with her beauty a very uncommon degree of sense and discretion, met me with a low curtsey and a smile of derision. "So," she said, "M. de Rosny, not satisfied with furnishing me with evidence, gives me proof."

"How, Madame?" I said; though I well understood.

"By his presence here," she answered. "An hour ago," she continued, "the King was with me. I had not then the slightest ground to expect this honour, or I am sure that his Majesty would have stayed to share it. But I have since seen reason to expect it, and you observe that I am not unprepared."

She spoke with a sparkling eye, and an expression of the most lively resentment; so that had M. de Perrot been in my place I think that he would have shed more tears. I was myself somewhat dashed, though I knew the prudence that governed her in her most impetuous sallies; still, to avoid the risk of hearing things which we might both afterwards wish unsaid, I came to the point. "I fear that I have timed my visit ill, Madame," I said. "You have some complaint against me."

"Only that you are like the others," she answered with a fine contempt. "You profess one thing and do another."

"As for example?"

"For example!" she replied, with a scornful laugh. "How many times have you told me that you left women, and intrigues in which women had part, on one side?"

I bowed.

"And now I find you—you and that Perrot, that creature!—intriguing against me; intriguing with some country chit to——"

"Madame!" I said, cutting her short with a show of temper, "where did you get this?"

"Do you deny it?" she cried, looking so beautiful in her anger that I thought I had never seen her to such advantage. "Do you deny that you took the King there?"

"No. Certainly, I took the King there."

"To Perrot's? You admit it?"

"Certainly," I said, "for a purpose."

"A purpose!" she cried with withering scorn. "Was it not that the King might see that girl?"

"Yes," I replied patiently, "it was."

She stared at me. "And you can tell me that to my face!" she said.

"I see no reason why I should not, Madame," I replied easily—"I cannot conceive why you should object to the union—and many why you should desire to see two people happy. Otherwise, if I had had any idea, even the slightest, that the matter was obnoxious to you, I would not have engaged in it."

"But—what was your purpose then?" she muttered, in a different tone.

"To obtain the King's good word with M. de Perrot to permit the marriage of his son with his niece; who is, unfortunately, without a portion."

Madame uttered a low exclamation, and her eyes wandering from me, she took up—as if her thoughts strayed also—a small ornament from the table beside her. "Ah!" she said, looking at it closely. "But Perrot's son—did he know of this?"

"No," I answered, smiling. "But I have heard that women can love as well as men, Madame. And sometimes ingenuously."

I heard her draw a sigh of relief, and I knew that if I had not persuaded her I had accomplished much. I was not surprised when, laying down the ornament with which she had been toying, she turned on me one of those rare smiles to which the King could refuse nothing; and wherein wit, tenderness, and gaiety were so happily blended that no conceivable beauty of feature, uninspired by sensibility, could vie with them. "Good friend, I have sinned," she said. "But I am a woman, and I love. Pardon me. As for your *protégée*, from this moment she is mine also. I will speak to the King this evening; and if he does not at once," Madame continued, with a gleam of archness that showed me that she was not yet free from suspicion, "issue his commands to M. de Perrot, I shall know what to think; and his Majesty will suffer!"

I thanked her profusely, and in fitting terms. Then, after a word or two about some assignments for the expenses of her household, in settling which there had been delay—a matter wherein, also, I contrived to do her pleasure and the King's service no wrong—I very willingly took my leave, and, calling my people, started homewards on foot. I had not gone twenty paces, however, before M. de Perrot, whose impatience had chained him to the spot, crossed the street and joined himself to me. "My dear friend," he cried, embracing me fervently, "is all well?"

"Yes," I said.

"She is appeased?"

"Absolutely."

He heaved a deep sigh of relief, and, almost crying in his joy, began to thank me, with all the extravagance of phrase and gesture to which men of his mean spirit are prone. Through all I heard him silently, and with secret amusement, knowing that the end was not yet. At length he asked me what explanation I had given.

"The only explanation possible," I answered bluntly. "I had to combat Madame's jealousy. I did it in the only way in which it could be done: by stating that your niece loved your son, and by imploring her good word on their behalf."

He sprang a pace from me with a cry of rage and astonishment. "You did that?" he screamed.

"Softly, softly, M. de Perrot," I said, in a voice which brought him somewhat to his senses. "Certainly I did. You bade me say whatever was necessary, and I did so. No more. If you wish, however," I added grimly, "to explain to Madame that——"

But with a wail of lamentation he rushed from me, and in a moment was lost in the darkness; leaving me to smile at this odd termination of an intrigue that, but for a lad's adroitness, might have altered the fortunes not of M. de Perrot only, but of the King my master and of France.

F. ANSTEY
(THOMAS ANSTEY GUTHRIE)
B. 1856

A CANINE ISHMAEL

(FROM THE NOTES OF A DINER-OUT)

"TELL me," she said suddenly, with a pretty imperiousness that seemed to belong to her, "are you fond of dogs?" How we arrived at the subject I forget now, but I know she had just been describing how a collie at a dog-show she had visited lately had suddenly thrown his forepaws round her neck in a burst of affection —a proceeding which, in my own mind (although I prudently kept this to myself), I considered less astonishing than she appeared to do.

For I had had the privilege of taking her in to dinner, and the meal had not reached a very advanced stage before I had come to the conclusion that she was the most charming, if not the loveliest, person I had ever met.

It was fortunate for me that I was honestly able to answer her question in a satisfactory manner, for, had it been otherwise, I doubt whether she would have deigned to bestow much more of her conversation upon me.

"Then I wonder," she said next, meditatively, "if you would care to hear about a dog that belonged to—to someone I know very well? Or would it bore you?"

I am very certain that if she had volunteered to relate the adventures of Telemachus, or the history of the Thirty Years' War, I should have accepted the proposal with a quite genuine gratitude. As it was, I made it sufficiently plain that I should care very much indeed to hear about that dog.

She paused for a moment to reject an unfortunate entrée (which I confess to doing my best to console), and then she began her story. I shall try to set it down as nearly as possible in her own words, although I cannot hope to convey the peculiar charm and interest that she gave it for me. It was not, I need hardly say, told all at once, but was subject to the inevitable interruptions which render a dinner-table intimacy so piquantly precarious.

"This dog," she began quietly, without any air of beginning a story, "this dog was called Pepper. He was not much to look at—rather a rough, mongrelly kind of animal; and he and a young man had kept house together for a long time, for the young man was a bachelor and lived in chambers by himself. He always used to say that he didn't like to get engaged to anyone, because he was sure it would put Pepper out so fearfully. However, he met somebody at last who made him forget about Pepper, and he proposed and was accepted—and then, you know," she added, as a little dimple came in her cheek, "he had to go home and break the news to the dog."

She had just got to this point, when, taking advantage of a pause she made, the man on her other side (who was, I daresay, strictly within his rights, although I remember at the time considering him a pushing beast) struck in with some remark which she turned to answer, leaving me leisure to reflect.

I was feeling vaguely uncomfortable about this story; something, it would be hard to say what, in her way of mentioning Pepper's owner made me suspect that he was more than a mere acquaintance of hers.

Was it she, then, who was responsible for——? It was no business of mine, of course; I had never met her in my life till that evening, but I began to be impatient to hear the rest.

And at last she turned to me again: "I hope you haven't forgotten that I was in the middle of a story. You haven't? And you would really like me to go on? Well, then—oh, yes, when Pepper was told, he was naturally a little annoyed at first. I daresay he considered he ought to have been consulted previously. But as soon as he had seen the lady he withdrew all opposition—which his master declared was a tremendous load off his mind, for Pepper was rather a difficult dog, and slow, as a rule, to take strangers into his affections, a little snappy and surly, and very easily hurt or offended. Don't you know dogs who are sensitive like that? I do, and I'm always so sorry for them—they feel little things so much, and one never can find out what's the matter, and have it out with them! Sometimes it's shyness; once I had a dog who was quite painfully shy—self-consciousness it was really, I suppose, for he always fancied everybody was looking at him, and often when people were calling he would come and hide his face in the folds of my dress till they had gone—it was too ridiculous! But about Pepper. He was devoted to his new mistress from the very first. I am not sure that she was quite so struck with him, for he was not at all a lady's dog, and his manners had been very much neglected. Still, she came quite to like him in time; and when they were married, Pepper went with them for the honeymoon."

"When they were married!" I glanced at the card which lay half-hidden by her plate. Surely Miss So-and-so was written on it?—yes, it was certainly "Miss." It was odd that such a circumstance should have increased my enjoyment of the story, perhaps—but it undoubtedly did.

"After the honeymoon," my neighbour continued, "they came to live in the new house, which was quite a tiny one, and Pepper was a very important personage in it indeed. He had his mistress all to himself for the greater part of most days, as his master had to be away in town; so she used to talk to him intimately, and tell him more than she would have thought of confiding to most people. Sometimes, when she thought there was no fear of callers coming, she would make him play, and this was quite a new sensation for Pepper, who was a serious-minded animal, and took very solemn views of life. At first he hadn't the faintest idea what was expected of him; it must have been rather like trying to romp with a parish beadle, he was so intensely respectable! But as soon as he once grasped the notion and understood that no liberty was intended, he lent himself to it readily enough, and learnt to gambol quite creditably. Then he was made much of in all sorts of ways; she washed him twice a week with her very own hands—which his master would never dream of doing—and she was always trying new ribbons on his complexion. That rather bored him at first, but it ended by making him a little conceited about his appearance. Altogether he was dearly fond of her, and I don't believe he had ever been happier in all his life than he was in those days. Only, unfortunately, it was all too good to last."

Here I had to pass olives or something to somebody; and the other man, seeing his chance, and, to do him justice, with no idea that he was interrupting a story, struck in once more, so that the history of Pepper had to remain in abeyance for several minutes.

My uneasiness returned. Could there be a mistake about that name-card after all? Cards do get rearranged sometimes, and she seemed to know that young couple so very intimately. I tried to remember whether I had been introduced to her as a Miss or Mrs. So-and-so, but without success. There is some fatality which generally distracts one's attention at the critical moment of introduction, and in this case it was perhaps easily accounted for. My turn came again, and she took up her tale once more. "I think when I left off I was saying that Pepper's happiness was too good to last. And so it was. For his mistress was ill, and, though he snuffed and scratched and whined at the door of her room for ever so long, they wouldn't let him in. But he managed to slip in one day somehow, and jumped up on her lap and licked her hands and face, and almost went out of his mind with joy at seeing her again.

Only (I told you he was a sensitive dog) it gradually struck him that she was not quite so pleased to see him as usual—and presently he found out the reason. There was another animal there, a new pet, which seemed to take up a good deal of her attention. Of course you guess what that was—but Pepper had never seen a baby before, and he took it as a personal slight and was dreadfully offended. He simply walked straight out of the room and downstairs to the kitchen, where he stayed for days.

"I don't think he enjoyed his sulk much, poor doggie ; perhaps he had an idea that when they saw how much he took it to heart they would send the baby away. But as time went on and this didn't seem to occur to them, he decided to come out of the sulks and look over the matter, and he came back quite prepared to resume the old footing. Only everything was different. No one seemed to notice that he was in the room now, and his mistress never invited him to have a game ; she even forgot to have him washed—and one of his peculiarities was that he had no objection to soap and warm water. The worst of it was, too, that before very long the baby followed him into the sitting-room, and, do what he would, he couldn't make the stupid little thing understand that it had no business there. If you think of it, a baby must strike a dog as a very inferior little animal ; it can't bark (well, yes, it can howl), but it's no good whatever with rats, and yet everybody makes a tremendous fuss about it ! The baby got all poor Pepper's bows now ; and his mistress played games with it, though Pepper felt he could have done it ever so much better, but he was never allowed to join in. So he used to lie on a rug, and pretend he didn't mind, though, really, I'm certain he felt it horribly. I always believe, you know, that people never give dogs half credit enough for feeling things, don't you ?

"Well, at last came the worst indignity of all : Pepper was driven from his rug—his own particular rug—to make room for the baby ; and when he had got away into a corner to cry quietly, all by himself, that wretched baby came and crawled after him and pulled his tail !

"He always had been particular about his tail, and never allowed anybody to touch it but very intimate friends, and even then under protest, so you can imagine how insulted he felt.

"It was too much for him, and he lost the last scrap of temper he had. They said he bit the baby, and I'm afraid he did—though not enough really to hurt it ; still, it howled fearfully, of course, and from that moment it was all over with poor Pepper—he was a ruined dog !

"When his master came home that evening he was told the whole story. Pepper's mistress said she would be ever so sorry to part with him, but, after his misbehaviour, she should never know a moment's peace until he was out of the house—it really wasn't safe for baby!

"And his master was sorry, naturally; but I suppose he was beginning rather to like the baby himself, and so the end of it was that Pepper had to go. They did all they could for him; found him a comfortable home, with a friend who was looking out for a good house-dog, and wasn't particular about breed, and, after that, they heard nothing of him for a long while. And when they did hear it was rather a bad report: the friend could do nothing with Pepper at all; he had to tie him up in the stable, and then he snapped at every one who came near, and howled all night—they were really almost afraid of him.

"So when Pepper's mistress heard that, she felt more thankful than ever that the dog had been sent away, and tried to think no more about him. She had quite forgotten all about it, when, one day, a new nursemaid, who had taken the baby out for an airing, came back with a terrible account of a savage dog which had attacked them and leaped up at the perambulator so persistently that it was as much as she could do to drive it away. And even then Pepper's mistress did not associate the dog with him; she thought he had been destroyed long ago.

"But the next time the nurse went out with the baby she took a stick with her, in case the dog should come again. And no sooner had she lifted the perambulator over the step, than the dog did come again, exactly as if he had been lying in wait for them ever since outside the gate.

"The nurse was a strong country girl, with plenty of pluck, and as the dog came leaping and barking about in a very alarming way, she hit him as hard as she could on his head. The wonder is she did not kill him on the spot, and, as it was, the blow turned him perfectly giddy and silly for a time, and he ran round and round in a dazed sort of way—do you think you could lower that candle-shade just a little? Thanks." She broke off suddenly, as I obeyed. "Well, she was going to strike again, when her mistress rushed out, just in time to stop her. For, you see, she had been watching at the window, and although the poor beast was miserably thin, and rough, and neglected-looking, she knew at once that it must be Pepper, and that he was not in the least mad or dangerous, but only trying his best to make his peace with the baby. Very likely his dignity or his conscience or something wouldn't let him come back quite at once, you know; and perhaps he thought he had better get the baby on his side first. And then all at once his mistress—I heard all this through her, of course—his mistress suddenly remembered how devoted Pepper had been to her, and how fond she had once been of him, and when she saw him standing, stupid and shivering, there, her heart softened to him, and she went to make it up with him, and tell him that he was forgiven and should come back and be her dog again, just as in the old days !——"

Here she broke off for a moment. I did not venture to look at her, but I thought her voice trembled a little when she spoke again. " I don't quite know why I tell you all this. There was a time when I never could bear the end of it myself," she said ; " but I have begun, and I will finish now. Well, Pepper's mistress went towards him, and called him ; but—whether he was still too dizzy to quite understand who she was, or whether his pride came uppermost again, poor dear ! I don't know—but he gave her just one look (she says she will never forget it—never ; it went straight to her heart), and then he walked very slowly and deliberately away.

" She couldn't bear it ; she followed ; she felt she simply must make him understand how very, very sorry she was for him ; but the moment he heard her he began to run faster and faster, until he was out of reach and out of sight, and she had to come back. I know she was crying bitterly by that time."

" And he never came back again ? " I asked, after a silence.

" Never again ! " she said softly ; " that was the very last they ever saw or heard of him. And—and I've always loved every dog since for Pepper's sake ! "

" I'm almost glad he did decline to come back," I declared ; " it served his mistress right—she didn't deserve anything else ! "

" Ah, I didn't want you to say that ! " she protested. " She never meant to be so unkind—it was all for the baby's sake ! "

I was distinctly astonished, for all her sympathy in telling the story had seemed to lie in the other direction.

" You don't mean to say," I cried involuntarily, " that you can find any excuses for her ? I did not expect you would take the baby's part ! "

" But I did," she confessed, with lowered eyes—" I did take the baby's part—it was all my doing that Pepper was sent away—I have been sorry enough for it since ! "

It was her own story she had been telling at second-hand after all —and she was not Miss So-and-so ! I had entirely forgotten the existence of any other members of the party but our two selves, but at the moment of this discovery—which was doubly painful—I was recalled by a general rustle to the fact that we were at a dinner-party, and that our hostess had just given the signal.

As I rose and drew back my chair to allow my neighbour to pass, she raised her eyes for a moment and said almost meekly :

" I was the baby, you see ! "

MORLEY ROBERTS
B. 1857

THE MIRACLE OF THE BLACK CAÑON

In that part of British Columbia called the Dry Belt, where rain is seldom and scanty, the whole landscape looks barren and desolate. Most of the creeks are bitterly alkaline, the shallow lakes are encrusted on their white edges, and when they dry in a hot summer their deposited soda glitters afar off like a mirage. What settlers dwell in its barren parts are few, and work with cattle or horses which find a living in the long, dry plateau. East and west are the mountains, and beyond them on either hand the rainfall is heavy. Here and there in this country are Indian settlements and reservations. Their inhabitants live their own semi-pastoral lives; they rear horses, and at times hunt and fish. But whether they are whites or Siwashes, they are all poor: there is no great natural reward in such a desert.

And years, many years, before the great railroad came to change the aspect of ancient things, the Miracle of the Cañon happened. Those who were the forerunners of the iron way beheld it, and to this hour those who remember the wonder and terror of that great hour, speak of it with awe, and curse the onward course of the returned river.

The Black Cañon itself is not terrible or imposing. It is but a narrower space where the steep iron-bound banks are set close together; the rocks are not perpendicular, nor does a tormented river run at unfathomable depths beyond the sunlight. But about it is the very horror of dry barrenness—it is an unspeakable place of thirst. For a mile from the sunk river on either side sharp rocks jut out forbiddingly, parting the thin soil; they are rent and gapped and broken; their jagged fangs are yellow as an old wolf's; they cut the hands of such as stumble along blindly seeking the stream, which drops at its nearest below the thirsty touch and angers natural desire. On either hand, north or south, the aspect of the spot is bitter—it gives no welcome, and no one dwells close by; it is a place of prickly pear and stunted cactus ; sour grass with tough broad-bladed leaves has usurped any tenderer herbage ; not a tree gives a moment's shadow in the hot noon. Sand and alkali are on the breath of the wind, and beneath, the splendid, cruel waters on the river run blue till they grow sullen and shadowed in the cañon. In the terror of the summer season it is a portion of open hell, as though there the punishment of some cosmic crime were fixed for ever.

But in the sullen depths lay the gold of a world's generations, and men hungered, as they have always done, on the barren edge of the impossible, desiring the rainbow gold of a river of death.

On the north side of the cañon's upper end was a mighty bluff some three hundred feet high. Its riverward surface was barred and banded with red and with yellow. Down its side it was guttered with wind-driven sand—it weathered and crumbled day by day. Yet the hardest strata were at its height ; it beetled and overhung. Sometimes portions broke off and plunged into the stream, which there began to deepen and grow black ; their dust made a sudden yellow patch in the water, and was then swept down in foam.

At the very base of this bluff was a layer of sandstone soft enough to scoop out with a knife ; under that again was a thin line of semi-crystalline fracture. In that there were gaps ; it was bent and distorted by the superincumbent pressure of the tens of thousands of tons above it. In one place close to the swirling stream was a little hollow cave, in which it could be seen how the strata sloped to the river. When the stream was high the cave was hidden, but at a low stage it appeared black to those who looked across from the southern side.

And a month before the miracle two men sat on the opposing bank, staring sombrely into the waters.

" This place is accursed," said the younger of the two, " and I feel like a damned spirit myself. We are cast out of the borders of the earth."

The elder man smoked quietly. Yet even he kicked his heels against the rock on which he sat, and his brows were drawn down ; his teeth clenched his pipe's heavy wooden mouthpiece.

" It's no good wailing and gnashing your teeth," he answered ; " I don't, and I've more to draw me away than you. We must put the survey through somehow, and trust that a paradise will open up for us when the work's done."

But the young fellow made queer, ugly faces.

" And in the meantime we must grit our teeth on alkali dust, and dig prickly pear spines out of our hands and feet, and oil the blisters on our noses, and thank God for giving us our beautiful work. Oh, Lord, what a fool a man is ! Here we are bursting our insides in a desert, and all the time there are South Sea island beaches and places where a man can lie in the shade and suck bananas! I'd rather be a nigger!"

He fidgeted with his fingers, and part of his face twitched two or three times till he brushed it uneasily with his hand.

"A nigger—not you!" said Quin quickly. "Only on Sunday, when we don't work, the evil spirit gets you and idleness knots up your nerves, and you don't sweat to relieve your mind."

Harry Payne shrugged his shoulders and gnawed his lip.

"Is it natural to work this way? By thunder, no! We take it on as we would old rye—just to get blind and not care. Then it's tumble into the blankets and sleep the sleep of the drugged. And next day again and again."

He sprang up excitedly and pointed down into the river.

"And look, Quin—here, here right underneath us, there's enough gold to buy ease and power and peace for a man's long lifetime!"

"But no man's long life can help him to it," answered Quin, smiling. "You can't wingdam this river. It would cost ten thousand dollars to get a dollar out. In this kind of country you must look for that. It's no kind of use—you might as well go at a safe with your finger-nails. Nature's like a bank. Did you get mad in San Francisco when you passed one?"

"No; but there were compensations."

"Boy," said Quin solemnly, "don't butt your brains out on the impossible. It's easier to rob the biggest bank in the States or out of them than to burgle here."

But Harry lay down on his stomach, and stared into the river.

"If it were only mine—a little of it! I can see the gold at the bottom," said he.

"It's all mixed with mud and sand," answered Quin literally; "you can see nothing. You'll be having the worst kind of gold-fever if you watch it. This is no sort of a place to get kinks in your brain. You mind yourself, boy. Think of something else. Come, let's go back to the camp and grub."

Harry grunted uneasily, for he could hardly take his eyes from the selfish water.

"Hog and hominy," he growled—"sow-belly and molasses! Well, it's all of a piece."

But they stumbled over the rocks to their white tents, and after dinner they slept, and woke feeling slimy all over and bad in their mouths; and then they smoked and growled and cursed the long hot day down into the west. For the misery of idleness was on them all, and the thoughts of far pleasure came to embitter them. Their day of rest was no boon. Even as they prayed for it to come so they were glad to see it go.

It was the same to them all; whether to Quin and Harry Payne, the bosses, or to Shaw and Liston and Willis, the men, the time was a burden.

" We've been here for years in this hell of dust," growled Willis. And the others snarled at him and reduced his exaggeration to exact days. They quarrelled and spoke sick words, for the alkali in their throats dried up kindness. Even Quin was hard put to it not to jump on their necks.

" Damn you, men, what's the good of taking it so? Be men—not snarling cayoots! Did you come across the mountains to look for a soft seat? And did you reckon that the land of the Chinook was all roses? D'ye think I'm having a lovely time?"

" Roses—roses!" growled Liston. " Prickly pear I know, and alkali and dust I know, but—roses! Such flowers don't fit with the bronze Klootchmen around here. The wages are well worth the work."

He grinned at his clumsy inversion. But gold got back into the talk.

" Do you really reckon there's much gold in this allfired cañon, Mr. Quin?" asked Shaw, the youngest of the crowd.

But Harry Payne answered him, and as he spoke in a high key the greed of wealth crept into the haggard lines of his young face, and avarice puckered his bloodshot eyes.

" Gold? Why, man, it's full of it! And away down to the end of the Fraser Cañon it's one long gold-trap—one almighty sluice-box! From the Forks down here, from here to Yale! D'ye know how they worked Boston Bar? Oh, God, that was just one riffle in the boxes cleaned up! And here we are grubbing in flames and eating ashes while the dollars drift under us."

He rose and walked up and down like a caged bear. He took his hat off and threw it down to catch the cooler evening air upon his brow.

They were all sitting round the camp-fire; even the Chinese cooks were close by, and each squatted on a skillet or on an inverted empty tomato-can. As their idle eyes followed Payne almost mechanically, the flames gleamed on lean, brown faces. Overhead the cool stars shone; there was a heavenly breath of air coming from the north. But Payne walked back and forth, back and forth, muttering. Presently he broke out again.

" Oh, boys, but just think of it! Just to dam this river and turn the stream——"

" Where?" asked Quin sardonically.

" Where—where?" said Payne, with irritation. " Why, it's just a dream! Turn it back through the hills, cut a tunnel for it, and run it into the Columbia."

" Up-end it by hand," cried Shaw, laughing—" shove it into the Peace River and capsize the stuff out ! "

" While you're about your dreaming, Payne," put in Liston, " why don't you dream a good 'un ? Find a big quicksilver mine and run the mercury into the river. Flood the bed of it, let it sneak down into every ledge and crack, and suck up the gold till it rolls thick and you can anchor a dredge in a quiet pool, like the one at Yale, and scoop out thousands of tons of amalgam."

" Holy Mackinaw ! " cried Willis, and they all laughed.

" Aye, but it's a big notion," said Liston, pleased with his own imagination. " Who'll rob your sluice-box then ? You won't need to set watchmen with shot-guns to fill up sluice-robbers and sneaking Chinamen with lead. All you want is your quicksilver mine, and the capital will roll in."

" You bet ! " said Payne eagerly. " For the gold's there—it's there."

And Quin looked at the boy from under his shaggy eyebrows. Though he tried to turn the conversation, it was to the full as hard to turn just then as the fatal river. For Payne was set heavily in his fixed mind. He dreamed of it and spoke in his dreams.

But when Quin got a show he spoke to Liston quietly.

" Say, you're not a fool ; and you're a man, too, among boys. Don't egg Payne on to guff too much of this river. He's half crazy as it is."

Liston nodded.

" Why, sir, but I did begin to have a kind of a kinkle that he was a bit cranky on it."

" I've half a mind to send him down to Savona or the Ferry," muttered Quin to himself ; " if he gets crazy or has the fever here, it'll be bad for his folks in Victoria."

But Payne turned cunning, and when Quin shut him up angrily, hoping that he would give him an excuse for sending him away, the young fellow said nothing at all. He was preternaturally keen, and fathomed Quin's mind. So he held his tongue. Yet in his spare time he sneaked off to the river and sat opposite the great bluff.

And now his child-like religion came back to him. He carried a Bible in his pocket, and read it at intervals. And a big notion was born in his brain. It grew marvellously, like a gourd—it overshadowed obstacles ; he walked in foreseen triumph and prayed happily to God. It ran out of him in words—he talked to himself. And then a bitter revulsion came.

" I'm a weak, miserable, and sinful wretch ! I hate myself and this place ! And it holds me ; but even when we shift further I shall be crawling down here again. I shall end in the river. It draws me ; moth and flame—moth and fire. Gold in it, and ease and rest."

He put his hand to his head and screamed.

" Oh, this awful, awful sun—it's in my brain and burns ! "

He crawled to the dangerous verge, and dropping on hazardous chance, scooped up water in his hat and cooled his head.

On the bank he prayed.

" Oh, Almighty God, be merciful unto me, and let me look into the bottomless pit of it, where I see the gold—the gold. Dry it up as Thou didst the Red Sea, to let me pass through out of this bloody Egypt. Thrust the hills into it."

And, looking up, he called in the noonday sun to the glaring northern bluff as if it were alive and sentient, itself a god. He made a fetish of it—myths sprang in his rotting mind like toad-stools on sick earth at hot midnight.

" Fall down, fall down, and stay the river ! "

And as he rose wildly he saw Quin come striding across the rocks. He cunningly composed himself.

" What's this, Payne ? " said Quin angrily. " Are you going clean crazy ? "

" Well, Quin, haven't I a right to come here in the dinner-hour if I like ? " he asked, almost humbly.

" You've no right to make this row harder for me to hoe than it is," said Quin, quietening. " This notion of yours will do for you yet. Let it be, man ! Come back, or I'll have to send you down home. My son, I think the heat's too much for you."

But Payne looked at him appealingly.

" No, no," he said, almost cheerfully, " I'm all right—quite right. I'll not come here again. I'll sling it—I swear I will ! "

And he went back to work. But the madness clung to him and cracked his skin ; it was in his harsh hair. He never looked straight at any man, but insanity sat secret in his dilate pupils.

But outwardly he sang through the day and made no mistakes. That night some teams camped close by. At one o'clock in the morning he went out and sneaked two boxes of dynamite from under the cover of a waggon. He cached his find carefully, and when he crawled into the open tent he laughed silently at Quin's peaceful face turned to the quiet moon.

In the morning before breakfast he wrote a letter to a store-keeper in Yale. He went out to work cheerfully, and spoke no more of the gold hidden in the cañon. But he never looked at Quin, and spoke hardly at all. On the fifth or sixth day a small parcel came for him, which he opened in secret. He put its contents in his breast-pocket, and grinned with joy.

" It's just a prayer—a great compelling prayer," he shrieked thinly in his mind ; and all day long he chuckled when he was alone, " I've got the power now."

But he trembled very strangely, and his hands shook. In all his limbs came a fleeting aura, as though something breathed upon him.

That very night he stole out of the quiet moon-litten camp, and finding the hidden boxes, he carried them, slung together, with great labour up the river-bank. He shook so much and his limbs seemed so little under his control that he had to rest every hundred yards ; but at last he came to a broader, quieter portion of the stream across which a taut rope was stretched. A crazy boat built by some man as a first attempt lay in a rocky recess. It was made fast to the rope by sliding rings, and could be pulled across the dangerous ferry by another rope that lay in the water, while a coil made fast to the shore from which it started paid itself out of the stern as it went.

Payne put his dynamite in the boat and pulled himself across the swirling stream. He sang and chattered and laughed as he pulled. When he came to the further shore he took his burden again and stumbled painfully down stream under the high, round moon, which gave him his own shadow for a companion to which he could talk. And soon the great bluff loomed up, and then it hung over him, and blotted out the moon, blinding him for a minute with opaque shadows that again grew pellucid and then transparent once more for his trembling, doubtful feet. He laid down his heavy burden and sought for the little cave, which looked like a black patch at noon from the river's further bank.

When he found it he returned for his boxes, and on laying them down in the cave's mouth he prised off the lids with a heavy knife. The cartridges lay there packed in sawdust. He took them out one by one and touched them lovingly.

" If only Quin and the boys knew," he said aloud, and above the low perpetual hiss of the waters his voice echoed with his very accent, and went whispering down the cañon's gap. He looked up suspiciously with his head on one side like a listening bird, and, being reassured, he screamed with high-pitched laughter, that came back mixed and mingled in a chorus of dissonance, and ran off chuckling inaudibly. But Payne now took no note of aught but the dreadful strength under his hands. At last he emptied the boxes, and poured the sawdust into the water, which was black below him, while here and there in the distance a moon-sparkle leapt off the broken edges of two meeting swirls. Then one by one he packed the cartridges into the recesses of the cavern. Yet he kept a single cartridge, and partly stripped off its covering.

" Now the fuse and the cap ! " he muttered, and took from his pocket that which he had sent to Yale for. Pressing the end of the fuse in, he nipped the cap a little to make it hold, and thrusting his fingers into the dynamite to make a deep hole, he put the cap in and squeezed the soft explosive about it again. He put that cartridge among the others, while the long length of fuse ran wormlike out of the cavern, the mouth of which he closed with broken rocks. He rose up and clasped his hands.

"Oh, God, be merciful to me—be merciful!"

As he turned, his quick mood changed; he laughed at the personal, hateful river, and then cursed it, laughing.

"I have done it! And now let them laugh. For the river shall be dry and the waters shall stand in a heap."

He lay down on a flat rock which was under water in the early summer, and, rolling over like a caressed cat, he hugged himself with odd, choked chuckles.

"To-morrow I shall be rich—rich! And it's mine—mine—not one shall share it with me! It shall be all mine—the river-bed as far as it runs dry. And then Quin will be sick of himself—the beast!"

Sitting up, he made mouths at Quin, and nodded familiarly to the moon, that hung like a Chinese lantern from the bluff's edge, and he winked at his own squat shadow.

"To-morrow I'll do it. No; I'll keep it till Sunday—till Sunday; and all the week I will think what I shall do with the gold."

He coiled up the loose end of the fuse, and hid it carefully from any man's sight, though he knew well that no man ever went there; and by three he was back in his camp-bed. But he neither slept nor needed to sleep, for his brain ran down an increasing slope, and his jumbled thoughts were like the Gadarene swine, with an abyss below them, and perpetually a thrill and a tremor shook his flesh.

During the remainder of the working week he lived in concealed frenzy, cunning of look and speech. He calculated hugely the wealth that even one day's work in the dry cañon would make his. He saw the poor world at his feet, and trod on air.

But Quin was himself sick in his mind at the long heat and his own troubles, so that he noticed nothing. He had a wife and children in California, and his heart hungered for them hourly. He almost prayed for some catastrophe to end the work, so that he might go back to them with a conscience clean of avoidance of duty. Since Payne worked quietly he thought no more about him or the river, dismissing it from his mind.

Yet when he woke on Sunday in the early dawn he saw the boy had gone. A note lay on the bed.

"What's this?" said Quin sleepily. As he deciphered it in the dusk he sprang up. The letter ran thus:

"Quin, mind what I say. For I know that the Lord of Hosts is behind me. This is what I say. The river and its gold, from the great bluff down to the Fraser, is mine. It is all mine—the gold and the bed of the river. And when the bed runs dry, as it will to-day, all that is taken out is mine. At six there shall be a sign and a wonder, and the miracle will happen. I have prayed. The big bluff will fall into the river. And the water will stand in a heap. And the children of Israel will find the gold. For their day's pay I will give them a hundredth part. Each day the same till the water returns. Amen."

And Quin ran out.

"Willis—Liston—Shaw!" he called, and the men came half naked from their tents.

Above the eastern mountains the dawn was very pale golden rose.

"Payne's gone raving mad," cried Quin; "he's away, and has left me a letter saying that the bluff is going to fall into the river, and that the gold in the dry bed is his. Hunt for him, you! I'll go to the river myself."

And in a few minutes he was on the edge of the rocks at the bank. He called hopelessly in the dim dawn, but he was answered faintly.

"Is that you, Payne?" he shouted.

Then he saw a dark figure sitting on the other side.

"It is I. Who calls the chosen of God?"

Quin stamped on the iron rock.

"Don't be an accursed fool!" he cried. "Come back, man! What's gone wrong with you? What the hell are you doing there?"

Payne rose and rebuked him.

"Do not blaspheme God, or the works of God. I have prayed for the waters to be stayed, and He has put the power in my hands. The river will run dry, and the gold is mine." He threw his hands up into the air crying, "Mine—mine!"

"He's mad—mad!" said Quin.

"As you have come I will wait no more," cried Payne, and he stooped down. Yet he rose again. "Quin!"

"What?" said Quin.

"Get you under cover, or run, for the bluff will fall into the head of the cañon even now."

And Quin saw him light a match. It spurted flame in the shadow of the cave's mouth, and then he saw Payne run like a goat along the hazardous edge of the river. As he went he signed with his open hand to Quin to lie down, to go, to hide.

Across the stream the one who waited and wondered saw with his keen eye a little pale smoke and perhaps creeping fire.

"What's he up to?" he asked, and then an inkling of the possible truth flashed on him. Without staying, he turned and ran and lay down under a great rock.

And suddenly there was a mighty crash that deafened him. The whole earth trembled. To Quin it seemed that he was lying on something hollow, that had been smitten from below by a giant's hammer, and for a moment he felt sick; then rocks and gravel flew past him or splintered on his shelter; the air was full of sand and dust that choked and blinded him. He rose and staggered and fell down.

And meantime Payne, escaped from the very pit, blind and mad with furious excitement, his mind spurting flame, his brain overturned, went screaming hand over hand across the river in the creaking boat.

"The dry places shall be filled with water and the rivers shall be dry places. For the sea is in the hollow of His hand."

He ran headlong for the camp. The other men were lying half stunned near the river. The blast had smitten them as they went running.

"By the holy frost, what's happened?" cried Shaw when he rose.

And Liston scrambled to his feet. They found Willis insensible with a cut on his head, and while they were attending him Quin came up.

But the great bluff stood yet in its ancient place, though Payne's god had torn away a buttress and dug a mighty hole into the dipping strata. Though the surface of the bluff was more concave, yet it had not fallen for all the awful blow dealt its foundations. And by now the river ran blue once more; the yellow patch of the fallen debris had been swept down.

And to the four men came Payne, singing.

But as they stared at him open-mouthed, awed and uncertain, he looked past and above them, and saw the great bluff gleam out in the arisen sun. His face went distorted, and his left hand twisted to his ear uncontrollably; his eyes turned into his head, and he fell grovelling. In the aspect of his stricken face was a curse on the works of God and the ways of Him. And within an hour he was raving on his bed in the fevered horror of madness, and the men were hard put to it to hold him down.

Meanwhile, from this place and from that, camp and house and ranche, men came to their disturbed camp to inquire as to the reason of the sound which had run across the plateau at dawn. They came galloping, and at noon there were thirty men with Quin opposite the rent and splintered bluff.

"Dynamite, for sure," said one man, "for the sound of it was like a sudden clap, not the lifting roar of powder, and powder would have hoisted the bluff off its roots."

"Where did he get it?" asked Quin, who was bewildered. But none answered, and the various talk ran on.

" Did he reckon—the madman—that the river would be dammed by the bluff even if he had fetched it down ? "

Quin nodded.

" By the powers," cried an old miner, " but it's an almighty notion and only a crazy lunatic could have tried it ! "

They argued hotly in the rising heat whether enough could come down to block the river, and, granted that were possible, how long the dam would hold against the increasing waters. Though some took one side and some the other, the very imagined chance of robbing the river-bed inflamed their minds, and the desire of wealth got hold of them all alike ; and they stood for unnoticed hours in the burning sun, with the heat coming doubly from the rocks beneath, and from the mighty bluff opposing them.

" Hark ! " cried one man suddenly.

" It is nothing," said his neighbour.

" It is distant thunder," said a third.

And their voices rose again.

Suddenly the very earth beneath them shook like an ill-built house, and there came a crack like a heavy rifle-shot, and after it a great grinding noise, that stayed their blood and made them pallid.

" Look ! look ! " cried Quin—" it moves—it moves ! "

The man next him cried " No, no," but even as he spoke the overhung edge of the bluff split and fell roaring into the torrent, beating it into spray that blinded them, and in the spray were a million wild rainbows.

But when the spray died slowly down there was an increasing roar, in which shouted words were dumb gestures, and the whole mighty bluff moved.

" Run, run ! " they mouthed, and some ran and stayed again, and some stood petrified.

And with a grinding noise that was a terror of itself, the whole higher half of the bluff and hill behind it went steadily into the river. Thrusting the water aside, it strove like a decree of God, strong of accomplishment, even to the shadowed rocks of the hither side. Through the narrowing gate the water foamed turbidly; but at last the gap closed, and the calm river stayed against the silent obstacle.

The men sighed, awe-struck, and again held their breaths. But then the desire of gold took them, and they ran all ways for all things that might help them to the riches under the sinking waters.

It laid hold of Quin too. There came a vision to him of home, seen through a mist that hid the place he hated ; he flushed burning red, and went white as foam. Now he might make a year's work in one sole hour.

" Quick," he cried to his men—" all our things—pots or pans or skillets—anything that will hold water or scoop mud! Quick, or these others will sweep the camp clean!"

They ran to their tents like wolves after a deer. Willis, with his head bandaged, was sitting by Payne. At the roar he had risen, and turned faint. But now he ran with the others, and left the wonder-worker rolling and raving and rolling again.

They were the first back to the west end of the cañon, and they found the river empty save for pools. It was a ghastly, weedy chasm, difficult of access, slimy, hideous with crawling insects in the holes and crannies. Here and there a stranded bewildered fish flapped desperately. They dropped a rope and lariat in the gap, and slid down.

"It's share and share here!" cried Liston.

They agreed on the word spoken.

"Then let Shaw stay here to hoist the buckets."

He went down and stripped there, throwing his shirt and jacket away.

"Is the most gold here?" asked Willis.

But they worked where they stood.

Then the men who had been with them galloped back with buckets and scoops and all things they could find. The news ran like fire in dry grass; women and children drove up in carts with their household utensils; each moment others dropped into the cañon; in half an hour the black banks hummed. The Siwashes and their Klootchmen came with the whites; Chinamen worked with them. And as the drying river told those down below, buggies came furiously driven to the richest place. All along to the Fraser, men were in the river-bed, greedy of sudden wealth.

And he who had wrought this, and accomplished the impossible hopes of toiling men, lay parched and fevered and all alone. His lips cracked and bled, and he yelled in a narrow tent of a great world opened to him.

"It's all mine—mine!" and the tent fly flapped idly in the heated air.

He sang the doxology, "Praise God, from whom all blessings flow."

But in the cañon they cursed awfully, and were afraid, toiling under the dam against which the waters rose and rose still. On its edge one more fearful than the rest had stationed his old mother, and she was shaken with terror for her son. She watched the water as one would watch fire at sea.

"See if it breaks out under. Say when it reaches the top," they had told her; but though she wagged her head in feeble assent, she was without faith in her own sight. In dread of her judgment, she crawled at last upon the dam itself, and wailed querulously to deaf ears below to say whether they thought it would stand. But no able-minded man was there. Who would pay him his price that day of most immortal days ? "

As each increased his pile of the drift which held gold, suspicion grew, and with it fear. Men doubted their partners, and glared angrily at each other on slight provocations. But the greater fear above them of the rising water cooled most contentions. And yet in the midst of them was Panic crouching, known, hidden and unseen. A chance palsied motion of the grey-haired woman on the dam sent them flying more than once. They returned, worked, and some prayed.

" Oh, God ! Oh, God, how long ? "

Then on the height of the piled earth there sprang a white figure naked to the bitter sun.

" It is mine—mine, and all the wealth of it from here down even to the river's mouth ! "

And the mad hero of the slidden mountain chanted dreadful joy of his riches, urging his men beneath to labour. In their ears he was as the buzz of a fly. But behind him, and against the barriers, the very quiet waters rose inch by inch ; each distant hill sent aid. For Nature was outraged and robbed—her secrets laid bare. As the madman sang, the pressed waters penetrated into every crevice, seeking every way, while a white naked insect yelled articulate blasphemy against the making of the world and the laws that hold matter in space.

" It is mine, and strong for ever ! "

But now the backed-up waters began to spread on the lower terrace above the natural river. Every moment brought more power to bear upon the unnatural barrier. Even the old woman saw it. She turned and clambered down to the ancient rocks, for the man whose fair flesh was scorching in the sun terrified her, as the unaccustomed sight before he came distraught her fixed and senile mind.

" My son ! my son ! " she wailed.

But her boy down below strove desperately as the others strove. Not a man but left bloody finger-prints on the rocks ; some paddled in blood, who, cursing for want of things to carry the river drift away, had stripped off their long boots in desperation. The lust for gold sent them wild : some cheered, some sang.

But others looked up and said, " How long ? "

For themselves they worked, but for none other than their own, and natural mercy left them. At one rich ledge two tramps fought unnoticed. The stronger beat out the brains of the weaker, and robbed him of his stolen bucket.

And the white genius of this sudden black inferno yelled congratulations to the burning skies, praising the Lord with fevered incantations.

Once again the workers fled and returned, and fled again, to come back once more. But down below Quin and his fellows toiled unmoved.

" Oh, there's millions—millions here ! "

They spat blood and sweat, and worked blackly grimed and half naked. But at the dam's dry foot the waters began to chuckle, and turbid springs spurted suddenly. The mad boy, wrapped in flames, looked not behind.

" It's mine—it's mine. Oh, God ! Oh, God ! "

Then he turned and saw the gleaming lake behind him. Thrusting his hands against the hot air, he cursed and commanded the encroaching waters, that rose even to the dam's height and began to pour over. The word ran like thunder in the echoing chasm, and the men fled, stricken with white fear. Some cried, " No, no—not yet ! " even as they ran.

And the miracle-worker cursed his God at the motion under his feet, at the fear of poverty returning, at the loss of unmeasured hope.

" It moves—it moves ! " piped the idiot woman, who had lived out her mind's life in that awful hour ; and she picked idly at the withered flesh of her dry hands.

But he who was above her heard, and shook his clenched hand at the clear sky.

" No, no, no ! " he cried, as the cañon edge was crowded with his men.

They clambered up the hanging ropes ; they fought desperately for foothold, and pulled down those who had advantage. Only the brained man lay motionless in the slime, while his slayer, fearful of some terrible return of sane justice, grinned sickly on the bank.

Then the great dam moved and surged with a grating noise, while the rivulets below gushed dreadfully, and after one long-drawn moment of expectation it gave way, and, with a roar that drowned the cries of the maddened crowd, it yielded wholly to the river that swept back into its ancient channel for ever, or till the end of long generations yet unborn.

But in the bitter surge and lifted crest of it he who had wrought the miracle was borne down like a foam bubble unregarded. His fellows stood awe-struck and motionless for a long, long minute.

And then the order of the natural world returned.

MORLEY ROBERTS

THE YOUNG MAN WHO STROKED CATS

STORIES, like plants, do not begin: they grow, and what folks are apt to call their beginning is when they break the fertile carth and show themselves. So in common parlance Tom Meredith's story began what time a ragged youth came up the pathway to the front door and rang the bell, when Tom was at breakfast with his father and mother.

" A beggar, I fear," said Mr. Meredith.

" Rather cheeky to come to the front door," said Tom.

" I hope he isn't hungry," sighed his mother.

And the maid who opened the door was very lofty with the ragged youth.

" You should go to the back," said she with her nose in the air.

" I does what I'm paid for," retorted the ragged one. " Does Mr. Thomas Meredith live 'ere ? "

He was carrying a basket, quite a dainty basket, and it was tied with a pink ribbon. It caught the girl's eye just as she was prepared to say that her young master was not likely to see beggars at nine o'clock in the morning or, for that matter, at any time. It would have been untrue, but that would not have mattered.

" Is that for Mr. Meredith ? " she asked.

" Yus. And it's a cat," said the young fellow, lifting the basket up and peering in through the interstices.

" Who's it from ? "

" I dunno. A young lidy give me a tanner to tike it to Mr. Thomas Meredith as lives 'ere. She p'inted out the 'ouse, and went away in a kerridge."

" If you'll wait a moment I'll speak to him," said the girl. She went to the breakfast-room.

" If you please, Mr. Thomas, there's some one says he has a cat for you," she announced.

" A cat for me ? I've ordered no cat," said Tom. But no one would have been surprised if he had ordered one, for men are most properly divided into those who own dogs and those who are owned by cats, and it was notorious that Tom Meredith belonged to the smaller but more distinguished order.

" Oh no, sir," said the girl, " but the young man says that a lady in a carriage gave it to him and paid him to bring it here."

" How odd," said Tom's mother, eyeing him anxiously. So far she had had no reason to do so.

" Very odd," said his father. " Bring the cat in, Jones."

" And tell the man to wait," said Tom. He knew no girl likely to present him with a cat, or with anything else for that matter. It was not that he despised them, but he was very busy, and keeping romance deep in his heart he found them nowadays very unromantic.

Jones brought in the basket, and, as she entered, there arose from it a pitiful wail. Tom got up, took it from her, and putting it on the table opened it. There instantly climbed into view a wild-eyed Persian kitten, little more than a month old. It was the colour of Chinchilla, and probably, as Tom knew, of high lineage. So far as one could tell its points at that age it was perfect.

" Humph," said Tom's father.

" Very rummy," said Tom.

" Give it some milk," said his mother, and while the two elders watched it lap, Tom went out to the hall door.

" Who gave you this kitten ? " he asked.

" A young lidy in a kerridge says to me, says she, ' Do yer warnt to earn a tanner,' and I says, says I, ' Oh, it ain't likely, is it, miss, and what do you think ? ' And wiv that she gives me the basket and a tanner and says, ' Tike this to number 10 and say it's for Mr. Thomas Meredith.' And as I opened your gyte she drives off."

" What was she like ? " asked Tom.

" Pretty, but very pile," said the youth, shaking his head. " And it was a one-'orse kerridge, and there was a nuss with 'er."

" A nuss ? " asked Tom.

" In uniform," said the youth.

" Here's a shilling for you," said Tom.

" Blimy, but you're a gent," said the ragged one. And as he went away he put the shilling and the sixpence on his hand and looked at them with his head sideways all the way down the path. And Tom went back to breakfast.

" There was something in the basket, Tom," said his mother.

" What ? " asked her son.

She gave him a plain card. On it was written in a round hand " For the Young Man who Strokes Cats."

" You don't know who it is, Tom ? " she asked.

" Haven't the least notion," said Tom with perfect honesty.

" You found out nothing from the boy ? " asked his father ; " didn't he know her name ? "

" No," said Tom.

" Somebody has fallen in love with you at last, Tom," said his father.

" I daresay it is some old lady who has noticed you always speak to cats," suggested his mother.

" A very silly habit," said his father.

" But this one is too sweet," said his mother. They sat down and watched the baby Persian finish his milk. When it was done he looked up at them and finally walked straight to Tom.

" I shall call it Korban," said Tom. For Korban means " it is a gift."

And Korban climbed up his coat and lay on his shoulder, purring feebly. There was a far-off look in his new master's eyes, and his mother knew that he was wondering who the giver might be, and her heart was a little hostile to the stranger, as all mothers' hearts are.

Tom was twenty-four, and there was perhaps no young fellow in Kensington who had been less troubled by love. In spite of his passion for cats, which are properly indoor or domestic deities, he was essentially an outdoor man, so far as the City permitted him to be and spending all his spare time on the river or some golf course he gave small attention to those who might have smiled on him. And yet the time now came when spring and youth and the thoughts of love came altogether. As the gift of the Unknown purred on his shoulder, his heart was moved. For the unknown is the land of romance always. He knew that he was found pleasing in the eyes of a stranger, and he flushed a little to think of it. There is no more wonderful or disturbing thing to youth.

So days went by, and the others in the house forgot how it was that Korban came to be theirs. But Tom did not forget, and when he came home tired he often sent for Korban, who grew quickly and was exceedingly agile and very round and furry, and every day more obviously of high lineage.

" Who sent you to me, Korban ? " he asked, as Korban pursued his own tail, or rolled over, or walked sideways loftily, or spat at some other imaginary kitten evolved from his inner consciousness. " I wonder who she is."

The pretty pale young lady, reported by love's ragged messenger, assumed many shapes in his waking thoughts, and sometimes in his dreams. But though the spring was in his heart she could not endure, and when Korban was a month old, began to fade from his thoughts. Yet he was still the Young Man who Stroked Cats on his way to the City. He was acquainted with many of them, and though he did not know it one was a relative of Korban. He was a very gracious and dignified Persian King, to whom Tom gave the name of Artaxerxes. Artaxerxes, blue-haired and yellow-eyed, a creature of smoke and fire, of grey jade and topaz, sat upon a wall and received tribute daily, looking past his worshippers' heads with subtle shining eyes like those of an idol staring over priests in an Eastern temple. And she who was the priestess, the pretty pale creature of Tom's fading dreams, saw him offer worship at the Persian King's throne, and when he had gone by she sent down for Artaxerxes, who came reluctantly and yet was gracious to her. So she stroked the fur that Tom had stroked, and she buried her face where his strong hands had been, and the King endured this ritual uncomplainingly, for she was always good to him.

When another month had passed and Korban began to acquire some of the imperial dignity which his lineage assured to him, Tom Meredith was alone in the house, for his father and mother were in Italy. Yet he was not alone, for Korban was with him, sitting on his knee, while his master smoked and dreamed, with a book of adventure lying on the floor beside him. He wondered why it was that some had adventures and others had none, and why the world was so foolish as to order its dull life to avoid them. He forgot that the gift of Korban was an adventure and might have been a great one if he had sought out the giver. And perhaps the world is wise, for true adventures are rare, and he who seeks may never find them. But to others they are a gift.

The purring of Korban became strangely loud, and Tom Meredith fell asleep. For a cat is a sorcerer of sleep and may procure it for the wakeful. And how long he slept he knew not, but he woke suddenly with the sound of a telephone bell in his ears, and Korban was on the table where the instrument stood, looking at it with startled eyes. Tom reached out his hand, and yawned and put the receiver to his ear.

Upon the magic instrument, which some use so grossly and without wonder, many voices are hard and untuneful, as if the little souls of the speakers had not strength to travel. But others are still sweet, full of character and music, and the voice that Tom heard was one of these though it was not strong. It was assuredly a feminine voice and suggested, he knew not how, fragile beauty and tenderness.

" Are you Mr. Tom Meredith ? " asked the voice.

" Yes," said Tom, " who are you ? "

" Be patient, young man," said the voice with a little tremor of laughter in it ; " before I tell you that or anything else, tell me if you are very busy, or if you have time to talk with a—ghost ? "

He knew this was an adventure and he sat down at the table before he answered.

" No, I am not busy. Still——"

" Do not make excuses. Sit down. Are you comfortable ? I

want to speak to you, and if you are not comfortable how can I speak ? "

" I am sitting down," said Tom. " Now tell me who you are and why you want to speak to me."

" I—I am a woman," said the voice.

" Your voice tells me that," said Tom.

" I hope it sounds a nice one," she said. " Yours is very kind and strong. And now I want to ask you a strange question. Are you a very, very honourable man, Tom Meredith ? "

" I—I hope so," said Tom.

" Then if you are very honourable, noble sir, you will promise me something, will you not ? "

" What am I to promise ? " asked Tom.

" Honourable sir, you are cautious. But I shall not ask you to do anything. All I want is your sacred promise not to do something."

" I promise," said Tom.

" Then you swear by Bast that you will not try to find out who it is that speaks to you."

" Who is Bast ? " asked Tom, wondering.

" She was Bubastis, which is her great name, the wife of Pthah and the goddess of Cats," said the voice. " Do you swear by her ? "

" I swear," said Tom. " And yet I wish so much to know."

" I am glad you wish it, honourable sir, but having sworn by our goddess you cannot break your word, for if you break it you will be torn to pieces by all the cats of Kensington, a very numerous and honourable company. Would that not be dreadful ? "

" Very dreadful," said Tom, " but might I not know how you found out I was likely to regard this goddess with awe ? "

" Are you not the Young Man who Strokes Cats ? " she asked, and then of course he knew that Korban was her gift to him.

" Then it was you who sent me Korban ? "

" Honourable sir, worshipper of Bubastis, you have a fine gift of naming cats. Is Korban beautiful ? "

" I think he is more beautiful now," said Tom. " He is listening to us. He is a wonderful cat and very wise."

" I am glad he pleases you," she said. " But now, kind and honourable sir, I must not waste your honourable time with cats. I want to say much and cannot."

" Say what you will," said Tom.

" May I speak to you at night when the mood takes me, good kind sir ? "

" You may," said Tom.

" I shall not trouble you long," said the voice ; " perhaps it will only be a little while. Then I am going away."

Her voice seemed melancholy.

" Where are you going ? " he asked, and she said, " Ah, I do not know." And then she added suddenly :

" Do you wonder that I, a stranger to you, should want to speak to you, sir ? "

Tom blushed and was glad no one saw him.

" I—I don't know," he stammered. " Sometimes I have seen strangers I could have spoken to. Are you alone, kind voice ? "

" Quite alone," said the kind voice, sadly, " but for you, dear sir, I'm quite alone. Else I could not speak. You must tell no one that I speak with you. It must be our secret."

" I will tell no one," said Tom. " But tell me why you want to speak to me. Have we ever met ? "

There was a little gurgle of faint laughter in his ear.

" Who knows ? Perhaps at the shrines of Bubastis, great years ago. I shall not tell you if we have met. But do you not think it was a beautiful thought of mine to speak ? Many of us are lonely, and there is no shame when this beautiful instrument helps us. Have you ever heard of a lonely woman who wrote beautiful letters to a man she loved, a man who did not know her till she died ? "

" I never heard of her," said Tom. " Then are you lonely ? "

" Very lonely," she said. " All of us are lonely, but some are more lonely than others."

" Why did you have this thought for me ? " he asked.

" I shall not tell you yet, if you cannot guess, honourable and kind and dull sir."

" Am I so dull then ? " he demanded quickly.

" I meant modest, kind sir, so please forgive me."

" Just before you rang I was thinking how dull it was in London with the big world calling outside," said Tom.

" You wanted an adventure, sir. We all need adventures to keep our blood sweet. I will be your adventure. I will steal away your heart. You do not know who I am. I may be near you, the girl next door, or a countess in Park Lane ; I may be so beautiful that you would fall down and worship, or so ugly that you would say, ' Poor girl.' I may be a waitress where you have your lunch when you go to the City, or even a typewriting girl, or a queen, or a little girl that is going away, or any strange woman with wild thoughts in her."

" I am sure you are strange and sweet," said Tom.

" Yes, I am very sweet, and exceedingly beautiful, and I would refuse kings if you asked me. And I shall speak to you every night, Tom."

It thrilled him strangely to hear his name spoken and know what was in her heart.

"Tell me what you are. Have I ever seen you? You might tell me that?" he asked.

"You may have seen me, who can tell, since I have seen you at my palace window. I think you have seen one that I love not a little. But not so much as you, honourable sir."

"Then—then you love me?" he asked.

"Dear simple kind honourable sir, do you think I could speak to you like this if I did not love you? Incredulous modest sir, of course I love you, and have loved you for many months, long before I sent you my Persian gift. Are you glad or sorry?"

"I—I cannot answer you," said Tom. "It's rather strange, you know, isn't it?"

"That's why I like it," she said, and it seemed to Tom that her head was on his shoulder and that they sat in the dark in some secret room while she told him her heart. "We women never get a chance of saying first without shame 'I love you,' and yet often women's hearts are so full of love that they would die to speak. Am I not old and wise and sweetly shameless, kind sir?"

"If you speak like that I—I shall never see you," said Tom with a sudden fear in his heart.

"Oh, dear honourable sir, tell me why you say that."

"You will not let me if——"

"If I am so bold, dear sir? How wise you are! Now listen and you will hear me clap my hands."

He heard her clap them and heard her faint laughter.

"Why do you laugh?" he asked.

"Because you are wiser than you were. Tell me, dear sir, have you ever loved any girl devoutly?"

"Never," said Tom, "not devoutly, you know. Of course I've thought I loved some one every now and then."

"Then love me," she said, "and make my little mad adventure a real great one. Till I go away it will be very much for me, and I will hang roses on this blessed instrument that has given me such power as no girl ever had. I wonder if I am the first who has spoken like this. Tell me, dear sir, am I the first and do you love me?"

"You must be a strange girl," said Tom; "I think you must be the very first to have done this. But how can I say I love you?"

"Hard and cruel sir, why not say it? Can it harm you? You love no one and yet love must be in your heart, sleeping. But you do not hate me?"

"Oh no," said Tom, "of course not: what stuff to think so. I wish I could see you. What shall I call you?"

"You must make a name, inventive sir. Before I knew yours I made many for you."

"Tell me what they were," said Tom.

She laughed. " I can't tell you all of them. But once you were The Boy who Doesn't Want to go to Business, and then you were The Young Man who Strokes Cats. And also The Little Girl's Morning and Evening Tonic, and finally the—Beloved. Am I not shameful, dear critical severe sir ? "

" Oh no," said Tom, " I think you must be a very amusing girl."

" If I saw you I shouldn't be at all amusing. I should shrink into my shell of pearl, in which all nice little girls keep their souls, and you would not have patience to coax me out of it. But now I am free and can say what I like, and if I blush, dearly beloved, you can see me do it. Free souls are as sweet as flying butterflies, but shut-up souls are drab little things, such as they become when they close their wings. But have you sought out a jewel of a name for me, rich sir, explorer of the language of love ? "

" I don't seem to be able to think of one," said Tom.

" What do you think of Ermyntrude ? "

There was a little laughter in her voice.

" Oh no," said Tom.

" Or Gladys, or Yolande, or some name a yard long," she suggested.

Tom liked none of them.

" Then ' the Poor Girl ' might do," she said. " Say the Poor Girl for the present. And now there is some one coming. Good-night."

" I'll call you the Dear Unknown," said Tom. " But tell me one thing. Are you—ill ? "

" They say so, but some day—I shall not be."

There was strange melancholy in her voice, and Tom knew it. He was learning things very fast.

" And now, sympathetic sleepy sir, I must say good-night. Will you speak to me to-morrow ? "

" Oh yes," said Tom, and as he spoke it seemed to him that he heard some one else in her room, a dim ghost of a voice. And when he spoke again he received no answer. But the sound of her voice was in his ears like the murmur of waters, and he wondered about her and also about himself, until midnight heralded a new day.

He hoped to dream of her but did not. Dreams were for the daytime, and through the long hours he thought of her, wondering how it was that she so affected him. He loved no one, but was ready to love, and the thought of the unknown, the " Poor Girl," of her laughing yet melancholy speech, moved him deeply. More and more he wondered where she lived, knowing that it must be near him, and on the way he took when he went daily to the station. She had called him the Young Man who Strokes Cats, and he had caressed many of them. Besides the Persian he had made friends with a ferocious yellow Tom, with a tabby, and with one delightfully absurd white creature who possessed two large black spots on one side, three on the other and an irregular blotch on his head. If the people who were owned by this cat were of the right sort they undoubtedly called him Pierrot. And besides these friends of Tom's there were also others, to say nothing of his own, a magnificent striped tiger who so far scorned to notice the existence of Korban.

" I shall ask her what her cat is like," said Tom cunningly. And that day he paid particular attention to every cat he saw. But Artaxerxes he did not see. That noble creature sat on a back wall and disdained the worshipping universe.

A modest youth—and youth is always modest under cover of its self-protecting blatancy—must always wonder when a woman loves him. To be the chosen one out of the world is a strange glory, and it half blinds him. So it was with Tom Meredith. And his story was stranger than any he knew. The unknown's voice was the actual voice of romance ; it swept him from the commonplace world into a very paradise. This was magic indeed, and he waited for the magical night like any lover, with impatience and with dreams.

When ten o'clock struck at last he was in the library, almost in darkness, for the room was only dimly lighted by the shaded lamp on the desk. As he waited with the standard telephone upon a little table at his side he was conscious of a fine tremor, an expectancy and apprehension of the nerves, which moved him strangely. His nature, awakening not at the sight of the Beloved but at her far-off melancholy voice, brought so magically to his ear, felt the wonder that is in all things, and was eager and yet afraid. He could not yet say he loved her, but the pulses of his heart responded to her delicate music in the darkness of a great adventure.

And then at last the bell rang. He lost the world he sat in and entered magical woods.

" Are you there, adventurous sir ? "

" Magician, it is I."

" How sweet of you, sir Knight. All day I have wondered whether you would answer when I called for help under your castle walls."

" I've thought of you all day, sweet stranger."

Her romantic heart called to his and gave him words to speak with.

" Of the Poor Girl, who is perhaps so ugly that she cannot bear to be seen by him she adores ? "

" I know you are beautiful, little girl. For even now your voice has music in it. It's—it's a harp in a dark wood."

He almost blushed to say so poetic a thing.

" I thank you, musical and dear sir. You must always think me beautiful, and never being undeceived you may carry me in your heart when——"

" When what, dear witch ? "

" When I am—dust," she answered. Even the hard magic of the wire could not destroy the melancholy with which she spoke.

" Oh, shall I never see you, dear witch ? That's hard."

" I think it will be never, sad-voiced sir. But to-day I saw you. How many wild cats did you stroke, absurd kind sir ? "

" Many," said Tom. " I cannot pass one without addressing it humbly and soliciting its favours after the manner of a poor tradesman who requests the favour of your esteemed orders. Your cat and mine, Korban, is with me now. He has another name as well. My little sister calls him Boffles, because, as she explains, he is very boffly and a muffly chunk as well as being a soggy buster."

" Kiss her for me, she must be a dear thing."

" And what is your cat like, unknown ? "

" I will tell you, cunning inquisitive sir. He has fur all over him and four legs and a tail and sharp teeth and when he is pleased he purrs loudly. He is in fact a typical cat."

" Wicked elusive one, you make him out no more than a furred mammal."

" Ah, I mean to be the secret lady and my cat must also be secret. So when I am—dust, and you are married, you will love me. In those days when you are dull and that hateful she, your wife, is also dull (as I'm sure she will be), you will think of me and my little bell will ring and we shall be off again into the magical forests. Then every speck of my dust will shine like stars, dear Tom."

" Your dust, your dust ! Why do you speak so ? Are you ill ? "

" Yes, medicinal sir, so ill that Time is no longer the half-brother of Eternity as the healthy folk think him."

" Oh, child, do you mean that you——"

" Yes, sorrowful sir. They all say so now, not in words but in gentle looks and sorrowful ways."

" You mean you are dying, dear one ? "

" That's true, pale sir. My hands say so if nothing else did."

" I must see you, once, once ! "

" If you could have done so when I was beautiful ! But now you would be grieved, and I'd have you remember me as your mind will make me, a golden lass among roses and lilies. For only in your heart, which begins to love me, shall I be beautiful again."

" I *do* begin to love you. Is there no hope ? "

" So little, gloomy sir, that I trust it not, nor think of it, and now I am glad. For when hope spread her wings and flew out of my window I went to look after her and saw you again, and I knew the bright bird had left me a feather as she went. Being as it were already dust I could speak to you, for no one has ever loved me with a man's heart, and I desired to be loved a little before my enemy came, dear sir."

" I—I love you," said Tom.

" Grieve not, my blessèd lover. I've come by magic to make you unhappy. And yet you have been loved. That's something."

He knew it was a sacrament, the greatest of all.

" It—it is much."

" Do you remember, dear sweet sorrowful sir, that when a poor girl was crushed in a railway accident and lay dying on the stained grass, a stranger came pitifully to help her ? She said, ' Do not move me, but kiss me so that I shall know before I die that some one has loved me.' Had some writer made that out of his heart I should have said the thought was genius and that a great man wrote it, but it was the death cry of a poor little girl that no one had kissed. Will not the kiss the stranger gave her warm his lips for ever ? "

It was as if something broke inside Tom's heart. There were tears upon his cheeks.

" And I shall never kiss you, never, never."

" I kiss you, dear one, with my heart," she said, " kiss me with yours."

She spoke no more that night. But Tom Meredith knew that he loved this voice of a dream, this mystic white rose of love in the valley of Shadow. He saw her given to him and yet reft away, a vestal devoted to the pale fires of the sterile deity Death. She went with him daily, and the sound of her voice was in his ears marvellously, and he waited for the night impatiently and his friends wondered about him. One keener than the others said he was becoming religious, and maybe it was true. If religion be not love, love is ever religion, and the heart knows it.

And the white maiden was happier now, and those about her said she grew better. Hope sprang again in their hearts, though she had none. She thought this chosen love of hers the full accomplishment of her life, and she thanked destiny and her own courage and what Gods there are for its flower, which was, it seemed, all that her life should grow. Some one beyond her own home would remember her, and she was glad that he was strong. For many know that immortality is remembrance.

The instrument by which she spoke to him stood near her bed or by the window when she sat there. For some it was an instrument of commerce, or of idle talk, but for her it became sacred, and she decorated it with flowers daily. When Artaxerxes came to see her she endeavoured to make him bow down to it, as if it were some ancient God of the Persians or a fetish from Bubastis which even kingly cats might worship. To no one but Artaxerxes did she speak of her lover. But it seemed that Artaxerxes understood, for a wise cat knows everything.

" This morning he stroked your royal fur, my Persian King," said the white maiden, " and he wondered if I belonged to you, great monarch. These yellow eyes of yours behold close those dear eyes of his. No one knows but you and me, my cat. It is our secret, a high adventure."

On the coasts of death and life are many adventures, and in many iron shores are havens. It may be that her belovèd helped her when she seemed past help. " Man doth not yield himself to the Angels, nor under Death utterly, save by the weakness of his will." His thought for her was strength. She reached out and leaned upon him.

So the night came and the hour when her soul shone like Hero's lamp across the water.

" Belovèd ! "

He answered :

" Dear child ! "

" Patient sir, how went the day with you ? "

" I thought of you, you."

" That's sweet of my belovèd ! "

" I cannot believe there is no hope for you, my child."

" They still hope, though I do not, and to-day there came another stranger to see me."

" Tell me. Did he say anything ? What did he say ? "

" Very little, dear sir. But he sat by me a long while and twisted his eyebrows over me, and I knew he was thinking. My old doctor left him with me. He was a strange man, neither big nor little, but strong, and he had a face which reminded me of some one. I can't think who it was. Then suddenly he told me something to make me laugh. Then he was silent again, and nodded to himself. Then he looked at me and smiled and said I was brave. He laid his hand on my forehead and went away."

" And yet said nothing ? "

" Nothing. Oh, now I remember that he was like, really just a little like, Napoleon."

" I shall hope for you. I seem to see you clearer every hour."

" Ah, dear sir, I saw you very clearly this morning. I have a glass that brought you near to me. I know the colour of your eyes now."

" What is the colour of yours, belovèd ? "

" I can tell you that. They are brown with little specks of red in them, as if they were a red-brown opal, if such a thing could be. They used to be very merry. But yours are blue, sir."

" So they say, child. But what I want to know most is your name, dearest."

" I will not tell you that. Not even now. I am for you what I shall be, a spirit and a thought. If my voice ceases for you it will be a grief, but not the bitter wound it might be. If you knew my name, sir, you would not rest till you saw me, for you are strong and determined, and then you would say I was like a sad Cheshire Cat with nothing but a wan little smile left for you. Think of me as young and beautiful and strong and gay, as I once was, with a lovely voice. May I not tell you what I was, now I'm so old, oh, so old and wise ? "

" My dear one."

She heard his voice break a little, and then he spoke again.

" The telephone is by my bed now, beloved. After eleven o'clock you can speak to me there. If the night is weary, call for me."

" That will be strange—and sweet. Good-night, dear sir."

For the nurse came to her and she would not share her secret with a soul. She smiled to herself and endured the hours. But he dreamed of her and seemed to see her plainly, though in the morning he could not remember her face.

In the morning a little parcel came for him. In it there was a miniature of a girl with brown eyes, in which he seemed to see specks of fire. And his imagination made it like the lady of his dream. But if it was hers, as indeed it should be, it must have been painted years before, since it was the face of a young girl, very sweet and bright and vivid.

" It is she," said Tom, and he knew that he loved her indeed. He showed it to no one, and kept it near his heart, waiting for the night-time to thank her. So the day went and darkness came, and she rang to him at last.

" Dear is that you ? " he asked.

" Yes, fair sir, it is I."

" I got what you sent me."

" My dreams ? "

" The little picture. It is beautiful."

" Some hateful girl who loves you has sent her picture. Burn it."

" It is yours, I know."

" I admit nothing, sir, nothing whatever. Should I be so forward to do such a thing ? It is true I said I loved you, but I am only a voice, and a voice without a face is no more than a thought. Is she sweet to look at, this wretched girl you speak of ? "

" She is quite lovely."

" Ah, I hate her. Perhaps I was like her once. But, dear one, put her aside and listen."

" I am listening."

" I have news for you, good sir."

" What news, little girl with the brown eyes and red specks ? "

" Napoleon came to see me again to-day, and he told me three absurd stories. I think it absurd for Napoleon to come here and stare at me and tell me funny things. One was about a little Jewish boy whose grandfather asked him to get well and promised him money if he would be quick about it, and the little boy, who was no more than seven years old, said, without opening his eyes, " How much ? " That is the only one I remember, for afterwards the little Emperor said he was going to stop thinking and do something."

" Oh, what, child ? Tell me, tell me."

" He says it is to be a punishment for being ill. He tells me it is very wicked to be ill and an immoral scandalous perversity to show no signs of getting well. That's what the severe Emperor says, so I am to have awful things done to me. I hope not with boiling oil. But I feel sure there are knives and chloroform in it. And the little Emperor rubs his imperial chin and says I shall get well."

" My dear, my dear ! "

" Do not hope too much, sir, for I know better. At any rate I know what a chance it is and know that he knows it. I was very impudent to him and called him Napoleon. I said, ' You know it is a chance, Emperor, a teeny weeny chance,' and he replied, ' Little girl, you mustn't know too much or I will have your head cut off. I am going to defeat the enemy. This shall be my Austerlitz.' And he laughed. But all the same it may be Waterloo."

" No, no, child, you shall not think that. When is it to be ? "

" The very next day after to-morrow, belovèd. My cat is with me, Tom. You stroked him to-day."

" Very annoying and wicked belovèd, tell me what that cat is like."

" Young man, he has four legs and a tail, and is a green tabby with blue and crimson spots. I think he ought to have a prize."

" His mistress ought to have one, I think. When we meet at last I shall certainly begin by beating you."

" How delightful to think we have got so friendly without having seen me ! But no, kind sir, I know you better. You might have been a horrid suspicious person and been rude when I rang you up and said I loved you. But you were very nice about it, and if Napoleon is defeated you can say, ' I made the little girl happy at the last and she went away into the White Country blessing me ! ' "

" Don't, belovèd ! "

" My dearest, my blessèd, I have made you unhappy. But you have given me courage. Without you to think of I do not believe Napoleon would have persuaded me. It would have been easier to —sleep. But always I love you. You will speak to me to-morrow night and in the morning ? "

" Yes, yes," said her lover.

" My nurse comes, Tom. She wonders who it is I speak to when she is away, but I smile at her and will not tell. Good-night, dear one."

When he said good-night there were tears in his eyes and his voice was broken. So was his sleep, for he dreamed he saw her buried. And again she was by his side, veiled. At five o'clock in the morning he went down to the library and brought up to his bedroom a history of Napoleon's campaigns in which he read the story of Austerlitz. When he came down to breakfast his father said he looked a bit pippy and his mother declared he was losing his appetite, but being English, he replied stolidly that he was only just a little " off it." But he wondered at the blindness of those who loved him, and their ignorance that a miracle had been wrought in their midst. A hundred times he looked at the smiling picture that she half denied was hers. Would he ever see her face to face, or would she die in silence, going out into the night, into the strange land she called the White Country ?

The day ended in heavy wind and rain, and he went upstairs early. It was only a little after ten o'clock when she spoke to him.

" This is my last night before—it, dear Tom. All day long, belovèd, I have been watching the clouds and listening to the wind. And the wild sunset was beautiful. How strange it is to think I may never again see one, never hear the wind in the trees ! But I am happy."

" My dear one," said her lover, " but are you not cruel ? "

" Cruel, Tom ! Am I ? "

" I cannot see you and I cannot speak. Oh, it is hard to speak like this. Let me come to you. I will speak to your people. They cannot refuse me or you ! "

" If I get well you shall see me. I promise that. And if not, think of me as the little girl whose picture you have, the little girl who loved you. You will remember me when others have forgotten and I'd have you remember me."

" I shall remember. But how shall I know, child ? It may be days before you can speak to me."

" Long days," she sighed, " but I have written two letters already, Tom, and one is for you. If it is not Austerlitz after all for the little Emperor you will get what I have written to you. I am quite happy and not afraid. For I know you love me."

" I shall love you always."

" It's sweet to hear you say it. Have you that strange wild girl's picture ? "

" It is in my hand."

" Kiss the little girl's picture, dear. I was like her once, and now I do not hate her for looking so well. Have you kissed it, dear sir, my lover ? "

" Yes, I have kissed it."

" Then that's good-night, I kiss you, belovèd. And at nine to-morrow I will speak to you once more. You'll be there ? "

" Yes, dear one."

And again she sighed " good-night," and then silence fell between them. That night he did not sleep till dawn, and then only for an hour. At six o'clock he rose and went out into the Gardens, walking there till eight o'clock struck. As he came back up the street he stopped and spoke respectfully to Artaxerxes, who sat at the receipt of his customary adulation and was very gloomy and grand about it. He also talked more familiarly with the spotted creature who was doubtless called Pierrot. He was neither grand nor gloomy but somewhat vulgar. He almost stood on his head with anxiety to be made much of, and he held up his chin to be scratched. For this is the cat's delight, and the human who does not know it is graceless, and Bubastis knows him not, nor his kindred, nor anything that is his.

And at nine o'clock the telephone bell rang and she spoke to him.

" Dearest one, Napoleon is in the house, so good-bye, my lover, till life comes back or till Eternity."

" I—I pray for you, my belovèd," said her lover.

" My dear one."

And silence fell between them like a heavy curtain. But he whom she loved did his day's work and remembered nothing of it afterwards. For the outward world was less than a dream of a dream, and even as he thought of her he knew she might be dead.

As he went home he looked fearfully at every house, wondering if the blinds of one of them might be drawn down. But there was no sign of death about any, and fear lessened within him though the night was one of wild visions and sudden wakings, in which it seemed the bell of the telephone rang for him. Yet when he started up there was always silence.

On the second day of his ordeal he spoke again to Artaxerxes, and very suddenly he knew the big Persian was hers. For as he bent down to the cat a little odour came up to him, an odour which was sharp and yet faint and sickly, the smell of ether or some powerful drug such as Artaxerxes might have brought from her sick room if he had but now left it.

" She lives here," he said. It was but five houses down the road from his own home. Though there was nothing to confirm his belief he was sure of it. And lifting Artaxerxes in his arms he set him on the wall and stroked him, and once more the faint deadly odour was in his nostrils. So another day went on, and the silent night passed. At dawn Tom went out and all the houses still slept. But at her house the blinds of the upper storey were drawn and the windows were open. On the sill of one window sat the Persian King, looking eastward.

" It is her room," he said.

That day he would not go to the City but walked in the Gardens. And when he went back at mid-day he saw a car come to her door just before he reached it. He seemed to know the face of the man who got out of the car. And yet he was a stranger. But as this stranger went up the garden path to the house door Tom remembered the face that was in his mind. It was that of Napoleon. This was the little Emperor going to see her. So Tom waited, and after a long time, for the minutes were heavier than hours, Napoleon came out of the house and Tom went up to him and said, " Will she live ? " For he drew his bow at a venture.

" I hope so," said the Emperor gravely.

" I thank you," said Tom, but he could say no more, and went away. For he knew Napoleon was not yet sure of victory.

Whether the great man came again the next day or not, he could not tell, for by an evil chance he missed him. But at night he dreamed that he saw Napoleon as he is depicted in the last phase of his strange life, when his spirit was like a candle guttering in the wind. And the Emperor was gloomy, for it was, so Tom dreamed, the anniversary of Waterloo. And when he woke he knew that the spirit of his dream was aware that the day was the eighteenth of June and his heart sank within him at the omen. But he fell asleep again, and her white spirit came to him saying she was dead and could now be his for ever. Yet once more she left him and he woke again, and found it no more than midnight, and he was certain, as disturbed souls are, that his fears had come true. She would speak to him no more. And with the thought of " no more " in his heart a heavy lethargy fell upon his spirit, for this certainty brings a dreadful peace to the spirit of man. There were tears upon his cheek, when this heaviness overpowered him, as though he were an unhappy child who had fallen asleep weeping.

But once more he woke suddenly. And there was cold sweat upon his brow and the hair of his head stood up. He tried to cry out " my belovèd, my belovèd," and could not.

The telephone bell was ringing.

EGERTON CASTLE

1858–1920

MOON'S GIBBET

" BUT it is from Moon's Gibbet, at the further end of Hamildon Down," the landlord at the Crown posting inn on the Shaftesbury Road was saying to an inquisitive stranger, " that you fetch the finest view. It's the down just above Penistone—any one there will tell you the nearest way to Moon's Gibbet. But you'll find it a stiffish climb, sir."

Moon's Gibbet ? I had never heard the name. But in conjunction with Hamildon Down the sound of it evoked an all too well-remembered picture painted in sombre colours on the dim background of the past : started to flight, like awakened birds, a whole host of hateful memories.

So, the record had been preserved ! It had become an accepted local name, after all these years ! I walked up to the large-scale hunting map that hung on the wall, and unerringly found the spot, Hamildon Down. . . . I knew it well. There, on the white, tear-shaped space denoting by its closed contour a high, barren knoll, sure enough ran the italics : *Moon's Gibbet.*

The inquisitive stranger had departed. I turned to the talkative host.

" An odd name," said I, assuming some simplicity. " They used, I know, in the old time, to raise gallows on the hill-tops. But why moon ? "

" There was," said the man readily, " a gallows once on Hamildon. I saw it myself, as a boy, with a black rag swinging from it like a scarecrow. I heard father tell as how that was the last man ever hung in chains in these parts. Years it was a landmark for the countryside in the Vale. Father knew the man. His name was Moon."

" Moon . . . ! " I repeated. And the landlord, flattered no doubt by my listening interest, went on, as he cleared the table :

" The man was well known in the Vale. The Moons were yeomen folk near Penistone. They've all been gone : there is not a Moon left in the county. They were well-to-do enough, it seems. As a boy I heard tell of them—hunting and sporting with the gentry, and looking almost like gentry themselves. But the son was a wild kind of chap, and one day he was took up on a charge of murder. No one ever knew the rights of it ; but, at that time, as you may have heard, sir, they did hang folk, in a manner of speaking, almost for the fun of it. Some said there was a maid in it, and it was a fair fight. But in the end they brought it in highway murder—it was on the Shaston Road—on the evidence of a fellow, the man's own cousin, who was known to be no friend. And hang him they did, at Shaston ; and then they brought him to dangle, tarred and in chains, on the top of Hamildon, well in view of the road where they said the murder had been done. That's how they did it in those days. It was soon after that that the Moons left the country ; and, they do say, also the informing chap. He never was seen again in these parts—which was as well for him, perhaps, for, after the trial, every one, I heard tell, was giving him the go-by. The gibbet's gone, too—oh, these twenty years ! But, as I was telling the gentleman just now, where it stood is the finest view this side of the Stour."

"Yes, I'll go," I said, as if answering an invitation. It was the conclusion, expressed aloud, of a singular conflict in thoughts of my own.

The landlord marked something odd in my manner : I felt him eyeing me with curiosity as I sallied forth from the Crown without another word, and dreamily made my way up the wide street towards the Shaston Road.

I am now what juvenals must call an old man, for I am moving through life on the reverse side of fifty. To one still sound of wind and limb, and in mind still liable to certain enthusiasm—still inclined to the cult of ideals—mere number of years does not spell age in the same sense as it does to young people. But, in one respect, no doubt, the true test of decline in me is upheld : I am more prone in my musings to dwell on memories than on projects, to revive old impressions than seek for new.

There is one impression of my young days, however, the memory of which I have at all times, and always with dismay, striven to ward off. An impression ? A dread adventure, I should say, holding every tragic possibility of consequence. Adventures have a way, especially in the guilelessness of youth, of dropping on a man and wrapping themselves round him as the giant boa from its high ambush on its unsuspecting victim. This one has become a skeleton in memory's cupboard, locked away from my life, never wilfully gazed on these thirty years or more. But it will, at times, obtrude its haunting ; and then it never fails to raise in my soul a breathless doubt as to the share I have taken (benevolently enough, as God is my witness) in a dark night-deed.

To-day, however, I boldly live with it again, face determinedly its vexing features. Why? I can hardly say. It is perhaps that the host's account, jejune as it was, of the man in chains has unexpectedly made plain the story, the fathoming of which I have shunned with such invincible reluctance. They say that, sooner or later, murderers yield to the impulse of revisiting the scene of their deed. It was the mere chance of travel that brought me to-day to this neighbourhood; yet under some such impulse I, in all my consciousness of innocence, find myself tramping this road, amid scenery which ranks among the most beautiful in England, but which has ever remained in my mind's eye hateful and sinister.

An hour's walk, first along the Stour and through its fat water-meadows, past the greystone mossy villages, then up the steeper roads, wood-shadowed, that lead to the higher ground, brings me at last, at a certain sharp bend, in view of the steep rise of this same Hamildon Down on which my eyes have not rested these five-and-thirty years.

There it springs, with strange suddenness, a high bluff, and towers, grey and barren, over the teeming green of the Vale land; there threatens against the white clouds its strange crowning outline of Danish earthwork, barely softened by ten centuries of weathering. This end of the hill—a boldly advanced spur of the Downs, a sullen, silent wilderness, untenanted by any living thing save the crows and the visiting seagulls—descends sheer upon the inhabited land. The highroad from the north splits against the promontory, sending on one side a minor branch to lose itself into a mere track among the high grounds of the Chase, and, on the other, skirting the foot of the scarped face, almost at the exact line of parting between the cultivated land and the irreclaimable waste.

Yes, it was a well-chosen spot for a gibbet. Our forefathers were adepts in such matters. From miles ahead, along the main road, the knoll and its parapets cut the southern view; from the Vale on one side, and the Chase on the other, it is seen as a dent on the sky-line. And when, against the blue, the gibbet raised its sharp thin post, with the significant black bundle swinging in the never-failing breeze, its menace to law-breakers must have been wide-reaching.

So, his name was Moon . . . !

It was on the close of such a day as this, windy and threatening of more wind, that I stood on yonder knoll—five-and-thirty years ago. I had reached it along the crest, on the farther side, from Sarum, by the sunken track, grass-grown but still distinct, which tradition ascribes to Danish days. I was then in my early twenties (it was the autumn of the Waterloo year), engaged on surveying for Arrowsmith, who was planning his new large-scale maps. The triangulation was night work: signal flares were combined to rise simultaneously at a stated hour on selected high spots of the Western Downs, and the angle measures were taken with the new perfected theodolites.

Near the spot assigned to me for that night, the very lip of Hamildon bluff, I found a new feature in the landscape—a gallows tree, with the pitch scarcely set into the wood, and the short length of chain dangling from the cross-arm untouched by any rust. A long ladder was propped against the post in obvious and ominous readiness. As I laid out and adjusted my implements, against the fast-rising darkness, I praised my fate that, in this wild, lonely place, with all its eerie tokens of old hauntings, the revolting structure should still want its burden.

The sky was overcast with lowering storm-clouds, and before the twilight had deepened into black night the breeze had increased to a vicious blow. I lighted my lantern and fixed it on the theodolite, which for better steadiness in the wind I had established close to the ancient parapet. I looked at my watch, devoutly hoping that my comrades, yonder away on Tod Hill, Browndown, and Ashcombe, would be as punctual as myself, so that I might leave the place before the coming squalls. The appointed time was nigh; I set fire to the oil of my cresset. The blaze darted out, and, bent level by the gale, flared with a roar. Almost at the same instant, at three distant quarters of the surrounding murk, appeared where I expected them answering points of light. Forthwith, with all eagerness, I took my angles, checking them repeatedly, and entered them in my note-book. Then, satisfied with the accuracy of my own work, I packed up my instrument again, put out my lantern, and, stepping over the highest parapet, crouched down on the reverse side to seek such shelter from the cutting wind as it might afford. The flare was calculated to burn some twenty minutes; though my task was done, I had to let it burn itself out, according to convention, in case the others should require the fuller length of time.

I had not waited there many minutes, the distant specks were all three still conspicuous on the surrounding black, when a medley of faint sounds—a clicking of iron and confusion of voices—startled me from my contemplation. I rose and peered over the earthwork. The cresset still gave its bright light. I gathered the scene at a glance.

A cart and pony stood now close by the gallows tree, and a pair of rough-looking men were actually engaged upon fixing to the chain that which it had been waiting for. One of the men, with arms raised above his head, supported the corpse's iron-cased legs, letting the feet rest upon his shoulders. The other, high up on the ladder, appeared to be adjusting the neck-chain with special care. His work accomplished, he came hastily down the ladder and busied himself with the cart, preparing for immediate departure, while his companion stepped up to the cresset, near my place of concealment, and began examining it curiously as he warmed his fingers at the flame.

"That will have been provided by him," he said enigmatically, with a jerk of the head towards the Vale.

The man of the cart, drawing close in his turn, plucked him by the arm.

"And a danged stupid thing to do, anyhow!" he said with a curse. "But that's his look-out. Hurry along, mate."

They mounted their cart again, without having noticed me, and rolled away with much application of whip. That I should not have heard them coming was due, no doubt, to the high wind which, even now as they sank again into the night, swept away all sound of hoof or wheel.

The scene had been like a dream episode. And, indeed, the whole of what followed that night was more like the course of an intermittent nightmare than any sequence of realities: a chain of sensations hateful to the soul and to all the senses, racking to sight, to touch, to hearing—aye, to smell! To this day the odour of pitch retains a nauseating horror.

For a minute or so I remained gazing with stupid mournfulness at the black figure which had begun to sway violently and with dismal creakings. Then, on a sudden impulse, I bounded over the parapet and rushed to the flare; it was already beginning to wane, and I had no other thought but to fly the accursed spot before it should go out.

Through a pause in the wind there fell from above a sound that made every hair of my body bristle with terror: a groan so lamentable that it was as a revelation of hitherto unimaginable suffering. The horror of it stopped me dead in the very gesture of plucking the cresset from the ground. And, as I stood, turned to stone and glaring fixedly before me, out of that darkness into which men and cart had melted, a new form bounded into the circle of light. A man, old, but tall and powerful, bareheaded, whose grey locks flew back in the wind from a deep-lined face, whose eyes, small and eager under bushy brows, were now peering inquiringly at me, with an intentness that brought a new kind of terror to my soul. In two strides he was by me.

"It was you gave those signal whistles just now?" he asked, panting, for he had been running, and he was not of an age when running comes easy. "Say it was you!" he repeated with a fierce anxiousness.

" No——" I stammered in bewilderment.

At the word, suspicion flashed into the small eyes; upon the shaven lips, grey even as the stubbly cheek-bone whiskers, and parted by labouring breath, came a twist of murderous anger. I verily believe that the next instant he would have been at my throat, when no doubt I soon should have been hurled down the scarp. But once more the lugubrious sound fell from the gibbet head. At this there came a look on the man's face that stabbed me to the heart; it drove all fear away, leaving nothing but a passion of pity. In a second he had turned and was up the ladder, had thrown one arm round the swaying body, whilst the other was working above his head at the hook of the chain. And, as he laboured frantically—so a man would to snatch another from torture—he threw out hoarse, appealing words:

" Harry, boy! It's me—your dad! Courage, boy! I'm near, Harry!" To which came in answer another groan of the damned. I stood, palsied, unable to think.

After some futile attempts at the hook, he turned his head.

" In the name of God . . . !" he called, with a kind of sob, and I awoke to reason again. I ran up to the hanging man, seized the tar-smeared legs, and, resting the feet on my shoulders (even as I had seen the hangman's mate do a few moments before) raised the stiff, iron-cased body till its weight was removed from the chain. Then I saw it fall sideways into the father's arms. The next moment we had it laid on the grass.

" Thank God . . . thank God!"

The words came unconsciously from the old man, like irrepressible gulps, as he busied himself in a frenzy of succour. For me he had not a thought. First of all he plucked from the face as far as the forehead something black that came off like a skin, and I suddenly realised that the hangman and his assistant—through what means bribed it was bootless then to surmise, but in obvious collusion—had mercifully done the tarring of a still breathing body over the cotton cap and not over bare face and head.

The cresset light was sinking low, but I could see that here was a young face. Heaven forgive me, but I doubt if, in the ever more acute agony of returning consciousness, the youth would have echoed the spasmodic " Thank God!" of the old man. He lay on the grass—a broken thing it seemed, only held together by the cruel irons—his eyes closed as if dead, but shaken by those dreadful sighs.

The rushing wind had for some time brought with it stinging drops of rain. Presently we were assailed by a drenching shower, and the flare went out with startling suddenness. On the instant the old man rose to his feet and dashed into the night. But, before I had time to recover from my dismay, the faint light of a lantern appeared a few yards off, and he was returning, lustily pushing before him a hand-cart over the rise of ground where—I understood all then—he had left it to run forward on noticing me by the side of my cresset.

It seemed as if we could communicate with one another without speech. In silence, as he tenderly raised the youth by the shoulders, he motioned to me to take up the legs. We stretched the pitiful body, still in its clinking fetters, upon the cart ; the father doffed his coat, which he rolled up for a pillow, and muffled his lantern once more. Then, without a word, we moved away.

For nigh a quarter of an hour, pursued by the tempest, we pushed and pulled side by side in silence, following the gently descending track, till we were stopped by a denser black mass rising indistinctly against the murk of the night.

"The house," said my companion, and went forward to open the door.

Only when we were safely within with our burden, the door clapped to and the wooden bolt shot, did he uncover his light. It was a poor, low-ceiled cottage room. On the hearth, close to a sinking wood-fire, a pot was simmering. In a corner recess stood a kind of bed covered with dun-coloured blankets, and by its side a table with bottles and crockery. There was a low door at the far end, and another on the left near the bed.

"Your house ?" I asked in astonishment, for the old man was dressed in the cloth and linen of the well-to-do, and his speech, for little that I had heard of it, was that of the fairly educated.

"My shepherd's cottage," he answered briefly. "He is away. We are safe here."

It was in this sordid abode, on the edge of the wild down, with the tempest howling around us, that we two, strangers to each other, ministered to the reviving corpse. The loathsome cap was finally removed not without trouble, for it stuck cruelly to the bruised back of the neck. The body-chains were loosened and flung aside with sinister clank, the evil-smelling tarred clothes stripped off, and the anguished body laid between the blankets. The father had no attention, no eyes, no ears but for his son ; never spoke a word but of encouragement to him ; as for me, a gesture sufficed.

A faint hue of life flowed back to the lad's cheek, and his eyes showed a fluttering tendency to open. The old man, with infinite precaution, raising the limp head, was trying to pour some warm broth down his throat, when above the din of the storm came a sound of knocking, unmistakable, peremptory, threatening.

My heart stood still. To the old man's face sprang a terror that sickened me. Yet he did not lose his presence of mind. He blew out the lantern and moved to the door, just as, under a furious kick, it flew open, the bolt shattered.

A gust of wind rushed into the room; the embers burst for a second into flame, and revealed the figure of a man peering in from the threshold. The intruder bore a distinct family likeness to my unknown accomplice, but was of much younger years. His clothes, of country cut, like those of a sporting yeoman, were drenched; his head was bare, and his face shone with the wet. As to his countenance, it was one of hatred and fury; his eyes, during the brief flash from the hearth, had found, and fixed vindictively, the helpless figure upon the bed.

"I knew it! . . ." he snarled with a kind of triumph. He walked in on this, closing the door again and placing his back against it. "I knew it!"

All but complete darkness had fallen once more about us. By the faint glow of the embers I could just discern the two erect figures. For a moment there was silence within. Then from the door came the words, in bitter implacable tones:

"What's the good of it? He'll only have to swing again!"

"You never would . . . you never would . . .! After what you have done . . .!" the old man stammered in a strangled whisper.

"Would not I? Trust me, my friend! And it's gaol for you, now, and for all concerned in the job. Oh, I had a queer doubt, after I'd found out you'd been earwigging the topsman, over there at Shaston! I thought I'd go and see to the hooking up with my own eyes. But I lost my way, and when I got there the gibbet was bare!" From my corner I could hear him chuckling. "But no matter," he went on, "it's all the better joke. And here I stick, to see it out. You are in for it now. You and all concerned," he repeated.

There was a long pause. It was as if I could hear the old man, in the dark, eagerly thinking. Presently he reached out his arm gently, plucked me by the sleeve towards him, and whispered close to my ear:

"He hasn't seen your face—wait there."

I felt myself pushed through a door, which was on the instant bolted behind me. I stopped a moment where I stood, lost in rueful reflection. The newcomer's triumphant and menacing tone, his minatory insistence on "all concerned," had struck in me the chord of a new anxiety. I leant an ear; but the room was on the exposed side of the cottage, the wind roared overbearingly down a chimney and rattled the casements as with human hands; the rain lashed the panes loud and sharp almost as hail. I could hear nothing from the next room, but once a thud or two, as of the door beating in the wind, and, for a moment, what sounded like the growls of grappling dogs. Then deep silence. Then, after a long interval, an occasional click of iron, nothing more. I gave it up. Resigning myself, not without a heavy weight of doubt, to my circumstances, I struck a light, discovered an end of tallow candle, and surveyed my prison—a pent-ceiled room, half kitchen, half wash-house. There was no outer door, and the window was too narrow to allow of an exit except under desperate conditions.

A small cask could be descried in a corner. The sight of it reminded me that I was feverishly thirsty. On the window-sill gleamed a white and yellow mug ; I filled it, hoping for water. But it was mead, sweet and heady. The two cupfuls I drank with greed almost instantly went to my head, vaguely disturbing the balance of my thoughts, but not without some kind of gratifying relaxation. After another meditative wait I once more went to hearken at the door, but could distinguish no sound but a confused shuffling and again the clinking. Impelled by a new boldness, I struck the door with my palm, and instantly rose the old man's voice with a startled, angry sharpness :

" What are you doing ? Stop where you are ! " Then, in a more conciliatory tone, " I will let you out when all is safe."

There was in the latter phrase something odd, of which my slightly dizzy brain could then make nothing. I sat down on a bench and waited.

I must have fallen into a doze, for I opened my eyes with a start to stare straight into a lantern that was thrust close to my face. The old man had entered without my hearing him, and was gazing down on me with a strange, inscrutable look that sent a shiver down my spine.

" My son is dead," he said without preamble. His voice was husky and faint, his eyes were wide open but expressionless, like those of the sleep-walker, and there was a fixed grin upon his lips. " My son is dead," he repeated, now with a faint note of impatience as I stared without a word. " The shock has killed him—you understand ? "

" The man—— ? " I stammered.

" The man ? " Again the mad grin bared the speaker's teeth. He made a wide gesture towards the Down. " He's gone ! He's gone ; we've paid the debt, you see—since my boy's dead after all. But you heard him. . . ." There was a rising insistence in the strained voice. " Had we not better, since the boy is dead, after all . . . take him back ? "

" To the gibbet ? " I cried, aghast.

" Ah—you heard what he said ! 'Tis gaol—for all concerned." His tone had now changed to one of wheedling that fairly revolted me. " Hadn't we better take him back ? When I thought he could live, I risked it. I thought I could do it alone—but you know I couldn't have done it without you. And it's gaol for me—and you, if it's found out. For me and you too. Think——" Whilst the voice was seeking persuasion, the small eyes shot out suddenly a kind of threat, instantly repressed. "Think," he went on. "It must not be found out, must it? And since my boy is dead, and you know I can't do it alone——"

He put his hand upon my arm. I recoiled with unreasoning aversion. I had been promptly sobered, but it did not require any further argument to make me see clearly that the horrible work must be yet more horribly reversed. This tampering with the execution of sentences was a dangerous experiment indeed. I was known to be on the hill that night. He saw acquiescence in my face and heaved a sigh of relief.

I followed him into the other room. The bed was empty. On the floor lay a long, loathly object; the gibbet's burden was ready clothed in the tarred garments we had been at such trouble to take off, ready shackled in the irons which it had been a matter of so much ingenuity to take to pieces. The dark cap was tightly drawn over the face.

A sickness overcame me as I pictured to myself the scene between the three . . . and one of them a dying man! the scene that must have taken place in this room whilst I waited imprisoned in the next; the cruel blow of the words, "Why, he'll only have to hang again!" (yes, it was more than enough to end a less shattered vitality); and the horror of heaven knows what bargain, subsequently made between the distraught father and a relentless hater: a bargain in which I also was being drawn, to the carrying-out of which, indeed, I was about to lend my help.

The old man was eyeing me intently. I pulled myself together and nodded. I had no words.

And thus, once more, we loaded the cart and pushed it, now in the teeth of the wind, up the sunken path to the knoll. The rain had ceased, and many patches of starry sky could be seen. Not a word was spoken until we reached the foot of the gibbet, which now, together with the fretwork of the ladder, rose conspicuously sharp against the faintly luminous heavens.

With curt directions to me, now and again, my accomplice went through the repellent task hurriedly, almost brutally, while I felt the awe of it tremble in every sinew, and the pity of it burn my throat. Then he once more reached the ground; he stood a moment gazing at the swaying and creaking burden of the gibbet. Then, with a kind of mad movement of rage, he pushed the long ladder, which fell with a dull thud, and turning to me:

"We may go," he said in a hard voice. "They'll come to fetch the ladder away to-morrow."

Mutely again we made the return journey together. He lustily, as before, pushed the cart, and I tramped by his side, glad enough to have seen, as I thought, the conclusion of an unchancy episode, yet wondering in a disconcerting manner at the callousness now displayed by him whom, but an hour or two before, I had heard sobbing over his son's body.

At the door of the cottage he broke silence. But it was not, as I had expected, to thank the stranger.

"This night's job is not a thing ever to talk about—you'll understand that, of course," he said, with a transparent affectation of calm. "The less said the better—for both of us, isn't it? And the sooner we part, also, the better, I'm sure. I won't ask you in again. Better not to know more of each other. We're in the same boat about this job," he insisted.

At this my rising irritation broke out.

"Oh, I don't wish ever to see you or this place again, be assured of that!" I cried. "I only want to take my apparatus—my telescope and dial thing, man, that I left in the room within," I repeated in louder impatience as he drew back a step in obvious dismay.

"Yes—yes," he stammered. "I understand. Stop there; I'll bring it out to you. But you won't come in, will you? You'll stop there, outside."

He pushed open the door, and the interior of the room was visible, flickeringly illuminated by firelight. No sooner had he done so than he gave a strangled exclamation, an involuntary yell of fear, which, in spite of my tacit promise, brought me with a bound beside him to the threshold. The old man, his nails clutching his cheeks in a gesture of despair, saw me with the side of his eye, but his gaze was fixed on the youthful shape sitting limply by the hearth, wrapped in a shepherd's cloak, stretching both his bare feet and his black hands to the fire.

"Harry! Harry!" moaned the father. "Why did you come out?"

"The cold—dying of cold. . . ." The boy uttered the words painfully, in a husky whisper, glanced towards me with lustreless eyes for a moment, then turned his face again to the fire.

There was a pause, filled with seething thoughts.

"Then, the other man——?" I said, almost in a whisper, pointing upwards to the Downs over my shoulder.

"The informer?—Yes," he answered. "The false witness! As God sees me——" he began with a rising voice.

I waved my hand forbiddingly:

"The less said the better—your own words!" My voice was thin, toneless, as one seems to hear it sometimes in nightmare. But, of a sudden, with a vehemence strangely like that of the old man himself : " I am innocent of all intent," I cried, " God only grant I may forget ! I will not judge you ! "

And, seizing my tripod, I rushed into the night once more ; struck the downward path, and only drew my first breath of relief when I had left the sinister desert of the Down above me, and again trod the living land of the Vale. There the wind was less boisterous, and I could hear the strokes of eleven dropping, slow and peaceful, from some unseen church tower.

All these scenes come back to me this day, in vivid pictures of strong light and shade.

So, his name was Moon ! I had never attempted to find out the name. But the landlord was mistaken in one thing : the Moon who was sentenced at Shaston for highway murder was not the last man that was hung in chains on Hamildon Down.

SIR ARTHUR CONAN DOYLE

1859–1930

A STRAGGLER OF '15

It was a dull October morning, and heavy, rolling fog-wreaths lay low over the wet, grey roofs of the Woolwich houses. Down in the long, brick-lined streets all was sodden and greasy and cheerless. From the high buildings of the Arsenal came the whirr of many wheels, the thudding of weights, and the buzz and babel of human toil. Beyond, the dwellings of the working-men, smoke-stained and unlovely, radiated away in a lessening perspective of narrowing road and dwindling wall.

There were few folk in the streets, for the toilers had all been absorbed since break of day by the huge, smoke-spouting monster, which sucked in the manhood of the town, to belch it forth, weary and work-stained, every night. Stout women, with thick red arms and dirty aprons, stood upon the whitened doorsteps, leaning upon their brooms, and shrieking their morning greetings across the road. One had gathered a small knot of cronies around her, and was talking energetically, with little shrill titters from her audience to punctuate her remarks.

" Old enough to know better ! " she cried, in answer to an exclamation from one of the listeners. " Why, 'ow old is he at all ? Blessed if I could ever make out."

" Well, it ain't so hard to reckon," said a sharp-featured, pale-faced woman, with watery blue eyes. " He's been at the battle o' Waterloo, and has the pension and medal to prove it."

" That were a ter'ble long time agone," remarked a third. " It were afore I were born."

" It were fifteen year after the beginnin' of the century," cried a younger woman, who had stood leaning against the wall, with a smile of superior knowledge upon her face. " My Bill was a-saying so last Sabbath, when I spoke to him o' old Daddy Brewster, here."

" And suppose he spoke truth, Missus Simpson, 'ow long agone do that make it ? "

" It's eighty-one now," said the original speaker, checking off the years upon her coarse red fingers, " and that were fifteen. Ten, and ten, and ten, and ten, and ten—why, it's only sixty and six year, so he ain't so old after all."

" But he weren't a new-born babe at the battle, silly," cried the young woman with a chuckle. " S'pose he were only twenty, then he couldn't be less than six-and-eighty now, at the lowest."

" Ay, he's that—every day of it," cried several.

" I've had 'bout enough of it," remarked the large woman gloomily. " Unless his young niece, or grand-niece, or whatever she is, come to-day, I'm off ; and he can find some one else to do his work. Your own 'ome first, says I."

" Ain't he quiet, then, Missus Simpson ? " asked the youngest of the group.

" Listen to him now," she answered, with her hand half raised, and her head turned slantwise towards the open door. From the upper floor came a shuffling, sliding sound, with a sharp tapping of a stick. " There he go back and forrards doing what he call his sentry-go. 'Arf the night through he's at that game, the silly old juggins. At six o'clock this very mornin' there he was beatin' with a stick at my door. ' Turn out guard,' he cried, and a lot more jargon that I could make nothing of. Then what with his coughin' and 'awkin' and spittin', there ain't no gettin' a wink o' sleep. Hark to him now ! "

" Missus Simpson ! Missus Simpson ! " cried a cracked and querulous voice from above.

" That's him," she cried, nodding her head with an air of triumph. " He do go on somethin' scandalous. Yes, Mister Brewster, sir."

" I want my morning ration, Missus Simpson."

" It's just ready, Mister Brewster, sir."

" Blessed if he ain't like a baby cryin' for its pap," said the young woman.

" I feel as if I could shake his old bones up sometimes," cried Mrs. Simpson viciously. " But who's for a 'arf of fourpenny ? "

The whole company were about to shuffle off to the public-house, when a young girl stepped across the road and touched the housekeeper timidly upon the arm. " I think that is No. 56 Arsenal View," she said. " Can you tell me if Mr. Brewster lives here ? "

The housekeeper looked critically at the newcomer. She was a girl of about twenty, broad-faced and comely, with a turned-up nose and large, honest, grey eyes. Her print dress, her straw hat with its bunch of glaring poppies, and the bundle which she carried had all a smack of the country.

" You're Norah Brewster, I s'pose," said Mrs. Simpson, eyeing her up and down with no friendly gaze.

" Yes ; I've come to look after my grand-uncle Gregory."

" And a good job too," cried the housekeeper, with a toss of her head. " It's about time that some of his own folk took a turn at it, for I've had enough of it. There you are, young woman ! in you go, and make yourself at home. There's tea in the caddy, and bacon on the dresser, and the old man will be about you if you don't fetch him his breakfast. I'll send for my things in the evenin'."

With a nod she strolled off with her attendant gossips in the direction of the public-house.

Thus left to her own devices, the country girl walked into the front room and took off her hat and jacket. It was a low-roofed apartment with a sputtering fire, upon which a small brass kettle was singing cheerily. A stained cloth lay over half the table, with an empty brown teapot, a loaf of bread, and some coarse crockery. Norah Brewster looked rapidly about her, and in an instant took over her new duties. Ere five minutes had passed the tea was made, two slices of bacon were frizzling on the pan, the table was rearranged, the antimacassars straightened over the sombre brown furniture, and the whole room had taken a new air of comfort and neatness. This done, she looked round curiously at the prints upon the walls. Over the fireplace, in a small, square case, a brown medal caught her eye, hanging from a strip of purple ribbon. Beneath was a slip of newspaper cutting. She stood on her tiptoes, with her fingers on the edge of the mantelpiece, and craned her neck up to see it, glancing down from time to time at the bacon which simmered and hissed beneath her. The cutting was yellow with age, and ran in this way :—

" On Tuesday an interesting ceremony was performed at the barracks of the third regiment of guards, when, in the presence of the Prince Regent, Lord Hill, Lord Saltoun, and an assemblage which comprised beauty as well as valour, a special medal was presented to Corporal Gregory Brewster, of Captain Haldane's flank company, in recognition of his gallantry in the recent great battle in the Lowlands. It appears that on the ever-memorable 18th of June four companies of the third guards and of the Coldstreams, under the command of Colonels Maitland and Byng, held the important farmhouse of Hougoumont at the right of the British position. At a critical point of the action these troops found themselves short of powder. Seeing that Generals Foy and Jerome Buonaparte were again massing their infantry for an attack on the position, Colonel Byng despatched Corporal Brewster to the rear to hasten up the reserve ammunition. Brewster came upon two powder tumbrils of the Nassau division, and succeeded, after menacing the drivers with his musket, in inducing them to convey their powder to Hougoumont. In his absence, however, the hedges surrounding the position had been set on fire by a howitzer battery of the French, and the passage of the carts full of powder became a most hazardous matter. The first tumbril exploded, blowing the driver to fragments. Daunted by the fate of his comrade, the second driver turned his horses, but Corporal Brewster, springing upon his seat, hurled the man down, and urging the powder cart through the flames, succeeded in forcing a way to his companions. To this gallant deed may be directly attributed the success of the British arms, for without powder it would have been impossible to have held Hougoumont, and the Duke of Wellington had repeatedly declared that had Hougoumont fallen, as well as La Haye Sainte, he would have found it impossible to have held his ground. Long may the heroic Brewster live to treasure the medal which he has so bravely won, and to look back with pride to the day when in the presence of his comrades he received this tribute to his valour from the august hands of the first gentleman of the realm."

The reading of this old cutting increased in the girl's mind the veneration which she had always had for her warrior kinsman. From her infancy he had been her hero, and she remembered how her father used to speak of his courage and his strength, how he could strike down a bullock with a blow of his fist, and carry a fat sheep under either arm. True that she had never seen him, but a rude painting at home, which depicted a square-faced, clean-shaven, stalwart man with a great bearskin cap, rose ever before her memory when she thought of him.

She was still gazing at the brown medal and wondering what the "*dulce et decorum est*" might mean, which was inscribed upon the edge, when there came a sudden tapping and shuffling upon the stair, and there at the door was standing the very man who had been so often in her thoughts.

But could this indeed be he? Where was the martial air, the flashing eye, the warrior face which she had pictured? There, framed in the doorway, was a huge, twisted old man, gaunt and puckered, with twitching hands and shuffling, purposeless feet. A cloud of fluffy white hair, a red-veined nose, two thick tufts of eyebrow, and a pair of dimly-questioning, watery-blue eyes—these were what met her gaze. He leaned forward upon a stick, while his shoulders rose and fell with his crackling, rasping breathing.

"I want my morning rations," he crooned, as he stumped forward to his chair. "The cold nips me without 'em. See to my fingers!"

He held out his distorted hands, all blue at the tips, wrinkled and gnarled, with huge, projecting knuckles.

"It's nigh ready," answered the girl, gazing at him with wonder in her eyes. "Don't you know who I am, grand-uncle? I am Norah Brewster from Witham."

" Rum is warm," mumbled the old man, rocking to and fro in his chair, " and schnapps is warm and there's 'eat in soup, but it's a dish o' tea for me. What did you say your name was ? "

" Norah Brewster."

" You can speak out, lass. Seems to me folk's voices isn't as loud as they used."

" I'm Norah Brewster, uncle. I'm your grand-niece come from down Essex way to live with you."

" You'll be brother Jarge's girl! Lor', to think o' little Jarge having a girl."

He chuckled hoarsely to himself, and the long, stringy sinews of his throat jerked and quivered.

" I am the daughter of your brother George's son," said she as she turned the bacon.

" Lor', but little Jarge was a rare un," he continued. " Eh, by Jimini, there was no chousing Jarge. He's got a bull pup o' mine that I gave him when I took the bounty. You've heard him speak of it, likely ? "

" Why, grandpa George has been dead this twenty years," said she, pouring out the tea.

" Well, it was a bootiful pup—ay, a well-bred un, by Jimini! I'm cold for lack of my rations. Rum is good, and so is schnapps, but I'd as lief have tea as either."

He breathed heavily while he devoured his food.

" It's a middlin' goodish way you've come," said he at last. " Likely the stage left yester-night."

" The what, uncle ? "

" The coach that brought you."

" Nay, I came by the mornin' train."

" Lor' now, think o' that! You ain't afeared of those new-fangled things! To think of you coming by railroad like that! What's the world a-comin' to ? "

There was silence for some minutes while Norah sat stirring her tea and glancing sideways at the bluish lips and champing jaws of her companion.

" You must have seen a deal of life, uncle," said she. " It must seem a long time to you! "

" Not so very long, neither. I'm ninety come Candlemas, but it don't seem long since I took the bounty. And that battle, it might have been yesterday. I've got the smell of the burned powder in my nose yet. Eh, but I get a power o' good from my rations! "

He did indeed look less worn and colourless than when she first saw him. His face was flushed and his back more erect.

" Have you read that ? " he asked, jerking his head towards the cutting.

" Yes, uncle, and I am sure you must be proud of it."

" Ah, it was a great day for me! A great day! The Regent was there, and a fine body of a man, too! 'The ridgment is proud of you,' says he. 'And I'm proud of the ridgment,' says I. 'A damned good answer too!' says he to Lord Hill, and they both bust out a-laughing. But what be you a-peepin' out o' the window for?"

" Oh, uncle, here's a regiment of soldiers coming down the street, with the band playing in front of them."

" A ridgment, eh? Where be my glasses? Lor' but I can hear the band, as plain as plain. Here's the pioneers an' the drum-major! What be their number, lass?"

His eyes were shining, and his bony, yellow fingers, like the claws of some fierce old bird, dug into her shoulder.

" They don't seem to have no number, uncle. They've something wrote on their shoulders. Oxfordshire, I think it be."

" Ah, yes," he growled. " I heard as they'd dropped the numbers and give them new-fangled names. There they go, by Jimini! They're young mostly, but they hain't forgot how to march. They have the swing—ay, I'll say that for them. They've got the swing."

He gazed after them until the last files had turned the corner, and the measured tramp of their marching had died away in the distance.

He had just regained his chair when the door opened and a gentleman stepped in. " Ah, Mr. Brewster! Better to-day?" he asked.

" Come in, doctor! Yes, I'm better. But there's a deal o' bubbling in my chest. It's all them toobes. If I could but cut the phlegm I'd be right. Can't ye get me something to cut the phlegm?"

The doctor, a grave-faced young man, put his fingers to the furrowed, blue-corded wrist.

" You must be careful," he said; " you must take no liberties."

The thin tide of life seemed to thrill rather than to throb under his finger.

The old man chuckled. " I've got brother Jarge's girl to look after me now. She'll see I don't break barracks or do what I hadn't ought to; why, darn my skin, I knew something was amiss!"

" With what?"

" Why, with them soldiers. You saw them pass, doctor—eh? They'd forgot their stocks. Not one on 'em had his stock on." He croaked and chuckled for a long time over his discovery. " It wouldn't ha' done for the Dook!" he muttered. " No, by Jimini! the Dook would ha' had word there."

The doctor smiled. " Well, you are doing very well," said he. " I'll look in once a week or so and see how you are!" As Norah followed him to the door he beckoned her outside. " He is very weak," he whispered. " If you find him failing you must send for me."

" What ails him, doctor ? "

" Ninety years ail him. His arteries are pipes of lime. His heart is shrunken and flabby. The man is worn out."

Norah stood watching the brisk figure of the young doctor and pondering over these new responsibilities which had come upon her. When she turned, a tall, brown-faced artillery man, with the three gold chevrons of sergeant upon his arm, was standing, carbine in hand, at her elbow.

" Good morning, miss ! " said he, raising one thick finger to his jaunty, yellow-banded cap. " I b'lieve there's an old gentleman lives here of the name of Brewster, who was engaged in the battle of Waterloo ? "

" It's my grand-uncle, sir," said Norah, casting down her eyes before the keen, critical gaze of the young soldier. " He is in the front parlour."

" Could I have a word with him, miss ? I'll call again if it don't chance to be convenient."

" I am sure that he would be very glad to see you, sir. He's in here, if you'll step in. Uncle, here's a gentleman who wants to speak with you."

" Proud to see you, sir—proud and glad, sir ! " cried the sergeant, taking three steps forward into the room, and grounding his carbine while he raised his hand, palm forwards, in a salute.

Norah stood by the door, with her mouth and eyes open, wondering whether her grand-uncle had ever, in his prime, looked like this magnificent creature ; and whether he, in his turn, would ever come to resemble her grand-uncle.

The old man blinked up at his visitor and shook his head slowly.

" Sit ye down, sergeant," said he, pointing with his stick to a chair. " You're full young for the stripes. Lordy, it's easier to get three now than one in my day. Gunners were old soldiers then, and the grey hairs came quicker than the three stripes."

" I am eight years' service, sir," cried the sergeant. " Macdonald is my name—Sergeant Macdonald, of H Battery, Southern Artillery Division. I have called as the spokesman of my mates at the gunners' barracks to say that we are proud to have you in the town, sir."

Old Brewster chuckled and rubbed his bony hands. " That were what the Regent said," he cried. ' The ridgment is proud of ye,' says he. ' And I am proud of the ridgment,' says I. ' And a damned good answer, too,' says he, and he and Lord Hill bust out a-laughin'."

" The non-commissioned mess would be proud and honoured to see you, sir," said Sergeant Macdonald. " And if you could step as far you'll always find a pipe o' baccy and a glass of grog awaitin' you."

The old man laughed until he coughed. " Like to see me, would they ? The dogs ! " said he. " Well, well, when the warm weather comes again I'll maybe drop in. It's likely that I'll drop in. Too grand for a canteen, eh ? Got your mess just the same as the orficers. What's the world a-coming to at all ! "

" You was in the line, sir, was you not ? " asked the sergeant respectfully.

" The line ? " cried the old man with shrill scorn. " Never wore a shako in my life. I am a guardsman, I am. Served in the third guards—the same they call now the Scots Guards. Lordy, but they have all marched away, every man of them, from old Colonel Byng down to the drummer boys, and here am I a straggler—that's what I am, sergeant, a straggler ! I'm here when I ought to be there. But it ain't my fault neither, for I'm ready to fall in when the word comes."

" We've all got to muster there," answered the sergeant. "Won't you try my baccy, sir ? " handing over a sealskin pouch.

Old Brewster drew a blackened clap pipe from his pocket, and began to stuff the tobacco into the bowl. In an instant it slipped through his fingers, and was broken to pieces on the floor. His lip quivered, his nose puckered up, and he began crying with the long, helpless sobs of a child. " I've broke my pipe," he cried.

" Don't, uncle, oh don't," cried Norah, bending over him and patting his white head as one soothes a baby. " It don't matter. We can easy get another."

" Don't you fret yourself, sir," said the sergeant. " 'Ere's a wooden pipe with an amber mouth, if you'll do me the honour to accept it from me. I'd be real glad if you will take it."

" Jimini ! " cried he, his smiles breaking in an instant through his tears. " It's a fine pipe. See to my new pipe, Norah. I lay that Jarge never had a pipe like that. You've got your firelock there, sergeant."

" Yes, sir, I was on my way back from the butts when I looked in."

" Let me have the feel of it. Lordy, but it seems like old times to have one's hand on a musket. What's the manual, sergeant, eh ? Cock your firelock—look to your priming—present your firelock—eh, sergeant ? Oh, Jimini ! I've broke your musket in halves ! "

" That's all right, sir," cried the gunner, laughing ; " you pressed on the lever and opened the breech-piece. That's where we load 'em, you know."

" Load 'em at the wrong end ! Well, well, to think o' that. And no ramrod, neither ! I've heered tell of it, but I never believed it afore. Ah, it won't come up to Brown Bess. When there's work to be done you mark my word and see if they don't come back to Brown Bess."

" By the Lord, sir," cried the sergeant hotly, " they need some change out in South Africa now. I see by this mornin's paper that the Government has knuckled under to these Boers. They're hot about it at the non-com. mess, I can tell you, sir."

" Eh, eh," croaked old Brewster. " By Gosh ! it wouldn't ha' done for the Dook ; the Dook would ha' had a word to say over that ! "

" Ah, that he would, sir," cried the sergeant ; " and God send us another like him. But I've wearied you enough for one sitting. I'll look in again, and I'll bring a comrade or two with me if I may, for there isn't one but would be proud to have speech with you."

So, with another salute to the veteran, and a gleam of white teeth at Norah, the big gunner withdrew, leaving a memory of blue cloth and of gold braid behind him. Many days had not passed, however, before he was back again, and during all the long winter he was a frequent visitor at Arsenal View. He brought others with him, and soon through all the lines a pilgrimage to Daddy Brewster's came to be looked upon as the proper thing to do. Gunners and sappers, linesmen and dragoons, came bowing and bobbing into the little parlour, with clatter of side-arms and clink of spurs, stretching their long legs across the patchwork rug, and hunting in the front of their tunics for the screw of tobacco, or paper of snuff, which they had brought as a sign of their esteem.

It was a deadly cold winter, with six weeks on end of snow on the ground, and Norah had a hard task to keep the life in that time-worn body. There were times when his mind would leave him, and when, save an animal outcry when the hour of his meals came round, no word would fall from him. As the warm weather came once more, however, and the green buds peeped forth again upon the trees, the blood thawed in his veins, and he would even drag himself as far as the door to bask in the life-giving sunshine.

" It do hearten me up so," he said one morning, as he glowed in a hot May sun. " It's a job to keep back the flies, though ! They get owdacious in this weather and they do plague me cruel."

" I'll keep them off you, uncle," said Norah.

" Eh, but it's fine ! This sunshine makes me think o' the glory to come. You might read me a bit o' the Bible, lass. I find it wonderful soothing."

" What part would you like, uncle ? "

" Oh, them wars."

" The wars ? "

" Ay, keep to the wars ! Give me the Old Testament for chice. There's more taste to it, to my mind ! When parson comes he wants to get off to something else, but it's Joshua or nothing with me. Them Israelites was good soldiers—good growed soldiers, all of 'em."

" But, uncle," pleaded Norah, " it's all peace in the next world."

" No it ain't, gal."

" Oh yes, uncle, surely ! "

The old corporal knocked his stick irritably upon the ground.

" I tell ye it ain't, gal. I asked parson."

" Well, what did he say ? "

" He said there was to be a last fight. He even gave it a name, he did. The battle of Arm—Arm——"

" Armageddon."

" Ay, that's the name parson said. I 'specs the third guards'll be there. And the Dook—the Dook'll have a word to say."

An elderly, grey-whiskered gentleman had been walking down the street, glancing up at the numbers of the houses. Now, as his eyes fell upon the old man, he came straight for him.

" Hullo," said he, " perhaps you are Gregory Brewster ? "

" My name, sir," answered the veteran.

" You are the same Brewster, as I understand, who is on the roll of the Scots Guards as having been present at the battle of Waterloo ! "

" I am that man, sir, though we called it the third guards in those days. It was a fine ridgment, and they only need me to make up a full muster."

" Tut, tut, they'll have to wait years for that," said the gentleman heartily ; " but I am the colonel of the Scots Guards, and I thought I would like to have a word with you."

Old Gregory Brewster was up in an instant with his hand to his rabbit-skin cap.

" God bless me ! " he cried, " to think of it ; to think of it."

" Hadn't the gentleman better come in ? " suggested the practical Norah from behind the door.

" Surely, sir, surely ; walk in, sir, if I may be so bold."

In his excitement he had forgotten his stick, and as he led the way into the parlour, his knees tottered, and he threw out his hands. In an instant the colonel had caught him on one side and Norah on the other.

" Easy and steady," said the colonel as he led him to his arm-chair.

" Thank ye, sir ; I was near gone that time. But, Lordy, why, I can scarce believe it. To think of me, the corporal of the flank company, and you the colonel of the battalion. Jimini ! how things come round, to be sure."

" Why, we are very proud of you in London," said the colonel. " And so you are actually one of the men who held Hougoumont ? " He looked at the bony, trembling hands with their huge, knotted knuckles, the stringy throat, and the heaving, rounded shoulders. Could this, indeed, be the last of that band of heroes ? Then he glanced at the half-filled phials, the blue liniment bottles, the long-spouted kettle, and the sordid details of the sick-room. "Better, surely, had he died under the blazing rafters of the Belgian farm-house," thought the colonel.

"I hope that you are pretty comfortable and happy," he remarked after a pause.

"Thank ye, sir. I have a good deal of trouble with my toobes—a deal of trouble. You wouldn't think the job it is to cut the phlegm. And I need my rations. I gets cold without 'em. And the flies! I ain't strong enough to fight against them."

"How's the memory?" asked the colonel.

"Oh, there ain't nothing amiss there. Why, sir, I could give you the name of every man in Captain Haldane's flank company."

"And the battle—you remember it?"

"Why, I sees it all afore me every time I shuts my eyes. Lordy, sir, you wouldn't hardly believe how clear it is to me. There's our line from the paregoric bottle right along to the snuff-box. D'ye see? Well, then, the pill-box is for Hougoumont on the right, where we was; and Norah's thimble for La Haye Sainte. There it is all right, sir, and here were our guns, and here, behind, the reserves and the Belgians. Ach, them Belgians!" He spat furiously into the fire. "Then here's the French where my pipe lies, and over here, where I put my baccy pouch, was the Proosians a-comin' up on our left flank. Jimini! but it was a glad sight to see the smoke of their guns."

"And what was it that struck you most, now, in connection with the whole affair?" asked the colonel.

"I lost three half-crowns over it, I did," crooned old Brewster. "I shouldn't wonder if I was never to get that money now. I lent 'em to Jabez Smith, my rear rank man, in Brussels. 'Only till pay-day, Grig,' says he. By Gosh! he was struck by a lancer at Quarter Brass, and me with not so much as a slip o' paper to prove the debt! Them three half-crowns is as good as lost to me."

The colonel rose from his chair, laughing.

"The officers of the Guards want you to buy yourself some little trifle which may add to your comfort," he said. "It is not from me, so you need not thank me." He took up the old man's tobacco pouch and slipped a crisp bank-note inside it.

"Thank ye, kindly, sir. But there's one favour that I would like to ask you, colonel."

"Yes, my man?"

"If I'm called, colonel, you won't grudge me a flag and a firing party?"

"All right, my man, I'll see to it," said the colonel. "Good-bye; I hope to have nothing but good news from you."

" A kind gentleman, Norah," croaked old Brewster, as they saw him walk past the window ; " but, Lordy, he ain't fit to hold the stirrup o' my Colonel Byng."

It was on the very next day that the corporal took a sudden change for the worse. Even the golden sunlight streaming through the window seemed unable to warm that withered frame. The doctor came and shook his head in silence. All day the man lay with only his puffing blue lips and the twitching of his scraggy neck to show that he still held the breath of life. Norah and Sergeant Macdonald had sat by him in the afternoon, but he had shown no consciousness of their presence. He lay peacefully, his eyes half-closed, his hands under his cheek, as one who is very weary. They had left him for an instant, and were sitting in the front room where Norah was preparing the tea, when of a sudden they heard a shout that rang through the house. Loud and clear and swelling, it pealed in their ears, a voice full of strength and energy and fiery passion.

" The guards need powder," it cried and yet again, " the guards need powder."

The sergeant sprang from his chair and rushed in, followed by the trembling Norah. There was the old man standing up, his blue eyes sparkling, his white hair bristling, his whole figure towering and expanding, with eagle head and glance of fire.

" The guards need powder," he thundered once again, " and by God they shall have it ! "

He threw up his long arms and sank back with a groan into his chair. The sergeant stooped over him, and his face darkened.

" Oh, Archie, Archie," sobbed the frightened girl, " what do you think of him ? " The sergeant turned away.

" I think," said he, " that the third guards have a full muster now."

SIR ARTHUR CONAN DOYLE

THE LAST GALLEY

Mutato nomine, de te, Britannia, fabula narratur.

IT was a spring morning, one hundred and forty-six years before the coming of Christ. The North African Coast, with its broad hem of golden sand, its green belt of feathery palm trees, and its background of barren, red-scarped hills, shimmered like a dream country in the opal light. Save for a narrow edge of snow-white surf, the Mediterranean lay blue and serene as far as the eye could reach. In all its vast expanse there was no break but for a single galley, which was slowly making its way from the direction of Sicily and heading for the distant harbour of Carthage.

Seen from afar it was a stately and beautiful vessel, deep red in colour, double-banked with scarlet oars, its broad, flapping sail stained with Tyrian purple, its bulwarks gleaming with brass work. A brazen, three-pronged ram projected in front, and a high golden figure of Baal, the God of the Phœnicians, children of Canaan, shone upon the afterdeck. From the single high mast above the huge sail streamed the tiger-striped flag of Carthage. So, like some stately scarlet bird, with golden beak and wings of purple, she swam upon the face of the waters—a thing of might and of beauty as seen from the distant shore.

But approach and look at her now ! What are these dark streaks which foul her white decks and dapple her brazen shields ? Why do the long red oars move out of time, irregular, convulsive ? Why are some missing from the staring portholes, some snapped with jagged, yellow edges, some trailing inert against the side ? Why are two prongs of the brazen ram twisted and broken ? See, even the high image of Baal is battered and disfigured ! By every sign this ship has passed through some grievous trial, some day of terror, which has left its heavy marks upon her.

And now stand upon the deck itself, and see more closely the men who man her ! There are two decks forward and aft, while in the open waist are the double banks of seats, above and below, where the rowers, two to an oar, tug and bend at their endless task. Down the centre is a narrow platform, along which pace a line of warders, lash in hand, who cut cruelly at the slave who pauses, be it only for an instant, to sweep the sweat from his dripping brow. But these slaves—look at them ! Some are captured Romans, some Sicilians, many black Libyans, but all are in the last exhaustion, their weary eyelids drooped over their eyes, their lips thick with black crusts, and pink with bloody froth, their arms and backs moving mechanically to the hoarse chant of the overseer. Their bodies, of all tints from ivory to jet, are stripped to the waist, and every glistening back shows the angry stripes of the warders. But it is not from these that the blood comes which reddens the seats and tints the salt water washing beneath their manacled feet. Great gaping wounds, the marks of sword slash and spear stab, show crimson upon their naked chests and shoulders, while many lie huddled and senseless athwart the benches, careless for ever of the whips which still hiss above them. Now we can understand those empty port-holes and those trailing oars.

Nor were the crew in better case than their slaves. The decks were littered with wounded and dying men. It was but a remnant who still remained upon their feet. The most lay exhausted upon the foredeck, while a few of the more zealous were mending their shattered armour, restringing their bows, or cleaning the deck from the marks of combat. Upon a raised platform at the base of the mast stood the sailing-master, who conned the ship, his eyes fixed upon the distant point of Megara which screened the eastern side of the Bay of Carthage. On the afterdeck were gathered a number of officers, silent and brooding, glancing from time to time at two of their own class who stood apart deep in conversation. The one, tall, dark, and wiry, with pure, Semitic features, and the limbs of a giant, was Magro, the famous Carthaginian captain, whose name was still a terror on every shore, from Gaul to the Euxine. The other, a white-bearded, swarthy man, with indomitable courage and energy stamped upon every eager line of his keen, aquiline face, was Gisco the politician, a man of the highest Punic blood, a Suffete of the purple robe, and the leader of that party in the State which had watched and striven amid the selfishness and slothfulness of his fellow-countrymen to rouse the public spirit and waken the public conscience to the ever-increasing danger from Rome. As they talked, the two men glanced continually, with earnest anxious faces, towards the northern skyline.

" It is certain," said the older man, with gloom in his voice and bearing, " none have escaped save ourselves."

" I did not leave the press of the battle while I saw one ship which I could succour," Magro answered. " As it was, we came away, as you saw, like a wolf which has a hound hanging on to either haunch. The Roman dogs can show the wolf-bites which prove it. Had any other galley won clear, they would surely be with us by now, since they have no place of safety save Carthage."

The younger warrior glanced keenly ahead to the distant point which marked his native city. Already the low, leafy hill could be seen, dotted with the white villas of the wealthy Phœnician merchants. Above them, a gleaming dot against the pale blue morning sky, shone the brazen roof of the citadel of Byrsa, which capped the sloping town.

"Already they can see us from the watch-towers," he remarked. "Even from afar they may know the galley of Black Magro. But which of all of them will guess that we alone remain of all that goodly fleet which sailed out with blare of trumpet and roll of drum but one short month ago?"

The patrician smiled bitterly. "If it were not for our great ancestors and for our beloved country, the Queen of the Waters," said he, "I could find it in my heart to be glad at this destruction which has come upon this vain and feeble generation. You have spent your life upon the seas, Magro. You do not know how it has been with us on the land. But I have seen this canker grow upon us which now leads us to our death. I and others have gone down into the market-place to plead with the people, and been pelted with mud for our pains. Many a time have I pointed to Rome, and said, 'Behold these people, who bear arms themselves, each man for his own duty and pride. How can you who hide behind mercenaries hope to stand against them?'—a hundred times I have said it."

"And had they no answer?" asked the Rover.

"Rome was far off and they could not see it, so to them it was nothing," the old man answered. "Some thought of trade, and some of votes, and some of profits from the State, but none would see that the State itself, the mother of all things, was sinking to her end. So might the bees debate who should have wax or honey when the torch was blazing which would bring to ashes the hive and all therein. 'Are we not rulers of the sea?' 'Was not Hannibal a great man?' Such were their cries, living ever in the past and blind to the future. Before that sun sets there will be tearing of hair and rending of garments; but what will that now avail us?"

"It is some sad comfort," said Magro, "to know that what Rome holds she cannot keep."

"Why say you that? When we go down, she is supreme in all the world."

"For a time, and only for a time," Magro answered gravely. "Yet you will smile, perchance, when I tell you how it is that I know it. There was a wise woman who lived in that part of the

Tin Islands which juts forth into the sea, and from her lips I have heard many things, but not one which has not come aright. Of the fall of our own country, and even of this battle, from which we now return, she told me clearly. There is much strange lore amongst these savage peoples in the west of the land of Tin."

"What said she of Rome?"

"That she also would fall, even as we, weakened by her riches and her factions."

Gisco rubbed his hands. "That at least makes our own fall less bitter," said he. "But since we have fallen, and Rome will fall, who in turn may hope to be Queen of the Waters?"

"That also I asked her," said Magro, "and gave her my Tyrian belt with the golden buckle as a guerdon for her answer. But, indeed, it was too high payment for the tale she told, which must be false if all else she said was true. She would have it that in coming days it was her own land, this fog-girt isle where painted savages can scarce row a wicker coracle from point to point, which shall at last take the trident which Carthage and Rome have dropped."

The smile which flickered upon the old patrician's keen features died away suddenly, and his fingers closed upon his companion's wrist. The other hand set rigid, his head advanced, his hawk eyes upon the northern skyline. Its straight, blue horizon was broken by two low black dots.

"Galleys!" whispered Gisco.

The whole crew had seen them. They clustered along the starboard bulwarks, pointing and chattering. For a moment the gloom of defeat was lifted, and a buzz of joy ran from group to group at the thought that they were not alone—that some one had escaped the great carnage as well as themselves.

"By the spirit of Baal," said Black Magro, "I could not have believed that any could have fought clear from such a welter. Could it be young Hamilcar in the *Africa*, or is it Beneva in the blue Syrian ship? We three with others may form a squadron and make head against them yet. If we hold our course, they will join us ere we round the harbour mole."

Slowly the injured galley toiled on her way, and more swiftly the two newcomers swept down from the north. Only a few miles off lay the green point and the white houses which flanked the great African city. Already, upon the headland, could be seen a dark group of waiting townsmen. Gisco and Magro were still watching with puckered gaze the approaching galleys, when the brown Libyan boatswain, with flashing teeth and gleaming eyes, rushed upon the poop, his long thin arm stabbing to the north.

"Romans!" he cried. "Romans!"

A hush had fallen over the great vessel. Only the wash of the water and the measured rattle and beat of the oars broke in upon the silence.

"By the horns of God's altar, I believe the fellow is right!" cried old Gisco. "See how they swoop upon us like falcons. They are full-manned and full-oared."

"Plain wood, unpainted," said Magro. "See how it gleams yellow where the sun strikes it."

"And yonder thing beneath the mast. Is it not the cursed bridge they use for boarding?"

"So they grudge us even one," said Magro with a bitter laugh. "Not even one galley shall return to the old sea-mother. Well, for my part, I would as soon have it so. I am of a mind to stop the oars and await them."

"It is a man's thought," answered old Gisco; "but the city will need us in the days to come. What shall it profit us to make the Roman victory complete? Nay, Magro, let the slaves row as they never rowed before, not for our own safety, but for the profit of the State."

So the great red ship laboured and lurched onwards, like a weary panting stag which seeks shelter from his pursuers, while ever swifter and ever nearer sped the two lean fierce galleys from the north. Already the morning sun shone upon the lines of low Roman helmets above the bulwarks, and glistened on the silver wave where each sharp prow shot through the still blue water. Every moment the ships drew nearer, and the long thin scream of the Roman trumpets grew louder upon the ear.

Upon the high bluff of Megara there stood a great concourse of the people of Carthage who had hurried forth from the city upon the news that the galleys were in sight. They stood now, rich and poor, effete and plebeian, white Phœnician and dark Kabyle, gazing with breathless interest at the spectacle before them. Some hundreds of feet beneath them the Punic galley had drawn so close that with their naked eyes they could see those stains of battle which told their dismal tale. The Romans, too, were heading in such a way that it was before their very faces that their ship was about to be cut off; and yet of all this multitude not one could raise a hand in its defence. Some wept in impotent grief, some cursed with flashing eyes and knotted fists, some on their knees held up appealing hands to Baal; but neither prayer, tears, nor curses could undo the past nor mend the present. That broken, crawling galley meant that their fleet was gone. Those two fierce darting ships meant that the hands of Rome were already at their throat. Behind them would come others and others, the innumerable trained hosts of the great Republic, long mistress of the land, now dominant also upon the waters. In a month, two months, three at the most, their armies would be there, and what could all the untrained multitudes of Carthage do to stop them?

"Nay!" cried one, more hopeful than the rest, "at least we are brave men with arms in our hands."

"Fool!" said another, "is it not such talk which has brought us to our ruin? What is the brave man untrained to the brave man trained? When you stand before the sweep and rush of a Roman legion you may learn the difference."

"Then let us train!"

"Too late! A full year is needful to turn a man to a soldier. Where will you—where will your city be within the year? Nay, there is but one chance for us. If we give up our commerce and our colonies, if we strip ourselves of all that made us great, then perchance the Roman conqueror may hold his hand."

And already the last sea-fight of Carthage was coming swiftly to an end before them. Under their very eyes the two Roman galleys had shot in, one on either side of the vessel of Black Magro. They had grappled with him, and he, desperate in his despair, had cast the crooked flukes of his anchors over their gunwales, and bound them to him in an iron grip, whilst with hammer and crowbar he burst great holes in his own sheathing. The last Punic galley should never be rowed into Ostia, a sight for the holiday-makers of Rome. She would lie in her own waters. And the fierce, dark soul of her rover captain glowed as he thought that not alone should she sink into the depths of the mother sea.

Too late did the Romans understand the man with whom they had to deal. Their boarders who had flooded the Punic decks felt the planking sink and sway beneath them. They rushed to gain their own vessels; but they, too, were being drawn downwards, held in the dying grip of the great red galley. Over they went and ever over. Now the deck of Magro's ship is flush with the water, and the Romans, drawn towards it by the iron bonds which held them, are tilted downwards, one bulwark upon the waves, one reared high in the air. Madly they strain to cast off the death-grip of the galley. She is under the surface now, and ever swifter, with the greater weight, the Roman ships heel after her. There is a rending crash. The wooden side is torn out of one, and mutilated, dismembered, she rights herself, and lies a helpless thing upon the water. But a last yellow gleam in the blue water shows where her consort has been dragged to her end in the iron death-grapple of her foemen. The tiger-striped flag of Carthage has sunk beneath the swirling surface, never more to be seen upon the face of the sea.

For in that year a great cloud hung for seventeen days over the African coast, a deep black cloud which was the dark shroud of the burning city. And when the seventeen days were over, Roman ploughs were driven from end to end of the charred ashes, and salt was scattered there as a sign that Carthage should be no more. And far off a huddle of naked, starving folk stood upon the distant mountains, and looked down upon the desolate plain which had once been the fairest and richest upon earth. And they understood too late that it is the law of heaven that the world is given to the hardy and to the self-denying, whilst he who would escape the duties of manhood will soon be stripped of the pride, the wealth, and the power, which are the prizes which manhood brings.

ACKNOWLEDGMENTS

To the following Authors for their courtesy and co-operation in permitting the inclusion of the stories that bear their names :

Sir Arthur Conan Doyle ; Rev. S. Baring-Gould ; Mr. Thomas Hardy ; Mr. T. Anstey Guthrie ; Mr. Egerton Castle ; Mr. Morley Roberts, and Mr. Stanley Weyman.

To Mrs. Robert Barr for permission to reprint two stories by her late husband.

To the following publishers who have kindly agreed to the use of the copyrights specified under their respective names :

Messrs. Chatto & Windus, St. Martin's Lane, London, W.C.

"How Jones got the English Verse Medal," from *Humorous Stories*, by James Payn ; "The Marriage Plate," from *Pipistrello*, by Ouida ; "The Reverend John Creedy," from *Strange Stories*, by Grant Allen ; and "An Alpine Divorce," from *Revenge*, by Robert Barr.

Messrs. Methuen & Co., Ltd., 36 Essex Street, London.

"Genefer," from *Furze Bloom*, by S. Baring-Gould ; "Gentlemen : The King !" from *The Strong Arm*, by Robert Barr ; and "A Straggler of '15," from *Round the Red Lamp*, by Sir Arthur Conan Doyle.

Messrs. Macmillan & Co., Ltd., St. Martin's Street, London.

"The Melancholy Hussar" and "Absent-mindedness in a Parish Choir," from *Life's Little Ironies*, by Thomas Hardy.

Mr. Eveleigh Nash, Covent Garden, London, W.C.

"The Young Man who stroked Cats," by Morley Roberts.

Messrs. Thos. Nelson & Sons, Ltd., 35 Paternoster Row, E.C.

"The Last Galley," from the book of that name, by Sir Arthur Conan Doyle.

Messrs. Hutchinson & Co., 34 Paternoster Row, London.

"The Miracle of the Black Cañon," from *The Great Jester*, by Morley Roberts.

The Oxford University Press, Amen Corner, London, E.C.

"Mr. Whittaker's Retirement," from *More Pages from a Journal*, by Mark Rutherford.

Messrs. Cassell & Co., Ltd., La Belle Sauvage Yard, E.C.

"The Clockmaker of Poissy," from *The Memoirs of a Minister of France*, by Stanley Weyman.

Mr. William Heinemann, 21 Bedford Street, London, W.C.

"In the Permanent Way," by Flora Annie Steel, from the volume of the same title.

Mr. John Lane, The Bodley Head, Vigo Street, London, W.

"The Dumb Oracle," from *The Twilight of the Gods*, by Richard Garnett.

Mr. T. Fisher Unwin, 1 Adelphi Terrace, London, W.C.

"The Adventure of Three Sailors," from *The Honour of the Flag*, by W. Clark Russell.

Mr. John Murray, Albemarle Street, London, W.

"Moon's Gibbet," from *Chance the Piper*, by Egerton Castle.

Messrs. Longmans, Green & Co., 39 Paternoster Row, E.C.

"A Canine Ishmael," from *The Talking Horse*, by F. Anstey.

Made and Printed in Great Britain by
Hazell, Watson & Viney, Ltd., London and Aylesbury